NECROSEAM CHRONICLES | BOOK THREE

PEARL OF EMERALD

NECROSEAM CHRONICLES

Other Books by Ellie Raine
Nightingale

*Forthcoming

NECROSEAM CHRONICLES | BOOK THREE

PEARL OF EMERALD

ELLIE RAINE

Pearl of Emerald
NecroSeam Chronicles | Book Three

Copyright © 2018 by Ellie Raine

Cover Design by Fiona Jayde
Interior Formatting by Tamara Cribley
Author Photograph by Melissa Giles Photography
Map © 2018 Ellie Raine

Printed in the United States of America

ISBNs: 978-1-7320415-0-9 (Hardcover), 978-1-7320415-1-6 (Paperback), 978-1-7320415-4-7 (Ebook)

Library of Congress Control Number: 2018946774
First Printing, Edition I: 2018

Published by
ScyntheFy Press, LLC
www.ScyntheFy.com

For information about special discounts available for bulk purchases, sales promotions, fund-raising and educational needs, contact ScyntheFy Press at: www.ScyntheFy.com/contact

For special bonus features and up-to-date news, visit the official NecroSeam web site: www.NecroSeam.com

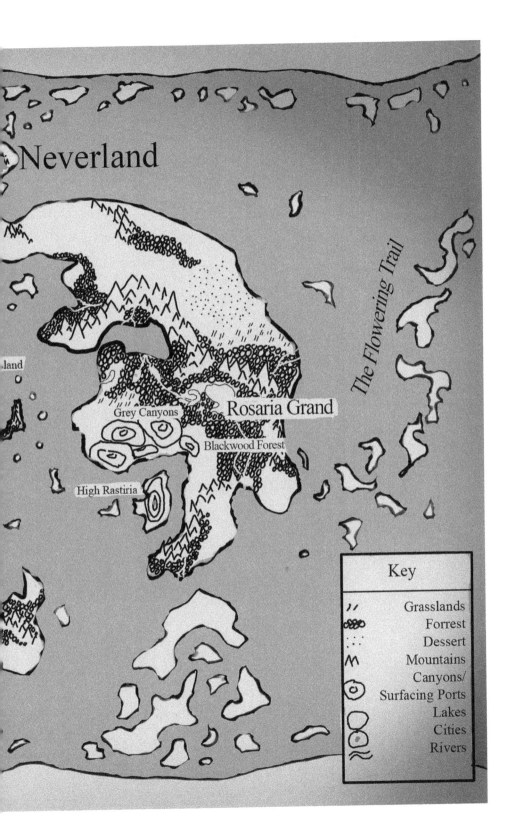

"I should have listened, Father.
"She'd warned me of this, told me this would happen. I heeded her then,
yet once the moment came, I thought I could change it... Fool, was I.
"Fool I still am."

—The King of Dreams, 2092 A.B.

PROLOGUE
KING DREAM

506 YEARS PRIOR

Screeeeee…

The scrape of a steel blade dragging on stone screamed thinly, and the soft points of my fox ears brushed my neck with each heave of breath.

I didn't wish to peer round the open doorframe. I didn't wish to see what was there, not in person. The vision of what currently lay inside was clear enough through my Third Eye; the stink of death profuse.

There were bodies strewn about the floor, nobles and servants alike. Not even royalty was exempt. The Queen of Ocean hung impaled against the wall; the King of Sky lay dead at her feet, his scarlet wings plucked from his back. His daughter's head had been removed and rolled beside her father's limp arm.

I only hoped to Gods my daughter Myra—my little Myra—hadn't seen. This slaughter was not for the eyes of such a small thing.

The vision burned in my Third Eye, though I was looking through someone else's point of view. I could hear the scraping blade both behind and in front of me, listening with two different sets of ears, but only Seeing through *his* eyes. His stinging, bleary eyes, wet and misty, glaring at the man with the golden crown.

The king's lion ears were grown and curled back, his glittering golden robes the only garb left unstained in the ballroom. He had no sword, but outstretched a hand and evoked his rock Hallows to the nearest blade that lay discarded on the ballroom floor, the weapon lifting in the air and flying to his grip.

The protagonist of my vision felt a tug at his own sword, and saw the king was attempting to rip it from his grasp. Black veins spewed from his hand onto the blade suddenly, the mirrored surface shrouded in stringy poison.

He gave the king a look that said, *take it now, if you dare.*

The king's expression fell, dismissing his Terravoking lest he grab the poisonous blade and bring his own death.

"Madman," King Adam growled, his timbre disgusted. "You're a damned madman."

The killer kept his dragging pace, his poisoned blade scratching the floor behind him. His gaze went placid, more machine than man, with but one mission.

King Adam's bronzed face paled at the look. "Why...?" he asked. "Why torment me further...? I've lost Genevieve—I've lost our *child*—what more do you want?!"

The blade whined over the marble quietly, the killer as silent as the dead men and women he stepped over.

Adam's voice shook. "All this, over a damned dismissal...? Good Gods, Doctor, if I'd known a lunatic was buried within, I..."

"Where?" the doctor croaked, his feet slowing to a halt at last.

The king kept his distance, blinking. "What?"

"Where is he?" His voice was a meager whisper, exhaustion and pain—*crushing pain*—weighing down his soul. "Where is my son?"

The narrator's memory flickered with bloodied walls—pooling floorboards—the red dripping, dripping, dripping from her open neck—

Agony writhed within the surgeon. He remembered her smile, her entrancing green-eyed leer, her laughter—her blood, painted on the wall of their home—*your failure's payment* glowing hot against the wood—her scattered pieces tossed about like morbid scraps—her head hung from the wall by her silken, Grimish hair—her heart carved out of her naked, appendage-less body and placed between her legs—

Fury *ripped* through the surgeon's blood again, his vision flooded with tears and blocking my view of the king, but oh, the man's neck had never looked so tempting to *wring* the breath out of...!

Yet he knew now was not the time to grieve. He could mourn her when their son was safe.

He'd seen King Adam not hours ago, his golden locks and coin-like eyes glinting from under his cloak as His Majesty fled from the streets with the youngling in tow.

The doctor focused on the present at hand, his cheeks wet as he screamed, *"Where is my son?"*

His roars echoed through the ballroom, heard mostly by dead ears. Barely a moment lapsed before he came for the king in a wild rage—

The first *clang* of swords sang from inside, and my Third Eye suddenly slammed shut, my own perspective swimming back into focus.

I hurried to look through the doorway, watching the two men trade blows. The surgeon had the advantage: Kael's Infeciovoking was not something Adam had ever fought against. Now, seeing the surgeon for myself with my physical eyes was more sickening than having Seen through *his* view. The state of the ballroom was the same as the vision. Every speck of crimson that oozed from the floor, every stale stare still caught in a silent scream, hadn't changed. But Kael's face, full of fury and sorrow, each thrust with the sword deadlier than the next, the anguish ripping from his cries…

I cupped my mouth as my eyes misted. "Gods help us…"

Their swords collided and held for too long. Kael's poison-infested blade spread its black veins onto Adam's weapon. The veins seeped into the king's hands and rooted into his fingers, which went rigid as his weapon clattered to the floor.

Kael turned his blade downward and thrust its tip at Adam's chest, but the king rolled away. The surgeon's blade cracked the marble instead. Kael lifted his weapon for another strike, but he staggered when the floor beneath him began to quake. Adam had evoked his rock Hallows onto the marble under Kael's feet and lifted the man off the ground.

It was only a distraction, I noticed, as the king's blackened hands shined with gold light, perhaps in an attempt to heal the infection with his remedy Hallows.

But Kael sprang off the floating piece of floor and *plunged* his sword downward. Adam hadn't had enough time to heal. He saw his attacker too late.

Kael's blade sank into the king's shoulder, the black veins rooting deep in his soul. His Majesty collapsed onto his back with a scream as veins crept over his skin.

Kael removed his soaked blade and towered over the fallen king, whose golden eyes peered up at the surgeon in a shiver.

"Why…" The veins spread to his throat, Adam shaking violently like a rabid feral. Foam bubbled from the corners of his lips and dribbled onto his beard… then, suddenly, his glassy eyes looked past Kael. "Ana… belle…?"

Kael turned, searching for what the king had been staring at, yet didn't seem to notice anything. But from my place by the door, *I* could see a tiny, golden-haired lion girl hiding behind a pillar.

Ana!

What was that blasted girl doing in here?! And without her disguise?!

Keeping hidden from Kael's sight, I snuck inside and ducked under a table, making my way to the girl. I couldn't risk going into Aspirre to get to her. There was no guarantee that I'd come back outside unseen. Even with as much practice as I've had, there was no perfecting that kind of coordination. Especially when they kept changing the layout of this damned castle every few years.

My sheltering table came to an end, and I peeked out from under the decorative cloth. Kael had his weapon raised above the king. He asked once more, "Where is my son?!"

The king's only reply was a gurgled sputter, drool slipping from his slacked jaw.

Kael snarled, "If you've so much as *touched* a hair on his head—!"

Kael leapt back when a scythe nearly tore through his neck. He staggered to regain his footing and saw his newest opponent: Death King Ysthavon.

As the two crossed blades, I crept from pillar to pillar toward Anabelle. She waited two pillars away. But there was an older boy with her, perhaps in his twelfth year. The boy wasn't what I would call handsome, especially not with his face contorted with sheer horror at what was happening.

My gaze narrowed at this newcomer. I didn't like strangers seeing Anabelle. And they *never* saw her without a guise. I went through much effort to make the world believe Adam's daughter had died at childbirth, I wasn't about to have it ruined by some stray lion cub.

When I hurried behind the next pillar, I hissed, "Ana!"

Ana gasped and found me. I held a finger to my lips, then waved for her to come to me. She took a step in my direction.

"Anabelle…" the dying king wheezed again from his place on the floor. "My Ana… You came. Dream said you'd come today. He said you'd come…"

Ana hesitated, then glanced at me before turning round and going to the king.

"Ana…!" I hissed after her, but she ignored me. *Damn Land and his reckless, recycled soul!*

I went to the pillar she *had* been behind, exchanging a glare with the older boy she'd left behind.

Ana was whispering to the king. Her father. She'd only just learned who he was. This was not the reunion I had planned. You'd think I'd have Seen it coming. *Some wise oracle I made.*

Then there came a straggled grunt from the balcony outside. I turned, noticing the curtain was drawn halfway, snow blowing inside with the chilled wind. Slowly, I walked over.

The white flakes dusted my cheeks as I came to the curtain, the scent of ice eerily serene compared to the stink of death inside. Another sound came behind the curtain, a struggle of air.

I peeled the cloth open.

Two men stood on the balcony. One gripped the hilt of a dripping, thin sword; the other gurgled from that very sword being lodged in his throat. The dying man, King Adam's chief military general Accursius Lysandre, swayed limp into the arms of his murderer: his own brother. Accursius's breath choked as the sword was shoved into his throat further. The snow speckled red around them.

Accursius's killer gave a low chuckle. "For all your precious foresight, you never were the brighter half, brother... I suppose we each have our *talents*." He grunted and ripped the sword upward, slicing open his brother's neck and kicked him to the ground. The snow fell lightly over the body like a soft veil.

"Macar...?" I whispered.

He turned to me, and I shuddered. Something had changed in that stare. Behind his blood-splattered glasses, his eyes were no longer wide and curious, eager to learn the mysteries the world had to offer. His lust for knowledge had curdled into lust of a different sort.

He smiled like a lunatic. "Ah! Dream, my friend. I wondered when you'd arrive for the show." He kicked his twin's boot with a grin. "What do you think? I dare say I've finally gotten the best of this brute. Perhaps it wasn't the most graceful of executions, but I think with practice, grace will come more naturally."

I stood in silence, my bones numb to the freezing snow and gentle breeze that batted against my robes.

Macar frowned. "Dream? Are you that amazed?"

"Macar..." My lungs quivered painfully, tears hitting as I realized I'd made a grave, *grave* mistake. "What have you done...?"

"What have I done?" He laughed, using his tunic to wipe blood from his spectacles. "Why, I'm doing precisely what I swore to do when you knighted me, Dream." He replaced the lenses on his nose and his lips split with a fang-filled grin. "I'm doing what's necessary."

MARINCIA

FAE'SHON NAYÛ,

A WESTERN ISLE OF THE FLOWERING TRAIL

1

JAQ

PRESENT DAY

"Nate?" I asked Master Lucas's bear-eared vassal, Nathaniel. He, Aiden and I were flattened on our stomachs on the snowy floor of our ship's upper deck, stealthily peering through the gaps in the railing behind the helm. Aiden kept his wings tightly folded as his mouth twisted in thought, the bird shifter squinting in deep consideration. I flicked Nathaniel a sideways glance. "What're we doin' here, exactly?"

Nate pointed with his scraggly chin and stabbed a thick finger at someone waiting below us on the lower deck. "Ye see that lass down there?" he rasped quietly.

I pushed up my glasses, squinting like Aiden. There were a bunch of our crew members down there—that reptile lady from Nulani, Rochelle; Tavius' orange-haired mom, Sirra-Lyn; Sirra's teenaged apprentice with the black pig-tails and bear ears; The twins' rabbit-eared vassal, Vendy, chucking snowballs at anyone who passed by...

"Which one?" I asked, scratching my scaled nose.

Nathaniel grunted, "The black-headed lass—with the tails."

"Sirra's apprentice?" I said, watching the student Healer get smacked by one of Vendy's powdered balls. "Or, uh, I guess her *Da'torr* or whatever. Sirra said her name was Lëtta."

Nate gave a low, suspicious mumble, "Well, I be thinkin' miss Lëtta looks *mighty* familiar, see..."

"Ya think ya know her?" I asked.

Aiden muttered from his other side. "Nathaniel thinks she's his descendant."

"Aye." Nate ran his fingers over his black beard, one round bear-ear swiveling to the side speculatively. "See, back when I were alive, I went down the Flowering Trail across Marincia, like we be doin' here."

Aiden chuckled. "Yes, as a *ship merchant*."

Nate glared at him sharply, and after Aiden made a zipping motion over his lips, the bear turned back to me and went on. "See, our ship had docked on Tel'net Brunn, somewhere 'bout 200 years back. n' this wasn't no safe town, ye see, a man couldn't walk those streets without his pistol. This be back when guns with powder weren't just antiques in rich lords' display cases. Shotri weren't around to put 'em outta worth yet, so they was expensive pistols and gun powder—shot like a canon blast from yer hand, real loud, n' all ye got in the mates were these tiny lead balls called—"

"Bullets," I finished for him. "Nate, I've taken history lessons."

He shrugged. "Can't keep up with the times, lad. Anyway, aimin' those things back then was a right hassle. No fire to burst over the targets, no lightnin' shootin' over their limbs and freezin' 'em—but Bloods, they could kill a bloke quick if yer aim was sure."

Aiden scoffed. "Bows were still better. You could get your arrows back from the poor sods, at least."

"Ye feather-brained dolts never liked a good ol' musket. Woulda put yer arrows outta commission fer good, if'n ye didn't make those Shotri." Nate shook his head, getting back to his story. "Anyways, I was in town and met a pretty little lass there—she was a Landish bear, see, wantin' to see the world, now that ships were made better and safer for travelin'. She was bein' robbed when I walked on her street, she was, so I shot the bloke and got her belongin's back. She ended up wantin' to join me crew, since we was… uh, merchants… an' all."

I snorted. "Uh, huh. Merchants."

He scowled, but sniffed, continuing, "Well, the lass a'came me first mate in the end. When our ship went down with that bloomin' storm, I thought she sunk with it. But *that* little lass." He pointed at Lëtta. "Looks just like her. 'scept she's got my Grim hair. An' she's got my Grandad's Necrovoking, we had both that an' Pyrovoking in the line, see."

I idly scooped some snow into a pile on the floorboards. This white stuff was weird. It was cold and wet, and it made this fun little crunching noise when you pushed on it. I started poking holes in the icy powder while scrutinizing Nathaniel's face and then Lëtta's.

"Have ya tried askin' her?" I offered.

Nate frowned. Then he shoved to his feet.

"Ey!" He called down to the lower deck, getting the three doctors' attentions. He stabbed a finger at Lëtta. "Little lass, do ye know who yer… uh, great-great grandmother was?"

Lëtta's bear ears dropped slightly, asking in her fluid accent. "Two greats?"

"Aye. Whoever was the first t' come overseas to the Flowering Trail."

"Oh, you mean great-great-*great* grandmother Darcy." She put a hand on her hip and shifted weight, her thin pigtails waving in the snowing breeze. "Grandmother said she was first mate on a merchant ship."

"Hah, *hah*!" Nate slapped a hand on the railing. "I bloomin' knew it. The lass's name was Darcy, too, it was—'ey, little lass, that was *my* ship she were on! Yer alive 'cos 'o me!" He laughed boisterously.

One of Lëtta's bear ears perked, and she called up. "You're great-great-great grandfather Nathan?"

Nathaniel elbowed Aiden in the ribs when the bird rose beside him, the bear still guffawing. "Ye hear that, feather-head? I'm a tri-great grandfather!" He crossed his arms over the rail and grinned. "Ey lass, I always wondered what happened to Darc. I thought she be a siren down in the sea, singin' to starfish for the last hundred years."

Lëtta rubbed a snowflake from her cheek, humming. "Grandmother said she was shipwrecked and washed ashore on a piece of driftwood."

"Ah! That lucky duck. I tried swimmin' me'self, but ended up sinkin'. I was right lucky the Reapers found me soul a'fore I rotted down there an'…"

They talked up a storm, trading stories, when I saw the rest of our ship-mates were coming outside from the cabins. I pushed to my feet and wiped off the melted snow from my hands and coat, then slid down the stair rail to greet Alex and Tavius.

Alex saw me and tucked one hand into his baggy breeches' pocket, his other hanging in a sling while his still-healing collarbone was wrapped in new dressings. "Ah, Jaq," Alex greeted with a head toss. "There you are."

"We goin' out to the docks yet?" I asked. "Herrin mentioned something about a tavern earlier."

"He said the same thing to us," Tavius agreed next to Alex. He wore a thick, stuffy coat today, looking like a waddling, sea-green marshmallow. He must have had three layers under there, and his lanky black hair was hidden under a warm hat that hugged his skull and trapped his ears. Despite the layers, the poor sod still shivered.

In contrast, Alex wore a thinner, burgundy cardigan with a woolen cowl, the sleeves pulled up to his elbows to reveal his grey-haired arms, like he was too hot. I grinned, noting it was same number of layers *I* was wearing. *Yeah, we Grimlings are pretty used to the cold, thanks to the caves.*

Alex swept his gaze toward the docks, watching the bustling merchants and marching Wavecrashers, web-eared shifters going about their day around our ship. There were even some people swimming in the ice-cold water, seeming unfazed by the chill as their scaled legs melded together in the water and shifted into long fish-tails, diving in and disappearing into the ocean's depths.

Man, this place is cool. Weird, sure, but still cool.

Alex sighed and muttered, "Herrin also said he had something to tell everyone. It sounded important."

I cocked an eyebrow. "Important how?"

"Death if I know." Alex shrugged, tossing his properly combed head to the ramp that led down to the docks. "I suppose we won't discover his intentions until we arrive. Come. Willow and Lilli went ahead, and Xavier is staying behind for a time. He'll meet us there shortly."

I paused, my brain backpedaling. *Oh, right. They weren't sharing a body anymore.* They could actually be in two different places again… Bloods, this was going to take some getting used to.

I grinned. *Something to look forward to, I guess.*

My feet crunched snow as I followed Alex and Tavius to the docks.

Some people from our ship walked down the ramp behind us, not part of our main crew. They were the handful of refugees from Y'ahmelle Nayû we'd rescued a month ago. Ringëd was with his parents, babbling in Marincian with the rest of their huddled group.

Bloods, there were so few of them. Out of an entire island, roughly a dozen survived that Fera attack.

They passed the three of us and we followed behind them. As we stepped off the docks and strode through the snowy city, we passed through the Reaper district—

A black blur soared past my face, startling me and making my foot slip on a patch of ice. Tavius caught me before I hit the snow and pushed me to my feet again, but several more black blurs streaked around us.

I whipped my head every which way, trying to get a good look at the things. "What the Void are these?" I demanded, dodging another flying creature.

They were the size of ravens, their heads and beaks kind of resembling them too, in a weird way. Their "wings" wavered like a translucent veil in the wind as the flyers seemed to bob up and down off the air and float by all the crowded Reapers' shoulders. They had tails that were shaped like a crow's, but they looked more like fins, and the Bloody things had gills on their necks.

Alex hummed curiously. "Ah, these must be those Seacrows I read of in my cultural studies textbooks."

"*These* are Seacrows?" My eyes followed one as it smoothly bobbed past my face, like it was swimming in air. "Bloods, I've never seen one in person… but they're all over the place here!"

Alex shrugged. "We're in the Ocean realm. Most Marincians are fish shifters, so it makes sense that Marincia's Reapers would receive messengers who could travel in the water with them."

One "flew" by Octavius's head and he ducked out of its way, both of us staring after it and breathing, "Cool."

Ahead of us, Ringëd stopped to speak with a Trixer from this district. I thought about listening in, but even if I could hear them, I figured I still wouldn't understand since they were still talking in the local tongue. Whatever it was, it looked serious.

Then Ringëd hugged his parents and walked off, leaving the refugee group with the Trixer, who led them into the station.

I crossed my arms. "Guess this is where our refugees are relocating for now?"

Alex rubbed his chin. "I wondered when they'd decide to resettle... Or perhaps this was the first island whose duke accepted their pleas?"

"Prob'ly the latter," I said. "If it were up to the refugees, I bet they'd have settled on the very next stop after Y'ahmelle Nayû."

Alex grunted, agreeing, and we followed Ringëd toward the tavern Herrin had asked us to meet him in.

2

XAVIER

"Xavier, you *have* to drink it," Bianca insisted, one of her rabbit ears lifting as she stared me down like a feral leopard transfixed on an enormous ball of yarn. She shoved the glass of blue-green liquid into my skinny hand. "Go on! You're not getting off this ship until I see you drink all of it."

I grimaced at the suspiciously radiant tonic, swirling it in the glass. "Didn't I drink enough of this disgusting swill this morning?" I complained, scratching at my thick, scruffy beard. "I think my throat's had enough abuse. Death, whiskey would leave less of a burn."

The rabbit girl put fists at her sides. "Do you want to use your legs again? Your immune system will only accept this elixir for a couple months, if you're lucky. We need to use it while it still works on you. Muscle regeneration is a slow process on its own, but this stuff will speed it up. Now *drink*."

My nostrils cringed at the pungent stink leaking from the flask's rim. I whimpered, "But it tastes like crow piss—"

"*Xavier.*" Her glare sharpened as her long, orange ears lifted in warning. "With the state you're in, I'll have no problem overpowering you to force it down your throat anyway."

I deflated, glancing solemnly at my twig-like limbs. Even under the long-sleeved coat and trousers, the boney things announced themselves like an embarrassing, rude relative spouting politics at a holiday reunion.

I sighed and muttered a curse, then steeled my taste buds and chugged the tonic. My eye sockets burned, the spiced mixture draining down my throat in a hot yet unsettlingly cool prickle. It wasn't quite liquid exactly, more of a thick syrup that steamed up my nostrils and ears. When the flask was finally empty, I thrust it on the nearby table with a hard *clink* and hacked over my knees.

Bianca beamed and patted my head, picking up the flask. "There we go," she praised. "That wasn't so bad, was it?"

"What in Void is *in* that?" I coughed, thumping my still-prickling chest.

A sly grin rolled over her lips, and she winked. "You don't want to know."

I grimaced—

Snip!

I nearly flinched at the sound of clipping shears behind me, suddenly feeling someone's fingers run through my shoulder-length hair.

Snip! Snip! Snip!

I carefully inched my gaze over a shoulder. Sirra-Lynn was back there snipping away at my frayed strands with a contented smile on her lips, her orange cat ears flicking.

"Erm," I began awkwardly in my chair, clearing my throat. "Mrs. Treble?"

"Oh, don't mind me," she hummed in a cheerful tune. "You looked like you could use a trim, so I thought I'd go ahead and give it a quick cut before you went out."

I sighed and gently pushed down her hand. "Mrs. Treble, please. I *am* grateful you've looked after my body for so long—truly, I am—but I thought we'd already discussed certain… privacy boundaries?"

She paused, her eyes growing distant as though her mind was in a fog. "Oh." Her voice was faded, almost saddened. "Uh, r-right. I guess I just… haven't really gotten out of the habit, huh?" She sheathed her shears into the pocket of her doctor's coat, lowering into a chair beside me and offering a small smile. "Got to admit, I've never had a Souless patient wake up with their soul back. Can't say I'm having an easy time adjusting. Maybe I should find a new routine."

I smiled in kind, then fished into my trousers' pocket and produced a string, tying my unfamiliarly long hair into a tail to free my sweaty neck. I wasn't accustomed to having so much *warmth* there. Though, I was thankful it hid my scrawny neck, to a degree. The new hair and puckered, aged scar running down my right eye were strange and new, but by Nira, this was *me*. I wasn't borrowing my brother's body anymore, and the long hair served as a constant reminder that, for the first time in years, I was my own man. No longer a parasite.

It was a small, glorious reminder that I *existed*.

"Are you enjoying your time with your family again?" I asked Sirra, shifting the subject to something more pleasant.

She chuckled. "You bet, Howllord. Though, I wish Connie would have joined you all when you came to Y'ahmelle Nayû. So far, she's the only one I haven't seen."

"She elected to stay in High Everland," I said, my head wavering. "She's safe, I assure you. My parents are housing her and keeping her well-guarded, being the sister of their graduated student."

Her laughter brightened. "That's right, Rochelle told me about his random apprenticeship after you all first visited her in Nulani. I was pretty skeptical of you all finding us, to be honest, but...well, I'm glad it worked out for the best."

"You and I both, Mrs. Treble." I produced my silver pocket watch from my silken vest's pocket. "Ah, it's nearly time to meet with Herrin and the others in town. I'd best be off."

I fetched my ornate cane that was leaning against the nearby desk and grunted while pushing myself up.

From her desk, Bianca saw how slow I was moving and asked, "Do you need your crutches today?"

I secured my grip on the cane's silver handle and waved her off with my free hand. "No, this works fine now." I wobbled with the first step, my skinny legs still so *despairingly* weak. I had to grasp the cane with both hands for balance, but it was better than when I'd started out.

Just three weeks prior, I'd needed Kurrick to carry me around everywhere. I couldn't even use the crutches for too long before my arms gave out. If not for those disgusting tonics, I would still be that far behind. Thank the Gods we had so many Healers on our ship.

I fumbled my way to the opened door of the clinic room, stopping to turn back to Bianca. "You're meeting us there, aren't you?" I asked her.

She was still at her desk, fiddling with medical tools. "Maybe. Why?"

"Well, as I mentioned, Herrin has something important to tell us. He thought everyone should be there." I held my breath before adding. "And I think Alex would... er..."

One of her rabbit ears folded down. She didn't look up from her tools and remained silent.

I cleared my throat. "You know, I don't think Alex had properly conveyed his situation with, er, *Lilli*..."

"Has he now?" She muttered flatly, fiddling away with her tools.

"Well, Alex isn't exactly the most verbose when it comes to his personal affairs. But I think it's worth noting that my engagement to Willow wasn't the only arrangement our parents made in our youth—except, Alex hadn't learned of *his* until months ago."

Her rabbit ear lifted slightly, and she peeked over her shoulder. "It was arranged?"

"Much to his distaste, yes. But as a friend and brother, I would suggest discussing such things with him—"

"Come back for your next appointment in a few hours, Xavier." Her tone suggested the conversation was over, and she returned her attention to her tools.

I sighed and rubbed the beard at my jaw, hobbling out of the cabin with my cane clicking over the ship's floorboards.

Ever since my soul returned to my body, she and Alex had been avoiding each other like feral moles to sunlight. Now that my brother and I were separated, I guessed she didn't have an excuse to see him anymore, except to check on his injury. And even then, it was usually Miss Ana or Sirra-Lynn who tended to him.

But they aren't the only ones gaining distance, are they? My mood dripped depressively. I'd barely seen Willow these past weeks. She'd never visited during my physical therapy sessions with the Healers, she'd never stopped in to check on me…

When I first returned to my body, I expected to be pushing her off and complaining that she was too invasive. Now, I would *prefer* that problem. She may as well be a phantom, only showing her face at dining hours—if I was fortunate. *Doesn't she care? Is she ashamed of me?*

I paused my hobbling, glancing at my scrawny legs that hid under my warm trousers. My mood sank even further, like a sorry lump of coal plummeting into the abysmal ocean floor. *Bloods, even I'd be ashamed of me.* I needed to regain my strength before she completely lost interest and chose someone more… well, *more*, as her husband. Someone like Matthiel.

Gods damn it.

I clunked onward, muttering curses, but relaxed once I made it to the outer deck. There were cold, white flakes swirling around me now. The fluffy shavings piled onto the floor and blanketed the docks below.

We'd just reached the island of Brulettóe Sry'leaux, a Marincian province that was part of the Flowering Trail. The Trail was a very long sequence of isles that stretched from the west coast of Everland to the *east* coast of *Never*land. It was the safest and easiest path toward the second continent, where we could make frequent stops to restock our food and supplies.

One of the snowflakes hit my nose. I blinked several more from my lashes, and was sure by the chilled spots on my scalp that my hair was about to be cloaked.

This 'snow' was so strange. Stranger than rain. It looked like ash, yet it was cold. It was nothing more than ice that fell from the sky like some giant glacier was waiting up there past the clouds. It just didn't make sense. But, well, now that winter was here, at least we didn't have to deal with the blasted heat anymore. The winds cutting past me now reminded me of Grim, in fact. Of *home*.

The thought of the caverns was lead in my stomach. We'd been away for so long, I'd all but forgotten what the caves were like.

A rough caw came from above. I spied my messenger raven, Chai, soaring down to me. He perched on my shoulder, his black talons gripping gently over my grey jacket. He nuzzled his beak against my sunken cheek, and the touch brought a surge of warmth, our Bond synchronized and strong.

"Have your wings grown back already, Chai?" I leaned on my cane and scratched at the raven's neck, rousing a coo from him. "You've gotten ahead of me. I'll have to hurry and follow your example."

Chai croaked and fanned his tail feathers, flapping up to soar toward the clouds. I breathed in the bracing air, imagining the white flakes were instead Grim's floating lights. For only a moment, I let myself pretend I was home. Home with Jaq. Home with Lilli. Home with Alexander... Home with Willow.

When the illusion faded, I grudgingly exhaled and leveled my gaze, looking over the ship.

There was someone at the railing, watching the snowfall in silence. I noticed my birthmark of three black diamonds was glowing softly from my left hand—something Alex and I were growing far too accustomed to when around this extra passenger.

"King Dream?" I called, clipping my cane against the ship's snowy deck. "I thought you'd gone ahead with the others?"

The blue haired boy was staring past the horizon, his azure eyes glazed at the flurry of snow. He hadn't seemed to hear me, so I hobbled beside him. "King Dream?"

His eyes fluttered, and he looked at me as if unsure of where he was. "Ah," he said as his lips quickly slid into his usual, stale smile. "Xavier. I was waiting for you."

"Were you having a vision?" I asked. I was accustomed to those blank looks by now. Between Ringëd, Linus and Oliver, they'd become commonplace among the Seers on our ship. Even Willow had shown those signs during the few glimpses I'd seen of her. She wouldn't tell me what she'd Seen, however. She wouldn't tell me much of anything these days.

Dream hummed ponderously. "No. Not a vision. I was... reminiscing."
"On?"

For the first time since he came to stay with us, I saw his ears begin to sprout azure hair, his fox ears nearly taking shape. He didn't let them grow fully and hastily had them recede back to normal in a fogged sigh.

"A past mistake," he whispered, so quiet I almost hadn't heard. "I am an old man, Xavier, despite this young face. Many days have I collected mistakes. On a white day very much like today, I'd seen the fruits of the greatest mistake I'd ever made."

"What mistake?" I asked.

His lips hung with that empty smile, and he patted my shoulder. "Look at me rambling while the others are waiting—come. Enjoy the snow and the sea. It isn't every day you Grimlings see either one, is it?"

"I think I've seen enough of the surface seas for one lifetime," I mumbled and followed him down the ramp onto the frosted dock.

I knew he'd averted the question, but I'd grown accustomed to *that* as well. King Dream often said cryptic things without explanation. Alex hated it. I couldn't say I fancied it any better, but on our first week out at sea, Willow had advised we ignore it. According to her, her grandfather was always on about something from the past. And he had quite the past to tell—two-thousand years of it.

"King Dream?" I began when we touched the dock. There was something else bothering me about him. I'd kept it to myself during our travels, but perhaps now would be a good time to ask?

The young man gave a soft hum. "You needn't bother with formalities, Xavier. I'm not your average royal. And you may as well be my grandson-in-law, soon enough."

If Willow doesn't lose interest before then, I thought broodingly. That pit began to fester in my stomach again, but I pushed it away to focus on my question. "Er, yes, well… There's something I don't understand."

"Yes?"

My cane caught a hole in the wood and I fumbled to pull it out, regaining my balance before turning back to him. "Willow mentioned you look so… *young* because you live in Aspirre. And time doesn't exist there."

"Mm. Yes. And?"

"And you only visit on rare occasions to the physical realms, usually for a few hours to preserve yourself for future eras."

"Yes. But I don't think I'm following where this is going, Xavier."

"What I can't understand is…" I puffed to catch up when I'd fallen behind, and he slid my free arm over his shoulder to help me keep pace. I panted. "Why… why are you here now? *Physically* here, for so long? If you only age when you come out of Aspirre, how do you intend to keep yourself from growing old and dying if you're out for months?"

He laughed. "I only preserved myself to meet you and your brother. Now that I have, there isn't much need for this old king to keep living, don't you think?"

That was only more puzzling, and I took my arm off his shoulder to walk for myself, fatigued though I was. "To meet *us*? You haven't known us very long when compared to your extended lifetime."

"You'll understand after tonight," he said simply, his lips curling as though genuinely excited.

I prodded. "Understand what, exactly?"

He smiled thinly and walked on, leaving me hobbling with my cane to catch up, Chai soaring above to follow.

3

WILLOW

Dressed in velvet black, Xavier waited before the towering Willow of Ashes.
He was a few years older, jaw lined with a trimmed, grey beard and above his head was a silver skull-crown. His wedding band and diamond earring shimmered in the glow of the cool, Fallen Light that was trapped in the lantern at his feet.

Alexander stood beside him, cloaked in white and arms crossed before his chest. Watching. Waiting.

Xavier strode to me and took my fingers. The Crest on his left hand gleamed bright and brilliant. The same was happening to Alexander's Crest on his right hand.

Xavier lifted my chin and pressed his lips to mine, whispering, "It's time, love. If I'm to protect you both, we can't wait any longer." He stepped aside to make way for me, still keeping my hand in his as he gazed at the Willow of Ashes, white flakes fluttering around us. "Can you give the Call, and awake the Relic…?"

"Da'torr?"

The swirling ash turned cold, the flakes melting on my cheek as the vision dripped away. I wiped away the snow coating my lashes, the present time bleeding into focus.

I was on the Marincian island again. The deep blue and indigo buildings collected snowfall on their seashell roofs, the scaled, web-eared locals bustling through the streets of their beautiful city. The roads here were not straight, I noticed. They weaved between ponds and plant life like waves in the water, winding and bending around iron benches and trickling fountains.

"Da'torr?" one of my newest vassals, a winged ghost woman named Rossette, asked again. "Are you well?"

I turned to her, pushing down the memory of that vision—the one that has replayed again and again this past month; the one I've begun to remember with more clarity; the one that haunts me now most frequently.

"I'm fine," I told her, gazing at the clouds that cried snow. The crystals dusted my disguised, grey hair, and I clutched the music watch around my neck. "I was only lost in thought."

My second, web-eared vassal, Nikolai, cocked his ghostly head at me. "*Haux ga'fezette val, Da'torr?*"

"<Nothing important, Nikolai,>" I replied in his tongue. "<I'm only tired, I suppose—>"

I gasped when a wad of snow burst over my head with a frozen splash.

Little Oliver was grinning at me from across the street, his wings fluttering excitedly. "Got'cha!" he boasted and stuck out his tongue. "That's ten points for me, Auntie Low!"

I smirked, dusting off the snow from my head. I found myself thankful Oliver called me by that name. It would keep the local fish-shifters from discovering me. Drawing attention from this city's Reapers wasn't wise if we wished to keep our travels hidden from our enemies. Who knew what would befall this realm if Everland's king came with warships—or worse, if Cilia followed us again with her rotted army. *Nira let us be free of that demon*, I prayed silently to the Mother Goddess, remembering the burning ruins of the Y'ahmelle Nayû with a choked heart.

Oliver began to gather more snow, no doubt intending to throw it at me again. I hurried to bend down and scooped my own wad of fluffy powder. Chuckling, I launched mine one second before he did, but I missed terribly and his shot was a direct hit to my now frozen nose. He burst into laughter and prepared another ball—but Vendy had swooped in and chucked her own ball at his feathered head in a flurry of bright giggles. The two began a war, and I ducked and dodged any projectiles that came my way before Lilli flew down from the sky and picked Oliver up, her prim brow creased in a scolding glare.

"Oliver!" She clipped, and briskly stormed off with him slung over her shoulder, her leather wings giving a strict flap. "What have I told you about leaving your Auntie Low be? Come, we're already late for dinner."

She hauled the whining child off as Vendy's face scrunched up in a pout and followed them away. Two others from our party, Linus and Matthiel, came from around a fountain and watched the three disappear into a tavern at the foot of the hill.

Linus hummed curiously. "She seems to be taking her new motherhood rather seriously, eh?"

Matthiel snorted. "A little too seriously, if you ask me. If she plans to adopt the urchin, I at least hope she's brought up the matter with Alexander."

Linus' head tilted as both men headed for the tavern themselves. "You don't think she has already?"

"Doubtful." Matthiel lifted his chin in a sniff. "I've known Alexander for some time. Had the subject been broached, we'd likely be hearing nothing but yelling from the both of them over…"

They descended the hill without noticing me. Which I didn't mind in the least.

I still wasn't comfortable around Linus. What he'd done in that prison when I first met him in Lindel was unforgivable. *But then… what Galden and his knights had done was also unforgivable.* The knights Linus killed that day may have very well committed crimes against the Death Laws as well. *But that still didn't give Linus the right to kill them.*

I sighed, head shaking. I supposed we *were* at war with Everland now. Things have been changing far too quickly for me to discern what was right anymore. It seemed there was nothing I could do but accept Linus's alliance… We've allied with stranger forces anyway.

Glancing left, I found our hooded shark man who was leaning against the tavern's wall, watching the crowd in silence. His pupils shined white under his hood, and wrapped in a cloth over his shoulder was a long, bulky object—which I knew was his Spiritcrystal-forged trident.

Hecrûshou was one of Marincia's Demon Kings. We'd met him on the now ruined island of Y'ahmelle Nayû, where he helped us fend off Cilia and her horde. He was now escorting us through our travels across the Flowering Trail in case Cilia decided to follow us, or if any other Necrofera decided to pay us a visit. I was still trying to wrap my head around him. We Reapers knew so little of their hierarchical societies. Interviewing Hecrûshou had certainly opened my eyes to an entirely new, hidden world I otherwise never would have learned of.

I rubbed my head, my hair still wet from the snowball Oliver had hit me with, and lowered myself onto a nearby bench. I watched as the others from our group came into the street and went into the tavern one by one, sometimes in pairs, sometimes in huddles of three or four. Ringëd was one of the last to trot into the tavern, seeming to have completed his task of seeing our refugees settled.

No one noticed me sitting here. Though, neither did I make a move to approach anyone. I hadn't been in much of a sociable mood as of late. With all the visions, the wars, the sinking feeling that we would meet Cilia again soon; Xavier constantly off with the Healers to oversee his physical therapy, and my

Bloody *Grandfather* traveling with us—physically with us!—for the first time since I've been born, I couldn't help but feel like I needed time to myself. Time to think, to assess our next move and our ever-thinning options. There seemed to be too much chaos in the world and not enough time to calm it.

I sighed, fox ears growing. But they perked when music began playing from a small group of bards near one of the beautiful ponds on the winding streets. The musicians were dressed in golden robes with high collars and fox-fur cowls. My brow furrowed at their attire, glancing around to see that most everyone was wearing similar golden garbs.

And now that I looked, it seemed the Marincian citizens were in an oddly cheery mood. But why? The types of songs the band was playing and this sort of clothing were only ever seen during…

I stiffened. Then quickly caught the shoulder of a passing local. "*Hol'loit?*" I asked the fish woman in her tongue. "<I'm afraid I've been out at sea for some time. My days have blended together. May I ask what day this is?>"

The woman's webbed ears flapped delightedly as she answered, "<Oh, little Grim one, poor thing! So far from home… you've come on a happy day. It's the 60th of Stoneheil. Remember to pay homage to Shel, little Grim one."

She smiled as she left, and I sat in shock. *Bloody Death! It's Rebirth Day?* Had I been on the surface for that long? *Oh, will I ever see the caves again…?*

A twitter came from the sky, and my tiny messenger crow, Jewel, fluttered to my extended finger. She chirped in a shiver, and I chuckled when she hopped to my shoulder to keep warm under my falsely grey hair—

"*Willow…*"

I halted, my lungs catching at the soothing voice that rang in my ears.

The world shifted and changed, the cold snow disappearing and replacing with ash. The island morphed into the Weeping Woods, the Willow of Ashes looming over me as its crystal leaves twinkled with the Requiem's melody.

"*It's time,*" Xavier whispered. "*Can you give the Call…?*"

—A hand clasped my shoulder and I jolted, barely stifling a yelp.

Xavier withdrew his hand and gave me a worried look. "Darling? Are you well?"

He was very thin, his long hair pulled back in a tail. The beard at his jaw was trimmed messily, but the veiling hairs helped his sunken face look less… well, *frail.*

"I…" My head raced to remember where I was—or rather, *when* I was. "I'm fine."

"Has the cold gotten to you?" His skinny fingers touched my brow, his face scrawled with concern. "Bloods, you're burning up." He turned to my two ghostly vassals who waited on either side of the bench. "Has she been acting ill today—?"

"I'm a Pyrovoker," I interrupted and peeled his hand away gently. I had to take care with him now, weak as he was. "Our body temperature is naturally higher than others. We've had this conversation before, mind you."

"When?" he grunted, sitting beside me on the bench and keeping his cane close at hand.

"Oh, I don't know," I said, thinking back. "Do you remember the time I..." I paused. "Oh... that's right. You wouldn't remember without your memories."

The hollow bags under Xavier's eyes darkened further. He hunched over in a long, fogged sigh. A lock of my long, disguised hair blew between us, and he lightly caught it between two fingers, his stare morose.

"First you tell me of the time I discovered your hair was made of ash," he began broodingly. "And now you tell me of a *new* time that I'm sure I don't remember either." He let the wind pull my hair free, and he cupped his hands. "Why must I always be *told* these stories of my own youth? Why can't I remember them myself? I thought..." He grimaced and fell silent, sitting back.

I placed a delicate hand on his boney shoulder, his thick coat not enough to hide his lack of muscle. "You thought what?"

"I thought once I found my body, the rest of my memories would return," he admitted, crossing his arms and yielding to a slight shiver. "Yet here I am: separated from Alex, my soul finally where it should be—but I'm no closer to remembering the past that was ripped from me." He kicked at the snow, the icy powder bursting onto the street.

I kept my tone calm. "They'll return when they return, Xavier. You cannot force it. They'll come when you're reminded of them... well, unless you *have* the memory in hand and a Somniovoker is around to give it to you."

His brow furrowed, turning to me with mismatched, questioning eyes. "Wait a moment. What of that first memory you brought when you surfaced to find me? The one of us in the palace orchards? Where did you get it again?"

I blinked. *That memory?* Bloods, it felt like ages since then, I'd all but forgotten. Between discovering Xavier and Alexander had been sharing the same body, fighting off Cilia and her hordes, watching Lindel be crushed to ruins by a colossal Stonedragon, Lilli and Jaq being locked in that desert prison, Xavier finding his body again—it was a wonder *he'd* remembered it.

"My grandfather gave it to me," I said, recalling. "He said he'd found it wandering in Aspirre..."

"—*Can you give the Call...?*"

My mind compressed, vision fuzzing.

Xavier's bearded face flickered beside me, the snow around us shifting between cold flakes of ice and warm specks of ash—

Xavier clasped my face, jerking the scenery into focus again. "Love?"

I blinked and pressed a finger against my throbbing temple. "Sorry, I… I suppose I'm not quite awake today."

"It was a vision, wasn't it?" he accused suspiciously. "I've caught your eyes drifting off like that all month. When do you plan to tell me what your Third Eye is showing you?"

The scene thrummed against my memory again, Xavier's older face waiting before the ancient Willow—

"It-it's nothing you ought to concern yourself with," I stammered, shaking the vision away again.

He folded a boney arm over the back of the bench and turned to me fully. "You know, Alex isn't here to overhear our conversations anymore. If something's bothering you, you're free to tell me. We can keep it between us."

"I know. But I…" My lips pursed. "Thank you, Xavier. But there are too many things happening, and I'm having some difficulty sorting through them."

"You don't have to sort through them alone," he said, his look almost pleading.

The vision came to mind again, my chest clenching. *It's time*, he'd said, *can you give the Call…?*

"It isn't your burden to bear," I whispered. Despite my natural heat, the frozen air cooled my skin anew, and I turned away to hide a shiver. "You have enough concerns of your own, Xavier. In the state you're in, you needn't take on mine."

He was silent beside to me. I peered over my shoulder and winced at his tight expression.

"Willow." His gaze had hardened suddenly, as though offended. "Is *the state I'm in* changing your mind about our union?"

I stared in shock at him. "Why would you ask such a thing?"

He leaned back on the bench and breathed out through his nose. "I'm little more than twigs right now, Willow. In a single instant, I went from 'trained Death Knight' to 'can't even piss without help'… And besides, I haven't had much chance to see you in weeks. The few times you're around, your mind is elsewhere. You haven't even worn your vines *once* since we left Y'ahmelle Nayû."

Oh. I supposed I'd been forgetting those lately. I hadn't thought there was much need to wear my engagement-vines on the ship. When we went to port, I simply forgot, having fallen out of habit.

As for distancing myself, I only wanted to give him space so he could focus during his therapy sessions. And then there were the war plans I had to review when Prince Cayden, Mother Alice or my father sent word to me overseas about the progress. I've been working, studying, training, plotting, strategizing, and playing diplomat almost non-stop all month. How much time in between had I seen Xavier? I couldn't count very many times... *Nira, have I been too distant?*

"Xavier." I clasped his spindly fingers. "I'm sorry. I haven't changed my mind. I've just been so busy... I'll try and see you more often on the ship. And I'll try to remember my vines."

He lifted an eyebrow. "And will you tell me what's wrong when your mind leaves the rest of us?"

"I'll... try," I offered.

He gave a sigh, then kissed my hand. "I suppose I'll have to take what I can—"

A soft chuckle came behind Xavier, and I only now noticed Grandfather Dream was standing there. How long had he been listening?

"I believe I know what's wrong." The young king gave that empty smile of his. "Don't worry, dear. We'll explain everything. Come along, now. We have a very long conversation ahead of us."

Xavier and I exchanged uncertain glances, then followed Grandfather down the snowy hill and into the tavern, the ghosts of Rossette and Nikolai trailing behind us.

4

XAVIER

The smoky tavern was brimming with boisterous locals as we made our way through the cramped aisles between tables.

The many eyes of these fish-shifters followed us as we passed, their webbed ears flicking in suspicion while still keeping conversation amongst their comrades. The fish-shifters' faces still looked humanoid, their noses defined with smooth, handsome crooks to them, but their scales were flatter than the reptile shifters, and they had a beautiful sheen to their tanned hues.

Marincians were said to be a sophisticated people, but I hadn't known the extent of that claim until now. Even with all the noise, there seemed to be a sense of refinement in their heightened voices; an elegance in their gestures, crude though they were. It seemed if there was one thing Marincians took pride in, it was how gracefully they could insult one another.

King Dream led us to a private room in the back of the tavern, drawing the seashell-curtain open to allow Willow and I entry before he let the shells fall back into place in a delicate clatter. Dream's soul-blind eyes hadn't noticed he'd closed the curtains on Rossette and Nikolai's ghosts, but the specters didn't seem to mind as they phased through the shells without complaint.

Alexander, with his left arm hung in a sling, was the first to straighten in his seat when we entered, his previous scowl softening at the sight of me. "There you are."

I was still growing accustomed to seeing my brother face-to-face again. Somehow, it felt unnatural. "I had a short doctor's appointment first," I said. "My apologies for keeping you all."

"At least you're here now." Alex pulled out the empty chair beside him. It was apparently mine.

Ringëd rose from his seat to help me set down my cane and led me to the chair, his feral ferret scuttling down from his shoulder to crawl onto the table, sniffing at the cooked sea-snails and oysters that waited in wooden bowls. Ringëd's wife, Mikani, was here as well alongside her father, Mr. Treble. Octavius and Neal sat beside him, arguing over elbowroom as their messengers, Shade and Ace, croaked irritably from their chair backs.

Ana and Kurrick sat in the middle of the long table nearest the curtain, the lion pair silent and brooding as always. Lilli sat at the corner of *our* side of the table, little Oliver in her lap. She, Zylveia, and El were having trouble feeding the boy a seaweed-salad, which he scrunched his nose at and made a disgusted face every time they brought the two-pronged fork to his mouth. Jaq sat to their left beside Alexander, snickering at the women's limited success.

Willow's two spectral vassals floated to the corner of the room behind Octavius and Neal. Linus, Vendy, and Matthiel were leaned against the wall, as there were no seats left for them.

I didn't see Dalen, nor Aiden, nor Nathaniel. A quick inquiry to Alex told me the three were out shopping for more supplies. Since this was our last stop before sailing to Marincia's capital, it was imperative that we stock up on the food and goods we'd drained during our latest voyage.

With the help of Alex and Ringëd, I lowered into my chair, prompting Jaq to nudge my boney arm with his elbow.

"Took ya long enough," Jaq grunted. His sandy hair had grown long during our time on the surface, and it fell to his neck in a shaggy tangle. "Can we get this started already? I'm sick of being kept in the dark about whatever's going on. These guys won't talk at all."

He was referring to Ana and Kurrick across from him. The crimson-eyed girl blushed at the mention and shrank in her seat, her knees pulled to her chest as her lion ears folded down and her tail curled at her bare feet. Kurrick only scowled at us, as per usual. Kurrick had distanced himself from Alexander and me over the last few weeks, but today he seemed especially closed-off.

Willow, seeing Lilli had reserved a seat for her, came around the other end of the table and sat beside the bat girl. But at the head of the table stood our scholarly host, Herrin, who rifled through a large stack of papers and muttered to himself in hastened breaths.

King Dream rounded the table toward Herrin, but the young king paused when he reached Ana. He placed a gentle hand on her shoulder. "Ah, Ana," he hushed with a smile. "Cheery birthday, my dear. I'm afraid we haven't been on land long enough for me to find a proper gift, but rest assured, I'll find something before we leave."

Willow's gaze grew curious at Ana. "It's your *rae'u shelic*?"

Ana's head ducked under her shoulders, her bronze face flushing pink as she nodded meekly.

Willow clasped her hands in delight. "Oh, what a lucky date to celebrate a *rae'u shelic*. Is it strange to share a Day of Birth with the lost ruler you wish were still alive?"

Ana's gaze flicked away, denying a reply. Kurrick's chest rose in a long breath as he folded his arms, seeming unsettled by Willow's question. Had they found it a slight on their belief? The way Willow had worded it *did* suggest she didn't believe the Relicblood of Land was still alive. I couldn't say I disagreed with her, but neither would I have implied as much in front of them. I'd have feared Kurrick would pound a hole in the table—or my skull.

Dream strode to the head of the table where Herrin was still shuffling through papers, oblivious to the rest of us.

Dream cleared his throat. "Herrin?"

The scholar jumped, his brown wings stretching in a start. "I—what?"

"Everyone is now present." Dream smiled his usual, detached smile. "We may begin."

Herrin's head snapped to Alex and me. He swallowed. "R-right! Okay... uhm—"

The seashell-curtain clattered open when a latecomer entered.

Bianca stepped in and let the curtain fall closed behind her in a noisy twinkle. Alex stiffened in his seat as she came to stand beside Matthiel and leaned against the wall, crossing her arms. She glared at Alex, snorted, then nodded at Herrin to signal she was ready for him to continue.

Herrin scratched his feathered hair and took a quick breath. "Okay. Good. So—uh, thanks for coming you guys."

"Why are we even here?" Neal questioned, pounding an impatient fist on the table as his messenger, Ace, picked at his master's untouched plate of cooked sea-snails. Ace decided he didn't like it either, apparently. "Spit it out already! We've been here long enough."

"Right." Herrin swept up his stack of papers, glancing at Alex and me. "Well, I'm going to tell you guys a story. It's one you've all probably heard. I'm going to start by telling you the version you know, and then I'll tell you the *real* version. The full one. So don't interrupt when I go through the beginning."

We all stared at him, skeptical as he cleared his throat and read from the pages before him. "Chapter One: The Children of the Relics'..."

THE CHILDREN OF THE RELICS

The time before the Relicbloods has been described as chaos.

All shifters within the five realms lived in constant fear of the demons that lurked about the lands. At the time, the shifters had no way to defend themselves, for no weapons existed that could kill the beasts. Be it wood, stone, or metal, the demons could not be stopped. This disaster had the Gods furious and heartbroken to see Their children slaughtered. They decided hence to share Their energy with us.

Since the only known way to kill the Necrofera was for another demon to rip out its heart, it was rare for a soul to return to Nira. But once a rotten soul was released, it dissipated into the Void to be Cleansed by the Goddess before She recycled its energy—this time, with a new gift to offer.

To these few souls, the Gods gifted a Blessing which allowed the soul to harness one elemental ability, referred to as the Hallows.

If a soul was given an element by Shel, that shifter would be given either the Hallows of rock, plant, or remedy.

Souls given an element by Ushar would possess the Hallows of wind, rain, or storms.

Rin would bestow the Hallows of ice, water, or pressure.

Iri passed on the Hallows of sleep, illusion, or prophecy.

And Nira spread the Hallows of death, fire, or infection.

Since the Hallows must be evoked from the soul, these Blessed shifters were known as Evocators. And now that the world had these Evocators, the shifters could ward off the demons. But to the Gods' dismay, these abilities were not enough to kill the creatures, unless one evoked the Hallows of infection.

The Pyrovokers, however, learned that a demon could be prevented if the corpse was burnt to ash and the bones were ground to sand. But this proved itself a difficult task. Every speck of muscle had to be burned; every brittle bone had to be crushed. And although it prevented the Change, no ghost appeared afterward, as we know would otherwise happen today. This had been a time before ghosts were discovered, all having been trapped in their corpses to rot or be imprisoned in ash. Historians today speculate the souls may remain trapped to this day.

A more reliable solution did not exist until one Necrovoker explored Grim's mines and discovered a mineral known as Spiritcrystal. This new crystal could touch a shifter's NecroSeam, yet not affect living or dead skin. The miner forged the crystal into scythes and distributed them across the realms. For the first time, ghosts began to appear from their corpses and live out their afterlives. Fewer demons were forming even though shifters were still being killed. These new weapons proved so successful, it was advised that every shifter possess one. But once the demons were no longer as great a threat as they'd been before, shifters began to misuse the Spiritcrystal scythes—and their Gods' Blessed Hallows.

Thus erupted the Great Wars, beginning the era known as The Time of Discord.

Everland's Terravokers began forming guilds of the strongest men who proclaimed themselves the protectors of their villages. At first, they carried out their duties justly, but their hearts soon darkened and they instead used their authority to gain temptation's desires. Women were raped, homes were pillaged, families were broken—greed was prosperous for those privileged with magic and crystal weapons.

Droughts were frequent and deadly, shifters driven hungry as locust and famine devastated the farmlands. The droughts were caused by the Sky realm's selfishness—the birds of Culatia so engrossed in their games that they did not realize they were stealing the moisture from the other realms' air and parching crops of much needed rain.

In a race to survive, the Everlanders were forced to steal from other farms to provide for their loved ones. But while they sought to pilfer crops, they were afraid of summoning Nira's wrath if they killed those they robbed. So, instead, many used the scythes to release a shifter's soul and avoid committing murder.

Day and night, shifters' NecroSeams were cut before their time, and many lay empty in the streets, their soulless bodies slowly wasting away.

During this hazardous time, the Sky realm worsened the already rampant horrors plaguing the Land realm with their dangerous games in the storms they created. Not only were they denying certain lands their rain, but the regions they doused were flooding by storms, desolating countless civilizations and drowning much of the populace.

But Everland was not the only realm victimized by Culatia's reckless games—Marincia's islands were disturbed with typhoons and unwanted currents caused by the harsh winds that destroyed their surfaced homes, their underwater caverns rattled below.

Fed up with the Sky realm's dangerous playing, the fish-shifters began a blood-lusting hunt for any Culatian they captured, seeking retribution for the lives their perilous tournaments had taken. Thus, war erupted between the Sky and Ocean realms, their battle sweeping the Land realm into further turmoil as tsunamis and hurricanes ravaged Everland's exposed shores.

However, while the three tangling realms were absorbed with their vengeful wars, each shared one common enemy; one that, much to their outrage, lived among thems in all realms.

Despite their hatred for their foreign adversaries, it was the Dream Walkers who dominated their ire.

Though no shifters were born within the Dream realm itself, those who evoked sleep Hallows were often used as spies by high officials and kings, and so a wide-spread distrust had already formed for the Somniovokers in each of the physical realms. Thus, out of great odium and fear, the Dream Walkers were killed on sight without trial.

This proved to be a terrible mistake.

Now, the shifters were in danger of having their souls die in their sleep. The goodhearted Somniovokers who were still alive formed guilds in secret, wanting to protect the defenseless dreamers, but knew they'd be slaughtered if caught.

As for the Death realm—though the Grimlings were hidden from the chaos above their caverns—they had their own horrors to survive. Whether it be the demons that came to eat their souls, those who reaped those souls before their time, the cataclysmic eruptions caused by the surface wars above them, the slaughtered Somniovokers who could not save everyone's dreaming souls, and the bands of Pyrovokers who scorched villages to ash, it seemed nothing would ease the Grimlings' suffering.

With such devastation suffocating the lands, the Gods decided order had to be set, else They watched Their world wither and die.

And so They created five new shifters, birthed by mortal mothers in each of the realms.

These were the Children of the Relics.

They were shifters borne with crowned marks who evoked all three of their realm's sacred Hallows.

For Everland, there came Land, a Golden Lion cub who emerged from his mother's womb beneath the colossal petals of the Blossom of Gold.

Culatia was given Sky, a Scarlet swallow who was hatched under the wing of the Phoenix of Scarlet.

Marincia had Ocean, an Emerald Seadragon who was born in the icy pools of the Pearl of Emerald.

Aspirre housed Dream, born encircled within the Orbs of Azure.

And Death was birthed within Grim under the weeping branches of the Willow of Ashes.

When the Relic Children were first discovered, they were seen as the chosen rulers of the realms, acknowledged for their crowned birthmarks and respected for their mastery of all three Hallows...

5

XAVIER

Herrin finished the opening chapter, and as he flipped through the stack of papers, I raised an eyebrow.

"We've already read this," I said. "I certainly didn't hear anything different."

"That's because there was nothing different," Alex snorted and stretched back in his seat. "Why are we really here, Herrin? You don't expect us to stay and listen to a *Choir* reading all day, do you?"

Herrin glared at us, his brown wings folding tight. "I'm getting to the different part. That was just the introduction."

We waited for him to find the page he searched for, and once he did, he grinned and snatched it up. "Here—this was one of the pages that survived the water damage from the original text. This is a later chapter."

Alex and I stared at the wrinkled paper. Depicted there was a young man's image—a shadow-haired figure with two sapphire eyes, and two marks of black diamonds below his knuckles on either hand. This was the picture that eerily resembled Alex and me, had we been born as one person. We'd seen it on the ship a month ago, before Kurrick callously tossed it in the ocean and destroyed most of its contents. I'd nearly forgotten about it after all that had happened afterward.

"This," Herrin said and pointed to the unnerving picture, "is *The Legend of the Shadowblood.*"

Alexander muttered, "And that's supposed to be some mixed version of us, is it?"

"Er, yeah, actually." Herrin shrugged. "Sort of."

My brother picked at his half-eaten snail dish, propping his cleanly shaven chin up with a fist. "And how do we know you didn't sketch that yourself?"

"Actually," King Dream interjected behind Herrin, "I painted it sometime around my... oh, what was it, my seventeenth year? Or was it one hundredth?"

All heads turned to the azure haired boy. Willow was the first to protest. "You couldn't have painted them *thousands* of years before they were born, Grandfather."

"I did my best." Dream sounded affronted. "It's not as if I expected them to be twins."

I rubbed my eyes. "You're not making sense."

Dream clicked his tongue, glancing helplessly at Herrin. "You see? I never know what to say. How do I explain these things? It's all here in my head, yet for some reason, it becomes tangled and knotted by the time it tumbles off my tongue."

"That's because you've got too many timelines crammed in there," reasoned Herrin. "But you have to remember that we don't know everything you do. We haven't lived that long, and we don't see multiple versions of the future on a daily basis, so we only understand things that've happened within an isolated period of time. See, I was thinking of skipping the featured chronicles of you and the other Relic Children and starting with—"

"Will someone get to the Bloody point already?" Alex snapped.

Herrin straightened and cleared his throat. "R-right. Well, the next few chapters are... sort of... about you two."

We waited for him to expound, and his lips pressed into a line. "See, when the Relic Children were born, one of them—"

"Me," Dream added cheerfully.

Herrin went on as if Dream hadn't interrupted. "... had a recurring vision. A bad one. It told of the downfall of the Relic Bloodlines... and it told of the End."

I pressed. "The end of—?"

"*Hol'loit!*" a spritely, scaled waitress exclaimed when she drew back the clattering curtain of our room and peeked inside. "Eez much good for now time, *Rouluêzi?* Needing *ze bevruji?*"

I waved her off, some of our group shaking their heads and others Deathly silent. The waitress kept her pleasant smile regardless. "Ah, eez good to hear! Call if needing somzing, zank you!"

She let the seashell curtain fall when she disappeared, and I heard her muttering in Marincian, questioning why she always got the tiny-brained foreigners.

I turned back to Herrin, keeping my voice down this time since the intrusion was a reminder that we weren't alone in this tavern. "What do you mean the end? The end of what?"

Herrin shrugged. "*The* End. Of everything. Life, death, *existence*."

"And just how would that happen?" Alex asked doubtfully.

"It will be brought by the Lightcaster," Herrin explained, providing zero context of what that entailed.

"The what?" Alex and I asked in unison.

"The Lightcaster," Dream repeated in Herrin's stead, sliding out a different drawing from the stack of papers.

My brow furrowed at the new picture. This one was of a man barely older than us, with bronzed scales and long fangs. It looked almost like... *Macarius?* But his hair and eyes were awash with different, patched colors.

Dream's eyes grew distant at the picture. I almost thought he'd decided to remain quiet until he said, "When I was very young, I'd Seen a number of visions. Being but a child, I hadn't known what they meant. The most frequent was of one man whose hair and eyes were patched in many colors. At the time, I couldn't be sure who it was. But I see you've already recognized him."

Willow interjected. "But who *is* the Lightcaster? Who is Macarius?"

"Macar..." Dream cast down his gaze, seeming to remember where he was. "He's proclaimed himself the Lightcaster. He will be the one to bring the End, according to the foretelling."

My stare flattened. "What foretelling?"

"*One will save,*" Dream recited. "*One will ruin. One will defend, or cometh the true End.* These are the words Iri has hissed in my dreams for the past two thousand years. The ones who will save and defend are the Shadowblood. At the time, I questioned the double mention, but when I discovered there were two of you, that part became clear. The one who will ruin, as you've probably guessed, is the Lightcaster."

"But how will he ruin?" I asked. "And how are you sure it was really Iri speaking with you? Many oracles have had prophecies, who's to say yours was really given by the Time God?"

Dream's brow cocked. "Considering Iri is called my Soul Father by quite literally every Harmonist on the planet, I'm genuinely surprised you're questioning me on this."

I pursed my lips, seeing his point.

"Regardless," he continued, "the words are true. I've Seen the visions. The Lightcaster will kill us. All the Relicbloods will fall—Rojired, Zylveia, myself... Willow." He flicked a sharp glance at his granddaughter. "Macar will kill us to gain his Blessings. And then once he has them, everything will End. He'll create Sanctuary, and that will be that."

Alex groaned, rubbing his face. "You've stopped making sense again. What is Sanctuary?"

"Sanctuary is what Macar hopes to build. It is his utopia in Aspirre, absent of time and will be, he believes, a safehouse that will protect us from the imminent calamity."

Alex rolled an impatient hand in the air. "And this is terrible because…?"

Dream gave a thin smile. "I'm not sure."

We both stared at him. "You're 'not sure'?"

"My visions only ever showed the Lightcaster cloaking the world in a blinding flash and then… nothing." His fanned his hand out to give a visual. "Everything Ends there. Why or how, I can't be sure. But each possible timeline leading up to it ends the same. With nothing. Only *one* possible route is the one with any future left in it."

"And that's the one where you kill the Lightcaster," Herrin finished, dangling the page with that eerie picture of us on it. "Or, *both* of you, I guess. I don't think you were supposed to be twins."

My fingers drummed over the table, stomach churning with a disturbing weight as I slowly processed all this. "So," I said, my tone gritty. "You want us to kill Macarius?"

"Yeah," Herrin shrugged. "That's the idea."

"Mm hmm. And, er, *why*? Can't anyone kill him?"

"You guys are the Shadowblood," said Herrin simply. "Opposite of the Lightcaster. He gets his Blessings by different means than you."

"What Bloody…" Alex hit a fist on the table. "Blessings?! Different means?! Blast it, you keep saying these things, but you've yet to explain any of it!"

"Well." Herrin sucked in a breath. "You know how people say that the Relicbloods' gifts—their combined set of Hallows—can't be transferred or given to anyone outside the Bloodlines?"

Zylveia's red wings fluffed at that. "Ees because this ees the true thing. Transfer no possible otherwise."

"Actually," Herrin contradicted. "Er, Your Highness Sky… those from *your* Bloodline aren't the original descendants of Sky."

Zyl's head lifted, befuddled. "What you mean, book-bug?"

Herrin ignored the insulting nickname she'd given him, though his nose crinkled. Then he circled a finger in the air. "Haven't you ever wondered why the God of thrill is a Skydragon, but his 'son' was a swallow? Well, that's because Ushar's son wasn't a swallow. Sky was a *dragon*, according to the original text. When I asked Dream about it, he said some things happened with the original Bloodline, the last king was challenged then defeated, and the power was transferred to the winner of the duel—who was a swallow shifter."

Zyl's scarlet eyes widened. "I never be hearing of this thing! You being sure, book-bug? What proof?"

Dream lifted a hand. "I was there for the transfer myself. Actually, not only me. Willow was…" His hand waved toward Willow, yet he stopped himself midway. Willow frowned at him, puzzled, and Dream seemed to realize something and began again with a new breath. "The last king of Sky's original Bloodline was… less than sane, to put it lightly. I suspected there'd been a bit of inbreeding, and the result was a madman on the throne. He implemented insane laws throughout Culatia, caused terrible disasters with the storms he created, forced his people to fight to the death *within* those storms for his enjoyment…" Dream grimaced and shook his head. "Needless to say, his subjects were furious. Zylveia, the day your ancestor challenged Sky's Bloodline and stole the throne, the Culatians worshiped him. It was the dawn of a new era, where the storms were once again tamed and the games regained their thrill. They wanted to forget the dark days and erase the royal dragons from history altogether. And thus began *The Choir's* first revisions."

"But…" Willow looked bewildered. "How did the swallow gain Sky's Hallows? Just by winning a duel? That Kael man supposedly killed *Land's* Relicblood, and he clearly hadn't gained the magic. He's still just an Infeciovoker."

"Ah, but Kael hadn't killed the king in front of Land's Relic," Dream said. For a moment, I thought I saw his eyes flick to Ana. The girl's head ducked solemnly in silence while Dream closed his eyes and went on. "You see, when the challenging swallow killed the dragon king, the Phoenix of Scarlet had been watching."

I frowned. "He'd found the lost Relic of Sky?"

"At the time, the Relics weren't lost. And strictly speaking, they still aren't today."

"*Grandfather*," Willow hissed and rose from her seat, aghast. "We aren't to speak of such things—"

"It's all right, Willow." Dream waved her down. "I appreciate your discretion, but there's no longer a need for it. It was I who told the Bloodlines to keep the Relics hidden. Now, I'm giving permission to make them known again—at least, to those currently present."

Both Willow and Zylveia looked dumbfounded.

"Let me explain," said Dream. "Zylveia, the moment your ancestor discovered the secret to transferring a Relicblood's power, I realized this was how the Lightcaster would gain *his* Blessings. All he had to do was take a member of the Bloodline to their corresponding Relics, shed blood, and the Relic would give the Lightcaster his own magic. This could be done with all the Bloodlines until he gained all fifteen elements of Hallows."

"All fifteen?" I echoed, skeptical. "Impossible. One man couldn't handle that many elements at once."

"He wouldn't have the stamina to evoke them all," Willow agreed. "I have six, and I'm terrible at over half of them."

Dream's head wavered. "Well, dear, don't take this personally, but your stamina isn't... well, it isn't anywhere near Macar's level. I've never in two-thousand years met a man with as much Hallows' potency. He is, opinion discarded, a prodigy of Somnio and Decepiovoking—and I don't doubt he could make balancing fifteen elements look like child's play, given time to prepare."

Willow's glare narrowed at her grandfather. Despite his warning, she very clearly *had* taken it personally.

"In any case," continued Dream as he tiredly rubbed his forehead, where his crowned Dream mark was displayed, "once I learned how power could be transferred, I'd hoped to prevent the Lightcaster's coming by hiding the Relics from the public. With time, only the Relicbloods knew of them."

Alex and I exchanged sidelong glances, and we turned to Willow. Her stare edged at us.

"Willow?" I began, suspicious. "Had *you* known of this?"

Her fox ears grew, tone guarded. "It's... forbidden to speak of the Relics," she said at last, a begrudged glare shooting at her Grandfather.

"And our marks?" My teeth sharpened, throat rumbling angrily. *Even after what we'd talked about,* I thought bitterly, *she's still keeping things from me? Doesn't she trust me?* "Do you also know why our marks reacted to the Willow like this?" I demanded and lifted my left hand to show her the Crest, which had been gleaming the whole time—as it often did when around King Dream. "The music your amulet plays is the same song the Willow chimes. That's where the Requiem comes from, isn't it?"

"How do you know of...?" Willow sounded horrified. "I've never mentioned any of this!"

"We've been to the Willow," Alex said. "Our marks led us there the night Xavier disappeared."

"But you couldn't have!" She gawked at me, holding shocked fingers to her lips. "I... Why hadn't you *said* anything?"

I snorted. "Funny. I was about to ask you the very same thing."

She matched my pointed glare. Why did she look angry? I wasn't the one keeping things from her.

Alex gave me a questioning look and awkwardly tried to fix my answer for the both of us. "We never had time to tell anyone." He leaned back in his seat and adjusted the straps on his sling. "When we returned to the palace, it was already in flames and... well, you know the rest."

Dream seemed confused for a moment, holding up an uncertain finger. "You've already been to the Willow of Ashes?"

"Yes," Alex and I answered in unison.

"What happened when you stood before it?" Dream leaned closer now, and we promptly drew back at his suddenly intense stare.

"Er..." Alex squirmed. "Well... nothing. Our marks only led us there."

"But finding a supposedly 'Lost' Relic of legend was pretty impressive, I think," I added. "Not that I remember actually being there yet. I only have memories before and after."

Dream's tongue clicked. "Then you didn't gain those Blessings so early..." His hands pressed against the table beside Herrin, slumping over in thought. "I'd hoped the process would be as simple as simply being *taken* there, but... well, I suppose it never worked with the Orbs, either, had it?"

Herrin's face drained at him. "You don't know how to give it to them?"

"I'd never Seen how," Dream lamented. "I only Saw them at the Relics. But, then... perhaps..." He slid a hand into his billowing sleeves and pulled out three glittering, blue globes. "I haven't tried *this* yet, have I?"

Alex and I stared at the beautiful orbs. They had a strange glimmer to them, deep and vibrant, the faint swirl of misty clouds storming within. When Dream held them out, our marks' constant glow brightened.

"What are those?" I asked, mesmerized by their beauty.

"The Relic of Aspirre." Dream kept a close watch on our marks. "These are the Orbs of Azure. But how to go about it? Mentally thinking it doesn't seem to be working... perhaps aloud then?"

We stared at him as everyone else marveled at our glowing marks. Dream seemed to come to a silent conclusion and pounded once on the table, straightening. "Right then. No harm in trying." He cleared his throat.

Then began to sing.

Sleep
Dreamest thou of me

It was a slow, wavering lullaby, the notes drifting and gliding along with Dream's wavering head.

Breathe
Mine ears beg thee to sing
May 'ere mares be repelled from thee
Pray, sleep
And dreamest thou of me

One of the Orbs began to pulse with light.

Drink
Ye faerie the river's mead
Sweet
And cherished thou shalt be

The single orb flashed into a solid glow.

Let morning sleep till moonlight flees
Pray, Drink
Ye faerie the river's mead

—the left diamond of my Crest shifted blue, making me yelp and stumble from my seat. Alex shot out of his chair in shock, his own Crest brightening azure on the same left diamond.

Dream's lips stretched into a grin, and he held the Orbs closer to us. My brother and I shuffled back against the wall, I on the floor and Alex standing above me in bewilderment.

Weep
Ne'er for the ones who bleed
Sweep
Thine tears how fierce they cling
May lashes free such ill tidings
Pray, weep
Ne'er for the ones who bleed

Another globe solidified with light, and my Crest's *right* diamond shifted blue—as did Alexander's.

The rest of our company rose from their own seats and backed away. Willow crouched beside me with splintered eyes. "G-grandfather!" Her voice shook. "Stop...! Whatever you're doing—!"

Sleep
Dreamest thou of me
Breathe
Mine ears beg thee to sing
May 'ere mares be repelled from thee
Pray, sleep

Willow lunged for Dream in a panic. "Grandfather—!"

And dreamest thou of me...

The final, middle orb glittered and cast the room in a blinding white light. "GRANDFATH—!"

6

XAVIER

~~~~~~~~~~

Screaming…

All I could hear was screaming…

My eyes cracked open. I was lying on a rocky terrain. Outside. The tavern had disappeared.

Where was I?

Pushing up, I heard Alexander grunt to my right.

The screams echoed all around us. The sky above was… shattering? Yes, *shattering*, fracturing with thin lines, the fragile shards raining down like glass as tremors ruptured the ground, the world trembling. From the cracking sky, black, sand-like beasts poured down, piling on the ground below and taking ever-shifting forms.

Noctis Golems? These were the demons of Aspirre, weren't they? Our Dreamcatchers had explained as much some months ago… *Months?* Why had that seemed wrong? Somehow, it felt like years since I'd first learned of the golems. *Many* years…

The golems blanketed the landscape, swallowing and clouding anyone who dared to breathe in their presence.

I stumbled to my feet—but stopped cold.

I could walk. Easily. My limbs weren't thin and weak, but well filled and strong. My surprise only lasted several fleeting seconds, then quickly drained away until I… until I…

What had I been surprised about?

"Xavier!" A strained voice called behind, tearing my attention back to the chaos.

Willow was running toward me across the broken cobblestones. She seemed… older, somehow. She had silver wedding-vines clipped to her ashen hair, connected at the brow by a diamond droplet. The image itself seemed faint. It was visible, yet somehow translucent and blurry.

"Willow," I breathed in relief, rushing to meet my wife halfway—

I skidded to a halt, bemused. *Wife?* When had we wed? I… why couldn't I remember our…?

"Xavier!" Willow shouted, panting for breath. "Xavier, you must hurry—!" she choked into silence.

Her lips parted, a small breath escaping as she tried to speak, though it was only silence. A line of red peeled across her throat. The line thickened and began to drip with a dark, sticky ooze.

Blood leaked from her lips, and she fell into my arms, her hair flaring around us.

My heart screamed. "*Willow!*" I collapsed to my knees as she dropped, and I desperately kept her head cradled to my chest, clasping her face, the luster fading from her gaze—

She vanished from my arms, like a bubble popping from the breath of a whisper.

The world fuzzed, flickering for a moment. When it solidified again, the terrain had changed. I was in some sort of arena. A colosseum in Grim.

The sky was still broken and shattered, black patches blotting out sections of Grim's clouds, like a glass painting that had been fractured and its pieces had fallen out.

The Noctis Golems poured in from the broken fragments once more, tearing through the screaming mass of shifters who disappeared down the beasts' sandy throats.

Shaking, I scuttled backward—and my hand touched something.

I twisted and found my fingers had brushed someone's boot. It belonged to a blonde, scaled figure lying next to me. The figure was limp and slumped over his stomach.

"Jaq?" I called hesitantly, reaching for his shoulder. "Jaq, what is going on? Where are…"

I rolled him over. At Jaq's temple was a large, wet gash, his black eyes stale and hollow.

"Z-z-z…" Alexander's voice suddenly shivered from behind me. "Xavier…?"

My brother had moved from the last place I'd seen him. Now he was some feet away and clutching the rabbit-eared corpse of Bianca in his arms. His cheeks were wet with tears, a straggled noise squeezing from his tightened throat.

There were *several* corpses cluttered around us. All were familiar. One was Octavius… and Lilli, Matthiel…

Alex looked sick, pulling Bianca's corpse tight against his body. The gushing hole where her eye had been stained his silver, captain's armor he was suddenly wearing. "Wh-wh…" His lungs quivered, gasping in a sob. "What is this…?"

A sudden lance of ice shot past my head—and plunged into Alexander's chest.

He gave a pained, shocked gurgle—my own chest exploding in a phantom agony alongside his. My brother's grip loosened around Bianca, and he collapsed beside her.

"Alex!" I lunged out to grab him—but something drove into my back, piercing out from my sternum. I sprawled over the ground, coughing blood. My cheek stuck to the wet ground as I wheezed for breath that wouldn't come.

Looming over me was a man with patched hair, colored in red, gold, green and white; his eyes were splotched similarly. *I know that face…* The scaled man smiled, his fangs unfolding and dripping with satisfied venom.

Macarius slid the sword from my back, raised it… then thrust it over my neck.

… you can change it…

The child's whisper echoed in the abyss. A faint, blue glow radiated from a misting fox that sat poised before me, its long tail wavering at its hazy paws.

Take my Blessings, it said.
Use them wisely…

"… have you *done*, Grandfather?!" Willow was shrieking above me as I came to.

The ringing voices were dim, but they slowly shifted into focus as the tavern's room dripped into view.

Willow was absolutely livid, holding a hand to my head as she glared up at King Dream. "Telling them about the Relics is one thing, but giving the Call in front of everyone here? What have you done to them?"

My throat cracked a grunt as I pushed upright. Just as I raised a hand to my throbbing head, I caught a glimpse of my Crest.

It had changed.

The three black diamonds were now azure, with two sharp arrows encasing them, a crown resting above it. The Dream mark faded almost the second I beheld it, and soon the Crest returned to its normal, blackened state.

"What in Void…" I breathed, my throat sore.

"…was that?" came Alex's equally stunned voice beside me. He was sitting against the wall and staring at his own Crest.

Something felt different. Something felt… *full.* Just a little more than normal.

"Thank the Goddess!" Willow squeezed the air from my lungs in relief. "Are you all right, darling?"

The image of her throat pouring with blood came to mind, and I grew sick, pushing her at arm's length. "I-I'm… fine." I forced back the memory. *Was* it a memory? I clutched my still blistering head. "What happened?"

Bianca shoved her way through the crowd and came to check both my and Alexander's pulses at our necks.

—My point of view shifted. She was reading from a medical text., studying the pictures that described how to check the pulse of an unconscious patient and where such points could be located on shifter anatomy—

I blinked, and the room returned, my eyes feeling unfocused and stale. What in Void was that?

Alex let out a holler next to me and shoved Bianca back.

Everyone stared at him.

"Alex?" the rabbit asked carefully, looking at me as well. I tried to banish the memory of Bianca's gouged-out eye staining Alexander's armor, but it burned back to mind with every blink. "Guys?" Bianca tried again, waving her hands at us. "How many fingers am I holding up?"

She held three fingers up for me, and two for Alexander. We answered accordingly, though our voices were faint.

"What happened?" Willow asked and put a gentle hand on my arm.

—Pain flared at her knee, cursing in Grimish, not caring that her father was watching.

"You mustn't let your focus stray, Willow," her father advised, picking up the wooden scythe she'd dropped and handed it back to me—to her. "Steady your emotions. The moment they falter in battle is the moment you've lost control. Let the scythe bend with you, it is an extension of yourself—

I shook my head, regaining my perspective and blinking hard.

Willow's hand was still on my arm, and when I swayed, she steadied me and scowled up at Dream. "What did you do, Grandfather?"

Dream's smile was excitedly wide, for once looking genuine. "Hopefully, what I had meant to do." He crouched before Alex and me, inspecting us. "How do you feel?"

"A… a bit…" I began, searching for the right words.

"… different," Alex finished, rubbing his chest.

"And the Crests stopped glowing around the Orbs," Dream noted curiously as we pushed to our feet, Willow handing me my cane. "That must mean the reserves have been filled…" He paused when he saw Alex was rubbing his eyes. "Something wrong, Alexander?"

"I…" Alex sounded unsure. "Will everyone be quiet? I can't hear myself think…"

Concerned glances were exchanged around the room. I answered him, "No one's said any—"

"Stop," he barked, shoving everyone aside as he drifted forward. "Just Bloody stop…!"

He stormed to the clattering curtain, but the waitress from before came inside and blocked his way. "*Hol'loit!*" she greeted. "You be needing of ze—?"

He shoved past her, his hand brushing over the waitress's scaled shoulder. She dropped to the floor.

Alex flinched back in a yelp. He stared in horror at the woman now lying on the floor, motionless, the hand that had touched her trembling.

Alexander's glare was petrified at Dream. "What did you do to us?!"

"Be calm!" Dream waved his hands in a pacifying motion. "She's only asleep! You'll have to learn how to control it—"

"Control what?!" My brother's eyes glazed as if looking somewhere else, flicking every which way as his breathing grew ragged. He clutched his grown wolf ears and shook his head. "Shut up, shut *up*…! Everyone shut the Void up! I can't…"

"Alex?" I clipped over to him with my cane, but he jerked away, shaking. His eyes were wide and wild. My brow furrowed. "Alex, what is it? No one's said anything—"

"I-I can't… see…" When he finally focused on Dream, his teeth sharpened. "I don't want to hear it, bastard! Go tell your prophecy to someone who gives a damn!" Alex stormed out.

Lilli was quick to rush after him, but I stayed behind, staring at the slumbering waitress on the floor. The others were staring along with me, murmuring amongst themselves.

Dream sighed and absently took an oyster from his plate, sucking it out with a wet slurp and muttered under his breath, "Blast, already so strong… This will not be easy."

I stammered. "Is she… is she really asleep?"

Dream *slurped* another oyster, answering. "Either that, or she's dead. I highly doubt the latter."

I knelt to the waitress, prodding her with a hesitant hand. "Miss…?" I whispered.

There was no reply. Only gentle breaths.

Had Alex really done this? I wouldn't have believed it, if I hadn't seen it myself. *Death…* I clasped a hand on the waitress's arm. "*Sefwit? Dan'tam…*"

Something fuzzed in my chest like cotton. The sudden fluff poured down my veins and leaked out my fingers in the form of blue lights. The Dream mark reappeared under my knuckles. The lights sank into the woman's scales, and moments after, her lashes fluttered open. She frowned when noticing she was on the floor and pushed up, clutching her head and gazing round the room of aghast faces.

My hand recoiled, and I jolted to my feet. "Wh… what did I just…?"

Dream hummed. "So, that's how it is, eh… Right then. Come, we ought to fetch your brother before he drives himself mad." He grabbed my arm and pulled me outside—

"What is that?" a child questioned in fright, shivering as he clung to the skirts of a tall woman.

The point of view was through the boy's eyes. He was so short, the woman beside him loomed over him like a magnificent tree. He barely reached her waist.

The child stared at a gleaming speck of light that was falling gently to the ground. The woman chuckled and bent to pick the lad up, her long white hair draping to the cobblestones. His chilled skin was soothed by her warmth, as though heat radiated from her very soul.

"That," said the woman as she hefted him, "is a Fallen Light, Dream. Pray tell, is this your first visit to my caves?"

He was too bashful to admit this was his first time 'out' since he could remember. Already fifteen, and how had he spent his years? Hiding in Aspirre, obscured in secrecy from the shifters whom his Dreamcatchers had called his 'siblings'… Not that he'd minded hiding his existence. Void, if his knights weren't hunted, killed, and run out of the kingdoms, he would be hiding yet. The physical realms were so unknown… so frightening. But he had to save his Catchers from extinction. Speaking with his so-called siblings seemed the only way.

"It's quite all right, Dream," said the woman. "I admit I have yet to visit your own realm, exempting slumber. Here." She shifted her hold of him and leaned him outward as the Falling Light glittered down. "Catch it."

Dream hesitated, cupping his hands and holding them out for the light. He shut his eyes and cringed, feeling a soft chill hit his palms. He peeked open an eye. The ball of light hovered there, a fog hazing around it.

"It's so cold," he whispered, fascinated.

The woman hummed. "The lights are what keep my caverns cold. It's speculated that Grim would be overheated without them."

Dream marveled at the glowing wisp in his hands. "I... never knew the real world could be so... beautiful..."

"Would you fancy to keep it?"

Dream's lungs filled with delight. "Can I bring it to Aspirre?"

"If you wish." She chuckled. "Though, I cannot speak for how long it will remain lit. They fade over time. But why don't we fetch a lantern to house it? My gift to you, my dear, little, older brother."

A gift. His first gift, from the physical plane. He smiled and pressed the wisp to his chest, ignoring the cold it brought him. "Thank you, Death... No." He peered up at her through a veil of tears. "Sister..."

The scene faded.

My eyes refocused to my own perspective, making me feel cross-eyed for a time. It didn't take me long to realize I was outside in the snow. Someone was clutching my arm and dragging me forward. It was Dream. The *older* Dream.

He was looking this way and that, muttering under his breath about finding my brother.

What in Death had I just seen...?

"Ah!" Dream exclaimed, his feet leaving prints in the snow until he stopped beside Alexander, who was crouched before a wall, facing away from us and panting heavily over his knees. Lilli crouched beside him, hovering a hand over his back, but not touching.

She glanced up at me helplessly. "I-I don't know what's wrong," the bat stammered. "He doesn't want me to touch him."

I wobbled with my cane and lowered next to him. "Alex?" I laid a hand on his back.

"—Alexander." An old professor at the academy flapped Alex and my test papers in front of us. "You are right handed, and so you write with a forward slant." He glanced away from me—from Alex—to look at Xavier... at me... though, I wasn't looking through my own view. "Xavier, you are left handed, and write with a straight slant."

The professor set both of our exams on our desks with a resounding thump. "Half of these answers are written in a straight slant, and half with a forward slant. You both have been swapping tests when you get to an answer you don't know. This is cheating, boys—"

Alex shoved me back with such ferocity, I lost hold of my cane and fell to the snow, my clothes getting soaked. He shivered as he glared at me, looking traumatized.

"Did you see...?" he choked.

"I... I remember that." I shivered myself, but mostly because I was thrown in the wet snow. "But it was different. *I* was..."

I was looking at myself, in that memory, I realized. *It was all wrong.*

Dream knelt between us. "You're Seeing visions through others' eyes. No need for alarm."

"There is *great* need for it!" Alex growled, clutching his knees to his chest. "I want it gone! I want it all gone, their emotions, their sight, their thoughts…! Gods, make it stop…!" He hunched over and groaned as if in pain.

Dream tapped a finger to his chin. "The Hallows must be bursting out from the sudden release. Like a drain freed of a blockage… I suspect it will settle over time." His gaze flicked to me. "Xavier? What are you Seeing with your visions?"

"Visions…" The word felt numb over my tongue. It sounded wrong. But then, what else could I have been seeing?

I watched my brother tremble in the snow, not sure what to do. Whatever he was Seeing, it was different from me, otherwise I would be just as shaken. I unwrapped my cloak and laid it over him, hoping the extra layer would help quell the tremors. Touching him, it seemed, would only make it worse for both of us.

"I don't know," I told Dream, pausing when remembering the scene in Grim I'd witnessed with him moments before this. I started again. "Did you… catch a Fallen Light with Death when you were young? Your first gift from this plane?"

Dream fell silent. I could tell a thought was streaming through his mind, but it flew by so fast, barely a few seconds passed before he shuffled away from me and murmured, "Past assigned to *you*… noted."

He took Alexander's arm and hefted him over his shoulders. My brother flinched at the unwanted touch, but was shivering too profusely to push Dream away.

"Come along," Dream grunted under my brother's weight. The lanky king didn't seem to have the strength to hold him for very long. "Let's finish this discussion over a fire, shall we?"

7

XAVIER

～∞～

"Well?" Jaq questioned, pushing his scaled finger over a piqued Alexander's brow.

Alex muttered. "You're thinking I need a shower."

"And?"

"And… I'm not saying the rest, Jaq."

"Come on," Jaq egged. "How do I know ya didn't just guess that? Gotta hear the rest of it, to be sure ya ain't fakin'."

Alex sighed and closed his eyes, adding in a grumble, "And I smell like sweaty, feral dingo balls."

Jaq heckled and slapped his knee. "You said it, not me!" He took a moment to laugh before finishing with a grinning sniff, and he rubbed his nose. "Death, guess ya really do have a new element."

"They have three new elements, actually," Herrin corrected as he spread his papers over the ship's hardwood floor, the pages lightened by the hearth we all surrounded.

We'd relocated back to our ship at the docks, those from the tavern surrounding us around the hearth. Herrin was sandwiched between our two rabbit girls: Bianca scribbling notes of her own and glancing over the hawk's shoulder as he gathered his papers and documents, and Vendy lying on her stomach and pinching each leaf of paper by the corner in inspection, squinting a confused eye at them as if determining whether or not they had mold.

Lilli and Oliver lounged in an indigo chaise, Matthiel in the cushioned chair beside them. Neal, Octavius, and Dalen had their backs against the wall while Ringëd and his wife sat cross-legged on the soft rug, and Claude leaned against a nearby work desk.

Herrin had trouble keeping his wings from flapping in excitement and blowing his carefully placed papers away from him. They also blew Vendy's long braid into her face and caused her to spit out the hairs ruefully. When Herrin gathered his papers again, he said, "Supposedly, they have *all* of Dream's Hallows now."

"Indeed they do," agreed Dream in a trilling chuckle. Blast it, the man was thousands of years old, yet he was lying on his stomach and kicking his feet in the air like a child. "The only gifts we haven't tested yet are weaving objects in Aspirre and Decepiovoking. But this can come later."

I sat beside Willow, staring at the Crest on my knuckles. "So…" I began, "you think we can suddenly muster new elements?"

"I don't think," he said. "Can't you feel the change? Feel that somewhere within you, new wells have been filled?"

I did feel it. It was strange and warm in my chest, a new cottony fuzz waiting to be released. Chai rested on the floor at my stretched feet, and he lowered his head onto my boot, his wings fidgeting.

I stared at my Crest again. *Was this the reason Alex and I weren't given normal Death marks?*

"It would explain why our Crests change," I said. "But why is this happening at all?"

"And how do we get rid of it?" asked Alex desperately.

Dream only smiled. "You can't. Once you've gained the elements, they will stay with you. You'll gain the rest as we go along."

Willow reached for my hand, but I quickly moved it away before she touched. She seemed affronted, retracting her hand with a wounded expression.

I cleared my throat. "Perhaps not this moment, love… at least until I know I'm not going to See anything with everyone I touch?"

She glared at me. "You can't honestly expect me to believe you're Seeing visions?"

I scratched my neck. "I don't know what else it could be."

"Necrovokers don't suddenly become Seers in the blink of an eye!" She rose in a fury, her fox ears growing. "It isn't possible! You're only hallucinating, something in those sea-snails you ate must have poisoned you."

"When you were a little girl," I said, keeping my voice soft. "You hit your knee with a practice scythe and dropped it. Your father picked it up and said if you allowed your focus to wander in battle, you'll have already lost."

Her stance faltered. "I haven't dropped a scythe since I was seven…" She squeezed her eyes shut. "I must have told you that story and forgotten."

"Your grandfather's first gift from Death was a Fallen Light."

"Yes, he's told me that story as well."

"No one told…" I sucked in a breath, calming. Then I offered her my hand. "Just this once. Think of a memory. Something that you've never told to anyone. Not a single soul."

She didn't give me her hand right away, staring at my fingers as if they would rip it off her wrist.

"Please?" I whispered.

She clenched her jaw, indignant… but she sighed and finally took my palm.

… What was she doing?

She sat huddled against the alley's cool brick wall, thankful the darkness hid her from the stray wanderers on the streets. She'd only packed a few belongings, no one but Jewel to accompany her. She'd barely made it past the palace gates before realizing how stupid her plan had been.

Perhaps Lilli had been right; even if he was still out there, staying here would be wisest. She bit back her tears, clutching her chest as if to squeeze the burning knot out of existence, and started back toward the palace. He knew where to find her. She only had to wait a short time…

The scene faded, and the cabin came back into view, the fire crackling from the hearth.

"Months after I…" I trailed off, casting down my gaze. I took both her hands this time, thankful another scene didn't appear. "You were running away. To find me. You made it past the gates, but then turned back. No one knew you ever left."

She fell Deathly quiet. Judging from her dawning expression, I took it she believed me now. She plucked her hands from my grasp, holding her fingers as if to find security from this living nightmare.

Lilli's brow puckered in bewilderment. "But I don't understand. Why do you suddenly have these new elements? How is it possible?"

"They are the Shadowblood," explained Dream. "It is what they were born to do."

Herrin sifted through his papers on the floor and held up that picture again—the one of Alexander and me merged together. "When Dream had a vision of the Lightcaster," said the scholar, "he *also* had a vision of his opposite. The Shadowblood is supposed to be the Gods' Champion. The one who will gain all elements of Hallows, just like the Lightcaster, but use them to protect the Relicbloods instead."

"Champion?" Alex's teeth sharpened. "We don't want this headache. Pick someone else."

From the cabin's corner, Kurrick grunted. "Would but we could, believe you me."

I turned to Dream for help. "Can't you give these elements to another shifter? Someone who has the time? We're in the middle of two wars here."

"This is the very reason your wars exist." Dream tapped a finger over his knee ponderously. "And the choice was never mine, nor anyone else's. It was the Gods who chose you both, thus why they marked you with the Crest."

I massaged my eyes. "I... I don't know if I can believe this."

"I know I can't," muttered Alex. "Where the Void is all this coming from? You can't just pull this out of the grey and expect everyone to accept it as fact."

Dream lifted an eyebrow. "You've already Seen through my eyes, Alex. I know you've felt my resolve, because *I've* felt you feeling it with my own vision."

Alex grimaced. "Are you *capable* of saying anything normal, or are you always set to 'the most ridiculous answer' option?"

"I'm glad you're keeping a sense of humor," Dream sighed. "I know this is difficult to grasp. I would have explained everything when you were younger, but I didn't think it the right time."

"And you decided now was the right time?" I asked skeptically.

"Now is the only time left." He lifted to his feet and started for the door, his voice ringing with a new, hollow tone. "You needn't stray from your current course. The Ocean Palace is where you must go next, regardless. You will get your military aid, but you will also get much more than that. I only suggest you hide Zylveia when we arrive."

Zylveia, who had been listening from the room's cozy chair alongside El, folded her scarlet wings. "*Re?*" she questioned. "Why this ees?"

Dream paused under the doorway to glance at her. "Your father believes the Ocean King has kidnapped you. Ninumel fears war drums will sound any day now. If you were discovered there at Marincia's capital, it would not be pleasant. Best you stay out of sight once we arrive." He circled two fingers over his temple. "Now if you don't mind, I'd personally like to leave sooner rather than later. My wife is already *in* the capital, and I'm afraid of what she'll do to certain lower regions of mine if I make her wait any longer."

His eyes slitted at Alexander and me. "Rest well, both of you. You have my Hallows now, but there are still four more sets to gain." He turned, but stopped. "Ah. And one other thing, Xavier."

I watched him cross the room and open a trunk that was off to the side. He pulled out a large, mirrored globe, and tossed it to me. I fumbled to catch it from my place on the floor.

"What is this?" I asked, turning the sphere over and gazed curiously at my stretched reflection.

"Your memories," Dream said. "Happy Rebirth Day."

Dream left, his footsteps fading from the hall outside.

I stared at the mirrored globe in my hands, blinking like a feral fish that had grown legs and discovered land.

"Did he..." I began, dazed. "Did he say *memories?*"

Alex came round to stare at the globe, frowning. "What does he mean?"

Willow peered over my shoulder. "Bloods, that's the largest memory holder I've ever seen."

"Memory holder?" I asked, turning the mirrored sphere in cautious inspection.

"They're compartments that Somniovokers have sealed an enchantment into, to hold memories." She ran a thumb over the mirrored surface, finding two sealing runes etched neatly into the glass. "Strange... this particular one has two enchantments. But usually a second rune means the holder has kept the memories trapped inside, to keep them from wandering or returning to the memories' owner when opened..."

"Excuse me?" I lifted the globe to look at the twin runes. They were three rings of gradual sizes, looking like targets. "Are you saying he *kept* my memories from coming back to me?" Anger fumed, and I glared at the open doorframe where Dream had disappeared. "Then, it's *his* Bloody fault—?"

"No," a soft voice whispered from the back of the cabin. Miss Ana stepped forward, her fingers tangled in knots. "Indeed, it was Dream who housed what memories of yours he found... but the intent was not to keep them from you. They were to protect them."

"Protect them?" I clipped. "From what exactly?"

"From the Noctis Golems," she whispered. "Aspirre's demons have been known to prey on wandering memories if they wander outside of a Somniovoker's protective barrier. Once a memory is eaten by a Golem, they never return to the owner—they are gone. For eternity."

A short silence followed. Then I scoffed. "You don't expect me to believe that nonsense? I've never heard of these... these *golems* eating memories. Death, I'd only learned of the Golems themselves not months ago."

Willow lifted a hand to interject. "Actually, she speaks the truth. In my youth, my mother had briefly taken me through Aspirre and shown me what the golems do with the memories."

My head snapped to her, incredulous. "What? Then why in Death's name haven't I heard of this before now?"

Willow simply shrugged. "Somniovokers have been feared and hated for thousands of years—in any realm. While my grandfather had seen to their protection and worked tirelessly to mend the hearts of society's distrust, not much has changed since the Time of Discord. They may not be hunted anymore, but the hatred still remains. Dream Walkers tend to keep their abilities hidden, so you can understand that disclosing certain information about Aspirre would give them away. It's hardly public knowledge."

I pawed at my beard, a sinking anxiousness rolling my stomach. "Then... Then what of my memories?" I stared down at my stretched reflection in the globe, then turned to Miss Ana nervously. "Have any of them been eaten?"

Ana cast down her gaze. "I am not certain... Dream collected what he could, yet there is no definitive evidence to support either theory. Even if any memories have not been eaten, we also do not know if Macarius had discovered them and taken them for himself."

"Why would *he* take my memories?" *Bloods, how more nerve-wracking could this be?* First I discovered my memories had been locked away, some of them may have been eaten by Bloody dream-demons, and now there's a chance someone who wants us dead has stolen some? This was too Bloody much for one day.

Miss Ana squeezed her knuckles tighter, pursing her lips. "There... was another, whose memories were lost in Aspirre, centuries past. While Macarius was trapped in the subconscious plane, he had thieved those memories and locked them away from their original owner. From what I understand, he is likely using them to control her still today."

"Her?" Alexander interrupted, raising his hands in protest. "Wait a moment. You claimed this woman lost them centuries ago. Do you mean to tell us she's still alive?"

Another hesitant pause from Ana. "No. She... has been dead for a long, long time."

Willow's fox ears curled. "You speak of Cilia."

Ana nodded. "When she had Changed, her memories scattered, as all demon's memories are wont to do. Dream was too late to find them, but he knew Macarius had stolen them."

I lifted my brow. "He was sure it was Macarius?"

"Yes," Ana said. "It was because of the single memory Dream *had* found of Cilia's. Truthfully, it was an ungrounded fear when Cilia's body had first vanished from her home. But once Dream found the memory, his suspicions were confirmed."

From the rug by the hearth, Jaq scratched his head, muttering, "Bloods, ya sound like ya were there yourself."

Ana blushed.

Willow put hands on her hips, her gaze suspicious. "Bloody Void, you *were* there, weren't you? That's why you think of my mother as a sister. You were with my grandfather and his family when this all transpired?"

Ana's blush deepened, but she nodded softly. From the back wall, Kurrick started for her, an intense look painting his face, but Ana raised a gentle hand to stop him.

"It's all right, Kurrick," she hushed, cupping her hands as her tone turned melancholy. "Yes. I was there to witness the events, young though I was."

Kurrick's scarred face wrenched in an uncomfortable scowl at Ana. Nevertheless, he kept his mouth shut and set his jaw, folding his arms with an indignant snort.

Willow pressed a contemplative finger to her lips. "Death below... To have lived so long with a clean soul, my grandfather must have kept you in Aspirre with them all this time..."

"Er, hang on," I said, frowning. "How is that possible?"

Willow shot me an edged glare. "The *how* of it doesn't concern you."

"Oh, but it does, I should think," Ana contradicted. Her lion ear flicked, fluttering her looped earing. "They've seen the Orbs of Azure. They've been given its Blessings. As such, I think it appropriate—essential, even—that they know the Orbs allow one to enter Aspirre physically."

"How *dare* you speak of...!" Willow stopped short, a thought running through her eyes. She squeezed her lids shut and knuckled her brow, chewing on a mutter. "Of course you know of the Bloody Relics... if you've been with my grandfather, you must have been influenced by his impressive lack of propriety..."

Ana hummed quietly. "I suppose you're right... I am sorry if the mention upsets you. Dream was my foster father, and he has told me much of the Relics in Myra and my youths—"

"Foster father?" Willow echoed, her brow raising. "This is the first I'm hearing of this! Why would he take *you* in, of all people? I mean no offense, Miss Ana, I'm simply astounded—Grandfather has lived for two thousand years. He must have met, quite literally, *millions* of orphans in his lifetime. Why would he choose you, then?" Willow approached Ana with a Deathly intense glare. Though she was far shorter than the lioness, Willow still seemed to intimidate the poor woman, who scuttled back a step in a meek cringe as Willow demanded, "Who exactly *are* you?"

Ana shivered, her lion ears folded in terror, her breathing growing jagged as she glanced round the cabin at all the eyes set on her. She cowered backward, bumping into Alexander. She caught his accusing sneer, and let out a squeak—

Then she bolted for the door and fled to the hall, vanishing.

"Ana!" Kurrick called, shoving Alexander aside to follow after. "Ana, wait!"

He disappeared next, cursing beyond the doorframe.

I twisted to where they left in confusion, awkwardly tugging at my tunic's collar. "Er... Well. That was... interesting."

Willow rumbled. "*Infuriating*, more like. Who in Bloods *are* they?"

I sighed. "I don't know. But." I lifted the mirrored globe, a smile cracking in my reflection. "I suppose I have other concerns at the moment, don't I?"

Alex cocked an eyebrow. "So then... how does it work?"

My brief cheer snuffed. "Oh... I don't know." I found the silver latch of the compartment's lid and slid it open.

Inside gleamed a cluster of bright balls of light. They resembled the Fallen Lights of Grim, as though someone had collected several dozen of them in the caverns and piled them together. Each shone with varying brilliance, some small specks and others the size of ghostly, radiant apples. I supposed the different sizes meant the length of the memory.

I marveled at the cluster, lost for words. *These are my memories*, I thought in awe, a newfound delight fluffing my chest, *Finally. I finally have them.*

"There are so many," I murmured, hovering a hand over them. Part of me was scared to touch them. Would they pop like delicate bubbles? What if I crushed them and couldn't return them? "How do... how do I..."

Alex swiped his hand into the lights before I could do so myself. They passed through his fingers like smoke. Alex frowned and rubbed his fingers contemplatively.

"Odd," he said, "If we can't touch them, what are we to do with them?"

"Death." I reached in to feel for myself, curious if they would be cold like the Fallen Lights—

They yielded to my fingers, tumbling soundlessly over each other like large, disturbed marbles. They felt like nothing. There was no sensation on my skin, no temperature, no pressure... it was as though I were moving light.

Testing, I plucked a fair-sized one from the pile and inspected it in wonder.

Alex piped, "Why can *you* touch it?"

"I don't know," I mumbled, turning it in my fingers. "Curious..."

"Very curious," agree Willow, plucking one from the pile herself. "Neither of you should be able to touch these. Only Somniovokers should be able to."

She sighed. "But I suppose the fact Xavier *can* touch them means you truly have gained Dream's Hallows…"

I took a hesitant breath, then experimentally lifted the light to my brow. "I don't suppose I could just…"

I felt the light sink into my skull—then the cabin was sucked away.

"What are you doing up there?" I called.

The grey-haired girl quivered over the stone wall. She pulled her charcoal strands away from her face, finding me below her.

Judging from her glittering butterfly broach and diamond-encrusted amulet round her neck, I assumed she was a young Howless—and with the way her arms shook, I also assumed she hadn't mean to get stuck up there.

The girl looked stunned when she saw me. She was staring at my eyes. Not surprising. I supposed heterochromia was hard to ignore.

"Before you ask." I put fists at my sides. "I'm not blind on my right eye. The color is just gone."

She blushed. "I didn't mean…"

"I'm used to it. Now what are you doing on my fence?"

Confusion puckered her brow. "Your fence?"

"Yes, well, I only arrived a few hours ago, but it's still my house."

I eyed the small pond by my feet. White-and-grey koi swam in the clear water, a slight breeze rippling the surface in glassy ringlets. Floating in the pond was a broken tree branch, and the tree it once belonged to loomed over the wall from the other side.

I inched away from the water, careful not to fall in. If I were to dirty my ivory suit and gloves, Mother threatened to take away Alexander and my hero figures. We were hosting guests tonight and she wished for us to look our best. I didn't know who was visiting, but Mother was Deathly serious that Alex and I behaved ourselves.

So, 'roughhousing' was out of the question… along with anything mildly fun. But we had to do something to pass the time, so my brother and I had gone to venture our new grounds instead, splitting up to see who could find the most interesting thing.

And I think I just won. I grinned at the grey-haired girl. "Given the branch in the pond," I began, "I take it you climbed that tree and fell on the wall after it broke?"

She nodded, looking embarrassed. "I didn't mean to intrude. I wanted to see where Jewel was going."

"Jewel?"

She pointed at a canary-sized black bird fluttering by my head. That was the crow that'd led me here.

"Is this your messenger?" I asked.

"No," the girl muttered sarcastically, "she's a little house pet I'd taken a fancy to. Are you sure you're not blind in that eye?"

"Yes," I chewed. "I only thought it was curious… Most Reapers don't get their messengers until they're older. You're far too young to have a messenger."

"I'll be nine in three days, I'm not a lost little kit," she insisted.

The crow, Jewel, buzzed up to her Reaper, chirping in scolding tunes. The girl bit her lip and glanced down at me. "Uhm, I'm a bit… stuck."

I smirked. "You don't say?"

"Could you fetch a ladder?"

"It's not that high a fall, is it? Can't you jump?"

Her onyx eyes splintered in horror. "I can't jump! Do you want me to die?!"

"You won't die." I stifled a laugh. It really wasn't that high, was it? "Look, it's only what, fifteen feet? You won't even get a scrape."

"I am not jumping."

I shrugged and stalked off. "All right. I guess I'll see you tomorrow—"

"NO!" she wailed. "Wait, all right! I'll… I'll jump. But you have to catch me."

"Honestly, it's not that…" Her sharp glare froze my tongue. I cleared my throat. "All right… Fine." I held out my arms in a sigh.

Her gaze narrowed. "You won't drop me will you?"

"Hmm." I tapped a ponderous finger to my chin. "You know, now that you mention it, I am a terrible catch—"

"Swear you won't miss," she clipped. "I'll die if you drop me! And-and you'll be responsible! Everyone will know!"

"You won't die," I laughed. "And I won't miss. I was only joking—"

"Swear it!"

I rolled my eyes, but raised a fist to my chest and gave an ostentatious bow, muttering. "I swear with the Mother Goddess as my witness that I won't drop you, miss… um…" I stopped, realizing I hadn't asked this. "Sorry, but what was your name?"

She looked suspicious, but answered. "Willow."

"Very well, Howless Willow," I held out my arms again, waiting for her to jump. "Ready when you—oof!"

She dropped like a stone, her chin nicking my brow and her knee sinking into my stomach. I lost footing and sent both of us splashing into the pond with a cold ka-plunk! The fish rushed away from us, a bubbled curse escaping my lips before Willow and I gasped up for air. Our clothes were stained with green and brown sludge as we coughed water.

"Th-th-there…!" I stuttered, the chilled water making my teeth chatter. I cringed when hearing she was still coughing. "At least I c-c-caught you, didn't I?"

The scene dripped away, and the cabin fell into view again.

I was staring at the ceiling now, on my back. And *Bloods* my skull throbbed like Death. I groaned, trying to push myself up, but my boney arms quivered and flopped back to the floorboards.

"Death..." I moaned, clutching my still-pounding head. "What happened...?"

Willow hummed above me, crouching as she pulled me into a sitting position. "You fell," she explained bluntly. "Might I suggest choosing a *smaller* memory if you plan to remember them whilst standing?"

She helped me to my wobbling feet and fetched my crutch. I took it hurriedly and leaned into it, stabilizing my footing. I blinked at her. Then laughed.

She cocked an eyebrow. "I take it the memory was an amusing one?"

"It was how we met," I chuckled. "You were stuck on a Bloody wall of all things. I thought you were a wandering Howless, your hair had been disguised in grey."

She paused, her breath catching. Then a smile split her face in slow delight. "Y... yes! I'd been training illusions with my Mother that day." Her smile faded. "You... hadn't even remembered that?"

"Not until now." I searched the floor for the mirrored sphere of memories I must have dropped. "Where has that thing gone off to?"

Alexander grunted behind me. "It's right here." He handed it to me, the lid closed now, and rumbled in warning, "Though, given your little tumble, I should think it best to wait for sleep before doing that again."

"Again..." I stared at my distorted reflection in the sphere, watching my bearded lips curl into an eager smile. "Bloods, there will be *many* 'again's."

8
OCTAVIUS

I poked at the plate of food on the long table in front of me, listening to the creaking floorboards as the ship swayed and bowed in the waves.

I was alone, except for Shade, who picked at his own meal beside me. We'd set sail some hours ago, and everyone was already asleep as far as I knew. The galley was a dark den right now, with nothing but the sound of waves outside and the moaning boards to keep me company.

What in Land was up with the twins now? They were some kind of... what, super Evocators or something? One minute they were normal Necrovokers and the next they just up and *poof!* and suddenly have Dream Hallows? *Bloody crazy.*

They'd gone to their cabins after all the excitement, both of them looking sick. But even aside from the new Hallows, there was something else weird with them. Whatever happened when they passed out at the tavern couldn't have been good. It had both of them looking at the rest of us like... well, like ghosts. It was creepy. If they were really seeing visions or whatever, did they see a bad future?

Footfalls padded from the spiraling stairs, making my grown cat ears flick.

It was that hybrid cat-jay girl, with the long, blue wings and snowy white cat ears. *Zyl's friend, El.* She stopped when she saw me sitting here. I had my cat ears recede in a long sigh, turning away and propped up my chin with a fist. El was the cute Culatian girl who'd been eyeing Neal all trip. He'd been bragging about it. It was kind of annoying.

A spike of oxytocin suddenly prickled behind me, my Infeciovoking fizzling. When I looked back again, the cat-eared girl was there and looking flustered. Her wings were pinned tight to her back.

"Y-ye..." she squeaked, her walnut face turning super red. *"Hemn El tov... ye, ye... ültrolo?"*

"Uh." I scratched my head. "Sorry, but I don't, uh, speak Culatian."

"My..." She strained to pronounce each syllable. "N-na*me*... ees... El." She beamed, looking proud of herself, and waited for my response.

I didn't know what else to do but shrug. "Yeah. I know. Her Highness Sky already told us."

One of her cat ears folded down, not understanding me. I tried again, "Uh, I'm Octavius." Her eyes brightened. "*Tu sekel El!*"

"Er, right... You, uh, want something to eat? Is that why you're down here?" Her head cocked. "*Re?*"

"Food." I stabbed the fish I was eating with a fork and waved it around to show her. Shade gave a questioning croak at her. "This stuff?"

"Ah!" She nodded quickly. "My na*me* El!"

"Heh, yeah... You already said that—"

"I f-*food* mu-ch *li*ke eet!"

"Right, okay." Bloods, she was just so damn *cute*. "My dad's the chef though, and he's already gone to bed... but I guess I can make something real quick if you want?"

"I food mu-ch *li*ke eet!" She smiled wide, pleased with herself.

I tried not to laugh and pushed to my feet. "Right. Give me a sec."

I went to the small kitchen at the back, found a clean skillet and put it on one of the open-flamed stoves. El came to watch as I opened the icebox in the back corner and picked up a few frozen meat options off the large stack of fish we'd gotten from the island. I held up a slab of catfish to show her, unwrapping some of the covering paper. "You want this one?"

She had that blank stare again, like she didn't know what I was saying. I held up a salmon slab next, unwrapping the paper. "What about this one?"

Her yellow eyes sparkled. "*Gillecht! Mey, mey, mey!*"

"Salmon it is," I said and set it aside, putting away the rest of the fish—

"*Neche!*" she interrupted, pointing to a sack of octopus meat I was about to put back. She held up two fingers. "*Rutteit, pas Zyl. Tis?*"

"You want this, too?"

She nodded. "*Pas Zyl.*"

"Oh—right. For Zylveia. Makes sense..." I looked around for a set of matches on the counter, but didn't find any. I searched the floor. Still nothing. "Sorry, El." I rubbed my neck. "I don't know what I did with the matches... Can't really cook anything without fire."

She blinked. "*Re?*"

"Fire," I said again, pointing to the stove and giving an exaggerated shrug. "I can't find the matches."

"Ah!" She snapped her fingers—which burst with a small flame as the Death mark on her forehead gleamed bright. "*Venni ach lis?*"

I gawked. "You're a Pyrovoker?" Bloods, I knew she was an Imbrivoker, but I thought her second Hallows was Necrovoking... *Guess I'm just getting used to corpse-raisers around here.*

I watched El put her now enflamed hand under the stove, letting the fire catch, and withdrew it in a toothy smile. "*Hembech?*"

I grinned. "Uh, yeah. Thanks."

I went to cooking. El shied back as she waited, watching me. I was getting kind of self-conscious with her standing there. How do I say *could you give me some space* in Culatian? How do I say it politely?

When the meal was done—maybe *too* done, some of the edges were burnt—I skewered the fish and octopus on thin sticks. I wasn't exactly the best cook. I never figured out how Dad did all of that fancy stuff. He kind of left before he could teach anyone other than Mikani... well, whatever. He was back now. Him *and* Mom.

The thought had me smiling when I gave El her orders. "There you go. All done."

"*Sayiu!*" El cheered and took the skewers. She bowed with her wings fanned out. "Th... than-k*iew*... Be... ry... Mu-*ch!*"

With that, she rushed up the stairs, her bare feet thunking overhead and making me chuckle. *Weirdo.* I started putting the cookware away. *But that's why she's so damn cute. Bloody Neal, why did HE have to snag her attention? The lucky bastard.*

"That was precious," someone purred overhead.

I glanced up. Mom was there. Well, her *ghost* was there. The specter sat on the overhanging lamp, and gently floated down to me, landing in a hushed silence. She smiled with her translucent lips, one cat ear flicking. "I think she likes you."

I leaned over the counter. "She probably thought I was Neal... wait, weren't you resurrected before? Did it end already?"

"It's been two weeks," Mom reasoned. "That's as long as Lëtta's Hallows can last right now."

"So..." I hesitated. "Where's your corpse?"

Her lips peeled into a snickering grin and she pointed to the ceiling. "It collapsed in the hallway up there. I can't move it and Lëtta's asleep, so I guess it's staying up there until someone wakes up to use the bathroom." She gave a snorting laugh and slapped her translucent knee. "Gardener, I hope I get to see their face when they trip on me." She motioned to wipe a non-existent tear from her eye and calmed down in a sigh, shooting me a playful look. "So, are you going to ask that girl to dinner?"

I lifted an eyebrow at her.

She shrugged. "Just a thought."

"Mom, I'm glad you're back, really, but…" I let out a stream of breath. "You've been gone for a *while*. I'm not sixteen anymore."

"Almost twenty-three, in Watermein." she smiled. It was a heavy, sad smile. "I never stopped counting, you know. Not for any of you."

I scratched the scruff at my throat. "But you and Dad can't keep treating us like you've been here the whole time. For Land's sake, Connie was only ten when both of you left. A *lot's* happened. Too much changed while you were gone to act like everything's normal again."

She touched my face, her white hand cold and rippling over my skin. "I know, honey… We didn't want to leave. Your father did what he had to. And I…" Her face fell. "I did what I had to, for your friend. He was so young when we found him—almost your age, at the time. And they wanted to throw him back in the ocean and let him drown, I couldn't just…"

I gripped her ghostly fingers. "I get it, Mom. And I'm glad you did. Xavier's my friend. It was one of my ancestors who tried to kill him anyway, it's only fair that one of *us* tries to save him, right?"

She smirked, then motioned as if to ruffle my hair even though her hand didn't make contact. "I guess that's one way to look at it. Shel, where did that confidence come from? You were still hiding in the back of every room when I last saw you." She floated to the stairs, her voice solemn. "You were right, it looks like… You're not that shy teenager anymore. I need to remember that I'm talking to an adult now. A knight, no less."

She chuckled to herself while floating up the stairs, and I was alone again, listening to the creaking floorboards as Shade fluffed his feathers.

ZYL

TRANSLATED FROM CULATIAN

I stared at the shiny communicator and scrutinized its many gears and buttons. I stared at it like a pesky bug; like an annoying gnat that wouldn't leave me alone until I swatted it away. I *hated* gnats.

I hated ships, too. Always rocking over fish-waters and making me sick… I hated being sick. But most of all, I hated what I had to do now.

I was alone in the crow's nest. If I had to be anywhere on this annoying boat, I preferred to be up high near the clouds. Snow had been falling since we left the island, the white flakes collecting in cold cushions around me. El was off somewhere, probably to get food. I wasn't sure if that yellow-eyed chef was still awake, though. Most everyone was asleep now. I'd borrowed this com from the scowling twin just before *they* went to sleep. I really didn't want to do this…

But I have to.

I sucked in a breath, held it, and inflated my cheeks like balloons while dialing the numbers. After hitting *send*, the projected screen blipped in front of me and swirled in the center. I blew out the breath just before my father's green-feathered servant, Tryle, answered from her travel-com.

I guessed the lantern light at my feet illuminated me enough, because she shrieked and dropped the com as if it'd bit her. She quickly retrieved it and stared wide-eyed at me. *"Princess Zyl?! Is it really you?!"*

I gave an exaggerated grimace, as if I'd gotten a good whiff of something rotten. "Yeah. Hi, Tryle. Is Pops there?"

"Yes! Yes, he is!" She must have been skipping because the palace halls were bouncing behind her on screen. *"Thank the Archer's wings…! The fish king released you?"*

"I wasn't 'released' from… ah, never mind. Just get my dad already." I paused, having a better idea. "Actually, Tryle, stay there. Don't get him. I want you to relay a message for me. Can you do that?"

"Of course, Your Highness!" She saluted, fumbling with the communicator. *"Anything!"*

"All right, good. Listen close. The Ocean King didn't kidnap me, Bloody idiot. I left on my own to find Roji. There's no way I'm taking Big Brother's throne while he's still alive out there somewhere, so I'm getting back Sky's *real* heir. So tell Pops to quit with the war talk. If he wants a war, tell him to go against Everland. They already pushed out the Reapers, how long will it be till that fake king kicks *our* knights out, too?"

"I… I'm not sure your father would agree to—"

"Just shut up and listen, Tryle. Tell him to back off on the Ocean King. He didn't kidnap me—but I'm sure as Sky going to find his sister, who *did* kidnap Big Brother. Now go tell that old fart what I just said. Don't call me back. Bye."

I slammed my thumb on the *end* button before Tryle could protest, and the screen blipped off.

I groaned and flopped over the edge of the nest, wings flattening at my sides. *Sky, that took a lot out of me.* Oh well. At least it's done, and I didn't even have to face Dad. That Bloody idiot—threatening war because he thinks *I've* been kidnapped? Tch. No stupid fish is smart enough to nab me. What does he think I am? A hatchling?

I pulled out my crimson, glass ocarina from the pouch strapped to my belt. I sighed, the glass comfortably cold under my fingers, and played the flighty tune of the *Winds of The Storm*.

"Zyl!" came the chiming voice of my Aide from below, interrupting my playing.

El flapped into view and perched by my head on the nest's railing. Her blue-and-white wings tightened behind her, creamy legs swinging over the edge. One of her white cat ears flicked at me as she chewed on a skewered salmon. She gave me a second skewer with grilled octopus. "Did you talk to him?" she asked after swallowing.

"Close enough." I took the snack and ripped off a piece, chewing. "Ah gave uh messuge t'Tr'le. All's gud now."

"Yay!" El giggled and stretched high with both arms and wings, then play-fully fell on her back against me. "I don't like war. War isn't fun. War is scary."

I grunted and took another bite of octopus. I was glad to see she was back to her old, bubbly self again. After we got her out of that damned prison, she hadn't quite bounced back all the way. I was starting to miss her sprightliness.

El gave a swooning breath on my back, stretching out. "And guess who I found in the galley?"

I swallowed and grinned. "Your Reaper cat?"

"Yeah!" She threw up her hands. "He was the chef tonight. It was just him, too, we were all alone together!"

I held back a chuckle. "How did he take your order? Neither of you under-stand each other."

"Well, no… but—but he ended up making me food anyway!"

"Eh." I examined the skewered octopus and noted the burnt edges. "It's not as good as the older cat's cooking."

"I guess not…" She admitted. "But! He's a Reaper, not a chef, so that's okay. Right?"

I laughed. "Sure. Have you been practicing those Landish words I taught you?"

She straightened upright. "Yes! I used them tonight. I said, *my name El. I food much like it!*"

I snorted a heckle. "That doesn't make much sense in Landish."

"But he made me food. That means he understood, right?"

"He probably guessed by the context." I fanned a hand at her. "I'll have to teach you more words."

"At this rate, I'll be talking with him in no time!" She smiled up at the snow-fall with determined eyes. "Just you wait, Reaper-cat. You'll understand me soon."

Oh, El. I sighed, shutting my eyes. *We don't even know how long this will last.*

I wanted her to be happy, but I had a mission to see through. I would get back Culatia's true heir. I would find my brother. Dad was as good as dead right now, so I didn't have much time left. Roji needed to be the next king.

Because I sure as Sky wasn't going to be queen.

9

XAVIER

TWELVE YEARS PRIOR

"Xavier?"

I glanced up from my book. Jaq was staring down at me from above the gravestone I sat against. I'd been so absorbed in my studies, I hadn't noticed him come into my family cemetery.

The young viper's nose scrunched at me. "Ain't it rude to sit on someone's grave?" he asked.

"He said it was all right." I glanced at my great grandfather's ghost who floated beside me. He smiled and nodded his agreement. I added, "So long as I keep him company, that is."

Jaq shoved his hands in his pockets. "Huh… So, uh, you guys busy? Where's Alex?"

I closed my book with a soft *thump*. "I don't know."

He looked genuinely surprised. "Since when don't ya know? Did ya have a fight?"

"Mm. No. I just needed to study. The clouds were pretty today and it wasn't too cold, so I thought reading this section outside would be nice."

"Weird. Never thought I'd *ever* see ya alone."

I lifted to my feet and stretched in a yawn. "You can't expect us to be each other's shadows every waking moment. Home is about the only place we can relax and find some space. We only stay close in public so we won't become open targets."

"Open targets for what?"

"For beatings," I said, sighing. I watched a beetle scuttle over a blade of grass, the bug dipping and rising as the grass bobbed in the cavern winds.

I bent to watch its wavering journey, crouching over my knees. "Some months before we met you," I murmured, "my family attended a festival in the main square. Mother and Father were giving an announcement to the people, and Alex and I were watching from beside the stage."

My tone soured. "We got into an argument. We argue often, about most things. He thought I'd been too soft on a Howless in our class, thought I shouldn't have stopped his hand from slapping her for calling our father a murderer that morning. We started bickering, and he ran off into town.

"At first, I didn't want to go after him. I was furious that he *always* resorted to violence at the first sign of conflict. He never thinks about the consequences, he simply lets his anger rule him..." My throat tightened, a shiver running down my spine. "But then, I... I felt something. There was a sharp pain in my ribs, like I was being kicked. I wasn't sure what it was, but somehow, I knew that..." I clenched my fists. "I *knew* he was in trouble."

Jaq hovered over me, questioning, "What happened?"

"I found him being kicked and beaten by the other children in an alley. He wasn't moving anymore, there was so much blood..." My voice fractured, remembering the red staining my brother's unmoving face, seeping between the cobblestones, his body eerily still...

Tears stung, I felt them drip down my face as my chest clenched sick. "I thought they'd killed him. I thought my brother was dead."

Jaq was silent above me. The wind swept through the cemetery, and I inhaled, wiping my lids.

"That day," I said, "when he finally woke up, we made a promise. That we'd never leave the other alone like that again, no matter how bad our arguments grew. We were born together, and we would die together... and we've kept to it since."

Jaq rubbed his neck, not seeming sure how to reply. He settled with a meager, "Oh..."

I breathed in again, letting the last of the memory trickle away from mind as I smiled and tucked my book under an arm. "Now then—enough about that. Did you want to find him? He might be studying also, but we can ask if he wants to take a break."

"Uh, yeah." Jaq followed at my side as we left the cemetery. "I heard some Screen actor was visiting town, everyone's pretty hyped about it. Wondered if you guys wanted to check it out with me."

"You mean Gabriel Lockner?" I asked.

"Yeah, that's the guy."

"You may as well stay for Father's social tonight. Howllord Lockner is the guest of honor."

Jaq halted in his tracks and went bug-eyed at me. "Seriously?"

"Yes," I chuckled. "He isn't just an actor. He's a retired Reaper, and a friend of my father's. He's visited quite a few times before—"

Jaq snatched my shoulders and shook me. "You privileged, lucky, spoiled little rich kid!" He laughed in a thrill. "Let's grab your other half and tell Bianca!"

He grabbed my arm and dragged me toward the manor, hollering excitedly as I tripped along behind him in a chuckle.

Willow laughed when the memory faded around us.

"How cute." She smiled. "So, you've known Jaq for that long?"

I lay beside her on the soft field of grass my subconscious had created within Aspirre. The Dream realm was a strange place indeed—but I was thankful it allowed Willow to use her Somniovoking to hop across everyone's dreams to come visit my subconscious tonight. If I'd known she could do that, I would have pleaded that she visit from the start of our voyage. Perhaps this could be a simple way to make up for lost time between us.

"We've known him since our first year of classes in the Academy," I explained. "Not that he was enrolled there with us. We caught him stealing our lunches one morning in the school yard."

"Curious." She hummed. "That wasn't how I imagined your meeting."

"Sometimes things happen in unexpected ways. Next memory?"

She shifted her legs over the grass. "I came here to spend time with the present you, not the past you. You were the one mewling that you felt neglected. We have all of our voyage to give you the other memories, and besides..." She crossed her legs and gave me a narrow glance. "I wanted to ask you something. About what my grandfather told you."

"Which part?" I muttered, rolling on my stomach and folding my arms. "There were a lot of things said."

"Specifically... about your new Dream Hallows."

I lifted my left hand to stare at the three black diamonds. "I'm... not up for broaching that. Ever since we woke up from that... THING..."

"Thing?"

I picked at the grass. The last thing I wanted to do was revisit that first scene Alex and I shared. Revisit the deaths... "Never you mind. Alex and I only saw something. None of it was real anyway, only a nightmare. Everyone was back to normal afterward."

"Then it was a vision?"

I stifled a tremor. "Gods, I hope not."

"Were you and Alex at the Willow of Ashes?" she asked, suddenly eager. "Were you asking me to give the Call?"

My brow lifted at her. "No… But that's oddly specific. Is that what you've been Seeing when you daze off lately?"

She flushed. "I didn't know what to make of it… But after what Grandfather said, I suppose that's how you'll gain Death's Hallows?"

"You actually believe all this?"

She shrugged. "I don't know what else to believe anymore. Between your Dream marks, and that vision I keep Seeing…"

"And about that." I sat up. "Why have you been keeping so much from me? You knew the Willow of Ashes wasn't lost, you've been Seeing visions of us there, yet you said nothing. Don't you trust me?"

"That isn't…" She took a breath and started again. "It was forbidden to speak of the Willow to anyone outside the Bloodline. Even spouses, mind you. I couldn't help that one. As for the vision… I suppose I should have mentioned at least something… But if I had, I would have broken the oath of silence about the Willow as consequence. And for the record, you still haven't told me your own vision yet. Bloody hypocrite."

"Only because I don't want to worry you. That's different."

"If you can't trust me with knowing your visions, how do you expect me to trust you with mine?"

I snorted and went back to picking at the grass, peeved now. I wasn't about to tell her of that horrible scene. I hoped to Gods it wasn't a vision. If that's what our future looked like, I would rather stay in the present.

A faint rumbling sounded above us suddenly. Grim's overcast clouds had darkened and changed to storm-like formations. A light rain soon dribbled on my nose. The droplets stayed at a minimum, thunder no louder than a calm grumble.

Willow held up a hand to shield her eyes from the leaking water. "Xavier? Why the glum weather now? What are you brooding over?"

Ah, right. My subconscious reflected my mood in Aspirre. Well, I considered, at least this was better than the alternative. Before I found my body, I always dreamt of dying. Thank Bloods those dissolved when I returned to normal.

Her expression softened when I didn't answer. "Does it have to do with your vision?" she asked.

"Don't call it that." I stopped picking at the grass. "Could we talk about something else?"

She stretched onto her stomach, twiddling her fingers, which shone with blue light as she wove a strange, canopy-looking object on a pole. We learned from Neal and Octavius that those contraptions were called 'umbrellas'. Apparently, they were used to ward off rain.

Willow held the umbrella over our heads as plunks of rain applauded from the top. She hummed. "All right. We'll talk about something else. Have you tried to use Somniovoking yet?"

I mumbled, "That wasn't what I had in mind."

"But I'm curious. Have you woven anything while in Aspirre?"

"No," I chewed indignantly.

"Why don't you try? Here, weave me a flower."

My head rolled back in a groan. "Willow…"

"Your fiancée would care for a flower. Are you denying her such a simple gift?"

I clicked my tongue. "I… I don't know how. I wouldn't even know where to begin."

"Take your hand like this." She laid her free hand over mine and pushed it to the grass.

"This is ridiculous," I muttered.

"Close your eyes."

Sighing, I complied. I heard her murmur in my ear next. "Imagine a flower. Think of my favorite one."

"Right." I paused. "And, er… that would be…?"

"Candle Lily," she said, thankfully not angry that I hadn't known. I felt her breath on my neck, a chill running down my flesh as she went on. "Think of the flower. Keep the image focused. Find the well of Hallows within you… and evoke."

I inhaled—then stiffened. I actually felt it. A gentle wind swirled coolly from my chest, draining down my arms. It leaked from my fingertips like icy water from a hot spout. The warmth from our intertwined fingers made the thought of the flower fizzle. I was focused on something else now.

A bright flash glowed outside my closed lids, and I peeked in time to see a blue light fade from my palm. Willow released my hand, and I saw the crowned Dream mark blacken and return to its original tri-leaf of diamonds over my knuckles.

Willow held her breath and lowered the umbrella when the rain ceased its downpour. Grim's clouds returned, twirling with Floating Lights. From under my palm, I felt a small flutter, and freed the black-winged butterfly underneath.

The butterfly batted to Willow's nose in a cheerful silence and took flight, circling us. Willow smiled. "That isn't a flower, Xavier."

"No." I grinned. "But I thought you'd like it. Odd, though, I'd meant for it to be blue."

"You realize this proves you have Somniovoking? That would have been impossible, otherwise. Your Dream mark even appeared."

I stared darkly at the Crest on my hand. A response wouldn't come to mind.

The black butterfly landed on my resting hand, staring up at me. I exhaled through my nose. "What I'd Seen in that vision…" I didn't look away from the butterfly's batting wings. "Everyone was dead. The sky shattered to pieces. Jaq and Bianca were corpses, and Lilli… you…"

Willow rested a hand on my shaking arm. She struggled to form a reply, but eventually gave up and leaned against me in silence.

"If that's supposed to be our future," I whispered, watching the butterfly take flight again. The clouds began swirling into storm-formations once more. "We have to change it. Don't we?"

"Yes," she said, soft as the rumbling thunder. She gripped my hand and said nothing more.

ALEXANDER

The floors moaned in the darkness as I lay in bed, staring at the ceiling.

Sleep decided I wasn't worth it, apparently. I thought this was Xavier's problem. When did it become mine?

Grumbling, I left Jaq and Xavier, who were sleeping on stacked beds set at the far wall, and made my way to the halls. I wasn't sure what I was looking for. Just roaming, waiting to tire. But it didn't seem possible at this point. All those conflicting perspectives finally died away after a few hours, but that first vision Xavier and I Saw… Seeing that… *THING*…

I shivered, pushing away the thought of the corpses—of our friends.

At least Xavier had a whole batch of missing memories now to distract himself with. And he had Willow to help him through it, if needed. Where did that leave me? What did I have to distract myself with—?

Something scampered by my feet, making me start and stumble to the floor. My left elbow gave a sharp *crack* against the wood, and I bit down a pained scream. Through clenched teeth, I seethed, "What in Death…!"

A series of soft snickers came from the feral ferret that scurried up to my face next. *Ah. Ringëd's damned pet.* "Kurn, you Bloody pest…!" I pushed myself over my knees, and the ferret's throat clicked, resting a paw on my leg in apology. "My arm was nearly healed, and now this…" I seethed again to bear the dull pain, and the ferret scuttled off down the hall, disappearing.

"You all right?"

I jolted, my head snapping up.

Bianca was standing under her suddenly opened doorframe. Her rabbit ears were draped to her neck, dark face sullen in the light of the candle she held.

I shoved to my feet and turned away in a blush. "Fine…"

She shuffled out to the hall. "Let me see your arm."

"It was merely Kurn and his antics." I headed down the hall as quick as my legs would carry me. She was the last person I wished to see right now. I couldn't stand watching that damned scene replay over and over again at the sight of her face, speckled with blood, one of her eyes hollowed out and…

I hurried on.

She caught me by the sling. "Will you come here? Hold still."

She grabbed my left hand and *yanked* it out of the sling, the pain nearly sending me to my knees. The ache in my collarbone was dull, but it still splintered like Void.

Bianca set down her candle and took out a needle from her pocket, pricking my fingertips.

"Ow, *ow!*" I winced and tried to jerk away, but her grip was too strong. "Stop that—!"

"Reaction time is good," she noted, putting the needle away. She started massaging the sealed gash at my collarbone, and the pain had me cringing against the wall.

"Turn around." She whirled me by the weaker shoulder before I could reply. My teeth sharpened and gritted when she massaged the exit wound in my back as well. My claws grew and pinched against my balled fist. Her fingers finally moved away from the scar and started working to my shoulder joint, testing its flexibility.

Now that the pain was gone, I *thunked* my forehead against the wall, panting. *Damn that woman…* I let her work the rest of my arm, my eyes drifting closed. Maybe I'd let her do what she wanted. Just a bit longer…

"You can't leave…"

I remembered that time again: the day she left us in Grim.

The Surfacing Port swelled with noise as Grimish shifters bustled through the station, hydraulics and whistles hissing in clamorous echoes. Bianca was a step away from her pod's stairs; a step away from leaving for Nira knew how long.

"Please," I remember pleading, grabbing her hand to stop her from boarding. "Don't go?"

Her orange rabbit ears drooped to her neck as she sighed and shook her head. "I have to, Alex."

My eyes stung and misted. "Why…?"

She gently pulled her hand free, seeming hurt to do it, but bit her lip and held strong. "I have a future to build for myself. You three are already off training with your Reaper duties, and what do I have here? I'm not a soldier, Alex. I'm a Healer. A tonic-brewer. And if I'm going to train as hard with my tonics as you three train with fighting demons, then I have to go where that opportunity is. There's nothing for me here."

My voice tightened. "I'm here..."

She blinked at that, her brown cheeks blooming pink as she took a breath and said, "What if I give you a gift before I leave?"

I tried to stop the pain from shaking my chest and rubbed my eyes. "A gift...?"

"Close your eyes," she ordered.

Swallowing, I complied—

A pressure suddenly came to my lips, so gentle my brain was late to register what was happening. I shut my eyes tighter, now Deathly determined not to let Xavier see from the psyche. I reached to touch her face, tracing to the back of her neck, returning the push that brought so much warmth and thrill and thrumming shock that knotted my soul in coveted tangles. Only when her presence poured away did I open my eyes again.

She flushed with a smile, her long ears folding back shyly as she turned to leave up the steps—

"Wait!" I caught her by the waist and reeled her in for one last embrace, squeezing her close, memorizing her warmth and the flowery scent of her hair. "Come back for me," I whispered. "I don't care how many years it takes. I'll be here. Xavier and I will be separated, and I..." I tightened my grip on her waist. "I'll have vines for you..."

In the present, Bianca's massaging fingers had reached my hand. Her pace slowed, and I craned back to gaze at her. Her ears were still folded down.

"I'm sorry," she said at last, breaking the silence. "I didn't know your engagement was arranged... Xavier told me it was set up before you and me even..." She paused, her gaze lowering. "Sorry... I know you nobles have obligations like that a lot. I just..." She sighed. "I'll back off."

She dropped my hand and headed back to her room.

"Wait." I snatched her wrist before she could leave. "That's it, then...? Are we... are we really...?" I couldn't finish, my throat cinching shut.

Her stare was empty. "You tell me, Alex. You and Xavier are back to normal, but you still haven't called off your arrangement with Lilli. I've seen how you look at her. If we had anything before..." Her eyes started to well, and she pursed her lips. "It's obviously gone, for you."

"No," I bit back my tone, quieting. "Please. It's not what you think."

"Then what is it?" She demanded, her rabbit ears folding back angrily.

"I..." How to say it? I'd never told anyone before. I didn't want to remember. "I made a promise to someone."

Bianca had no reply. She lingered there, waiting for me to expound. My left shoulder started throbbing again, and I seized it to stop the trembling.

"I watched her mother die," I whispered. "I... I watched her soul deteriorate. I had her blood on my hands, I watched her..." My breath choked. "All she asked of me was to watch over Lilli. To keep her safe. I've already failed, with Tanderam. If I call off the arrangement after that trauma..."

Bianca stared at me for a long moment, then bent to pick up her candle. "Then I'll make it easy for you. She doesn't need this. *I* don't need this. You can keep your promise..." She exhaled slowly. "Goodnight."

The last word held a haunting resolve; a final note.

A last, gutting decision.

She disappeared into her room, leaving me alone in the hall. My stomach shook, and I leaned into the wall.

—*My point of view changed. I was now looking through the eyes of someone crouched on the other side of the wall, their tears blurring their view. There was a raven on this person's lap, cradled in slender, pale arms as the sound of a girl cried softly. I could feel her pain, feel the confliction wringing her chest. She'd heard everything. She held tight to her raven and called softly for her mother.*

The image faded, and I caught sight of the blue glow coming from my right hand. The crowned Dream mark was there, quickly fading to the original Crest of black diamonds. I turned to face the wall. *Damn it.* She'd heard everything...

"Lad?" Nathaniel, our resurrected captain, questioned behind me. I hadn't heard him approach. The black-haired bear shifter put his thick hands at his sides. "What ye be doin' up? Ye ain't taken to sleep walkin', have ye?"

Behind him followed my two resurrected vassals, Dalen and Vendy. Dalen scratched his feathered hair and pushed his candle out to better see my face. "You feelin' all right, *Da'torr*? Ya look paler than usual."

"Yeah." Vendy winced when she peered at my face. One of her brown rabbit ears lifted as the teenager pulled her long braid over a shoulder. "Maybe skipping your beauty sleep wasn't such a good idea, yeah? No offense or anything, *Da'torr*."

I smeared a hand over my face and sighed. "Of course, Vendy, why would anyone take offense to such comments..." I drifted back to my room, steps lethargic and absent. "Regardless, I... I was just heading back to bed. I suggest you all do the same soon."

They all looked confused, but shrugged and walked on as I shut my door and curled into bed, wishing that Iri would show mercy and have me wake up realizing this was all just a terrible dream.

When morning came, I realized He hadn't answered. Bianca had made her decision.

I crawled out of bed and slunk down the hall, hesitating before rapping my knuckles on Lilli's cabin door. In short time, she answered, cracking the door open just enough to peek half her face out.

"Oh." She sounded disdained, the one eye of hers I could see red and glassy, her black hair tangled and frayed about her brow. "Alex..."

I gritted my teeth. She'd heard everything last night. And yet, she wasn't speaking a word of it. Had she nothing to say? I glanced over my shoulder and ran a hand through my hair. After a long moment, I muttered, "I... I know I promised to give you an answer regarding our arrangement once Xavier and I were separated. I've failed to do so. But I've decided that..." I held my breath. "I... will accept our union..."

I nodded tersely, spun on my heels, and stomped off. I didn't want to look back to see what expression she held, so I hurried down to the galley. My appetite was spoiled already, but I needed something to do. A distraction.

To my relief, there were others in the galley. Not many, only two, but perhaps it was better that way. I wasn't in the mood for crowds. I saw neither Xavier nor Jaq, but I supposed they'd both been asleep when I left the cabin, so I shouldn't be surprised they weren't here. Herrin *was* present however, along with Dream. The blue-haired king righted in his seat when I came down the spiraling steps, a wide smile plastered on his young face as he chimed brightly, "Alexander!"

There was something about that eager smile that made me stop cold. Then I remembered the nightmare from yesterday at the tavern, remembered everything Dream had just dropped onto us, and I turned right around to trot back up the steps. I decided that Dream and Herrin were the *last* two people I wanted to see after all.

"Ah, hang on!" Dream called after me, and I groaned when I heard his bare feet thunk up the stairs after me. I stormed down the hall, and he kept pace at my side, still smiling. "Did you test your new Somniovoking last night?"

I growled, making a point to avoid eye contact. "Go bother someone else."

"Ah, forgive me." He was having trouble containing his chuckles, and slid his arms behind his back. "You must understand, I've waited a very long time for this. It goes without saying that I'm excited."

I glowered at him. Then I noticed something peculiar on his chin and knitted my brow. "Even your facial hair is blue?" I asked.

His bare feet slowed to a stop. I watched him reach a befuddled hand to his chin, rubbing experimentally. "Shepherd!" he gasped, scratching with more vigor. "I have *whiskers!*"

He whipped out a communicator from his trouser pocket and dialed a number. Before long, a rust-haired fox woman came on the screen of light.

"Crysa!" Dream all but exploded as he scratched at his short chin hairs as if to show them off. "Do you see it? It feels like I'm wearing a feral lamb on my face! What do you think? How does it look?"

He drifted down the hall, seeming to have forgotten me. I could still hear him prattling, "Why yes! I *do* see a bit of crow's feet by your lids! Beautiful, Dear. You and I will have our own collection of wrinkles in no time at… oh, you have another surprise for me? Well, what is… when I get there? Blast, woman, you'll torture me all trip. Could I guess? Is it a…"

He went back down to the galley, bombarding her with a list of guesses that bounced through the walls.

I rolled my eyes and dragged my feet down the hall. Perhaps Jaq and Xavier had woken…

10

XAVIER

I took another wobbling step forward without my cane—
My weak legs toppled under me and I hit the floorboards again with ungraceful *thunk, thunk, thunks*! I grunted, pushing up to sit, my lungs blistering with heavy pants.

"That was better," Alex encouraged. He crouched down to thump my sweaty back. "You went 38 whole steps without the cane. That's grand progress."

I was far too out of breath to reply, sprawling on my back and feeling the ship sway soothingly.

"Come on." Alex pulled me up by the arm and slung me over his shoulder. "Again."

"I… I need a break," I wheezed.

"Not until you've reached fifty steps. That was today's goal."

"Alex, please…!" I buried my face in my hands and groaned. "My legs feel like they're on fire!"

"Oh, it can't be that terrible—"

I shoved a hand over his chest, violet lights shining from my palm as my Death mark gleamed over my left knuckles. In a heaving grunt, I yanked out his soul—and pulled it into *my* vessel.

Alex's body collapsed in a loud *clack-ca-THUNK*, bringing me with him since he was no longer supporting me. From the floorboards, I set my jaw and pulled my soul into the psyche, forcing Alexander *out* as I now watched the outside world from the small, circular window in this empty abyss of my own psyche.

I heard Alex groan, and noted that my view was still focused on the cabin's ceiling, immobile.

I hummed from the psyche. *"What's the matter, Alex? Can't you stand up?"*

"You... Bloody... bastard..." He sounded as hoarse as I had felt not seconds ago. "I can't move."

I grinned. *"Oh, it can't be that terrible."*

"Ha, ha, ha..." he muttered sourly, then craned his head to inspect his empty body. It was crumpled and snoozing soundly beside us. He grumbled. "I better not find any bruises later..."

The door creaked open suddenly, and Alex's view flicked to Jaq and Octavius who'd appeared under the doorway. Jaq's brow furrowed when he found Alex's body snoring softly on his side, and he lifted an eyebrow at me—or, technically at Alex, since he was *out*.

"The Void are ya doin' in here, mates?" asked Jaq. His voice was more amplified than I expected, so I presumed Alex's wolf ears had grown. Well, *my* ears. *Ha!* Him, using my ears this time. I could get used to that change of pace.

Octavius shuffled inside next. "I thought you guys were glad to be separated?"

Alex remained on the floor as he growled. "Xavier was making a point. And that point has been *made*, now could you put me back already?"

I floated into the psyche's window, pulling myself outside to the physical world as the psyche was sucked away, and Alexander took my place inside. Taking control of my sore muscles again, I pushed into a sitting position. Luckily, I was far better practiced at navigating my weak limbs than he, so I could at least find the strength to move, sluggish though I was.

I evoked my Death Hallows next, violet lights streaming from my fingers as I pressed against my chest and felt the thrumming sensation of touching Alexander's NecroSeam within my heart. In a long stream of breath, I peeled his soul from my vessel, then delicately replaced his detached soul into his own body and stitched his NecroSeam to his heart.

My brother's eyes fluttered open, and he sat up, rubbing his shoulder tenderly. "Bloody bastard..."

"It's only fair," I considered. "I know what it's like in *your* body, but you hadn't been in mine yet, had you?"

"And I suppose this makes us even, then?" he asked flatly.

I laughed. "Not in the least. You'd have to spend six years in my vessel for us to be square."

He scowled. "I should hope you don't want that as much as I don't."

"Obviously. But I can enjoy your suffering within my speculative imagination."

Jaq leaned on his bunk's pillar. "I still want to know what all that's like, anyway. Can you only bring each other in there? Or have you tried with anyone else?"

I scratched the beard clinging to my face. Its scraggly warmth had grown on me, no pun intended. I smirked. "Actually, I *haven't* tried, Jaq. Do you wish to test it? I'm sick of everyone talking about our Dream Hallows, it'd be a refreshing change of pace to use my original element again."

"Death yeah!" Jaq eagerly moved from the bed and *thumped* onto the floor in front of me, sitting cross-legged like an excited child awaiting a long-desired story from his mother.

Octavius lingered by the bunk, skeptical, but seeming intrigued.

Jaq glanced round the room as if assessing where he would land from his sitting position. Once he was satisfied with his predicted landing area, he breathed in deeply, then released it in a sharp exhale. "Okay. Go."

I chuckled and evoked my Hallows, violet lights streaming from my hand once more as I pushed against Jaq's chest. "Enjoy the ride."

I *yanked* out his soul.

JAQ

As Xavier pulled me out, I gasped for breath, but my lungs didn't fill up. For the first time in my life, I forgot what *touch* felt like. I apparently didn't have to breathe, and the woody smell of the ship disappeared. The mates were all ghostly white now and tinted in shades of grey even though *I* still had color left on my scales when I looked at my hands. I mean, they were see-through, but they still had color.

I laughed, delirious. *"Co-ho-hoo!"*

Xavier grabbed the glowing NecroSeam from inside my translucent chest, and I jolted. Holy *Bloods!* His hand was freakin' warm. It was the only sensation I could actually feel.

His fingers wrapped around my Seam, which was still intact, and he pulled me over to him.

I sank into his skin—and everything went pitch black.

Then light suddenly spilled from some circular, window-thingy above me. Everywhere else was dark as Void. *Hm.* I didn't know where in Death I was, but I had an idea. Empty, black, and endless? Yep. Sounded like how the twins always described the psyche.

I laughed, rubbing my hands together. *"Oh man, this is so cool!"*

"Well," I heard Xavier say from… well, *everywhere*. His voice bounced and reverberated from all directions in the abyss. "Welcome to the psyche. That's where I'd been living half the time for the past few years."

"Roomy." I looked up at the ray of light glowing above me. *"How do I get to the window thingy?"*

"Just think of moving toward it," Xavier suggested.

"All righty." I thought to move upward, and was surprised how easy it was to float up to the window. I looked out of it and saw Alex and Octavius were staring from the other side, both looking either scared or curious.

"So, this was your view, huh?" I grunted. Six years of wondering, and I finally got to see it for myself. The window kept blinking, the view moving around the room on its own. It drifted to the floor where I saw myself—my body—snoring on my back and drooling a little.

"Yeah," I heard Xavier sigh depressively. The view rose to a higher level, and I guessed that meant he'd stood up. "Did you want to try switching out here?" he offered.

I looked around, accidentally turning full circle in the void. *"Uh, how do I do that?"*

He chuckled. "Here…"

I yelped when something tugged at me, like some kind of vibration pulling me toward the window. I cringed when it pulled me all the way through—

The physical world slammed back to existence, so hard I stumbled and had to grab the nearby desk to keep myself standing. My lungs hurt, and I wheezed for breath that I suddenly needed again, my stick-like arms quivering to hold me up over the desk.

"W-w-whoa…" I held a hand up to inspect it. *Bloods,* I thought, *no scales. Just smooth, mammalian skin.*

I could feel my ears *move,* then. They were getting warm with new fur as they stretched outward, and every sound was suddenly bursting in my eardrums louder than before. I pinched the new coned tips experimentally. "Ho, ho!—I have fur on my ears!"

I heard Xavier heckle from my thoughts. *"Yes, how otherworldly, eh?"*

"This is so cool!" I tried to take a step for the door, but my knees wobbled weakly and almost toppled right then and there. I lunged for the bedpost to keep myself up. "Seamstress prick me, Xavier! I can barely feel your legs!"

He grunted from my thoughts, *"Tell me about it."*

I found his cane next to me and grabbed it, hobbling out to the halls. This thing was hard as Death to maneuver. It kept wanting to slip right off the floor if I didn't put enough weight on it.

"Where are we going?" Xavier asked from my thoughts curiously.

"Where do ya think?" I grinned wide, finding the door I was looking for and threw it open. "Hey, Bianca! Check it out!"

In the clinic cabin, the rabbit was alone and in the middle of heating a beaker with green liquid. When I burst inside, she lifted up her dirty goggles and turned my way.

"Oh, Xavier." She lowered into a nearby stool, yawning. "You can't be out of that muscle-growth tonic already? I just gave you more this morning."

I couldn't stop myself from snickering, clipping inside with the cane. "He ain't out of it. And bet'cha can't guess what *we've* been doin' today."

Her brow bunched up so intensely, creases streaked her forehead. "Why are you talking like…"

Her stare went stale at my toothy grin, and she gasped, rushing to pull open a drawer. She fumbled to get her rose-rimmed, soul-seeing glasses out and slid them over her eyes. She abandoned her experiments and came to grab my face, lifting my eyelids with a horrified yet fascinated look.

"Holy Bloods!" she cried. "*Jaq?* Is that you in there? Xavier's eyes aren't black!"

I laughed. "Cool, right? Turns out he can do this to *anyone*, not just him and Alex."

Bianca went to get a notepad from the counter, finding a fountain-quill and shaking it until a sputter of ink squirted out. She started scribbling. "So—so can Xavier put souls into *other* people, too? Or just inside him?"

"Dunno," I hummed, scratching my—*beard?* I blinked after feeling the coarse hairs at my jaw. Man, this thing was soft! Lucky bastard. I could barely grow a few whiskers on my chin. Why did Alex always want to shave his?

"*I haven't tried that,*" Xavier said from my thoughts, answering Bianca's question.

"He says he hasn't tried," I relayed.

I cringed when she shook my shoulders. "What in Death is he waiting for?! Xavier, get out here and put Jaq inside me!"

"Uh, Bianca…" I heard Xavier roaring with laughter in my head. "Ya do realize what that sounded like, right?"

"You know what I Bloody meant!" She let me go, tapping an impatient foot. "And I'm serious. We need to know what your limitations are with this soul-removal Evocation. I mean, what if you can put *multiple* people in one vessel?"

Xavier was silent from my head for a minute. Then he said, "*I hadn't thought of that.*"

I yelped when I was sucked back into the psyche, my view confined to that lonely window again in the abyss. *Damn, that was fast.* Looking out the window, it looked like he didn't even stumble, either. I guessed he'd had six years more practice than me, though, so that made sense.

The bottom part of my window lifted. Was he smiling?

"Care to find out?" I heard Xavier ask Bianca.

He used his cane to ease himself to the floor and motioned for Bianca to join him. She flopped down in front of him, grinning like a little girl about to get *five* scoops of ice cream. "Let's do this!"

Xavier removed her soul and pulled her into his chest.

"HAH!" I heard her voice cheer in triumph from *really* close in the abyss. Then I was squeezed from behind. *"It worked! We're both in here!"*

There she Bloody was, the orange-haired rabbit girl floating in the blackness alongside me, wheeling loop-de-loops and giggling like a five-year-old.

Xavier's view through the window flicked at the ceiling, chuckling delightedly. "You are?"

"Yeah!" She giggled and kept flying loops in the black expanse. *"Bloods, I've always wondered what it was like in here! Heh, heh! This is fun!"*

Xavier's tone was brooding. "Only if you aren't trapped in there for years."

I rubbed my chin—my bare, scaled chin—and gave a thoughtful hum. *"How many people can you cram in here at once?"*

Xavier flicked his view to the left, then pushed himself up with his cane. "Let's find out, shall we?"

MATTHIEL

"You want to do *what?*" I asked the frail madman skeptically.

Xavier was grinning like an imbecile from outside my cabin door, the scar over his right eye wrinkling slightly over his cheek.

He explained once more, "Take out your soul and place it in my body with the others."

"That's what I thought you said." I massaged my temple desperately. My messenger raven, Paschal, gave a grumbling croak from my shoulder. "And, er, *how* many people are in there, then?"

Xavier paused, then glanced at the ceiling. "Head count, please?" He stood in silence for a moment, then answered. "Five, at the moment. There would have been six, but Alex declined."

"I can't imagine why," I muttered. "I'm inclined to follow Alexander's example, thank you."

Xavier shrugged. "Suit yourself—"

His eyes switched to a lime green, his grin turning smug. "You're missing out, man."

They switched again, this time to brown, and Xavier's hobbled posture turned feminine as he inhaled an inspired gasp. "I just got the *best* idea, Xavier!

Let's find Willow!" He paused, listening to something, then scowled. "Aw, come on! I don't want to be the only girl in here. That's not fair."

His eyes switched to a slightly darker shade of brown and his shoulders suddenly turned rigid. "Uh, why was *I* pushed out? Crap, how do I… No—wait! Let me write this down! The other Enlighteners would want to hear about…!"

He—they—clipped down the hall with Xavier's cane.

I stared after them, bemused. *How I lost Willow to that twelve-year-old is beyond me.*

EVERLAND

LINDEL

NEW ALDAMSTRIA

DRINELLE

11

MILANN

MONTHS PRIOR

"*Kh-khaoh…!*" I coughed and tripped on a crunched piece of road, smoke still really thick even though the fires were put out days ago.

I couldn't breathe good, and I couldn't see good neither. I sniffed, rubbing my cracked ewe horn and wiped off the soot that got stuck to my fingers.

Mum was dead. So was Da. They were squished by a falling building when those big dragons came by and stomped everything down.

Mum… I pulled my coat tighter, my chest hurting bad.

It never felt no better after Mum kilt my bird… I didn't even get a chance to name it. And it really, really *hurt* to remember. It hurt, hurt, *hurt…*

I hiccuped and dragged an arm over my runny nose, wiping my cheeks dry. And now Mum and Da are gone, too. It all just *hurts…*

Phweeeeee!

I got a good jump when a train whistle screamed.

I saw smoke puffing from the car's chimney by the crumbled station up ahead. Some people in white cloaks were yelling for people to get on. Wasn't those Reapers? Like the missy with that little birdy from the parade?

Maybe I should find her? I wondered. *Maybe the missy Reaper could tell me what to do now?* I betted one of those Reapers on that train would know where to find her, too.

The train was floating forward now.

"W-wait…!" I fumbled after it, the smoke leaving a trail from the chimney—

Rrrhhhh….

My legs froze stiff at the growl, and I looked back.

There was a black *thing* behind a felled-over streetlight. I couldn't see it no good through the smoke, but there was black sludgey stuff like snakes sneaking over its skin. It had small ewe horns, but it was a big thing, and it was always *moving*, with big, glowing white lights for eyes.

I shivered when it stared right at me. That was one of those demony monsters. Like on the screens. Like the Missy Reaper kilt…

Chun-chun-chun-chun…

That train up ahead was almost out of the station, floating away.

"Wait…!" I bolted for the station, running from the monster—

The demon bleated and jumped, slamming on top of me. I screamed, pinned on the street. The demon didn't have claws, but its skeleton-like hands scratched my stomach.

I kicked it off, crying at the bleeding sting, and scurried around the corner.

Then something glowy caught my eye. It was blue and shiny, stretched wide and curved to a sharp point. I picked up the shiny thing by the long stick it was on—I had to rip it out of red fingers still holding it from under a pile of stones—wiped my eyes and sniffed big.

The missy Reaper had a thing like this! I saw it on Screen, she hit the demons with it and they were kilt.

A new shriek tore from around the corner, and that same demony monster came running in, knocking over boxes and crumbled stone.

I sniffed again, holding the shiny Reaper-thing tight. *Just like the missy did.*

If I didn't kill it, it would kill me. I just had to cock it back like the missy did, wait for it and…

It jumped for me. I screamed and swiped the shiny, pointy end at it, right down the middle.

Something *snapped* and the thing dropped, curled up… and the black stuff started dripping off it, misting upward and disappearing.

I did it. I was breathing so hard, my chest hurt. *I-I did it! Just like the missy Reaper!*

My knees hit the cracked ground and I heaved, feeling sick. *I-I need to go.* The train was already gone, but I could follow the tracks. I had to go soon, too, or more demons might show up.

I pushed up, keeping a super tight grip on the glowy weapon—

My thumb brushed over a ripple-looking mark on the stick part, and it glowed gold. Then the thing shrank into a tiny ball the size of my hand. It still weighed the same, though, so my arm dipped to keep it held up. *Weird.* Do all the Reaper thingies do that? I pressed the mark again and kept the weapon shape in case I needed it on my walk.

I twisted back to the demon I kilt. The black sludge had all dripped off and disappeared.

And now I was staring at my Mum.

12

PRINCE CAYDEN

Stay calm, I reminded in silence. *Calm. You were the captive of the enemy. The Reapers held you prisoner for months. You were bruised and bloodied, tortured for countless days in a dark, disgusting dungeon. You are relieved to be set free. You are happy to see Father soon.*

I repeated the thoughts on a loop, attempting to believe them. Hopefully, it would project outwardly.

My steps were rigid as I walked through the snow-ridden square of Everland's capital, the crowd of stunned citizens parting to make way for me and the lovely Yulia, who was escorting me to the center. She wasn't here physically. The Somniovoker had created a phantom doppelganger, here to show my father that the Devouhs had willingly handed me over via their servant. Or, daughter? Niece? I wasn't sure how Yulia figured into the Devouhs' lives. The way they interacted, there wasn't a clear line between family and employee. Was that simply how it was with private Dreamcatchers? I didn't recall Father being so close to his own Somniovokers. But then, this was Father we were talking about.

My hands were strapped with fake dampening-gloves and shackled together, purely for effect. I wore tattered rags that were covered in soot and blood, just an extra bit of depth that told our false story. My eyes were wrapped in a thin fabric to give the illusion that I was blinded, though I could see well enough through the brown filter.

Father stood in the center of the square on a wooden platform. In his grasp, only able to touch him due to the special gloves Father wore, was the ghost of Lord Apsonald. I could only see him myself because Lord Lucas had carefully attached a silver button with an enchantment rune into the fabric over my eyes.

I had my face craned down to look at my feet, but my stare lingered on the translucent viper. *Apson.* My teeth threatened to sharpen, and I commanded the muscles in my lion ears to yield before curling back. I was supposed to be tired and frightened. Not on the verge of ripping out Father's throat. I kept my round ears folded firmly down.

Behind Father hung a large vision-screen that loomed over the square. On the screen of light was Linus, the goat wearing the garb of Land's Servant. My garb. It made his eye color olive and his hair a lighter shade of brown, as it did for me when I had donned the uniform.

There were reporters with recording devices swarming Yulia and me now, bulbs blinking from vision-corders and shouts erupting from the crowd, but I ignored them. My gaze was solely on Linus from the screen. We had planned for him to pose as the rebellion's leader for this, though he was overseas with the twins.

Damn you, Linus. He'd just finished telling me he'd never leave my side again, and the moment I needed him most, what did he do?

"Cayden." Father's amplified voice broke my thoughts. "Is it truly you? It's no trick?"

My throat scratched. "No trick, Father. They value the soul of the Roarlord."

He gave a brisk toss of his head and ordered a pair of guards to check. The two Raiders wary of Yulia. When she stepped from my side, they came to touch my shoulder, informing Father that I wasn't a phantom created by an illusionist. They checked me for any enchanted items as well, in case I was someone else made to *look* like the prince. They removed my blinding cloth and confirmed no such items were found, having overlooking the small button on my covering cloth.

Father blew out a relieved breath and glanced over his shoulder at the large screen of light. His gloved grip was tight on what looked like, from my now soul-blind eyes, thin air. I presumed that was Apson. "I see you've kept your word, Servant," Father said.

"Indeed I have," fuzzed Linus' voice on the screen, his masked face shadowed under the wide-brimmed hat. *"And I expect you to follow suit, Galden. One released son for one released soul."*

"Of course, of course." Father nodded in a bobbing motion. "I'll release Apson, as promised… but *I* choose where and to whom. You understand, I cannot simply give you an informant so willingly."

Linus' eyes slit behind his mask. *"Then where do you choose?"*

A wicked smile rolled over father's lips as he handed nothing—supposedly Apson's ghost—over to nearby guards, who also wore specialized gloves to keep hold of the specter. "Right here," Father said, "In this square. I intend to make a show of it. You see, Servant, we've captured one of your beloved Necrofera. I think Apson will make a fine meal for the beast."

The crowd began cheering around me, my weak voice drowned. "Father…"

"*Galden.*" Linus' tone was a heated. "*You gave your word.*"

"Which is what I offer," Father chuckled. "You asked me to release Apson in exchange for my son. Well, I'm releasing him."

"*And endangering your own people by bringing a Necrofera into the city?*" Linus growled.

"I assure you, the beast is contained. The only danger will fall on Apson." He turned to the guard who held the invisible ghost. "Return the prisoner to his cell. We'll retrieve him once we begin the feeding." He nodded toward Yulia now. "And take that dirt crawler with you. She's the High Howllord's girl, I'd recognize that face anywhere."

Yulia didn't flinch when a Raider reached for her arm. His grip met empty air, and he blinked when she smiled. She then phased backward through a bystander and disappeared into the crowd.

Father shouted orders to find her, and my 'rescuing' guards hurried me up to Father's side. He then hurried me toward the awaiting hover-coach that was decorated with royal flags.

"Are you hurt, Cayden?" Father asked as he sized me up and down with worried eyes. "Do you need a Healer? Captain! Take him to the royal Healer immediately."

"Father, I—" I was dragged into the coach, the door slamming behind me, and the feral horses were whipped into motion. We headed up the winding, mountain path toward the palace, and I watched as the guards whom I knew held Apson's ghost marched into a different coach that hovered down a separate road.

Apson, I thought furiously, my teeth gritting, *where are they taking you?*

Hours later, I stood alone in the expansive bedchamber with iced limbs. I hadn't moved away from the door since the servants had closed it behind me.

The gold-lined room was exactly as I remembered: unnecessarily large without enough furniture to fill the hollow gaps of space. Shel, I'd hoped to be rid of this infernal box for good. Yet, to my ever-bubbling vexation, here I was.

Well, at least we'd planned for a trick like what my father had pulled. And now it was time to proceed with that plan and find the lady Yulia's copy.

I sucked in a slow breath, balled my hands as I scanned the nostalgic room one last time, then cracked open the door. I saw no guards or servants in the corridor, so I stepped out.

I hoped I'd given enough time for Yulia to come here after she'd—if all went well—followed the coach Apson had been carted off in. Now the only question was, where to find her—?

"Cayden?"

I cringed at the feminine voice behind me. It was vaguely familiar. When I spun around—

A Roaress trapped me in her arms and squeezed my ribs mercilessly.

"A-ah!" I tried to sound pleasantly surprised, my smile cautious as I registered the intruding woman's face. "Lady Revinna…!"

I'd almost forgotten about her. Had she been the woman I was courting last? Or was that Diane? Blast it all, I'd been away for so long, I thought I wouldn't have to worry about these women anymore.

Then again, now that I looked at her face, I supposed I didn't have to worry over this one. She had gold wedding vines dangling from her hair, a violet gem hanging from the centerpiece at her forehead. She'd apparently gone and married some other Roarlord while I was gone. Fancy that.

She released me to clutch my hands, her brown eyes rimmed red as if she'd battled with tears for months. "I've been so worried," she said, her voice a gentle quiver. "When I saw you were released on the Screens, I came right away."

"Did you?" I drawled dully. "And does your husband know you're here, Revinna?" Perhaps the reminder would guilt her into leaving faster. I hadn't much time to spare, Apson's afterlife was at stake.

Revinna chuckled and wiped her eyes. "Yes. He knows." She tugged me along the corridor. "Come, come! You must be hungry. Your father has arranged a dinner in celebration."

I grimaced. "Has he, now…"

I broke away, sure to hunch my shoulders and wince back as if my weeks of 'torture' had had a permanent effect on my social habits.

She gave me a careful glance and retracted her hand. "Cayden?"

"I'm sorry," I said, adding a morose undertone to my voice. "I don't think I'm quite up for… dinners."

Her brow arched in sympathy. "Oh. Yes…" She seemed to contemplate a thought in silence for a moment, then shook her head. "It won't be a public event. I promise. Your father only wishes to see you back with the family."

"Tell my father I'll join him another day." I started to retreat back to my chambers. *Damn it.* I'll have to wait for her to leave, then find Yulia later tonight.

I'd only taken two steps before Revinna snatched my hand in a panic. "No, please…!"

I raised a brow. She looked frightened, her grip shivering and lion ears practically stuck to her jawline. "Please," she said again. "He's expecting you. If I tell him you won't come…"

My eyes fell to her hands. I saw large, dark welts littered in yellow rings along her knuckles and puffy veins.

"Revinna?" I began slowly, scrutinizing the rest of her. It wasn't noticeable right away in the dim corridor lights, but now that I paid more attention, I noticed there were bruises coating her arms and neck, and a mess of scars trailed her collarbone. They looked like claw marks. And they looked recent. "Gardener sow me," I whispered, anger bubbling. "What has he done to you?"

She whispered. "Please. Don't disappoint him. Please…"

My teeth sharpened. I gripped her hand with gentle fingers, minding the welts, before storming down the halls with her in tow.

I shoved open the dining hall's doors. "*Father.*" My voice ruptured against the echoing walls. "Would you care to explain what…"

The words died on my lips. At the long table were all of my blonde sisters, my single little brother—and my mother and father. It wasn't the number of people in the hall that had me pause. It was how each one of them were stiff as month-old bread. My sisters, young and old, were rigid in their seats, the younger ones quaking and looking on the verge of tears. They weren't tears of joy that I'd returned, I wagered. All had the same dark welts that Revinna housed, their skin scarred red and purple. Even my youngest brother had marks on his cheek, along with a split lip.

My mother was the worst sight. She had more scars than bruises, the red tracks streaking from her face down to her chest, scabs caked and cracked over her neck. There were small specks of blood seeping from under her gown's bust on the right breast.

Mother's hand shook as she dipped her spoon into her soup, but she stopped to glance at me when I entered. The others had turned their heads to me as well, but not a soul stood to greet me.

Father was the only one to rise, his cheeks drunkenly red as he laughed in delight. "Cayden! Good, good, you came!"

He waved for everyone to stand, and they promptly obeyed, chair legs softly scuffing over the carpet. Father didn't seem to notice that they didn't take a step further while he himself came around the table to take my shoulder, chuckling. From my peripherals, I saw Revinna cringe away from him.

"I had the servants bring a seat for you," said Father as he dragged me to the nearest end of the table, opposite him and Mother.

There were, in fact, two empty seats there. I was still in shock at the sight of my mother and siblings that I absently lowered into one.

"And, of course," Father continued, waving for Revinna to join me as he went back to his own seat. "Your wife will be at your side, as she should."

My gaze ripped away from my siblings, focusing on him again. "Wife?"

"Your welcoming gift." Father's smile stretched wide as he dug into the flank of pork on his plate. "I knew you'd need a grand gift when you returned. Something to help you forget whatever horrors those demon-mongrels put you through." He belched and wiped the juice from his lips with a kerchief. "I signed the papers for you a month ago. We'll arrange for your ring and stud to be ordered later. For now, you can fully enjoy your first night back." He guffawed and slapped an entertained hand on the table.

Servants came to refill his wine, and they poured me a goblet of my own, then filled up Revinna's as she took the seat beside me. I regarded the woman with a hard expression, and she returned a chilled gaze. She tried a smile, but it soon vanished, replaced with a mixture of shame and fear.

I watched as everyone resumed their meal. *Dearest Shel.* My father had always been mad, but has he completely lost what little sanity he had left? And all because I'd left…

I saw movement to my right. A white-haired head phased through the wall. *Yulia.*

I cleared my throat and rose slowly. "I… e, excuse me, Father. I haven't had such… splendid food for months. My stomach needs time to… adjust. Please, excuse me…"

Anger fumed in Father's eyes, but he nodded, cursing those monstrous dirt crawlers as he glugged more of his wine.

My eyes met Mother's one last time, her haunting stare begging me not to leave. I cast my gaze down and forced my legs to move. *I'm sorry, Mother. I have a vow to keep.* When I was alone in the halls again, I let out my breath, my chest a sickened knot.

"We must hurry," Yulia's wispy voice murmured beside me, her phantom copy appearing from within a stone pillar. "They have the Fera locked in the same cell as Apson. The live feeding is scheduled for tomorrow morning."

I hit the wall. "*Tonight.* We have to speed up our plan, I can't wait a whole damned month. He dies *tonight.*"

Yulia cast down her gaze, nodding. She raised no protest.

But Father's death would have to wait a few hours more. Apson, I knew, had to be freed first. Even with the king dead, the brainwashed citizens would likely riot over an assassination and go on with the 'feeding'.

I stalked down the corridor with Yulia, avoiding any passing servants or patrolling soldiers. Yulia followed close and hid within pillars as I led us to the library, shutting the doors behind me.

There were countless shelves towering the room, one large window set at the back, though its curtain was drawn to hide the night sky outside. There was a fire set in the hearth, its embers crackling in the resounding silence. I'd always loved this room. Hardly anyone ever came here anymore. The Gods knew Father never set foot in here, and it had been one of the only sure places I could escape when I was younger; escape and spend hours with Linus.

My fingers traced the dusty bindings along the shelves, remembering those times. How long ago had that been? I must have been ten, perhaps eleven? Those were better days. We'd wasted so many nights to meet here outside of our double-life with the rebellion—when my predecessor, a man named Gerard, was Land's Servant and not I.

Gerard had taken me in when I came to him as a cub, despite my lineage. I'd begged to join his ranks, to see my father killed for all he'd done to my family. Gerard passed me onto the others as his son and apprentice, to keep them ignorant of my royal title. Gerard truly was like a father to me—more so than my real father. The others never learned of my true identity—save for Linus. Within the first week of his recruitment alongside his father into the resistance, Linus had attended a palace social and bumped into me in this very library. His prophetic Hallows had Seen that I was Gerard's apprentice. I'd expected him to hate me for my blood, for being the son of the false king we sought to dethrone... yet he simply shook my hand and laughed, commending me for fooling him so well.

I finally found the lamp I was searching for. It was set into a bare space on the wall of the palace. I flattened my palm against the stones beside the lamp and evoked my rock Hallows, golden lights streaming from my fingers and sinking into the stones.

The wall rumbled and ground to life, and I heaved, pushing back as much of the stone as my muscles would allow. I grunted as the stone ground its way out of place, then dismissed my Hallows. Inside the now opened wall was a dark tunnel. It was one of the many hidden passages in the palace. These tunnels were connected at many entry points throughout the grounds, built in case the royal family needed to escape from attacks. Most entrances, like this one, were only accessible to Terravokers to better prevent others from following. As far as I knew, no one had used them in years, save for myself.

I slid inside the tunnel and took a torch from the rounded walls, going to the library's hearth to light it. These tunnels hadn't been refurbished in so long that the lighting was still archaic.

I stepped back into the tunnel and kept the torch in front of me, closing the entry point behind me. Yulia's copy walked through the wall then and stood beside me.

I glanced at her. "Where was Apson sent?"

"To a cave along the eastern mountainside," she said, "outside the castle grounds."

I nodded and started down the passage with Yulia. I knew the way to the eastern mountains, luckily. There wasn't a direct route there from these passages, but there was one exit two miles away from our destination. I checked the chipped-away signs at each fork in the tunnels and led us on the right path. Before long, we reached a dead end where a ladder led to a ceiling door. I climbed up and unlatched the rusted, metal lock on the door, then shoved against it. It took some effort, but after three more heaves, the door swung open, the snow that had weighed it down flooding off to the side.

I lifted myself out of the tunnels and reached a hand down to Yulia, but remembered she was a copy. She couldn't touch anything. I peered down into the tunnel and called, "Can you… er, float up here, Howless? Like a ghost?"

"Ghosts cannot float higher than the living can jump," she replied, climbing up the ladder. When she reached the top, she rose to her feet beside me and continued, "Though, you were right: we are similar to the ghosts. Copies can gain lift off of objects if they wish, and fall downward *through* objects as well. We simply cannot fly."

I hummed. "Curious. I'll have to remember that."

We traversed the snow-ridden mountain path to the cave Yulia mentioned, the Howless leading the way this time. It took nearly an hour to reach, but we soon heard voices up ahead and slowed our pace. I hid behind a dried up tree while she phased within its bark. A number of armed Rockraiders stood outside a cavern's entrance. They had a firepit nearby, one of the Raiders was tending to the charring logs.

"I-I-I don't like this," one of the soldiers stuttered, quaking in his armor by the cave's entrance. He flinched at every guttural bleat that screeched from within. "I didn't sign up for demon duty."

His superior grunted and slid a new log into the firepit, a spray of embers puffing. "Keep your willie dry over there, Lorn," the captain grunted. "It's barred up, it's not going to escape."

The shaking Raider cringed when the hidden beast gave another haunting cry from the depths of the cavern. "B-but it's not natural…!" he squeaked. "Did you hear how many men that one thing ripped up before they got it in that cage? I don't want to be around if it gets loose!"

"For the love of Shel, Lorn," the captain groaned. "It's not going to…"

Yulia's phantom stepped out from the tree, and the captain saw her. He jerked to his feet, pulling out his sword. "What in Bloody…! D-Dirt crawler!"

The other guards turned to the commotion, and all but one hurried after Yulia as she baited them away from the mouth of the cave. The single Raider left was the shivering man, Lorn.

I grinned and picked up a large, stray rock from the ground, using my Terravoking to morph it into a make-shift helmet to hide my face. It was rough against my skull, but stretched thin enough that the weight was evenly distributed. I was no smith like Henry, but I thought it was a fair job, rushed though it was.

I stepped out from around the tree. Lorn spotted me. He jumped in a start and raised his oddly radiant sword before him.

"S-stay back!" His voice cracked at the last word.

I stretched a hand to him and evoked my rock Hallows, prying the weapon from his fingers with a sharp tug and catching it by the hilt. I turned the glowing-blue blade in inspection.

"Spiritcrystal," I observed. It was incredibly light. The bluish sheen was beautiful against the blade's mirrored surface, though it wasn't quite bright enough to light the surrounding area. The firepit's flames were even glinting off the smooth metal more brilliantly than its natural gleam.

I rapped my knuckles on the blade's flat face experimentally, the metal ringing in return. "So, it can touch skin, which rules out a pure-crystal blade. Must be alloyed with… Hm. Feels like Olium?" I supposed the Rockraiders have been taking the Reaper's jobs now. Just how many of these weapons had they stolen over the years? Hopefully, Henry would have that data for me in town. He'd entered the capital a month before us to claim refugee status and opened a forge here. I hoped he gathered enough information in that time.

I blithely bobbed the flat side of the sword over my shoulder and approached the Raider.

"Well, Lorn," I sighed in my gravely, disguised voice that I often used for Land's Servant. "Why don't we play a little game? We'll call it, *I set the beast loose, and you catch it.* Sound fun?"

Lorn's face fell. Then the Fera inside shrieked and made him duck, the man crying out in terrified sobs as he scurried down the mountain.

I chuckled. That was almost too simple. Normally, I would have slit his throat before giving a warning, but it hadn't felt appropriate this time. I wondered why? Had my months with the Reapers sapped me of my bloodlust? My head shook. Such a strange influence they were.

I crept into the cave and kept my head low, raising my glowing sword. There were no torches in here save for the one around the curve of the tunnel, the light's edge barely reaching me. As I closed in, I braced for other awaiting guards, pressing my back against a shielding stalagmite and perking one lion ear to listen. There was no sound. None except the demon's gurgled bleating.

I craned my head around the rock to look. There was the beast, caged in a barred, iron box just big enough to fit it. It had curled horns, the tips dripping black muck onto its equally slurping skull, limbs disjointed and cracked in unnatural angles. The thing lurched in its cage, growling furiously as the chains rattled with every violent thrust against the bars.

Looking past the cage, I found a slumped figure lying on the cavern floor. It was a corpse. It looked slightly aged with no blood to be found save for the crusted flakes covering its torso. Its scale-skinned head was a foot away from its neck, its sandy hair clumped with dirt and snow. *Apson's vessel*, I noted silently as my lids narrowed. *His soul should be nearby.*

I searched the area more intently and soon found two pairs of floating, glowing shackles. Their lights radiated with such brilliance, they seemed to shimmer like rays of moonlight. These were pure Spiritcrystal, no question. And judging from their hovering positions, they were locked around Apson's invisible wrists and ankles, from a sitting level, I guessed.

I reached into my trousers' back pocket and withdrew a soul-seeing mask I'd brought with me before coming to the capital. I donned it under my stone helmet and then took out a gold earcuff, which was enchanted to allow me to hear ghosts as well, and slid it on one of my lion ears. Then, cautiously, I pushed off my shielding stalagmite and crept toward Apson's now visible spirit.

The ghost glanced up when I neared him, looking confused.

"It's me, Apson," I hissed and crouched beside him, glancing at the raging beast in the cage. It snarled at me and snapped its fangs, and I shivered before jerking my attention back to Apson.

The ghost's bleary eyes focused on my hidden face, sounding exhausted. "Cayden…? What are you doing here?"

"Retrieving my general." I reached for his glowing chains, but my fingers passed through without contact. My tongue clicked. "Blasted Spiritcrystal…"

I evoked my rock Hallows instead, a golden light spewing from my hands. His shackles soon radiated with the same light, and I focused on wrenching the chains apart.

Land's Blade! This crystal was slippery. It was worse than manipulating metal alloys. I couldn't even feel my Hallows grip the damned stuff it was so elusive. I ground my teeth, dismissing the magic. I wasn't familiar enough with this crystal to form so much as a dent. It seemed I'd have to find another way.

I frowned and lifted the alloyed sword I still wielded. *Well*, I considered, *it's worth a try.* I ordered Apson to lay his shackles on the dirt and stretch the chains taut. He did so, and I speared my blade through one of the links, then told Apson to pull. It took some effort, but the chains snapped. Grinning at our success, we did the same for his bound ankles, and the newly freed ghost floated to his translucent feet beside me.

"Come," I said in a hush, grunting while heaving his corpse over my shoulder and, holding back a gag, scooped up his head and tucked it under my arm. Lord Lucas had been damned adamant about collecting *all* of Apson's remains when we went over the plan. His body was heavy, but I managed to regain balance and stepped for the cave's entrance, panting. "I'm to bring you to the transport squad Lord Lucas assembled at the mountainside," I told Apson.

Avoiding the demon still rattling in its cage, we fled the cavern.

The guards still hadn't returned, as I supposed Yulia still had them distracted in the mountains. Only *my* feet crunched through the snow and left prints as we started through the woods. Apson's limp toes dangled at my ankles as I lugged the corpse on my back, and his ghost floated beside me to scan the terrain for enemy soldiers.

I'm not holding a corpse, I thought repeatedly, trying to keep focused. *I'm just carrying an unconscious man on my back... with his head tucked under my arm.* I could feel the tips of his long fangs scratching my elbow, and I grimaced. *Lucas, you morbid bastard, there had better be a good reason for this.*

"Cayden," Apson's ghost began as we trekked round a rocky bend. "Does your Father know? About Land's Servant?"

I hefted his body over my back to better balance him and grunted. "Not unless you've told him, Apson."

"I would never." He sounded affronted, the soul's scaled face hardening. "If you haven't noticed, I lost my head over keeping your secret."

The reminder made my stomach sink. And, annoyingly, it made my fingers remember they were holding the very head he spoke of. I pushed down the last thought. "I'm... sorry, Apson," I said. "I shouldn't have let you come back to Father. He seems to have lost more than his sobriety since I left."

The ghost snorted. "Galden's always been mad. He simply never had the convenience to display it until now."

And now it's displayed on my family. Anger boiled, but I was distracted when my boot slipped in the snow. I didn't fall, but Apson's corpse slid down my back an inch, and I quickly lifted him back up and nearly dropped his head in the process.

I tightened my grip and regained footing, blowing out a breath. Hopefully, I didn't sound too disgusted in front of Apson's watching ghost.

We kept to the snowy path, and after nearly half an hour, we reached the pass where Lucas's transportation squad waited in the shadows. They'd brought a Storagecoffin to house the corpse, and one of the female, Grimish Reapers used her Necrovoking to store Apson's body inside.

I was still panting from the hike when they readied their horses to leave. Yulia approached, her feet sinking in the snow. This was the *real* Yulia. The physical one. She nodded to me, as did the antlered Dreamcatcher, Jimmy, who stood beside her.

"Is this Apson's spirit?" Lady Yulia asked, glancing to Apson's soul. "Forgive me. I can only see the shackles."

"It's him," I confirmed and turned to Apson. I slid off my stone helmet, keeping the soul-seeing mask and earcuff on. "Apson... There is so much I need to answer for, but not enough time to do it. You were my friend for longer than you even realized, and it's because of me that you've ended up this way. So, it's my responsibility to take your place in the palace."

The ghost looked horrified. "If you stay, your father will..."

"I've lived under my father's roof for over two decades without him figuring me out. I can do it again, only this time, it won't be for as long." A growl slipped through my throat, and I squeezed the hilt of my glowing blade. "I will kill him, Apson. I will put an end to the nightmare."

I glanced at the Dreamcatchers, holding out my sword to Yulia. "Howless, this is yours now. I picked it off a Raider."

Her pale hands hesitated, but she took the sword nonetheless. The fox seemed surprised at how light it was. She glanced at Jimmy, as if asking for an answer he didn't have, then returned her gaze to me in a blush. "Dream's knights aren't meant for combat," she said, her voice a delicate wisp. "Not in the physical realms. And it is against the Fourth Law of Death for anyone but Reapers to have it. I-I can't take this."

She tried handing it back to me, but Jimmy clasped her shoulder. "Keep it," he said. "It'll be handy if we run into demons on the way back. We can give it to the High Howllord when we get there."

I nodded my agreement, and she fell quiet, staring at the blade as if afraid it would come alive and snap at her.

They departed with the squad of Reapers, and I was left behind, staring after them under the rocky pass. The archway shaded me from the moonlight, and I pressed a hand to its side.

I knew this pass. Many nights I used to come here, on the outskirts of the capital, looking out to the roads leading out. I remembered dreaming of leaving, back then. I remembered the urge to walk down this path, to start over under a new name, to be lost in obscurity among the common masses. I would have committed to it, had Linus met me here the night he'd fled; had he not abandoned me.

I reached for the green bead in my pocket, drawing it to my face in a long sigh.

"Linus?" I pinched the bead between my fingers as I watched the retreating caravan, the group growing smaller and smaller as they descended the mountain path. "Did you know, back then? What would happen to my family if I left Father's side?"

I'd grown accustomed to these one-sided conversations. I'd had them for nine years, cursing his name, questioning him, pleading to Shel that he was still alive. And he'd heard them. Every one, so long as I had this bead. It had once been a gift, when we were boys. We both had one to link us to his visions. It had been our method of communication, though if only *he* could hear me. I never minded. We'd worked with the resources we had.

I palmed the bead. "I will kill him, Linus. I will see my father dead for what he's done."

I started back toward the palace, my boots leaving deep prints in the snow.

I pulled away the hidden tunnel's stone wall with my Terravoking, slinking back into the palace library and making sure no servants had seen. The room, it seemed, had been left alone while I was away, the hearth's soot and charred wood still uncleaned.

I quietly shifted the stones back into place to hide the passage's entryway and plucked a book at random from the shelves, then strolled out. If anyone noticed I'd been absent, I could simply say I'd lost myself in a book.

I kept the book held at my side and paced my steps evenly, stalking through the corridor toward Father's chambers. I didn't want to seem rushed, but neither did I want to dally. A brusque gait was best here. I could claim I had an important thought to discuss with Father, something I'd just read about that was worthy of discussion.

When I arrived at the proper door, I halted, seeing my mother was being escorted by three Raiders down the hall.

"Mother?" I called, looking from her to the door where she normally would be sleeping. "Where are you going?"

She turned and saw me past the guards. Her brown eyes lit up. "Oh, Cayden…" She held her breath after looking at the guards again, as if reminded she was being watched. "I have a different room, now. For my… protection, from the rebels…"

"Yes," came a different voice I didn't recognize behind me. "Her Grace is being heavily supervised. You needn't be concerned."

I craned back, my brow furrowed. Staring at me was my father's Second Hand, Roarlord Wales. His face was the way I remembered, crooked nose and wide face with curling ram horns at his temples, but that voice… it was deeper. Gnarly. And the accent was different. I could swear it almost sounded like… *Like the twins' accent,* I realized. Where the 'e' and 'h' sounds were more of a sharp hiss, clipped at the top. Grimish. *Wales isn't Grimish…*

"Are you," I began suspiciously, "Feeling sickly, Wales? You sound out of sorts…"

His expression didn't falter, and he pulled down his shirt collar to display a long gash running down his adam's apple. "A rebel soldier caught my throat with his blade," he rasped in that foreign accent once again. "The Healers did what they could to repair the damage."

"I see…" It was an obvious lie. The wound could perhaps be an illusion, as could his entire physique. But then, who was this man, really?

I spotted a golden wedding ring on his finger, along with a diamond stud in his left ear. *I wonder…* I reached for the ring, humming. "I don't recall you having a wife, Wales—"

He jerked his hand away and hissed at me. *Hissed.* Like a Bloody cat. Wales was a ram.

"You've been away for some time," he growled. "Much has changed, Your Highness."

"Indeed it has." I glared at him for a moment, but shook my head. I could uncover this imposter later. I had greater concerns tonight.

I went for the latch to my father's door, but 'Wales' blocked my way. "The king is not to be disturbed," he said.

"I only wish to speak with my father," I said. I could later claim an assassin came after both of us and fled. I'd have to cut a gash into my arm somewhere. "It's a private…"

He pushed me back, and something shocked over my skin at the touch. I couldn't see anything on his hands, but I could swear I saw tiny black veins fester over my chest, my hairs standing on end as my heart thudded painfully. It only lasted a fraction of a second, but it was enough to freeze my limbs. *What in Nirus…?*

A heart murmur? Had it skipped a beat? I couldn't have been that overexerted… Had he done something?

"Your father is under strict supervision as well," he said. "As are you, my lord." He waved for a cluster of passing guards to surround me. "Return to your chambers, Your Highness. Your protection is our highest priority."

"What…" The guards barricaded me within a tight circle, just like what mother had had, and they marched down the corridor with me entrapped. "Wales…!"

He was obscured by the men guarding me when we turned the corner. *Damn!* Could I brawl my way out of this? I could just kill the guards, kill Wales, and get to Father in a matter of minutes. My fists clenched. *But then, there would no doubt be witnesses.* I'd be exposed as Father's assassin. Our plan to have me crowned as king would be ruined, and would only exacerbate the war against the Reapers.

Fine, I decided grudgingly. Father lived tonight. But by Gods, I would see that man dead at my feet, one way or another. I just needed more time.

The guards stopped in front of my chambers. I tugged on my long sleeves, gave an indignant snort, and threw open the door—slamming it shut and turned the latch. But I stiffened when a soft gasp sounded behind me from inside the room. Inching back, I found someone was in my bed.

"My lord." The intruding woman bowed her head. She was dressed in a thin, silken gown that only barely covered her breasts, her thighs exposed to show that she, it seemed, wore nothing else underneath. Her bruises darkened an alarming amount of her bronzed skin.

"Revinna," I hesitated. "Right…" *My 'wife'. Damn it all.* She was no less a prisoner than the rest of us, under Father's claw.

Her blush was slight when she gestured to the bed. I remained where I was.

"Tell me," I said. "Did you have any say in this marriage?"

She glanced away. Shook her head.

"Then, my father forced it upon you?"

"I…" She flushed further, rubbing her arm uncomfortably. She hadn't anything else to say.

"Well, then." I went to the chair by the fire, reclining and lacing my fingers over my chest. "I'm sorry he's brought you into our family horrors. You can rest easy, tonight. I'll not claim someone who didn't ask for it."

"I-it's all right." She sat higher on the bed, crawling over the edge. "I really do care for you, Cayden. I always have. I may not have asked for the marriage, but I…" She smiled shyly. "I am thankful that it's you."

I stared at her. "Excuse me?"

She climbed off the bed and perched on my lap, taking my hand and placing it *high* atop her leg. I discovered that, indeed, she wore nothing under that gown.

"I'm saying," she cooed in my lion ear, tracing my chin. "I *want* you to claim me."

Oh, LAND no. I seized her by the shoulders, and for a moment she looked elated, but her face fell when I pushed her off my lap and stepped away.

"I can't," I said, pinching my nose and failing to stifle my grimace.

She sounded baffled. "But why?"

"I can't take advantage of you like this," I lied. "It just isn't right."

"But I'm all right with it. I want this, Cayden."

"Well, that doesn't mean I…" I stopped myself, knowing *I don't want this* would have sounded cruel. Instead, I sighed and added an extra bit of defeat into my voice. "I need more time. I've only just escaped my chains…"

She deflated, retreating to the bed. "Oh… yes. Yes, of course…"

I shook my head, inwardly groaning in relief.

Father, you damned bastard. Well, at least one thing was certain: He's earned himself a quicker death.

13

JIMMY

The sound of crunching snow woke me up, a brightness filling my closed lids. My nose finished the last of its gargled snore and I rubbed my face while stretching up to sit. "Like I can help it, freezing my ass off." I yawned, continuing where Yulia and my conversation left off before my copy disappeared out here. "Just because you're quiet as a feral mouse doesn't mean jack. You live in the cold, so you're immune."

Yulia gave an elusive smirk next to me in the wagon's open back, her feet dangling with her ankles tucked over one another in a spritely pose. "I suppose you have a point," she said.

"And you might not snore," I went on, "but you can't keep to your own space. Every time I move over, you end up trailing me till I'm out of space again."

Her porcelain-perfect face blushed slightly. "I am sorry for that… Perhaps the cold does get to me, eventually." She glanced out the wagon to the horizon, laying her hands over the wrapped bundle that was the Spiritcrystal sword over her lap. She blushed a deeper red. "You're very warm…"

That even made me flush a little. *Crap.* It was getting awkward again. Why the Void did she have to say that? If she wasn't so Gods damned beautiful, it wouldn't be so hard to get it out of my system already; to just up and make a move and get whatever rejection or acceptance over with.

Rules, I reminded. *You have rules, damn it.*

I blew out a breath, sobering up. No commitments. Not to anyone. A night of fun with past girls were all right, but I'd have to be an idiot to seriously see anyone a second time after what happened with Sarin.

The name made me sick to my stomach.

I leaned on my arms at the back of the wagon, the noise from our fully awake caravan clattering with armor and soft chatter from the escorting Reapers.

I wagered we had another few hours before Yulia took her shift, when the second half of the group went to sleep during the day.

I had one leg tucked to my chest and the other swinging lazily over the edge of the wagon. The snow had a glossy sheen to it, the morning sun spreading over the mountain peaks and making everything a blinding white.

New Aldamstria had disappeared yesterday, but we still hadn't reached the bottom of the bordering mountains. It looked like we'd left the path overnight. I didn't know exactly when that happened, I should have noticed it when my copy was out here while I was sleeping, but my conversations with Yulia were so Bloody distracting…

Rules, I reminded again more sharply. *Sarin. Don't forget.*

I glared at the retreating mountain peaks, shoving the memory out. From my peripherals, I saw Yulia lean forward and cock her head at me.

"Jimmy?" she asked softly, her wispy tone careful. "Is everything well?"

"Yeah," I grunted, "Yeah… just remembering some things."

"Is that what it usually is, when you look distant?"

Usually? Damn it, how bad did it look? I didn't know what to say, so I just shrugged.

Her voice turned sympathetic. "May I ask…?"

"It's nothing big." I scratched between my elk antlers. "I, uh… I guess I'm just being sentimental, you know? I'm still getting used to all this."

"'this'?"

"Being out in the open. Having people know what I am without being driven out of town." I clicked my tongue and stretched my neck. "I should have taken a private gig sooner. Being a local Dreamcatcher is hard… always having to do your job without a damn person knowing how much you work to help them. And the minute you tell *one person* you're a Somniovoker, they tell the whole bleeding city, and just about everyone you know tells you to either hike it or wake up as a drenched ghost in the river."

Her brows arched back. "Oh… I'm sorry. Is this what local Catchers often face?"

"Yeah. Too often. But most of them aren't stupid like me and tell their fiancée everything the night before their wedding."

Her face contorted. It was the first time I ever saw the slightest line crease her forehead. "What happened after you told her?"

I kicked my dangling leg as a distraction. "She didn't say anything at first. She just went 'oh', had that look on her face like I was a serial killer, and walked out. I tried to talk to her the next morning, but her family wouldn't even look at me. My friends wanted nothing to do with me either. Eventually, word about my dream Hallows got around town, someone nearly burned down my family's house and I ended up shipping out of there in less than a day. I started over in Lindel, and that was fine after a while, but then *that* place got smashed to bits by a giant dragon and ravaged by demons." I exhaled through my nose. "But I can't go back home again. And all because I thought someone would actually accept that I was a Dream Walker, no questions asked... But I guess it's hard to sleep next to someone that can toy with your subconscious, huh?"

She put a hand on my knee, looking so heartbroken it made my chest hurt. "I'm so sorry," she hushed. "That's so... horrible..." She dropped her eyes to the snow. Did she look guilty? Embarrassed? She was blushing a subtle pink when she started again. "I never thought of how hard it was for the local Catchers. I've only ever known the Devouhs. They've always treated me like family. I've been so fortunate they allowed me to watch over their dreams, and they've even given formal payment for my services after I was knighted."

I stopped kicking my feet, frowning. "*Allowed* you? They didn't hire you?"

She hummed, a smile stretching over those smooth, slender cheeks. "I was too young to be hired legally. Any service I gave was my free choice. I wouldn't even accept payment for acting as the twins' caretaker when they were infants."

Infants? Those two were in their twenties now, weren't they? "Yulia," I started, confused. "How old were you when you met the Devouhs?"

"I was twelve," she said.

"You've been with them that long? And your family just let you walk out?"

Her smile went flat. "My family..." She clenched her fingers over the wrapped sword in its scabbard. "My... husband... couldn't exactly protest."

"Bloody... you were married that young?" My stare went wide at her. "Was it one of those arranged things?"

Her head shook. "It was my choice to accept his offer. My house was in a financial crisis. My mother passed away when I was very young, and at the time, my father had been imprisoned for failing to pay overdue property taxes. My marriage held the promise of Father's release. So, of course I accepted."

"Well, what happened to the guy?" I asked. "I don't see any vines in your hair right now. Did you divorce him?"

"No." Her words had a dark undertone as her white fox ears grew. "Lord Lucas ripped off his head."

Silence strangled the wagon, the escorting Reapers still chatting away outside as the horses snorted and clopped through the snow.

My throat went dry, not sure what in Void to say to that. "I'm sorry..."

Her next smile was laced with the most haunting mix of disgust and pleasure. "I'm not."

She slid off the wagon, pulling up her winter cowl as her grey face went back to her normal, soft expression. "I think I shall check on Apson," she declared and disappeared behind the wagon's canvas.

MARINCIA

YU'NN QUISETTE,
CAPITAL OF THE OCEAN REALM

14

XAVIER

I hobbled down the ramp with my cane, Alexander helping to steady me as we touched the dock.

We were dressed more regally today in white coats and vests with deep emerald cloaks to shield us from the cold snow. The last island we'd stopped by weeks ago had a few noble outlets, and Willow had taken it upon herself to buy us all appropriate clothes for our audience with Marincia's king.

Willow herself followed after us onto the docks, the Death Princess wearing a warm, velvet black gown and cloak, the fox-fur hood long and draping down. She let her hair keep its ashen color today, braided around her face and tied back with the black-ribbon and bell. Her gown was not quite authentically Grimish, but instead a strange merging between the Death and Ocean realms' fashions. The texture was embossed with smooth, ripple-like scales and lined with elegant swirls. And, to my delight, her silver engagement-vines dangled from her hair.

When she stepped beside me, a grin tugged my lips. "No disguise today?" I asked.

Her head shook, patting Jewel's head, who twittered from the princess's shoulder. "We're here to plea to the Ocean King about assisting us in the war. If we're to make his audience, I had best represent my father appropriately, hadn't I?"

"Well, you certainly look the part of a queen. Minus a crown."

"I found what I could. Shall we?"

I grinned and, with a flashy wave of my arm, tossed aside my cane. Then I held my arm out for her to take. "I thought you'd never ask."

As expected, she drew in a stunned breath. "You don't need it?"

"Bianca's tonics really do work fast. It's only been a little over fifty days so far. Between those disgusting drinks and the constant physical training, perhaps I'll even gain the weight back and start building more apt muscles?"

"One thing at a time, darling," she chuckled as her arm slid happily around mine, and we strode forward. "I was growing suspicious when you first complained you didn't see enough of me and then disappeared for the last four weeks yourself. Is this what you've been up to?"

"I wanted to surprise you."

Alex snorted next to me. "More like he didn't want you to see him fall on his posterior every time he took a step."

I shot a rueful glare at him when Willow chuckled.

Alex was in a more cheerful mood, at least. Or perhaps 'cheerful' was the wrong word? Ever since announcing he'd keep his engagement with Lilli, he's seemed a bit... hollow. I don't know exactly what happened with Bianca, but he was slowly starting to accept that she'd made her decision. Very slowly.

King Dream soon swept past us, the azure-haired boy taking the lead.

"Ah, Xavier!" Dream greeted brightly. "Glad to see you're walking on your own again. Come along! The Ocean Palace is this way!"

Willow stared in shock at her young grandfather. "Hang on. You're wearing *proper attire* for once?"

Indeed, Dream's usual, grody sweater had been replaced with sleek, orange silks and an alabaster cloak that shone with intricate designs that truly made the garb look fit for a king. He even wore a white-gold crown atop his azure locks today, small bells jingling delicately from the rim. His curly bangs were combed aside to reveal the crowned Dream mark on his brow and, Bloods be good, even his shepherd's crook had been sanded and rid of its stray splinters, the bell tied to its hook ringing with each gesture Dream had made.

Willow pinched his cloak with fascinated eyes. "I don't think you've *ever* worn anything so fine since I've been born! Why make the effort now?"

Dream still smiled his stale, practiced smile. "Dear, you're here to negotiate military aid for a war. This is quite a serious matter and even *I* understand that we should use any means of social acceptance available to us. Believe it or not, your grandfather wore formal robes for similar meetings in his youth during my siblings' days of conquest. Of course, I was far *smaller* then... and Death would typically scold me if I didn't wear what she'd picked for me... hmm..." He cocked his head at Willow. "It's funny, this isn't the first time I've come to such negotiations with you, is it? Yet I'm the only one who remembers."

"Yes, well," Willow huffed. "Such things are to be expected when the rest of us actually *age* so we can be reincarnated after we die. You've yet to do either, Grandfather."

"Hmm. Point taken." Dream turned on his heels and began forward again, the bell tied to his crook jingling.

I followed him with Willow in arm, but Alex stopped in his tracks and turned back toward the ship. "Wait," he said. "Are the others not joining us?"

"I suggested they stay in town," Dream explained. "Wander, if they liked. Only royalty and the Shadowblood need to speak with Ninumel."

Alex and I ignored the 'Shadowblood' mention. He always called us this now. It was growing rather tiring, to be frank.

We carried on, following King Dream and his jingling crook.

Marincia's capital was so different from Everland and Grim. Snow was, apparently, the usual forecast here, far below Nirus's equator. Instead of a normal, rocky island, we strolled on a large mass of ice—a glacier, Nathaniel had called it. Beautiful things, the way they reflected this strange, colored torchlight along the weaving streets. Their torches weren't made of fire here, but of gleaming stones found within the ocean's dark depths. They called them Heliogems. They came in three mesmerizing colors of emerald, sapphire and ruby, gleaming against the clouded night sky.

Monuments of the Gods were erected outside different temples, and as we found our royal hover-coach, which had been waiting for us along with several scaled servants, we admired each statue with awe. The most dominant God here was, of course, Rin, the God of beauty and water. His monuments depicted Him in either His human form, trident in hand, or His dragon form, with long whiskers waving at His sides as He swam through invisible water.

As we rode up the windy, wintry path toward the palace in the distance, we passed by blocks of Wavecrashers: this realm's honored knights. Row by row, the royal guards shouldered long tridents and donned scaled, dragon-shaped helms with matching plate. The legwear, however, only covered the outside of their thighs and calves. *Was this to leave room for their tails when they shift?* I wondered.

The captains of each squad rode on the backs of strange, white beasts, their snouts clouded with hot breath against the chilled air. The creatures' heads were flat and spiked like icicles that shot backward, their long tails dusting away snow in their wake and large front feet chipping at the ice as if to clear a path for easier travel.

Alex, Willow and I watched from our carriage window as two of these strange creatures plowed through the snow in front of us, clearing our way.

"Are those Frostdragons?" I asked.

Dream hummed from the opposite bench. "Of course. This *is* the Ocean realm. You've already seen a Bindragon as well, thanks to Hecrûshou."

Alex rubbed his chin. "Then what of Marincia's third type of dragon? What of the Seadragons?"

Dream grimaced. "Hope that you *don't* see those anytime soon."

Alex and I stared at him, baffled and a little unnerved at what that could mean.

We finally reached the gates and found the palace itself was an entrancing sight. It had curved roofs and pointed, balled spires, edges ribbed like the spikes of a dragon's back. It was enormous, looming over us with Heliogems set in the stones.

Many scaled Footrunners and Ocean Knights stood at attention within the gates of the palace, spears and tridents poised with pride. Once we were let into the pooled courtyard, we saw several fish-tailed shifters lounging in the steamy water, relaxing quietly with a sophisticated air about them. Our party took the dry path around the pool, watching curiously as every fin-eared head followed us.

We finally found our way into the palace, and Dream informed the master-servant of our arrival. When he announced his and Willow's title, the woman's scales went white and hurried down the corridor—splashing into another pool on the left. I wasn't sure why she did that. Was there a water-tunnel leading somewhere else in there? This realm was so odd…

After some waiting, the master-servant returned, her fish-tail turning back to scaled legs once emerging from the pool. She led us to a glass pod set into a hollowed column. It was something of a lift, by the looks of it. Gears and springs pumped to life as the woman pulled a lever—which caused another handle to push out of the wall, and she began cranking it in a circle to make us descend into the surrounding water below. I'd guessed this lift was powered manually, instead of electrically, since there was so much water around us. It was probably a safety measure.

The spherical lift lugged down the crystal clear water, the glass allowing us to see the many feral fish swimming in large schools alongside the half-humanoid shifters. The water vanished and was soon replaced with a layer of smooth ice, and before long, the lift slowed to a clattering stop.

We filed out, now finding ourselves in a large, pooled throne room. The tiled walls were dressed in green, potted plants and flowers dangling from various awnings. At our feet were circular platforms floating above the watery floor that made a path from the lift to the wide platform up ahead where the web-eared, mustached Ocean King awaited.

King Dream stepped ahead of us onto the platforms, smiling at the scaled king while stretching his arms in a warm gesture. "Ninumel!" He spoke the Marincian tongue as smoothly as taking a breath. "<Thank you for seeing us, my graceful friend!>"

King Ninumel watched us approach his slippery island and sat back in his throne, one of his green brows lifting. "<You come so formally announced, Dream. Usually, you just pop into existence right at my tail without warning. What's the occasion?>"

"<I thought formalities were called for this time, since I came with your other guests.>" Dream gestured to Willow, Alexander and me. "<You've met my granddaughter, Willow—"

"<I've been to Serdin's realm often enough to recognize that long hair,>" Ninumel propped an arm on his throne and craned down to look at Willow. "<Your father said you'd be coming. I hear you want help fighting the dual-war with Everland and the Necrofera?>"

Willow gave a polite curtsy, speaking Marincian. "<Indeed, Your Grace. I've come to request military aid for the war effort.>"

"<I've already told your father that I need my Wavecrashers here. I may be on the brink of war myself with Culatia if that damned feather-fool still thinks I have his daughter. Which, I'd like to make clear, I *do not*.>"

Willow cupped her hands in front of her. "<I full-heartedly believe you, Your Majesty. But we would only request a minimal portion of your troops. Just a few thousand around the coasts of Everland would be enough.>"

"<Young lady, you can't expect me to give up so many knights at such a critical time. It would paint a target on my head for Rojired to take advantage of. He'd take my brief vulnerability as an opportunity to attack—>"

"<And how long will it be before Everland comes for Marincia?>" Alexander blurted, impatience reverberating his throat. I winced next to him as he went on, "<Galden hates all the Relicbloods. Death, Dream, probably Sky soon enough—if he wins this war, where do you think he'll go next? They'll take your knights captive, enslave your people as they're doing to ours, kill anyone whose Bloody *hair* isn't Everlandish… you'd have to be a damned fool to risk that fate on your people—>"

"<What he means!>" I interrupted hastily, seeing Ninumel wasn't taking kindly to that last part. "<Is that while your feud with Culatia is certainly dire, you can't ignore the second threat that looms just behind it. We have many of our Reapers here on your islands, if Everland *were* to invade, you'd have our full support. All we ask is that you help us in our time of need now.>"

Ninumel's gaze fixed on me, looking both confused and curious as he glanced from me to my brother. "<You two. You're familiar… I know those strange eyes.>"

Willow hesitated, gesturing to me first. "<Why, yes, Your Grace. You've met the twins a number of times—nearly a decade ago when you visited the Death Palace. This is my betrothed, High Howllord Xavier Devouh, and his brother, Lord Alexander. They are the sons of my father's Eyes and Low Everland's commanding general.>"

"<I thought your betrothed was dead?>" Ninumel craned down to peer at me warily. "<He isn't one of those walking corpses you Necrovokers bring with you, is he?>"

"<No, no,>" Willow assured. "<He's very much alive. And he is more than qualified to speak his mind on matters of war, being the son of Grim's general.>"

Alex was about to open his mouth, but I shot him a warning glance and shut him up. With his Gods awful diplomacy, he'd sooner get us a one-way ticket to Marincia's watery dungeons than convince Ninumel of anything.

Alex's wolf ears curled back in annoyance, but he held his tongue as I stepped up to address the Ocean King myself. "<Your Majesty Ocean, as I said before, your help could not only bring *our* victory, but yours as well. And even if we don't succeed in this war, our Death Knights will stand beside your Wavecrashers in any following invasion by Everland. And should *Culatia* strike, as you so fear, our Reapers will… help *defend* your waters. Though, against the Sky realm, I'm afraid anything beyond housing the homeless and wounded would cross our neutrality treaty with Culatia. Only against Everland can we fully take arms alongside you.>"

Ninumel twiddled one side of his drooping mustache in great thought, his free fingers drumming the arm of his throne. "<You speak sensibly enough, Strange Eyes,>" he deliberated. "<And while I thank you for the offer, I fail to see how it's your place to promise me anything. Military aid would be provided by your wife-to-be. You should know the spouse of a Relicblood has no say in such things.>"

"<With all due respect, Your Majesty,>" said Willow, "<it seems you don't understand how Grimish culture addresses such matters. When the king or queen of Death is in power, their spouses are their partners and greatest advisors. Neither husband nor wife stands idle at the ruler's side as a mere object used for breeding an heir. They rule *with* us—as is the will of the Seamstress, with any husband and wife, lord or beggar.>"

She began pacing, her hands weaving in thoughtful gestures. "<It is true that, as Grim's future queen, I will have the final, absolute say in these things.

But I am not forced to come to decisions on my own regarding any one topic should I seek counsel with my husband. And because Xavier is the first son of Low Everland's current, commanding general, he has vast knowledge and background on the subject of military policy and foreign treaties. I fully agree to the terms Howllord Xavier has proposed. Grim will honor its vows, under watch of the Goddess Nira, and witness to the holy Artist, Rin.>"

I stepped past Willow and stopped right at the steps leading to the throne. "<We ask again, Your Majesty,>" my voice was humble, but gruff. "<Will you send troops to secure Everland's coasts? Or will you have our people suffer this dual-war alone? Will you allow Galden's Raiders to conquer us, kill our children, rape our women, imprison our Brethren, and seek the death of our Relicblood?>"

Ninumel scoffed. "<That pretend-king isn't stupid enough to kill a Relicblood.>"

"<Galden is not the mastermind behind this war,>" Willow warned. "<He is a puppet, manipulated by a man who wishes to kill all Relic Bloodlines—including your own.>"

This made him laugh. "<One man, killing all Bloodlines? Madness.>"

"<It won't be madness if we allow him to build his army of demons and ignorant soldiers. From what we've gathered on the man, he's been whispering in Galden's ear, and is not an intellect to be taken lightly.>"

"<If our king falls at the hands of such a man,>" I joined. "<He'll only have three targets left. Refusing to help stop him will pave the way to your own death.>"

Ninumel sat unblinking, the last of my words hanging in the humid air. All were silent. What was he looking for, in my stare? In Willow's? A sign of deceit? He wouldn't find any. His face was hard with inspection, his webbed ears fluttering momentarily. The seconds ticked away until Ninumel finally grunted and leaned back in his seat. "<You seem confident this mysterious 'manipulator' is out to kill us all.>"

"<He is,>" I nodded toward Willow beside me. "<He nearly had my betrothed killed by one of his cohorts months ago. One of his former allies has turned against him and joined us, told us his intentions.>" That wasn't exactly how Claude came to stay with us, but it was close enough to the truth. Best to keep it short. "<Please, Your Majesty. We're not only trying to stop our Reapers from dying. We're trying to prevent another set of Great Wars. We'll be living in our *own* Time of Discord if we do nothing. We have to stop the anarchy this madman seeks to create.>"

His lids narrowed. Then he glanced at Dream, who only nodded gravely. Ninumel let out a breath. "<Well... King Dream hasn't objected, so... I'll trust

the Great Oracle's judgment. But I fully expect that aid you promised in the future, if that feather-headed idiot invades my waters.>"

Ninumel pushed off his throne and started down the steps, walking past me and nodded to Willow. "<I will set a thousand Wavecrashers at each naval port along Everland's coasts. But no more. I'll discuss the matter with my generals. In the meantime, you may stay here until you feel ready to set sail again. Good evening, and may Rin bring calm waters during your future travels.>"

He waded into the pools around us, his scaled legs shifting into a dragon's tail, and disappeared below.

"Well!" Dream clapped his hands. "Here I thought *I* was going to do the negotiating. It seems I didn't have to do anything."

We were soon led up the lift by a helpful, fin-eared servant woman. Dream stepped off on the first floor and went to make a quick com-call—he wouldn't say to whom or about what—and left Alexander, Willow and me in the lift. The servant brought us to the third floor of the domed structure, stopping at one of the guest suites. She gestured toward the door, speaking Landish as if she couldn't wait to practice it on us foreigners. "Suite for tu here, jes? For tu!"

"Well," Willow sighed and lifted to her toes to kiss my cheek. "This would be you and Alexander. I'll see you in Aspirre, love. We'll have another Memory session, if you'd like?"

"I would." I smiled, walking inside with Alex following—

"*Ueiwa!*" the servant gasped and blocked Alexander's way. She crossed her arms to form an 'x' across her chest. "No tu *men*! Ees no allow! Shame, shame!"

Alex's brow furrowed. "He's my brother."

"Ees no allow!" she repeated. "No even brozer! Yu want arrest? Yu like dungeon? No! Brozer have room down zis way."

She grabbed Alexander's wrist and dragged him down the hall, twisting so she could smile back at Willow and me while waving an encouraging hand. "Ees O-K for yu tu, no worry! Zis room for *Yujanne!*"

Yujanne. Lovers. The second she uttered it, she ducked around the corner with Alex and disappeared.

I went rigid, Willow and I left alone outside the door.

"Er…" I cleared my throat behind a bashful fist. "What happened there?"

Willow looked just as baffled. "Death… I've heard Marincia has a low tolerance for homosexuals, but I thought my tutors were jesting when they said it was illegal for those of the same sex to stay in one room together. The law even extends to siblings? How strange…"

I rubbed my neck. "Well, that certainly changes things a bit. What, er, what do we do now?"

She smirked over her shoulder. "We do the polite thing and adhere to their laws. Come, *min yujannëd*. We can start your Memory session now?"

"Ah, well—*khmm, hmm!*—actually..." I slid in front of the door and opened it for her, leering doggishly. "What do you say we make some... *new* memories instead?"

She sauntered inside and gave a devious chuckle. "Why, what *ever* did you have in mind, darling?"

I shut the door, turning the latch, and reeled her in by the waist. "Let's just say my legs aren't the only thing I've gained use of." I tasted her neck, trailing up to her ear and whispered, "I can demonstrate, if you like? *Min Yujannit...*"

"—Oh," someone hummed by the lit hearth, making both of us jump.

King Dream was there, inspecting the room up and down and seeming lost. "Strange. This used to be part of the corridor... I'll have to update that in Aspirre."

Willow's fox ears sprouted at the same time as my wolf ears. She broke away from me and stormed up to the intruder. "Grandfather, *what* are you doing in here?"

"Erm, sorry dear..." He laughed weakly, rubbing his knuckles. "I didn't mean to interrupt... but I'm afraid I have to steal your betrothed for a few hours. You can have him back once we're finished, but I'm afraid we're adhering to someone else's schedule. Xavier? If you please?"

He waved for me to comply, but I stayed put and glared at him. "To do what, exactly?"

"To get what we came here for in the first place." He reached into his billowing sleeve and took out the Orbs of Azure. "But first, let's retrieve your brother."

A blinding flash hit my retinas, and I shielded my eyes with a hand—

The room vanished, along with Willow.

When I came to, Dream and I were now alone in... was this the palace hall?

"Let's see," hummed Dream. His hands gleamed blue as strings of light zipped about him in a sandy storm, tiny azure grains clumping to form solid objects. "Five windows, a balcony, fireplace, bed on the west end facing the east wall..."

One by one, walls appeared along with furniture, the corridor's marble floor replaced with the same soft carpet that had been in the last room.

"And that should be enough," concluded Dream, wiping his hands as if they'd been covered in dust. He inspected the new room with a scrutinizing eye. "I can add more later, I suppose... Now then." He spun on his heels—er, no. He was floating

in midair, his bare feet crossed like an excited child awaiting the fair. "Let us fetch your brother, shall we?"

He floated past me. The door opened on its own to let him pass as I fumbled to match his pace.

"What did you just do?" I gazed about the corridor, the space of the pillars and windows nearly identical to Ninumel's palace, but there were very subtle changes in decoration. "We're in Aspirre, aren't we?"

"Of course," said Dream ahead of me, spinning while still hovering in the air. "I've taken you into Aspirre before, if you recall. When we retrieved your body."

"Yes, but there had only been floating roads in a black abyss," I protested, gesturing to the palace surrounding us. "There are buildings in Aspirre?"

"Well, not naturally," he admitted and bobbed his head to the side. "Somniovokers can create permanent structures and cities here. You'll find them in more populated areas in the physical realms. It makes traveling between planes far simpler. Do you have any idea how easy it is to get lost in here? Now come, we'd best not dawdle. We're on a schedule."

He floated ahead, and I hurried to keep pace.

ALEXANDER

In the dimly lit room of my private suite, I glared at myself—at my copy.

I'd been dragged in here by that blasted servant woman, all because of some idiotic law. Not sure I was in any mood for sleeping, I'd thought I may as well pass the time with something... instructive.

Copies were strange. I'd discovered I could summon them a few nights ago. It was part of my half of the Somniovoking, according to Dream. We already learned Xavier could weave objects in Aspirre—I tried, but couldn't—so, I supposed that meant I was the only one capable of making copies between the two of us.

I hated to admit it, but these new Hallows were growing on me. They were new and... and, well, *exciting*, if unwanted. But I wasn't much experienced with these copies, so I figured since I was alone now, I may as well make use of the time to... well, to talk to myself, essentially.

"So, you're not vindictive for any reason?" I asked my copy. He was an exact replica of myself, sitting in the chair opposite to mine and giving me a flat, mismatched stare.

"No," grunted my phantom, crossing his arms in a scowl. "I already went over this. I'm us. *You.* However you want to address it. I'm not a new, created being."

"How would you even know? If you are me, then you know just as little as I do."

"I'm at least aware that I'm *not* the original. I know what I feel right now."

"And that is?"

"A connection to you, I guess. To us. Whatever. It's not as if I'm tangible anyway." He waved a hand through the table beside him, his skin fizzing without contact. "Can't assume I'm the original if I can't touch anything."

"And individual thoughts? Anything new that I wouldn't have thought myself?"

"Unless I *wouldn't* think this self-interview is a waste of time, then no. Still my thoughts. Still my decisions and reactions to whatever situation arises. Am I done, or did I still need some entertainment?"

I grumbled irritably. "Wouldn't you know that answer, if we shared thoughts?"

"We apparently don't share thoughts until I come back. They stopped syncing when I summoned me. I've branched to separate histories now."

"This is getting convoluted..." I raised a hand to have my copy warp into a ray of colored light and flash into my palm, the following headache burning with the new memory it'd collected.

It was disorienting as Death. Now I had *two* perspectives of the same conversation. This Evocation was going to be complicated—

—*Watching through someone else's eyes, I saw the back of my own head stiffen. The viewer was curious at my sudden stillness, he and another figure waiting for an opportune moment to announce themselves. But then, he wondered if he even needed to.*

The image faded, and my own point of view took command again. I growled, venturing a guess as to who was watching me. "Where in Death do you keep coming from?"

I twisted round the chair to see the azure-haired boy lingering by the fireplace. Xavier stood beside him and looked ready to question how I knew they were here, but Dream gave a hum instead. "Familiarizing yourself with your visions? Have they calmed?"

"Thankfully, yes... How do you keep popping in on people without opening locked doors?"

"I don't usually enter through doors, unless protocol demands it." He waited for me to rise before pulling out the three Orbs of Azure from his billowing sleeve and pointed to the middle sphere. "The Orb of Present allows one to venture into the subconscious realm both physically and spiritually. In other words, anyone holding it can vanish from this plane of existence for a time."

"Apparently, you've vanished too long to remember what privacy is. What do you want anyway?"

Xavier answered that one. "He wants to take us to Ocean's Lost Relic."

"Right." I massaged my eyes. "That business."

"Come along." Dream headed for the door. "We'll take the conventional route this time. We have to meet someone first, and I wish to give them enough time to arrive."

He walked out through the door this time, and with a simultaneous shrug, Xavier and I trailed after him.

15

XAVIER

⁓⁓⁓

Alexander and I were led to the castle gardens. Or, what I supposed counted as a garden in Marincia. It was mainly pools and oceanic vegetation neatly lined with various plants that I didn't recognize.

I was surprised to find Herrin waiting for us under an iron archway. He was speaking with a web-eared woman, and clinging to the woman's hand was a young, scaled boy with long green hair and emerald eyes. On his exposed clavicle was a crowned Ocean mark, so I assumed the boy was King Ninumel's son, and the woman his wife.

"…wonderful to meet you, Archchancellor," the queen was saying to Herrin in well-spoken Landish. She seemed mesmerized and curious while inspecting the hawk's brown-feathered wings and young face. In her free hand, she clutched a tattered version of *The Choir* against her scaled bosom. "Queen Crysalette has told me much of you."

Dream chuckled as we approached, cupping his hands. "Veyazelle, *Ruddïmne Duer*, what a great pleasure to see Marincia's greatest scholar tonight. And she doubles as one of our Enlighteners, no less."

Queen Veyazelle smiled at the blue haired boy and drew him in for an endearing embrace, kissing his cheeks in greeting. "*Oscha, aquasé min tres*! The Little Blue King has finally come to see me after so long!"

"Still on with that name, eh? No one's called me that in over a thousand years, Veya."

"Then you never should have told me about it." She wagged a webbed finger at him, smirking. "And you still look a good twenty years my minor, so by my standards, the name still fits. But I hear from your wife that you plan to stay out in the conscious realms now? Because of what's coming?"

"Indeed I do." His smile broadened to a more sincere curl. "Crysalette and I can finally grow old, if all goes well for the Shadowblood."

The tall woman peeked over him to look at Alexander and me, blinking as if noticing us for the first time. She held a stunned hand to her lips. "*Oscha halel...* just as *The Choir* showed! As if you'd torn the page in two..."

"Interesting, isn't it?" Dream nodded to us as we stepped closer, and he gestured to Herrin. "This is why I sent for Herrin to retrieve you and your son. Fuérr here will be the one to give the Call, as I mentioned on com earlier this week."

"Of course." The queen knelt to the little boy who looked no older than six, and she scooted him toward us. "Fuérr, *min ringëd, tu sans pap'ur ques Shad'oui Genglit. Ye* Xavier, *et* Alexander. *Hanni'liu "babi lett"!"*

"*Babi lett,*" the child prince mimicked obediently. His fin-ears flicked bashfully while he stared up at us with wide, emerald eyes.

"*Babi lett,*" Alex and I greeted back, our response more uncertain.

Dream chuckled delightedly at us, but his eyes soon snapped up when a newcomer approached us. He outstretched his hands and exclaimed, "Crysa! My dear, how I've missed that lovely, aging face!"

A rust-haired fox woman sashayed toward us with a grin, leaving prints in the snow behind her as she held her cloak tight against her eye-opening bust. *Good lord.* From her delicate face to her graceful toes, that woman looked exactly like Willow, save for the hair and eyes. Now I saw where the Death Princess got her voluptuous genes.

"Dream, darling." His wife, Crysalette, waved in a flourish while still keeping her cloak wrapped over her body. She seemed suspiciously keen on hiding what was under there. "Always the flatterer. Ah, and look at you! Your whiskers have grown a half-centimeter since last we spoke. A dressed chin is most becoming of you, dear."

Dream beamed and scratched at the small patch of blue stubble under his lip. "You think so? It doesn't seem to want to expand any further. I'm still no match for Xavier, at the moment... but never mind that." He clapped his hands. "Now! About this 'surprise' you've been on about. I think I've figured it out."

Crysalette's brow perked. "Have you, now?"

"I most certainly have," he bragged. "I had a vision of you knitting again. You've made me a new cloak for this winter weather, haven't you?"

She hid a chuckle behind a prim hand. "Not quite, dear."

Dream's smile fell. "No new cloak?"

"Not this year, I'm afraid." She unwrapped her covering robes and put a hand on the small, bulging bump stretching her belly. "I'm using my yarn for someone else this time."

Dream stared at the bump. We all did. I expected him to say something, but he kept to his staring. His face was an unreadable, blank slate.

Then, at last, he pointed an absent finger at her, asking, "Is it mine?"

"He ought to be," she huffed. "He's been giving me rather colorful dreams all month, as Myra did."

Dream knelt in the snow, inspecting the bump and poked at it lightly. His expression was still blank. "*He.* Hmm… So this is the son Willow mentioned…" He glanced up at his wife. "How long has he been in there?"

"It started swelling almost a week after I left Aspirre. It's the first time in a few hundred years I've actually been out in the physical world this long, so I suspect it simply hadn't time to grow until now."

"How strange…" He put an ear to her belly. "It's been so long since that vision, I'd nearly forgotten… When did this happen, exactly?"

"You know, I've been pondering that," she said, putting fists at her sides. "We've already concluded that conception is impossible within Aspirre, since internal aging freezes the process. So it had to be during a time when we were *out*. And the last time we were out long enough to conceive was that fortnight we spent in Culatia, after Sky Queen Aroura's party of 1756."

Dream rose and rubbed the sparse hairs at his chin in deep thought. "We did have a lot of wine that night."

I offered a flat stare at both of them. "You've been pregnant for nearly four centuries?" I questioned, baffled. "As if he's been in some sort of stasis until now?"

She shrugged. "These things happen."

"No, they don't," Alex and I said at once.

Dream stared at her belly one last time, then broke his blank expression at last with a toothy grin. "Wonderful!" He kissed his wife and turned to me in a laugh. "Xavier, it seems you'll be having a little uncle-in-law soon."

That was perhaps the oddest thing anyone had ever said to me. "Congratulations… I suppose."

He kissed his wife one last time before Crysalette wrapped herself in her cloak and let out a short breath. "Well, now that that's been taken care of. Herrin, Veya? I'm feeling rather peckish. Why don't we discuss Enlightener matters over a warm meal? The Shadowblood has business with the young prince here."

Herrin scratched his neck awkwardly. "Uh, s-sure…"

"But of course!" The Ocean Queen interlaced her hands in a swoon. "An expecting mother must keep up her strength!" She knelt to her son and kissed the boy's head, patting his cheek. "<Go with the blue king and the champions, Fuérr. You know the way. Be blessed, Rin's Beloved.>"

She rose, bowed to us in deep thanks, then walked away with Herrin and the Queen of Dreams, chatting fervently about the coming baby.

"I don't understand," I murmured as the little prince, Fuérr, came to grab Alex and my fingers in each of his tiny, webbed hands. He was marveling at our matching tri-leaf of diamonds over our knuckles. I glanced at Dream. "Why is the prince taking us?"

"We thought you meant for Ninumel to do all this?" Alex added. "Why replace him with a child?"

Dream wafted a flighty hand at us, still staring after his wife with a smile stuck on his face. "Oh, I was never expecting Ninumel to take you there. He's far too close-minded to believe everything he was taught up until now was a lie—or rather, a revision. We were lucky my wife decided to make Veyazelle an Enlightener and teach her about you both. Fuérr is a good young lad. And he just so happens to house my brother Oscha's soul, so he is perhaps the best candidate for the task now that he's old enough to give the Pearl its Call. Are you ready, Fuérr? *Shatu deaux?*"

Fuérr nodded eagerly, seeming happy to be given such a great responsibility, and pulled Alex and me out of the gardens by our fingers.

16

HERRIN

H oly. Freaking. *Bloods.*

The palace library was gigantic! Way bigger than Everland's ever was.

Rows and rows of bookshelves as tall as whole trees loomed over me, their headboards carved like lapping waves, the corners and edges trimmed in emerald and gold dragons that slithered rhythmically over the wood as if to protect the thousands of books those shelves fostered.

In the back of this expansive room, there was a curling staircase leading up to a second level that, as I could see over the wood railing, had *another* thousand or so books. There were covers of every color, every condition: some tattered, some new, some covered in dust and some titles almost completely deteriorated.

I dragged my fingers over a row, picking one up that was labeled in Marincian, and then in Landish: *What the Stars May Mean for Nirus's Future.*

"Land…" I marveled at the thick text, palming the cover that was speckled with glittering stars and painted pictures of the other planets that surrounded Nirus which you couldn't see outside a telescope. "There's got to be every Bloody book that ever existed in here!"

The Ocean Queen chuckled and raised a scaled hand to her smooth lips. "That is the goal, one day. Unfortunately, I doubt it's an achievable one."

"If it is, then this would be the place to do it." I opened the astrology book, twisting my mouth. All the text was in Marincian. *Damn.*

I thumped it shut and turned to the two queens. "Is there any chance I can borrow these and have them translated?"

The Ocean Queen's webbed ears folded to her head when she smiled. "Of course, Archchancellor. I can have whichever ones you like fetched in the Landish versions within a week."

I stared bug-eyed at her. "Really?"

She hid another chuckle and nodded, her deep violet, fin-like hair falling over her shoulder. "Yes, really. Any you like."

"Th… thanks!" My hands started collecting books left and right, balancing the growing stack with my other arm.

This place was amazing! The crisp perfume of old pages and dried ink mixed with the oaken scent of wood and smoky charcoal from the hearth that was snapping with red embers. There were fancy cups on hot-stone tables, warm coals wafting with heat inside the middle as the drinks atop it spilled steam. Cushioned chairs and couches and chaises and ottomans were scattered artistically over the deep jade carpet.

On the domed ceiling was a painted mural of twinkling stars, enlarged planets, wavering dragons swimming between them in the empty blackness of space, atmospheric clouds trailing down to the walls and melting into Nirus and all its countries.

It began with the Sky realm, their floating islands and tall, window-covered buildings painted under billowing storms. A colossal, Scarlet Phoenix was shown flying through the nimbus and spitting enormous bolts of lightning onto a towering, conductive rod.

Below the islands was the Ocean realm's beautiful waters, the rounded adobe and seashell buildings curved like the waves they were placed over. Enveloped inside an opened, white clam rested an Emerald Pearl, the globe glittering from inside an icy cavern.

The two continents of Everland and Neverland were depicted on opposite walls, their square, flat-roofed buildings painted in gold, yellow, and lavender colors. The Dancing Desert swirled in a storm of sand on the right wall, and a luscious forest bloomed with flowers on the left. On both murals was a large, Golden Blossom the size of a full-grown shifter.

And deep, deep, *deep* below the Land realm's ground, waiting on top of the first crust, was Grim. The fabled Willow of Ashes wavered with white leaves in an unseen wind, obscured by a light fog that crept into the spikey, gothic buildings and cemeteries that made the Death realm's cityscape.

Well, that was *four* realms. I didn't see the fifth anywhere: the Dream realm. Crysalette's home.

Then again, most of Aspirre didn't look much different from the starry void at the very top of the ceiling, did it? I'd been in there myself—physically!— because of King Dream. But I guessed most people only saw Aspirre in their dreams. They usually didn't see what was outside those isolated city and subconscious areas; they didn't see the sandy demons that loomed outside our dreams. Waiting. Watching… gnawing hungrily for our souls…

I shivered.

Pausing my book collecting, I glanced over at Crysalette. "Uhm, Your Majesty Dream…?"

She smiled. "Please, Herrin, just Crysa will do."

I flushed. "Uh, r-right. Crysa…" Bloods, I still couldn't get used to her casual attitude. She was royalty, for Land's sake. "Well, uhm, back on Y'ahmelle Nayû… Dream took a lot of us into Aspirre. *Fully* in there."

She hummed. "You wish to know how he could do such a thing?"

"I already asked him. It's because of the Orbs. But, well, he didn't really explain much about the, uh… the golems."

She nodded, her tone dampening. "Not much is known about the golems. Not even by us, unfortunately."

"But why aren't they listed in any demonology texts?" I questioned. "I've read dozens of those books and not one of them *mentions* Aspirre has anything dangerous in it except nightmares."

"Most shifters don't believe they exist outside their dreams," she explained. "Only Somniovokers know the truth of the Noctis Golems. But those without that Hallows believe them myths and legends, nothing but a scary story to make children behave."

"But what *are* they? Are they dreaming Necrofera?"

She laughed. "The Necrofera cannot enter Aspirre. They do not dream. They merely remember. Even we cannot enter their subconscious, if they even have one."

"So where did the golems come from? Can a soul rot while dreaming?"

"Not to our knowledge. None of our Dreamcatchers have ever reported such a thing happening, at least."

"But it doesn't make sense!" I protested. "Did they just pop in out of nowhere? Dream's lived in there for two-thousand years. He's got to have learned *something* about them?"

She shrugged, sighing. "Unfortunately, Dream is just as clueless. He asks those same questions even today, all of which are left unanswered. All he knows is how to avoid being mauled by them. Killing them is impossible, we've found. Not even Spiritcrystal can hurt them. The only thing to do is keep them out."

"But that can't be the only solution. There's got to be a way…"

She chuckled and took both my shoulders from behind, steering me along the colossal shelves. "Well, if you find one, Herrin, do let us know. In the meantime, we have business to conduct with your other Enlighteners, Archchancellor."

I blinked, the stack of book wobbling in my arms and threatening to slide off my velvet blue robe's sleeve. "Uh… *Other?*"

She turned us to a large sitting cove and looked over my wings. "Good evening, everyone!"

My legs went stiff.

There were nearly two dozen people sitting there. And all of them were staring at me.

I almost dropped the books, my wings folding tight to my back. The scaled men and women rose to their feet in confusion.

"Arch..." One of the older women began, squinting behind her glasses as her webbed ears flicked. "Chancellor...?"

I swallowed the knot in my throat. "Uh... h-hi..."

They all looked at each other, as if checking to see if they all saw the same thing.

A shark man cleared his throat and approached me first. He extended a hand to me. "Archchancellor, I am Ruthën Torlique, Zouthern Yu'nn Quisette's chief Enlightener. It eez a pleasure to meet you at last..." When he took my fumbling hand, he hesitated. "Though, I muzt admit... You are... *younger* zan expected..."

They all murmured their agreement.

My face warmed. "S-Sorry. I can't really help my age."

His scaled lips tugged a grin, then he burst in a laugh. "Zis eez true! Pleaze, forgive. It waz juzt surprise."

The others made rounds to shake my hand, making me balance my stack of books with one arm in the process. Apparently, I was super underdressed for this meeting. All I had on were a plain shirt and breeches hidden in a too-big robe to keep warm, a buttoned flap at the back to make room for my wings.

I counted twenty-three people here, all Marincian. The last woman who shook my hand had stringy, purplish hair that was tied in a tail and sat high on her skull. She didn't have scales, but did have webbed ears like the others. And judging from the thin, membrane-looking translucency of her hair, I guessed she was a jellyfish shifter.

"Marvelous meeting you at last, Archchancellor," she said in a light accent and bowed. "I am Azölle Lo'loit, of the Rolgun island east of here."

That was a weird one. I asked, "You came all the way here from a different island?"

"But of course." She lowered into a plush chaise and raised a cup of tea to her lips. She took a sip, then smiled eagerly. "You travel with the fabled ones, yes? You know the Shadowblood personally."

"I—"

"Indeed he does!" Crysa came from behind me and swiped the Storagebox I had strapped to my belt under my loose robe. She shoved her hand inside and plucked the ledger of loose papers, scriptures, and notes I had stored in there. "And he's worked hard this past month to scribe their stories for you all to read!"

My pulse choked in my throat. "Wh... B-But...!" I reached for the ledger, but Crysalette deftly swung her arm aside and handed it to the jellyfish woman, who preened joyously and started scanning the pages with shameless gusto.

I blustered. "W-wait! It's just a rough draft, it's not even organized, or edited, or...!"

Crysa patted my head. "It'll do fine, Herrin."

The jellyfish gasped, holding up the first page. "My grace! This is true? They shared one body for so long?"

The others started murmuring curiously, taking other pages from the ledger and reading themselves.

"Uh..." I blushed. "Well, yeah. Xavier had this ability and..."

"You call them by their first names?" A man asked, baffled. "Artist paint me, you *must* be close!"

"W-well, they're my friends. And my brother is one of their vassals. See, they're Necrovokers, originally."

"And it's true they have Dream's Hallows now too?" a woman asked.

Crysa gently pushed me into a seat in the middle of them all, handing me a cup of hot coco.

"Yeah," I said, hiding an embarrassed lip twitch by taking a sip of the coco. Bloods, I've never had so many people looking to me for answers. "Every Hallows they get seem to be split between them. It's really just a theory at this point, but it should be proven or disproven after tonight when they get their Ocean Hallows."

Breaths were drawn throughout the group.

One man asked. "Is that where they are now? Receiving their Hallows from...?"

"Mm-Hmm." I took another sip. *Wow, this stuff was good.* I was starting to relax a little more, sinking further into my chair. "Ocean's incarnation is taking them to the Pearl of Emerald."

17

XAVIER

On we walked through the icy streets of Yu'nn Quisette, our only light coming from the Heliogem-torch Dream had gotten from one of the palace walls. It was a ruby-hued light, gleaming bright and pure with a warm radiance that spilled onto the ice and reflected subtle jewels of newly red snow over our cloaks.

Little Fuérr pulled Alexander and me by our fingers, and we walked until the city was nothing but a speck in the distance. Now we were surrounded by the overwhelming mountains of ice that were so tall, their peaks were shrouded behind clouds. Soon, we came to a fragmented area on the icy floor where ocean water parted the land and blocked our path.

Fuérr released our fingers to dip his small feet into the freezing water, and his scaled legs merged into a dragon's tail. He lowered waist-deep in the water, not seeming to care about the harsh temperature. I guessed his scales gave him some resistance to the cold. Either way, it was impressive that he didn't even flinch when diving under.

Alexander, Dream and I waited for him on the surface. A few seconds passed until Fuérr resurfaced and frowned at us. "*Eui, sette mul toi, Shad'oui?*"

Alex and I glanced at each other, then answered, "<We can't go any further...>"

The boy's mouth twisted. "<That's why you dive, silly Shadows. You won't find the Pearl out here. Just look at your marks.>"

We saw our Crests were aglow now, one diamond pointing out to the dark sea. Fuérr wafted an expectant hand at us. "<Come, come! Mama wanted this done before Papa realizes I'm out of bed. I don't want to be Iced.>"

Alex raised an eyebrow. "<Iced? What does that mean?>"

"<Forbidden from the water for a time. It's not fun, being Iced. So come, hurry and dive.>"

"<We'll freeze to death,>" I protested, kneeling over the edge to feel the frosted water with a hand. "<We may come from cold caverns, but our water was never chilled with an island of *ice*.>"

"<Not to mention, we can't breathe underwater,>" Alex added. "<We don't have your gills, *or* tail. Dream, can't you just bring us into Aspirre and have us pop in next to it?>"

Dream gave a brooding glower. "I would, but we would end up outside of it, in the water. The Relics have a strange barrier around them—even the Necrofera are warded from them somehow. I've never found a way to get to this particular Relic without getting wet. Best to bear through it and try to keep up with the boy as much as you can. Follow your marks if you get lost, that might help."

"Might?" we questioned.

Dream, seeming practiced at this particular trek, stripped his clothes down to his undergarments. From a sack he'd brought with him, he pulled out three pairs of strange, soft-rubber suits and put one on, tossing the other two at us.

"What are these?" I asked, following Dream's example and stripping to don the strange suit that hugged my arms, legs and torso. It was thankfully warm.

"Thermal wet suits," Dream said. "There isn't much else we can do to prevent hypothermia." He stretched his arms and leapt off the edge, splashing headfirst into the water.

He emerged again with chattering teeth and a hard gasp, flinging the water from his blue hair and grown fox ears. "N-n-never gets-s-s any eas-s-sier..."

I clicked my tongue, cursing before zipping up my wet suit and yelped while dipping into the freezing water. Alex wincingly did the same.

"<Finally!>" Fuérr huffed, his tail slapping against the water. "<Come, it's this way.>"

The little prince slithered down, spraying us with icy flecks in his wake. Dream took a deep breath and plunged after the boy. Alex followed next, and I was last to go under.

If not for Dream's ruby torch, I would hardly be able to see anything. Alex and my marks did gleam ever brightly here, but it wouldn't have helped us see the streaming fish flying past us, nor the stray pillars of ice shooting from the abysmal floor.

The need to breathe was terrifying, the chill having our breaths seep out in involuntary bubbles.

"<Here, Shadows and Dream fox,>" Fuérr's voice echoed in wavering tones through the water, as if his throat had shifted to speak like no mammal could ever achieve under here. "<In case you fur-growers didn't get enough breath.>"

From the boy's hands came a green glitter of Hallows, and with a frivolous swat, the water around our heads spilled away, forming a sphere of air that we could breathe in.

Satisfied that we weren't going to suffocate, Fuérr nodded and sped ahead, leaving the three of us fumbling to swim after him. Damn that tail of his—I felt like a feral monkey tangled in vines. Alex and Dream weren't fairing any better, but somehow we stayed within sight of the child. I suspected Fuérr was slowing his pace for our sake.

After what felt like hours of swimming, Fuérr suddenly dove deeper. We hurried after him, pulling ourselves farther and farther downward, my ears popping as the pressure rose and my muscles became heavy.

The water grew colder. My skin numbed under the wet suit, and I tried to keep up with the others, but because I'd only regained my strength to an average level, only Alexander was able to push on ahead. His collected years of Reaper training far outshined mine—because it had been *his* body we'd shared those six years.

I called after him, but he couldn't hear me. The water between our personal bubbles must have stifled me. I fell farther and farther behind, Dream struggling alongside me. For a two-thousand-year-old king, he was a slender thing. Strangely, he had a similar, spindly physique as I had myself.

Dream and I had to stop mid-swim as a school of fish flew in front of us, and we bumped arms trying to swat them away—

"It is with great pleasure…"

My point of view fell away, the cold waters disappearing and replaced with someone else's gaze.

"… that I present you with the Dreamcatchers' garb," the new narrator announced, his pride feeling inappropriately heavy.

What had gotten into him lately? Sure, he hadn't known the boy long, but this was the first friend he let himself have in the last fifteen-hundred years. After watching everyone he was ever close to grow old and die without him, he'd made an effort to avoid this sort of thing.

When had he let himself get carried away? Had he been that starved to find companionship? That desperate to share his ancient history and tight-lipped philosophy…?

Oh, it didn't matter. He had made his decision. Was it foolish? Perhaps. Impulsive? Certainly. But he didn't care anymore. He was tired of isolating himself, all for a doomed schedule of which even HE didn't know the date. What if his new choice changed that damned vision anyway?

"Congratulations." The narrator smiled and handed a folded, azure robe to the *adolescent cobra before him. "Welcome to the Brotherhood, Macar."*

Macarius returned the smile—a warm, sincere gesture—and bowed. "Thank you, Your Majesty. Sire. I will carry the title with honor…"

I was hurtled back to my own point of view when Alex grabbed my arm.

My brother lugged me forward so I could keep pace in the freezing water, and I saw Prince Fuérr had done the same for a rather pale Dream. The blue king's horror-stricken eyes were locked onto mine, his fox ears grown and folded to his neck.

What had I just seen?

"<Sorry,>" Fuérr said in his strangely rippling voice, tearing my attention away. "<I forgot the pressure gets higher down here.>" He evoked green Hallows from his small hands, and the water around us brightened.

The pressure soon eased from my muscles. I guessed he'd switched to Pregravoking. I'd never seen this type of Hallows before, but I'd always wondered how it would be useful. Now, I was glad as Death those Evocators existed. Without the heavy pressure bearing down on us, Alex and I could continue through the water more easily. Alex still had to pull me along to keep me within sight, and Dream was dragged by Fuérr, but it was better than being crushed by the incredible weight of the ocean.

We eventually began rising toward the surface. Fuérr swam higher and higher, his movements becoming more excited and erratic until we finally surfaced from a small opening at the floor of a glacier, *inside* the formation.

There was no other way in, it looked like. *And that means no other way OUT,* came the grimacing afterthought. We would undoubtedly have to go through that again when we were done here. *Brilliant.*

We all flopped out of the pool and puffed over the icy floor to rest our sore muscles.

Fuérr giggled at our exhaustion, the boy's tail shifting back to legs when he lifted himself onto land. "<Fur-growers are so silly in the water. I've never seen worse swimmers.>"

"<Again,>" Alex wheezed, raising a finger. "<No tails. Spoiled little…>"

"Alex," I interrupted, lifting my left hand. "The Crests."

He looked at his right hand, seeing his Crest was gleaming brighter now, like mine. The left diamonds were pointing us down the icy cavern, where we saw refractions of multi-colored light glistening. More Heliogems.

"<Here,>" Fuérr urged. "<The Pearl is this way. You'll like it. It's very pretty.>"

We started to follow as he hurried on, but I glanced back to see Dream had hesitated behind us. He took a moment to let his fox ears recede, sucked in a calming breath, and came up beside me.

"Xavier," he said, so quiet that only I could hear. His azure eyes stayed focused ahead, his throat burning. "Don't *ever* look at my past again."

He walked ahead with Fuérr, leaving me rigid alongside Alexander.

18

XAVIER

Silence befell the caverns, save for Fuérr's lighthearted humming as he marched over the icy surface and weaved between the sharp stalagmites as if it *wasn't* incredibly slippery in here. Like Dream and Alex, I had to tread with more care.

Step by step, I tested the next piece of ice with the pad of my foot, checking for traction before following the young prince through the crystalline cavern.

The towering walls stretched high and wide, so large you could quite possibly fit an entire village in here. And yet, it was empty. Void of life, void of *death*, void of anything save for ice, ice and more ice.

I wasn't sure how long we walked. Fuérr's singing voice bounced off the enormous, glittering ceiling as the little dragon danced to his own, Marincian ballad.

> *Jeaux chad'naît faquer'joul*
> *Jan'nasch trët Oscha*
> *Ma'tu aqua goul'joul na min*
> *Foi min lül ga'jin*
>
> *fëttscha min Söl praul nawhil*
> *Min ma'tu M'älmerre*
>
> *Ît Tët Fae Pas Flouflusé*
> *Jan'nasch trët Oscha…*

In his watery language, it was pristine and beautiful, reverberating off the crystal icicles that rang in harmony.

Fuérr would look over his shoulder and walk backward every so often to make sure we were still behind him. Then he would smile wide and sing that same ballad, dancing to and fro as if caught in a trance.

Soon, he led us into a wide hollow. Here, there were raw Heliogems shining from the walls and sprinkling the frosted hollow with a quilt-work of blue, violet, green and ruby lights.

But those were mere rocks compared to what was towering in the center of the hollow.

Crystallized ice flowed like an enormous wave over our heads, frosted and glittering in the multi-colored light around us. It was shaped like a clam, but it must have been three stories tall.

My Crest of diamonds was shining bright now, the pulsing having grown to a solid gleam. Alexander's mark was doing the same.

"<The Pearl is here,>" Fuérr beamed and touched the icy clam's shell, evoking his Hallows.

The shell ruptured and groaned, responding to Fuérr's Glaciavoking and began to open.

Inside was the largest, greenest pearl I've ever seen in my life. It shimmered as if coated in a layer of jade frost, a cool steam misting from the clear pool that the dazzling globe floated on.

"Beautiful," I murmured, taking in its ethereal majesty. My guts twisted, awe-stricken. This coldness, this *frost* filling my chest…

Something was here, watching us. Every standing pore on my flesh quivered as my knees grew weak under the divine weight I could feel swelling the entirety of my being.

Small. I felt so small, so miniscule in such a presence.

I let the weight push me to my knees, and I bowed. "Rin bless us with Your graceful presence," I whispered in prayer.

He was here. He watched, He waited—He beckoned.

Alex knelt in a silent prayer beside me, his breath fogged as he gazed upon the lost Relic of Ocean. It was moments later when he found his voice. "What happens now?"

Dream lingered off to the side, nodding to the little prince. "Fuérr? <It's time to give the Relic its Call.>"

Fuérr took an excited, preparing breath and clasped his hands together, facing the Pearl.

At first, he did nothing. I craned my neck to see his face, but all I found was true, absolute calm. Then, his lids peeled open. He outstretched his arms. From his hands shined emerald lights, swaying and streaking in hypnotizing swirls.

Fuérr began to dance.

His movements held such grace, it was hard to believe he had any bones. His lithe feet skipped and flowed over the ice; his arms bowed and wavered like a river, his head held high and proud like a refined artist losing himself to some silent music. But then, I could swear music *had* started playing.

A quiet ring echoed in the hollow from somewhere, one note at first, until several more joined to form a resonating chord. It wasn't until Alex nudged my side and pointed at the enormous ice-clam that I found the source of the notes.

All this time, Fuérr's dancing Hallows had been making the pool of water ripple under the Pearl. Some of the liquid had been lifted into hollow stalagmites and were spiraling up at such a frequency that sound had started pouring from various holes like a strange, watery flute.

The tune was that same ballad Fuérr had been singing in the cavern.

Fuérr's dance intensified, his verdant eyes now wide and unblinking. He looked possessed, as if reading the next steps on a manual we couldn't see. His hand would jerk up, and the pool would slosh upward after it. He would bow and circle in place, and the pool would swirl under the Pearl.

The colossal sphere started to glow. As did our marks, the very left diamond now a solid emerald green.

The prince lifted a foot and *slammed* it down, jingling the overhanging icicles. Some of the shards broke apart and started raining down on us. We reached up to shield ourselves, but Fuérr cast them aside with his Glaciavoking and added them to his dance. The bits of ice formed a gossamer wind around him as he kept in rhythm, the water flutes growing louder.

The right diamond on our Crests bled green now, like the first.

The entire cavern quaked. The flutes wailed in the haze that encircled us. The frosted wind bit at our bare skin as our wet hair tossed every which way while the prince conducted the flow of air and directed the streams of floating water.

The tempo accelerated, rising into a powerful crescendo, the storm threatening to sweep us in its beautiful rage. Alex and I braced ourselves on a stalagmite to keep from being blown away, screaming, the final diamond on our Crests changing green…

My scream turned ice cold, as if my lungs had been blasted with frost.

I coughed out fog, my hands gleaming with emerald lights, and I felt something fill a spot in my soul. It was from that spot that the lights poured out my fingertips. I tugged at the spot until it all burst out at once and then…

Blackness.

Screaming... Gods, stop the screaming...

My lids flew open.

The cavern was gone. It was no longer ice cold. There seemed to be no temperature at all, here.

The sky was fractured and shattering in sharp fragments, people of every race and shift rushing from every direction, running from the sand golems who engulfed those who had been too slow.

I backed into someone—met Alexander's gaze. It held the same question I was thinking.

Here again?

Our friends' corpses were scattered round us like before. Though, they were in different places now. Willow wasn't among them.

I searched for her, and finally spotted her white hair in the distance. She was holding a small bundle of something with one arm, though I couldn't quite see what it was through her draping hair.

She saw me and rushed for us, screaming. "Xavier—!"

Something lanced through my neck, clogging my windpipe, the shock coming before the pain.

I collapsed to the ground and could barely hear Alex gurgling beside me as darkness smothered my vision once more.

... This is no time for games.

The voice echoed in the blackness. Then an emerald light gleamed and glittered from the serpentine Seadragon wavering around me.

Take my Blessings, it said, its voice lilting and wavering as if underwater. Use them with grace...

The ice cavern dripped back into view.

I was lying on my stomach with my arms stretched out. I watched my Crest of black diamonds change to a crowned Ocean mark, glowing emerald over my knuckles. Alex stirred beside me.

I saw Fuérr's dancing had slowed, the water flutes' rings diming with his decreasing pace until he came to an elegant ending pose.

The boy's head craned back to us. "*Bezrït, Shad'oui?*"

My Ocean mark faded black, the original tri-leaf of diamonds returning over my knuckles. A constant chill ran over me from the inside now, my teeth chattering. "*Bez-z-zrit-t-t...*" I shivered to Fuérr, sitting up.

Dream knelt to inspect us, humming. "How do you feel?"

I heard Alex give a straggled cough. "Like I'm drowning, but still breathing."

Dream eyed me next. "Xavier?"

"C-c-cold." I shivered, clutching my arms to find an escape that wouldn't come. "S-s-s-so... c-c-cold..."

"Curious," Dream mused, rising.

Fuérr glided over to us and asked something of Dream, but I couldn't hear it over my knocking teeth. Gods, it was freezing. Before, it had merely been external, but now it felt as if my very blood was made of ice.

I huddled over my skinny knees, gooseflesh prominent even from under the hair on my legs *and* the thermal wet suit. My bones were ice, my brain was ice, my chest, my throat, my tongue, *Death*, I needed it *out*...

I gave a cold, steamy gasp when my Crest changed to the Ocean mark, my fingers leaking emerald lights. And with it came a stream of frost.

I could *feel* the moisture in the air around me, every tiny particle that brushed against my cheeks and floated around my hands. The coldest spot in my chest pulsed along with my heartbeat, its chill dripping out as I pushed on it mentally and guided it down my arms then out my palms.

The air crystalized around my hands. It hadn't come out in any particular shape, but it radiated from the center of my palm in all directions, spikes and curves forming as the coldness of that spot inside me drained away.

I was beginning to warm again. But only slightly.

When I cut off the Hallows, I laughed and marveled at the strange, lopsided ice figure that hovered in the air—

It dropped to the floor and shattered. I stared at the rubble. "What happened?"

I turned to Alexander. A small mass of water had formed over his palm, but was now splashing down over his hand. He frowned and glanced at me in turn.

I could tell by his expression that he'd had the same thought that came to my own mind, and both of us concentrated on doing what the *other* had done.

I thought to create water, perhaps combine the particles of moisture as I'd done with the ice...

But nothing formed. I only made another block of ice, deformed and mis-shapen. *Well, at least it's something.*

I moved my hand to the left, wanting to move it to ask Dream about—

The moment my hand drifted away from the block was the moment it dropped and, once again, shattered. I glowered at the sparkling shards.

I tried again, creating the ice, but had the same result when trying to move the damn thing. It wouldn't move from wherever it had formed. I exhaled, determined, and tried one last Bloody time…

I created another hunk of ice. Then, it finally stayed in place in front of my hand. I grinned, but my lips fell when the block jerked away from me on its own accord. I watched it hover before Alexander now, who was heckling at the thing. He apparently had no trouble moving it.

I scowled at him, my wolf ears growing as he smirked back at me.

Dream clasped a hand on my shoulder. "He's finding it hard to control his own water. Why don't you see if you can't help him, hm?"

One of my ears lifted, and I called out, "Alex? Can you make that water appear again?"

Alex seemed to guess the reason I'd asked and set aside the ice piece. He scowled at his hands until they shined green, and slowly, glassy liquid dripped into existence in front of him.

I reached for it and focused all my attention on draining out my Hallows, the Ocean mark shining from my hand as a sudden, satisfying vibration met my glowing fingertips. The water quivered before Alex. I couldn't help but laugh in delight and tugged the water in front of me, looking at my wavering reflection in the suspended, fist-sized droplet.

"How interesting," Dream said.

I shivered, the coldness that had seeped out of me returning, and I let the water splash to the icy floor to rub my shoulders. "C-c-can we make a f-fire in here?"

Dream's head tilted. "Not unless any of us are Pyrovokers, or brought mate-rials that are impervious to getting wet. Come, we're finished here. There will be fires in the palace hearths."

Alex came to help me to my feet. He looked cold as well, but not nearly as frozen as I felt. The moment he touched my arm, he recoiled. "Death's Head! You're cold as ice. Can you even make it back through the water?"

"H-h-hopefully…" My skin trembled under the wet suit.

Fuérr came and gripped two of my fingers, smiling. "*Bezrït, Shad'oui.* <You will adjust to your new temperature. It is how ice-makers are. For now, cast out the ice to keep warm during the swim.>"

Not knowing how else to reply, I nodded, letting the boy lead me out of the frosted hollow and back to the entrance pool we'd come from.

Alexander came beside me, warning, "Stay close. If your arms give out, grab onto my back."

"R-r-right." I sucked in a breath and evoked ice onto the floor, letting the coldness drip out of me as warmth mercifully returned.

We dove.

The freeze crashed over me, sucking dry what little warmth I had just gained. I flailed in the water, bones chilled to ice, and what in Death was this *feeling*?

I felt like a finger wriggling in a leather glove. Squeezed, though gently, from skull to heel. The water felt thicker than before.

It hadn't felt like this on the way here. Everything was different. Almost... *alive*.

I opened my eyes.

All I could see were bubbles. Then Alex came into view, holding a hand over his mouth and nose, along with Dream beside him. Fuérr had already swam ahead of us, his newly grown dragon tail wavering.

The young prince's hand shined green as he created three pockets of air around each of our heads again and gave us a means to breathe as we followed behind him.

We were all lagging drastically this time. Though, I suspected Alexander was only back here with us to keep an eye on me.

We swam for what felt like an hour. Fish of all shapes and sizes zipped by, reflecting the ruby light of our Heliogem torch with their glittering scales. I saw two eels weave below me, a stingray gliding gracefully overhead, and a strange, bulky creature with a hard shell scuttled from a hole in a rocky pillar that we rounded.

Dream, I noticed, was staying a fair distance away from me. Anytime I was forced to swim an inch toward him to avoid a tall reef or passing school of fish, he lurched back in a flinch. As if afraid I would sting him.

I focused on keeping up, concentrating on each kick and stroke.

But something *still* felt odd. Being in the water, hugged by it tight from every direction, it was like being swallowed by some enormous beast, its throat fitting perfectly around my skin. I felt my hands push against the water the same way I'd felt the humid air around me back in the hollow. It had been nagging me since we dove under, but now it was impossible to ignore.

I wonder...

Curious, I pushed on a new reserve in my soul. My hands gleamed emerald, and the Ocean mark appeared on my left hand. I stroked the water—

I was launched forward.

The sudden force of the re-directed water propelled me straight ahead, closer to Fuérr as Dream and Alex were left behind. I looked back to see they'd both stopped in surprise, and grinned.

This time, I let the Hallows pour out of me freely, from hands *and* feet, pushing and pulling on the water. In time, I swam just as easily as the prince. No physical strength needed.

Fuérr laughed, watching me flow *with* the water instead of inside it, and he beamed.

"<There you have it, Shadow!>" His chuckle wavered and rippled through the water between us, barely piercing through my air bubble.

But Fuérr's face suddenly fell, his finned ears dropping when his gaze moved to something behind me.

Rrrrrrraaaaaa....

A strange, trilling ring came from behind.

We spun as the ringing cry grew louder. Then from the darkness came a pair of shining, jade eyes.

Three rows of tall, sharp teeth came into view when a giant, snake-like creature let out a rippling shriek, its scales flaring around its smooth face.

Fuérr squeaked. "<Seadragon!>"

The dragon's serpentine body writhed as it sped toward us. Its shriek gurgled and bubbled, razor teeth long and packed tight in its blackened gums.

Alex and Dream turned tail and scrambled to swim faster. Fuérr darted backward, grabbing Dream by the arm and evoked his water Hallows to propel them forward.

I hurried to do the same and grabbed Alex, then *pushed* the water under us. I wasn't as fast as Fuérr, even still. I also wasn't as fast as the feral Seadragon. I pushed on, but the serpent's long snout was right at our feet.

Then a *second* dragon streaked in front of me, its slender body wavering and thin fins rippling in a blur of bubbles.

The second creature weaved under us, coming to meet the first, both spiraling for us.

Others came slithering from the dark depths and curled around reefs. Some had begun fighting each other, but most were still focused on their prey.

Then, I heard Alex give a scream from within his muted air-bubble, and his hands shined emerald.

The weight of the water suddenly turned heavy.

Bloods, I may as well have been pushing rocks as our speed decreased drastically. My ears were pounding. Did Alex increase the water pressure somehow? He must have been using his new Pregravoking to do it.

I craned back to see his hands were still glowing and outstretched at the Seadragons. Good Gods, the things were *retreating!* Their tails zig-zagged away into the darkness, back to where they came from. They must not have fancied the pressure.

Then again, neither did we.

I choked on a pained gasp, my body being crushed. *Death, if Alex doesn't ease up...* I forced my pulsing neck to twist back to Alex. Why wasn't he stopping? —*Oh.*

One look at his distressed face and flailing hands told me enough. I put my water Hallows on pause and I tried a different reserve to evoke: *pressure.*

I squeezed my lids shut, focusing on the water that pushed snuggly against my skin. I let out the Hallows in a long, forced breath.

A green light bloomed from behind my closed lids. The pressure dissipated, and I opened my eyes. The crushing water was now light and malleable again. I could move about easily.

Alex and I shared a small, relieved laugh, and I pushed us upward.

When we emerged to the surface, we found Fuérr and Dream waiting for us by the icy shore where we'd discarded our clothes earlier. Alex and I panted over to them and pulled ourselves on solid ground.

"I..." I wheezed, shivering when the coldness returned. I found my now snow-covered clothes and dressed quickly, wrapping my cloak on tight. "R-r-really... don't want to do that ag-gain."

Dream replaced his own clothes and chuckled, his breath fogging and teeth chattering. "Hopef-fully, you won't hav-v-ve to. C-come along. Let's-s-s find a Blood-dy fire."

19

ANABELLE

The ship swayed smoothly over the waves, gently rocking the clinic cabin. From the window, I could see flakes of snow drifting over the docks and cityscape of Marincia's capital.

I stood wrapped in a warm, woolen shawl, sipping the steaming tea that Bianca had been kind enough to brew for all of us here. She knew 'just the thing' to make cold weather comfortable, she had told us. Her skin may have been a warm, surface-brown, but her Grimish upbringing was apparent even in her sharp accent.

Miss Rochelle was here with us, along with a fully resurrected Sirra-Lynn. We had just tended to Lord Matthiel, who had requested a tonic to rid him of his nausea. Jaq had been a frequent visitor for the very same tonic this past month.

Now, I watched as Sirra-Lynn spoke to her *Da'torr* with her husband, the couple intertwining fingers. "…and our home was destroyed in Everland," Sirra explained to Miss Lëtta. "Claude has nowhere to go when this is over, and the kids are old enough to be on their own. He's asked if he could join us, *Da'torr*… Would you mind if we made room for him?"

Claude hastily added, "I can be your personal chef, if that helps?"

The teenager twirled one of her black, thin pig-tails with a contemplative finger, chewing ponderously on her gum. "Sure," she said, her Marincian accent trilling and watery. "Why not? Our old home would have been too small, but who knows how big the next one will be? But." She flicked her black-lined eyes at Claude. "You must be aware, sir, that Sirra is bound to me until my Seam is cut. I may be her apprentice doctor, but even after my training is complete, she will follow me wherever I go. The Bloodpact cannot be erased."

Claude's tone was gruff. "I understand. I go where she goes. Now that our kids are safe and know what they're doing, they don't need me around anymore. And I don't want to live alone. Not without Sirra."

The girl smiled, pausing her gum chewing to sigh wistfully. "How sweet… Very well. This will be the plan."

"Thank you, Lëtta," Claude breathed in relief and hugged the girl, walking out with her and Sirra excitedly. "So, for future reference, what's your favorite meal? I should probably start getting used to…"

They left the cabin, and Rochelle smiled after them, wiping a small tear before returning to grinding her herbs. I noticed Bianca was focused on a different task. She was reading from a large text, the same I always found her nosing through. As she read, she carefully extracted some type of clear liquid from a vial with a small dropper. She wore her usual goggles and protective gloves, seeming cautious while dripping the liquid into a different beaker, which was also filled with a clear solution.

When the two chemicals intermingled, the result was a hazy, red color. When she lifted the glass with a pair of tongs and set it over a burner, a puff of smoke burst lightly from the beaker's brim.

I stepped up to her, whispering, "What experiment is this?"

One of Bianca's rabbit ears lifted as she hunched over the counter to observe the mixture's reaction through her thick goggles. "I want to make a line of acidic Splashspheres and globes," she explained. "The text says they used to put the solution in waterskins with holes in it, but with today's use of Metaglass, which we use for Shockspheres, Flamespheres and all that, I think it'll be way better to use it as Shotri ammo."

I nodded my approval. "Ah, I remember the waterskins. You mentioned then that the men would return complaining of being burnt themselves, if they'd been careless with it." I chuckled. "An update of your previous design will be appropriate for the new era. I like it."

She stared at me through her goggles, quiet for a moment. "Mine? No, I read about it in the Alchemist text." She uplifted her goggles and picked up the heavy text to show me the passage she meant.

"Yes," I said. "You wrote all your designs and practices down so you would not forget them when you were born again. At least, that is what you said when I asked."

Her expression faltered. "Wait a minute… You think *I'm* the Lady Jilume Herdazicol?"

"Of course. I wouldn't mistake the soul of my old teacher. You even share her visage."

"I what?" She grabbed the book and flipped to the back with peculiar vigor.

She stopped on a page that held a painted portrait with the caption *The Lady Jilume Herdazicol*. I smiled brightly, pointing at the nostalgic brown face whose orange hair and rabbit ears were draped over her shoulders with a sense of wild refinement.

"You see?" I said. "You look so much like your old vessel. It seems your bloodline carried such resemblances throughout the ages."

Bianca's eyes were wedged open, perhaps out of shock?

"But… but I…" Her brow crinkled further. "I never knew my real family." She rubbed her temples, as if experiencing a horrific migraine. "Then… wait, then that opening note was for *me*?"

My head cocked, curious. "Opening note?"

She fanned the book's pages back to the very front, running her fingertip over the elegant script.

"The author's note," Bianca explained while I read over her shoulder.

Author's note? Mistress Jilume never mentioned adding this.

To my future incarnation, it read, *you will not remember our discoveries and experiments when next we're born. To combat this, I've compiled our formulas in one place so that we may continue our research and perhaps even improve upon it. I know not what new technologies your era's sciences hold, but I trust we will find ways to incorporate updated revisions to these practices, if able.*

Post Script: If by chance we were to meet our ward, Anabelle, I would very much appreciate a due 'hello'. I expect she will still be around for some time. I wonder if Sir Kurrick is still stitched to her coattails, as it were?

Here's to the future,

The Lady Jilume Herdazicol

My lion ears dipped in shock. "*Mistress…!*" I cried softly. "Why would she risk such a mention…?"

Bianca pressed a hand over the book, her gazed pricked with accusation. "You *are* that Anabelle, aren't you? You even said she was your old mistress."

"Why would she…" I scanned other pages, searching for anything more she may have risked including. Yes, there was indeed more! Land's Blade, there were journal entries and various notes of me, of my own discoveries and questions to her.

"Mistress, why hadn't you mentioned…?" I whispered, more to myself. All this time, yet I never knew; never thought to look.

Bianca squinted an eye at me. "Well, I guess now it makes a little more sense how you'd still be alive even though this was written in the 1800s. If the Dream family adopted you and kept you in Aspirre for hundreds of years, that solves one mystery. But I've *got* to know. Why did King Dream take you of all people in? You kind of ran out of the room before answering that."

"Please, Mistress!" I bit back my panic and peered over my shoulder at the other doctor present. Rochelle was thankfully paying us no mind, the lizard woman preoccupied with shaking a vial of medication.

I blushed and returned my attention to Bianca, whispering, "I am sorry. I'd said far too much those weeks ago... Please, there is only so much Dream wishes me to reveal and..."

Bianca lowered her quill in disappointment. "Oh... so I should ask *him* about it?"

I sighed. "Try if you wish, though I doubt he'll say much more than I. Perhaps... perhaps one day soon, I shall tell you all. But this is not that day. Please, forgive me."

I bowed and strode out to the halls before she could reply, and I steadied my nerves. Keeping silent was proving more challenging, now that Kurrick and I have been out of Aspirre this long. It was a record for us. And to have found the reincarnation of my beloved Healing instructor, only for her to stay ignorant? It was torture. I missed Mistress Jilume terribly. Her death took nearly a full century to accept. But then, she's here again in different flesh and upbringing. And being near Bianca has been incredibly comforting...

I sighed, a small smile tugging my lips as I strode down the swaying corridor.

The others were bustling around the ship today, many footfalls and hollering voices sounding off everywhere I turned.

My feet suddenly paused when someone—that hybrid cat-jay girl—seized my arm.

"Zyl?" asked El, her white brow furrowing in concentration to say the next words in Landish. "Yu... s-*seeee*... Zyl?"

My head shook, and El deflated, her wings bowing hopelessly as she went to ask the next person she found. That next person was Neal.

"Yu *seeee* Zyl?" she asked him as well.

Neal displayed a leering smirk and propped himself uncomfortably close to her against the wall. "Sorry, no Zyl. But I've been looking for *you*, little kitty. Birdy. Whatever... You think sometime you'd wanna..."

She walked around him, going to Aiden to ask after Zyl instead.

Neal looked utterly dumbstruck. I hid a chuckle. Perhaps rejection was a rarity for him.

Aiden explained he hadn't seen the Sky Princess either, and so El sighed and started down the stairs that led to the galley. But she flinched when Octavius trotted up, and she ran out of the hall in a furious blush.

Octavius blinked after her, shrugging as he started toward his brother.

"What the Void was that?" demanded Neal, swatting his brother's shoulder chidingly.

Octavius's face pulled with confusion. "What was what?"

"Bloody bastard, doesn't even notice! Of all the Bloody…" Neal shoved past him and went to a nearby door, where that feral ferret, Kurn, was scratching at the door and snickering in a whine. Neal picked up the ferret and knocked, turning the knob. "Hey, Ringëd, Kurn wanted in—"

A woman shrieked, followed by puffs of fire that shot at him from inside. Mikani and Ringëd barked obscenities at the intruder.

Neal slammed the door shut, looking horrified as he patted at his singed clothing. "Uh, *khm-hmm*, right… honeymoon."

Octavius heckled when Neal made his way back, the ferret still in his hand, and I let slip a laugh myself. Oh, but I was growing rather fond of this family. They were so different from mine, yet held so much similarities. *Myra and I used to tease one another often, didn't we?* I reminisced in silence. Then my mood dripped depressively. *Oh, how I do miss my sister…*

Once the hall was clear of traffic, I took my opportunity to keep moving.

I reached the outer deck and my boots crunched over snow. I found Kurrick sitting on the rail by the ship's edge, his legs cast overboard and his lion tail swishing in rhythm with the boat's sway. I took a seat beside him, and he acknowledged me with a quiet glance before returning his eyes to the snowy night sky.

I watched the gentle flurries with him in silence, listening to the lapping water beneath us and feeling the chilled breeze on my face. There was music playing below us from an opened window, orange light radiating out of the room. The music sounded like a stringed instrument, the strummer murmuring a solemn tune.

> *Long ago, with times discord, there came the Children of Relics,*
> *One for each realm they came to be the rulers thought angelic…*

My heart grew heavy. That was the Ode of Hope. Linus had been singing that song more often lately, hoping that his lost Relicblood would hear it… that *I* would hear it.

> *From Land to Death, beginning and end,*
> *Land, Sky, Ocean, Dream and Death…*

The song played on, his voice growing melancholy as Kurrick and I listened.

"It always reminds me of that time," I whispered, watching the white flakes flutter over the sea. "The snow, I mean."

Kurrick grunted. "It is not a time well forgotten."

"The Day of Revival is approaching. Whether they are prepared for my return or not." My gaze fell to Linus' window again, his song soft and gentle. "Do you think they will accept me?"

Kurrick snorted. "If you mean specifically Cayden and Linus, I do not doubt they'd kiss your feet if you were a feral platypus."

I hid my chuckle behind a hand. "Perhaps... And they seem to have already accepted you as well."

His head snapped to me, his amusement gone. "There is nothing of me to accept." He stepped down from the rail. "You are a queen, Anabelle. Queens do not belong with kitchen boys."

"You've been a knight far longer than you've tended to kitchens." My voice rose irritably. "You've never left my side since that night, why would you even speak of doing so once I'm queen?"

"It was not my choice to be your keeper," he growled. "Dream had all but taken me captive, and only because I'd *seen* you that night. I knew you existed. And my punishment was five hundred years in a timeless void."

"You weren't the only prisoner in Aspirre, Kurrick. Do not mistake that. Everything we've been through, everything you've ever said to me, do not dare say it was all torturous. I've known you too long to know when you lie."

He glared for a moment, then cast down his gaze. "It doesn't change any-thing... I am not suited to be a king, Ana. There are others who were bred for such things... Better you wed Cayden than a kitchen boy."

He left the deck, walking inside with heavy shoulders.

I glanced at my dangling feet. Linus still sang the Ode of Hope below me.

Better you wed Cayden, Kurrick had said. Didn't he know? Cayden's heart lay elsewhere.

I sighed, lifting my legs to unstrap my boots. I placed them on the deck and stood barefoot on the railing, summoning my Arborvoking from my feet to use the wood as an anchor. With this, I walked down the side of the ship. Once beside Linus' window, I sat, still using the cold, wooden planks as anchors, and hugged my knees.

Long ago, with Bloodlines passed, the king of Land had been our cost,
Without a king, the land is lost, cracked and broken, torn and crossed...

I remembered the snow from that night. I remembered the kitchen boy, the music… the dying face of my father.

One day he will return we know, the rightful throne will be obtained…

I wrapped myself in my cloak and buried my face in my arms, wishing to forget.

"Miss Ana?"

I flinched. Linus had stuck his head out the window. His beaded dreads clattered softly in the gentle breeze, his dark goat horns and braided goatee collecting snowfall as he peered at me with a puzzled brow.

He held a worried tone. "What are you doing out here? And, er, *how* are you out here?"

I whispered, "There are… metal bearings within the ship's structure." While there *were* such bearings, I actually wasn't pulling against them now. I would have been far too heavy, they would have likely uplifted. "I am using them as anchors."

He smiled wanly, chuckling. "Terravokers… Cayden used to sit at my window like this, when we were boys." His expression turned crestfallen, and he folded his arms on the windowsill. A green bead was clasped between his thumb and forefinger, and he turned it thoughtfully. "He's infiltrated his father's palace successfully and freed Apson. Though, he's discovered his family is in far more danger than anticipated… he's finding it more difficult to kill his father and take the throne than we'd anticipated." He sighed. "Every second he stays, he risks exposure and… and death…"

"Do not yet grieve," I said. "Cayden will return. Galden will meet his end and Everland will be free of his tyranny one day soon."

"A wonderful future." His smile returned, but only for a moment before it fell once again. "Miss Ana, could I ask you something?"

"Yes?"

"The true heir… well, he may be our lost Relicblood, but I've come to wonder if he wants to return. Do you think he seeks to unite us, or does he simply feel obligated?"

My lips pressed into a line, deliberating my answer with care. "It could be… a bit of both, I should think. If *I* were the heir, it would pain me to see what we've become, and I would wish terribly to correct it…" My shoulders sagged. "But then, I wouldn't be sure I could. I would fear that my followers wouldn't accept me after such a long absence."

"You think he would fear such a thing?" His brow lifted in surprise. "Why?"

"Well…" I blushed. "What if he is not what we expected? The Ode we sing of him, the legends we've told for centuries, I should think it reasonable for him to be worried we'll be disappointed once he reveals himself."

He grunted. "That is an awful lot of pressure for one shifter, eh? I hadn't even thought he could be riddled with self-doubt like the rest of us. I just… Well, I'd thought he would show himself when we went to war with Galden."

"Perhaps the time is not yet right?" I watched the snowfall over the water. "He will come. One day soon, he will show himself. His true self… But I hope he does not disappoint us."

Linus snorted. "Don't spout such blasphemy. He could be a mere beggar in the streets, but he will still be our king. So long as he stands with us during our hardships, nothing about him will be a disappointment."

I flushed, a small smile pulling my lips. "Ah. I… suppose so…"

Still, came the brooding afterthought, *I hope you still believe so when that day comes.*

20
ZYL

I sidled against the wall of an alley, ducking through the dark streets on this icy island, my breath fogging with each pant. I had to be sure my hood stayed up as I dashed from shadow to shadow, avoiding as many Heliogem-lamps as possible and kept my wings pinched down tight. They itched to stretch, every nerve on the appendages screaming at me to skip all the incognito horseshit and fly over the damned buildings in one go.

Don't be stupid, I told myself, hustling past the trident-wielding guards at the palace gates when they were distracted with a change in work-shifts. I forgot to ask King Dream or Willow for one of those illusion-infused earrings. If any of these algae-eating fish saw my scarlet wings, there'd be serious trouble.

Especially if any of the Stormchasers stationed here saw me. Bloods, forget being imprisoned by some slithering kelp-for-brains, I'd rather drown than be sent home. If Big Brother isn't there, then I sure as Void won't be either.

I snuck behind pillars of a weird, pooled courtyard, where a bunch of snotty looking fish women were drinking tea and chatting in that 'we're-better-than-you' toned language of theirs. It was so weird, the way their words rolled off their tongues like eels lapping water. Some said it was a sensual language. Romantic, even. *Bah!* They could do with a few harder syllables, at least. Something more definite. Not that slurred, tripping babble they called a language.

I finally made it out of the courtyard, circling the perimeter of the palace. There was a hole in the wall just a few yards above me: a circular window. I risked the short flight and hopped inside it, scrambling behind a statue of Rin as two Marincian Footrunners patrolled past me. When they were gone,

I tiptoed along the corridors, glad when finding an air vent big enough to fit me and my wings, and unhinged its cover to climb in.

Slugging through the narrow paths, I went over the plan in my head:

One—sneak into the Ocean Palace undetected. *Check.*

Two—search for Big Brother.

Three—if he *is* here, grab him and lug his stupid tail feathers back to Father, and avoid being crowned Culatia's queen yourself.

Four—Live out the rest of your days playing games and saying SKY NO to the mountain-heavy responsibility Father keeps trying to dump on you.

I highly doubted Roji was here, but I couldn't stand staying on the ship and not bothering to, at the very least, make a quick search. I mean, I was right here. I wanted to make sure I didn't miss any nook or cranny.

I wished El were here with me, but I didn't want to risk her being imprisoned, like what happened in Everland. I thought it best if she stayed on the ship.

I continued my crawl in the cold vents, but stopped after hearing voices. I wriggled toward them to better hear, lying over a wiry vent to see—

Bloody Sky! It was the Ocean King himself!

It looked like he was having some serious conversation with a military-looking fish, both speaking that annoying, drooling babble in low tones. *Tch. Boring dragon.* They weren't doing anything interesting, so I started back on my way.

But I paused when a dial tone fuzzed on the screen in front of the Ocean King, interrupting his conversation. The screen was scribbled with swirling letters that I couldn't make out behind my wiry window. The king sounded confused, then gave the screen a blubbered command.

I nearly yelped when my father's dark, tawny face appeared on Screen.

"Ninumel, this is your last Bloody chance!" Father roared at the dragon, feathers falling from his head when he stabbed a finger at the screen. Our master-servant, Tryle, was cowering at his side, translating for him in hurried Marincian babble. *"Either release my daughter, or I will take her from your dungeons!"*

My teeth barred, cursing under my breath. "That Bloody idiot!" Did he not get my message I gave to Tryle? And what was with Garrach over there?

Garrach was the blue-feathered jay standing beside my father, half of him off-Screen. He was my father's Hand. Something was off with him, though. His usual 'all's good' expression—even in the most stressing moments—was twisted and warped with something more… scheming. He was whispering something in my father's ear, so low, I couldn't hear it. My eyes squinted at him. *What is he talking about over there?*

Ninumel had to wait for Tryle to finish her translations before stammering in a rage, shouting in Marincian again. Tryle translated on Screen, her voice meeker than the king's. "For the last Gods damned time, Rojired, I do *not* have your daughter! And you wouldn't dare attack while the Relicbloods of Dream and Death are housed here as my guests!"

My father's brow furrowed at that, clearly confused, but his befuddlement soon turned to anger. *"Don't think me a fool, tail-licker! I'd just spoken with Serdin not a day ago. He's still in his Grimish caves, and—"*

"I wasn't talking about Serdin, you sickly old bigot! His daughter is here with her grandfather."

"What in Sky are they doing there?"

"That is none of your business, is it? Go squawk to someone else, Rojired, I already told you I don't have your daught—"

The vent I was pressed over rumbled, and I froze. I felt the metal sliding under me.

Ninumel voiced a questioning growl—

My vent *CRASHED* down. I hit the floor in a startled squeal, bits of ceiling dust clouding in my wake. I coughed, head shaking to gain some clarity, then stiffened.

Ninumel was staring down at me with wide, astonished green eyes. But what really had my wings drop was my father's furious stare. And his rupturing voice. *"Zylveia...?"*

I cracked a weak grin, which faded in a swallow. "Uh. Hi, Dad..."

21

WILLOW

~~~~~~~

I sat on the edge of the bed in my disappointingly empty guest suite, cupping my chin. *Damn it, Grandfather*, I thought furiously. *You had to take him and leave me here to die of boredom, didn't you?*

Granted, I expected to have a private room to myself when I arrived, but after being delightfully surprised that I could for once spend a night with my betrothed, I'd had my expectations heightened. And then ripped from me in the same moment. *Damn you, Grandfather. Damn you.*

I sighed again, this time more broodingly. Then a ghost passed through the door. It was my Marincian vassal, Nikolai.

"*Da'torr?*" Nikolai asked. "*Bezrit?*"

"*Bezrit, Nikolai*," I said drearily.

His translucent fin-ears flicked. "<You seem tired.>"

"<I am,>" I grumbled, arms and legs crossing over the bed as I fell back on the plush mattress. "<I am tired of sorting through war documents, I am tired of making endless com calls to my father and Lord Lucas, I am tired of delegating, and I am tired of *waiting*.>"

"<Ah.>" He chuckled. "<In other words, you're bored?>"

"<Terribly.>" I rolled my head to the side to look up at him. "<How are you and Rossette fairing on our latest stop?>"

"<Rossette is still roaming the palace with the twins' vassals. I think she is enjoying herself, to an extent. She says she is thankful you haven't resurrected her in this winter weather. She doesn't like the cold.>"

"<And you?>"

"<Oh, I love the snow, Mistress.>" He gave a pale smile, and for a moment, he really did look like an adolescent boy. So young. And yet, his life had already ended, just years ago, as he'd told me.

I sat up again, glancing at him questioningly. "<Nikolai... I've been meaning to ask you something. Since you and Rossette are to be my vassals now, I feel I should know how you both died.>"

He scratched at his scaled chin soundlessly. "<Rossette once told me she fell from Culatia. She was traveling with her parents on an airship during a storm and was blown overboard. Her wings were too small at the time to carry her back to the cabin. She died at the foot of a valley in Neverland's forests.>"

I shuddered. "<So, she experienced my worst nightmare...>" I couldn't imagine falling that high. I was terrified while falling from that clock tower back in Everland, and that was miniscule compared to Culatia's altitude.

"<As for me...>" His tone grew distant. "<I ran away from home. I lived on a neighboring island of Y'ahmelle Nayû and took a ferry in secret to the waters. But the ferry was overrun with Necrofera when we neared Everland's shore. The other passengers were slaughtered, but I had my Glaciavoking to help me. It didn't kill them, and I bore many wounds, but I managed to swim to the docks before I bled out and died. And then, after a while of seeing nothing but blackness, *Da'torr* Janson came and cut my NecroSeam.>" His lips pursed, glancing away.

I decided to shift the focus. "<Why did you run away from home?>"

He gladly took the redirection. "<My parents wanted me to be a gallant Wavecrasher, and to fight for the Relicblood of Ocean. I did not. I wanted to be a painter.>"

"<You paint?>"

"<I do.>" He preened, but was soon crestfallen. "<Though, it's been some time since I've picked up a brush, or have even seen a canvas...>"

I touched the specter's shoulder, his see-through skin rippling under my fingers. "<Then I'll find you supplies in town. I would love to see one of your paintings.>"

His finned ears flapped brightly at that—

—Nikolai vanished suddenly, along with the room.

I jolted at the abrupt change, glancing round to see I was now in the palace hallway. And yet... I peered down. I was still sitting, though the bed that I could still feel under me was nowhere in sight.

"What in Nirus...?" I whispered, beguiled.

"...is what I'm saying, Lashün," a voice echoed from down the corridor. "You and Kchavefv must sort out your differences, else I fear the realms will suffer."

A second voice snorted, replying in a heavily accented Landish. "Eez not Kchavefv I have problem wis. Eez hiz fazer. Culatia will be better off when ze soul of Sky eez back on hiz srone."

A chuckle from the first voice. "I don't doubt that. You and Skrii were always loyal when you were Oscha, despite your arguments. What I'm saying is…"

The men themselves came into view, striding side by side down the hall. One man had emerald hair and eyes, along with scaled skin. A crowned Ocean mark was displayed on his neck.

The second figure, I discovered, was no man, but a boy. He seemed to have just entered adolescence, his face smooth and round. He had curly hair that draped just to his chin, and my breath iced at the azure shade of his strands. It was the same blue as his eyes, a crowned Dream mark at his brow.

"Grandfather…?" My voice was hushed.

The boy halted and glanced my way, his face brightening. "Oh. It's you. You've finally come to say hello again?"

A vision, I realized. This must have been a past vision, since Grandfather was so young. Then, whose eyes was I looking though? Who was Grandfather seeing?

The young Dream's head cocked, his curly hair bouncing at his chin. "Well, you've certainly taken your time, this round. How are things in your era?"

I stayed silent, listening closely to what this mystery person, whose perspective I viewed, would reply with.

The young Dream hummed. "Something wrong?"

There was still silence. The scaled Ocean King lifted a brow at my grandfather. "Dream? Whom do you zpeak to?"

Dream's answer was blithe. "Death."

I froze stiff.

"Death eez in her caverns," contradicted the Ocean King. "Zere eez no one zere, Dream."

"It's not our Death," Dream amended. "She is a different incarnation, yet to be born. My granddaughter, believe it or not."

My lungs went cold. "You can… see me?" I asked. I wasn't viewing this through someone else?

He seemed puzzled. "Is this the first of your visions?"

"You call this a vision?" I awkwardly rose from my invisible seat, noting with a pat to the non-existent cushion that the bed was still physically there. "I… I don't understand. How can I be in my own vision?"

"Interesting. It seems the tables have turned, eh?" He chuckled, folding his arms. It was so strange, hearing Grandfather's voice sound so… so adolescent. It scratched and cracked in some places, as if he were going through puberty and his throat was in the midst of changing to the slightly deeper tenor I was accustomed to.

"Nira…" I breathed, "has this happened before?"

"Yes." The youngster shrugged. "Only, very rarely. It's been quite some time since you last appeared."

"What sort of vision *is* this?"

"A shared one," he explained. "You are having a vision of the past while I am having a vision of the future." He laughed. "You know, this was your own explanation when I first saw you. It seems we've come full circle." He turned to the Ocean King. "Excuse me for a moment, Lashün. It's not every century I see my unborn family."

Grandfather walked off and waved for me to follow at his side, and we left the Ocean King standing rigidly behind us.

Grandfather's footsteps echoed through the corridor, and mine, I observed, made no sound. My bare feet still felt the soft carpet underneath. Dream hummed again. "So, tell me: Is it still 2103 for you?"

"Yes…" I paused. "What year is it… here?"

"1426. Now, I saw you were sitting on, well, nothing earlier. May I ask what it was?"

"Oh. Er, it was a bed."

"A bed? So, they end up building a room here…"

"Grandfather?" I rubbed my knuckles uncertainly. "Exactly how many of these… er, shared visions have… *we*… had?"

"Quite a few. Now." He clapped his hands in excitement. "These visions never last long, and you haven't had a chance to tell me this, so I'll be quick— will I meet your grandmother soon?"

My brow furrowed. "Grandmother Crysa?"

"Crysa…" His eyes seemed to slide into a daze. "I'll have to remember that… And when will I see her?"

"I suppose…" I said, calculating, "not for another century, roughly."

His expression soured, but he went on regardless. "What will she look like? Is she beautiful?"

"You said she was the most stunning creature you'd ever set eyes on."

"What is she like? Do we get along?"

"From what I've seen, yes."

"How many children will we have, exactly? You're the only one who's ever shared these visions with me thus far, I haven't even seen your mother. Are you the only family I have left in your time?"

"Not at all. My mother is still with us, and I'm even about to have a new uncle."

He frowned. "Your uncle will be born after you?"

I shrugged. "You live quite a long time."

"Fascinating…"

"Grandfather, will this not change your future?" I questioned. "If I tell you so much…"

"Willow." He smiled, it was a genuine one. "If my future were subject to change, I wouldn't have Seen you in the last thousand years at all. I wouldn't be Seeing you now. It seems that regardless of what you tell me, you will always be in my future."

I sighed. "I don't understand… why are we Seeing each other like this?"

"I already told you my theory on that. But then, if this is your first shared vision, I suppose you haven't heard it yet… how curious."

"Grandfather, I still don't under—*ouch*!" I slammed into something solid, though there was nothing in front of me. I rubbed my aching nose and put a dazed hand on the invisible wall. "What in Death…"

His head tilted. "Ah, that's right. You're in a room. You must have run out of space in your time."

"In my… are you telling me I'm physically walking in Ninumel's guest chamber right now?"

"Ninumel? Is that Oscha's future incarnation?"

"No, his son is the new incarnation…" I blinked when Grandfather began to fade, the entire corridor losing opacity. "What's happening?"

"Dash it all," he muttered, then sighed. "Well, don't be a stranger, Granddaughter. I'd like to see more of you, if you can manage. I'll see you at the turn of the millennium…"

—The corridor slammed into inexistence, and before me now was the large wooden door of the guest chamber.

"*Da'torr?*" my spectral vassal, who'd disappeared during the vision, questioned from the bed. He looked concerned.

Death. If I really had been walking around here in this time, I must have also been speaking to seemingly no one, in Nikolai's perspective. I must have looked like a madwoman…

—A sudden wave of coldness spilled into the room, and I gasped when three figures flashed into existence right in front of me.

"G… grandfather?" My feet were rigid when I saw the blue haired king, his hair dripping wet. He wasn't young anymore. Well, not *as* young, as in the vision. "Grandfather, I've just had the strangest vision! Do you remember..."

I belatedly noticed Prince Fuérr stood behind him, the boy lifting to his toes to better see me. Alexander and Xavier stood beside the child, each of them soaked from head to foot. Had they been *swimming*? In this weather?

Alexander didn't seem to mind the temperature, but Xavier's teeth were chattering terribly and his breaths were fogging drastically thick. He quivered like a rabid thing and wrapped himself tight in both his and Alexander's cloaks.

"Xavier?" I went to pressed a hand to his sunken cheek. "Mother of Death! You're freezing!"

Xavier sighed in relief at my touch, leaning into my palm. "And you're burning. Come here." He opened his layered cloaks and wrapped me in with him, shivering. Gods, his skin was like ice against my Pyrovoker's heat.

Grandfather Dream went to the hearth and snapped his fingers at me. "Willow, we need your fire. I don't see any matches."

I struggled to free a hand out of the cloaks. Xavier had too tight a grip on the rest of me, clinging like he would die the second we parted. I summoned a puff of orange fire with my free hand and dragged myself and Xavier toward the hearth, lighting it.

We sat before it in a huddle, Xavier's shoulders relaxing at last.

My gaze narrowed at Grandfather. "What did you do to him?"

"Fuérr gave him his Blessings," he said. "He'll be cold like this from now on, I'm afraid. It's the trait of a Glaciavoker."

Nikolai floated over to us, agreeing, "<That's actually right, *Da'torr*. That's why I'm naturally cold when you resurrect me.>"

Alexander raised an eyebrow. "Then why am I not cold like that? We've already seen that I can control ice."

"Xavier *creates* the ice," explained Grandfather. "You manipulate already *existing* ice. It's vastly different. The creator taps into his cold soul to manifest it through the Hallows. With your Hallows split, it seems the trait only affected the creator."

Xavier pressed his hollow cheek against mine and grumbled, "When am I supposed to grow accustomed to it?" "Give it time," said Dream.

Little Fuérr wrung out his long, emerald hair and hummed. "<It won't take long, I think. At least the Shadow won't hurt from frostbite or die of being too cold. Ice Makers don't get those.>"

Xavier's chill radiated over my warm cheek, and I thought I saw a sliver of steam creep between us. "Fascinating..." I murmured. "Then, Glaciavoking is much like Pyrovoking. Is it the same for the other creating-type Hallows? Like Aqua and Astra? Or even Infecio?"

"Infecio is different, actually." Dream scratched his neck. "In a way. They have the infections within their souls, ready to be used, but this prevents them from catching most infections themselves. They have a built-in immune…"

He trailed off when shouting came from outside the door. It was faint, probably a floor below us, but whomever caused the ruckus sounded absolutely livid.

"Is that Ninumel?" I asked and left Xavier by the fire to head for the door, my fox ears growing to better hear.

I strode through the hall, hearing the others' footfalls behind me when I hurried down the staircase. The commotion bounced from the main hall, and once I descended the steps and saw what was wrong—

I gasped and screeched to a halt, Xavier and the others bumping into me. Herrin and Grandmother Crysa had come as well from a different hallway with the Ocean Queen. When Prince Fuérr spotted his mother, he went to cling to her skirts. His finned ears folded in fright as his father's booming voice ruptured through the hall.

"*Pschal frettre-reng'el!*" Ninumel screamed at Zylveia, who inched away from him rigidly. "<You idiotic, feather-headed *fledgling*! Your dementia-ridden father is already a madman, and now he's an *angry* madman!>"

Zyl's scarlet wings draped in fright, and she stuttered in her own language. "*O-oy oy, lovt—*"

"*Mauén foi! Foi, foi, foi!*"

Zyl spotted me by the staircase then—and she darted behind me. "<H-Hey—Willow, can you tell this crazy fish to back off!>"

I stood agape, both of them still squabbling incessantly, Zyl hollering insults next to my fox ear until I pushed her away and roared. "ENOUGH!"

The hall fell silent, my echoes lingering.

I glared murderously at Zyl from over my shoulder and hissed under my breath in Culatian. "<What in the five realms are you doing off the ship?!>"

Zyl blubbered. "<I-I-I just wanted to see if Big Brother was here!>"

A growl slipped through my throat. *That damned, foolish girl!* I stepped toward Ninumel, changing my tongue to Marincian. "*Haux vo'laux?*"

"<What happened,>" Ninumel sneered, "<is that *that Bloody idiot* barged in on a com call I was holding *with her father!*>"

My face fell. "Oh, Death."

"<I swear on my life, Death, I did *not* know she was here—>"

"<I believe you whole-heartedly, Ninumel,>" I assured and raised pacifying hands. "<I will speak with Rojired and quell his anger—>"

"<Rojired has already declared war!>" The scales on his face flared, his eyes livid at Zyl. Then he flicked his gaze to me. "<I'm sorry, young Willow, but I cannot spare any troops for you until after *my* war is resolved! But do I still have the Reapers' assistance when Rojired strikes?>"

My sharpened teeth gritted. "<I promised you aid, and I will stay true to my word. But.>" I pointed to Zylveia, my fox ears curled back. "*I* will take that one back to her father before he sets one talon on your waters. And when he calls back his armies, I hope you'll stay true to *your* word?>"

"<In a tail-flap!>" Ninumel huffed. "<Just get that thing out of my palace! I have to prepare for a Gods damned war!>" He stormed off round the corner, cursing to himself.

Once he was out of sight, I spun on my heels to glare at Zyl, fury bubbling.

Zyl shrank away and hid behind Xavier. "*R-re? Re kegntcha mot glecht ĕlos?*"

"Xavier," I growled, my eyes narrowing.

Xavier promptly pulled away from Zyl and stood at attention beside me. "Alexander."

He stepped to my other side in reply, glaring daggers at Zyl.

My next words came in a low rupture, and I switched tongues to Grimish so only they would understand me. "*A'halaa Yeyt.*"

They both seized her by either arm, the Sky Princess tensing in panic. "Willow?!" She cried in Landish. "What doing?!"

"*Begna yeyt k'laven ysch kachesch,*" I ordered of the twins. "*Liz ul p'laven.*"

They both nodded tersely. "*Thoul'beahl trinn.*"

They hauled Zyl out of the palace, the swallow kicking and screaming as I followed behind.

"*Tovt!*" Zyl screeched. "*Tovt, tovt, tovt…!*"

Zyl's hands suddenly burst with electricity, and the twins yelled in pain when they were shocked stiff, dropping to the floor. Zyl broke into a run and fled outside before spreading her wings and taking flight.

"Death!" I hurried to the twins, who were still convulsing over the ground with bolts of static popping over their muscles.

They recovered slowly, Alexander sitting up first in a curse as he glared out the doors where Zylveia had disappeared. Xavier had more trouble rising, his arms still on the thin side, and I helped lift him to his feet.

"Are you both all right?" I asked, slinging Xavier's arm around my neck to help steady him.

Xavier puffed. "Fine. We have to find her."

Alex clicked his tongue. "We don't have wings."

"No," Xavier agreed, "but we have a vassal who does. Dalen." He glanced at the ceiling now. "We need to resurrect you. There's been a complication with Her Highness Sky."

Grand idea, I thought, and looked back at Nikolai's ghost, who'd followed us down here. I tapped into my own mental connection with Rossette. "Rossette, please come at once to be resurrected."

Right away, Da'torr, came her voice almost immediately.

I went ahead and resurrected Nikolai's body, which had been held in his Storagecoffin strapped to my thin waist-belt. Once I sewed his soul into his newly risen vessel, Rossette's ghost appeared, as had Dalen's. I resurrected her and even pushed more of my Hallows into her bones to age the girl by several years. If she was going catch up to Zyl, her wings had to be more matured.

"The Sky Princess is gone," I told her. "She's taken flight somewhere, and we need to take her back to Culatia. When you find her, Rossette, restrain her and return her to the ship. We will be waiting there."

Rossette bowed. "Yes, *Da'torr*."

The twins had finished sewing Dalen to his resurrected vessel, and both winged vassals took to the air. I led us out of the palace, and Nikolai trotted to my side, sounding uncertain. "*Da'torr?*" he asked. "<Why was I also resurrected?>"

"<In case I need your ice, once Zyl is brought to us,>" I explained. "<Rossette's Astravoking will make her resistant to Zyl's lightning, but the same can be said for Zyl. If we're to keep her from flying off again, we may well need to freeze her wings for a time.>"

He nodded in understanding, but looked dismayed, his gaze dropping.

I pursed my lips, guessing at what he was thinking. I put a hand on his scaly shoulder. "<I'm sorry, Nikolai. Once we have Zyl, I will find your painting supplies, as promised.>"

His finned ears flapped up and his smile returned as we headed back towards the ship.

FUÉRR

TRANSLATED FROM MARINCIAN

Death left with the Shadow, storming out in a very big hurry.

Was that red bird Sky's sister? I know Papa mentioned she was missing from home. What was she doing here?

"Come, Fuérr," Mama hushed and grabbed my wrist. Why was she shaking? "Your papa and I have some… things to take care of… And it's well past your bedtime."

I started to follow her. But Dream put a hand on her shoulder.

"Wait, Veyazelle," he said in our language. His accent was almost flawless and pretty, not like the Shadow's woodenness with some vowels. "There is something I meant to tell you both. I'd thought I would have more time here before revealing this, but with the current circumstances, I'm afraid my schedule has been cut short."

He spoke in his own language now. Landish words were so stiff and strange. Not pretty at all. There was no smoothness to them, just hard, solid sounds like the words were pounded by a hammer.

Whatever was said, Papa didn't like it. His scales reddened on his face, and he started shouting.

Dream said something else quietly, then took out a pretty blue orb. What was *that*? My eyes widened at the sparkling ball. Was that his Seeing Stone? Mama said a lot of oracles use them. But this was a the prettiest I've ever seen, much shinier than the boring ones in story books.

Images started moving in the ball. I tried to see, but Dream turned himself to block my view. I scowled.

Mama watched whatever the ball was showing. She looked scared. Then she started crying. Why?

Papa's eyes were misting also, but he still looked angry. He ground his teeth real slow, breathed in, and let it out with tightly closed lids. He whispered something in Dream's language, sounding sad.

Dream put away the pretty blue orb, and Mama knelt to me.

"Fuérr?" She said softly, shivering. Was she cold? "You're going to go with Dream on his boat. With the Shadow. And you're going to keep them safe for us. Okay?"

I frowned. "Where are we going?"

"You're going to Neverland."

"You're not going, Mama?"

Her head shook, and she wiped at her wet eyes. "No. No, I cannot come with you. But I'll be here when you return." She started crying, her voice squealing tight.

I hugged her. "It's okay, Mama... I'll go. Don't be sad..."

She sniffed, still crying, and held me tight. "Come. Let us pack your things quickly, before they leave."

She rose and I took her fingers, following her upstairs as Dream and his orange-haired lady came. Both of their furred ears were showing, draping down with their heavy heads.

22

CILIA

I emerged from the cold seawater, but only up to my eyes. The Reapers' ship was still at port and most of their crew still bustled onboard. From this distance, I couldn't see exactly who wandered by on the deck, but I knew he was there somewhere. My descendant. The one who shared Kael's face.

Kael…

I found a large boulder of ice surfacing from the water nearby and lifted onto it, staring at the ship's deck and hoped to see my descendant again. I knew he wasn't Kael, not after five hundred years. Kael was long dead by now. But then, could his soul have been reborn? Perhaps as my descendant?

My thought was pushed aside when I felt a heavy Weight lean against mine. It wasn't tangible, just a hefty push against my soul. It matched my Weight almost exactly. *Then it isn't HER…*

"Cilia," a watery voice rumbled beside me, "I thought I made it clear what would happen when next we met."

I turned, finding a shark-tailed man with fin-like, indigo hair staring at me from the edge of my ice boulder. His white pupils gleamed bright in the darkness, reflecting off the snowfall. My cat ears grew and curled.

"Last I recall, Hecrûshou," I said smoothly, letting him see just how unconcerned I was. "You wanted me Cleansed."

He began reaching for the clothed trident at his back. "Indeed I did."

I stopped him with a clawed, wagging finger, and a grin rolled over my lips. "We're not in your territory anymore, Dark Lord. We're in La'lunaî's waters now. Your make-believe 'Laws' bear no meaning here. And how would the southern queen react to seeing me dead at her doorstep? She is something of a friend to me, lest we forget."

Friend was a generous term, in all honesty. La'lunaî tolerated me. She once said she found me amusing; her little kitten. That was perhaps the closest thing to 'I don't feel inclined to rip your black heart from between your ribs', for her. But Hecrûshou didn't need to know the details.

I flicked my eyes at him, deciding to add, "Not to mention… well, I don't think I need to remind you of your last argument over boundaries with her. Especially while you still wield that offensive thing on your back."

He grimaced and withdrew his hand from the wrapped Spiritcrystal trident. "I… recall that argument, yes… But then, La'Lunaî is not here. We would have felt her Weight, were she near. Hers overshadows ours tenfold."

"True," I hummed. "But she has lessers watching us as we speak. They will no doubt inform her, in time."

He growled sourly, turning his attention to the ship's bow instead. "What do you seek, with them? Why pursue so relentlessly?"

"I should ask you the same, Hecrûshou. You've never taken it upon yourself to serve as bodyguard for any Clean One. Why start with them?"

"It is the Death girl." He held a tone that lulled with hopeful stupidity. "Never has the Grim ruler showed any interest in working with us. Never have they considered to grant us citizenship, to give us rights that were ripped away from us simply because we died. They've never listened, nor stopped to realize that we could be a great asset to them. But that one." He nodded to the ship, though the girl wasn't there. "She listened. She changed her mind. If that one is to rule next, think of how it could change the world as we know it. A new era is about to dawn, Cilia, of that I assure you."

I snorted. "Idealistic idiot. I'd forgotten how righteous you could be."

"And I, how callous *you* could be." His gaze narrowed at me. "And you seem to have picked up a Clean One of your own. Who is the cobra? You appear to be taking orders from him, yet I recall you vowing to never be any-one's whore again."

"That is my own concern." My teeth sharpened, and I let him see—

But my cat ears picked up a voice spouting orders from the ship. Hecrûshou lifted his gaze there as well.

It was the Death girl. Her white hair almost blended with the snow as she stormed onto the deck. Those brothers were behind her also, looking furious.

My throat clicked. "Damn it, there they are." Macarius expected me to bring those two back without heads. I glared at Hecrûshou. *How am I to act with the shark monitoring me?* Could I risk another battle with him? I suppressed a growl and glanced at the deck again—

The breath left me.

More of the crew had come out to see what the noise was about, and among them I found not one, but *three* cat shifters with ink-black hair and green eyes. Two I knew from before, the boys who were allied with the Reapers. The third was a woman I hadn't seen before, but she looked... *Shel's golden blade.* I could swear she had my face. Though her hair wasn't as stunningly grey as mine, hers was far darker, matching the hue of her... brothers'? Cousins'?

My pondering evaporated when a fourth cat emerged to join them.

It was *him.* The very man I was looking for.

I rose on the ice boulder, and Hecrûshou swam to my front as if to block me. "I cannot allow you near them." His voice was grating. "The Death girl is not to be touched."

"I don't care about her," I spat, holding my gaze on the man. Could he be Kael, reborn again? How would I know for certain? There wasn't much I remembered of my husband; the Voice.

Macarius refused to tell me anything without 'earning' it. All I had to remember Kael by were a few glimpses of his face. He always smiled at me. Always had the gentlest laugh... He loved my cakes, the apricot specifically, it was his favorite. He would wear ivory coats often, some sort of medical uniform. Had he been a doctor? Oh, why couldn't I remember...?

My vision blurred when my eyes began to well.

From my peripherals, I saw Hecrûshou follow my gaze, the shark sounding sympathetic. "Ah... so, that is why you linger." The water sloshed when he sat on the ice at my feet, his tone soft. "They speak of you on occasion. Your descendants. It's still astounding your line has been carried on for so long. I watched my own line die centuries past... I hadn't even known you had family left."

"Neither had I." I sat on my haunches and pulled my legs to my chest, watching the man with Kael's face listen to what the twins were saying, their words muffled by the rising winds.

The gale was growing more violent, bitter against my burning cheeks and creating steam as the flurry fell faster. It seemed a sudden blizzard was on its way, the waters lapping higher on our rock.

"Cilia," Hecrûshou prodded quietly. "Why are you a lapdog for that cobra? What has he promised you that you don't already have?"

A tear spilled from my lashes. I didn't bother to break its path. "My memories."

There was a notable silence from him. When next he spoke, he sounded baffled. "You still haven't...?"

"No," I whispered, pain clenching my chest.

"But how? For so long... even I regained mine after the first twenty years."

"You had your family to remind you." My tone was bitter, cat ears curling. "I had nothing. *Nothing.* For five hundred years, I thought I would never remember." My fists tightened. "But then, I found Macarius. I don't know how, but he knew me when I was alive. Even though his soul is clean. And he has my memories."

"Of course..." He murmured with an intense look. "Only Somniovokers can hold memories. So, he is manipulating you with a prize that rightfully belongs to you originally..."

My voice fell. "I... just want to remember someone. Just one man. I don't need anything else."

"And then? What will you do?"

"I don't know," I admitted, resting my chin on my knees and sighing. "Even if I remembered him, I know I won't see him again. He is long dead. But then, if his soul was reborn..." I gazed longingly at my descendant. A new warmth bloomed in me, far stronger than any heat my Pyrovoking could ever bring.

Hecrûshou grunted. "You speak of Kael?"

My thoughts cracked and split. I gawked at him, voice floundering. "H... h-how do you know that name?"

"He has spoken of him, your descendant. He claims to have seen him with his own eyes, to have traveled with him. He says Kael was your husband. And that he still lives today, working with the snake you call Macarius."

"That's impossible." My tone fractured. "Macarius would have said..."

"What reason would he have to tell you?" he challenged. "You have been fooled, Cilia. Were it not so, I should think this Macarius would have returned all of your memories by now."

"He only hasn't returned them so I won't fall into an eternal slumber."

He blinked at me. Then the bastard laughed. "Is that what he's told you? Good Gods, girl, the worst that will happen is you'll be asleep for a day or two. The only danger that awaits you is tangled hair!"

My cat ears draped to my neck. "How do you know?"

"How do you think I regained mine? My uncle was a Somniovoker, the one who first found me after I'd Changed. He helped me collect what he found in Aspirre and gave them to me all at once. I assure you, there is no 'eternal slumber' to fear."

Gods. I never even... My throat clicked. "And Kael? You think he is alive after five centuries?"

"You claimed Macarius has lived for so long, why shouldn't such a possibility lie with your lover?"

I stared at him. Then my nerves shattered.

Idiot! I cursed to myself, my teeth sharpened furiously. *Damned, idiot girl…!*

"My descendant," I clipped, fury rising along with my impatience, "does he know anything else? Where Kael would be, if he is truly alive?"

Hecrûshou shook his head. "Claude knows nothing since he left them. I suspect only Macarius would know that answer."

I rose once more, the flurrying wind whipping past me and throwing my hair back as steam rose off my hot skin.

"Thank you," I said, hushed. "I… I know an apology is beyond acceptable. I cannot take back what I've done. But from here on, I promise you. I am no threat to you."

His gaze narrowed at me. "What will you do now? Confront him and ask for Kael?"

"I cannot trust his answer," I said, head shaking. "But… perhaps I can buy you and the Reapers time. I'm afraid I must still follow you. You all may help me force Macarius to *take* me to Kael, if possible."

"You could simply threaten him with your army," he pointed out.

"Macarius is far too clever for that. He'll know I won't kill him until I find Kael. He is no good to me dead, for now."

"And once you've found Kael? What do you plan to do then?"

My smile was absent of its usual cruelty. For once, it held genuine cheer, imagining the day I would find Kael again. A strange emotion swelled, something I'd assumed I'd never feel again: *Hope.*

"I'll return to my isle," I answered, "with my husband. And I will mount the snake's head on my wall."

23

ZYL

*T*hat bitch!

The flurries raged over the city, snow thrashing everywhere as I flew over the round buildings and dodged the stray Stormchasers flying into the blizzard's nimbus. They were shouting commands, desperate to stop the icy storm that crashed in on them out of nowhere.

It was my doing. My snow. I couldn't help it, my heart was pumping so fast, I couldn't keep still, I couldn't hold in my Imbrivoking. *Willow,* I thought feverishly as the wind tossed my tears aside, and I wished I hadn't left my goggles on the ship. *You backstabbing bitch!*

She was going to turn me in! She was going to bring me back to Dad! That had to have been what she was babbling about in that weird, Grim language. Otherwise the twins wouldn't have tried to haul me away. *Damned, self-righteous BITCH!*

I gasped when I almost flew straight into a tall tower, and my wings reflexively spread to slow my pace before I crashed into it. I fumbled onto the tower's open balcony, shoving past multiple Stormchasers who stood inside here. I blinked through ice and tears. Was this a Chaser's roost? *Archer shoot me.*

The lingering Chasers were now staring at me, their wings rustling in the chilled gale. There were a fair mix of Landish and Culatian knights here, all transfers who'd been sent to this Marincian station.

"Princess…?" One blue-feathered knight breathed in Culatian, his grip tight on his bow as he went bug eyed at me. "Princess… Zylveia…?"

I hurried the Void off the roost, my wings pushing against the growing wind. It was freezing, but I couldn't stop. I couldn't go back. Not until I had Roji…

I rubbed my eyes dry and kept flying, trying to see in the veil of snow. Where was I? Damn it, if I just had my goggles, I—

A winged guy shot out of the ice and grabbed my arm. It was the twins' dead-thing, Dalen. I ripped my arm away and sped ahead, but then *Aiden* glided in front of me to block my way. He hurtled a gust of wind to push me back, but I heaved a countering gale back at him. With him distracted, I dove under him, barreling through the clouds and snow, the sharp ice hitting my almost numb face.

The younger, green-winged girl of Willow's came into view then. She was coming at me from the right, and I rushed out of her way when she almost tackled me. Her hands sparked with electricity, lightning clapping all around me as she tried to trap me. But I had lightning of my own, feeling the charge of each bolt before they came, and dodged each one before zapping my own strings at her. She dodged just as easily, but it slowed her down.

I flapped into overdrive, puffing, the storm now out of my control and thrashing my wings every which way. Sky, I was getting dizzy. There was no telling which direction I was flying anymore. But on I flew, it felt like hours. Maybe it *had* been hours. Was I flying in circles? It was impossible to tell. I still had to dodge the occasional spire and lightning rod, so I knew there was still a city beneath me. But was it the same city, or did I fly to a different island? Gods, where was I…?

My feathers were icing over, and I could feel myself losing altitude. I had to land, and soon, or else I'd freeze over and fall to my death. But at least I'd lost the others in the blizzard. I hadn't seen any of them for a while.

I spotted a circular glow radiating from within the storm and hurried toward it. It was a clock tower. There was a small opening underneath it, with huge, iron bells that were crusted with frost. I landed inside and puffed for breath, shivering in the cutting wind as my wings wrapped around me to keep warm.

"Zyl…!" A faint voice shouted over the rushing wind, and my head snapped up. The voice called again, "Zyl!"

El 's figure illuminated from a few yards away. There was a warm glow flickering from her hand like a tiny beacon in the darkness. Her fire struggled to stay lit in the blizzard, licking violently between her fingers as her Death mark gleamed white on her forehead. Her scarlet Sky mark shined from her bare foot, too, her Imbrivoking Hallows creating a small pocket of calm air around her.

I was shaking inside the tower, wanting to calm my own air, but my nerves were trembling along with my arms. The blizzard was too strong even for me now, and I was *so* cold…

"Zyl." Her tone quieted when she soared closer, her cat ears draping to her neck. She touched down inside the open tower beside me. "You have to stop this blizzard. The Chasers are getting overwhelmed—"

"I can't." I shuffled away from her, my back meeting one of the supporting pillars. I felt cold inside just as well as out, the panic pouring out. "I can't stop it. I'm sorry. S-sorry..."

My feathers went stiff in the ice and I shivered, sniffling. "Please," I whimpered, "don't take me back. Don't..."

El sighed and enclosed us both with her wings, wrapping one arm around me as she kept her fire lit with the other. Her skin was hot and searing against my back. She was so warm... like being at home by the fire, falling asleep as Big Brother read me stories... He would carry me to bed, tuck me in... it was more than Dad ever did.

My eyes stung, El's face blurring behind water. "I... j-just wanted..." My skin quaked, and El held me tighter to warm me up. "To f-find... Roji..."

"I know," she whispered. El cradled my head to her shoulder, just like Roji used to do. Just like Roji...

The pain gushed out my eyes, my lungs squeezing. El only stroked my hair, leaving me to my crying and gave me her warmth.

I didn't remember falling asleep in her arms.

24

XAVIER

~~~

The storm finally settled, the ship rocking to a steady swell at last.

Alex and I breathed in relief and released our hold of the mast, and I saw Willow let go of the rope she'd used to steady herself.

Dream had fastened himself to a nearby net, and Crysalette held one hand to the stair rail while her other was wrapped around… Prince Fuérr? What was *he* doing here?

Oh, never mind that now. There were far more pressing matters.

We all clambered to the edge of the deck to check the horizon. There were still a few stray clouds, but the sky was relatively clear now, the stars glittering in the overhanging void and a stream of vibrant green, aurora lights wavered between them. The moon was in a crescent shape tonight, just a small, thin slit glowing in the night.

The island had disappeared. The blizzard had blown us off the docks somehow. But didn't we anchor the ship? Had something broken the chain? Either way, we were certainly not where we had been. Not a speck of land could be seen from any direction.

"How far have we drifted?" I asked, glancing at Alex.

My brother glared at the waters and brushed off the stray flakes of snow that had clung to his short hair. "I don't know. We'll need a flyer to scout our location."

"All our airborne personnel are looking for Zylveia," I said. "Save for Lilli."

Willow stomped over to us and wrung out her long hair. It had been drenched by crashing seawater during the storm. Her clothes were soaked through as well, much like ours. My beard was still dripping water onto my chest, but I ignored it. Our sudden isolation was far more alarming.

Willow's fox ears were still grown and they curled tight to her head when she scowled at the sea once more, her brow wrinkling with severe creases. "I'll find Lilli," Willow volunteered. "If the others return with Zylveia, restrain her."

"That didn't work the first time," protested Alex. "She'll electrocute us again."

"Then... I leave it to you, Xavier." She cast me a cold stare. "The moment you have her, take out her soul. Separate it from her vessel."

I stared at her. "Don't you think that's a bit... drastic?"

"That idiot girl just started a war that my father has been trying to pacify for years. If her Hallows is too much for us to keep her captive, then we must do whatever necessary to sever her magic connection with her vessel. A soul cannot cast anything without a physical medium to release it. Separate her soul. We'll keep her body tended to while it sleeps."

"For how long?" I asked.

"Until we take her back to her father. However long that takes, provided that blizzard she conjured didn't blow us too far off course. Damned, foolish girl and her tantrums..."

She stormed inside, still wringing out her hair as she left a trail of water in her wake.

I hunched over the railing and cupped my hands, hitting my brow with my knuckles. "Now I wish I never discovered that Evocation."

Alex leaned his back against the rail beside me. "If you hadn't, we'd still be fighting for elbow room in the same flesh. But Willow is right. Zylveia must be kept under control. She can't be causing storms whenever her emotions explode... And she has to return to her father. It's the only hope we have to stop their war."

"I know," I said. "I only wish *I* didn't have to do it. Can't I teach someone else?"

"No one else can. They've all tried, after we left Y'ahmelle Nayû. You were in therapy when they tested it."

I looked at the Crest of diamonds on my left hand. Though the blizzard had subsided, I still felt that strange chill running through me; the ice that coated my soul, crystalizing with every breath.

"I don't want these Blessings," I said quietly. "I wanted a normal life after I found my body. I was fine with my halved Necrovoking, fine with the normal path of a Death Knight."

He hummed, thunking his elbows on the railing. "You wouldn't have had a normal path either way. You know what your betrothal with Willow will eventually make you."

I shuddered, but not from the frost. "I'm... aware. I've always been aware. Not that I wanted that path, either."

"But you will be king. Everything she'd discussed with Ninumel will happen eventually."

"King." The word was thick on my tongue. "It sounds wrong. I'm not a king, Alex. I'm not groomed to rule, I'm groomed to fight."

He shrugged. "You've always been the diplomat between the two of us. You take after Father in that sense. I'm not the best with delicate words and compromises… That's always been your strength, and it seems appropriate for a ruler."

The coldness crept to my chest, and I folded my arms on the rail. "I suppose I understand why Zylveia doesn't want her throne. It's a heavy burden. I want nothing of it myself."

"Well," he considered, rubbing his bare chin. "If you really don't want that responsibility, then there's nothing for it. You have to leave Willow."

I gave him a piqued, sidelong glance.

He took that as my response and chuckled. "Then I'm afraid you'll have to live with it. *Sire.*"

"Bloods," I groaned. "Don't you *ever* call me that."

"How else will you acclimate yourself to it?"

"From everyone else." My tone dropped to a more severe grumble. "Anyone else. Just not you. Void, Jaq can call me whatever he damn well wants, but I'll not hear it from you. I swore an oath to my brother, not my servant. With whatever happens, I need you there as my equal, as it's always been."

"Xavier." He shook his head hopelessly. "I won't be your equal when you're king. But I'll be there if you need me. I may not rule with you, but I'm damn well going to die with you, even still."

I nodded since my stomach was sinking too far to reply.

Then a dripping splash came from below the deck, followed by a Marincian curse as a shark-finned figure leapt onto the ship's edge, his blue hair tossing over his shoulders as the clothed trident was slung over his back.

Hecrûshou crouched on the railing, his white pupils shining from within the darkness as he rasped, "You nearly drifted too far from my watch. Perhaps next time, I should board during a storm."

He stepped onto the deck, his dripping clothes adding to the puddles on the hardwood. "What happened?" he asked. "The storm was unnaturally sudden. The work of an Imbrivoker, I assume?"

My wolf ears grew. Just thinking of Zylveia's damned tantrum made my blood boil… "Do you know how far we've drifted?"

"The closest land mass with any supplies is the eastern coast of Neverland."

"Neverland?" Alex echoed. "Culatia's capital won't be above there until Eyesinder. Bloods, it'll take months to get Zylveia to her father."

"How close are we to the continent?" I asked the Demon King.

Hecrûshou crossed his arms. "It will perhaps be a four week journey. I hope you have enough supplies to survive that long out at sea."

"I hope so as well," I glanced at Alex. "Do you think our new Aquavoking can push us to land faster?"

He shrugged. "It's worth a try, if Hecrûshou assists. We can ask Aiden to help with the wind as well."

"Grand." I rubbed my eyes. "Maybe we can make it in a fortnight, if we're fortunate. Once we reach Neverland, we're finding the first city with a Stormchaser station and requesting an airship to Culatia."

Alex snorted. "Neverland only has one Chaser station. In the capital, just like Everland. Same with the Reapers there."

"Well, this just keeps getting better," I muttered. "Fine. We may as well see this queen who wanted to speak with us there. She's offered aid for our battles against Everland, perhaps we can alleviate two wars along the way."

"It seems like a fair plan," wagered Alex. "It's not as if we have much choice at this point."

The deck vibrated behind us, many feet thunking onto the wood suddenly. Our winged scouts had returned.

El was in front, carrying an unconscious Zylveia in her arms, the Sky Princess's wings wrapped round her body as if to keep warm. El looked dismayed when she approached me.

"P... pl*eees*." She struggled with the pronunciation. "Keep... s-*saeevv*..."

Alex and I nodded, and my brother took the swallow from her. It was a feat in itself to find a comfortable hold with Zylveia's large wings, I noticed her bones were digging into his chest. I followed him as he took Zylveia into the cabin and brought her to the infirmary, startling the two Healers on duty when he laid her on one of the beds.

Willow came inside soon, probably having heard that Zylveia had been found. She stood between Alex and me, all of us gazing down at the slumbering girl with mixed emotions. Alex was blank and unreadable, Willow stern, and I... uncertain.

I glanced at Willow one last time. "Are you sure this must be done?"

She nodded. "I'm afraid she can't be trusted, otherwise. She will be given great care, don't doubt that. This is only temporary."

A new voice suddenly added, "I'll watch over her dreams."

Dream had entered behind us. His gaze was remorseful, yet determined as he looked upon Zylveia and nodded to me.

I inhaled deeply, then let it out in a smooth stream. I held a hand to Zylveia's dark chest and evoked my death Hallows, my Crest changing into a Death mark as black light shined from my palm. I felt her NecroSeam vibrate, the thread pulsing along with her heartbeat.

"I'm sorry," I whispered, and pulled out her soul.

I left the clinic cabin with heavy feet.

Well, it was done. What a grand gift I have, toying with people's souls…

"What," I heard Willow clip down the hall. "Is *he* doing on this ship?"

I rounded the corner, finding her staring at the little Ocean Prince, whose shoulders were gripped by Crysalette. Dream stood beside them, his expression dour.

"I asked Ninumel if Fuérr could join us." Dream didn't look the least bit sorry. "And he agreed."

"Why in Nira's sorrowed name bring him with us?" Willow threw her hands up desperately. "He's only a child, Grandfather! He should be with his parents. What were you thinking?"

"Had we left him there," said Dream, poignantly quiet. "He would not have a future left."

The halls grew still. Crysalette bowed her head, patting Fuérr's long, emerald hair and laid it neatly over his shoulder, hushing him when he inquired in his language what was being said.

I stepped beside Willow and asked, "Someone would have killed him, you mean?"

Dream nodded solemnly. "If he stays with us, he lives. It was the only path where he survives."

Willow gazed at little Fuérr, biting her lip. Then she sighed and turned away. "Very well… I'll let the others know we're housing the child prince. Bloody oracles and their damned Third Eyes…"

As she left, Lilli passed her in the hall with Oliver following at her heels. Willow disappeared round the corner, and Lilli looked at me in question.

I nodded to Prince Fuérr. "The Ocean Prince has joined us for this journey, it seems."

Lilli's brow knitted. "Oh… I see…"

Behind her, Oliver peeked round her waist and blinked at little Fuérr. His eyes grew wide with thrill. "Fuérr!"

Oliver leapt in front with an exhilarated laugh, jumping up and down with boundless energy. "It's actually Fuérr! Finally, finally, finally!" He grinned at the little prince and pointed. "Heehee! You're so little! And ya *still* look like a girl."

Fuérr scowled at him, his mouth twisting in confusion. He clearly hadn't understood.

I scratched my scruffy chin and cocked a brow at Oliver. "Do you know him, then?"

"Fuérr's my best friend!" He giggled, wings fluffing as he grabbed Fuérr's hand and wheeled him around excitedly. "Or, he will be, when we're big!"

When they came to a stop, Fuérr wobbled, looking dizzy. Then he was seized by the arms and shaken vigorously, Oliver laughing. "Are ya comin' with us, Fuérr? Are ya, are ya? Mama, can he come with us?"

"He'll be coming with us to High Neverland," I assured. "We're not sure for how long, but we expect it will be for some time."

"Yeah!" Oliver bounced over to Lilli and wheeled her around while Fuérr staggered to regain his balance. "Can he stay with me, Mama?"

Lilli hesitated. "We don't have any more room in our cabin…"

"We can get our own room, right next to ya! That one's not bein' used, I looked!"

"I…" she began, "I suppose it should be all right…"

"Yeah!" Oliver fluttered back to Fuérr, snagging his wrist and tugging him along down the hall. "Let's get ya moved in! I call top bunk…!"

Fuérr was dragged against his will around the corner, sputtering for the owl to slow down in Marincian.

"Well," I chuckled and folded my arms as Lilli held an uncertain expression beside me. "This will certainly be an interesting trip."

ZYL

TRANSLATED FROM CULATIAN

"Roji," I called through the palace halls, the comforting sounds of thunder rumbling outside as rain applauded on the windows. "Rojiiiii…!"

I heard his chuckles echo from somewhere in this room, but the sounds bounced too much for me to figure out where it was coming from. I put fists at my sides. "I can hear you, Roji! Just come out already!"

His snickers were poorly stifled, and this time, I heard it coming from above. I glanced up and found Big Brother lying lazily over the chandelier, grinning down at me. "Well, you found me," he chuckled and curled a finger to egg me on. "Come and catch me, if you can, lil' sis."

"That's not fair!" I cried, hopping and flapping my tiny wings, but not catching any air. "I can't fly yet…! That's cheating, Roji!"

"We never established the rules, now did we?" his laughter bounced around the corridor for everyone to hear…

My eyes were slow to peel open.

Normally, I would have rolled over on the bed and engulfed myself in the blankets, but I didn't feel a bed under me; I didn't feel any blankets around my shoulders. And now that I thought about it, I didn't feel *anything* touching me. Not even the cold, freezing air I remember passing out in.

"El…?" I croaked, rubbing my eyes and moving forward. Weird. It was like I woke standing upright, my feet were already in the right position to walk. And walking didn't feel like anything. I may as well be gliding over the damned… floor…

I stared at my feet. My *see-through* feet, which hovered over the floorboards. My head snapped up, the cabin awash in white and grey tones, not a speck of color visible except for myself.

I screamed.

El quickly threw open the door. "Zyl?!"

She was panting and wearing glasses. They looked familiar. Weren't those the rabbit doctor's glasses she used to see ghosts?

My shoulders went rigid. *Ghosts.*

"A-a-am… am I… d-d-dead?" I moved to walk over to El, but my feet swooped forward before I could take a step and I glided over the floor without making contact. I shrieked at the sudden speed and ran into her—*through* her. I phased through the door too, and El had to walk back out to meet up with me. My voice trembled. "Oh, great Ushar, I'm actually dead!"

I gasped for breath, but didn't feel any air reach my lungs.

"Zyl." El waved her hands in a 'calm down' motion. "Don't worry. You're not dead. Xavier just took out your soul for a while, so you wouldn't cause anymore storms."

I gawked at her. "What! But I…"

"<You've endangered two entire nations,>" a familiar woman's voice clipped in Landish down the hall. Willow's newly colorless figure strode up to me, her usually pretty face ugly with creases from her glower.

She stopped in front of me and crossed her arms, switching her language to Culatian. "You've proven to be too emotionally unstable to be trusted with your Hallows. I just ended a com call with King Ninumel, and the tally for the injured during your little tantrum-blizzard are in the thousands. You'd better thank Death there were no fatalities, but rest assured, I will not risk another disaster like that simply because you're too immature to handle responsibility."

I growled. "You're one to talk, Willow. You left your palace just like me."

"*I* didn't leave to avoid my duty as future queen."

I crinkled my nose up in the air. "Oh, that's right. You left to 'save the people from the demons.'" I curled my fingers sarcastically, snorting. "Please. I know you left to find your dead boyfriend."

That obviously hit a nerve because her brow twitched. "He wasn't dead. And I planned to return afterward."

"So do I, after I find Roji."

"Well, I… it's not as if… *argh*, never mind! Arguing with you is useless. It was my grandfather Dream who asked me to leave, regardless. I didn't surface on my own impulsive accord."

"Neither did I!" I stamped a foot—or would have, if my foot hadn't phased through the wood without sound or contact. "Dream was the one who told *me* to leave and look for Big Brother, too."

She paused at that, one fox ear flicking up. Then her throat clicked angrily. "Did he now?"

The floor creaked behind us.

We craned to see the young king in question was frozen mid-step there. He was posed like he was trying to sneak away quietly, but had just been caught.

Willow growled in Landish. "<Grandfather…>"

A nervous laugh slipped from Dream's lips. "<Oh, er, hello dear! I, *khm-khmm*, I was just going to check on your grandmother…! Please excuse me—!>"

"<Grandfather!>" Willow barked, stopping him in his tracks. "<Did you tell Zylveia to leave Culatia?>"

His head wavered. "<Well… If I hadn't, she'd likely be dead by now.>"

"<Grandfather,>" Willow warned, "<if this is some cheap excuse…>"

"<It's true!>" He insisted. "<The same people who would have come for you would have ended *her* long before they would have come to Grim. Why do you think I sent her away before you?>"

"<What are you talking about!>" Willow threw her hands up. "<Cousin Felix has no reason to kill Sky's Relicblood!>"

He looked genuinely affronted. "<Not Felix,>" he corrected. "<Granted, he had a *slight* chance of killing you in Death's Duel, but if he failed, the others would have come and finished you in two years' time. *Zylveia*, however, would have lost her head but months ago had I not sent her off. Her father's days were shrinking as it were, I needed to be sure at least one heir was safe.>"

"<And the first heir of Sky?>" she asked. <Don't you dare tell me you sent him off as well?>"

He looked morose. "<I'm afraid not. Even *I* don't know where he is. He himself could very well be dead.>"

That was a sharp stab to my gut. "You," I squeaked. "You think Big Brother's dead?" My wings dropped, though their usual heaviness wasn't there anymore. "But I... I came all this way..."

Dream quickly amended in Culatian. "Ah, I'm not certain of it, Zylveia. I was simply stating that it's possible—not that I believe he's dead, but it's not outside the realm of plausibility—"

"<Grandfather!>" Willow hissed, trying to discreetly jerk her head at me. She must have noticed my eyes were misting—or, motioning to mist, since I didn't have any physical tears.

Willow sighed hard, then waved Dream away. "<Go tend to Grandmother. See how my uncle-to-be is fairing... but we are not done here.>"

Dream unceremoniously turned a corner out of sight. Willow's tone softened when she looked back at me. "Zylveia, I'm sorry. My grandfather isn't the most graceful with such discussions."

I was shaking. "Is... *is* Roji dead? I thought he left with the fish-girl, I didn't even think about..."

She started to reach a hand to me, but retracted it back. Then she decided to clasp my translucent shoulder after all, her fingers actually making contact in quiet ripples. It was like pressing against water: she could touch it, but also push through if she put in the effort.

"I'm sure your brother is safe," she murmured. "And... I suppose you had a fair point. Perhaps you and I did leave for similar reasons. Grandfather may have told me that finding Xavier was for all of our benefit, but... all I could think of back then was finding him alive. When I learned it was a real possibility, I didn't care about anything else."

She let her hand drop, stretching her neck. "But my leaving the palace caused far too much trouble. If I'd stayed in Grim, that Demon Queen wouldn't have been able to use my image to trick the Everlanders into going to war with us. So then, I suppose... we've both started wars."

I sniffed, wiping my nose more out of habit, since it wasn't actually running. "But it wasn't your fault the demons were killing everyone."

Her lips broke into a small grin. "No. It wasn't. And neither was it your fault your father decided to wage war against Ninumel. You didn't wish for a fight. Yet..." Her gaze sharpened, though her eyes were glazed with remorse this time. "I still must take you back to your father."

"Why?" I cried. "It's not like *you're* going back to your caves."

"If my return would ensure my nation's victory and preservation," she said, "then I would absolutely descend to Grim again." She sounded sad now, muttering. "If I'm speaking truthfully... I *want* to go home. But that is not what's best for my country, at the moment. Gathering more allying troops against Everland is the way I can help my people now. My father has the palace secured down below, so I must secure the situation above, as his representative. You, on the other hand." She pointed at me. "*Must* return to your father. No one may have died in that blizzard you created, but don't doubt for a moment that this war your father has declared will bring more deaths than your storms could produce in a single hour."

My voice trembled. "I never wanted this."

"I know," she lamented, turning to leave. "But your father has brought it upon us, regardless. And the only way to stop it is for him to see you in front of his old, senile eyes himself. I'm doing what's best for my people, no matter how much I dislike it. You will do the same for yours. Willingly or otherwise."

She started to walk off.

"Why do you even care?" I spat, my ghostly hands balling. "Culatia has nothing to do with 'your people'."

Willow looked back at me, her expression eerily blank. "*Mu thechat necros yettek,*" she said in that weird, Grimish language. "*With war comes death.* Make no mistake, Princess of Sky. When your people fall, they will come to me. They will become my people, and the fate of their afterlives will be in my hands. It is absolute; there are no exceptions. For, you see, every soul meets Death... They all meet me, in the end."

She left the corridor, leaving me floating there in silence alongside El.

NEVERLAND

ROSARIA GRAND,
CAPITAL OF THE EASTERN CONTINENT OF LAND
BLACKWOOD FOREST

25

QUEEN SYREEN

"This chain of schools was built before the two continents were split," Headmistress Lysandre explained as she led me through the carpeted halls of the Lysandre Boarding Schools alongside her armored daughter, Genevieve.

Both women had brown scales coating their skin, their hair a dry bark color. While the Lady Lysandre wore a silken, maroon gown that shimmered with floral designs at the hem, Genevieve was fully plated with rose-gold armor adorned with ribbons and celebrating badges to mark her as the captain in my honorguard. The captain strode beside me in silence, ever alert, even when relaxed with her helm tucked under her arm as it was now.

The hall we strolled through was lined with numerous portraits of previous headmistresses, and as we approached the end, two men's faces hung here as well. Both men were scaled with brown hair, though the first man had fading grey streaks, aging him over his successor, who I assumed must have been his son.

"There were many locations spread across Everland," continued the headmistress, "before Neverland seceded from the original country of Everland."

"And there were men leading the schools once?" I asked, gesturing to the last two portraits.

"For a short time, yes." She clasped her scaled hands before her. "Things were far different in the late sixteenth century, as my husband could tell you. He is an astounding historian. More than just a handsome face. In fact, these last two portraits are his ancestors: the founder himself, and his son." She nodded to the second portrait, which showed the younger man. He seemed quite young to be leading a school, but then, those were indeed different times. She smiled and tapped the nameplate, explaining, "This one not only shares a name with my husband, but *looks* remarkably like him as well. The resemblance is unmistakable."

I hummed, inspecting the sharp, scaled face and noting the spectacles over his eyes suited him well. The nameplate read *Macarius Lysandre*. "These are the founder and his son?" I asked. "They taught at this building?"

"Oh, no, Your Majesty." She chuckled lightly. "All locations of the Lysandre Schools hang up these two portraits. Since we are a co-ed school, it gives the young boys hope that they can accomplish anything the women can. Equality has always been our aim."

"That's quite progressive. Most men that I know cannot read, since society has deemed it improper."

"Which is why I ask if you wouldn't mind encouraging the notion, Majesty? We value Neverland's education, and we believe a studied nation is a strong nation. Discouraging half the population from scholarship seems, with all due respect, outrageous."

I nodded. "I agree. I'll speak with my advisors on creating promotional mandates. I suppose I can push other schools to follow in your footsteps and allow boys to attend the same classes as the girls."

"Thank you." She sounded beyond grateful. "It would be wonderful to have other schools incorporate the changes we've had for centuries. Did you know, they say the first of our buildings was in the lost city of Aldamstria itself, and the halls we walk in now came but months after? There are many locations throughout Everland, Culatia, and Marincia as well I hear, and…"

We passed by a classroom, where I overheard a lecturer reading from a tome. "… and the Lightcaster shall bring truth to all," she said. "Truth of the past, truth of the Relicbloods, and truth of their oppression. The day will come where we the people will band together and fight those who hold our leash; those who think themselves our betters. But, as the Caster teaches, the Relicbloods are not Gods. They are shifters. They bleed as red as our own blood. And yet, they think themselves higher than our honored queen…"

We left the building and stepped out to a lovely breezeway. The many pergolas were wrapped in lively green vines and beautiful flowers, the lingering patches of snow melting under the sunrays that glittered over the school grounds.

"Headmistress," I began, "What is this talk of a 'Lightcaster'? I've been hearing the name more often as of late, though there have been different opinions of her role."

"*His* role," she said, "The Lightcaster is said to be a man. He is the one who will bring the world truth, as legend has it. He is among us now, somewhere, though his face has yet to be uncovered. He brings our school news of what is truly happening in the other realms, like a messenger with a higher purpose. They say he will be the one to combat the Shadowblood, in time."

"The Shadowblood... Those twins." A smile pulled my lips, remembering those grey, handsome faces and peculiar eyes. The ones who were said to possess Hallows strength unlike any other. "But why would the Lightcaster wish to combat them? I've heard many a sermon lately speak of their power. The rumors say they've already gained other Hallows elements they weren't born with. They say they are a force for good."

"He is a force for the *Relicbloods*." The word came out as a disgusted sneer. "Don't believe those fools, Majesty. The Shadowblood will bring our End. He will only help the Relicbloods bring our world to utter destruction through their tyranny. They're already glorified by the resistance who seeks your very death, Majesty."

I hesitated. "I have realized this. I simply believe I can convince the Shadowblood to ally with us instead of the Relicbloods. I've arranged a meeting with them at the palace. They will dock within the week, along with the Relicbloods of Sky and Death."

"Is it wise to bring the enemy into your home, Majesty?"

"Oh, I've devised a plan once they arrive. Worry not. Those Champions will see that they've allied with the wrong side, given time." My grin was lusting. "Wait and see, headmistress. I will show the world that those outside of the Relic Bloodlines are superior. I will make claim of their champions and have that power in my ranks."

And, I chuckled to myself, *in my bloodline.*

I bid the headmistress farewell and left the school, Genevieve and I taking a private coach to the palace. When we arrived, I glided through the courtyard, walking with Genevieve at my side. My personal guard's rose-gold plate glinted off the window's light so brilliantly, it contrasted her matte, walnut brown scales.

"Is your mother always fretting so?" I asked Genevieve.

She was a quiet one, I've noticed. She hardly said a word unless prompted. Now, she gave a soft breath and said, "When it comes to the Shadowblood, Mother can be riled. She stands firm to the belief they can only serve the Relicbloods."

"Well, she'll come to believe otherwise when I'm through with them," I said, anxious as we approached the dining hall.

I found my darling younger brother, Hugh, there. Though, he wasn't sitting at the dining table enjoying a meal. Instead, he stood away from the table and gripped a wooden sword while encircled by a cluster of guardswomen. They all had wooden practice swords as well, and Hugh glared at each of them, tapping his foot with his arms crossed over his chest. He did not look pleased.

When he spotted me, his grown lion ears perked.

"Sy!" he called, prompting all the guards to kneel before me. "Can you tell them to stop going easy on me? They won't actually fight, they're only holding out their swords for me to swat at."

One of the guards, still kneeling, spoke. "We did not wish to harm him, your grace."

I sighed and laid a hand on the woman's shoulder. "Thank you, Sil. But it seems my brother needs more of a challenge." I ruffled Hugh's bouncy blonde hair, smiling when that crow of his swooped down to alight on his shoulder. I stroked the bird's feathers. "He's simply too talented. Lady Lilac chose the soul of a true warrior, didn't she?"

Hugh stood taller at that, Lady Lilac rubbing her skull against his cheek encouragingly.

"Now, Hugh," I said as I put a hand at his back and led him out of the dining hall. "I know you're excited for the Reapers' arrival this week—"

"I've been training really hard," he interrupted in excitement. "I've practiced every day, for months. I'm actually going to meet a prince who can fight!"

"A prince?" I inquired. "No, Hugh, there are princesses on their way. The men among them are knights, not royalty."

"But one of the twins is to marry the Death Princess. That will make him a prince someday, won't it?"

My step staggered. "One is… betrothed to her? Where did you hear this?"

"The Reapers on the grounds spoke of it," he explained in an admiring swoon. "They say he has a power like none have ever seen! He can remove the souls of the living at his will and leave their NecroSeams unscathed and their bodies sleeping!" He let out a heavy breath. "I want to be a strong prince like that. One who can fight. I want to ask him how he got his power."

I stopped to collect my wits. I'd originally planned to claim both brothers; had assumed they were unspoken for; had thought they were simply escorting the Death Princess as her guards. But one was engaged to her? One with the power to manipulate *living* souls?

My teeth sharpened and ground. Such power *must* be in my future bloodline! If the Death Line gained that strength, overpowering the Relicbloods would prove near impossible!

I stood in silence, ponderous while drumming fingers over my arm. *One holds the power to raise the bones of giants,* I contemplated, *and the other removes souls at will…* I needed the complete set. Their genes would perhaps be weakened, if separated.

I blew out a breath and walked brusquely down the hall with Hugh and Genevieve.

"Well, dearest brother," I said with a vicious smile. "You may ask him your questions when he arrives. However…" I knelt to him, hesitant. "Promise me you won't leave the palace to pursue some dangerous Reaper knighthood? I allowed Lady Lilac to roam free as she pleased, and I've even arranged for your defensive lessons, but now that Reapers are coming here—with their future queen, no less—they may entice you to leave me. If you did, I…" A sickened weight pulled down my tone. "I don't know what I'd do. We've lost both our father and mother, you're all I have left of our full-blood family. I do not wish to lose you as well."

Hugh shook his head. "I'm not going to leave, Sy. I don't want to fight for the Death Relicblood. I just want to help people, if I can. I just wanted to ask the other prince what I could do here in the palace for it."

I smiled, relief flushing my knotted chest. "Well, tell me what he says, hm? I'll arrange for anything you need." I patted his shoulder before rising, and continued down the hall with Genevieve.

The matter of the 'prince' and his betrothal would be hazardous to my original plans. Should I move to claim him, the princess would no doubt step in. I would need to tread with care. Perhaps I could convince him that I was the better choice? And that was assuming the second brother wasn't spoken for as well…

Fine. Change of plans. A smirk rolled over my lips, a chuckle slipping out. *One way or another, I'll have acquired two new lapdogs before this event is over.*

MARIAN

I rushed through the flower-littered streets, passing all the ladies and their husbands in the market square and rushed into the alleys.

The chapel was just in sight.

With a swift duck under a woman's heavy crate of pears and a quick flutter with my wings over a handsome boy's feral dog, I tucked my new book tight to my chest and bounded for the chapel doors—

I skidded to a stop, two inches away from slamming my nose into the wood grain, my long, cleric robes flaring around me. I puffed while ripping the doors open, then rattled it shut, exhaling as I pressed my back and wings against the doors. *It's finally here!*

I grinned and looked at my prize. The book title read:

*The NecroSeam Chronicles: True Tellings of the Shadowblood
and Their Journey Across the Realms.*

Scribed and narrated by Chief of Knowledge, Herrin Tesler,
Archchancellor of the Enlightener's Guild

"—Marian?"

My head snapped up. Mother Thane was stepping down from the altar, breaking her morning prayers to meet me.

The elderly priestess was in her finer robes this morning. The sunlight barely spilled in from the single, stained-glass window on the flat ceiling, marking the early morning hour. Yet despite the fact it was barely seven in the morning, Mother Thane was here as always, fully dressed and preparing for her Songday sermon. Her long brown hair was braided and draped over her shoulder, falling to her waist, and her curling sheep horns looked newly polished.

"Marian," she said, cupping my face with worry swimming in her milky, blue eyes. "You've been running through town again, haven't you? Has something happened?"

"Not yet," I panted, letting her comb her thick fingers through my feathered, auburn hair and pick out the stray flower petals that had stuck there in my hurry. "But something will, Mother Thane."

"You've had another vision?" she asked.

I threw open my satchel, rifling through *Choir* texts and loose-papered notes, and pulled out my crystal orb. "Look here! The Shadowblood will be here within ten days' time."

I showed her the vision of the shadow-haired twins, their grey faces displaying within the orb that depicted the champions of legend walking through the halls of their ship.

"They're finally coming!" I preened, hopping excitedly with fidgeting feathers. "A lifetime of Seeing those two *after* their travels, and that future is at last catching up to me! I knew I Saw their faces for a reason, Mother, I *knew!* And, and…!" I fumbled to show her the new book I'd acquired. "Look! This tells of their life, it's written by the Archchancellor Enlightener himself! He travels with them, on their ship. Oh, I *must* meet him, Mother Thane! Crysalette had said such great things of him."

Ever wise and always questioning, the Queen of Dreams had said, *never takes the first answer and always strives to dig deeper to find the truth…* Lord Herrin must be a sage of a man. I imagined a wise old priest, his face wrinkled with years of wisdom and unequalled experience, a grey beard trickling down his chin, perhaps. Oh, what stories he could tell of the outside world; of the other kingdoms…

Maybe even invite me to join them on their travels? I dared to dream in silence. I'd never been outside this city, away from the chapel. I hoped they needed an oracle. It would be a great thrill to use my Blessing openly, instead of hiding it as if it were some stigma.

Mother Thane chuckled. "And meet him you will, child. When they arrive, go to those of your guild. I imagine they are just as excited to see your Archchancellor as you are."

"Oh, they are. I've just come from Mrs. Elliot's shop. She'd gotten this book from overseas, Crysalette had given it to Enlightener Veyazelle to have it printed and distributed across the realms. There's to be a gathering in Mrs. Elliot's bookshop with the Archchancellor when he arrives with the Shadowblood."

"Then I suppose I should expect you there," Mother Thane said. "There's naught I can do about your Enlightener business, but I can send word to the rest of the resistance that the Shadowblood is coming. They're said to lead us to our lost Relicblood. If this is true, then we can't trust the queen with them."

"I think you're right." I held a hand to my collarbone, slowing my breath. "There was more to my vision, Mother. Something is going to happen when they arrive. There will be fire at the palace. Chaos, screaming, smoke…"

The memory of the vision flickered behind my eyes, my heart pounding. I shook it away. "I cannot See what will come out of the rubble. But we must do something. Else, I fear the Shadowblood will end their journey within those walls."

Mother Thane nodded, her lips curled in a dour frown. "I will tell Vanessa of your vision, child. Now rest. You're excused from Songday services tonight, to let your Third Eye settle."

"I…" My lips pursed, smiling. "Yes. Thank you, Mother." I bowed and swayed down the aisle through the chapel, drifting through the back into the dormitories.

Rest? Hah! How could I rest knowing that in a mere week, my long-anticipated future awaited?

There would be no rest today. Only reading.

26
FUÉRR

TRANSLATED FROM MARINCIAN

I bundled the stained sheets and blanket, rolling my wettened drawers inside to hide them from sight.

I hurried to change into dry breeches, trying not to wake up that annoying owl—Oliver, as he kept telling me. I don't know how he already knew my name. Maybe the Shadow gave it to him.

Hopefully, he wouldn't wake up while I found a place to wash these.

The pile of sheets was a wide load for my arms, but I managed to keep it crumpled without it all falling out. I slipped through the door quietly and walked out to the hall—

I froze.

Oliver stiffened in front of me, his toe poised in a mid-slink and that pet crow of his perched on his head. He held a similar bundle of sheets and blankets. When did he… he wasn't still asleep on the top bunk?

"You too?" He asked in his strange, rough language. I didn't know what it meant, but I could guess, since he was blushing as much as I was.

"Great," I muttered, scowling. If he tattled, I would freeze his tongue and snap it off. How do I say that in Landish?

I shoved a finger to my lips. He pointed to his own chest, then stabbed the finger at me as if telling me to not say anything either. I nodded, both in agreement—

A flush roared from the lavatory near us, and someone walked out.

It was that scaled, snake man with eyeglasses. He shuffled out of the lavatory in a yawn, his fangs showing, and he scratched his sandy hair. He stopped when he saw us.

He looked from the owl to me, and grinned. *"Didn't quite make it to the toilet, huh?"* He laughed in his garbled Landish tongue. How mean!

"Don't tell Mama," the owl pleaded in that same gibberish. Oh, I knew the word *Mama!* Finally, a word I understood in that stony language.

But that small victory twisted sick in my stomach. Why didn't Mama come with me on this ship? Oh, I hoped we didn't take too long to go back home…

The snake laughed again and waved for us to follow him down the hall.

Oliver went after him, his footsteps *thump-thump-thumping* over the hardwood, and I rushed to keep up.

The snake led us down to the bottom level of the ship, where the crew's laundry was hanging to dry. The owl and I mimicked him as he took one sheet and dipped it in a bucket of sudsy water, drawing it over some metal sheet with crinkled ridges. It made the oddest, ripping sound. He had a particular rhythm to it, almost like he was listening to a song.

Oliver scrubbed his sheets in a separate bucket, and I tried it myself in a third. My ears flicked when I drew my wet drawers over the metal sheet, making that strange noise. I laughed, running it over again. And again. And again.

It was like making music. Maybe not *pretty* music, but still music.

We finished in maybe an hour, and the snake helped us hang everything up on a string, pinning them in place with some strange wooden clips. Was this how the servants at home cleaned sheets? I never thought about it before. Maybe I would ask Mama when I came back.

Mama. I felt sick again. *Why* didn't she come with me?

My head snapped up, realizing the snake and the owl were starting back up the steps. I rushed after them, slowing in a sigh when I caught up.

Then my stomach made a very unpretty noise.

They both looked at me. My face heated. "Um…" I mumbled, rubbing my growling belly. "I, um… I'm hungry…"

"What'd he say?" Oliver asked the taller man in Landish.

The snake shrugged, muttered more gibberish with the owl, then he turned a different direction led us somewhere else.

Other people were walking around now. Apparently, the other travelers in their group woke up while we were washing the sheets.

The snake took us to the mess hall, where all sorts of smells drifted in the air, simmering food snapping from the pots and pans that were being tended to by that cat chef.

I was given a bowl of thick stew, the same as Oliver. We sat at one of the long tables, and the tall snake eased into a seat himself and slurped up his stew with loud noises.

Oliver copied his manners, sucking the stew out of his spoon with an annoying giggle.

Barbarians. I huffed and sat up straight, delicately lifting my spoonful of stew and tipping it to my lips like a *proper* gentlefish—

Something wet and sticky slapped my forehead.

Oliver snickered at me, his spoon held in a flinging pose. I touched my fingers to the stew he'd hit me with. *Ugh! It's in my hair!*

He cackled while I rubbed at the spot with an arm, shooting him an annoyed glare. *If only Papa could see this un-soft-fisted-cated bird.*

Papa... the sickness came back. But I stuck up my nose, lifting my spoonful again—

Another glob of stew slapped my nose. Oliver burst into uncontrollable laughter.

I flung my own spoonful at him and shouted, "What is *wrong* with—?!"

He hit me again, then again, giggling like a feral snowbird.

Annoying little...! I dipped my hand in the stew and smeared it over his face.

He made a *yuck* noise, wiping his face desperately.

I grinned, clearly having won this fight.

But I frowned when he started laughing, wiping his face with his shirt.

My brow furrowed and I muttered, "Why are you laughing if I won?"

He smiled at me and said, "Because it's fun!"

Fun? I thought crankily, *how could messing yourself up like that be fun—*

"Wait." I blinked at him. "I understood you."

The viper heckled when Oliver showed him his stew-ridden face, both jabbering away in their language.

I grabbed the owl's shoulder and turned him around. "You speak Marincian?" I demanded.

He laughed and pointed at my face, speaking his usual gibberish again.

"Do you speak Marincian?" I asked again with more force.

He babbled on in Landish and lifted a translucent strand of my fin-like hair.

I scowled. What was going on? Did he only know that one line? But-but he *answered* my question! He had to have known *that* line, too?

"Oliver!" a woman snapped suddenly from the stairway. It was that pretty bat lady. She came shuffling up to us and grabbed a napkin from the corner counter. She wiped Oliver's face with it, then wiped mine, even though I bent away several times. *"What have you mischiefs been doing down here?"* she chided in Landish. *"Swimming in your food?"*

She pulled Oliver out of his chair and lifted me up next, setting me next to him. She lifted a brow at the snake man, who was still busy heckling away at us.

She blathered a few sharp orders at him in their language, and he grumbled, stretching up in a yawn and motioning for Oliver and me to follow him. He led us up the stairs and down the hall, stepping into the washroom. It was already occupied by those two green-eyed brothers, who were using separate nozzles in the several open showers.

We disrobed and stepped in the tiled room, the snake talking to the brothers in their language. The two looked at Oliver and me and laughed, saying something else to the snake, who shrugged out of his clothes and turned on a third shower.

He slipped off a ring from his finger and set it over his clothes—

I gave a soft gasp. There were scars on the snake's forehead. Like cravings, in Landish. I didn't know what they said, but they were puckered and ugly, painful just to look at. Have they been there the whole time? Hidden by an illusion from the ring?

The snake caught me staring, and I blushed, then hurried to the corner where the filled tub waited. I crawled in, my scaled legs melding together and shifting into my dragon tail, and I splashed my face to rid it of the splattered stew.

I sank into the water up to my eyes, sighing bubbles as my gills let me breathe in peace from my neck.

How long have I been on this boat? A month? A year? Ten? More bubbles streamed when I grumbled. When am I going home—?

A giggle ripped up my attention. Then I lunged back when Oliver leapt into the tub with a large splash. He laughed and pinched my tailfin—making me stiffen. He jabbered in Landish and held out his arms as far as they could stretch, his grin pulled from ear to ear.

I flicked my fin away from his grubby hands in case he decided to snatch it again, and I grumbled. "You're really annoying..."

His grin worsened. "And you still look like a girl."

"I don't look like a—!" I froze, gawking. "You did it again! You *do* speak Marincian!"

His head tilted at me, like he was confused.

"Stop pretending you can't speak Marincian!" My tail splashed the water's sudsy surface. "I'm tired of hearing gibberish from everyone on this mismashed ship!"

"Mismashed ship!" he mimicked, laughing. The he paused and rushed out of the tub, running to his pile of clothes, then jumped back in the water. In his hands was a clear, rubber water-ball with sparkling blue glitter tumbling inside. He laid it in the water, the thing floating on the surface as it spun and made the glitter inside swirl like a lovely, lovely storm.

My eyes went wide. "Pretty…" I poked it with a webbed finger. The glitter tumbled at my touch, and I giggled. "Pretty, pretty!"

Oliver smiled and his fingers slid under the ball and lifted it over the water. Then a blue mark on his neck lit up, and his fingers started glowing. The glitter in the ball swirled and shimmered, then it… it made *shapes*. Crystal clear shapes with an entire scene playing in an icy background. Someone was laughing in there.

The person inside was a teenager with long, green hair and emerald eyes, webbed ears folding as he bent over his knees in a hard laugh. "You're still really annoying," the dragon chuckled in Marincian, shoving the viewer—the person whose eyes we were seeing through—off of him.

The narrator laughed. "And you still look like a girl."

I grabbed the ball out of his hand, but the images faded quickly.

"What was that?" I demanded, shaking the ball, trying to get the glitter to show that scene again. Nothing happened. "Was that… was that me? I was big!"

Oliver took the ball back and rolled it around his palm, watching the glitter swirl. *"Cool, huh?"* He said in his weird, blathering language. *"Mama gave me this so I could show everyone what I was Seeing. It also helps me figure out what's a vision and what's actually happenin' right now."*

I didn't have a clue what he was saying, but I only now noticed the blue mark on his neck. I'd seen those marks before, in picture books of oracles. He was a future-viewer? With a pretty Seeing Stone… or, Seeing Ball, I guessed. Stones weren't made of rubber. This must have been how he knew those few lines of Marincian—he'd seen himself saying them to me in the future. Even though he clearly didn't know what they meant yet…

"Fuérr?" someone called from the door.

I turned around in the water, seeing Dream come in. "There you are, Fuérr," he said in Marincian.

Where has he been? I'd needed a translator for the past three days, he wasn't anywhere in that time. I've been using the Shadows for that, if they weren't busy.

Dream waved for me to hurry out. "It's time for the Shadowblood's water training. I wanted them to get some practice in before we docked, if you'd be so kind?"

I sighed and pulled myself out of the water—my tail shifting to separate legs again—and stepped out to get a towel. "A short lesson," I said in a huff while drying my hair with the towel. "I don't feel like teaching today."

"Anything you can offer." He smiled, then vanished out to the hall.

I grumbled and patted my scaled face with the towel. "I see why Papa thinks he's annoying…"

HERRIN

Their training with the Ocean Hallows is going smoothly, I scribbled in my ledger, dipping the quill's nib into the inkwell. *Prince Fuérr is their primary teacher in their new elements. But helping him are Hecrûshou, our party's Demon King, who is instructing them with Aquavoking, and Nikolai, a vassal of Her Highness Death, who is schooling them in Glaciavoking.*

From what I've observed, they're moving along well enough. They haven't fully mastered any element save for their original Necrovoking, but they're progressing faster than the average Evocator with each one they gain.

The split nature of their Blessings seems to be their main advantage. They've already gained more elements than Princess Willow, the first in history to have more than three, and already, they've surpassed her own skills with the Hallows.

A part of me wonders if the Gods knew splitting the magic this way would help their strength. Maybe in truth, the Shadowblood was meant to be a pair all along—?

A low croak popped my concentration bubble.

I looked at the window. One of the ravens had perched there. This one had a scar running down its right eye.

"Oh," I chuckled, the raven flapping inside and alighting on my desk. It looked at the papers curiously, like he usually did when he visited. "Hey, Chai. Want to learn a new word today?"

The raven dipped its head, cawing and ruffling its tail feathers with excitement.

"All right, all right." I sifted through all the loose papers on the desk, looking for a good one. I singled out a leaf and pointed to the chosen word, clearing my throat. *"Careful."*

Chai croaked and repeated, "Care-*ful*. Care-*fuul*."

I laughed. "Nice. That one's a warning, like, uh… *danger.*"

"Dang-*er!*" Chai flapped his wings rapidly, his talons walking over the papers eagerly as he looked at each one. He touched his beak to a single word. "Dang-*er.*"

I looked at the word. "Heh. Yeah, that's right. That's *danger.*"

He preened, mimicking *careful* over and over, slipping in *danger* once in a while.

Then he stopped, glancing at one page in particular. It didn't have any words on it, but it *did* have a sketch there: a face painted in light water colors. It was a picture of Xavier, as he currently looked. It was something I commissioned Nikolai to do for me. His brother's face was next to him, but Chai only cocked his head at the first one.

He screech cheerfully at the sketch of his Reaper, and I laughed—

Then the bird grabbed the page with his beak and flew out the window.

"H-hey!" I rushed out the circular opening, reaching for him, but he already soared up a level and disappeared above the upper deck.

"Gods damn it..." I guessed it looked *too* much like Xavier.

I hurried out the door.

XAVIER

"Keep that stream steady," Hecrûshou warned. The demon sat slouched over the ship's wooden rail, one foot kicking idly as he oversaw Alexander and my Aquavoking training.

Fuérr watched us intently, the child's arms folded over his scaled chest. He had been the one to start today's lesson, again, but Hecrûshou was his acting assistant.

"Alexander," Hecrûshou called, "keep pushing the water out. Xavier only needs something to pull on. Don't worry about the shape this time. Only focus on *creating*."

Alex gritted his teeth, his stance wide as he held his hands out, a flowing stream of water leaking from the air over his palms as his fingers gleamed emerald. "What does it *look* like I'm doing?"

I smirked, rhythmically circling my own gleaming hands in the air and swirling Alex's water in hypnotic ringlets. "Squatting over a privy—?"

I was drenched in a sudden burst of water that he shot at me, the force so strong I was knocked on my back. The water I'd been controlling came splashing down on me all at once.

I sat up, heckling and wiping the water from my lids. "I think that's the most you've made in one hit!"

The others laughed around us as well, Nathaniel and Lëtta the loudest voices guffawing shamelessly from the helm. Well, good to see the two family members were bonding well enough.

Dalen and Vendy were out here as well, beside Jaq. Neal and Octavius had taken a seat on the opposite rail to watch us, cackling like spectators at a circus.

Nikolai chuckled politely off to the side. We'd already ended our Glaciavoking training with him, but he'd decided to stay and watch the rest with Hecrûshou and Fuérr.

"<No, no, no,>" Fuérr chided, stamping an irritated foot. "<We are training now! Training and playing don't mix. Play time is for later.>"

I pushed to my feet, sighing, then evoked my water Hallows and *peeled* off the water that had soaked into my clothes, forming a cloudy ball in the air before me. I'd missed a few patches, but I was overall dry.

Hecrûshou paused from the rail. "You can already separate water like that?"

I glanced at him from over my shoulder, keeping the murky ball of water held there in the air. "I tested it out two nights ago."

"That is an advanced Evocation..." The demon's glowing eyes narrowed. Then he reached over the deck and brought a new ball of seawater up, tossing it to me.

I dropped the first ball in a small splash and fumbled to catch the new one. This one was heavier, thicker than what Alexander had produced.

"<Extract the salt from that water,>" said Hecrûshou. Then he nodded to Fuérr, speaking in Marincian. "<If this lesson pleases you, Highness?>"

Fuérr nodded in a huff. "<A good lesson. Go on.>"

Hecrûshou looked back at me. "I do not want to see a single grain left floating in that sphere."

"I'll try..." I focused on the ball, stretching it thin.

One by one, tiny crystals dripped onto the deck. I managed to make a fair pile after a few moments, enough to spice three meals, I wagered. But there were still more yet—

Chai swooped down and snagged my shoulder with his talons, coming down so quickly the impact had me lunge back a foot, and I dropped the ball in a splash.

"Chai!" I clicked my tongue, the raven still flapping its wings excitedly. "What's got you in such a cheerful mood then?"

There was a piece of parchment in his beak. I took it, curious. "What's this?"

It was a sketched face. *My* face, with my long hair tied in a tail and thick beard hugging my jaw, my scar running over my right eye and cheek. *Hrm.* I had a feeling Herrin had something to do with this.

Nikolai's webbed ears fluttered off to the side when he caught a glance of the picture over my shoulder. "Ah?" Nikolai said, "That is mine..."

My brow raised in surprise. "Is it? Well, I'd say you did a fine job. Even Chai recognized it."

Nikolai smiled with such joy, I thought his scaled face would split.

Fuérr lifted to his toes, trying to see the sketch. He marveled at it and grabbed Nikolai's arm, pointing to the paper. "<You drew that? How pretty! Can you teach me? Can you?>"

Nikolai laughed warily. "<I–I suppose, if you want, Highness…>"

"Skill aside, I'm curious," I said, waving the sketch. "Why draw it at all?"

Nikolai started to explain, but a panting voice cut him off.

"I—*gasp!*—I asked him to…!" Herrin wheezed, running onto the deck from inside. He delicately took the sketch back from me. "I thought the Enlighteners would want to see an updated picture of you both, since you don't exactly look the same anymore."

"Ah." I scratched at my beard, grinning. That sketch made it look quite fetching on me, if I did say so myself. I supposed Nikolai took artistic liberties and cleaned up any stray hairs that littered my neck. He'd made my tangled hair look smooth and conditioned as well, my nose drawn strong and handsomely. Even my scar didn't look quite so jagged, he'd made it smoother, more refined. That was very kind of him. "I had a feeling you were behind it, Herrin."

Herrin offered a shrug.

"'Ey lads!" Nathaniel called from the helm's upper deck. "Best ye brace yerselves! We're comin' in on the docks there!"

I whirled about, gazing over the ship's edge and spying the port of High Neverland's eastern coast. It was approaching quickly, other ships and smaller boats going about their way in the water around us.

We did as ordered, holding fast to steady masts and taut ropes as our ship *thunked* two, three, four times against the wooden docks. Nathaniel shouted for some of our crew to tie down the ship, then stomped down to the lower deck and clasped both Alexander and my shoulders. "Ye two, come away with me down yonder. We got a few things ta settle a'fore ye see this queen."

Alex and I exchanged curious looks, but followed Nathaniel regardless. He jerked a thumb at Jaq, Octavius and Neal as well, motioning for them to join us for whatever fate awaited us.

"Why must we do this again?" I asked, shifting uncomfortably in the wooden chair, my arms folded under the sheet Nathaniel had wrapped around my neck. The cloth draped to my knees, and Chai gave a grumble from the curtain rail at the back of the cabin to voice his own distaste.

Alexander sat beside me with a similar sheet around him, Mal giving a single croak at his feet. "Bloody ridiculous," Alex muttered. "The rest of us haven't a fraction of what's on Xavier's face. Why were we dragged into this?"

The other men grumbled their agreement in their own chairs down the line.

Ringëd was slouched to one side of his seat, his arm exposed out of his sheet to hold a cigarette to his lips. "I want to know why we can't just do it ourselves," he said. "I brought my own damn razor, I could have been done with this an hour ago."

"Sorry, mate." Nathaniel's bulky figure loomed over the table in front of Alex as he swirled a brush into a bowl of cream. "Got'a be a clean, professional job. I been doin' this for a few hundred years, and Neverland's got it in their noggins that any hair on yer face is dirty. I had an old master up here once, it was damned annoyin'. Even the smallest cut or burn caused a mess 'a trouble. Now you lot are 'bout to see royalty. Ye want'a look yer best accordin' to their standards, if ye want to see any Leaflite knights helpin' yer war. Right, Feather-brains?" He glanced at Aiden's ghost, who was supervising in the corner. "Ye know what I'm sayin'? Ever been up here yerself?"

Aiden grimaced, his translucent wings bowing slightly. "I was born here, actually. I died here, too. Nathaniel is right, and that in itself should tell you how disgustingly crucial having a bare face is here. This is not Everland. And this is *certainly* not Grim, so I do hope you're prepared for a bit of a culture shock."

"More of a shock than Marincia had been?" challenged Alex as Nathaniel lathered the cream onto his jaw and chin.

Nathaniel's laugh was dark. "Much more, lad. Much more."

He rid Alex of his grey stubble, then came to do the same to my fuller beard.

I sighed mournfully as the blade scratched over my skin, leaving it bare and cold. Spring was already blossoming outside, but without the extra coat of hair on my face, it still felt a few degrees cooler, especially when added to my new Glaciavoker's chill.

Glancing in the mirror, my thin, dismal face was now exposed for all to see. Though my cheeks had filled significantly since my waking, they were still slender and sharp compared to Alexander's. *Had we truly looked the part of twins before this?* I rubbed a hand over my smooth chin, sighing again. I just looked so *frail*. I was damn well growing it all back after we were through here.

Nathaniel inspected me carefully and gave an approving nod before moving on to the others.

When they were all finished, he came back around to Alexander and gave his hair a trim around his ears. When finished, he came to me once more and untied the silken ribbon holding up my shoulder-length strands, combing them so they lay flat and spread. But he'd only just retrieved his shears when the door creaked open and Willow stepped inside.

She stopped under the doorway after spotting us in our chairs. She wore a thin black dress today, simpler than what she'd worn in Marincia's palace, but just as elegant. Though her bust wasn't exposed, the thin material displayed the curves and accents of her chest in tasteful detail. Her lips were painted an alluring dark violet today, and they frowned at me. "You're cutting it?" Willow asked.

I dismally shrugged from under my sheet. "It seems that way."

"Must you?" She came behind me and combed her fingers through my hair, inspecting me in the mirror on the wall. The jewels in her engagement-vines glimmered in the light. "I rather like it long."

I glanced up at her curiously. "Do you?"

"I think it suits you. But I suppose if it's necessary…"

"It's not." I shot a warning look at Nathaniel before he did anything with those shears. I took off the sheet and rose in a smile.

Alex snorted along with Jaq and Matthiel, but none of them followed with another word, and Nathaniel put his hands in the air in surrender. "Can't do nothin' the woman don't want. Right good instincts there, young sir."

Nathaniel went to trim Jaq's sandy hair next, the viper directing him to keep his long as well, the others chatting amongst themselves.

Willow cleared her throat and held a fist out to me. "A few things: one, I have something for you."

I curiously held out my palm and let her drop a silver ring into it. "An engagement ring?" I asked, blinking at the stunning, polished jewelry.

"The one I bought for you back then," She explained. "I asked Ana to resize it to fit you now. Strangely, there wasn't much to change. I'd first had it sized when you were fourteen, and it seems your six-year coma had stunted much growth in your finger."

I slid it on and admired its shine and noted the unfamiliar weight it brought. "But…" I protested, lost for words as I turned the ring over my finger. A pleasant cheer brightened my mood to feel its comfortable squeeze. "When did you have time to sneak my ring size?"

Her lips rolled with a sly grin. "I'd asked Alexander to measure it with a string while you were sleeping. I'd meant to give it to you when you returned to your own vessel." Her tone drained with a hint of guilt. "But I admit, I'd forgotten until recently… I'm sorry it's so late. I have your marriage stud with me as well, for… well, later."

"Yes… later…" *A time that wouldn't come soon enough*, I thought with an inward sigh. I examined the ring one last time before offering her a warm smile and kissed her hand. "Thank you, darling. This was wonderful surprise."

She smiled in kind, though bashfully. Then her eyes flicked away as if remembering something. "The second thing…" She looked back at the door as if conflicted. "Xavier, I wondered if… would you mind coming with me for a moment?"

Alex, being the first of whom Nathaniel had finished, took off his covering sheet and rose, brushing the stray hairs from his tunic. "Where does he need to be?" he questioned. "We still aren't ready to see this queen. We can't walk into her palace in our loungewear."

"This won't take long," she assured. "He only needs to…"

"To be putting me normal," came an accented voice behind me.

Zylveia's translucent figure phased through Willow, and her hybrid cat-jay friend came in after, meekly adjusting the soul-seeing glasses that Bianca had lent her.

I saw El steal a blushing glance at Octavius, who was busy having his hair snipped by Nathaniel now, and she quickly returned her attention to Zyl, who put her ghostly hands on her hips.

"She be saying ees good for putting me back, now," explained the Sky Princess. "So, putting me back."

I cocked a brow at Willow. "You're allowing it?"

Willow nodded, though her expression was begrudging. "For the time being."

"I not going run this time," Zyl said, circling an impatient hand in the air. "El be staying here, with or without me."

"Stay here," nodded El firmly.

"I not leaving her here alone. I… *ye, ye*… not being the good one, before…" She rubbed her neck. "But I talk with El. I see father and stop war with fish king. But we come back to find Roji *after!*"

"After after," agreed El in another nod.

Willow grunted and gave a one-shouldered shrug. "Fine. I don't care what you choose to do after, so long as the battle stops."

Willow led the way out of the hall, and Zyl, El and I followed her. Alex went the opposite way to dress in more appropriate clothes.

Willow lifted a gesturing hand while she walked. "We need to get Zyl back to her father as soon as possible, but the queen here has been urging us to see her for weeks now. I'm not exactly sure why she's so adamant about offering us her soldiers, but we need all the help we can get in case Zyl cannot calm her father."

"What does the queen want from us in return?" I asked.

Willow shook her head, Jewel twittering on her shoulder. "I'm not sure. Her servants refuse to disclose anything more."

"Then perhaps that's the catch. Whatever she wants from us may be more than we can offer."

"Unfortunately, there's only one way to find out." She sighed. "But we won't be here long, regardless. Perhaps a night or two at the most, and then we'll escort Zyl to the nearest Stormchaser station in town. But I admit, it will be too difficult to care for her if she's separated from her body while we stay here. I don't feel comfortable leaving her behind with the ship, especially since half of us are staying in the palace and the other half must go into town for supplies."

"Not to be mentioning," Zyl's soul muttered. "You might be needing of my lightning. I seen old queen of Neverland before, she not fun person. She ees... not the gentle one. You cross her, you be ready to fighting."

"I've heard that as well," admitted Willow. "But that was the old queen. This newer queen seems to have a few changes in mind for Neverland. Hopefully, they are changes for the better."

We filed into the clinic cabin where Zyl's sleeping vessel lay. All of our doctors save for Ana were here, tending to the Sky Princess. Sirra-Lynn, resurrected, was the first to notice us enter, and her scaled friend, Rochelle, lifted her glasses beside her.

I approached Zyl's vessel as her soul floated beside me, and I took her wispy hand in offering. I smiled thinly then glanced at Willow, who gave me an approving nod. Zyl's soul sucked in a breath, purely for ceremonial purposes I was sure, as I evoked my death Hallows and gripped her glowing NecroSeam with careful fingers. After dragging her back into her body and tying her Seam to her physical heart, Zyl's lashes fluttered.

Her physical face was now set in a grimace, as if feeling sick, and her scarlet wings drooped over the table when she heaved herself up to sit. Various cracks sounded when she stretched and swung her legs over the table, the result of being inactive for a month. I knew firsthand what waking up this way felt like, though I imagined my scenario had been worse. Six years would no doubt be far different than a single month.

I laid a hand on her shoulder. "Take some time to recover. Slowly."

Zyl nodded in a groan, rubbing her temples as if they were splitting. And if it was anything like my experience, they most certainly were.

After making sure Willow and El were staying by her, I left the clinic to change. It didn't take long, and once dressed in a more appropriate attire, I started down the halls.

The Queen of Dreams crossed my path along the way. Her belly had swelled even more in the last month overseas, and she had a delicate hand placed under it as if to keep it afloat.

"Ah, Xavier." She stopped and held out a balled hand to me. "Just who I was looking for. Dream and I have a few things to take care of in town, so we will not be joining you to see the queen. That being the case, we had these purchased for you."

She let the chained items fall into my open hand, the links hissing lightly.

Two glowing, metal spheres clattered into my palm. "Scythe-spheres?" I asked. Well, this day just kept getting better by the minute with all these new gifts.

"We think you've gained enough strength to wield them again," she explained. "And in times such as these, I'm sure I needn't tell you the importance of being armed."

I clipped the chains round my neck, the spheres hanging heavy from my clavicle. I couldn't help my pleased grin, the weight of the weapons bringing a sense of security I hadn't felt *once* since waking in my own body. "Thank you," I said in all sincerity.

"You're very welcome. Do take care." She nodded as she passed, her rust-orange hair tumbling over her shoulder. The woman truly did remind me of Willow. There were traces of her face in her grandmother, the shape of her eyes and the straightness of her nose.

She kept to her path and strolled behind me, but I turned and called, "Your grace?"

She paused and twisted, one thin brow lifting. "Still with the formalities?"

"Forgive me…" I stepped up to speak with her at a more private volume. "Er, Crysalette. While you're here, I wondered if you could explain something about…"

"My husband?" She placed a hand at her hip. "Not surprising. He may be the one thing everyone wants me to explain. What has he done this time?"

"It wasn't *this* time, so much as… *a* time." My fingers fidgeted. How should I word this? I wasn't even sure what to ask. I would have questioned Dream himself, but he'd been avoiding me rather strictly after we left Ninumel's palace. I'd seen him spend more time around Alexander, evading me like the plague. "Back in Marincia, I Saw something," I said. "A past vision, I think."

She didn't flinch, but I could see her eyes sharpen. "How far in the past?"

"I'm not sure. Has he ever told you that he was… friends with…"

"Macarius," she finished softly. It hadn't been a question. "Yes. I knew."

"Why would he associate with him? Didn't he know what Macarius would do?"

"There is something you must understand about my husband," she said. "Dream is a powerful oracle. But he is not impervious to mistakes. Seers may have detailed visions, but they may also have *vague* visions. It's not always the clearest view, and can take more deduction than one might think. Dream has had over two-thousand years of deducing what vague visions mean and don't mean. And he hasn't always been correct. In regards to Macar..." Her voice iced. "He feels he'd made the greatest mistake of his life."

"Did he tell you details? Of what happened during those years?"

"Xavier." She sighed, sounding tired. "Macar is not a subject to pry, with him. Dream made a mistake. And now, he hopes to fix that mistake. There is nothing more I can tell you."

She turned to leave. But she soon paused and called back. "Oh, and Xavier? Stay close to Anabelle. You will get the troops you need, if not the ones you expect."

She left the corridor, leaving me to my original path with a furrowed brow. *Anabelle?* That was a strangely specific suggestion.

Once I stepped off the ship and down to the docks, I found the others already waiting for me. Willow stood alongside her bat-winged Aide, Lilli; the Sky Princess beside her own cat-eared Aide, El. I didn't see little Oliver with Lilli, but after a quick inquiry, I was informed he was being watched by Linus as the two had already gone into town. Jaq was here as well, watching a flock of gulls flutter from the boardwalk's poles. Willow and my vassals were floating alongside us as ghosts, save for Vendy, who was currently resurrected and attempting to round up the gulls with stretched arms and an exuberant giggle— though they all flew off long before she reached them, much to her pouting disappointment.

Octavius and Neal trotted down after me, the brothers in the middle of an argument over the true meaning of 'a few' versus 'several', and Matthiel followed behind them weighing in on the debate.

Little Fuérr strode behind them while clinging to Ana's fingers as they walked down the ramp. Kurrick stepped onto the docks without a word behind them. My eyes narrowed at the lioness, who knelt to adjust the young prince's sea-green cravat.

Stay close to Anabelle, Crysalette had said. But why? Did Dream have a vision he wasn't telling us...?

There was a coach already waiting, along with a handful of royal Leaflite soldiers to escort us to the palace. Their captain saluted and bowed to Willow. "Your Highness Death," she said, straightening. "Our queen welcomes you and your company."

Willow nodded her acknowledgment. "Thank you. How long will our ride be exactly?"

"Roughly one hour, your grace. Please, enjoy the trip and be at rest. We've been assigned to see you there safely."

Willow thanked her again and filed inside the coach as the rest of us followed. Little Fuérr settled over Willow's lap, the boy sitting poised and excited as he glanced up at her and questioned, in Marincian, why Oliver wasn't joining us.

"<Oliver went to run errands with Linus,>" Willow explained in a grin. "<Are you disappointed, Fuérr?>"

The young prince flushed, turning his scaled nose toward the window. "<No! I'm glad that annoying sea-slug isn't coming...>" His reflected expression in the window told otherwise.

I chuckled, Willow and I exchanging a smirk.

The buggy led us out of the harbor and into the busy town, heading toward Neverland's palace in the distance. Willow peered through the window's curtain, and I glanced over her shoulder to see this new realm for myself.

Nira, it was beautiful. Barely First Spring, yet every tree was scattered with growing buds. Some were even in full bloom with bright, vibrant colors I'd only seen in textbooks. Grim's flowers and leaves were less saturated, and they seemed rather dull in comparison to these brilliant hues of pink, red and violet. The new-growth leaves were a brighter green than I was accustomed to as well, and just the sheer number of trees and brush was incredible.

Everland had been a dried-up wasteland with nothing but rocks for miles. Neverland seemed to be nothing but greenery, with hardly a bare stone to be seen. Indeed, the capital city of Rosaria Grand was remarkably... *grand*.

Lilli, who gazed through her own window on the other side of the coach, gave a marveling breath. "It's beautiful!"

"I've never seen such bright colors," Alex commented.

Matthiel shook his head, stunned. "Nor have I."

Jaq wiped his glasses on a kerchief, and when he replaced them over his eyes, he stared outside in amazed silence.

I noticed the buildings were primarily made of wood, dressed in hanging vines and sprinkled with flowers. The few stone structures seemed to be more historic than the rest, a few towering temples, the occasional school building or town hall, archways and defense towers that haven't seemed to be used in ages... It was so different from what we'd seen in Everland. Was this really the same realm?

The bronze and brown-skinned shifters bustling in the sunlight were no different from those we'd seen on the other continent, but the roles of Footrunners and Smithers seemed to be primarily assigned for women here. The other glaring difference was the men's fashion. Though their clothes were dyed with similar colors, their trousers were notably tighter round the calves, and the hems often stopped just above the ankle. Now that I looked, actually, everything was tighter. Like the fabric sought to squeeze the slender men's limbs into a new, unnatural shape.

The women's busts seemed to be strangely lifted as well, as if padded by something under their tunics and gowns. There were more trousers on the girls than we'd seen in Everland, and far more muscles than on any of the boys here. In fact, I couldn't spot a single man with *any* muscle, save for those wearing the Reapers' white cloaks or the Stormchaser's crimson uniforms.

We reached the palace gates within the hour, as estimated. Once we stepped out of the coach, our party was led to the flowery courtyard by a woman butler. Our guide didn't take us far, stopping near the back of the yard where a very tanned, lion-tailed girl stood under a vine-littered pergola.

Behind her was a line of five young boys, all poised rigidly straight and dressed in fine silks that were, like I'd seen in town before, tight around their torso and limbs. Only one boy in particular stood in front beside the crowned, teenaged girl.

The young queen's cropped hair hugged tightly against her skull, helping to showcase the many glittering earrings on her lobes and the gemstones that lined her throat in a sparkling necklace which matched the thorn motif of her brilliantly polished crown.

Willow placed her hands delicately in front of her and stood tall. "Queen Syreen, I presume?"

The girl smiled. "Indeed. You must be Grim's little cave princess."

I almost cringed; heard Vendy gasp a disbelieving curse behind me. *Barely a few seconds into the meeting and the Bloody queen opens with an insult?* I inched my skeptical gaze at Willow, but saw her attention was still dedicated to the queen. If Willow had been offended, she didn't make it known outright. But neither did she bow, nor even nod. She merely returned the queen's razor-sharp smile.

The young queen sized Willow up—or rather, *down*, making a point to crane her neck to loom over her. "You're not quite what I was expecting…" said the queen. "You're shorter than the Screens let on."

"And her grace is younger than I've heard," replied Willow, her hazardous smile frightening beside me. "I suppose we've both been misinformed."

The queen's eyes narrowed for only a moment, then she flicked her gaze to Alexander and me. "Ah! *You* two must be those illustrious twins. The Shadowblood brothers…"

Alex and I exchanged a cautious glance. Never mind how she knew that name, why did she sound as if we were only known by the title?

She strode past Willow and bowed to us humbly. "I've heard many a priestess speak of your talents. I am honored to have you as my guests."

"Thank you…" we said in unison, equally hesitant.

Matthiel leaned into my ear from behind and hissed, "Priestesses? Why would they speak of you?"

I muttered over my shoulder. "I haven't a damned clue."

A low caw sounded from the pergola, and a small black bird peeked its head from under the shielding leaves. It flapped down and landed on one of the young boys—the one standing in front. The crow gave more scratchy caws, making the boy blush as he tried to quiet it. He finally calmed the crow, and Willow's gaze turned delighted at him.

"Ah, a fellow Reaper?" Willow chimed and pleasantly clapped her hands as she approached the boy.

The lad flushed pink, his lips sealed shut. His crow ducked its head, attempting to hide itself in the veil of his wavy blonde hair.

Willow knelt before him. "And what might your name be, young sir?"

The boy gulped. "H… Hugh…"

"Pleasure to make your acquaintance, Young Hugh. And what shall I call your messenger, then?"

He couldn't hold back a small smile. "Her name is Lady Lilac, your grace. She found me some months—"

The queen stepped between them. "My brother is rather shy, Highness. He isn't one to speak with strangers."

Willow rose, looking at the queen with slitted vision. "I see…"

The boy, Hugh, glanced at me, then blushed and cast away his gaze. *For a boy who isn't one to speak with strangers*, I thought, *he certainly looked ready to chat up a storm with Willow.*

The queen gestured to all the boys now. "These are my brothers," she said. "All share half of my blood, save for Hugh, who is my full brother." She set endearing hands over Hugh's shoulders. "Hugh, dear? Why don't you take our brothers and be sure they have something nice to wear for tonight's ball—?"

"Ball?" Willow interrupted, baffled.

"Of course!" The queen clasped her hands eagerly. "I thought it a wonderful way to welcome you all to my land!"

"With all due respect, your grace," Willow said, "we haven't time for a ball. Our Reapers are facing two armies in Everland, and Culatia has just declared war with Marincia."

"I understand perfectly!" said the queen. "What you need is a well-deserved break from all the battles and trifling warfare. A relaxing night in my home will be a marvelous change of pace, I should think!"

"Your majesty, please. This is no game. You expressed interest in offering us aid—"

"And aid you shall have!" she assured in a chuckle. "I fully support your efforts to take down Everland's tyrannical king. It will present a great opportunity to unite our fair country again, as it once was in times of peace…! Oh, but such discussions can be had tomorrow. Tonight, we celebrate this beautiful alliance with Grim! Now please, do make yourselves comfortable in my home. My servants will bring you to your quarters. I will see you all tonight."

She nodded to Willow, then flashed a smiling leer at Alex and me. My blood chilled. I watched carefully as she turned and left with her brothers. Hugh lingered behind the pride, stealing a final, blushing glace at me before trotting after his sister and vanishing into the palace.

Zylveia's feathers ruffled. "Dumb queen not even look at Zyl."

Lilli rubbed her fingers nervously, glancing at Willow. "Are we sure this is a good idea?"

"No," murmured Willow. "But it seems we won't see any soldiers until after this party. Bloody child queen…"

She sighed and said nothing more of it as we followed the servants who'd come to escort us to our guest chambers.

27

HERRIN

I held a hand to my eyes to block out the sunlight.

Man, this sun was bright even for *me*. I had a feeling the Grimlings wouldn't like it all that much. But it did make the city look gorgeous. The rays lighting up the flat-roofed buildings made the stones shimmer and the wood glow, and the luscious greenery scattered around the streets made it look like we were walking through a forest instead of a modern, royal city.

The roads looked like they were built around the trees, feral sparrows twittering from branches, bees zipping by my ears, feral horses clopping by with braided tails.

I staggered behind the others on several occasions, just taking everything in. Land, I'd never *seen* so much green! So much color, so many flowers blooming all over the place, from windowsills to climbing vines on walls, to isolated gardens and parks, in pots, in vases, in women's *and* men's hair… Was this seriously the same realm as Everland?

Everyone from our errand group had drifted to different merchants and shops here in the bazar. Claude and his daughter focused on food supplies; Sirra-Lynn, Rochelle and Bianca went to apothecary tents—I overheard Bianca offering to trade and sell her own tonics for extra Mel—and the cute Lëtta, Sirra-Lynn's Necrovoking *Da'torr*, was jabbering away with Nathaniel and Aiden.

I sighed, staring at Lëtta. Her thin black pigtails were swept up by the breeze, every amused laugh and wavering hand gesture making her all the more alluring.

Damn it… When she first joined us, I was hoping to have a chance with her. But she's been lusting after Matthiel the whole trip. I've seen her swooning over him like a fangirl to an actor. *Bloody, spoiled, rich, pretty boy…*

Up ahead, Dream and Crysalette were browsing a tailor's selection of clothes. Dream had changed his hair with an illusion, making it a boring brown color. His crowned Dream mark was also gone, his bronze forehead smooth. My guess was, he wasn't up for being stared at. Or maybe he didn't want the city knowing the King of Dreams was here.

"Oh, this one is perfect," Crysalette said next to him. She was admiring a shimmering, golden dress that the tailor's shop had displayed on a headless mannequin. "I should think it will fit Anabelle well enough."

Dream cocked his hooded head at the dress. Then he pinched the dress's shimmering sleeve with two fingers, his eyes glazing for a minute.

"It will," he hummed, a thin smile stretching his lips. He glanced over his shoulder at Kurrick, who waited with crossed arms and a stern scowl. "You'll appreciate it, Kurrick. A fitting entrance for her."

Kurrick's lion tail flicked, not giving a response.

"Would you like a matching wardrobe?" Dream asked the surly warrior. "Or are you still planting your stubborn feet in the mud—?"

"I make my own fate," Kurrick ripped, leaving it at that.

Dream sighed then turned to the tailor. "We would like to purchase this gown."

The tailor lifted a pencil-thin eyebrow and sized him up. "Do you have the Mel for it?"

I tried not to laugh. I've gotten so used to Dream's grody sweater, I didn't think about what he looked like to other people anymore. Especially with his disguised hair, he looked like a Landish peasant.

Dream pulled out a money pouch from his Storagebox and handed the merchant the amount of beads that was displayed on the mannequin.

"Here you are," he hummed cheerfully. "And could you send it to the royal palace before tonight? It is for a woman named Anabelle, be sure to make that clear to the messenger."

Royal palace? I wondered. *Was that where Ana was?* I thought she just went to a different district for other supplies. Then again, I did wonder why Kurrick didn't go with her...

Beside me, Dalen was talking to our sister, Carrie, on com. She was giving an update about what was happening on the other continent. Man, how long had it been since we saw her and Rolen? We left them in the middle of autumn, but now it was already First Spring of the new year. On paper, it didn't seem like such a long time, but it felt like forever ago.

When Dream and Crysalette were done buying the dress, they came back to me.

"Herrin," Crysalette began. "Come along. We three have business with our Enlighteners here."

I followed behind them, a bell tinkling when we walked into some tiny bookshop. "Uh, right. How many will—"

Someone slammed into me, feathers fluttering in the air when I fell back on the cobblestones.

I pushed up in a daze. Some girl was on the ground too, rushing to collect books and papers she'd dropped. She was muttering frantically to herself and stuffing everything in her satchel, stacking books in her arms.

There were auburn wings folded to her back, her feathered hair tied in a tail with a green ribbon. She wore boring, ivory clergy robes, the collar climbing tall over her throat and long sleeves flowing down to her knees.

She looked like a mess, scuttling over the stones like a feral crab while collecting everything she'd lost.

Then a clear, fist-sized orb rolled over the ground. I picked it up, squinting at it. "A crystal ball—?"

The girl snatched it out of my hand and ran for it, shoving into three other people before taking to the skies and flying off.

I stared after her, blinking. What was *that* about?

Crysalette breathed lightheartedly above me. "Oh. There goes Marian."

I pushed to my feet, brushing off my now dirty shirt. "Let me guess," I grumbled, "Enlightener?"

Crysalette chuckled. "She's a rather funny one, isn't she? Strange, though, she flew off in such a hurry. I suppose she wasn't expecting us so early."

I searched the skies for her again, but she was already gone. "Should we go get her?"

"I'm sure she'll return soon." Crysalette smiled at the horizon and walked into the bookshop with Dream and me following after.

The shop was a scrunched building, its stuffed shelves bending in the middle and looking super close to toppling over from the weight. Crysalette led the way to a door in the back and knocked twice.

It opened a crack.

One beady, vein-festered eye peeked through and targeted me first. The person's one visible brow furrowed, then the eye flicked up at Crysalette.

"Your Majesty!" An old woman's voice croaked from the half-hidden face. Then the crone swung the door open fully to let us in. "Come, come! You're early, dear me. But Marian's run off."

Crysalette stepped in. "Yes, we saw her bounding into town. I don't think she recognized us, but I dare say that is my husband's fault."

I filed inside with Dream, and he took off an extra ring he had on his finger, his disguised hair bleeding blue again and crowned Dream mark showing up on his forehead.

"Forgive me for enjoying my privacy, darling." Dream pulled off his hood to reveal the rest of his azure head. "I assumed it wouldn't do to attract attention to your Enlighteners."

This room was crammed full of people. It was only big enough to fit twenty bodies, but I counted over forty.

The old woman who let us in eyed me up and down, grunting. "I suppose you're Her Majesty's servant, then?"

I scowled. *Servant?*

Crysalette laughed and patted my shoulder. "Oh, no, no! Herrin is here to tell you all of his recent scriptures, Elliot."

The cramped room went quiet. Bloods, everyone was staring at me now, like they did back in Marincia. Was this going to be a common thing?

"Herrin...?" The crone rasped, sliding on eyeglasses over her hooked nose. "You don't mean... Herrin Tesler...?"

I sighed, waving half-heartedly. "Hi."

The others started mumbling, mostly commenting on my age. *Great.* It was Marincia all over again.

Crysalette clapped her hands. "I suppose I forgot to mention he was young. In any case, this is your Archchancellor. He'll be telling you of the Shadowblood's recent developments, and I'm sure he'll be more than glad to answer any questions you have."

The crone frowned, but shook her head, murmuring. "Very well... oh, but— Marian was looking so forward to meeting you... Will you be here long?"

I shrugged. "That's up to Crysalette."

Crysalette tapped a finger to her lips. "Where has Marian gone, exactly? We do have business with other company tonight."

"Marian has gone to give warning to the rebellion," the old woman explained, moving to a window and drawing back the curtain. "The girl's had a vision. Not a favorable one either."

Dream spoke up now. "Ah, I have a feeling I know what she'd Seen."

I stared at Dream skeptically. "Hold up—Is something going to happen that I should know about?"

"Not to worry," Dream assured cheerfully. "We have a plan. Now, I think you should show them those wonderful portraits Nikolai sketched for you, and then..."

BIANCA

I handed the apothecary merchant my extra vials of Mundarian Root extract and took the spiked beads of Mel from her.

"Thanks," I said and packed up the rest of my beakers in my satchel and Storagesphere that waited inside. "So, business aside, I was wondering if you or any of your apprentices would be interested in joining the Alchemists' Guild?"

The woman cocked an eyebrow. "Never heard of it."

"It's new," I said. "We don't have a lot of members right now, but we're looking to expand."

Expand was a nice word for *exist*. Right now, the only member was the president—me.

The woman shrugged. "I'm already busy with the shop as it is. I don't need more work, and neither do my wards."

I sighed, dejected. "Oh… Thanks anyway."

I walked out, stretching tall and hearing my back pop into place with a series of cricks. My rabbit ear folded down, and I held a hand to my eyes to block out this relentless, burning sunlight.

Stupid sun. You'd think I'd be used to it after four years. Apparently not. Though, what would have happened if I grew up here, like I was supposed to? Would I have minded so much?

Did my real parents mind it? I bet they loved it up here. A lot of the locals did. What kind of family would we have been if Mom and Dad didn't find me alone up here and bring me to Grim? What *did* happen?

I tugged my hood over my face and went to look for the others as a distraction. Why was I thinking about that stuff anymore? I thought I was done with that stupid identity crisis in primary school.

It's Ana's fault. She had to go and say I was the new incarnation of the Lady Herdazicol—and that I looked just like her, too. They say the Mother Goddess likes to recycle souls in the same family line if she's able, so was it possible my family name—my *real* family name—was Herdazicol…?

My steps slowed, an idea hitting me. I pulled out my com, dialing Master Hendril's number and waiting for the device's gears to whirl and crank to life. The screen of light projected up and flattened in a wide rectangle.

Soon enough, Master's wrinkled, goat-horned head fuzzed into view. *"Bianca?"* His voice fizzled. The reception across the seas was pretty bad. *"Have you docked in Neverland?"*

"We have, Master," I said, biting my lip. "But I was wondering something… You know the Alchemist whose text you gave me? The Lady Herdazicol?"

"*Yes?*"

"Well, I was wondering if her family line was still here. Have you heard of any noblemen or women named Herdazicol in this age—?"

"*What's that, dear?*" His face wavered, the screen fuzzing with static. "*The— ignal is a—it terrible—ere.*"

"I-I was wondering if you knew any noble families named Herdazicol that are still alive!" I said louder, my ears folding down when a number of heads turned my way from the crowd.

His face fizzled back into focus, his voice clearing. "*Oh. Why, yes, the Herdazicols have been long time donors to various schools of medicine throughout the years.*"

My heart started pounding. "Are they rabbit shifters?"

"*Yes. But I don't know why you're ask...*" His creased face sagged. "*Oh.*"

He must have guessed it. I pursed my lips. "Do you know where they live? I wanted to ask if maybe... if maybe I..."

"*I'm... so sorry, Bianca.*" His tone was quiet. Too quiet. What did that mean? "*It had been so long, I hadn't even thought...*"

"They're dead." My stomach lurched nauseously. "Aren't they...?"

His eyes saddened from behind his glasses. "*There was an accident in their manor. Near twenty years ago. A grease fire, the Seekers said, the Herdazicols' bodies were found inside when the smoke cleared. But their daughter had gone missing.*"

"Was... was that me?" I asked, my gut thrumming anxiously. "Am I a Herdazicol, Master?"

"*I don't know,*" he admitted, scratching between his horns. "*But I'm ashamed I'd never considered the possibility...*"

I wiped a sleeve under my nose, taking in a calming breath. *Get over yourself, Bianca. You're a woman now, able to take care of yourself, thanks to your foster parents. Why did it matter who your real family was?*

Maybe it didn't. But some part of me—a *big* part of me—thought I needed to know.

"If they're dead," I said, "What about their souls? Were they reaped properly?"

"*I should think so.*"

"Then I can find their ghosts," I decided, my ears lifting determinedly. "When I get back to Grim, I can look for them. Ask them in person."

Master brightened. "*Yes, I suspect you can. Shall I ask the High Howllord here to request a search below?*"

"Can you do that?" I asked, thankful.

"*Of course.*" He smiled his old, wrinkly smile. "*I'll keep you updated. Nira send you luck.*"

"Thank you, Master." I hung up, pocketing the com and trying to calm down my thumping chest.

Bloods, what a day. I walked on, a weird mix of anguish and hope numbing my steps—

A loud *bang* suddenly exploded from a Smither's workshop, a puff of blackened smoke pluming from the cracks of a closed window.

Someone started hacking and shoved open the window to let the smoke spew out. A soot-covered face popped out next, the man stumbling out of the window to run to the well that waited by the stable yard. Horses whinnied and snorted as the man yanked up the well's wooden pail and splashed his face with the water, wiping at his blackened eyes. He dunked the pail back in the well to chug it down his throat next.

I glanced at the window he'd squirmed out of. The smoke was still hazing inside, but it thinned a little. I peeked in. There were tools and springs, gears and all kinds of cogs that I couldn't even hope to name. Weird.

"H-hey!" The man ran over and shut the window in my face, using himself as a shield to block me from looking inside. "What you lookin' at what ain't your business, uh? Shove off, go on. Mind what's yours."

He was pretty young, probably in his twenties. His frizzy hair was a honey blonde color, his brown skin covered in soot and something else that smelled like hot peppers and garlic.

I put a hand on my hip. "What are you doing with Jarrach peppers?"

He froze. "H… how'd you know it was…"

"It's a common Grimish curry. I'd know the smell anywhere." My brow furrowed. "But it doesn't look like you're cooking."

He looked down at his dirty, leather apron and thick gloves, then coughed and leaned against the window to act casual, rubbing at an eye—

He bristled, letting out a pained yelp and rushed back to the well, taking off his gloves and splashing his eye with water.

I rummaged through my satchel to take out a pair of goggles, handing it out to him.

"If you're going to mess with chemicals and oils," I said, "Wear these. I have extras."

He blinked through tears and water, his red eye squinting more than the other. When he took the goggles he sat down against the well and mumbled, "Uh, thanks…"

I crouched over my knees. "You a chemist?"

He rubbed at his eyelid, wincing. "A right poor excuse for one… Ma was prob'ly right, I oughtta stick with buildin' things, not mixin' em…"

I shrugged. "You get better with practice. Besides, it was only Jarrach pepper. I got some of that oil in my eye the first time I cooked with it as a kid."

He looked at me more closely now. "What accent you got there, lady?"

I still had an accent? Huh. "Grimish."

His brow scrunched. "You're a Grimlette?"

"Adopted. It's… a long story." *About to be longer.* I pushed down the creeping excitement. I could worry about that later. I looked at the window again. "What were you trying to make in there?" I asked.

He stood up and went to the window in a depressed sulk, opening it up and waving away the lingering smoke. "Nothin' specific. Thought I'd throw some things together 'n see what happens."

He crawled back inside through the frame, and I stuck my head in curiously. "Well," I hummed, "I think you proved it could make for a good defensive tonic, if you throw it at people's eyes."

His laugh was sarcastic. "Har, har, har. Have a good laugh, Grimlette?"

"No, really. See, you just have to…" I squirmed to fit inside, stumbling to the hardwood floor.

Huffing, I went to his work desk and inspected all the coils and springs that were scattered there. At the corner of the desk was an opened brewing text. It was Edition V of *The Lady Jilume Herdazicol's Advanced Tonic Brewing: Formulas for the Practicing Alchemist.*

I grinned. "I see you like my book."

He looked at me like I belonged in an asylum. "You look right young for a three hundr'd year old lady."

"That was a past me," I said smugly. Not that I was entirely sure Ana was actually serious about me being Lady Herdazicol reincarnate, but who says I *wasn't?*

He stared at me flatly. "You're the future self that looney went on about in her lil' note then, are you?"

"Sure am." Again: why not? "And I *did* meet Anabelle again. And Kurrick is still following her around."

"Oh, sure, sure…" He snorted. "I s'pose that makes me the new queen of Neverland."

I found his amateur chemistry set and carefully sniffed the bowl of liquid substance that was there.

"Ah." I took out my extra pair of goggles and strapped them to my face, slipping on my gloves. I found his glass stirring rod and swirled it in the mixture. "I'm guessing you heated it too quick?"

He blushed, glaring.

After pouring it all in a glass beaker, I corked it and set it over the open flame, turning down the heat.

"Let it boil *slowly*," I said, "otherwise, it'll explode like it did, and you won't have anything left to throw at anyone. When it's bubbling, stick it in an icebox. It'll be the most potent by then, if it's anything like cooking the curry. Jarrach peppers are weird like that. But this way, you can store it and light it up when you need it, without hurting yourself in the process."

He stared at me. "You do this a lot, Grimlette?"

I grinned. "Yeah. And this was a good idea you had here. I never thought about using Jarrach peppers, I've been using basic chili peppers. I should have thought of it, since it's from my own damn realm, but whatever." I lifted up my goggles. "What's your name?"

He scratched his chin. "Folks call me Red. Don't you ask me what it stands for neither, I ain't tellin'."

"Sure." My grin widened. "Well, Red. You have any aspirations in chemistry?"

He swiped a thumb over his nose, sounding sad. "Naw… Folks round here don't think a man's got the brains for it."

"Where I'm from, we don't care. You want a job?"

His look was suspicious. "Doin' what?"

"Re-founding a lost art." I folded my arms proudly. "I'm Dr. Bianca Florenne, chairman of the new Alchemist Guild. And I'm currently seeking new members. Travel fares and living expenses will be provided in full. Payment available with every tonic brewed. Must be content with constant traveling. Terms negotiable."

I extended a hand to him. He glared at it like a man staring at a wasp.

"So," he began, "you go round to other places a bunch?"

"Yep," I said, hand still hovering in front of him. "I don't expect to stick around any place for too long, till I get back to Grim."

"And you'll pay?"

"Help with chores and make good brews, then yep."

He smirked. Then squeezed my hand. "Deal."

28

OCTAVIUS

Shade picked at my wrinkled, silk-brown sleeve, probably feeling my annoyance with it.

Why were noble clothes so freaking *stiff*? How did all of these bluebloods move so easy in them?

I looked around our cramped guest room. It was a huge room, but with so many people in here, I was getting claustrophobic. Matthiel was at the wall-mirror checking over his suit, Jaq on the bed lacing up his sea-stained boots, Alex and Xavier wearing what they came in with—which was fancy enough anyway, even with the wrinkles—and lounging around reading from books they found on the desks. Fuérr sat in a pout by the open window and glared at the night sky, and Neal came out of the washroom and buttoned up his pants.

"I still don't understand why this ball is necessary," Matthiel scoffed, adjusting his collar-string.

Alex grunted and set down his book, rubbing his eyes. "It's *not* necessary. But I don't suppose this queen will give us her troops if we bow out, will she?"

Xavier grimaced and laid his own book over his face, his sigh muffled under the pages. "Likely not. How long must we stay here? And don't tell me we all have to share this one room the whole visit."

Alex snorted. "Was someone's night cut short with their fiancée in Marincia?"

Xavier laughed, but it sounded mournful, peeling the book off his face. "Honestly, I *hope* Dream pops into existence here and gives us an excuse to leave early."

I tugged at my high collar, mumbling from my chair, "I don't know… I'm kinda glad we finally get a break. I mean, how long has it been since we weren't either being chased by Necrofera, hunted by Rockraiders or were out at sea every freaking day for the past few months?"

Neal leaned against my chair's back, grinning. "I'm with Tavius. I feel like we're on vacation. May as well enjoy it."

Xavier sighed. "I suppose…"

He 'supposed'? Land, this was the first time we could sit back and wind down! Take a load off, breathe easy, and not worry about being killed. Couldn't they lighten up?

"Besides," I muttered, feeling Shade crawl up my head, "I've never been to a royal ball before."

They looked at me. They *all* looked at me.

"Oh," Xavier said, breaking the silence. He rubbed his neck. "That's right, you haven't… We're so accustomed to them, I forgot you may not be familiar with it all."

"Well, *I* didn't forget." I pushed off the chair, Shade fluttering from my head to keep balance. "And I'm going to enjoy this thing. Weird and abrupt or not."

Xavier smiled. "Perhaps you're right. We have been on the run from things that wish us dead. We should take this opportunity to rest."

Agreeing grunts came from the others in the room.

—*clack, clack, clack!*

We turned at the knock. I was closest to the door, so I went to pull it open. A servant woman was there, holding a bunch of paper-wrapped parcels that were tied with shimmering gold ribbons.

She bowed, handing the parcels to me. "A gift from Her Majesty Syreen."

"Uh…" I took the load, the paper wrappings crinkling over my arms. "Thanks—?"

She shut the door on my face, the wood slamming into my nose painfully. I winced and dropped the parcels, rubbing my nose tenderly. "What the Void…"

I saw the parcels at my feet, one of the gifts having been thrown out of its wrappings. I bent and picked up the bright red, satin fabric. "She's… giving us clothes?"

There was a parcel for each of us. But there weren't any names on them. Well, except for two.

I picked up the ones labeled *The High Lord Xavier Devouh* and *The High Lord Alexander Devouh.*

"Apparently these are yours," I said, holding them up to the twins.

Alex took his with a suspicious scowl, carefully unwrapping it. He held up the sleek pants. And blushed.

"What in Death is *this*?" he demanded, stretching away from the pants like they were covered in puke. "She expects us to wear this?"

The crotch area was padded so thick, it already looked like someone's junk was stuffed inside.

Xavier snorted a laugh. "Oh, look at that! The trousers are more endowed than the wearer—"

Alex grabbed his brother's 'gift' and threw it at his head. "I'll bet two Tallohs your suit is the very same—!"

Xavier's heckles choked off. The Crest over his knuckles turned blue and the crowned Dream mark shined for a second, then faded. When the parcel fell to the floor, I saw his haunted expression.

"Ah..." Xavier inched away from the parcel at his feet, clearing his throat. "So, that's what this is about..."

I frowned. "Vision?"

"Of a sort." His next smile was pressed tight as he kicked the parcel under the bed and tugged his vest. "But a *lot* of things suddenly make sense now."

ZYL

TRANSLATED FROM CULATIAN

I gasped in pain, the servant lady drawing back the strings of whatever-the-Void-this-was and damn near crushed my ribs into a single mass of bones.

"Off, off...!" I wheezed, barely able to breathe with this thing squeezing my chest. "Get it... off...!" My wings reflexively flailed, smacking the lady and forcing her to back away. I crumpled over, gasping. "Willow... h-help...!"

The Death Princess was wheezing herself, and I looked over in time to see her shoving back her own servant lady who'd just tightened the same damn thing on her chest. *"What in Death..."* she gasped to the servant in Landish, *"is this thing?"*

It was kind of like a binding strap for exercising and combat, but it was ten times tighter, built with some wire inside, and it pushed *up* everyone's breasts instead of strapping them down. It made my chest look like it actually had something there and made Willow's look downright unnatural. Those things were shoved together so tight, it looked like they'd burst. Sounded like they *felt* that way too, judging from her pained wheezing and failed attempts to untie the strings at her back.

Willow's servant put her hands on her hips in annoyance. *"It's basic fashion!"*

I snorted between pants. "It's a torture device for your tits is what it is!"

El, who'd been smart and wouldn't let those servants put one on her, had just finished untying Lilli's painful strings, and the bat let out a reviving exhale.

The hybrid came to untie mine next. The pressure vanished off my ribs, and I sighed. "Sky, thank you, El…!"

"I heard Neverland was weird," El mumbled, "But I didn't think it was *this* weird."

The twin's resurrected vassal, Vendy, hurried to untie Willow's straps, the Death Princess exhaling in relief. Willow waved away the two servants vigorously. *"Get those things away from us! What we brought will be fine for this blasted ball, just leave us be!"*

One servant rolled her eyes and left without a word and the other followed behind in a mutter. *"Foreigners. No sense of style…"*

When they were gone, Willow threw off the loosened strap, rubbing her nude pups tenderly. "Why would anyone make those a necessity in fashion?" she asked in Culatian, going to the Storagesphere she'd brought along and pulled out a thin, long gown, sliding it on. I rolled my eyes. *What a surprise.* It was black.

"Do you ever wear anything with color?" I asked, putting back on the short top and pants I was wearing before this stupidity started.

Willow tied the drawstring at her neck in a hum. "On occasion. Black is simply traditional for the Death family."

"I think you mean boring," I corrected. "Jade is traditional for my family, but you don't see me wearing it all the Gods damned time."

"Well, Zylveia, some of us heiresses actually intend to represent our country with pride." She sent me a low glance. "But I suppose you're not proud of being next-in-line for your crown, are you?"

I scowled. *Catty bitch.* I wasn't about to fall for that bait.

I glanced at the corner, where that Healer lioness was crouched with her bare back facing us. She was staring at a long-sleeved dress she held in her arms.

"Oy," I walked over, bending to look over her shoulder. *"You no change, too?"*

"*I…*" Her voice was a whisper, like always. Her shoulders hunched and she blushed. *"I hadn't expected to attend this ball…"*

I lifted an eyebrow. *"Then why you bring dress?"*

"Crysalette had it ordered for me," she said. *"She wishes for me to wear it."*

"You no wanting to be wearing? Ees pretty."

All right, so 'pretty' probably wasn't as fancy a word as I wanted in Landish, but it was the only descriptor I knew in that tongue. If I knew more words, I would have said, more accurately, it was the best damn dress out of any of us.

It was covered from bust to hem in gold sequin, shimmering in brilliant glints in the overhanging light. When she lifted the garment, it sent a glitter of dusting light over the fabric.

The other girls had noticed the sheen and came over, admiring the thing.

"*It's gorgeous,*" Lilli breathed, glancing down at her own, rose-pink gown in envy. "*Better than what I brought. Crysalette has a good eye.*"

Vendy smacked her lips in a grumble as she tugged on her plain, vermillion sundress, her brown rabbit ear folding over her loose, shoulder-length hair. "*Land, you're going to make me look like a country bumpkin. Remind me to stand next to someone else at this thing.*"

Ana's hands were shaking. "*I-I've never worn something so extravagant. I cannot wear this.*"

"*Oh, but you must!*" Willow knelt beside her and ran a hand over the layers of sequin in awe. "*How often a chance will you have to look like a princess yourself?*"

Ana sighed, whispering so softly I almost didn't hear. "*Like a queen...*"

My nose scrunched, shrugging before walking out to leave them to their changing. *Weirdo girl.* If it were me, I'd take the dress no questions asked. From lowly servant girl to beautiful Roaress, you'd think she'd jump at the chance to snag her bodyguard's eye like that. Whatever. Her choice.

I yawned and folded my arms behind my head, starting down the hall. I may as well find something to preoccupy myself with while I waited for El to change. I was fine in what I had on. It may not be fancy or even clean, but it wasn't like I had much option. And there was no way in Void I was going to be put in those constricting death-traps the Neverlanders called dresses. Bloody freaks, trying to shrink their ribs like a doll, just plain weird.

I passed someone in the hall then, the winged man stopping to stare at me. His face was grimy with dirt and oil, a pair of working goggles strapped around his neck. His overalls were ragged and wrinkled, pockets filled with all kinds of wires and clippers, large leather gloves rough and worn with holes in the fingers. He had a bag of small Shockvials in hand, a larger bag of bigger ones on his tool-belt, and a tube of what I guessed was even larger Shockvials slung over his back. He looked like an electrician, or a vial suppler. Or both.

His brown wings went stiff when I caught him staring, and I glared in annoyance. "*What you want, re?*"

He blinked like a stupid fish. "*Oh, uh... Nothing. Sorry.*"

I sniffed and started on my way again.

"*W-wait!*" he called after, "*aren't you...*"

"*Yea, yea, I Sky Princess. Buzzing off.*"

It took a few seconds before he finally skulked off, and I spun on my heels in a snort. *Stupid fish-eyed bird.* I sighed, deciding to turn around and head back to the room before someone else pestered me about my blood.

29

CILIA

A jolt hit my spine, prickling and numbing.

I quickly ducked into the nearest alley and shied away from the streetlamps that dotted the harbor's streets.

It's coming from the waters. I scanned the dark waves, a floating bell gonging in the lapping breeze.

There were two Weights there. Three? One flickered faintly, the first two drowning it out almost entirely.

I scowled at the harbor, looking past the Reapers' ship. "La'lunaî…"

"She isn't alone," a guttural voice murmured behind me.

I flinched, but relaxed. It was only Hecrûshou. He had apparently filched a new indigo coat and brown breeches, his hood drawn over his fin-like hair and casting his face in darkness. His glowing pupils burned white in the shadows, and that Spiritcrystal trident was wrapped in its usual cloth and strapped to his back.

"At least you're keeping your Weight suppressed," I muttered.

The shark shifter hunched over as he peered toward the harbor at my side.

"I'm glad you're wisely doing likewise," he said. "This isn't La'lunaî's territory. Yet that is her Weight, no doubt, accompanying two others. She keeps it pushing on us as a warning."

"A warning for what?" I asked, clutching my knuckles to keep them from shaking. "What have we done?"

Hecrûshou's tone dimmed. "Perhaps… she suspects we've paired for a coup against her?"

My face cracked in horror. "We wouldn't be so foolish!"

"I doubt she trusts us that wholly." His words ground rough like stones. "This does not bode well, regardless… Best we stayed under her radar."

"What if she finds us?" A tremor ran through my bones, and I stole a glance over my shoulder. "What if she's watching…?"

He clapped my shoulder, pressing as if to keep me from quivering. "Hold yourself together. Trembling before her will have you looking guilty."

"What should we do?"

He stared at the dark sea with narrow eyes, silent for some time. Then he whispered, "We seek shelter inland. There will be refuge waiting for us in the forests."

"You mean Miranda?" I asked.

He nodded. "Should La'Lunaî advance, Miranda is the only hope we may have to survive."

"Will we not look extra guilty of plotting a coup?" I tugged my hood over my face, crouching. Every clopping horse and heckling drunk had my pulse leaping now. "Meeting with her will seem as though we're rallying against La'Lunaî."

"We haven't much choice, I'm afraid." His glowing eyes peered down at me, a thought seeming to form there. "Regardless, there is another matter I wish to discuss with Miranda… have you spoken with her? Of your pasts?"

"Not of pasts," I said. "Our previous chats have been about territory. We merely agreed to split the continents between us."

"I thought as much," he muttered. "You say you first Awoke on what is now the Gyle Islands?"

I gave him a sidelong glance. "Yes… why?"

"Miranda Woke in the very same place," he said, "in that same era, when it was still known as Aldamstria."

My grown cat ears perked. "You think she knew me? When I was alive?"

"I suspect so." He crouched beside me and rubbed a thoughtful thumb over his lips. "She and I speak often. We are of like minds, regarding the Clean Ones… She once mentioned you looked familiar, when you first met. She didn't think much of it. But after hearing your story, I wonder if your matched Waking site is more than a coincidence."

I stared at him, heart pounding. *Could Miranda have answers for me…?*

Hecrûshou jerked to his feet suddenly. *"Oscha…!"*

I bolted upright, following his line of sight. "Wh-what is it? La'Lunaî?"

"No." He moved out of the alley, cursing in Marincian as he sprinted toward the harbor.

Bemused, I ran after him.

Then the unmistakable scent of smoke and burning wood hit my nostrils. The spiced smog was thin at first, but it thickened and blotted the streetlamps as we drew nearer to the harbor, our path headed for the ship that festered with climbing flames.

Land preserve us. It was the Reapers' ship.

30

HUGH

I slunk through the party guests that crowded the ballroom, my small tiara falling crooked as I bent and dodged the ladies' carelessly waving hands. Lady Lilac fluttered from my shoulder and cawed at them in annoyance, though she was left unheard—and I unseen—by the drunken ladies and their husbands. Though, perhaps it was to my fortune that they didn't notice me. It only meant that Sy had less a chance of catching me sneaking about.

I had been more than welcome to attend this ball, as Sy allowed, but if she knew the reason I wished to come…

I shook my head, focusing on my goal. Where was that Reaper prince? Had their company arrived yet? Or—Land's Blade, what if they'd already left? *They can't have*, I decided with a determined swallow. Lady Lilac's talons gripped my shoulder tighter. *They can't leave without taking me with them!*

I knew it would break Sy's heart, but there was no other way. If I was to see the world and become a warrior prince—just like prince Xavier—it wouldn't be by staying locked away in this prison castle as Sy wished of me. Perhaps one day, she would forgive me—

"*Oof!*" I bumped into a girl so suddenly, I was thrown backward and fell on my rear in a wince. Her drink spilled over my golden suit and Lady Lilac fumbled off my shoulder in a screech.

The girl hadn't fallen, but she *had* been startled when I ran into her, one of her brown rabbit ears lifting. "Oh, Bloods," she cursed and reached a hand down to help me up. "Uh, sorry about that."

I stayed on the sticky floor, my breath catching as I focused her brown face. *Land*, I thought in a blush, my chest melting at those warm, radiant eyes. Her brown hair cascaded in lovely waves over her shoulders, her vermillion sundress loose and wavy over her muscular shoulders and slender knees. But most of my attention snapped to the hefty blade waiting in a leather scabbard at her curvy hip.

Flushing, I took her offered hand and let her pull me to my now shaking feet. "U-um…" I stammered, my throat drying as Lady Lilac fluttered to my shoulder again in a small caw. "Th-thank you, Lady… erm…" I hesitated, hoping she would give me her name.

"Vendy," she said, placing a casual hand on her hip—the side without the sword—and cocked her head at my crow. "Oh, hey. You're that Reaper Prince from this morning."

I paused. "This morning? Then…" My mood brightened tenfold. "Then you're with the Reapers from afar?"

"Yeah." She plugged a finger in her long ear and turned it in an itching motion, squinting an eye in a hum. "I'm the twins' vassal."

My brow knitted. "Vassal?"

"Yeah. You know, dead people who serve Necrovokers for combat and other tasks in exchange for being resurrected, that kind of stuff."

I scratched my head. "Dead… people? But you don't look…"

"Resurrected," she grunted. "Like I said. It's a long story."

I blushed furiously. *Dead or not*, I thought with my heart in my throat, *She's still a vision…* I shook my head, focusing back on task. "B-but if you're with them, do you know where Prince Xavier is? I-I'm looking for him, you see, and…"

She cocked an eyebrow at me, one of her rabbit ears lifting. "*Prince* Xavier?"

I nodded vigorously.

"Uh…" She rubbed her neck, then took a breath and spoke to the ceiling. "Hey, *Da'torr* Xavier? Where are you right now?" There was a moment of silence, as if she were listening to something I couldn't hear, then she turned to me and said, "He's heading to the back of the ballroom where Princess Willow is—"

"Thank you!" I started in that direction—but paused, spinning back to her and gave her a blushing bow. "Thank you for your help, Lady Vendy… it was a… a pleasure meeting you." I whirled forward and snuck away before she had a chance to respond.

JAQ

"So, I've been to a few parties before," I muttered under my breath to Alex, looking over the ballroom with a furrowed brow. "But this is, uh… new."

Both he and Xavier murmured. "New. Yes."

Most of our group were standing off to the side and watching the Neverlanders dancing and chatting, enjoying the stringed quartet with an accompanying flautist trilling softly beside them.

The only normal thing was that the women wore dresses and the men suits, but everyone looked just a little... off.

The women's tits all looked smooth and padded, like they'd stuffed pillows in there and covered the nipples under even the thinnest fabrics. They had corsets, and those we knew about since some had been imported down to Grim, but even the men's doublets looked padded around the chest and crotch. It was weird as Death. I didn't like staring at a bloke's pants to begin with, but they were so tight, it was impossible not to see everything under there.

To my left, Octavius had his shoulders stuck tight to his neck. "Well, um," he said, giving a nervous laugh, "Now I'm glad we didn't wear the clothes those servants sent for us."

"Agreed," Xavier grimaced.

Alex crossed his arms. "I don't understand. Why do I find this country's fashion stranger than Marincia's? They barely wore anything there."

I grunted and scratched my scaled chin. "Probably because it made sense for fish to wear swim-conscious clothes. None of this padding stuff makes any damn sense."

"It does in a cultural sort of way," Matthiel considered behind me, though he sounded uncomfortable all the same.

I glanced back at him. "What do ya mean?"

"The parts that are stuffed," he began, lifting his glass of wine in a half-shrug, "are considered the most attractive, even in Grim. Bringing attention to them, outrageously sized and false it may be, is one way to, I suppose, suggest great fertility, which seems to be a status symbol here. Neverland is called the green country for a reason; its lands are filled with fertile soil the likes of which no nation has. Embodying every sense of this 'fertility' makes sense from a cultural standpoint, if you ask me." He scowled at the crowd. "Still, I'm glad as Death we brought our own garments."

"—Did they send you 'gift' wardrobes as well?" came Lilli's voice behind me.

I craned back to see her standing there with hands on her hips and bat wings tucked politely at her back as she looked me up and down. I did the same for her.

"Looks Grimish enough," I commended, pushing up my glasses to better look at her rose-pink dress. "I take it ya ditched the local get-up, too?"

"Swiftly," she practically bragged. "You should have seen the torturous contraptions they use as binding straps."

"Ya should have seen the men's pants."

"I'm seeing them now." She lifted a delicate brow at a passing Roarlord, offering a blush.

Alex looked behind her, questioning, "Where are the others?"

Lilli made a point to avoid his eyes, but answered anyway. "Zylveia and Vendy are taking advantage of the refreshment table. I'm not sure where Ana and El are, but Willow is speaking with the queen's general there in the back."

"Ah!" Xavier started over that way, letting go of that ring he'd been fiddling with all evening. "Excuse me, then."

I watched him rigidly make his way through the crowd to Willow. It seemed like he had something on his mind and didn't want to waste any time to tell her.

Alex stared after his brother in a mumble. "He's still acting strange."

"Still?" asked Lilli.

I shrugged. "He's been up-tight since we first got those gift clothes. Wouldn't say why, but he's actin' all traumatized."

"How odd…" She frowned after him.

"It would do him some good to tell us what the matter was," Matthiel glowered, knocking his wine back and draining the rest of his glass. He sighed at the empty cup and started walking to the drink table for a refill, muttering under his breath, "Always keeping these things to himself, the bastard…"

I saw El pass by him on her way over to us. The hybrid was wearing a simple crimson dress, the short skirt swishing just above her knees. When she tromped up to Octavius, who was still looking the other way where Xavier had gone, her cat ears perked and her blue wings dropped. She tugged on his arm, getting his attention.

"Uh?" Octavius blinked, seeing her. "Oh. Hey."

"El learn words more," she said. "Zyl teech to El."

"Uh, oh. Cool." Tavius went out of his way to sound impressed. "Yeah, sounds good."

She lifted her skirt a little, as if showing it off, and accidentally exposed more of her dark legs. "What yu think?" she asked brightly. On second thought, maybe it wasn't an accident. "Dress ees the good one?"

"It's… it's pretty, yeah," he said, blushing. "So… uh, are you used to these kind of parties in Culatia?"

She nodded heavily. "El like *röl'chauft* much much."

"*Ro…* uh, how do you say that?"

She went over each syllable, and soon enough both started exchanging words while pointing at new things around the room. I shook my head, grinning. *That's adorable.*

"Are you enjoying the evening?" a new voice sang to the left.

I had to make a double take. She wasn't there a minute ago, but that teen-aged queen somehow snuck up on us and was now standing real close to Alex, wearing an extremely low V-cut gown that slit all the way to her bronzed stomach. Her gold crown glinted from her head as she bent her neck to the side. "Did the suits I sent up not make it to your chambers, Alexander?" She didn't even look at Lilli and me.

Alex glanced at us uncertainly and scooted back. "We… felt more comfort-able in the clothing we brought." He belatedly added, "Your grace."

"Please." Her smile was full of sparkling teeth. "The Shadowblood is exempt of formalities. You may call me Syreen, if you prefer."

One dead-pan look at me said he didn't prefer.

She lifted up a glass of wine and offered it to him. "I've brought you a drink, in case you haven't quenched your thirst tonight. Please, enjoy the evening." She all but shoved the drink, though delicately, into his hand, placing a gentle hand on his arm and breathed over his neck. "Here is a place to relax and let go. Feel free to do as you please… to whomever you please…"

Her step swished as she left.

I cocked an eyebrow at Alex. He was frozen stiff, staring at his new drink.

After a minute, he flicked his eyes up, not looking at anything in particu-lar, and said, "Jaq."

"Yeah?" I asked.

"Find everyone and tell them to meet us back on the ship." His voice turned hauntingly guttural. "It's time to leave."

He walked off.

I scratched my nose, glancing at Lilli. I dropped the low-class dialect for a bit. "It seems you don't have to worry about this queen winning him over you."

Lilli hummed. "It's not because of me that he's rejecting her. He isn't mar-rying me for that."

I gave her a sharp look. "Hey now, if you think it's about Tanderam—"

"No, no. It's… a bit more complicated than that. He…" She trailed off, then just shrugged. "It doesn't matter."

"Hey." I nudged her with my elbow. "If anything's bothering you, I'm all ears, all right?" I tapped a finger over my forehead, where my 'Grimling' scar was hidden with an illusion, and winked. "Tanderam was Void. Everything else is easy. We got hides like turtle shells, ain't nothin' gonna crack it."

She let a small laugh burst. "Turtle shells *do* crack under enough pres-sure, Jaq."

My shoulders dropped. "They do?"

"Yes."

"Well, what if they were made of steel?"

"A Terravoker could simply manipulate it at will."

"Damn it…" I put hands over my waist. What was better than steel? Olium could be controlled, too. Wood? No. Spiritcrystal? That only protected ghosts…

She chuckled, laying a hand on my arm. "Thank you, Jaq, but…" She traced her fingers over my hidden scars, her expression saddening. "You're right. We went through Void, and we came out of it. So, you don't need to worry about me." She lowered her hand, smiling. "But thank you. You can be… surprisingly charming sometimes."

Her steps clicked as she left.

I scratched my neck, feeling a layer of snakeskin start to peel off. She said not to worry, but damn it, she looked so *down*. What the Void did Alex do?

I let out a breath through my nose and walked off, looking for the others. *Whatever.* I could pry details from Alex later. He looked way more worried about that queen anyway, so if he said to bail, then I figured we should bail—

CRASH!

I jolted at the shattering noise, seeing a circle of guests gasp and skirt away from one of the drink tables, which had collapsed after someone fell flat onto it. Oh, Death. That was Matthiel.

"Matt, ya crazy drunk." I rushed over and pulled the slumped nobleman from the pile of shattered wine glasses and spilled drinks, slinging his arm over my shoulder. "I thought ya only had three of those?"

"*Tffth…*" His bloodshot eyes rolled, then closed, and he pressed his cheek on my shoulder. "T-t-two… I *hafh* two…"

"Matt?" Bloods, he was shivering, his skin was like ice. I leaned him on my side and used my free hand to slap his face. "Matt? Ya still with me, mate?"

He sputtered something I couldn't make out, drool bubbling from his lips. "What?" I prodded.

"*Fffsss…. C-cwlf…*" He swayed, but managed to mumble, "C-cold… m'fire's… g-g-gone…"

He lunged down, and I strained to keep him from dropping. When I had him steady, I looked around the stained, wet floor and shattered glasses. *Wait a minute…*

He only had two of these? And Alex had been staring at *his* drink like it was going to jump out and bite his fingers off…

I grunted, "Aw, Death."

WILLOW

"And I wanted to know how many of your knights you planned to send…" I trailed off when the general Fangs of Neverland took another large glug of her strangely vibrant wine.

Her face was drunkenly red, words slurred in a flighty laugh. "Cave girl, you are funny." She belched and hit her chest to quell it. "Talking of wars and battle at a time like this? You are so tense." She squeezed my shoulder and guffawed. "Relax! You've been in those dark holes too long. Have a drink, find a man to bed tonight. There are plenty of handsome ones to go around here."

I lightly pried her fingers off of me, stepping aside as the woman twisted back and slapped a passing Roarlord's posterior. The lord flushed and shot her an affronted glare, and she chuckled devilishly as he hurried off. She followed him, boisterously hanging at his ear.

I groaned and massaged my eyes. Was anyone even slightly interested in what was happening overseas?

I stomped through the crowd, stepping outside to the balcony and taking the steps down to the gardens. My Storagesphere bounced from my chained waist belt as I descended, reminding me that it was there. I didn't trust the servants of this palace not to steal my belongings, so I'd brought everything with me. Not that I had much to bring, but of what I did carry, they were dear to me.

The lights and trickling fountains in the gardens were a good distraction from my ever growing fury. Between the insults, the blatant disregard for our dilemma, the disgustingly casual sexism, I was starting to wonder why I was even bothering with this queen. Her troops would be a great help, true, but Ninumel's armies could just as easily be a great help…

Not to mention, this queen seemed far more interested in Alexander and Xavier than with me. Perhaps too interested. I dared say it bordered on obsession… Was I imagining that? I was irritated and beyond angry right now, it was more likely my emotions were warping my sense of judgement… and that girl was giving Xavier more attention than I've admittedly offered him as of late… Perhaps my suspicions were stemming from my own insecurities?

I sighed, reaching for my Storagesphere that hung at my waist and pulled out the rectangular box that usually held my engagement-vines. I was wearing them now, but the diamond centerpiece still waited in the case, along with Xavier's marriage stud. Those items would remain in this box until our wedding.

Wedding?

How laughable. Even after we brought Zyl back to her father and quelled the tension with Culatia and Marincia, we still weren't going home to Grim for... oh, who knew how many years?

I shut the box and replaced it in my Storagesphere. It was so strange... As a girl, I'd thought my wedding would be filled with joy. I daydreamed that I'd be surrounded by beautiful things and enchanting people, the chapel bouncing with music and lively dancing...

Why didn't I care for it anymore? It all seemed superfluous now. After all the death and despair we'd faced, a wedding ceremony felt gratuitous. Even disgusting.

Not to mention, I thought dismally, *I may well drive him away before we exchange vows if I keep drowning myself in work.*

Perhaps everyone was right: I should enjoy this ridiculous ball. I should keep my head above the water, breathe easy for a change. Xavier may appreciate a dance, at the least.

I exhaled, leaning against a nearby statue of Shel—

—night flashed into day.

I yelped and pushed off the statue, staggering in the new, bright sunlight. The sculpture I leaned upon had changed as well. It was still the same as it had been, but now it looked cleaner, newer and practically glowing in the sunny rays.

I ripped my gaze round the garden. The flowers were all very different now, pergolas and fountains moved around from their previous placement. There were gardeners tending to the rose bushes. None of them seemed to notice me.

"This is a lovely summerhome, Garund," I heard a boy complement from not too far. "It's very close to the ocean. Makes for a beautiful view."

What in Nira's name...?

I peered around the statue. The boy in question was admiring the blooming vines that were wrapped around a wooden structure. The young man looked to be nearing his thirteenth year, his wrinkled, orange tunic contrasting the azure hue of his hair.

Grandfather? I rubbed my eyes desperately. Was this another shared vision?

I took a moment to collect myself before tip-toeing over, waiting behind a nearby sculpture to listen to the conversation he and another man were holding.

The taller man delicately cupped a violet blossom hanging from the vine in his hands, gazing at it with a gentle smile.

"Isn't it lovely?" the man whispered, so quiet I almost couldn't hear it. "Such vibrant colors, bearing so much life, so much growth... This land is far more fertile than Aldamstria's soil."

I had to stifle a gasp when he stepped into the sunlight. His golden hair shimmered in the bright rays, his petal-like strands curling playfully at his tanned cheekbones. His bare shoulder held a crowned Land mark, his lion tail hanging peacefully beside one leg.

Land?

Gods have mercy, I never thought I'd see that Bloodline in this lifetime. In *any* more lifetimes... Yet there he was: golden, brilliant, muscular, gentle, and everything the legends had written of him. This was the Lost Relic Bloodline, in the flesh.

Which meant I was in a time before it had vanished.

"Speaking of fertility," my young grandfather began, his voice dropping in a sigh. "Garund, I've come to speak about your heir. Or rather, the lack of one. You haven't even found a wife for yourself, and you're nearly twenty-five."

The golden eyed man tensed, blushing as he whispered. "I... I just haven't found the proper woman..."

"And you never will. I know your tastes lie elsewhere."

His blush brightened further under his bronzed skin.

Grandfather gave his formulaic smile. "I'm not judging you, Garund. All of Land's incarnations have preferred the company of men. The surprise has been spoiled for a thousand years. But, as I've told you every time, you must find a woman to bear your children. Do as you please behind closed doors, but your Bloodline must continue somehow, for you have no siblings to do so for you."

Garund's face fell melancholy, his voice softening. "I... I suppose I will think on it..."

"I'm glad." Dream patted his elbow, since he was too short to reach the man's shoulder. "Now come, show me the rest of your summerhome. I'm particularly interested in the dining hall right..." His eyes found mine from behind the sculpture, and his voice faded. "Ah... actually, Garund, why don't you go on ahead? I'll be there shortly."

Garund glanced at me with unseeing eyes, squinting in confusion, but eventually shook his head and left the gardens, casting his golden eyes to the ground in deep, bashful thought. There was something oddly familiar about him...

Grandfather Dream waved for me to come, and I slid out from behind the statue.

"Land preferred male company?" I asked. It may have been a rude question to open with, but blast it, I had so *many* questions and had no idea how much time I had to ask them all. My last vision dissipated so quickly, it was likely this would do the same.

"You're always surprised by it," Dream said, clasping his hands eagerly. "Well, it's good to see you again, Granddaughter. You've certainly taken your time, this round."

"You said the same thing last time," I commented.

His brow furrowed. "Last time? We barely exchanged three words. It wasn't exactly the most opportune time for a family reunion."

I stopped myself from questioning that, remembering that in my last shared vision with him, he was older. The vision I had Seen hasn't happened yet in *his* timeline. And whatever vision he was speaking of hadn't happened yet for me.

"Ah…" I said instead, looking toward the place Garund had left. "So… that truly was Land?"

"Of course." His head tilted. "You don't recognize his habits from your era's reincarnation?"

"My era doesn't have his reincarnation," I explained. "In fact, we don't have his Bloodline at all. It died near the end of the sixteenth century. We're the only four left."

Surprise overcame his youthful face. "You've told me before that Land is among you."

"Not from what I've seen."

He held a finger to his chin. "What year is it for you now?"

"2103," I said.

"Month?"

"Mid Zephril."

He hummed. "Earlier than last we spoke… Your timeline for these visions keeps declining, while mine climb forward. We seem to be crossing roads in opposite directions…" His arms folded. "Which means, from *your* perspective, you haven't told me of Land's new incarnation."

"So then… Land does live, in my time?" I asked, failing to hide my intrigue. "W-well, I… W-when will I see him?"

"You've said Land was hidden among your group all along, so I imagine you already have."

"He's among us?" My thoughts raced to collect all the men's faces from our party. No one that came to mind had such brilliant, glittering hair, such radiant eyes…

"He did seem familiar…" I strained, shutting my lids to concentrate. Think, woman, *think*. I've hidden my own hair and eyes from the world with illusions before, Land was likely doing the same. I couldn't rely on physical characteristics. Garund's mannerisms had reminded me of someone...

Bashful and sweet... I crossed out the members of our party that didn't fit. *A gentle smile... Speaks in shy whispers...*

My stare went stale. *Whispers.* And Garund's smile—it *had* been familiar.

"Grandfather," I began slowly, "does Land come back as a woman?"

He smiled. "See? You know her."

"Oh, Nira help me." *Idiot girl!* Idiot, idiot, idiot, idiot! "Anabelle."

—The sunlight fell into night once again, and the trickling fountains spurted with water in front of me.

"Bloody Death!" I whipped round, glaring at the glowing windows of the ball inside and heard the faint music of the stringed quartet and flautist swell.

Everyone seemed so calm inside. So at peace... As if world shattering knowledge hadn't just been revealed.

My heels clicked over the stone path as I started inside.

31

XAVIER

I hurried past the partying guests, heading for the balcony where I last saw Willow stalking out. I was almost there, but a woman slid in front to block my way.

"Howllord Devouh?" the woman questioned.

She was Landish with sun-browned skin and pale orange hair that tumbled in a glossy curtain over her shoulder. Her limbs were draped in a violet gown that was cinched at her waist and hips, a long slit trailing up her stocking-dressed leg.

I craned my neck to look past her. Blast, but this woman was tall. At this rate, I would lose track of Willow. "Sorry, I've no time for chatting at the moment. If you'd please…"

Her painted red lips rolled into a smile, moving herself in front of me wherever I stepped. "Howllord, my name is Vanessa Lauranet. I'm with Neverland's reporting station, channel eight, twenty-four-seven broadcasting of the latest news across, under, and above the globe. I'll only take a bit of your time—"

"I've none to spare, I'm afraid." I pushed past her. "I must speak with my Relicblood. Now, if you'll kindly excuse me."

I didn't bother to look back at her probably-offended expression and headed for the balcony again. I bumped into the flautist on the way. The musician's eyes followed me as I left, though they weren't resentful for me having just run into him. He only grinned, returning to his whimsical playing.

I hurried out to the balcony and looked over the railing, spotting Willow. Thank Bloods, she was walking this way. My feet trotted down the steps while she stormed up them, and I met her half way. "Willow, I need to talk to…"

"Not now, Xavier." She climbed past me.

I almost stumbled trying to keep pace. "Wait, you need to hear this! I had a vision about this queen and—"

"Xavier, I will hear about it another time." Her eyes were set hard at her destination. "Right now, I must find Ana."

"Ana?" I stopped at the top of the steps, calling after her. "Why Ana?"

She didn't offer me an explanation as she disappeared inside.

Chai flapped down by the railing, cocking his head at me. I felt his concern. He must have likewise felt my distress. I stroked his tattered feathers. "This is not the time for her to be distracted."

I'd had the vision the moment I touched those suits we were sent. I hadn't Seen much, but I did see through the queen's eyes as she sent the servants off to deliver them. She had specifically chosen Alex and my wardrobes to match. And the thoughts that streamed through her mind were indecent fantasies I *really* shouldn't have Seen.

A separate croak that wasn't from Chai sounded behind me. I craned back in time to see that boy prince from before hide behind the stairway post, trying to hush his crow. I stepped round it to face him, and he flinched.

"You're that young Reaper." I crouched down to his eyelevel. "Was it Prince Hugh?"

He flushed, either staring at my heterochromic eyes or my trailing scar that was slashed over my right brow and lid. He kept his mouth shut tight, but eventually nodded.

"Why are you hiding back here?" I had a different thought, then began again. "Are you following me?"

"S-sorry!" he said quickly, pursing his lips before asking, "Um... you're the prince-to-be, yes?"

I rubbed my mournfully smooth chin, lamenting my recently lost coat of hair. "I suppose." *Provided Willow doesn't change her mind,* came the brooding afterthought. With the way her attention constantly wandered away from me lately, it seemed a likely—and worrying— outcome.

But, I reminded silently and turned my silver engagement ring over my finger fondly, *if she'd changed her mind, she wouldn't have given me this now... would she?*

"And you know how to fight?" Prince Hugh asked, pulling me away from my thoughts. "Against demons?"

"Of course." I stopped and amended. "Well, I'm a bit... out of practice. But I've re-started my physical training with my brother, so I should hope I'll catch up to him again soon."

The boy looked at his sleek, polished boots and grumbled. "I bet he doesn't go easy on you…"

I cocked an eyebrow. "Your master doesn't give you a challenge?"

"I don't have a master. Sy doesn't wish me to swear fealty to Death's Relicblood. She's assigned me trainers in the sword."

"You should be training with a scythe." I lowered onto the step to sit, giving him a sidelong glance. "You say your sister doesn't wish you swearing fealty… but what do *you* wish, Hugh?"

A look of dismay washed over him. "I… want to be a knight… But Sy would never allow it. The moment I went in search of a mistress or master, she would likely banish them from the kingdom."

"Have you considered finding a master overseas?" I asked. "Or even underground, in Grim?"

"Well…" His face reddened again. "I had wondered if… if *you* could… that is, if you'll allow…"

That caught me off-guard. "You want… *me* to train you?" I asked skeptically.

He nodded, embarrassed, but resolute.

I scratched my head. "I suppose… I suppose I could, but my brother would be a more fit trainer. I've recently woken from a six-year coma. I have to retrain my muscles myself, it would seem rather strange for you to be training alongside me. The most I could offer would be supervising your instruction."

"I wouldn't mind that," he said, leaning closer in anticipation. "You at least know other knights that wouldn't let me win matches. And I fear I won't have another chance to leave here, I-I wouldn't know how to get to other kingdoms on my own."

I sighed and hunched over. "You really wish to leave your sister so eagerly?"

His excitement fell, looking ashamed. He cast his eyes down the staircase. "It's not that I wish to leave her… I want to leave this *prison*." He gestured to the castle. "These walls, this cage… If I stay here, I'll never make something of myself. Knight or otherwise. I'll simply die as 'Hugh, one of those princes who never did anything and whom no one cared about.'"

My heart hurt to see his sullen face. He'd said his sister would do anything to keep him here… after that short vision I had of her, I was inclined to believe him. I breathed in slowly, then let it out. "If you truly wish to join us… I cannot stop you. You are welcome, as our Brother Reaper."

Every inch of him seemed to lift. "And you'll train me?"

"We'll… see."

He latched onto me so suddenly, he knocked the wind out of my lungs. "Thank you!" He sounded absolutely elated. "Thank you, Master!"

I cringed. The word had an uncomfortable twang to it. But the boy leapt to his feet and ran inside with his messenger before I had a chance to say anything. I sighed, staring after him. What a strange young man.

Someone new walked out to the balcony then—and I jolted.

It was the queen.

I hurried to stand, keeping a fair distance as she stepped up to me with a lusting smile, holding up a glass of wine. "Good evening, Prince Xavier. Would you care for a drink?"

I didn't take the drink. "No, thank you. And I'm afraid I'm not prince of anything quite yet."

"Ah, that's right…" She still held the glass out to me, stepping closer as I backed down a step. "You're only engaged to the little cave girl. She is quite an adorable thing, isn't she? Tell me…" She moved down the steps, and I backed down farther. "With a girl so small, how does one such as yourself keep from breaking her in bed?"

I gritted my teeth, denying her an answer to that incredible invasive question.

"Oh, my…" She gasped softly, fanning a hand to her chest as if sympathetic. "Don't tell me you've not been claimed? How cruel of her, marking you in name and not in body…"

I was forced to step off the staircase when we reached the gardens. And *still*, she sidled closer. *Damn this woman.*

"I don't find this topic appropriate, your grace." I had my wolf ears grow and curl, making my displeasure clear. "I'd prefer to keep such things private."

"Ah, of course… I was simply curious." She held out the glass of wine once more. "I'll leave you to your evening, then?"

She held the glass out, lingering there. I saw she wasn't going to leave until I took it. Stifling a growl, I seized the stem.

—the waiter poured in the thick, clear syrup, doing the same for the other glasses before dripping in one spritz of red coloring. He muttered under his breath about the queen losing her mind, asking him to trick the guests into drinking this toxin—

I froze, still gripping the glass.

The queen had already turned to walk back inside, leaving me alone in the gardens. I quickly tossed the glass into the rose bushes, hurrying up the steps—

Alex slammed into me, knocking me back a few feet. When I regained my balance, he grabbed my shoulders. "Did you take a drink from her?" He questioned intently.

"Tossed it," I said. "I take it you Saw they were poisoned as well?"

"Not poisoned," he contradicted. "It's Yinklît Gel, the Hallows dampening sap. It's in the wine."

I gawked at him, disgusted. "She wants everyone to drink it? Why?"

"So no one else but her people will have access to their Hallows. There's more going on, Xavier. I Saw why we're actually here. She never intended to ally with Grim, she intended to claim *us* and use our armies to conquer Everland before conquering *Grim*."

My hands balled. "We need to find Willow and get out of here."

"I already told Jaq to gather the others."

"Good." I led the charge into the ballroom, shoving aside that damned reporter woman who came bickering at my ear the moment I stepped in. "Let's get the Void out of here."

MARIAN

Tft! Tft! Tft! Tft! Tft!

My boots hammered over the street, splashing into a puddle and soaking my long robes. "Iri, please…!" I panted, hooking a streetlamp and wheeled round for a sharp left. "Don't let it have happened already…!"

That vision was still fresh in mind: The fire on the docks, their ship lit by torches, the queen's women pinning it on the rebellion, the Shadowblood stranded…

My legs burned as I picked up speed, my long sleeves billowing behind me. I yelped when tripping on a low stone, but kept to my path.

These damned obstacles…! I felt like a grounded mammal, anchored to the ground. Oh, why did I fly around town all day? If my wings hadn't been so sore, I'd have flown directly there.

I took the next right.

Halted.

"No…!" I staggered at the top of the hill, knees quaking. Down below at the harbor, their ship was ablaze, the mast and sails burning bright above the dark waters.

"No, no, no, no…" The smoke reached up the hill, stinging my eyes and nasal passage. I choked on a cough and held a hand to my nose.

I'm too late.

My tears weren't simply from the smoke anymore. *I've failed…*

The Shadowblood was stranded. Whatever calamity awaited them at the queen's palace, they hadn't a means to flee by sea. *Which means their salvation now relies on the rebellion.*

Furious, I flexed my aching wings and hustled to soar over the city. If I could reach the palace in time…

I ignored my screaming ligaments and flapped at a deadly speed for the royal gates.

XAVIER

A passing waiter tripped over my foot.

His serving tray upturned, and Alex and I were showered with purple spirits, my chest hairs sticking in the mess.

"Shel!" The waiter bowed over and over, blocking Alex and my way when we tried to step around him. "I'm so sorry, my lords! Please, I'll fetch you a new attire!"

"Damn it!" Alex shoved him aside, trying to fling off the drink from his hands. "We need to wash it off!"

I followed after him, trying to wipe off the sticky liquid on my fingers. Blast, this wasn't good. We'd been doused in it, my feet were even soaked after it'd drained down my legs and seeped through my shoes.

Alex stopped abruptly and I ran into him, craning to see a servant woman had appeared in front of him.

"My lords," she said, bowing. "Her Highness Death requests your presence in private. She stresses urgency."

I breathed in relief. "Willow must know what's happening."

Alex nodded to the servant woman. "We'll see her immediately. Where?"

"This way, my lords." She bowed once more and led us out of the ballroom.

I peeled off my soaked vest, tossing it in the nearest potted plant and desperately wiped at my dress shirt. I grimaced, the shirt soaked through with the colored Yinklît gel. "Blast, it's not coming off," I growled.

Alex had done away with his long-sleeved doublet and was finding his own dress shirt underneath was just as damp. His wolf ears folded. "I hope to Gods the others didn't drink this."

A chill ran over me, though that was probably the cold gel's doing. Still, I had this terrible feeling… Could Willow have drunk one of those glasses? Was this why she'd called for us?

And this servant woman was leading us an alarming distance away from the ballroom. The music and chatter had died to mere muffles that echoed in the corridor. She led us up a staircase, going up two flights and headed down a dimly lit, carpeted hallway. My polished shoes sank in the soft brown fibers, the vacant rooms lining the narrow walls a bit unsettling.

"Alex?" I held my left hand to him, specifically the finger that wore my silver engagement ring, which was now sticky and stained red in the gel. My voice was guttural. "See if Willow is hurt. I want to know if we need to have Ana come tend to her immediately."

He grabbed my finger and enclosed his hand around my ring. His brow furrowed. "Hang on…"

The servant stopped at one of the doors and ushered us in. We stepped through the frame, but Alex was frowning. He looked at me warily. "Willow is still downstairs."

Ck-thack!

The door slammed shut behind us, and the latch turned from the outside.

I turned the knob, but it rattled, unyielding. Alex met my eyes, his pale face as dreaded as my sinking stomach felt.

"Oh dear," a flighty voice cooed behind us. "Someone seems to have gone for a swim in their drinks…"

My head inched back, and my shoulders locked.

Crawling over the single, large bed and arching her back to expose her bronze cleavage was the young queen.

Her dress's low collar left little to the imagination, her skirt's slit peeling away from one leg to show how bare it was past her stockings.

She rose like a feral snake, one hand dragging past her belly and the other climbing to her throat as she chuckled huskily. "What ever shall we do…?" Her hands gleamed with golden light, and the countless potted plants surrounding us began to quiver.

The leafy vines began to grow, sprawling out of their pots and curling over the crimson carpet. The girl rasped hungrily. "Why don't we get you out of those sticky clothes…"

Death. I sucked in a breath, letting the coldness in me build, evoking—

My ice stopped at my hands, not releasing. Panicked, I looked at my fingers. They were still soaked in the gel, solidified like cold syrup over my pores.

"Bloody Death—"

My ankles and waist were wrapped in the vines from behind, snapping taut. They dragged me to the bed, cinching me to the mattress on my back, my limbs spread.

Damn it…! I tried to wriggle free, to grab the scythe-spheres around my neck, but the vines tightened their grip, forcing a pained grunt from my crushed lungs. I heard Alex struggling beside me on the bed, but I couldn't turn my head to look.

The queen chuckled and loomed over me, smiling like a madwoman. She shoved her lips over mine, prying her tongue through and making my hairs stand on end.

I finally *ripped* out one arm from the vines, pushing her back. "The Death is wrong with—!"

New vines wrapped around my arm and pulled my hand into her open neckline. I tugged back, but these damned vines wouldn't let me move, curling between my fingers and forcing them to close around her breast.

"Oh, my," she purred, fanning a falsely aghast hand over her face as if to act bashful. "Why, my lord, we mustn't… but I suppose if you're so insistent…" She traced a manicured nail over my flinching jaw, tangling her fingers through my long hair and *yanked* my face into her bosom. "Why don't we have a little fun?"

32

ZYL

TRANSLATED FROM CULATIAN

I chugged down another glass of wine, tossing the glass carelessly aside on the drink table. This stuff tasted weird, but hey, if it did the trick, it did the trick. I had a good buzz going now, though I expected to be drunker than a divorced lord at a brothel by now, after so many of these glasses. I guessed this country's wine was weaker than Culatia's.

I shrugged. *Eh.* Just meant I had some work to do.

I chugged down another one.

El's giggling up ahead caught my attention. She was flirting with her little Reaper cat. It looked like she was having an actual conversation with him this time. Heh, good. So, the extra words I taught her helped after all. And look at that, it looked like he was actually flirting back. *Nice job, El.* They were both still shy, but it was a way better attempt than the last few times they'd 'talked'.

I put down my cup and scooted it over to join the other empty glasses I'd collected, sighing. At least her efforts weren't for nothing, this trip. *Damn it, Pops, why'd you have to start a Bloody war? You're getting in my way from finding Roji.*

—Someone lowered into the seat beside me, dropping his brown wings behind the chair's back and *thunked* his elbows on the table. "Some party, uh?"

It was the electrician from earlier today. He was still wearing his dirty overalls and goggles around his neck, but he'd removed his gloves. They were folded to his tool-belt now.

I glowered at him. "I'm surprised they let you in. They barely let *me* through, for wearing wrinkled pants."

"I just finished replacing a broken lamp out in the gardens," he explained. "No one's told me to leave yet, so I figured I'd stick around. You don't look like you're having fun, there, Highness."

"What do you mean?" I swiped a filled glass of the weird wine. "I'm having *loooads* of fun." I downed that glass and put it aside.

He took a glass himself and examined it. "What is this stuff, anyway?"

"Who knows? Spirits are Spirits."

He sniffed at it, grimaced, then left it alone. "Doesn't smell like any Spirits I've had."

I drank it for him, grumbling. "Yeah, these things are weak as Void, that's for sure…" I paused, realizing something, and turned to him. "You're speaking Culatian."

He grinned. "You sound surprised."

"I kinda assumed you only spoke Landish." I poked at my hair in a gesture. "Your feathers are brown and all."

"People have their secrets." He shrugged. Then his eyes narrowed. "Speaking of secrets… any particular reason you're down here, princess? Last I heard, your old man's going to kick the bucket soon. Your realm needs an heir, doesn't it?"

I slammed a fist on the table. "I am *not* the heir."

"That's what I heard—"

"You heard wrong. When I find my brother, we'll have the real heir back on the throne after Pops goes under."

He drummed his fingers over the table, cupping his chin with a propped up hand. "Looking for your brother, huh…" He wiped his hand over his mouth and breathed through his nose. "And you think he'll take over again? Just like that?"

"He has to." Ah, finally, the drinks were kicking in. My head started spinning, and I looked over at him with a heavy skull. Memories of Roji came flooding back, remembering when he left, when father gave his title to me… my eyes started to mist. "I can't be queen. I can't take Roji's crown. *He* is Sky. *He* has his Soulenergy. If I took over, I'd…" I dropped my head, mumbling. "I'd mess Culatia up…"

The electrician's face softened, and he scratched his head. He was about to say something—

The flautist from the band suddenly popped up out of nowhere and interrupted. *"Your High… oh, Land. How many of those have you had?"* he asked in Landish.

"Uh…" I turned in my chair to count the empty glasses, but the table spun and my head slammed into it, the world dripping and churning. *"Mnhnghhh…"*

What the Void? I couldn't move. My body weighed like a rock.

I heard the flautist curse. *"Blast it all, Zyl…"* He sounded familiar. Why did he remind me of Linus? *"We really could have used your Hallows."*

The electrician's voice was alarmed. *"What's wrong with her?"* he demanded in Landish. You know, he also sounded familiar… huh…

"Those drinks aren't wine." The guy who sounded like Linus hefted me off the chair, slinging my arm over his shoulder. *"Help me, will you?"*

The electrician hurried to take my other shoulder, and they rushed me out to the gardens.

WILLOW

I hurried through the crowd of cheerful lords and ladies, pushing my way toward the staircase in the corner.

I passed little Fuérr, who trotted at my heels. "<Miss Death,>" the child whined in Marincian. "<Miss Death!>"

He followed me up the stairs, my attention only halfheartedly dedicated to him. "<Yes, Fuérr?>"

"<I can't find the others,>" he said, worried. "<They're all gone, and everyone is so tall and no one speaks Marincian and—"

"<Stay with me if you wish, Fuérr, but bear in mind I have business to settle.>"

I noticed his face flushed with a mixture of relief and uncertainty. He nodded, keeping his scaled lips pressed to show me he wasn't going to be a bother.

The music was faded from the upstairs banister of the ballroom. With Fuérr straggling at my skirts, I scanned the floor for Anabelle. There was no trace of her. *How could I have been so Bloody stupid?* I cursed to myself. *All this time, she had been right in front of me!*

My fox ears grew and curled, heels clicking faster—but I almost stumbled when Oliver ran into me.

"Auntie Low!" Oliver tugged my long skirt urgently, his small wings fluttering. "You gotta come with me!"

Fuérr perked from behind me. "<There you are, you annoying sea-slug! Where have you been?>"

Oliver, not understanding a word Fuérr had said, grabbed the Ocean Prince's hand and tugged him along. "Come on, Fuérr! We can't stay here anymore."

My brow furrowed at the little owl. "Oliver, I thought Linus was watching over you tonight?"

"I am," came Linus' voice next.

I spun on my heels. Linus didn't *look* like Linus. He looked like the flautist from the band downstairs. "Are you wearing an illusion?" I asked.

"Your grandfather lent me an enchantment," he said, flashing a ring he now wore on his finger. "And I know you want an explanation, but we need to leave." He headed for the stairs, and Oliver tugged Fuérr along with them.

I followed, stammering, "I—wait! What's going on?"

Linus' footfalls thudded rapidly down the steps as we followed. "Neverland's rebellion is among us. They've come for the Shadowblood."

"The twins? But I... w-where are they?"

"I was hoping you could tell me that, princess. They're the only ones I have yet to find." He stopped at the bottom step and glanced warily at me. "You haven't had anything to drink tonight, have you?"

"No," I said. "Why?"

He breathed out in relief. "Thank Shel, you still have your Hallows tonight... come." He crept along the side of the crowded ballroom with rushed steps. "Her Highness Sky drank damn near twenty glasses of the stuff. Just one was enough to shut off her Hallows for the rest of the night."

My face contorted in horror. "You're saying those drinks are drugged?"

"It's Yinklît Gel with coloring."

My face cracked. "Death's Sorrowed Head!" *Was that what Xavier had been trying to tell me?* Bloods, I'd been so caught up with Anabelle, I'd ignored him again. Why did I keep doing this to him?

I shook my head, staying focused. *Priorities.* I can reflect and apologize after finding him.

We passed by Lilli, who spotted Oliver with me. She fumbled to keep pace with us.

"Oliver!" Lilli's bat wings twitched. "What are you doing here?"

The disguised Linus grabbed her shoulders and pushed her along. "Another time, Howless. Do you know where your fiancé and his brother are?"

She frowned. "Why do you sound like Linus?"

"Illusion," I clipped beside him. "I don't understand yet either, but we need to find the twins. Have you seen them?"

"No," she said, beguiled. "Alex left some time ago. He asked Jaq and me to find the others and leave for the ship."

"The ship is gone," said Linus. "It's been torched at the harbor."

I gaped at him. "You're saying we're trapped?"

"Unless we get to a Sky Port before this queen overtakes them all, yes."

"Mother of Death!" My teeth sharpened, and I increased speed. "Where in Void are those two?"

"I'll find them." Linus slowed to a stop, reaching for the engagement-vines dangling from my hair. He was silent for a moment, then his dark face paled. "Oh, dear... We should hurry."

I didn't like that implication. He led the way through the palace halls, the music muted and distant behind us while my pulse drowned out the rest.

I didn't know what sort of trouble they'd gotten into, but with Xavier's muscle development still low, I hoped to Gods Alex could at least protect him until I arrived.

"Oliver," Lilli hushed to the owl behind me. "Take Fuérr and find Jaq, will you? Stay with him. Can you do that for me?"

The boy nodded dutifully, then he trotted off the other way, dragging Fuérr along.

The rest of us climbed two flights of stairs, dashing into a narrow, dimly lit hallway. Linus halted in front of the last door, dropping to the lock and fiddling with a pin and blade. "They're in here," he said, his tools clinking within the lock. "Just give me a moment—"

"We haven't got a moment!" I shoved my hands on the wooden door, evoking my flames in a powerful rush of green fire. The wood crackled and burnt to charcoal, and I kicked the brittle remains with a satisfying *crack* before leaping inside with hands still enflamed, though they'd cooled to blue then orange, so I could reserve my strength.

Lilli came at my side, her dual-scythes at the ready…

But we paused. There were vines everywhere, green leaves varying in bloom and stems tangled all throughout the room.

Alexander was splayed on his back over the silken sheets of the single, luxurious bed, his limbs wrapped in those vines.

Beside him, a scrawny man was sitting up on his knees. his scarred, bare back turned toward us as his face was buried in the young queen's barely concealed bosom, his vine-entangled fingers clutching her slender waist and sensually exploring her open back.

His long-grey hair had been untied, and it fell to his shoulders when he ripped his head free of the queen's chest, green vines snapping off his neck, letting him gasp for air before more vines grew and latched round his throat once more. The stringy plants pulled his face into hers and fastened their lips. He was twitching, the plants ever twisting and reddening his grey skin as they squeezed tighter and slithered toward his trousers' drawstrings.

When we'd barged in, the queen pulled away from Xavier, turning to glare at us. "I thought I was clear that no one was to interrupt—!"

She gasped when she saw me. Given my pure, *blistering* rage, her horror was understandable.

"Oh." My throat seared, teeth sharpening. "You are *dead*, child."

I stormed forward, hands blazing with flames.

The queen panicked and shuffled back over the bed. Her hands lit with golden Hallows, and she sent a tangle of vines that cracked with enormous, purple-tipped thorns across the room, blocking me from them.

"These two are my claim, now!" clipped the queen, her lion ears curled as she feigned a calm and commanding demeanor. "Stealing the queen's consorts is an act of treason!"

"Consorts?" My snarl fractured further. "*Consorts?*"

That was it. This bitch wanted to die.

I hurled my fire at the thorny vines, burning them to a crisp, my fire dripping all the way back to their stems and catching on the carpet along the way. The scent of burnt fabric permeated, a small trail of fire flickering along the floor, but I didn't worry. This whole damned palace could burn for all I cared.

I headed for the bed, my hands still blazing. "That is my betrothed, you sniveling parasite," I snarled. "And I'll take him back, thank you."

"Take them and you get no army!"

I paused. Sneered. "What?"

She shoved off the bed to stand, taking a defensive footing. "They are all I ask for!" she said, "in exchange for my armies!"

I laughed. Was she making jest?

When she offered no reply, I fell silent, and my brow knitted. "This is why you asked us to come?" I questioned darkly.

"It's a simple exchange." She collected her wits again and ran a scoffing hand through her cropped hair, lifting her chin to act unmarred. "Unfair for me, even. You're getting the better deal." She slunk to the bed behind the twins, wrapping her arms around Xavier's neck and gliding her fingers over Alexander's hairy chest. "Several aiding armies, for two men. You'd have to be foolish to pass up such an…"

I kicked her sternum with such force, she slammed into the headboard, heaving from the blow and the new smoke.

"You'd have to be foolish to think I'd agree to something so ludicrous." I burnt the vines that constrained the twins, freeing them.

They gasped air back into their lungs, rubbing their arms and legs, and Alex was quick to withdraw his scythes. "Disgusting little…"

Xavier stumbled off the bed, holding a hand to the impressions on his throat in a wince. "Sorrowed Death, am I glad to see you," he panted to me, withdrawing his own scythes.

I pulled out my hair-stick and had my staved scythe materialize as the queen regained her breath and footing. Her dress was now covered in ash and burnt plant remains, the smoke growing thicker. My fire had caught onto the walls now and was spreading quickly.

A scream ripped from the queen's lungs when she charged for me, evoking her Hallows onto the headboard and fashioning herself an oaken sword.

I sidestepped her thrust and threw my fire at her, but she held up her blade in time to block. Though, with her weapon being made of flammable material, it caught my flames. She cursed, throwing it at me and forced me to dodge while she ripped apart more furniture to make a number of long, sharp spears, all aimed for us.

She thrust them down in a yell and we rushed out of the smoking room, hearing cracks and splinters behind us.

We dashed down the hall and hurried down the steps, crossing the corridors and running into the ballroom, startling a number of guests with our drawn weapons. But half of the said guests—those who didn't seem the least bit surprised by our alarmed demeanor—were wielding Shotri and swords, aiming them at the already-kneeling shifters who had their hands raised behind their heads in surrender.

I lowered my scythe. *What is all this?*

"Shadowblood," an orange haired woman in a violet gown called, cocking her Shotri and stepping up to Alexander and Xavier. She scrutinized their bare-backed attire, her expression hardened. "Just as Marian foretold… Are you hurt?"

"No," they said in unison. Alex asked separately. "Who are you?"

"Vanessa, wasn't it?" Xavier asked. He seemed to have solidified a thought. "Ah. So, you're not a reporter. You're with the rebellion."

The woman, Vanessa, saluted. "Yes, my lord. We suspected the queen invited you here as some sort of trap. We came to provide an escape and shelter."

I stepped beside her myself. "On behalf of Grim, we thank you. I heard our ship has been destroyed, and it seems we'll need a place to hide for a time."

She nodded to me. "Of course, Your Highness. We have people—"

Shouts came from around the ballroom, Leaflite knights rushing in and exchanging blows with the rebels scattered about. The ballroom's walls bounced with the sounds of clashing metal and cries of pain, the normal guests hiding under tables and trying to flee to the gardens in terrified shrieks.

"Guards!" came a ripping voice from the ballroom's entrance.

It was the queen.

She'd appeared under the doorframe, having accrued a new entourage of knights. She was hacking the smoke that plumed into the room behind her. "I want no prisoners!"

The extra knights charged inside, the rebels crossing swords and Shockspheres.

The queen's hateful glare was solely dedicated to me. "You… Little… *Cave leech.*" Her hands thrust out, gleaming with gold Hallows.

The potted plants scattered around the walls rumbled from their soil, their roots creeping through the cracked ceramics while the room became dressed in vines, leaves, and climbing branches. The opening to the balcony was sealed shut by the living growth, blocking our only exit. The hallway outside was now smothered in flames, smog pouring around the queen as she began cackling like a madwoman.

She shot the enormous tangle of vines and thorny branches at me—

But the plants came to an abrupt halt, snapping and curling in place as if struggling against themselves.

"Syreen Gretchen Lowery," a woman's voice boomed from the second floor's balcony. "It is time you stepped down from your throne."

Everyone stopped their brawling, craning to see who'd spoken. But I already knew the voice before looking.

Standing barefoot atop the railing was a woman in a glittering, golden gown. Her eyes were a bright shade of gold as well, her shimmering, metallic hair contrasting her red-tinted skin.

Anabelle.

Ana's hands were shining with Hallows as the plants in front of us squirmed in place, seeming to respond to her push.

The queen staggered, muscles straining against the tangle she'd created. But her vines wouldn't move to her will. She screamed, "Who are you?!"

"I am Anabelle Goldthorn." She stepped off the rail, her feet shining with Hallows.

Crack!

The crowd gasped as the marble floor shot up in low, grinding rumbles, forming a thick pillar just at her feet.

Crack! Crack! Crack!

Each dainty step she took brought a new pillar of stone, allowing her toes to pad softly down to us as she descended the massive, lopsided staircase. When she touched down to the ballroom's smooth floor, she stood tall and poised, her gown's countless sequin gleaming in the light as if dressed in twinkling gold stars.

"I am the queen of these lands your ancestors have stolen from me," Ana announced. "I am the last Relicblood of Land."

Murmurs erupted through the room.

Ana strode forward, still reaching one hand out to the tangle of plants as she approached our group. The crowd parted quickly to make a path for her, half looking frightened, and the other half awed. Vendy was amongst the mass and quickly snapped out of her revere to throw herself to the floor in a drastically low bow.

Ana paused when passing Linus next, who stared at her, frozen. "You…" he began, but the words seemed to flee from his mind.

Ana brushed her free hand over a bleeding gash on his shoulder, sealing the wound with her remedy Hallows. The nearby rebels heightened their murmurs, shuffling back and kneeling in prayer. Their opponents were too stunned at Ana to even notice their opening.

Linus' eyes began to mist. Without a word, he dropped to one knee and bowed his head in reverence.

Ana closed her eyes and breathed in slowly, then continued on her path, stopping in front of me.

"Sister Death," she greeted, her usual whisper now a confident, regal tune. It held the tenor of a queen.

"Sister Land…" My voice was not as confident. "You've certainly taken your time for this reunion."

"Five centuries is long enough," she agreed, glancing at me with remorse. "I… am sorry for my absence."

"Apologize later," I said. "We have other concerns."

She nodded, turning her attention to the stunned queen behind the tangled plant life.

The girl still pushed against Anabelle's efforts, but had gained no ground. In fact, I could see her feet sliding backward over the floor.

"You…!" The queen's hands began to shake, either out of fear or incredulity. "A lie! It's only an illusion…!"

Ana *slammed* down a foot, the crowned Land mark on her shoulder blade gleaming bright. The floor underneath her cracked and split, the fractures climbing toward the queen. The floor rumbled and caused the queen's step to falter, losing her control of the vines as a spike shot up from the marble and pierced through her calf. Red soaked her gown's skirt, the queen howling in pain.

She ripped her muscle out of the spike in another cry, stumbling over the floor as Ana approached her. With each light step Ana made, a new spike shot up from the floor, and the queen dodged and rolled away from each one in a panic.

"Queen Syreen," Ana announced loud enough for the entire room to hear. "I heed you step down. I have come to reclaim my lands. The Day of Revival begins now."

"H-how…!" She was trembling, screaming, "Your line is dead!"

"I exist to prove the contrary," said Ana, stopping before her. "Step down and serve in my ranks. I have a use for great swordswomen. Concede, and I gift you with life and honor."

The queen's sharpened teeth gritted, a growl clicking her throat. "Pretentious filth!" She reached for a fallen Shotri and shot a sphere so quickly, Ana was caught off-guard. She was hit and strained against the following sparks as the queen pushed to her feet, favoring her good leg, and roared. "I AM THE QUEEN!"

The ballroom burst into motion, the pausing fighters' inspirations rekindled. More guards filed into the ballroom from the gardens, some staying behind in the halls to quell the fire spreading inside.

Ana's shocks died after a few moments and she panted, resetting her footing and lifted her marble blade as I stood my ground beside her, my scythe lowered and ready. Leaflites came for Lilli and the twins, and they all sliced their way through them, Alexander helping Xavier when he was pushed back by a woman's stronger shove, both brothers felling her from both chest and back before clashing blades with more knights.

Trusting them to defend themselves, I rushed the queen alongside Ana. The queen shot more spheres at us, splitting us up. I swerved round to the queen's right while Ana swerved to her left, both of us slicing for her—

Clang-clang!

Someone had slid in front of our blows, blocking our strikes, and I saw the new woman was glaring dangerously at Ana and me from beside a nearby table.

The scaled knight swiftly seized a large bowl of the Yinklît drink off the table and splashed it over Anabelle, drenching her.

Ana flexed her hands, growling furiously with curled lion ears.

The opposing knight abandoned her metal armor, the plate clattering to the floor as she darted to the queen's side protectively.

"My queen!" she said, panting, "you are hurt?"

"I'm fine, Genevieve." The queen ground her teeth, trying to hide her limp.

A wooden pillar cracked nearby, the flames having spread and charred it. The column moaned and split at the top, then fell and slammed into the floor between us. The thick smoke was becoming choking. I saw the knight lift the queen in her arms and dash away, leaving us to choke on the smoke.

"Ana!" I hacked. "We—*Khauh-kha*—need to get out of here!"

Ana covered her mouth and nose with a hand, nodding as we turned and ran. The rest of our group joined us along with the twins, all of us heading for the vine-blocked doorway to the gardens. The twins cut away at the vines while Ana hurriedly rubbed her hands together, trying in vain to rid herself of the Yinklît Gel that knight had thrown on her.

I still had *my* Hallow at least, and I threw blue flames at the blocking plants, burning through the thick barrier.

A scream sounded behind us, a Leaflite knight charging for Ana with her blade raised high—

Linus veered in front of her with a stolen sword and plunged his steel into the knight's breastplate. She choked up blood and Linus shoved the corpse down, panting as he threw his gaze at Ana. "Are you hurt, Sire?"

I noticed Ana's lion ear twitched at the name. "No…" Ana coughed from the smog. "But my Hallows are blocked."

"Sire…!" That rebel woman, Vanessa, hurried over and saluted Ana, seeming frazzled and beyond awed. "P-please, let us escort you out! We have a safe passage in the gardens—"

Another column collapsed in a puff of embers behind us. My fire had finally done away with the vines blocking the doorway.

"Take us there," Ana ordered, turning to Linus next. "Assemble the other Grimlings and Reapers from our party. I expect to see them safely where next we take shelter. Use your Third Eye to find us."

Linus was still panting, but accommodating. "As you wish, my lady."

Vanessa led us out to the gardens while Linus took off to do as commanded, wood and flames crackling behind us.

33

HUGH

⁓

Lady Lilac and I rushed down the smoking stairwell in heavy pants, my cloak billowing behind me as I tugged the cowl firmly over my head to hide my face from scrambling servants and panicking Leaflites.

They were shouting about a fire in the ballroom. And by the thickness of this smoke in the stairwell, it was certainly spreading quickly.

Now's my chance to slip out unnoticed! I wasn't sure where this fire came from, but with everyone worried over the flames, I was almost guaranteed a convenient cover from Sy and the guards.

"—Get to the princes' chamber this instant!" I heard Sy shouting from the bottom of the stairwell suddenly. "Find Hugh and keep him safe, or so help me…!"

I quickly ran up the other way, Lady soaring by my head. I panicked when the guards' clattering footfalls drew nearer behind me. Hurried, I found an open, stone window in the stairwell and hopped onto the sill, then hung outside of it by my fingers. Lady Lilac flew out over my head.

The guards marched past me up the steps in a large block, and my knuckles screamed in pain, wishing the women would hurry and leave—

My fingers slipped an inch, and my claws grew in a yelp, skidding over the stone.

"L-Land!" I stammered as my heart blistered in my throat, my claws scraping down another inch. Lady Lilac screeched in the air over my head in worried circles. I swallowed and carefully lifted one of my hands to reach for the sill's inside—

My other hand slipped entirely off the sill, and I screamed, tumbling down with my cloak flying around me.

"Woah!" A girl's voice gasped not a yard below me—and I was caught in the arms of a rabbit-eared teenager.

I blinked at the girl's familiar, dark face, stammering, "L... Lady Vendy?" Then I noticed she was standing perpendicular to the tower's wall, her bare feet shining with a golden light that seemed to stick her soles to the stones, her sloppily-braided hair falling beneath her toward the ground. I panted, "You're a Terravoker?"

"Uh, yeah." She scrunched her nose at me. "Why are you jumping out of windows on this wing? The fire hasn't caught here yet, has it?"

I blushed. "Well, um... no. But my sister was on her way to find me and I'm sort of... running away with you all." I offered a nervous smile, my grown lion ears folding in embarrassment.

One of her rabbit ears lifted in question, but Lady Lilac suddenly soared down and alighted on her shoulder, cawing in a soft plead at her.

The Lady Vendy hummed in thought, then shrugged—lifting me slightly with the gesture—and snorted. "Well, good thing I came back for our stuff in the guest rooms. Come on, we've got a ways to walk."

HERRIN

Clang! Clang!

"H-Hey!" I pounded the chapel's iron knocker again, slamming it harder.

Clang! Clang! Clang!

"Is anyone there?!" I shouted at the doors. Dream and Crysalette still weren't even visible on this street. I'd flown over and got here first, but no one was answering the stupid door. "Hey! I-I'm looking for Marian Gulldread! Please, it's important!"

I kept pounding the knocker—

The doors squeaked open, and a fat, elderly woman looked alarmed at me. She lifted a tremoring hand to push up her glasses.

"Did you say Marian?" she asked, hushed. Her stare narrowed at me suspiciously. "Who is asking?"

"I'm Herrin Tesler," I said. "Archchancellor of the Enlightener's Guild."

The woman's crooked spine almost corrected itself straight. Her glasses slipped down her nose, and she quickly scooted them back over her eyes. "H... Herrin Tesler...?" she croaked. "The one who wrote those books of hers?"

"Yeah! That's me. Look, something happened in the palace and I can't really explain right now, but I have to find Marian."

"She isn't with you?" Her tone was worried. "She left to warn you all. She hasn't come back."

"Damn it..." I heard footsteps pelt the street behind me. Dream and Crysalette had finally shown up. I darted back and met Crysalette halfway. "She isn't here," I panted.

"Oh, dear." Crysalette was breathing hard too, holding her enlarged belly and taking her husband's arm for support.

Dream hushed her. "Darling, you mustn't exert yourself."

She waved him away and tossed back a lock of her sweaty, rust-orange hair. "I'll be... fine, dear..."

More footsteps echoed against the buildings. Octavius and Neal were sprinting over, waving their arms like a couple of maniacs. Oliver and Prince Fuérr were running with them. Behind the kids were Jaq and Linus, both lugging an unconscious Matthiel over their shoulders. *Oh, Bloods.*

"What happened to Matthiel?" I asked when they wheezed over their knees in front of me.

Jaq puffed. "He drank... some stuff..."

My stare went flat. "He's drunk?"

Jaq shook his head, inhaled as if ready to explain, but started hacking instead.

Linus answered. "The drinks at the palace were Yinklît gel with coloring. Matthiel only had two glasses, thank Bloods, but he'll need time to regain his Hallows. And his consciousness."

"Holy crap..." I murmured. What in Land happened at the palace?

Jaq's hacking died down, and he looked between me and the Dream couple. "Where's Bianca?" he asked.

"And my parents?" Octavius followed. "And Mika and..."

"I've found them all," came Kurrick's voice from around the corner. He stalked into view, bringing the rest of our entourage with him.

When Bianca's head popped into view from behind Kurrick, she saw Jaq lugging Matthiel and rushed to the unconscious man. "Death, Jaq!" she gasped, pressing two fingers over Matthiel's neck to check for a pulse, one of her rabbit ears draping down. "What happened to him?"

Jaq shook his sweaty head. "Long story." He spotted someone new at her heels. "Who's this?"

The newcomer, clad in overalls and hauling three huge bags, waved cheerily. "'ey, there, mate. Name's Red. Don't ask me what it stands for, I ain't tellin'.'"

Bianca absently tossed her head at 'Red'. "He's a new Alchemist recruit. Talk about it later?"

"Yeah," Jaq grunted, lifting Matthiel and starting forward with Linus. "Come on. We can't stay in the city for..."

"Guys!" A girl's voice shouted suddenly, gasping for breath. "Guys, w... wait up...!"

Vendy came running toward us, her messy braid flailing over her shoulder as she dragged a cloaked kid behind her by his wrist. The boy had a crow flying by his covered head.

When they reached us, Jaq groaned and smeared a hand over his scaled face. "Aw Death, now who's *this*?"

"U-Um," the kid began as he tugged his hood over his face nervously. "Lady Vendy says you're... you're with... Prince Xavier...?"

Jaq raised an eyebrow. "Uh... sure, kid. Why?"

"I-I need to find him." His grip tightened desperately on his cloak. His crow settled over his shoulder comfortably. "Vendy says you all can take me to him?"

Jaq looked at Linus, then at me. I only shrugged. What was *I* supposed to say?

Crysalette sighed and laid a hand on the kid's back. "Of course we can, dear. Come, we must hurry."

34

XAVIER

I pushed away a blocking branch through the dark forest as our new, pseudo-army trudged through with mixed emotions.

Some of the members were ecstatic and chatty, the rebels in particular murmuring about the sudden appearance of their lost queen. *Queen... Bah.*

I twisted back to see Anabelle farther back in the crowd. Her eyes and hair were newly golden now, surrounded by her new soldiers, including Neverland's resistance leader, Vanessa.

—I was smacked in the head by a low branch, my attention thrust back to the trek as I rubbed my throbbing skull. "Bloody lost Relicblood," I muttered to Alex beside me, "there in front of us the whole damned time..."

Alex snorted his agreement. "Tell me about it."

I looked ahead to be sure that electrician was still in sight, the one who was leading us. He carried Zyl, who was unconscious in his arms. As grateful as I was to have his help with caring for Zyl, I couldn't help but wonder why *he* was leading the pack?

Leaves and pine needles crunched under my boots as I left Alex behind to catch up to the electrician, asking, "Where are we going exactly?"

The winged man hummed. "My home. We're camped in the middle of Blackwood Forest."

"Is it safe there?"

"Yeah," he assured. "No one usually comes up here because of all the rumors about Necrofera. That's why they call it *Blackwood*. Everyone's too scared to come near here, but don't worry. We're well protected and the forest itself is so dense, it'd be easy for outsiders to get lost before they ever found us."

I murmured, "It sounds like you don't take to people very kindly?"

He cocked his head. "We like our privacy… but for this, I'm willing to make an exception. Some of your friends should already be there. I told Vanessa where to find it, and said to send some of her crew there with them. There's enough room, it's actually an old campground some old army built who-knows-how long ago, so there's a lot of huts and bunkers built in the trees."

"I see." I rubbed my neck. "Thank you for taking us in."

He shrugged, lifting Zyl in the process. "Don't mention it."

I glanced at Zylveia's unconscious figure and frowned. "Will she be all right?"

"I… don't know," he admitted. He sounded worried, holding her tighter. "If I knew what was in those drinks, I would have stopped her sooner. Zyl, *galect ültorofv*, you careless girl…"

"You're really concerned for her?" I asked.

He sighed, his wings drooping. "Yeah, well… it's my fault she's here, so I'm kind of obligated to watch out for her now."

"How is any of this your fault?"

Another shrug. "I left her with Dad. And she came looking for me."

That took me a moment to process. I slowed to a stop. "You…" Seeing he was leaving me behind, I hurried my pace. "*You're* Sky Prince Roji? Of Culatia?"

"Yeah." He sounded sapped of energy, like he couldn't care less about hiding his identity right now. "I'd take off the goggles with my illusion, but my hands are kind of full. Lil' Sis takes priority, you know how it is."

"I… but you…" I fumbled for the right words, dumbstruck. "You've been hiding down *here* all this time?"

"Surprise," he muttered. "Not exactly as dramatic a reveal as *Land* reappearing, but eh. I'm not really in the mood for showing off."

I stole a glance back at Ana again. "There are too many things happening at once…" I rubbed my temples, returning my attention to the disguised Roji. "How much farther is your home?"

"It's just up ahead." He threw his head forward in a gesture. "Mind the fence."

"Fence?" I looked ahead, seeing there was a wall of iron posts and copper wires strung across the forest. The closer we came to it, the more I could hear a soft humming sound.

He stopped in front of the electric fence and held Zyl out to me. "Take her for a minute, will ya?"

"Er, actually, I don't think I'm strong enough yet to—" I gasped when he dropped her in my arms, and her sudden weight nearly had both of us on the ground. Alex must have heard me struggling because he hurried over and took her from me.

"Don't strain yourself," Alex warned, hefting Zyl as he glared at the disguised Roji. I didn't think he'd heard my conversation with him earlier about who he was. Alex asked him, "What are you doing?"

Roji was reaching for the electric fence, placing a palm on one of the iron posts. "I have to deactivate it for everyone." His hands burst with a sudden spark of lightning, the bolts spreading down the post and across the thick copper wires.

The humming died into silence, and Roji removed his hand, walking over to a hinged gate and opened it with a loud squeak. "All right, it's safe now. Sorry about that, the fence keeps out any stray hunters and Necrofera."

Our entourage entered through the gate, and we found ourselves in the abandoned campsite Roji had mentioned.

The foliage blocked most of the moonlight, so the site wasn't easy to make out at first, but Roji went to a metal box and opened the case, flicked a switch, and lamps flickered to life throughout the camp. There were huts and small facilities both on the ground and in the trees, boardwalks trailing the high branches that wound all throughout the area. Moths began gathering at the dim lamplights, and Roji sniffed, putting fists at his sides as he grinned.

"The place was pretty worn down when we found it," he explained to me and Alex as the others took to exploring the site. "But Mini and I put in some work to get everything running again. There's electricity, plumbing, heating, you name it. I don't know how long you guys plan to stay, but you're welcome to take your time and gather your strength for as long as you need."

Roji took Zyl back from Alexander, nodding to us. "Figure out housing amongst yourselves. Don't go near the fence while it's running, power it down first. Showers and lavatories are off to the left there. If anything needs fixing, or you need some supplies, come talk to me or Mini."

He walked off with Zyl, taking her inside the largest, cottage-looking structure on the site.

Stepping out of the outdoor showers, I took one of the communal towels left on the wooden wall that separated the men's section and the women's. Not that they'd been assigned previously, it was something the others had decided somewhere along the way.

I dried off as best I could with the still-damp towel someone had used recently. It was a little disconcerting, but we had too many people and not enough supplies, so there was little choice except to share. Luckily, some of the rebels had thought to bring spare clothes and were handing them out to anyone who'd been drenched in the Yinklît gel, so there was a pile of loose trousers and large shirts on the foldable chair. I sorted through them, attempting to find the smallest sizes and finding they were still too large for me. I sighed, tying the trousers' drawstrings so they would stay on my boney beltline. I put the towel back over the wall.

Alex came out after me and dried off, rubbing the towel over his hair vigorously. "Thank Gods that electrician's family knows how to work with plumbing," he muttered, tossing the towel on the wall and went to throw on his own borrowed shirt and trousers. "I was starting to think we'd never be rid of that gel."

I grunted my agreement and strode toward the fire some of the others had made in the pre-dug pit. We both sat and warmed in the heat. Alex looked over the noisy site, both at the ground-level and the overhanging boardwalks in the trees.

"How long ago did those scouts leave to find Linus and the others?" He asked.

"It's been over two hours," I said, shivering. I cupped my hands and released my ice Hallows a little, trying to warm faster while also occupying myself with training. I'd been working with Fuérr over the weeks to form shapes with my ice. It was a complicated procedure, since I had to shape the ice *while* producing it.

I uncovered my latest creation and inspected it. It was blocky and rough at the edges, but overall, it looked like the shape I'd intended. It was a candle lily, without the stem.

Alex looked at the frozen sculpture and commended, "You're getting better. But why is it always a flower?"

"Fuérr suggested I practice with one shape until it's mastered before moving on to the next one."

His hands gleamed emerald as he released his own ice Hallows and lifted the frosted candle lily out of my hand. The ice glided over his fingers, and he concentrated while rearranging the shape into a simple, smooth ball. There were no dents or jagged edges this time.

"That one's far cleaner," I said, grinning. "I'm not the only one improving."

He grinned back, but it fell. "Why did you decide on such a complex shape, though? I picked a ball for its simplicity."

I brought up a knee and leaned an arm over it, shrugging. "I thought Willow would appreciate it."

"Ah." He propped his arms back to hold himself up. "And did she?"

"I... haven't shown her," I admitted. "I wanted to perfect it first."

"You're close enough now that she'd recognize it."

I began turning the ring on my finger absently. "I suppose."

We watched the flames in silence for a while, listening to the pop of firewood and the loud whine of crickets. I took a breath. "Alex?"

He flicked his gaze at me, waiting for me to continue.

"I…" I sighed. "I need more training with my physical strength. I can't keep relying on you and Willow to come save me anymore. I need to be there for you all, as you're here for me."

He hummed. "We'll get you there. But if you recall, I couldn't get myself out of that mess just as much as you, tonight." He shivered in disgust. "If the girls hadn't burst in, we would have both been that madwoman's playthings."

I grunted, hunching over the fire. His mention of it caused tonight's insanity to flit back to mind again, a shudder running down my spine. I had been seconds away from having a cherished moment I'd saved solely for Willow taken from me by a crazed, lusting queen—what was worse, Willow saw it all herself. I prayed to the Seamstress she didn't think I actually wanted to… to *mate* with that sick woman. I held my skinny knees in a sigh.

I hadn't expected Willow to blast down the door. I hadn't expected her to know where we were at all, let alone that we were in trouble, but I thanked Death she had. If she were in such a situation, could I have helped her just the same?

"Well." Alex scratched his nose. "Ana turned out to be the lost Relicblood of Land, we managed to invoke the wrath of a queen in heat, who has an army she'll surely send after us, *and* we destroyed part of her palace while once again involuntarily joining forces with the kingdom's resistance. I say our productivity is up ninety percent."

"We seem to have a habit of enraging Landish rulers," I observed morosely. I plucked a stick from the ground and prodded the logs, embers dusting in the air. "Is this ever going to end? Everywhere we go, we're either cast out or caught up in another country's feuds. We're caught in a cycle."

He quietly agreed. "It does feel that way."

"Are we ever going to make it back home?" I asked mournfully. "Or are we going to die before we get off this damned rock? And Willow and I…" I looked at my ring. My tone softened. "We'd planned to wed when we returned to Grim. But from what we've seen, all the fighting, the deaths… those visions of the sky shattering, everyone just a pile of corpses…" I gripped my ring, pain festering as I watched the fire. "What if we never make it back to Grim?"

The silence swelled. After a long moment, Alex exhaled and clapped my shoulder. "No one said you had to wait for Grim, Xavier."

I met his look. His grin was hollow.

Then shouts sounded near the edge of the site, breaking our attention. It sounded like Jaq.

Alex and I jumped to our feet, heading over. Jaq had been part of the missing group. If he was here, then the others would surely be with him.

We were soon close enough to see Jaq was hefting an unconscious man over his shoulder, alongside Linus. "Make room!" Jaq shouted at the gathering crowd. "We need Healers to do some work on this one!"

The man over his shoulder was Matthiel.

I totted up to them. "What happened?"

Linus grunted at Matthiel's weight. "He drank a fair amount of that Yinklît gel. It wasn't near as much as Zylveia, but it was enough to render him limp as a feral eel."

They carried him into one of the barracks, where rebels were hurrying to help however they could. Oliver flew in after them, and Bianca, Rochelle, and Sirra-Lynn darted close behind with bags of medical tools in tow.

I saw the Treble family walk inside the fence of our site next, Mikani and Ringëd among them. Nathaniel and Aiden's ghost came in behind them, followed by Herrin, Dream and his wife, and El.

"Yu see Zyl?" asked El once she spotted Alex and me, looking worried. "Can no find."

I would have answered, but someone else spoke instead. "Zyl's with me."

I craned back. Roji had appeared behind us. Now, though, he was without his disguise, dark of skin and red of feathers, his eyes a bright rosy color. Even in the dim lamplight, his scarlet hair seemed to flicker like sparks of red bolts, though I couldn't tell if that was a trick of the light or if it was naturally there. He was still in his work-overalls, however, so the change wasn't all that exciting.

Alex stared baffled at him. "Who are you—?"

El let out a shriek, jabbing a finger at him. "R–R–Roji…!"

He waved an unceremonious hand at the hybrid. "*A'li, El.* Guess you're still following lil' sis around, huh?"

"*Z–z–z–zit…*" El stuttered and scratched her head helplessly.

Roji massaged his neck and rolled his head back. Then he blinked, looking near my waist. "Hey now, *you* look familiar."

I frowned, twisting to see whom he was speaking to. Fuérr had appeared next to me, apparently. His webbed ears folded upward at attention when Roji had addressed him.

Roji rubbed his chin, inspecting the little Seadragon. "You look like my nephew," he mumbled. Then he spoke in fluent Marincian. "<You're Fuérr, aren't you?>"

Fuérr jolted stiff. "<You speak Marincian?>"

"<Sure do. I'm married to your aunt, little Ocean.>"

The child's brow furrowed. "<Auntie Mini? But Papa said she was stolen.>"

"<Nope. Left with me on her own free will. Come on, she'll want to see you taken care of.>" He switched to Culatian now, babbling something to El and prompting her follow him alongside Fuérr as they all disappeared into the cottage.

Alex gave me a dumbfounded look, throwing a thumb over his shoulder. "Was that who I think it was?"

"Sky Prince Roji of Culatia," I confirmed. "He's taking care of his sister."

Dream, who'd come to stand by us, rubbed the small, blue stubble at his chin. "So, this is where Roji was hiding…" He glanced at me. "Ah, Xavier. We picked up a stray on the way here. He was asking for you."

I raised an eyebrow. Who would be asking for me at a time like this?

Beside Dream, Crysalette murmured to a short, cloaked figure who hid behind her. "He's here," she said to the hidden figure. "You can come out now."

The adolescent boy carefully lifted his hood ever so slightly. He saw me and breathed in relief. "Master!"

I froze when the boy ran to my side. His crow poked its head out from under his hood, making it drop to the boy's shoulders.

"Hugh?" I questioned stiffly. *Mother of Death*, I groaned inwardly, *you've got to be joking.*

Alex shot me a perplexed glance. I gave him a look that said 'I'll explain later' and kept my attention on the young prince. "What are you doing here, Hugh?"

"You said I was welcome to join you if I wished," he said, panting. "And I wished. One of the palace wings caught flames, and I saw some of your friends fleeing. I thought if I followed them, they'd lead me to you."

Alex's eyes hardened, hissing to me so Hugh wouldn't hear. "Will his sister notice he's gone?"

"Better question," I muttered, cupping my mouth. "Will she assume he's with us and come after him?"

We shared a grimace. Well, everything else was going to Void tonight, why not tack this on the list of things that will surely get us killed later?

Hugh's gaze glided past us, the boy rising to his toes suddenly. "Shel Almighty! Who is *that*?"

I turned to look myself. Ana was there by one of the fires, surrounded by a circle of rebels. Vendy had hurried to her side and was speaking fervently with her, bowing every few seconds and blushing furiously. Willow stood beside the new Relicblood as well, waiting for Vendy to finish her gushing before the two royals began discussing something that seemed important, judging from their stern expressions.

Hugh's breath turned wistful. "Her hair glitters so brightly… like a field of golden flowers…"

"That is Anabelle," I said, pausing before adding. "She is the lost Relicblood of Land. Apparently."

"The lost heir does exist?" The boy stepped closer, trying to better see, but seemed too afraid to go much farther. "Amazing…"

"Ah, good," Dream said upon seeing Anabelle, walking over to the fire with his wife. "Things at least seem to have turned out well for her."

I watched the ancient couple stride toward Ana arm in arm, and Alex soon shook his head. "We should see what the meeting is about. It could be something we need to hear." He started after them.

I glanced down at Hugh. "I suppose you'll wish to listen with me?"

Hugh gave a sharp nod. I blew out a fatigued breath, then walked on and waved for him to follow. "Don't interrupt."

He straightened. "Yes, Master!"

ANABELLE

"And the prospect of imported troops?" I asked Vanessa softly.

"Unfortunately, my lady, we'll see little, if any." Vanessa's walnut arms crossed. "My scouts say every Surfacing Port to Grim has been sealed off and overtaken by the Leaflites. Same for the Sky Ports to Culatia."

"What of the Reaper and Stormchaser stations there?"

"Captured or killed, if they didn't flee." "Send search teams to seek out any knights who still live," I said. "They may be hiding amongst the civilians. Bring them here. We must cull as many numbers as possible with sympathizers. They are not forced to join, but welcome if they wish to aid in taking back the nation."

Vanessa bowed to me. "Right away, Sire."

She trotted off to deliver the orders to her comrades, the other rebels in the circle scattering to do the same.

Vendy straightened beside me and saluted, her rabbit ears flicking upright as though they would rip from her head. "Sire, what do you want *me* to do, Sire?"

I gave the girl a nervous smile. "Oh, Vendy… you needn't take orders from me. You have your *Da'torr* to protect, else they find themselves in trouble again."

She saluted again. "Yes, Sire! Right away, Sire!" She turned about face and started off… but stopped. Twisted back to me—and hopped over to crush the wind from my lungs in an overjoyed squeal.

"Oh, I *knew* you would come back!" She cried and squeezed tighter in a flighty giggle. "Thank you, Ana! Sire! Majesty—whatever you want to be called!

I wish... I wish my parents could have been here to see you..." The poor dear began sniffling, her eyes welling.

I hesitated, placing a hand between her rabbit ears. "Oh..." I whispered. I'd nearly forgotten her parents had been part of Everland's rebellion before they were hanged for treason. All in my name... their deaths were on my hands, because of my absence... so *many* were killed because of me.

I stroked Vendy's hair, tears hitting me, though I blinked them away. "I am... sorry for your parents, Vendy. Perhaps when I reclaim my lands, I will visit Grim and meet their ghosts?"

She perked at that. "You will?!"

My smile was wan. "I will. Consider this a vow, for their loyalty to the Old Kingdom."

Her eyes flooded with tears and she crushed my ribs again, then released me to rush back to her *Da'torr* as 'ordered'. They were walking our way regardless, but she made a point to gush her excitement to them along the way.

Before they arrived, Willow gave me a concerned glance. "We still won't have the numbers we need against Neverland's entire force," she said. "With neither Zylveia's nor my soldiers to back us, this coup seems doomed to fail."

"They are a small militia," I admitted in a whisper. "But they have already done so much. What they need is hope in the face of despair."

Kurrick, who'd been listening in silence behind me, let out a quiet breath through his nose, closing his eyes as if in thought. He hadn't spoken a word to me since he arrived at camp. He'd hardly cast his gaze in my direction. What was running through his mind? If only he would speak...

A series of feet crunched the pine needles nearby. Dream and Crysalette had arrived first, smiling with pride. The twins followed them, a young man at Xavier's heels. Linus was the last to join, staying the farthest back as if to give us space. None of them spoke a word to me, neither praise nor accusation. They merely watched, waiting.

"I..." I whispered, dropping my gaze. "I am sorry. For my deception... I am sure each of you has questions for me. You deserve answers."

Willow laid a hand over her hip, keeping her voice low. "Goldthorn. The family name of King Adam... Are you his daughter?"

The memory of my father's face came to mind, his eyes drying in his death. "Yes," I whispered, a coldness festering my blood.

Alexander did not sound convinced. "King Adam died five centuries ago. You told us this was near the time Dream had adopted you. I presume this is the reason he took you in of all people?"

"Yes," I said again, glancing at Dream and Crysalette. "I have stayed with the Sandist family in Aspirre, along with Kurrick."

"Why?" Xavier questioned. "Why would you make everyone believe your Bloodline died?"

"Land's continents have suffered immensely from the belief," Alex added with a curt thrust of his hand in my direction. "You've seen yourself what damage it's done."

I closed my lids, breathing deeply. "Yes. But there was no given date for when the Lightcaster's seal would be broken. Dream hid me in hopes of protecting me from the Caster, should he be released early and seek to finish what he began."

Everyone turned to Dream now. Willow tapped a finger over her hip. "Grandfather? What seal does she speak of?"

Dream folded his arms behind his back. "At the time of Adam's death, I didn't have many options, Willow. It was either stand helpless and allow Kael to kill me and my family, or seal him and his manipulator in Aspirre until the Shadowblood was born."

Xavier suddenly looked uneasy. "Until *we* were born, you mean?"

"Yes." Dream's expression was dark as he stared at the fire. "I'll be honest, I didn't know I could seal someone in my realm until that night. It was something Iri had shown me, in a moment of panic. I didn't know how long the seal would last. Anabelle had already been with us since her birth, I couldn't simply leave a child so small on her own while I waited in Aspirre for you two." He sighed. "So, I kept her hidden."

Willow let out a quiet snort, looking to me. "That certainly explains why my mother was like a sister to you."

My lips yielded a smile. "I still consider Myra my sister. Though, it has been some time since I last saw her. It hadn't been the same when she left to be with your father."

"I can imagine." Willow circled a finger over her temple. "I think that covers most of my questions for tonight..." Her eyes were rimmed red from exhaustion. "I don't know how long we'll be here, but I think we should all rest for now. There's nothing more we can do about that manic queen."

"Yes," I whispered, bowing to everyone. "I am truly sorry, still... I pray you can forgive me, in time."

I took my leave before any of them had a chance to reply. My heart drummed painfully, my breath barely contained. So many eyes, today. So much uncovered... I heard the footfalls of someone following me and inched my head back.

There were two men behind me. Kurrick on my left, and Linus on my right. Neither man looked at the other. Neither man uttered a syllable. They only followed me to my designated barracks on the ground-level, glancing over their shoulders as if searching for dangers in the dark.

We passed by Octavius and Herrin, both ceasing their wood gathering to watch me in silence. Ringëd and his wife did the same, Claude and Sirra-Lynn… Bianca… The rabbit's ears dropped in shock when she met my stare. *Mistress Jilume…* My gaze lingered on her a moment longer. *Please, not you.*

My vision blurred and I hurried into my barracks, shutting the door and sliding my back down it in misery. I let myself weep in solitude.

35

XAVIER

Alex scratched under his chin while watching Hugh roll open his cot, which the boy had tactically placed right beside mine in our crowded barracks.

"So," my brother began, flicking his gaze at me, "when did you find yourself an apprentice?"

I sat cross-legged on my own cot, stroking Chai as the raven nestled on my lap. The electric lamps in here were dim at best, and the only sounds came from whining crickets, belching toads, and the inside chatter from the others of our party who bustled about their bunks.

"I suppose, er…" I cleared my throat. "Tonight. He'd asked at the palace, before the wing went up in flames."

"I see." Alex lifted a brow at the boy. "Then I assume you disagree with what your sister is doing, Hugh?"

Hugh finished unrolling his cot and sat upon it, looking quizzically at my brother. "What is Sy doing?"

I rubbed my eyes. "Oh, Seamstress… Hugh, your sister has just declared war on Grim and Culatia. That's why we left so swiftly."

The boy's lion ears sprouted. "W-what? Why would she do that?"

"There's the question of the night," Alex laughed hauntingly, lowering to his back and folding his arms behind his head.

Dalen's ghost clicked his tongue from a nearby bunk's post. "I still say ya should've called me when the brawling started. I could'a gotten people over there faster."

Vendy, laying flat on her stomach over the top bunk above him and kicking her feet with a thrilled grin, wafted a hand at him. "Hey, don't sweat it. *I* was there at least, so it's not like they weren't protected."

"And where were ya when that crazy queen snagged 'em?" Dalen's ghost challenged. "All I'm sayin' is ya can't have too much backup, right?"

"Yes, well." I yawned, lying back and stared at the stars overhead through the worn hole in the ceiling. "Our lungs were being crushed regardless, we barely had the air to think at the time, Dalen. But we'll have to remember that if it ever happens again."

"Death, don't jinx us," Alex pleaded, covering an arm over his eyes. "We can file this night under one of the worst we've had up here."

Dalen laughed. "I'm surprised you're not used to it by now, *Da'torr*. What is this, the third time you've been driven out of someone's palace?"

"Ninumel didn't drive us out," Alex corrected with a raised finger. "He *politely* demanded us to leave."

Hugh glanced at Dalen in a frown, then addressed me. "Master? Who is this Dalen person you keep speaking to?"

"Ah, Dalen is our vassal," I explained. "He isn't resurrected at the moment, but his soul is with us, over there."

"You mean as a ghost?" Hugh's soul-blind eyes widened, still staring at the corner. "The ones that follow Necrovokers, like in the stories?"

"That's the kind," agreed Alex. "Your master and I share our vassals, since we have identical blood."

"Wow..." Hugh squinted at the bunk post still, as if trying to find Dalen, who chuckled at the boy's strange faces. Then Hugh's gaze moved to Vendy on the top bunk and he blushed. "So... so *you* would normally be a ghost as well, Lady Vendy?"

"Yeah." Vendy shrugged and rolled to her back, picking at her cuticles. "That's how you start as a vassal. But Bloods am I glad I was resurrected for *this* tonight!" She punched the air triumphantly and rolled to her stomach again in a giggle. "It was actually her! The lost Relicblood...!" Vendy sighed dreamily and deflated over her cot. "Thanks, *Da'torr*... you kept your promise, from our Pact. I got to see her. And *you* led me straight to her, from the Bloody beginning at that."

Alex hummed broodingly. "I suppose we did, somehow... though it was by her own doing that she joined us in the first place, I'm not sure if you can count us as having done *anything*."

Vendy turned up her nose. "Nope, it was all you. If you didn't take me as a vassal, I never would have seen it. I would have been stuck in Grim while all this happened."

Alex thought on that. "I suppose... that counts, yes. Then I'm glad we were actually able to keep our end of the Pact to you. Honestly, we assumed it would be a fruitless promise."

I chuckled. "Apparently, we were proven wrong." I absently turned the ring on my finger. Touching the cool metal dampened my mood, suddenly.

The last I'd seen of Willow, she was walking away from the firepit, not even having looked in my direction. She'd barely acknowledged me since we fled the palace. Had I done something wrong?

My ears grew fur, I felt them stretching to points. Death, perhaps she *was* angry about the queen having her way with me?

No. She saw we were tangled in her vines. She wouldn't have known to free us, otherwise. *Then why the silence?*

With a sudden impulse hitting, I stretched to my feet and went to the door.

Alex called after me, "Xavier?"

"I'm going for a walk," I said.

"Now?" He sounded skeptical. "For how long?"

I only shrugged, walking out. He didn't protest behind me. I needed to see her, that much I knew. If something was wrong, I intended to fix it now rather than let it fester, as she seemed to be determined to do.

Chai, perched on the railing outside our barracks, spotted me and flew above my head, following as my heavy steps vibrated the upper boardwalk. I climbed down the nearest ladder, heading for the private hut I knew to be Willow's. My knuckles hesitated over the door, then knocked lightly.

The one who answered was not Willow, but Lilli.

"Oh, Xavier." Lilli rubbed at her lids, yawning. Her black hair was loose over her shoulders in straight, even strands. I saw Oliver was snoozing inside. But there was no Willow.

"Where is she?" I asked. Of course Lilli would know whom I meant.

Lilli peered round the doorframe. "She went to the woods outside the gate. She said she wanted some time alone—"

"Which way?"

Lilli pointed, and I stalked in that direction. When I reached the fence, I noted its electricity was silent, presumably inactive at the moment, so I opened the north gate and treaded through the Blackwood Forest.

"Chai," I called, whistling and extended my arm to let the raven perch there. "Find Jewel for me?"

Chai gave an affirmative croak and flapped off my arm, leading the path through the wood. The campground's lights faded to darkness the further I went, twigs and dry leaves snapping under my bare feet. I hadn't thought to bring boots. I hadn't thought much of anything, at the time. I was quickly regretting that, my soles collecting blisters with each step.

Soon, the only light I had to guide me were the faint glow of my scythe-spheres and the cool wash of silver moonlight that filtered through the canopy of silhouetted leaves.

I followed the raven for some time, journeying deeper into the forest. The farther Chai led me, the more I worried.

What was she doing so far out? Surely, she wasn't taking such pains to avoid only me. She hadn't known I was coming, of that I was certain. Her visions were never so recent, nor so frequent to make any reliable scry.

I relaxed a little. So, I wasn't the problem. Something else was wrong, perhaps something out of my control… And she was isolating herself to drown in it. *Again.*

My wolf ears folded back, and I ducked under a spider's gossamer web. *Nira Cleanse me before I let her shut me out again.* It was time she started confiding in me, damn it.

Chai veered right, perching on a low branch and glanced back at me. He swept his beak toward the lake that waited behind the thicket of trees. Leaves crunched under my blistered feet as I made my way over, and I scratched under Chai's beak in thanks while scanning the lake.

It was a small body of glassy water, lily pads and wide-tongued grass blades curling over the mucky bed. There were several, smaller ponds littering the lake's crown. And floating at the lip of one of those ponds was a cascade of wet, ashen hair.

"What am I doing wrong, Jewel?" Willow's despairing voice rang in my amplified hearing. "First Anabelle, then that loony queen, Zyl is poisoned, *Prince Roji* appeared out of the grey…!" A splash sounded. "Why is the world cracking all at once? Every time, Jewel—*every Bloody time* I think I can relax, not have to worry that something or someone will plot to kill us, that I can for once spend a night in grief or in peace without interruption—*this* happens. Another, Gods damned war starts. Is it me, Jewel? Am I simply the kind of woman people see and think, 'now that looks like someone I could declare war upon'?"

Another splash, steam rising from her little pond. I saw her arms rise from the water and bend back over the grassy lip, which was barely wide enough to separate her pond from the larger lake.

A quick glance to the side showed me her tattered gown and jewelry had been cast aside in the grass.

I cupped a ponderous hand over my mouth, watching her head dip into the water. With a dripping slosh, she resurfaced up to her pale belly, her nude figure all but glowing in the moonlight, white hair draped down her slender back and curling over the sloshing water.

Well, well... With a mischievous smile, I disrobed and quietly slipped into the lake, using my Aquavoking to push myself toward her in near silence.

I reached the narrow, grassy lip that barely separated my lake from her pond as she gave a sigh.

"And I'm sure Xavier will be upset with me," she lamented to her songcrow, who sat in the grass and fluttered her wet wings. "It seems to be a growing pattern, for us... but I can't blame him, can I? I was lucky that girl only wanted to sleep with him—unforgivable as it was—but what if she'd wanted to slit his throat? She'd have done it long before I arrived. Anything could have happened, and I..."

She lowered back in the water, her tone dreary. "It's too much, Jewel. He's the damned *Shadowblood*, that's all I ever hear anymore. These visions are driving me mad as it is, how can I expect to hold a blasted wedding with all this... this absolute *mess* following us wherever we go?"

"Well," I hummed, startling her as I stretched my arms out of the lake and folded them over the grass between us, "we could skip the wedding, if you'd like?"

She gaped at me. "How long have you been there?"

"A bit," I grinned. "And I must agree: you do look like someone I'd declare war upon."

She glowered, sinking to her neck in the pond. "Well... I had planned to apologize for ignoring you again in the morning, but now that *that's* been spoiled, I suppose I've nothing left to say."

"You could say yes," I suggested.

She lifted an ashen eyebrow. "To what?"

"To marrying me."

Her stare went blank. "I thought you said you've regained most of your memories?"

"I have."

"Then you surely remember we're already engaged?" she chuckled. "Asking me again is redundant."

"Not if I'm asking for your hand tonight," I explained. "Right now."

Her gaze turned beguiled. "Right here?"

"Right here."

She tucked a lock of hair behind her ear, her brow creased in thought. "Well, I... I suppose I'm able to officiate us according to Grimish law. But then." She blushed, sinking to her chin. "Do you really wish to wed... naked?"

"As bare as a newly shorn lamb." I smirked. "If one is to wed with neither a ceremony nor an audience, what difference does it make?"

She hid her face behind her hands and laughed. "I don't know whether to be charmed or peeved with you."

"I suggest you grow accustomed to that, darling. I feel it'll be my husbandly duty to have you teetering between the two."

She leered at me sidelong and lifted her chest out of the water, folding her arms over her beading, glistening breasts. "You're sure of this, are you? You'll dash the theatrics? No priest, no gown, no suit, no dancing…"

"The only things we need under the watch of the Mother Goddess," I began and pulled myself out of the water to sit on the grassy lip, only my legs engulfed in the rippling surface. I placed a hand over hers. "Is ourselves. You, me, and our oaths."

"But it's so…" She paused, glancing aside thoughtfully, then sighed. "No, it's not sudden, is it? By rights, we should have wedded the moment the law changed and dubbed me of age. Even still, we should have wedded long before then."

"Which is why I've grown impatient." I gripped her fingers lightly. "I'd made a number of mistakes over the years, but… Bloods, I never should have let you believe I was dead. I should have contacted you. I should have let you know somehow, someway, that I was still waiting for you. I know it's taken me so long to remember everything between us, and there are still moments I'm missing, but in what I *have* regained… Well, I'll show you."

I reached over the grass and touched the surface of her pool, fingers spread as an azure light radiated from my palm. My crowned Dream mark shined from under my knuckles, and Willow pulled away as she gazed at the images now spilling over the water.

This was a trick Alexander and I had learned out at sea. The water could serve as a Seer's looking glass, and in the glowing surface, images appeared.

I sat hunched over my bedroom desk, snapping open and closed the velvet box of engagement-vines under the dim lamplight. Tomorrow, I was to present these to Willow at Festival, for her thirteenth birthday. In front of all those people.

I leaned back in my seat and clutched my fluttering stomach. Blast it all, why couldn't this be done in private? Our betrothal was none of the world's Bloody business…

"Ah!" a small voice gasped outside my veranda door, startling me.

Closing the box of vines, I went to slide open the glass door. Bloody Void! Willow was clinging to the veranda's iron rail for dear life, her eyes wide and brimming with terrified tears.

I stood baffled for a moment, then hurried over. "What in Death's name are you doing up here?" I hissed, pulling her onto the veranda.

She puffed over the grey stone, trembling. "I... I wanted to see you off before you left. Bloods, your room is higher than I thought..."

"I'm not leaving until the day after Festival, you daft bell." I plucked out the stray leaves from her white hair, guessing she must have climbed the vines alongside my wall. How she'd brought herself to do it was a mystery all its own, though. I grumbled, "Now I have to get you out of here without the servants seeing... Your father will have my neck if he knows you're in here."

"You let me worry about my father," she said, her little songcrow alighting over her head. I led her inside and slid the glass door closed, drawing the curtains as she brushed the twigs off her sleepgown. "What's the fuss about, anyway? You've snuck into my room hundreds of times."

"I wasn't scared Deathless of climbing back down the way I came." I rubbed my stinging eyes. How late was it? "Come, I'll fetch you a cloak. Perhaps I can get you through the kitchen door."

Her arms encircled me from behind, pressing herself to my back. "I'm staying here."

I sighed, leaning against her warm weight, a calm flushing over me. Damn that girl. She wasn't making this easy. "The servants will come in the morning," I said, more to remind myself. "If they find you in here, it won't be pleasant."

Her arms tightened round my ribs. "I won't have another chance to see you before you leave."

"You'll see me at Festival."

"That's not the same. Not like this." She released me to circle in front and squeezed my fingers. "Why do you have to go at all? I thought you left Low Everland permanently?"

"Something's come up with my grandfather. He's apparently fed up with being the king's Eyes, and my father has to interview candidates to find a replacement. I'll only be gone a short while. When business is done there, I'll come right back. You won't even notice I'm gone."

"So until then, I'm going to see as much of you as I Bloody well like."

I sat on my bed, smearing a hand over my face. "Relentless, you are... Willow, as much as I want you to stay, what do you expect will happen when the Dreamcatcher—your own mother, mind you—notices both of us are awake?"

"It's not as if we're doing anything immoral." She seated herself beside me, sinking in the mattress. "We're already engaged, anyway."

"That doesn't make it acceptable to our parents."

She kicked her feet. "Why do you have to leave? You can stay here with me, I can ask my father..."

"We've discussed this. My father wants Alex and me there with him, to learn from the experience. So, we're going... and that's that."

She was silent for some time, still kicking her feet broodingly. Then she whispered. "You won't forget about me?"

I let out a chuckle. "I'm not running to the surface or some exotic land far away. And even if I did, I would still come back. I'll always come back."

She bit her lip, Jewel twittering dejectedly from her head. "Swear it?"

I cupped her face to draw her in, stealing the heat from her lips. "I swear. I'll come back for you. You won't have to wait long…"

In the present, I lifted my hand from the water and the scene vanished, the brightness fading from my Dream mark as the original Crest returned under my knuckles.

Willow, the older Willow, hadn't dried her tears, if she'd noticed them at all.

I lifted her chin and gently took her lips, whispering, "I'm sorry… I broke my promise that night. I did not come back. And instead, you came to me. But I… wish to amend that vow. Even if I leave you again, I will always find you. And always, *always*, I will love you."

I kissed her fingers, a heavy fear draining my tone. "But here and now, I don't know what's going to happen. I don't even know if we'll make it back to Grim alive. I keep having that vision of the sky shattering every other night, watching Alex and Jaq and Lilli being butchered—watching *you*…" I swallowed, lungs growing cold. "Something is going to happen, Willow. I don't know when, and I don't know how. And I… don't think we'll be able to wed in Grim, as we planned. But blast me, I waited so long already, I will have you as my wife one way or another. It may as well be now." I retracted, my voice softening. "If you'll have me?"

She was silent for some time, perhaps deliberating… Then she sighed, lifting out of the water to perch beside me. Her lips took mine, her heat burning against my chill.

"Xavier," she said, "As far as I'm concerned, you're already my husband. I intend to spend the rest of my life and afterlife with you, however long or short it may be."

Her fingers were warm against my face, staving off my natural cold. I trapped her hand in mine, relishing the warmth.

"Then," I began, "It's settled. From this day on, under the watch of the Mother Goddess, I live with you as your husband."

Her new, dazzling smile was the most beautiful gift she could grant. "And I with you, as your wife."

When I stole her lips again, I drank in her fire, my cold fingers gliding down her neck. A wisp of steam rose from our touch, every taste an electrifying storm. My pulse tangled; *thrashed* into a strengthening zephyr I didn't care to tame.

I stole her body's sweet warmth and tried to memorize every smooth slope, every curve, every subtle shape her bones dictated under this supple flesh. I tasted her throat, my frosted breath fogging over her neck.

She pulled me down, lowering us to the grass, and my hunger seared hot and ravenous, wanting her, *needing* her, the throbbing ache insatiable as I cooled the burn from her lips and whispered in Grimish, *"Myel ma amya…"*

"Myel ma amya," she returned, and at long, long last, danced with me into bliss.

ALEXANDER

The vision of my brother and Willow, his new *wife*, dissipated, and I found myself back in the crowded barracks with the others. I was sitting upright on my cot with iron-stiff posture.

"They've done it," I said aloud, stunned. I'd had a feeling he would make the decision eventually, but I hadn't thought it would be so soon.

The others turned to me from their bunks, Jaq and Octavius pausing their game of cards from the floor.

Jaq pushed up his glasses and asked, "Who's done what now?"

"Xavier and Willow." I pushed to my feet absently. "They've wedded."

"What!" they all blurted and scrambled to stand, Jaq sputtering loudest. "When?!"

"Just now. They wedded alone."

"But that ain't fair!" Jaq cried. "I was supposed to be best man!"

I shot him a flat glare. "I beg your pardon, but that was to be *my* job."

"Well, now it ain't nobody's job!" He kicked a support beam, a dust of yellow pollen puffing up. "Gods dammit, that impatient bastard!"

Octavius scratched his head thoughtfully, mumbling, "Well, why not throw a party for them here at camp? We could just do it tonight. Not like any of us can sleep anyway, after what happened."

I rubbed my chin. "There's an idea… A reception of sorts would be appropriate."

"Appropriate and merciful," came a new voice from the suddenly opened doorway. Dream was there now, his face sagged with a mixture of annoyance and depression, his blue fox ears folded to his neck. "I Saw the same vision I believe you did. I was supposed to be there for my granddaughter's wedding! They've stolen that from me, but I'll be damned if they take away my dance with her!"

"Then we'd best hurry." I grinned and stalked out. "It seems we've much to prepare."

XAVIER

Crickets whined in their nightly symphony, the lake shining blue and brilliant under the moonlight, smooth as a mirror until the wind rippled its surface with silvery folds.

I watched in a drunken daze as my wife rose to dress before coming to sit beside me. She reached into her Storagesphere that she had set aside before our wondrous, *wondrous* love making. It had been so much more than I'd imagined. Years I'd waited, and Nira save me, it had been worth every miserable moment.

From her Storagesphere, Willow pulled out the elongated box that held her engagement vines and diamond droplet, offering it to me.

Still high on that last wave of ecstasy, I clipped the two vines to her hair, brushing the ashen strands to one side and enjoyed the taste of her lips again before connecting the diamond centerpiece over her brow.

Her smile brightened when she lightly touched the centerpiece, as if unaccustomed to its weight, and she took out a new, smaller box next, revealing the diamond marriage stud that was to be mine.

When she uncapped the backing to free the sharp end, a shiver spilled through my blood. She must have noticed because she asked, "Do you wish to wait for this one?"

I sucked in a breath and straightened in defiance. "No. I'm ready."

She nodded and evoked her fire Hallows, an orange teardrop sparking from her fingertip as she sterilized the needle and brought it to my left ear. I shut my eyes, teeth barred as I braced, and grunted at the brief pain that speared my lobe. It was over so quickly, I hadn't noticed her cap the backing afterward.

I lifted a hand to my newly heavy ear, which still throbbed slightly as I acquainting myself with the stud's foreign weight.

"Now then, Death Prince Xavier Ember," she said, rising as she reached a hand to me. "How does it feel to be a married man?"

"Shamefully overdue." I took her fingers and let her pull me to my feet, my smile feeling permanent. "Why had we waited so long?"

"Being trapped in your brother's body made for an excusable setback, I'd say."

I grimaced, finding my clothes on the grass and dressed. "Could we pretend all of that never happened? I'm my own Bloody man again, I'd like to forget the years I spent in inexistence."

She chuckled and looped an arm around mine, leading us back to camp through the forest, her marriage vines and centerpiece glinting in the patches of moonlight that shone through the canopy.

"How do you suppose the others will take the news?" She mused.

I snorted. "If they're wise, they'll go about their day as they otherwise would have. They all knew how long we'd waited, it should be met with no surprise or care that we…" I hushed, the sound of a bow drawing over a fiddle hitting my ears. It came from the orange glow of the encampment ahead.

No, it was more than the lone fiddle. The longer I listened, the more instruments came into existence. A flute, a tambourine, a few slurred voices singing as if in a drunken cheer. There was chatter all throughout, laughter, several voices piercing above the rest, which all sounded like members from our personal group.

Willow frowned. "I thought everyone had gone to bed?"

"As had I," I said, suspicious.

When we reached the electric fence, making sure the low hum of power was absent, I opened the north gate for Willow and me to walk through.

"Announcing the arrival!" a woman's voice cut through the crowd's chatter. That had been Crysalette. The orange-haired queen waved a hand in our direction. "Of Her Highness Willow and her newlywedded husband, Death Prince Xavier!"

Willow and I stiffened at the sudden wave of cheers that greeted us, and we were swept into the crowd by too many ushering hands to count.

"Wait now!" I protested as someone—Bianca—shoved me into an empty ring patch that our company had formed around us. "How… how in Bloody Death did you all find out?"

Willow grimaced beside me. "I bet I know how."

She was glaring at her azure-haired grandfather in the back of the crowd, a pleased smile decorating his face. At his side was my brother, his arms folded as he shot me a sly smirk.

Bloody Seers and their scrying visions. Exactly how much had Alexander spied—?

Jaq shoved me from behind and I all but fell onto Willow.

"Go on 'n dance already!" shouted Jaq, pounding a mug of foaming drink on the nearby table and spilled some with each impatient hit.

The music from before started again with a lively jig. I glanced at Willow, rubbed my neck, and we found ourselves laughing.

"Shall we?" I grinned, offering her my hand.

She took it with an ostentatious curtsy. "It would be my pleas—*oh!*"

I yanked her to me by the waist and twirled my chuckling wife with a jovial step, gliding her along as we spun to the beat of the clapping crowd.

36

SYREEN

I paced the charred remains of the ballroom, my lion tail whipping behind me. "Where could he be?" I growled, unable to discern panic from rage. "It's been two days, and Hugh…" My claws grew, piercing my own, clenched fists. I snapped my gaze at the Leaflites who were standing rigidly around me and screamed, "Search the town! Upturn every damned home and establishment!"

They saluted and left to do as commanded, leaving me to my pacing. Genevieve remained at my side.

Hugh… dearest brother…

I prayed to Shel he was unharmed. He couldn't be found in the palace, so I hoped it was a sign that he was still alive. Perhaps he was simply hiding, having been frightened from the massacre at the ball? *Or…* My lungs quivered with a sinking horror. *Perhaps the Reapers did precisely as I feared and stole him from me?*

My only comfort was knowing their ship was in ruins. They couldn't leave now without being seen by my patrolling women at the harbor. I'd originally planned to blame the fire on the resistance, to persuade the Reapers to help me exterminate those feral rats… but the rebels found them first.

No matter. My heart's fire blazed anew. *If they cannot leave, then they cannot take my brother with them.*

I snarled and withdrew the blade waiting at my hip, striking at a splintered pillar in a fury. "Every one of them will pay…!" My throat crackled hot with the vow. "If harm befalls my dearest Hugh, I'll rip out their hearts… The Relicbloods will find their Blood soaking my fingers!"

Genevieve neither moved nor spoke a reply. The viper woman merely did as she always did, standing at my side in wait of orders. I growled at her. "Genevieve, assemble my generals. We have soldiers to prepare. This false *Queen of Land* will be exposed for the fraud she is." My claws punctured my palm as the fist tightened. "And worry not, Hugh… I'll see you safe at my side again."

Genevieve bowed. "As you wish, my queen."

As she left, a feeble old man shied inside, lingering under the crumbled frame. "My… My lady…?" he stammered. It was Lornard, one of my man servants.

My burning glare made him flinch as I clipped, "*What?*"

"Th-th-th… there's a-a… a prisoner, in the dungeons, Majesty…" The mousey man was shaking, sweat beading at his unkempt brow. "The guards-women asked m-m-me to t-t-tell you… my lady…"

"What prisoner?" I demanded.

"She's…" He licked his lips, taking a new, deep breath. "They've reason to believe she's a member of this… Enlightener's Guild, Majesty."

My lion ear flicked. "The group who speaks of the Shadowblood?"

He nodded, keeping under the blackened frame as if he feared taking another step would sign his death. "Th-they think she is an oracle, also. Among her books and belongings, they found a crystal ball. And she bares a Dream mark on her back."

"Does she?" My lips curled hungrily. "Tell the guardswomen I wish to see this oracle."

MARIAN

Breathing hurt. My throat burned. I could only wheeze, like a broken flute sputtering noise. Was that drool dripping…? Or was it blood?

Crack!

I screamed, the skin on my back splitting open again under the leather whip. I squirmed, no longer piloting my limbs, but my arms were chained above me, clipped wings spread open with cinching ropes.

Another warm stream of liquid ran down my back, rolling over the length of my bare, bronzed skin.

Crack!

I heaved another feral shriek, my wheezing turning to crackles.

Though my ears were ringing, I still heard the dungeon's upper doors creak open, and my tormenter paused her work.

A girl walked down the steps and came into the flickering firelight. She wore a crown atop her cropped hair, her gown trailing behind her, adorned in colorful jewels and elegant beadwork.

She was smiling, like a mother would to her child.

Or like a stalking beast to its prey. I ground my teeth, ignoring the iron taste of blood.

The torturer behind me coiled her whip and came between the young queen and me, bowing. "My liege," she said, "She still refuses to speak."

The queen waved a gentle hand. "It's perfectly all right... I simply wish to speak with this one in private. If you'll allow, that is?"

The guard bowed again. "Of course, my lady. Call if I am needed. I will be at the door."

The queen nodded cheerfully, cupping her hands over her delicate skirts while she waited for the guard to stomp up the stairs and shut the heavy door.

"Now, then." The queen gave a flighty, smiling sigh, stepping toward me while upholding her unscathed poise. "My deepest apologies for my women's abhorrent treatment. You are a guest here."

I spat a red glob at her sparkling skirt.

She didn't flinch at the new stain. She only smiled wider. "I hear you were in possession of a few... questionable books? Ones that spoke of the Shadowblood?"

She waited for my answer. Waited in vain.

She paced the sullied floor, circling out of sight behind me. "And I see you do indeed have a Dream mark... Crystal balls are only needed for oracles, are they not?"

Land... What is she plotting?

She came around to face me, frowning. "You're not a very chatty girl, are you? Pity..."

She lifted a hand, which gleamed gold, and brought the thorny vines that were wilting in their pots from the ceiling down to us. The plants slithered and twisted, unwinding themselves into tiny, sharp slivers.

"I didn't wish to resort to such barbaric measures." Her smile now displayed pearly, predator teeth. "But I'm afraid I haven't the patience for conventional methods of extraction. My brother is missing. I believe the Shadowblood has taken him. Now, let me ask you, fair oracle: Where."

I squealed in terrible agony, the thorny vines puncturing through my hands and wriggling under my skin, thrashing and sliding like snake tongues as they climbed up my arms.

She reached into the satchel at her hip and produced my crystal ball, the one I thought I had lost, and shoved it into my hand as her throat ruptured a nasty sneer. "Is."

I screamed as the vines bit deeper, crawling to my shoulders and licking under the flesh.

"My Hugh?"

The vines ripped free.

37

XAVIER

I was stirred awake when a warm body shifted under me. Willow's long locks were thrown over her pillow, leaving her neck exposed and ripe for me to taste.

"Good morning," I whispered and kissed down her jaw, gliding a hand over her smooth belly.

My wife gave a drowsy hum when she rolled on her back and connected our lips. She smiled, reaching her fingers to the marriage stud in my left ear. "I see you haven't tired of these mornings yet," she said.

"I doubt I'll ever tire of them." I fastened our lips again, more voracious this time.

I rolled on top of her, making her chuckle.

"Why, darling," she said, a smirk crossing her face, "whatever could you want before you run off to training? Which, need I remind you, is in a few moments?"

"A few? Well, that's more than I was expecting."

She chuckled again and slid out from under me. "Save your strength, love." She went to the corner of our private barracks, where her tunic had been thrown aside the night before. I shamelessly leered as she bent to retrieve it. She slid the tunic over her head and pulled her long hair out of the collar, then caught me staring and grinned. "Xavier, really. You were groaning about your aching muscles last night, do you really expect me to believe they're already healed?"

"I'll be fine." I made a mental effort to stop myself from wincing while pushing up. Laying down hadn't felt so horrible, but now I was blisteringly reminded of my two-week training regimen with Alex. Though in truth, it wasn't nearly as terrible as the first few days. My muscles were growing conditioned to the routine, which was a good sign.

I went to trap her in my arms from behind, inhaling the scent of her throat. "For you, darling, I can ignore anything. Especially a little soreness…"

She sighed, taking my arm and *squeezed* the bicep until I yelped. She crossed her arms expectantly.

I scowled, wolf ears growing from the pain. "Fine… point taken…"

I went to the other corner to find my own clothes, half sulking and half biting down the burn in my legs as I knelt to inspect my discarded trousers. I supposed I was exhausted anyway. Alex had been drilling most of us these past weeks, and he did not hold back. I'd especially been worked like a dog, since I now had an apprentice to watch over *while* I was training.

Hugh was a dedicated student, but Bloods, he was severely sheltered and under developed as a soldier. It was hard enough to train myself in the state I was in, but to train two Reapers on the same muscular level? Death, it was tiring.

I blinked when Willow suddenly came around and crouched over my still-undressed lap. She herself still wore nothing save for her tunic.

"I believe these are mine," she said, taking the trousers I held and tossed them to the floor. "But I've decided I won't be needing them for a few moments."

My mood took a dramatic, and hardened, turn. "What of my 'aching muscles'?" I asked.

"Oh, you won't be using them." She pushed me to my back and mounted, grinning thirstily. "I'd say it's my turn to do the work, don't you think?"

"Death, I love you."

Her icy leer was mischievous. "Was that a curse, or were you calling my name?"

My reply came as a moan when she dipped.

OCTAVIUS

Neal threw down his last card and let out a smug laugh. "I win again."

The rest of us groaned and upturned our hands. Alex and Jaq started scooping up the cards and shuffled them again while Hugh sat cross-legged on the floor with us, the kid watching with that usual, fascinated look of his whenever a guy did anything remotely interesting.

I guessed to him we were just weird foreigners, which made us cool or something. Even though Neal and me were technically Landish, just like him. But only our skin color really showed that. And *we* didn't come from a matriarch.

Maybe what really had him so starry eyed was the fact that men were doing the same things as the women. Void, we were even bunking with them in all the barracks halls. The first time Vendy and El walked in, he was blushing so hard I thought he was sunburned.

Speaking of El…

I looked over my shoulder where her usual cot was. It was empty, obviously. She left some hours ago, her wings drooped when I saw her leave while everyone else was sleeping. She'd also been crying again.

My cat ears grew.

"Well!" Neal slapped his knees and lifted to his feet. "Drill's supposed to start in a bit. Where's our Death Prince?"

Alex shuffled the cards over the floor with a quick snapping sound, the corners zippering in a smooth cadence. "Late again, it seems," he noted. "If you wish to head down, we'll wait for him here for another half hour."

Neal shrugged and went to walk out. "Sure."

I pushed up too, following after my brother. "I'll see if El's there yet. Might need to get her from Prince Roji's again."

Alex nodded in understanding. "If we're not there in ten minutes, Octavius, start Drill for me. Like before."

"Right…" I walked out with Neal.

Alex sort of made me his stand-in drill instructor since day one. I had no idea why in Land he thought I was a good candidate—Neal and Xavier were way better at telling people what to do. I felt like a feral flounder squirming on a hook, fumbling with orders while the block members stared at me like I was speaking gibberish.

Well, I guessed to El, it probably *was* mostly gibberish… but she was learning a lot more Landish words, with our nightly vocab swapping sessions. She was teaching me some Culatian too, but I didn't know all that much yet. To her, I probably sounded like a toddler.

Neal walked alongside me down the upper boardwalk until we climbed down the ladder onto the field. We went to the usual spot, where most of our block members were gathered. Some of them were stretching, some relaxing and chatting, others looked like they were meditating on the patch of dirt… there used to be grass here, but we've been stomping all over it that it was totally worn down now.

Neal started stretching his arms across his chest and fell into the mass with the others. I craned to look at all the faces, but didn't see El. And if I didn't see her immediately, then she wasn't there.

She was always easy to spot: blue wings, white hair, cat ears, pretty walnut-brown skin, sunny yellow eyes, cute smile… Well, when she *did* smile. She hadn't been doing that all too much lately.

I sighed, looking at Prince Roji's house in the distance. Was she still over there?

Neal whistled suddenly, getting my attention. "Tavius," he said, then threw his head to the left in a gesture.

My eyes followed that direction. *Oh.* There she was.

Her back was facing us, blue wings draped so low her feathers were on the ground. She sat alone on a log by one of the doused firepits. My stomach sank to see her cat ears were folded down, her shoulders sagged.

I shoved my hands in my pockets and made my way over to her. When I was behind her, I heard a soft sniffle, and she ran an arm under her nose while staring at a bundle of pine-straw in her hand. She took her other hand and evoked her Pyrovoking, her fingers tipped with little droplets of flames, and set the bundle's end on fire. She didn't do anything with it afterward, just stared. Watched the smoke curl in the air in silence.

I leaned over her shoulder cautiously. "El?"

She jumped and rubbed her wet eyes. "*Ye, ye…* Tavii…"

She's been calling me that for a while. It took too much effort to say all those syllables at first, so it sounded awkward. And I liked the shorter name, actually. Especially when *she* said it.

"*Kegttcha…*" I said, trying to collect the few words I knew to form something coherent. "*Kegttcha… za… T'ollo?*"

All right, so I knew I butchered that, but it looked like she understood it.

"Am okay," she said. She was better at Landish than I was at Culatian. She smoothed back her hair, which was tied in a tail on the side of her head, and went back to staring at the burning bundle of pine-straw. "But yes… am sad."

"<Sad… of Zyl?>" I asked, sitting on the log beside her and folding my arms over my knees. "<She not is wake?>"

She shook her head, rubbing an eye. "No… still sleeping. Bianca not know if she ever wake up…" she choked off, then her face fractured and she fell onto my shoulder, crying.

I went stiff. *Crap. What do I do?*

I took a minute to let her bawl before awkwardly putting a hand on her back. "<Zyl…>" I said. "<is wake *three*.>"

She paused her sobbing a little, staring up at me with a scrunched brow. "*R-Re?*"

"<Zyl is wake three,>" I repeated. "<I doctor see checks. Shells tight hooker doorknobs.>"

She burst into a laugh, drying her runny nose. "Tavii." She hiccupped and kept giggling. "Tavii, that no make sense. What you try saying?"

I rubbed my neck and switched to Landish. "Uh, sorry… I was trying to say: Zyl should wake up soon. I checked on her last night. She's showing good signs of recovering."

"<Really?>" She sniffed loudly, wiping her eyes. Then she gave that cute smile and giggled again. "*Skrii*, that not what you said."

"Oh... what did I say?"

"I not know Landish words for it. But it funny." She stifled a chuckle behind a hand. *Shel*... Her eyes were glassy and a little red from crying, but she was so damn cute when she looked at me like that. I just wish it wasn't because I sounded like a four-year-old.

I gave up on trying Culatian for now, sticking with my own language. "What is that for?" I asked and pointed to the bundle of pine-straw she was still holding. The fire had almost reached her hand.

El shrugged and watched the straws burn away to the end. "It nice to look at." She said the rest of it in Culatian, but most of it I couldn't make out. I took a guess from her tone that it was important, though. Maybe watching it helped her calm down? Like a way to soothe herself?

I didn't want to look like an idiot, so I didn't say anything, in case I was wrong. I just nodded, pretending like I understood all that. Has she ever done that for me when *I* went on ramblings in Landish?

She stopped herself midsentence, blinking at me. I stopped myself from wincing. *Damn it, she caught me.*

She pursed her lips and tried again in Landish. "It help El... not be the hot one. See—" She took my hand and pulled it over the back of her neck, and I bit back a blush when a wave of heat washed under my palm.

"It too hot, being *Pyrovokit*," she sighed. "Letting out fire help to be cold. Just little."

My ears were thumping so loud, the constant static of menial germs was kicked out of my attention. Bloods, she *was* burning, and her skin was so *soft*... Her neck was skinny enough for my fingers to curve around the sides. Panicking, I had an impulse to rip my hand away, but she had it pinned there under her own hand.

This... I swallowed, my face getting almost as hot as her skin. ... *would be so much better if she knew what I was and STILL let this happen.*

But if she knew about my Infeciovoking, she wouldn't want to touch me at all. Land, what if she stopped talking to me altogether? *It wouldn't be the first time that happened.*

She let go of my hand, and I tried not to act petrified as I set it on my leg in a cough.

She scooped another bundle of straw up from the ground and lit that one on fire too, the Death mark on her forehead shining white.

"S-so..." I rubbed my shoulder, desperately thinking of something to say. "You really care about Zyl, huh?"

El's yellow eyes glazed over. "Zyl is… El's friend. *Only* friend. No one like El at home…"

I frowned. "Why not?"

"El not…" She shrugged with her wings, and then flicked her cat ears. "Normal. There only being birds, in Culatia. No cats, but visitors." She let the bundle of straw burn out and crossed her legs. "El's mother is being bird. But father… I not ever knowing father. He was visitor cat from Grim. El was… how say… mistake. So, no one at home like El."

"But why's it matter?" I asked. "Everyone should like you. I mean, you're sweet, you're smart, you're *really* cute—" I froze, shutting up. *Land, did I just say that out loud?*

She looked confused, one cat ear folding. "What word mean… 'cute'?"

"Um, never mind." I shot to my feet, giving her a nervous smile and threw a thumb toward the block. "Uh, how about we start stretches…?"

HUGH

My eyes flicked at Sir Alexander, who sat hunched over the floor with his gaze dipping and rising, as if trying to look at Sir Jaq across from him, Lady Vendy beside him, and the single card in his hand simultaneously.

Sir Alexander took his time, scowling and scratched at the stubble that had grown wild over his neck and jaw. After a time, his strange, blue-and-white eyes focused on Sir Jaq and he revealed his last card.

"Jester of Wings," he announced, throwing the tattered card over the one that Sir Jaq had placed before this.

Sir Jaq smirked and pushed up his eyeglasses, then placed *his* final card over Sir Alexander's Jester. "Jester of *Tails*."

"—Jester of FANGS!" Lady Vendy shouted and slapped down her final card over Sir Jaq's.

Sir Alexander cursed, looking to me now. "Tell me you have something higher?"

Sir Jaq heckled. "Won't do *you* much good. Ya ain't gettin' it back."

"Which is why it would warm my heart to see Hugh take both of them from you and Vendy, you cheating bastards."

I looked at my last card, flushing. It was more than a little unnerving to have them all staring at me so intently. Especially Lady Vendy…

"Um…" I took my last card and set it over Sir Jaq's latest play. "Prince of Fangs…"

"What!" Sir Jaq's glasses almost slid off when he crouched to look closer. "You gotta be Bloody..."

Sir Alexander let loose a satisfied guffaw, picking up the two lesser cards he'd won this round while I took the three Jesters and my Prince.

Sir Jaq and Lady Vendy were left with nothing in their hands. They had both lost the game.

Sir Alexander was still laughing. "Well, Hugh," he said and threw down his hand, scooping up the deck. "I have nothing that can beat that. You've won this round."

I couldn't help but beam. This was the first time I'd won this game. I only just learned it a week ago from Sir Alexander and Sir Jaq. It was the same old deck of playing cards I was familiar with, but the game itself was of Grimish origin.

From my understanding, the five suits were the usual: Claws, Wings, Scales, Tails, and Fangs. But for this game, that specific order was the ranking value, where Claws was the lowest and Fangs was the highest. Suit took first priority, and then its ranking identity was next: Page, Squire, Knight, Jester, Prince, Princess, Queen, and King. The goal of the game was to take the cards of the other players and end up with the highest ranks after going around and placing one card at a time.

This was my first time winning, and right now my blood raced with pride as Sir Alexander put away the cards, still laughing.

"All right," Sir Alexander said, pushing to his feet and drawing back the curtain of our small barrack's window. "Well, we've waited long enough. Octavius and Neal left... what, thirty minutes ago?"

"Just about," grunted Sir Jaq, who rose and stretched his scaled arms. Sir Jaq was very tall. It was one of the first things I noticed when Sir Alexander introduced him.

Sir Jaq gave a grin, displaying his long fangs. "Fifty crunches says our royal Death Prince got side tracked by his lower regions again."

"You think I'm stupid enough to bet against that while they're still on their honeymoon?" Sir Alexander snorted. "You must think me a damned fool."

"How long is that supposed to last, anyway?" Lady Vendy asked and stretched to her feet, her rabbit ears straightening as she pulled her long, brown braid over a shoulder. "It's been a couple weeks, hasn't it?"

Sir Alexander shrugged. "I've heard it can take a month or two, for some newlyweds. Even a year."

Sir Jaq hummed. "Should we go and steal him for drill?"

Sir Alexander scratched the stubble at his neck again, as if considering. "Just leave him be," he decided. "We are in times of war. He should be with his wife as much as he can."

Sir Jaq grunted his agreement while I sat blushing on the floor, my knees held to my chest.

Master had been staying in his own private barracks with his wife since we first arrived at this camp. He'd asked before if I wished to be housed with them instead, since I was his apprentice, but I declined exactly for the reason Sir Alexander had just mentioned. I would be beyond uncomfortable if I wedged myself into their private quarters, especially so soon after their marriage.

With me there, they would probably feel pressured to abstain from doing… well, what married couples were expected to do. The last thing I wanted was to prevent Master from spending those private moments with his wife. That's why I resigned myself to these quarters instead, with other camp members. Not that I minded. I may not have known hardly anyone in here when I first started out, but thanks to Sir Alexander and Sir Jaq, I was properly introduced to the rest.

Apparently, Master had come to Neverland with many an acquaintance. They were intriguing people, all from varying cultures and upbringings. There was rarely a boring moment in here.

Sir Alexander sighed and opened the door, golden glitters of morning sunrays spilling over his Grim-pale complexion. The dark grey hairs curling from his chest and arms may have dampened his chalky tint, but against the light, he all but glowed. Sir Jaq's scales were just as reflective when he stepped outside next. It was a stark contrast so Lady Vendy's dark walnut tone as she stalked outside next, her sword now sheathed at her hip.

When I followed out to the upper boardwalk after them, I glanced at my exposed arms. There was no such reflection to my bronzed, red-tinted skin. Though, the sunlight gave my complexion a subtle, more vibrant gloss.

Sy had always said how the sun enhanced my beauty… She said I was blessed by Rin to have such smooth, sun-kissed skin. *You will have hundreds of women fighting over you,* she'd tease and ruffle my hair, *you will be quite the precious catch, dearest brother…*

My chest felt like stone. *Sy…*

"Prince Hugh?" Lady Vendy called, pulling me out of my daze. One of her rabbit ears lowered in question at me. "Where'd you space off to?"

I swallowed a blush. Despite what Sy had said that day, I found that the one woman I actually *wished* to catch the attention of hardly treated me different from everyone else at camp… where I was from, the women were the ones to approach the men about a courtship. But Sir Neal informed me that Lady Vendy's culture in Everland expected the opposite. Perhaps if *I* approached her first, she would… maybe…

My stomach fluttered nervously, and I held my breath, evoking my Arborvoking over a nearby branch over the railing. The branch glittered with gold light and grew outward toward me, its leaves sprouting anew as a vibrant, violet flower blossomed from within the new growth.

I plucked the violet and thrust it out toward Lady Vendy, sputtering. "L-Lady Vendy," I gulped the knot in my throat. "P-p-please... accept this token... a-as—"

She slapped it out of my hand. I watched with a cracked heart as the violet fluttered to the boardwalk at my feet, then snapped up my broken gaze at her.

"Are you an *idiot?*" She said, horrified. And yet, I could swear her dark cheeks were flushed pink. "I can't Bloody believe you would...! *ARGH!*" She bit back a breath, then ran off over the boardwalk, leaving me stiff and hollow beside Sir Alexander and Sir Jaq.

Sir Jaq blinked after her. "Uh. Wow, that was harsh."

"Indeed," Sir Alexander murmured skeptically. He rubbed his stubbled chin in thought. "Commendable bravery, Hugh, for such forwardness... Odd though, I wouldn't have expected a reaction like that from her."

My soul wilted as I watched Lady Vendy descend to the grounds and stomp across the camp looking terribly livid now. "Had... Had I done it wrong, for her culture?" I asked shakily.

Alex hummed. "No, by all standards, such a gesture is even favorable in Grim. Perhaps... hmm. I hadn't expected this. Perhaps Xavier and I should have a particular discussion with our vassals that we neglected to broach..."

I sighed and watched Lady Vendy disappear into the cook's tent. *Well, so much for that attempt...*

I gazed over the boardwalk's railing, watching the camp members organize into their usual blocks. Some were stretching, others were clashing swords in an exercise, and some were training hand-to-hand combat. Stormchasers cast a volley of arrows at trees, Wavecrashers practiced routine stances and thrusts with their tridents, Reapers did the same for their scythes...

It really looked like a training ground for an army. *An army set on killing Sy.*

That stone in my chest grew mountainous.

"Hugh," Sir Alexander called. "Put it out of mind. Best you didn't dally. If you're late to drill, I'll have *both* you and your master carrying extra rocks during laps."

I jolted, seeing he and Sir Jaq were already making their way down the boardwalk. I trotted after them... but once I reached a second, intersecting path, I slowed to a stop. That was where Master's quarters waited...

"Hugh?" Sir Alexander called once more.

I pursed my lips, then said, "I'll be right there! If I'm late, I will bear my punishment."

I bowed respectfully, then jogged down the adjacent boardwalk. Lady Lilac came swooping over my head, flying ahead to the railing outside Master's quarters. There were two other messengers perched there. One was that tiny black ball of feathers that belonged to the Death Princess, and the second was a larger raven with a scar running down its right eye. That one was Chai—Master's companion.

Lady Lilac flapped beside Chai, fluffing her chest feathers proudly while the two began a croaking conversation, the tiny one twittering along with them.

I'd nearly reached the black birds when Master himself emerged from his quarters. His long, grey hair fell to his shoulders, shallow cheeks reflecting the sunlight off his marble-grey skin just like it had done with Sir Alexander.

Were they really twins?

Sure, they had the same pale complexion, dark grey hair and mismatched eyes, but that was the only similarity I could find. For one thing, Sir Alexander kept his hair short, and had far more muscle. Master was a slender man with a thin face and long hair. Overall, Master looked... gentle, despite the scar running down his right eye, much like his messenger's puckered wound. Master could be stern, as I've found out when I spoke out of turn or made a mistake, but outside of that, he had a softness to him. And for that, I was glad I'd chosen him and not Sir Alexander. Even outside of training, Master's brother could be strict, unkind and even rude beyond belief. Master was strict himself, but he was never unkind. Not that I'd seen, anyway.

When Master came out of his quarters, he was tugging on his tunic, covering his hollow chest and ribbed torso. His wife came behind him, tying on a jingling bell to her hair with a black ribbon.

When I trotted over, Master noticed me. "Ah, Hugh," he said. Then his brow furrowed. "I know I'm late, but that doesn't excuse you as well."

"I know, Master," I panted, a bit out of breath from the short run over. "I'll accept whatever punishment Sir Alexander finds fit."

"I'd prefer if his punishments weren't necessary at all." He crossed his arms, gazing down at me. "I'll allow it this once, as a warning, but I can't tolerate poor punctuality after this, Hugh."

"But you're *always* late, Mas..."

He lifted an eyebrow at me, and my tongue froze.

Drat. I did it again... I quickly amended, "Forgive me, Master. I spoke out of turn..."

"That you did." He drummed his skinny fingers over his boney arm. "You forget your rank, apprentice. My actions, while I admit aren't exactly commendable, are my own. They aren't an excuse for a ward to skip his training without permission."

I bowed, blushing. "I'm sorry, Master."

"Forgiven," he said, "for now. Next time, I'd rather you catch yourself before opening your mouth, if you can manage. If not… well, perhaps you'd like to spend drill standing on your head with your hands tied to your back in front of everyone?"

I promptly shook my head.

His wife hid a chuckle behind her hand. "I'll leave you two to your training." She winked at me. "Don't let him bully you too much, Hugh. If you ever want revenge, I can arrange something."

"Conspiring with my student, darling?" He took her fingers and brought them to his lips. "Perhaps I should find a fitting punishment for you as well…"

She laughed and started off down the boardwalk. "I look forward to it, love."

He smiled as she left.

Watching him made me smile, too. Master adored his wife. And she so clearly adored him. Could I have something like that one day? A wife that was not only a warrior, but a strong, caring woman who would look at me the way she looked at Master…?

With the way things were going with Lady Vendy, I thought miserably, *it likely would NOT be with her…*

Master took in a breath and exhaled, turning away from where his wife had left. "All right, Hugh," he said, "best we get to training before my brother comes up with a better punishment than he probably already has planned for us."

He walked ahead of me, and my legs spurred into action to keep up.

"Um!" I had to take longer steps to match his pace. "Master, there was something I wished to speak with you about."

He didn't slow, but gave me a sidelong glance as he pulled out a string from his pocket and tied his long hair into a tail. "Yes, Hugh?"

"I know you said before that we're trying to overtake the capital," I began, hesitating. "And I know it's a good thing we're trying to do… but what if…" I braced myself in case I was in for another scolding. "What if Sy steps down from the throne?"

I cringed when he looked down at me. But his voice was quieter than expected. "If she steps down?"

I nodded meekly. "If she agrees to give her crown to the Land Queen, then she won't be hurt, right?"

"If she agrees, of course she'll be spared," Master said, looking puzzled. "But it won't be that simple, Hugh. I know you care for your sister, but I doubt she'd be willing to part with her kingdom so easily."

"I can talk to her. She would listen to me. If I just explained why Queen Anabelle needs the crown, then…"

"Hugh." Master knelt to me. "These things aren't solved so perfectly. Your sister is a prideful woman—and a little insane, probably. Anything you say to her will likely be dismissed as lies that we supposedly told you."

"But I could—"

"Hugh." His tone held more edge this time. "Why are we fighting?"

I stood at attention, as practiced, and recited, "because Sy has declared war upon us."

"And why has… Sy… declared war?"

"Because she doesn't want to give up her crown to Queen Anabelle."

"That's what it has *become*," he corrected. "What was the initial reason she made the declaration?"

I blushed, glancing off to the side. "Because your wife wouldn't let Sy claim you."

"Precisely," he muttered, a hint of resentment in his tone. "Now, following that logic, what would we have to do to stop the fighting?"

I mumbled. "Let her claim you…"

"Wrong."

I blinked at him, baffled. "But you said that's why she started it in the first place?"

"It was the spark that drove her immediate decision," he agreed. "But that won't solve anything now. In truth, we discovered your sister had planned to not only claim us, but to slaughter the Reapers once we helped her conquer Everland. From there, she planned to move her now doubled troops into Grim and conquer *us* next, one Undercontinent at a time."

My shoulders tensed. "You don't know that."

"I wish we didn't," he grunted. "But my brother's and my prophetic Hallows showed us too many things about your sister we didn't *want* to know. After seizing control of Grim, I imagine she would have tried moving to the other nations as well, though that's merely speculation. The point is, Hugh…" His gaze grew drastically serious. "It was never about claiming us. That was her excuse, to mask her true intent. And her real reason is something we can't allow. She seeks to kill and conquer. We're sworn to prevent this however we can."

"But killing her would go against the Creed," I protested, willing back the water stinging my eyes. "Protect, defend, preserve and foster every life and afterlife'. Putting her to death would break the code, wouldn't it?"

Master stared at me for a moment, dumfounded. "You memorized the Creed?"

"Every line."

A small, proud grin fractured his lips. "I only wrote it down for you yesterday… It took Alex and me weeks to remember all of it."

"I was up most of the night studying." I hurriedly wiped away a traitorous tear.

"Well, if you meant to impress me, you've done it." He chuckled grimly, then sighed. "But the Creed is meant to remind us of our morals, should we forget them. Or, in this case, if we're forced to break them."

"But it doesn't have to be broken at all."

Master paused. "Let me ask you something, Hugh. You love your sister, don't you?"

I nodded vigorously.

"And I assume you love all of your brothers in the palace as well?"

"Of course." Though, I didn't know why he was bringing up my brothers.

"I want you to imagine a scenario," he said, lifting his hands as if weighing them separately, "where, for whatever reason, your sister threatened your brothers and tried to kill every one of them."

My eyes bulged. "She would never—!"

"Humor me. This is all hypothetical, but I need you to understand this."

I clicked my teeth shut, nodding broodingly.

He went on, "Pretend your sister went *completely* insane. Perhaps she was convinced your brothers had murdered you and covered it up, which may be why, in her hypothetical eyes, you disappeared. And now, seeking her delusional revenge, started slaughtering all of them one by one. Now pretend you walk in and see her killing off your brothers. So, herein lies the question…"

He raised one hand. "Do you sit back and allow her to kill them?" He raised the other hand. "Or do you fight her to protect your brothers?"

"I would… protect my brothers," I answered. "But that doesn't mean I would need to kill Sy. In such a scenario, wouldn't she stop once she saw I was alive?"

"That's assuming she'd snap out of her rage to see you in time. Sometimes, Hugh, things don't go the way we want. We can spare your sister if she chooses to relinquish her throne peacefully. That's our ideal outcome. But we have to account for the more likely possibility that she *won't*. It is entirely her choice… all we can do is pray she chooses wisely."

I glowered at my feet. "Maybe... maybe I could convince her to make the right choice. I could walk back into the palace, she would see it was me and listen."

"And if you meet any guards who might *not* recognize you so readily? While Lady Lilac follows you everywhere and marks you as a Reaper?" He gestured to Lady, who flapped over our heads alongside Chai.

"I could tell Lady to stay here," I said.

"Could you bring yourself to do that, knowing there's still a chance your sister won't listen? What if she attacks us here while Lady Lilac is with us, alone, and is put in danger?"

I wilted at the thought. Bloods, I hadn't considered that...

Master rose. "I can't stop you, if you wish to leave the camp and try to convince her... but I would prefer if you stayed. If she kept you there during an attack, and we were to invade the palace..." His brows arched worriedly. "I can't guarantee one of our own men wouldn't kill you, simply because he wouldn't know who you were."

My stomach twisted further. "Oh..." The more I thought about it, the more idiotic my plan sounded. But I didn't want Sy to die...

Sometimes things don't go the way we want.

Master had a point. Though, I wished he'd have picked a less farfetched analogy. Sy wasn't about to go on a murdering rampage with my half-brothers. But she *would* kill Master if given the chance. If she and Master were to fight...

"This is so confusing," I lamented, scratching my head. "It's getting harder to know what's right and wrong anymore."

Master smiled wanly. "I hate to tell you this, but it only gets harder with age. Nothing is ever as black and white as we would like... most times, it's the shades in between that get muddled in the complexity of it all."

Master placed a hand on his side, his look questioning. "So then, what are you going to do? Go back to your sister, or stay here?"

I pursed my lips, my palms growing sweaty. Why wasn't he angry with me? I was talking about leaving to see my sister. The enemy. I expected him to scream at me and call me a traitor to the Brotherhood... but here he was, giving me a choice to leave if I so wished. *Sy never gave me a choice.*

I held my chest high. "I'll stay. If Sy can be spared, then I can see to that here, if I'm able."

Master released a breath through his nose, as if relieved. He patted my back. "Then," he began, walking forward, "I think we've kept Alex waiting long enough. He has a terrible patience. Brace yourself for a brutal reprimanding."

Feeling as if a mountain had been lifted from my shoulders, I chuckled and trotted alongside him. "I think he'd punish you more than me, Master."

He cast me a curious glance. "Oh? And why do you think that?"

"Because my reason for being late is more excusable," I said, smirking. "I wanted advice on a perfectly rational, moralistic dilemma. You shirked drill because you were horny."

He halted, and I bumped into him. When I glanced up, I winced, seeing his face was stuck with a stiff, wicked smile. *Uh, oh.*

"Is that so, Hugh?" he hummed cheerfully, placing fists at his sides. "I suppose you raise a fair point. Perhaps I'll have to even out this unbalanced reprimanding?"

Before I could run, he grabbed me by the waist and slung me over his shoulder, his boney joint digging into my stomach. He stalked down the boardwalk with me squirming and kicking in a panic.

"W-wait!" I choked. "I'm sorry! I'm sorry…!"

He laughed. "What's that, Hugh? You want to be hog-tied and standing on your head for a few hours? Why, what a splendid idea."

38

XAVIER

"Forty-two!" The block members shouted as I dipped, straining to keep myself—and my brother who was lounging on my back—up.

"Forty-three!" They cheered when I pushed up and dipped again.

"Forty-four! Forty-five! Forty-six!"

A drop of sweat rolled off my nose. I dazedly glanced up, finding a few familiar faces. Octavius was nearest me, laughing as he helped keep count with the others. Neal was on the other side of me, obviously enjoying the show. Past my semi-circle of spectators, I even saw Dalen's ghost bent over his knees and chortling off to the side. Beside him were Aiden's and Nathaniel's souls, having a grand old time at my expense.

I would have been irritated, but I began chuckling myself when I saw my smart-mouthed apprentice. Hugh was upside-down keeping balanced with his hands and head while he leaned against a nearby wall. He was laughing at me along with the others.

"Since you obviously like your current position, Hugh," I called in a strained grunt, executing another push up. "I'll be generous. Let's tack on another hour against the wall."

Hugh's laughter quickly subsided, replaced with a distressed, upside-down scowl.

The block erupted with laughter, I even felt Alex quivering over my back. He shifted his weight over me and asked, "What did he do this time?"

I finished another push up. "Well, Hugh? Care to tell everyone what you said to me?"

Hugh's face grew a bright scarlet from his upside-down position, his teeth clamped shut.

"Go on, apprentice," I heckled in a wheeze. "Everyone's just dying to hear."

Hugh glowered, but reluctantly called out his answer. "I… I told Master he would be punished more harshly. Because his reason for being late was less excusable than mine."

"And what did you say my reason for being late was, Hugh?" I prodded. If he was brave enough to say it to me, surely, he could muster the courage to display his bravery to everyone else.

His blush deepened. "Because… b-because you were horny…"

A roar of laughter ensued, so extreme that Alex rolled off my back and dropped to the dirt, clutching his sides.

"Well, he's not wrong!" Alex gasped between guffaws.

I finished the last of my push-ups in a chuckle, then shoved to my feet. Alex needed more time to recover, still heckling on his back and shielding his eyes with an arm. After he calmed, I lowered a hand to him and pulled him to his feet.

"Your apprentice is hilarious," Alex wiped at a tear. "*Please* have him mouth off to you more often."

The rest of our small block of drill-mates had to quell their own laughter as Alex went back to his place at the front and clapped his hands sharply. "All right, all right! It's done. Our fair prince took his penalty. Now, for the rest of you."

The block members took their place in their usual lines, Octavius standing in the front row with me to my right, Neal to my left.

Behind me, El slipped into the second row in silence.

She looked morose as usual. She hadn't been very responsive while Zyl was still asleep from being poisoned. El visited her daily, from what I'd seen, and always came back looking drained. She barely said a word to any of us anymore, Culatian or otherwise. Octavius was the only person she seemed comfortable enough with at all. I imagined she wouldn't bounce back until Zyl awoke. *If* she did. The Healers couldn't be sure.

I heard El sigh behind me as Octavius and Neal still tried to stifle their laughter. These three, along with Alexander and Hugh, were my only familiar faces in this block. Everyone else were strangers: Neverlandish locals from the Reaper stations, Wavecrasher bays, Stormchaser roosts, and rebellion ranks. There were even two new men in the back, neither of them looking fit enough to be knights of any kind. Were they more Dreamcatchers? We'd been rescuing scores of them lately.

Luckily for us, that teenaged queen didn't only go to war with Grim. She went to war with *all* Relicbloods. That gave us more soldiers for our strange, mishmash army. We were rescuing new recruits from all over the continent, each city having been taken under martial law because of this new queen's royal mandate. Our camp was rapidly expanding each day.

"All right," Alex called loud enough for the whole block to hear, cupping his mouth. "Everyone on your backs! We'll start with—"

A large, snowy-white bird suddenly flapped over our heads, causing a mass of confusion behind me. I made a double-take at the clumsy fowl.

Its feathers were pure ivory from head to diamond-tail, its thick beak a faded pink, and its eyes were a hypnotizing, bloody red.

"Is that…" Octavius began, staring at the feral bird in awe. "A raven?"

The raven was still flapping frantically over the block, swooping down and causing a ripple of heads to dip each time it careened past. It seemed frazzled, its head darting left and right as if looking for someone.

Alexander clapped his hands and yelled. "Whose messenger is that?"

No one answered, but more heads ducked as the albino raven made another desperate swoop.

Alex barked. "Whosever companion that is, send it off! This isn't…"

Someone in the row behind me squealed in fright when the raven dove for her.

A blur of blue feathers went down as the girl dropped with the bird, which had landed on her shivering, cat-eared head.

El winked open an eye, uncurling herself slightly as the albino raven nestled into her white hair in relief, puffing from exhaustion. El sat in a daze. "*Re…?*"

A circle had formed around her, all of us staring.

The raven went limp between El's cat ears, the wheezing bird sliding off her head and into her lap. Then it blearily stumbled to the dirt. It was panting heavily, its small chest shuddering as its snowy wings flattened.

El's eyes glossed over. She reached a hand for the puffing raven. "*Y… ye, ye…*"

With delicate fingers, she scooped up the raven and cradled it. She looked at me, at Neal… then at Octavius.

"H… he*lp*." She suddenly burst into tears, and even she seemed surprised by it. Her breath went ragged, still looking at Octavius. "He*lp*…"

A resounding silence overcame the block.

I glanced at Alex over my shoulder. The Bloody idiot was stalk still, gawking at her.

Well. Looked like I would have to take charge here. I shot my head at Octavius. "Take her to Bianca," I said.

Octavius was just as frozen as Alex, his gaze wavering between El and me. "U-uh," he stammered, "does this make her…"

"A sister Reaper, yes, now stop gawking like a feral guppy and do something." I helped El to her feet, since everyone else was in too much of a damned stupor to do it themselves.

She was shaking terribly, a look of confusion, relief and pain contorting her face. Bloods, it was a face I knew all too well. I'd felt the very same when I rescued Chai.

She was still in tears, though she didn't say a word. She gazed at the albino raven, entranced as if staring at her own soul.

Dear girl... My heart ached for her.

"Octavius," I snapped, making him jolt. "Take El to Bianca. Now. This messenger might need medical help. I have a feeling it was one of the rescued ravens from Everland."

Octavius seemed to finally remember that his legs had functioning muscles. "R-right!" He took El's hand gently, blushing, but focused on his task and guided her out of the block.

ZYL

TRANSLATED FROM CULATIAN

I groaned awake, but kept my eyes closed. My lids didn't want to move. Everything felt numb. Bloods, this was worse than being put back in my body after a month.

I cracked my eyes open finally.

Froze.

There was a kid on top of me, her scaled face an inch from mine, staring at me with big, emerald eyes. Her hair was feathered and the color scarlet, matching the tiny wings that fluffed at her back.

The goblin's webbed ears flicked.

I screamed.

The goblin screamed with me, fumbling off the bed and ran out the door. "Daddy!" she cried, "Daddy...!"

I threw off the sheets and jolted to my feet. *Woah.* I wobbled when the room spun, falling back on the bed. *Okay, bad idea. Let's try that slower.*

This time, I took more care when standing, using the wall to hold myself up while I made my way to the opened door. Something smelled delicious, like frying meat. I could hear sizzling from the hallway. Whose house was this?

I crept farther down, that goblin's high-pitched voice getting louder.

"Daddy!" she said, it sounded like she was jumping, her feet making low thumping sounds. "Daddy!"

I peeked around the corner.

At the table was a green-haired fish woman spoon feeding a scaly, red-winged toddler. A long-haired fish kid was sitting next to her, kicking his feet and blabbering to the woman in Marincian. *Hey, isn't that Prince Fuérr?*

No one noticed me yet. At least, not until that little goblin tugged on the cooking man's pant leg and pulled him away from the stove, the kid's wings flattening with effort. "Daddy…!" she said again more urgently, pointing at me.

The father sighed and put down his cooking utensils, speaking in Landish. *"Mavis, for the last time, it's not going to be ready until I…"*

He spotted me, then went rigid. "Uh, Zyl."

My breath was ragged. "Roji…?"

He breathed out through his nose, grinning wanly. "Morning, Sis."

"Roji…!" My legs moved on their own, fumbling as fast as they could. I latched onto him, my stomach burning sick as my throat closed up and I started sobbing. "Ro-*hich*-ji…!"

He sighed, stroking my head. "Yeah… you found me. Good job, Sis."

Silverware and glasses clinked quietly at the table as Roji and his family ate their breakfast. Prince Fuérr was apparently the fish woman's nephew or something like that, so the little snot was here too.

I sat slumped in my seat, watching them. The hybrid toddler was in a wooden highchair and throwing most of her food on the floor, slapping the rest of it on her tray in orange splatters. That little goblin from earlier was sipping her milk while kicking her feet and staring at me with those big green eyes.

Her scaled mother was trying her hardest to make the toddler put some food in her mouth. Based on her green hair and eyes, I took it this mother was that Ocean Princess everyone's been talking about. Didn't I see her once, in Culatia? She looked kind of familiar.

Roji cleared his throat finally, breaking the awkward silence. "So. Zyl." He gestured to the other members surrounding the table. "This is my family." He motioned to the fish woman. "I don't know if you remember Dalminia, Zyl, but this is my wife. And the little artist there is Prylan." He then ruffled the feathers of the bigger goblin girl, grinning. "And you've already met Mavis."

Mavis kept to her staring, sipping her milk.

I pursed my lips. "So… the rumors were true? You left for… um… this?"

He rubbed a finger under his nose. "Yeah. Pops wasn't up for it when I told him Mini and I were getting hitched. He said either I needed to leave her and give up 'my stupid idea' of allying our countries, or I had to leave with her." He shrugged, chuckling. "Obviously, you can guess which one I picked."

His wife chuckled with him, using our tongue to add, "My brother would have been of like mind."

"So, we found a little place here in Neverland. Plenty of water down by the river, so Mini and the kids can swim and catch us some feral trout now and then, and enough storms come by here so I can collect some bolts and keep up the electronics." He spread his hands and raised them. "It's pretty nice here. Town's a couple hours away, so we get out privacy, but we also get our supplies if we need anything. I take up a few electrician jobs here and there to earn us some Mel on the side, too."

"So…" I sank in my chair. "You like it here?"

"Yeah." He rubbed his neck. "Look, Zyl. I know you came hoping I'd come back home, but I can't just pack up my things and leave my family here. Dad banished me for a reason."

"But Roji," I said. "Dad is dying. And when he does go, if you're not there, then I…"

"Will be queen." He ran a hand through his feathered hair. "And you don't want that?"

"It's your crown, Roji. You're the one with Sky's soul. Look, Dad's lost his mind, all right? He's gone to war with Marincia."

Both he and his wife lost their breaths. "He did what?" demanded Roji. "Why?"

I rubbed my shoulder, flushing. "I… sort of went with Willow to the Ocean Palace to look for you. Pops saw me there on a com screen, and now he kind of, sort of, *maaaybe* thinks Ninumel kidnapped me…"

"Did you call him?" Roji questioned skeptically. "You at least *tried* to tell him you weren't kidnapped?"

I set fists at my sides. "Of course I did. But every time I called, he kept getting whispers from Garrach, and then screamed that I was a lying illusion that the fish king conjured up to fool him."

Roji's elbows thunked on the table as he rubbed his temples. "Great. Maybe if *I* call…"

I snorted. "Pops isn't going to listen. He'll think Ninumel made *you* up, too. I don't know what in Sky Garrach has been telling him, but it ain't good when mixed with Dad's dementia. If neither of us are there, I get the feeling Garrach will take over, and the war's not going to end. The only way he's going to call it off is if one or both of us goes up there in person. And *I'm* not going back until you come with me."

"Neither am I, without my family," he countered. "And even *if* we went up there, you think these three won't be hurt for having Marincian blood? If he's at war, he isn't going to let Mini and the kids waltz in without them getting locked up or worse. We only had the money for one enchanted item with *my* illusion in it. We don't have anything for them."

I raised a finger. "The Dream King can give them disguises with his illusions. He came with us, you know."

He opened his mouth to protest, but shut it. Opened it again, shut it again. He vigorously scratched his feathered hair and grumbled. "You've got to be kidding me..."

Shouts burst from outside, all of us jumping. They sounded pretty close, just out the door.

Roji lifted from his seat. "Gods damn it, I told them to stay away from my house!"

I hurried after him when he threw open his door, hollering. "*Oy*, knock it off! Take it somewhere else!"

The men responsible didn't listen. I doubted they even heard Roji. Two men were in the middle of a brawl over the grass, surrounded by their peers, who looked split down the middle, cheering on their teammate and spouting curses at the other group.

The two guys fighting looked like a winged Stormchaser and a scaled Wavecrasher. Was that what their peers were, too? Where did all these people come from?

The featured two men were beating each other bloody, and Roji stormed toward them.

"I *said*—" He grabbed the winged brawler by his wingtips, yanking him out of the man-made ring. "Knock it off—!"

The Wavecrasher swung at Roji and clocked him in the jaw. It was obviously intended for the other guy, since the scaled idiot doubled back in horror when Roji sent him a sharp glare.

But Roji didn't say anything. He looked from the Stormchasers to the Wavecrashers, crossing his arms. "<What in Void is going on here?>" he demanded.

The Stormchasers dropped to their knees, scrambling to glue their wings to the ground.

"<S-s-sorry, Your Highness...!>" One stuttered in Landish. "<W-we didn't mean to bother you. These stupid *fish* started crossing our side of the camp, and—>"

"<Your side?!>" The beaten-up Crasher huffed, spitting a glob of blood at his feet. "<You don't have claim of land, here!>"

"<This is *our* Relicblood's site, so yeah we do!>"

Someone walked by me suddenly. It was Roji's wife.

Everyone hushed when the Ocean Princess stalked up beside Roji, all of them looking shocked as Void. My brow crinkled. They knew about Roji, but not about the Ocean Princess?

She was holding her hybrid baby in her arms, the tiny thing whining noisily. I flinched when that bigger kid of theirs, Mavis, clung to my leg, watching her mom from a distance.

"<Both of you have a Relicblood here,>" said Roji's wife. "<And stop this fighting. You're upsetting our children.>"

"<Our…?>" The beaten Wavecrasher's webbed ears folded down, staring at the scaled, winged toddler in her arms.

They were all staring, realization lighting their eyes.

"<Yeah,>" Roji said hotly, waving at his family. "<This is *our* home, so you follow *our* rules. Within this fence, there's no war between Culatia and Marincia. The only fighting that's going to happen will be between us and that insane queen. Got me?>"

The Stormchasers bowed, their shoulders locked like they'd been electrocuted. "<Yes, my lord…!>"

The Wavecrashers were more hesitant, but when they looked at the Ocean Princess, they copied the Chasers' examples and bowed.

Roji exhaled hard, scratching his neck in thought. Soon, I heard him mutter a curse, and he stomped through the group to head into the field.

I stumbled behind him. "Roji? Where are you going?"

He kept to his path through this… what the Void was this, some army camp? There were all kinds of people running around, some faces I recognized, but most I'd never seen before in my life. Where were we?

Actually, come to think of it, what happened to that palace? Why are we in the Bloody woods?

I hurried up to Roji. "Where are you going?"

"To talk to Anabelle," he said. "All the Sky Ports are under siege by this damned queen, so the only way either of us are getting to Dad is if we fly there ourselves and risk being shot down by every fucking country that's in war, or if we take the city back with Anabelle."

"Anabelle?" My nose scrunched up. "You make it sound like she's in charge of things."

"She… oh, right." He turned back to me, his face worried suddenly. "I almost forgot. Zyl, you've been asleep for almost twenty days now."

My legs went numb, slowing to a stop. "What?"

"A lot's happened since we got you all out of that burning palace."

"What?!" *What in Sky did I miss?* "I... why was I sleeping for so long?"

"You practically drank your weight in Yinklĭt Gel."

"I don't remember that!"

"It was in those drinks at the queen's party. Your friend Matt drank them too, but not as much. He woke up after the first three nights."

"Yinklĭt..." I stared at my hands. Was that why everything felt numb? I held my breath, evoking my wind Hallows.

Nothing came. Bloods, nothing even *started* coming. I tried again, straining my eye muscles glaring at my hands, thinking to make anything happen. Just one little puff? A small gale? Anything?

I felt nothing. Absolutely nothing.

"No, no, no, no..." Lightning? No... R-rain? No...

Now I was hyperventilating. Roji took my shoulders. "Calm down, Zyl. It's... probably temporary."

"Probably?!"

"Well, your doctor friends weren't sure..."

"Bianca!" I shrieked, running through the campsite. Please, Gods, let her be here, too. "BIANCA!!"

39

BIANCA

I watched Mr. Treble press a hand over Crysalette's massively bloated belly, touching different places over her maternity dress and humming.

"Well," Claude said to the rust-haired Dream Queen. He also turned to Sirra-Lynn, who was waiting off to the side. "Feels like it'll be within weeks, now. He's got a lot of movement going on in there, and he's fully developed. I'd say be on the watch."

Sirra helped Crysalette off the table. The queen winced slightly when she touched down, stretching her back with audible cricks.

"Thank you." Crysalette nodded to both Sirra and Claude. Then she twisted to the back of the room. "Do you hear that, dear?"

In the corner, Dream sat in a rickety chair, the teenaged king's bloodshot eyes half closed as his throat gave a hoarse *hmm*.

Crysalette tried again. "Dear?"

Dream was shocked awake, sitting straight up. "W-what?"

"The baby is due within weeks."

"Oh." His smile was delirious. After a minute, his eyes fluttered closed again and he fell back, hitting his head on the wall and yawning, "That's... mmn, wonderful, dear..."

He vanished.

I mean, *vanished*. The chair he'd just been sitting in was empty.

I gaped and pointed. "What in Void...!"

Crysalette sighed. "He's been up late, helping me. I imagine he's hardly found the time to get even an hour's sleep."

"But...!" I stammered, still dumbly pointing. "But he just... where did he *go*?"

"To Aspirre," she said, waving a hand as she explained, "it happens with one of the Orbs of Azure. If a Relicblood of Dreams is in possession of it, they are transported to Aspirre the moment they fall asleep. It had the same effect with our daughter, Myra."

"Is that safe, though?" I asked.

"We have plenty of Catchers here on camp, since the queen banned them from her cities as well. I believe we have enough barriers to keep out any unwanted Noctis Golems. Dream should be free to rest as he needs—"

"BIANCA!!" someone shouted outside.

We all looked out the opened doorway of our hut. The shouting wouldn't stop, getting shriller and more panicked by the minute. "BIANCA…!"

"That sounds like Zyl," I said, going outside. *Was she awake?* I ran through the camp, finding the Sky Princess, who was still yelling for me. "Zyl!" I hollered, waving. "I'm right here!"

Zyl spun and bolted for me, running into a guy along the way and almost knocked him over.

"Bianca!" She grabbed my hands, her arms shaking. "Bianca…! I-I-I can no…" She gasped for air. "Can no be evoking…!"

"Clam down, Zyl," I hushed, leading her back to the hut. It looked like she was having a panic attack. Did I still have that bottle of lavender extract in my supply bag? That might help her settle down a bit. "It's all right. You had a lot of that Yinklît drink. It just needs to pass through your system."

She let me guide her into the hut and I set her on one of the empty cots.

While I sifted through my bag to find the right bottle, she sniffled and wiped her runny nose. "R-Roji say 'maybe' get back? Why maybe?"

"Well…" I found the lavender extract and went back to her, squeezing the dropper to fill it. "There have been accounts of people in the past drinking enough of it to where they lose all access to their Hallows reserves. Like they'd completely clogged it, and they never got it back."

She paled. *"Re?"*

"But," I assured, holding up the dropper. "It's *extremely* rare. Now open up and lift your tongue, this will help you calm down."

She took a deep breath, nodding, and let me drip the lavender under her tongue.

"Try not to swallow it," I told her.

She made a disgusted expression, but shut her mouth and did her best not to swallow the bitter stuff… then her eyes shifted past me and lit up. She swallowed the lavender in a grimace and hopped off the table. "El—!"

Zyl paused when El and Octavius stumbled through the doorway. Neither of them looked like they noticed her. My long ears perked when I saw what El was carrying.

In the hybrid's arms was a snowy white raven, the poor thing breathing in loud wheezes. El was crying.

One look at Octavius's panicked face told me what was going on. One of my ears draped down. "You're kidding me?" I asked Tavius.

He shrugged helplessly. "Xavier thinks it might have been another rescue… he thought you should check on it, to make sure it isn't hurt."

"Right." Getting right to work, I reached for the bird.

"*Tovt!*" El yanked the raven to her chest protectively. She hiccuped and started babbling in Culatian between sobs, trembling.

Whoa. This was just like when Xavier found Chai.

"Hey, hey," Tavius hushed her and raised his hands. "It's okay. *Degtta. Zezet El mot rachre.*

El hiccuped again, her puffy eyes blinking at him. "*El mot…?*"

Octavius nodded, offering a wary smile as he held out his hands. "*Degtta. Befval…*"

El sniffled, but slowly handed him the raven.

His eyes went blank for a bit when he looked at the bird. Then he gave it to me. "She's exhausted, missing some feathers on her wings. I don't know how far she's been flying, but she'll have to rest, or she might die of fatigue."

"We'll make sure that doesn't happen." I cradled the now sleeping bird with particular care, smiling at El. Then I gave Octavius a sideways look. "Sounds like you picked up Culatian quick."

I caught him blushing just a little, and he rubbed his neck. "She's, uh… been teaching me some words."

El sloppily smeared away the water from her eyes, her cat ears perking when she finally noticed that Zyl was standing by the wall.

"Zyl?" El hiccuped. "*L-Loda?*"

"*Ûs…*" Zyl didn't look sure how to process all this. She mumbled. "*El…*"

She was cut off when El latched onto her, breaking into an even louder sob. "*Zyl Loda…! Zyl-Zyl Loda!*"

Everyone in the hut fell quiet, El's crying filling the empty space as she stood there hugging her newly woken friend.

I walked out of the hut to give them some space. Octavius left them alone, too, and trotted back to his drill block. I yawned and stretched, hefting my satchel over a shoulder. The empty vials and bottles tinkled inside.

This wasn't my main supply bag, it was just a smaller one I was going to use for getting more material. We were running low, and since it was my break, I figured it was a good time to start looking through these woods to harvest whatever they held.

I searched the camp for my assistant Alchemist, Red. Where was he? Bloody slacker, he'd better not be at the cook's tent again, or I'm going to…

Oh, there he was. He was using one of the soldiers to test out a new brew he'd apparently made. Looked like it was working pretty well. Smoke and flickering blue fire was spewing at the open target set in front of the soldier.

I grinned, calling out, "Hey, Red!"

Red whipped around, lifting up his goggles to find me. He smiled and waved, running up the hill to meet me.

"Hey, boss!" His goofy grin was smug and ridiculously proud. "Got a new batch all tested 'n everythin', like ya asked."

"Good to hear," I commended. "Look, can you help out the Healers with whatever tonics they need for a bit? I'm going to make a supply run."

He saluted lazily. "Sure thing, boss."

He ran off, eager as ever, and I crossed through the campsite, heading for Prince Roji who was himself heading for a group of familiar people doing a round of daily exercises.

Well, *some* were familiar. There were several blocks of them lined up, with one person leading each square at the front, shouting orders and counting the number of push-ups they were on. It looked like a real training camp of soldiers.

I noticed Jaq was leading one of the blocks, Lilli and Matthiel another, and even Ringëd managed one group. Most of the others were led by various rebels from Vanessa's people, and down at the end, Alex was the last block's drill sergeant.

Roji was heading for Alex's block, so I went that way myself, stopping off to the side to watch for a minute.

"96!" Alex barked, pacing the front of his block with folded arms. "97! 98! Xavier, get your apprentice in gear again! Everyone hold yourselves up while we wait for Hugh to rejoin."

Everyone groaned, pausing their upward position over the ground. Xavier was red-faced and panting heavily, sweating like a hog in the front row. He looked over at his student beside him, who was sprawled on the ground and wheezing. Xavier put his weight on one arm, which quivered, and he used the other to yank Hugh up by his shirt collar. The kid puffed and squirmed his arms back in position, completing the last two push-ups with Xavier pulling him up this way.

Alex continued, "99! 100!"

The block collapsed in a gasping heap, Hugh dropping the hardest of all of them. Xavier was second behind the kid, but it looked like he was doing a lot better than the first day. Suspiciously better...

Back when he started, Xavier could barely pull off twenty of those. Now he could crank out a hundred *and* on a single arm? I've even seen Alex sitting on him a few times too, and Alex I *knew* weighed at least 180 pounds. Something was going on.

Xavier got immune to the muscle-building tonic weeks ago... didn't he?

I watched Xavier with narrow lids, noting the slight definition in his arms that hadn't been there last week. *I wonder...* Maybe all his intensive training started an explosive reaction with the formula, if it was still in his system. It could have been sitting there, waiting for him to burn enough energy while it hid dormant during his days of rest. Was that even possible? I'd have to run some blood tests and figure this out.

When Alex saw Roji waving at him, he clapped his hands. "Break! Get some water. Afterward, find an available log from the pile and carry it during laps. Find the heaviest you can manage."

Xavier panted as he pushed himself up and rubbed his arms tenderly. Hugh was still wheezing on the ground.

Xavier tugged at the kid's collar. "Don't rest too long, Hugh," he said, helping the kid to his feet. "Remember, you have to keep moving, even if just a little. I let you off the wall early for a reason. Your body will adjust as your muscles strengthen... now go get some water. You're doing well."

Hugh nodded, exhausted, but looked determined as he wobbled over to where they were filling up canteens, which they'd stolen from town. Octavius and Neal, who'd been in the same block, went after him to fill up.

Xavier went to grab a towel from the short fence to the side, wiping the sweat from his face and neck. Princess Willow walked over then, handing Xavier a canteen of water. Like every day for the past couple weeks, she wore her marriage-vines over her forehead. The embedded diamonds were speckled with rainbow glints that shined in the patched sunlight.

After Xavier took the canteen and chugged it down, he kissed her fingers and watched her leave as she went to talk to Lilli down the line. Xavier smiled after her, his new marriage stud gleaming from his ear.

I sighed, smiling myself. It'd been a weird surprise when they suddenly decided to get the marriage over with. But you know... nothing's really changed. Now, it sort of just made sense.

With Alex now free, Roji walked up to him. I stepped up too, but waited to the side to let them talk.

"Got a minute?" asked Roji.

"Briefly," answered Alex. "What do you need?"

"Pull out all the Stormchasers you guys rescued and send them to me. Tell everyone else to do the same."

Alex looked suspicious. "Why?"

"I need to make plans with them. You guys are going to need some cover when you take over the capital, and Shatter season starts tomorrow."

Alex grinned. "So, you've decided to join us after all?"

"Well, I figured I didn't have much choice." He shrugged. "For one thing, my Dad apparently started a war with my brother-in-law, this new queen in town started a war with *Dad*, and most importantly, the bitch poisoned my lil' sis. She ain't getting away with that. Now where's Queen Land?"

Alex shook his head. "I don't know. Though, Willow may have some idea. She's over at the other block there, speaking with Lilli." He pointed with his chin.

Roji nodded, starting off that way—

"Wait!" I called to stop Roji. "H-hey! Uh…"

Roji paused, craning to me. Alex looked at me too, a little startled. I guessed he didn't notice me until now.

I went up to Roji and patted the satchel at my hip. "I need to make a supply run in the forest. Can you cut off the gate's power?"

Roji scratched his chin. "I guess… but don't take too long. I don't want to leave it off for more than an hour."

"I won't." I said.

Alex frowned at me. "You're going alone?"

"Yeah." I cocked an eyebrow. "So?"

He licked his lips in thought, then looked over at the canteen station and called out. "Octavius!"

The cat perked and came trotting over when Alex waved for him. "Yeah?" Octavius asked.

"Lead everyone into laps for me." Alex lightly patted his shoulder. "I'll be back in a few moments."

Octavius blinked after him as Alex came to stand beside me.

I muttered. "Where do you think you're going?"

"To make sure you don't get mauled by any Fera," he said, tugging the leather jerkin he wore over his tunic, complements of the scouts' latest raid in town. "Roji said he keeps the fence up to keep them out, so you'll need a Reaper there as a guard."

I snorted. "You guys go out of the fence all the time."

"We're already equipped as needed." He gripped the scythe-spheres at his neck, the things giving light clinks. "We don't leave without a scythe. Rule one."

I rolled my eyes. "Okay, but we have that Demon King following us somewhere. He'll keep them back."

"We haven't seen nor heard from Hecrûshou since leaving the palace. We can't rely on him to do anything right now. So." He put one hand at his side and gestured with the other. "Shall we, doctor?"

I grumbled, my long ears draping down. "Don't step on anything I need to harvest."

Roji led us to the east gate, using his Astravoking to turn off the electricity before letting Alex and me out, the two of us starting our trek in the woods.

"Nice of you to let Octavius lead drills," I said, moving a branch out of the way. "Would have thought you'd put Xavier in charge."

"I would have." He stepped over a tall root, and two scratchy croaks sounded when Mal flew down on a branch to follow him. "But Xavier can't keep up with some of them yet. I needed someone to be at the front of the pack. Plus, Xavier already has experience with leading a squad. I thought Octavius could use the practice. We're still short on instructors and Drill Sergeants, it's likely we'll need him as one soon."

"What about Neal? Isn't he already more fit than his brother?" I crouched to examine a patch of leafy weeds with bulbous, latticed blooms. *Clover.* I wasn't too low on that, but may as well stock up while it was here. I got out my tweezers and collected as many weeds as I could from the root up, shoving it in an available jar.

Alex stayed off to the side, watching me pluck the weeds. "I've asked Neal to run a different instruction," he admitted. "Being proficient in throwing knives is a skill only he and Octavius have. But it could come in handy if everyone learned. The more tools we can use, the better. Our numbers are growing, but I doubt we'll have nearly the number this queen already has."

"Smart," I commended and put my jar of clover in the bag. I rose and started forward again, exhaling.

This was nice, actually. Alex and I hardly talked anymore. I thought it'd be painful, but now I guess enough time had passed that it felt... well, neutral. I could live with neutral.

"So, what's new with you?" I asked idly, walking slower to let him stride next to me.

He shrugged. "I suppose... everything. Too many things are happening at once, I hardly feel like the same person anymore."

"I can imagine," I muttered. "New Hallows, new privacy standards without Xavier in there, the world is apparently Ending, and I might be a long-lost duchess from the surface."

His head lifted at that. "What?"

"My parents," I said, sighing. "My real parents. I found out they might have been the lord and lady Herdazicol, from up here. Rabbit shifters. Burned in a house fire some twenty years ago. Their daughter went missing. Might be me."

He looked totally dumbfounded. "Gods, Bianca. I… I can ask my father to search for their ghosts—"

"Master Hendril's taking care of it now. But thanks." I cracked him a smile, nudging his side with an elbow. "Maybe if I *am* a pure-blooded Roaress, I'll invite you to parties."

He laughed, a relaxed one. *Finally.* Things really were starting to feel better with us. Maybe we'd be all right after all.

I paused when I saw someone else up ahead. A head full of golden locks was hovering over a patch of plants.

"Ana?" I called, wincing when I remembered who I was actually talking to. "U-um, your majesty?"

The Land Queen's head whipped around to see me, her lion ears perking. She quickly rose and hurried to take my hands.

"Ana!" she pleaded, her golden eyes wide. "Please, just Ana. I cannot stand hearing my friends call me so formally."

Friends. I blushed. The lost Relicblood of Land—Void, Land reincarnate—called me her friend. "O… okay…" I mumbled sheepishly. "Ana."

Bloods, that made three—no, *four* Relicbloods I could call by name. Wait, no, Dream made five… I guessed Fuérr was technically Ocean reincarnate, too…

I coughed awkwardly and scratched my neck. "So, um… are you harvesting herbs, too?"

Ana nodded, her smile bright. "We were running rather low. And I… well, I needed a brief escape, to be alone."

"I don't blame you," I said. Everyone's been crowding her day in and day out. Though, I was surprised even her relentless guard dogs, Kurrick and Linus, weren't here with her. Guess she gave them the slip, too. Good for her.

I looked at what plant she was harvesting. Gasped. "Is that what I think it is?" I asked.

She glanced at the spiny plants shooting up from the ground. Their leaves were long and thick, curling wildly like a tangle of hair. Ana nodded and pulled out a leaf she'd torn off from her bag, peeling the outer layer to show the sticky gel inside. "Yinklît leaves," she said.

"What is that doing down here?" I questioned, skeptical as I went to the patch to marvel at it. "It's supposed to be native to Culatia!"

Alex put a hand over his eyes when he looked at the sky. "Perhaps some seeds fell here from the Sky realm, over time?"

"Oh, man, this is great!" I snapped off leaves left and right, stuffing as many as I could in my satchel. Bloods, there was so much…! "Guys, help me collect some of this!" I turned to Ana and grinned. "This might be just what I need to cure Zyl."

Ana returned my grin, but it fell when Mal started screeching from a branch above us. Alex went rigid, cursing and got out his scythe blades.

Then pine needles snapped behind us.

"What in Nirus," an elderly woman clipped, standing livid a few yards away and glaring at us, "do you think you're doing to my garden?"

My nerves froze over. The old woman had a walking cane in one hand, wearing a simple smock and apron. My ears dropped when I saw her pupils were glowing white.

More needles crunched around us, and I saw there were black globs with skeletal figures closing in on us now. Where in Void did they…?

Alex took a guarded stance and stood between us and the old lady, his wolf ears curled. "Don't." He shuffled back when she stepped closer. "You have a chance to walk away—*huah*!"

A tree root cracked to life and wrapped around his ankle, yanking him up so high, he was dangling arms-down in the air.

"Don't wave those dangerous things around my babies, young man," the old woman scolded and waged a glowing-gold finger. The motion shook the living root in turn, and Alex dipped and rose along with it.

She stroked one of the gelatinous demons on the head lovingly. "Don't worry, precious, this troublemaker will be dealt with… Lousy Reapers and their sharp toys."

Alex still had his scythes in hand, and I watched him curl up and hack at the root, splintering it and making him fall on his back. He scuttled to his feet, watching for any more roots this time.

"Well, go on!" the old woman spat, waving her cane at us. "Shoo! Go destroy someone else's yard, bleeding rats…" She turned and started shuffling away, bringing her posse with her.

Um… was that it?

Alex looked downright stupefied next to me. "Wh… what?"

The woman glared back at him, snarling with black liquid squirming over her face. "I said *leave!*"

"Miranda," a new, drawling voice called. I was getting dizzy, moving my head around so much. "If you wish to frighten them, don't drop the pretense that you'll kill them."

The old woman searched for the voice, finding a man wrapped in a hooded jacket leaning against a tree. He had a familiar, long staff wrapped in a cloth that was slung over his back.

Alex sighed in relief. "Where have you been, Hecrûshou?"

"Where have *I* been?" he countered, walking up to us with his hands in his pockets. "I wasn't the one to disappear after the incident at the palace."

"Well, what about the ship?" asked Alex. "Where were you when it was set aflame?"

"Wandering the town looking for new clothing to hide in. I can suppress my Weight all I wish, but if Shëfaux finds me swimming in his territory, there will be trouble for all of us."

The old lady rested her hands on her cane in a *hmph*. "I see you've finally caved and followed the Reapers out of your own territory, Shou."

"You should be pleased, Miranda," Hecrûshou said. "Their princess has accepted my proposal to recognize our kind as equal citizens."

The old lady scoffed. "Well, isn't that precious? You actually think she can convince others to give us fair trials before they slaughter us?"

"She can." Hecrûshou was practically gloating now. "She only needs the proper evidence that proves not all of us are out for souls." He motioned to himself, and then to her in offering. "The more on our side, the better?"

She scowled, glaring at Ana and me. We were still on the ground with our hands full of Yinklît leaves.

Jackal ears sprouted from the woman's head and her teeth sharpened. "Maybe if you tell these rascals to stop tearing up my garden, I'll consider it... Do you have any idea how long it took me to grow all those Yinklît plants? Months, Shou. *Months*. Blasted kids have no respect."

"B-but!" I choked, holding tight to the leaves. "W-we need these. Please."

She squinted an eye at me. "Why would you need those, girl? Have you got someone's Hallows to close up?"

"I need to make something to counter it," I said. "Something that will cure Yinklît poisoning, for my friend. And anyone else who might need it later during the war."

She lifted a bushy eyebrow. "What war?"

Ana rose beside me, brushing the dirt from her knees. "The war with Neverland's queen. We need a defense against what her soldiers will throw at us when we overtake the city. Please, our numbers are small, we need all the advantages we can find."

"And what makes you think I care about politics you Clean Ones entangle yourselves in?" she sniffed. But her gaze narrowed at Ana. "You have a strange brilliance to your hair, girl… and your eyes…"

I jumped up. "Yes! She's the, uh, Relicblood of Land! The lost one! Pretty important, and, um…!"

The woman tapped a long claw over her cane. "Land's lost heiress, eh…?" She squinted further, stepping closer to Ana until she was face to face with her. "What is your name, child?"

Ana's posture didn't falter. "Anabelle Goldthorn. Daughter of Adam Goldthorn, the late King of Land."

"Late indeed…" she said. "Show me your mark, should you have it."

Ana showed the woman her back and drew up her tunic, causing Alex to turn away in a polite blush. There, on her right shoulder blade, was a crowned Land mark.

"My stars and sky…!" the woman laughed, though it was more like wheezing.

The minute Ana put her tunic back on, the woman drew her in for a tight hug, startling the lioness. "After so long, you still live…! Little Ana!"

"P… pardon?" Ana asked, looking awkward in the old demon's grip. "Have we met?"

"Oh, my dear, my dear!" She chuckled, letting Ana go and patting her hand. She lifted a finger and winked. "I was a nurse in your father's palace, in the Old Kingdom. I was there for your birth, and there when King Dream came to hide you." She continued laughing, leading Ana by the arm deeper into the forest as Alex, Hecrûshou and I hurried to keep up.

"I am sorry," Ana whispered. "I do not remember you."

"Oh, you were such a little thing, you wouldn't remember me, *kheh, heh*! Now, I take it you're here to reclaim your father's lands?"

"I am."

"Good, good! Then, by all means, take whatever you need from my garden." She motioned to a large field in the middle of the woods.

My jaw dropped.

The sunlight glittered through the foliage and rained down on the plethora of plants and vines and flowers and weeds and *holy Nira so many colors!* There were even more patches of Yinklît plants. The expanse stretched on and on into the woods, I wondered if it *ever* ended. Butterflies fluttered all over the place, feral birds flew by and chirped like we were in a Bloody fairy tale. And what was better: *everything was something I needed.* There were no useless plants I couldn't make something with in sight.

"You're serious?" I was already out of breath, gawking at the old lady. "We… we can have any of this?"

She smiled a wrinkly old smile and nodded. "Anything you need."

I squealed and hugged the lady, then hugged Ana, and all but frolicked into the field with my satchel opened and at the ready. I was going to make *so* many brews—!

Something nudged my elbow.

I flinched and twisted back. *Huh…* There was nothing there, except for some weird, skinny tree.

I shrugged and went back to my harvesting, kneeling over a patch of Yinklît leaves and snapping them off one by one, piling them in my satchel—

Creeeeeeeak…

I twisted back again, my long ears standing and swiveling forward. There was still nothing there but that tree. *Wait a minute, wasn't it farther away before?*

Scrunching my nose, I glared at the tree over my shoulder, then went back to my harvesting. Weird Bloody forest and its weird Bloody trees—

A puff of warm air blew my hair forward, and I jerked around a third time. My brow furrowed. *What in Void was that?* And okay, now I *know* that tree branch was bent the other way before.

Scowling, I pushed up and stalked over to the tree. I put fists at my sides and leaned my head to the right, scrutinizing the bark patterns. What kind of tree was this? It wasn't one I recognized, that was for sure.

I scratched a nail at one of the trunk's notches—

The notch peeled open on its own. Now there was a horizontal, long pupil staring back at me.

The tree *sneezed.*

I screamed, tripping over one of its roots—which *moved*—and I fell back, crushing a Yinklît plant and getting sticky gel all over my arms. But I was way too focused on the *Bloody walking tree* to give a damn.

The tree had a face now, and it bowed its long, spindly neck so the thing could sniff my hair.

"G-g-guys…?" I scuttled back in a whimper. "W-w-what in Death *is this thing?*"

I inched my eyes to Alex, seeing he had been distracted with a limp green-and-blue striped weed and was only now looking my way. When he saw this damn tree was sniffing at me, his eyes splintered open and he shot to his feet.

"What in Death!" He fumbled over, his hand hovering over his scythe-spheres. "Bianca, get away from that thing—!"

I screamed when it's long, thin nose pushed into my stomach, the thing making some weird, creaking noise with its branch-like throat. Then it *pushed* me up off the ground, and I slid over its head and down its neck, catching myself on one of its sturdier-looking branches—horns?—and held on for dear life in a shiver.

"Alex!" I shouted, tightening my grip when the tree started moving forward with me on it. I managed to sit upright, now riding the damn thing backwards like a horse. "W-what do I do?!"

"Just…! Er, try and…! Erm…" Alex scratched his head, looking confused as Void while following at my side as close as he dared. His brow was furrowed, studying the tree as it stopped to graze a patch of wild clover. "Hrm. Curious thing, you are…"

"*Alex.*" I chewed. "Get. Me. *Down.*"

The idiot finally pulled me off and set me back on my feet. When Ana and that old demon lady came to meet us, I stabbed a finger at the grazing tree.

"What *is* this thing?" I demanded.

The old woman chuckled. "Don't get your ears in a knot, deary. It's only a Barkdragon."

I blinked at the living tree. "A real Barkdragon…?" I'd only ever read about them. *But if it's really one of them, then…* "Is it true their skin can grow any seeds you sow on them?"

The old lady hummed. "They can, if you can get it to stay in one place long enough to nurture it. But good luck with that. Only one doctor has been said to have tamed one, and that was over three centuries ago."

I yelped when the Barkdragon pushed its head on my shoulder, creaking happily as it sniffed at my hair, then sneezed softly. I laughed.

Huh. That's weird.

"This guy kind of feels familiar," I mumbled, testing out a stroke to its bark-like neck. These must be scales, shaped like that as a natural camouflage. Flat teeth and feeds on plant life, so obviously herbivorous… There was a mark on its left branch-like horn, like a burn scar, shaped like an oak leaf.

I ran a thumb over the scar. This had been from a branding iron, hadn't it? *Didn't I… Didn't I heal a mark like this once…?*

"Bazil," I whispered, my head feeling like cotton as the name formed out of nowhere. "You're Bazil, right?"

The Barkdragon's creaking turned into bright chirps, rubbing its head over my side and circling me like a horse-sized puppy.

Ana held an astounded hand to her lips. "Great Shel," she hushed, holding her fingers out for the dragon to sniff. "It *is* Bazil!"

I squinted an eye at the golden-haired lioness. "You know this guy?"

"Of course." Ana scratched under its neck. "The doctor who'd tamed a Barkdragon was the Lady Herdazicol. My old Mistress, in the 19th century.

She rescued Bazil from a settlement whose people used the dragons for labor. They live hundreds of years naturally, but if they are harmed or abused, they die rather swiftly. They are not strong enough to even pull carts, as the Landragons are. Many Barkdragons were worked to death in those days, leaving few left in the world."

I pressed a hand over the branding mark. "Poor little guy…"

Ana let a giggle slip. "I would say this proves I was correct." She looked right proud of herself, smiling at me like that. "Bazil recognizes you. Mistress Jilume's soul must have an unmistakable scent within you."

The old woman let out a cackle. "Well, small world it is indeed, eh? *Keh heh!*"

Alex gave me a helpless look. "What in Bloods is going on, Bianca?"

I smirked, climbing onto Bazil the *right* way and patted his neck. "I can't say I know for sure either, Alex. But it looks like I found myself an old friend."

CILIA

My claws dug into the tree I hid behind, watching that Reaper twin and the girls roam through Miranda's gardens. She and Hecrûshou were speaking separately off to the side now.

I'd come here with Hecrûshou, hiding in a stolen coat with a wide cowl. *Miranda is from Aldamstria?* My pulse blistered. *From where I lived?*

And she'd been a nurse. Why hadn't she told me this? Granted, I didn't see her often, but how could I not have known? If she knew me when I was alive, or even my husband… whom I remembered had been a surgeon in the very palace she spoke of…

I must speak with her. But I couldn't have the Clean Ones know I was here.

Pursing my lips, I glared at Miranda and 'nudged' her with my Weight. She went rigid that very moment, along with Hecrûshou.

Her head snapped to my hiding place, and I let her see me. She muttered annoyingly to Hecrûshou. "Don't tell me she's agreed to join you, as well?"

He crossed his arms. "She has a different goal in mind. But hers is a rather curious one."

I pushed my Weight harder at her to stress urgency. That black bird with the Reaper twin started squawking at me, but his Reaper quieted him, mumbling something regarding the two demons he already knew about.

Miranda released an irate growl and threw up her hands, heading to me. "Oh, all right, Cilia." Her tone hushed when she approached. "What do you want?"

I whispered. "You were a nurse at Aldamstria's palace?"

"I was." She put fists at her sides. "What of it?"

"Did you know my husband?" It was a struggle to stifle my choking heart-beat as I clutched the coat at my chest. "He… was a surgeon there. For King Adam. For her father…" I stole a glance at the golden-haired lioness gathering herbs in Miranda's gardens. I wouldn't have believed a Clean One could live for so long, but then, Macarius had. Could she have used the same methods, to live now? Like Kael…?

Miranda's wrinkled brow furrowed. "A surgeon…?" Her glare sharpened at me. "Was he a Grimish cat as well?"

I nodded, and her eyes grew wide, her brown skin paling. "Dearest Shel… I always thought you were familiar…" She extended an accusing finger at me. "You were Dr. Treble's wife, weren't you? Visited him on occasions at his work?"

My breath abandoned me. "I still don't remember much of Kael. Only small fragments. What do you know of him?"

"I know he was a monster," she growled. Her jackal ears grew and curled. "He butchered an entire court in a single night. Went Bloody mad. Poisoned everyone with his sick Hallows."

That's right… Kael was an Infeciovoker. Like my descendant.

"Not to mention," Miranda added darkly, "he killed King Adam."

My face fell. "But why would Kael…"

"He was a fine young man until that night," she scoffed. "Then the lunatic snapped after Adam dismissed him. The queen died while in labor, Kael was the doctor on duty at the time. The child was lost with her. The king went too far, true, banishing him from the kingdom, but Kael walked out of the palace gates and then…" She snapped her boney fingers. "He came back that night. slaughtered everyone. Went Bloody mad, he did."

I touched the scar running across my neck. "Went mad…"

"Cilia…" I remembered his voice sobbing over me in the darkness.

Miranda's gaze narrowed. "I take it he killed you as well, then? Probably that same night, I'm betting."

"No," I whispered, drawing my hand away from my scarred throat and balled my fingers, staring at the similar scars that were drawn across my wrists. "I had a different killer…"

Her brow creased. "Did you now? And who was it, then?"

My cat ears grew, folding down. "I… don't know."

In truth, I didn't know if Kael *wasn't* responsible. Of the few memories I had of him, I couldn't imagine him giving me these scars… for any reason. *But then*, I thought uncertainly, *why do I remember him begging my forgiveness…?* Forgiveness for what?

Miranda laced her fingers together, resting them over her cane. "I wonder... were you the reason he broke? He often spoke of his wife, too. Bloody much if you ask me. If he found you dead..." She inspected me. "And judging from your scars, you may well have been in pieces when he found you. Curious..."

I choked in a rush. "I think he may still be alive. A man named Macarius has my memories and—"

"Macarius Lysandre?" she asked, surprised.

I hesitated. "I don't know his family name."

"Is he a cobra shifter? Bit of a pompous asp? Somniovoker, illusionist?"

"Yes... By all accounts, yes."

She gave a single laugh. "That snake was always barging into the clinic. Thought he was entitled to go wherever he pleased, just because he was the royal Dreamcatcher and historian, the damned sociopath." Her teeth grew sharp. "You say he's still here? As a demon?"

"Not a demon. I don't know exactly how he's stayed alive, but he claims he was trapped in Aspirre these past centuries."

"Adam's daughter claimed the same thing," she pondered aloud, staring at the lioness in the fields. "If *she* is still alive, then I'm inclined to believe you're right about both Macar and Kael... I recall them disappearing suddenly after that night. Most of us survivors simply assumed they'd fled. Perhaps Anabelle could shed some light on this—"

"No...!" I drew up my cowl. "They can't know I'm here. Please. Macarius thinks I'm still following them under his order... If Kael is alive, then I'm sure the snake knows where to find him."

"And what happens if you *do* find that lunatic?" she challenged. "I hear you've been quite the busy demon queen this past year. Was it all to find him, then?"

I wilted at her accusing tone. She took my silence as my answer, scoffing, "Not so different from your husband, are you? A happy couple of serial killers."

"As if you haven't eaten your share of souls over the years, *Queen* Miranda," I snapped. "Don't pretend to be a saint now and throw *my* mistakes at me."

She growled, but softened her voice. "Then what is your plan? Find Kael and stop your murdering?"

"Only after I kill Macarius," I said. "He's exploiting me. And I suspect he's exploiting Kael in a similar manner."

"Likely," Miranda grunted. "The bastard was always sneaking about, conducting sick little social experiments." She shrugged and snorted. "If you keep to yourself, I won't alert you to Anabelle and her friends. But so help me, Cilia, if you even *point* a claw at any of them..." Her face slithered with black sludge, voice dropping. "I will tear you to shreds."

She spat at my feet and brusquely walked into her gardens, Hecrûshou nodding to me as he followed her.

40

ZYL

I watched El eat from her plate quietly. Her eyes were all puffy and red, her white hair mussy and cat ears folded down super low.

The chatter in the mess hall—well, *tent*, really—didn't seem to bother her.

Fuérr and his little pal Oliver were running around the tent, keeping under its shelter so they wouldn't get drenched in the torrent of rain coming down out there.

Roji and his family were here also, getting food from that baker cat. Roji said he decided to bring Mini and the kids out more, to help set a precedent between the Chasers and Crashers. *'They're gonna get it in their thick skulls that we're not at war with each other'* he said, *'they're gonna calm the Void down, shut up, and deal with it while they're on our yard'.*

I sighed. Today had been one emotionally taxing day. First I find Roji, then El gets a pretty white raven? *And my Hallows…*

I tried to tune into the storm outside, to feel anything… but I was still numb. I shivered, rubbing my arms and stared at my food. I wasn't hungry anymore.

"Another one?" I heard the cook ask skeptically from his place behind the serving table. He was talking to Willow. *"Haven't you already had two bowls, Highness?"*

Willow hummed, as if curious. *"I have. I don't know, I've been rather… peckish, lately."*

"Uh, huh." He scratched his thick beard. I guessed it'd grown while I was asleep, the last time I saw him it was only short stubble. *"You feeling okay?"*

"Fine," she said, lifting her empty bowl politely. *"It's only hunger, Mr. Treble. There's no need for alarm."*

"If you say… so…" He reached the ladle over to pour the stew in her bowl, but he paused. *"Uh…"*

Willow drew back. *"What is it?"*

"It… that, uh…" He cleared his throat, pouring her another scoop of stew. *"Nothing. You* are *really hungry. Come back for as much as you need, Highness."*

She relaxed, murmuring, *"You Infeciovokers and your 'static' senses…"* She walked back to her table and sat beside Xavier. Her new husband, apparently. Sky, so much stuff happened while I was asleep.

I twisted forward again in a sigh, folding my arms over the table and dropped my head. I went back to watching El across from me. She picked at her food, barely eating. The rain pelted against the canvas over our heads in a steady hush, soft rumbles purring from thunder.

The sounds reminded me of home. I closed my eyes, pretending I was up on the islands again. *Guess I'll be there soon enough anyway, I thought, But at least I'll have Roji with me.*

I smiled, watching Roji run after his goblin daughter around the tables.

You know what? I didn't need my Hallows. At least, not right away—I could wait to get them back. Bianca said she had what she needed to make me a cure. The important thing was that Roji was coming home. Fish family or not—Big Brother was coming *home…!*

I was still smiling like a five-year-old fledgling on her first flight run when I looked back at El.

But I winced, seeing El's dead-pan face was still oblivious to the world. Sky, you'd think this girl just came back from a funeral.

"So," I said, making her jump, her cat ears flicking straight up. "You've been quiet. Should I be worried?"

El's blue wings lowered behind her. "Oh, um… sorry." She rubbed at her eyes. "I'm just… I'm really glad you're awake, Zyl. I didn't know if you'd ever wake up."

"Well, I did," I grumbled, taking my wooden spoon and dunking the bits of potatoes into my stew idly. "And the world kept spinning meanwhile… How long have you had that new raven of yours anyway?"

El rubbed her shoulder. "Um… Well, Salfwy just came this morning. Just before you woke up."

"Salfwy?" I asked, rubbing my nose in thought. "Heh… 'snow'. Good name." I tapped a finger over the cracked wood of the table planks. "So… does this mean you have to be a Reaper now? How's all this work?"

El rolled back a walnut shoulder. "Willow said I don't have to be a Reaper if I don't want to. I mean, I'm already a Stormchaser, so…"

I popped a potato in my mouth, chewing. "Beff yur Reafer Caff iff hahhy bou'iff." I wasn't really sure if she understood me, but given her blush, I guessed she did.

"You think so?" She sighed, swooning with a flutter of her wings as she all but dripped onto the table, giggling dreamily. "He *did* look happy earlier, when he came by to check on me."

I swallowed the potato. "Yeah, I saw that bit. See you've been weaseling your way into his little heart since I've been gone. You even got him learning Culatian." *Even if he sounds like a stumbling toddler whenever he tries,* came the afterthought.

"Yeah!" She brightened, clapping her hands excitedly. "He's better than when he started off, at least. And he's been teaching me more Landish, so we can actually talk now. Oh, but there was one word he said that I didn't know." She smooshed a finger over her lips and puckered her brow. "And when I asked him about it, he got really shy and wouldn't tell me."

"He got shy, eh? What was the word?"

"He said I was... *Cute.*"

My wings straightened. "He said that?" I lunged over the table and shook her shoulders. "You're kidding! He actually said that? Oh, El, this is *perfect!*"

"W-w-what?" She looked dizzy when I let her up. "But... but what does *cute* mean?"

"It means cute, you adorable heart-thief!" I was giddy in my seat now. "It means he likes you!"

Her face went bright red. "Really?!"

"Really!" I grabbed her hands and squeezed in a victorious laugh. "It probably slipped out of him—which is even better! Oh, El, I can hear wedding bells already...!"

Her cheeks practically radiated with heat. "W-w-wait, slow down...! What if he just said that to be nice? He was trying to cheer me up."

"Don't be silly!" I ruffled her hair, then *thumped* back in my seat with crossed arms, folding my legs to perch on the edge of the seat in a grin. "I've been watching him all day since I woke up. He's totally into you."

"But how do you know?" She groaned and thunked her forehead on the table. "He hasn't made a move yet, as far as I can tell... and he doesn't know enough Culatian yet to *say* it, if he wants to do anything."

"Forget all that." I made a shooing motion with my hands. "You don't need words. Just gotta watch his body language, you totally got him hooked."

"If you say so." She sighed despairingly, propping her head up with a fist and smooshing her cheek. Her expression turned morose suddenly. "Maybe I should check on Salfwy... It's almost been an hour."

I hummed, watching her. She was really worried about that raven. Like it was more than a pet. Maybe it was? What did I know about Reaper stuff?

"Say, El," I said, my posture hunching. "About this raven business."

One of her cat ears swiveled forward. "What about it?"

Sky, how did I say it? "Well, Willow said you had a choice about what you wanted to do with yourself." I circled a hand in the air. "And you've been getting closer to your Reaper cat too…" I bit my lip. What was wrong with me? Why couldn't I say it?

I guess… I guess I didn't really want her to leave. But… I shoved the words out before I could change my mind. "I think you should take the Reaper gig and stay with the cat."

There—I said it.

El tensed, her wings stiffening. "You think so?"

"Definitely." My grin was weak. "I mean… I-I don't want to see you leave, but—damn it, it's *your* life, it's *your* choice. You really got a shot with the cat, and this raven's *gotta* be a sign from Ushar. Or, maybe Nira… But come on! What are the odds? You meet a Reaper cat, you actually get his interest, and *BAM!* You suddenly get your own bird that'll put you in the same line of work? It's *gotta be a sign.*"

Her ears drooped. "I… I didn't think about it that way."

"Well, I did." I harrumphed and took another bite of my stew defiantly. Hopefully, it hid the sound of my heart cracking in two. "I can't make the choice for you… but I want you to know that it's yours to make. I'll… be fine if you want to stay with him."

Her voice was so, so soft. "Are you sure?"

I stuck up my nose. "Definitely. Besides, I have Roji back now." The reminder brought back a smile. "I'll be all right." And that was the real, honest to Gods truth.

The smile that spread over her pixie face was probably the warmest I'd ever seen on her. Sky's Wings, El was in love. I sighed admiringly. *Yeah. She needed to stay.* She'd never be this happy again if she came back to the islands.

Her smile cracked into panic suddenly. "Sky, there he is…!"

I twisted back. Aha! The Reaper cat just walked in, drenched in rain water. His brother came in after him, flinging his arms to dry off and muttering to himself while his muddy boots squished over the wet grass in here.

El's Reaper went to get his fill of stew, and El mooned over the table as she watched him. His brother started for the serving table—stopped, spotting us back here. He grinned.

The brother abandoned the serving table and waltzed over to us. He leaned on our table next to El. *"Evenin' ladies."* He said in Landish.

I scowled at him. *"What you want?"*

He tossed his head at El. *"Got a proposition for Miss Cat-Jay."*

Proposition? I thought. What did that word mean again?

He went on, *"See, I'm starting a new class tomorrow. Recruiting whoever wants to learn to throw sharp things at people, fun stuff. Thought you might be interested, El, given your new Reaper status and all."* He leaned closer to her cat ear and muttered, *"Bet our dearest 'Tavi' would be pretty impressed if you tried out his style of fighting... It'd be our little secret. Come to the north quadrant first thing in the morning if you're interested. Night, ladies."*

He tipped his head, and waltzed back to the serving table, whistling to himself.

El's Reaper might be impressed, eh...? I rubbed my chin and lifted an eyebrow at El. "Interested?"

She was already starry-eyed. "I-I might... give it a try?"

We shared an excited giggle.

XAVIER

My wife took her seat beside me again with what was, I believed, her *third* bowl of stew.

"How are you still hungry?" Lilli questioned across from us, her bat wings flexing doubtfully. "You had five sandwiches for breakfast *and* lunch, and now all this?"

I grunted from my seat. "She has a point. Where is it all going, I wonder?"

Willow lifted her chin. "Your tone of surprise is unnecessary. I skipped all but one meal yesterday. My stomach is justifiably angry with me."

She was skipping meals again? I thought in a groan. *Nira, this woman...* "If I catch you drowning in your work again," I warned, "I will pull your head out of the water by whatever means necessary."

She tossed her hand at me. "Yes, yes, I'll be more mindful next time."

I wasn't so sure of that. This blasted woman had to stop neglecting her health, Death damn it.

The seat beside Willow creaked when Octavius sat down with his own bowl of stew. He seemed dismayed. Or perhaps exhausted?

Jaq, slurping his meal to my left, grunted, "Rough day, Tavius?"

Octavius sank his elbows on the table. "Yeah, something like that."

Neal seated himself across from him and smirked devilishly. "He's been cock-blocked all day by the newly woken Sky Princess."

Octavius glowered at him. "Piss off." He shoved a spoonful of stew in his mouth, chewing ruefully, his cat ears curled in annoyance.

But his chewing slowed. One ear revolved toward Willow. He stared at her as she finished her bowl, scrapping it clean.

She caught him looking, and her brow furrowed. "Yes?"

He stared for a moment more, his expression pointedly blank. Then he scooted his bowl toward her and rose. "Here. You can have mine."

Willow frowned at him. "Why?"

He shrugged quickly. Perhaps too quickly, I thought. "You feel like you're still hungry," he said. "I'll get another one."

"But I could just as easily get another—"

"Don't worry about it." He was already halfway to the serving table, calling in hushed tones for his father.

Curious... I gazed after him, my lids slitting as Octavius began whispering to his father in private. Damn this rain, though, I couldn't hear a word of it, even with my wolf ears grown.

A crack of thunder ruptured overhead, and the tent flap was thrown open by newcomers.

Herrin dripped inside, fluffing his feathers to rid them of the water. He didn't have much success. He stomped his way over in the muck to a table in the back corner where a group of his Enlightener members were dining.

"Any word yet?" he asked the bunch. Why did he sound worried? "Have they found her?"

The group solemnly shook their heads. There was a strange tension among the guild members. What was all this about?

Herrin's wings drooped dejectedly, and he slogged his way back toward the exit.

I caught his arm as he passed. "Herrin?"

His eyes focused on me belatedly. Clearly, I'd ripped him out of a brooding thought. "Huh?"

I murmured under my breath so the others wouldn't hear me over their own chatter, a light rumble of thunder helping to drown me out. "Is someone missing?"

His face wrenched in pained concern. "It's one of our Enlighteners. No one's seen her since we left the city."

That long? He'd helped many of them escape here in the past few weeks, I thought he'd found all of them.

"Do you think something happened to her?" I hushed.

He shook his head. "I don't know. But we're going to keep looking. Mrs. Elliot's the most worried. Marian is an oracle, she thinks if the queen gets a hold of her..." He swallowed.

I stifled a shiver. If that mad girl caught an oracle, I dreaded to think what she would do to pry the future out of her Third Eye. "Is there anything I can help with?" I asked softly.

"No," he sighed hard, rubbing his eyes. "The only thing you could do is the same thing the rest of us are doing and scout the city. But you'd be more recognizable." His steps were lethargic as he started off. "Thanks for asking... but don't worry. We have our own oracles already working on it. We'll find her."

He disappeared into the storm, the tent flap wavering in the harsh gale.

But passing him on his way out were Sirra-Lynn and Rochelle, looking remarkably hurried. The doctors walked inside and spotted me immediately.

Sirra-Lynn rushed to meet me, panting. "Your Highness? Xavier? We have a request."

"A request?" I asked.

"Yes." She looked incredibly anxious as she rubbed her knuckles. "Do you and your wife have a minute?"

I stomped into the medical tent and shook the rainwater from my hair, slicking it back to keep it from sticking to my face. Willow walked in after me, wringing her tied up, long locks over a shoulder.

"This way," Sirra-Lynn urged, grabbing a damp towel that had been hung on a rack by the entrance and dabbed at her wet face and neck. Rochelle had found a similar towel and done the same, following Sirra in near perfect step.

Willow and I followed skeptically. What was all this about?

In the back of the tent, I spied Bianca by the burners, as well as Alexander. He watched off to the side as she toyed with colorful tonics and bubbling brews, twisting a knob at a coiled tube to allow one solution to drip slowly into its beaker.

She was instructing the men and women of her new Alchemist Guild, all wearing comically large goggles over their eyes and protective gloves, most of which were covered in soot and I didn't even know what else.

Her first member, Red, was assisting the Mistress Chemist with her instruction, handing her vials and small, glass dishes and demonstrating stirring methods with a glass rod.

Alex watched her with a soft grin. Things between them seemed calmer now. More relaxed. And yet, he still had a certain... *look* while observing her lesson in silence. *Why was he doing this to himself?* I couldn't help but wonder. *Hadn't he accepted his betrothal with Lilli?*

At Alex's feet lay that snoozing, twisted tree: Bianca's hound-like Barkdragon. Bazil, she called him. His woody torso creaked and rose as he took a soft, sneezing breath through his branch-horned nostrils, then shifted slightly and curled there in his cushioned corner.

Bianca was jabbering something about 'isotopes' when one of her orange rabbit ears perked in my direction. She looked at me curiously, lifting her oversized goggles. Then she turned to her assistant and handed him the half-filled beaker she'd been displaying to her students.

"Take over for a bit, Red," she said.

The many bug-like goggles were now fastened to him. Suddenly finding himself in the spotlight, Red was true to his name and flushed scarlet, fumbling with the beaker as he struggled to continue his Mistress Chemist's lesson.

Bianca patted his shoulder with her oversized gloves and slipped them off before striding toward Willow and me. When Alexander noticed us as well, he walked at her side.

"Is everyone okay?" asked Bianca, one brow lifted in concern at me in particular. "You better not have overdone your training, Xavier."

I snorted. "Hardly. Sirra and Rochelle have asked that we join them for a... a discussion, perhaps?"

"What discussion?" She followed Willow and me as our guiding doctors turned into a connecting tunnel between tents.

Bianca's Barkdragon creaked awake from the corner, rising sleepily to follow Bianca like a loyal, feral horse. Its limber steps gave only the smallest groans, like branches rubbing together in a gale. I noticed there were bright green sprouts coating the dragon's back now, ones that hadn't been there before. What was Bianca growing?

Alex was the one to answer, "It's a curious reason. They've asked me to come and observe as well."

I grunted. "So, that's why you're here."

"I was told to wait until they found you," he explained.

I muttered under my breath so the women wouldn't hear. "And here I thought you stopped to enjoy the view."

He declined a response, flicking me a piqued look, which I met with equal weight. He snorted and turned his attention to the two doctors when they finally came to a stop in the corner of the new tent. Sirra-Lynn's teenaged Mistress Necrovoker was here, waiting for us.

Lëtta stood beside a lone patient bed where a man slumbered under the neatly kempt sheets. It wasn't any man I knew. His hands and arms were dressed in tubes that dangled from their insertion points within his walnut skin. A machine blipped with his heartrate at his side. They must have stolen the equipment from in town, I guessed.

Rochelle cleared her throat and stood at the foot of the patient's bed. "Thank you for coming," the reptile woman said to our little quartet, rubbing her spotting hands nervously. "We have a request for you, Xavier."

I scratched the beard hugging my jaw. "Only me?"

"Yes." She peeked over her shoulder at Sirra-Lynn, who nodded encouragingly. "We want to experiment a bit with your soul-removal Evocation. If that's all right?"

"I suppose." What on Nirus could it be?

Rochelle let out her breath and bowed in thanks, waving at Lëtta in the corner as if asking the girl to bring her something. "Thank you. Please, try and keep an open mind. We wouldn't be asking you if it wasn't relevant."

"Relevant to what?" I asked.

"To the Tailor's cause," Sirra-Lynn answered this time—taking the spectral hand of a ghost who suddenly phased through the tent's wall to join us.

The ghost had a familiar face. *The slumbering patient.* I glanced at the patient we surrounded, realizing what this was about.

My throat rumbled, "Your Seam was cut before your time?"

The timid ghost nodded.

I hefted my shoulders, arms folding. "And you wish for me to return your soul to your still-living vessel?"

Another nod, the ghost adding meekly, "If you can, Your Highness... I-I'll take my fate if it fails, according to law, but if there's a chance you *can*..."

I inhaled deeply, releasing a smooth stream through my nose. I then turned to Willow, lifting a questioning eyebrow to silently ask for her opinion.

She matched my pose and crossed her arms. "Well, I can't see how a test could hurt."

Alexander grunted his agreement, waiting beside a now wide-eyed Bianca who looked on the brink of exploding with newfound excitement.

I sighed, reaching a hand out to the exposed spirit. "Very well. A test we shall have."

The ghost reached for my extended hand, perhaps expecting a shake, but I bypassed his fingers and sank my hand into his cold, rippling chest.

My Crest shined with a white light over my left knuckles, changing into my Death mark, and from my fingertips poured violet wisps of light. The lights wove together, creating a temporary NecroSeam that latched like plant roots into the ghost's soul.

Then with the utmost delicacy, I dragged the soul to his breathing vessel, pushing the soul under his skin and conducting the lights to stitch themselves to the man's beating heart, much like a master seamster would a thread into leather.

Once I felt it stitch securely, I dismissed my Hallows, my Crest returning to its original, three black diamonds.

"It's done," I announced, stepping back to watch the slumbering patient carefully.

Everyone's breath hung at their lips, unlike the patient's, which remained even and steady.

I frowned, a bit disappointed at the lack of results. *I was sure it had attached successfully… Why wasn't he waking?* I blinked. *Waking. Ah.*

I walked back to the patient's side and cleared my throat behind a fist, switching to my dream Hallows and pressed a glowing-blue hand to the man's brow to wake him—

The man's eyes flew open. He jolted upright so swiftly, his skull slammed into mine.

Biting back a wince, I rubbed at my sore temple, but watched the man pat himself experimentally. He laughed in pure delight.

Sirra-Lynn clasped her hands together in victory, now in tears. "Shel bless you…! It worked!"

Alexander hummed as if impressed. "Death's Head. It was actually a success."

Willow tapped a considering finger over her lips. "A partial success… Xavier gave him a temporary Seam. It isn't by any means permanent."

"But it's something, isn't it?" Rochelle asked, hopeful as she pushed up her half-moon eyeglasses and addressed Willow. "Could this bring the Fifth Law of Death into consideration of a repeal?"

Willow studied the now sobbing patient with a wrinkled brow. She was silent for a long moment. She turned to me, as if to ask for my opinion.

I offered a small shrug. "If not a repeal, perhaps an amendment?"

"Perhaps," she agreed, looking troubled. She addressed the anxious doctors with a sure tone. "Such a change cannot be addressed without further experimentation. Thus far, Xavier is the only known Necrovoker able to accomplish this feat. Bring other patients you have under your care. Call for the other Necrovokers in camp and have Xavier attempt to teach them. If even *one* succeeds, then the motion has grounds to be brought to court."

The doctors cheered in relief, talking up a storm now as Bianca joined them in excited speculation.

But I grimaced at Willow. Her lips tugged into an apologetic frown.

Grand. I pushed my lids in with my thumb and forefinger, stifling an aggravated groan. *Just when I thought I couldn't be buried with any more work.*

MATTHIEL

This was pure madness.

I scowled at my violet-glowing fingertips, this damned Seam slipping and sliding off my assigned ghosts' chest without any hope of finding purchase.

What in Death was Her Highness expecting to achieve? None of us could do this! These were *living* souls, not deceased ones. Xavier was the Bloody chosen one—er, two—hand-picked by the Seamstress Herself. Of course *we* weren't going to make this miracle happen.

I stole a glance at Lilliana, with whom Xavier was attempting to provide instruction on this nonsense.

To my right sat Her Highness with her own assigned ghost, attempting to make her temporary NecroSeam stick to the slippery specter. She was not faring better than myself.

I sighed, admiring her long, wavering locks that tumbled down her muscular back, hearing her melodic voice murmur kind words of apology to the ghost before her. She listened to the ghost's story, of how her Seam came to be cut early. Her Highness looked on the verge of mournful tears. So caring, for every soul...

I flicked an irritated gaze at Xavier. *Prince* Xavier. How could he wed Her Highness without telling a soul? Death, I had been asleep for it all. She deserved a beautiful wedding—the most magnificent celebration to befit the blessed soul of Death. It was a disgrace to keep such a sacred union hidden from the public's eyes.

Yet, it's done. I sighed again, dismal. I supposed Her Highness would not have agreed to a private marriage if she hadn't thought it proper. Perhaps I should trust in her judgement, if not Xavier's.

I glanced about the circle of Necrovokers in the tent, all trying this daft experiment for themselves. There were so few of us. Lilliana, Willow... that odd girl who was Sirra-Lynn's Bloodpact Mistress *and* apprentice Healer... what was her name again? L... Lëtta? I've caught that one staring on several occasions. Though, she never had much to say. It was rather unnerving.

Looking past my assigned ghost, I scowled at the four individuals who, in my opinion, had no business being here.

The Enlightener teen sat in the back, scribbling furiously on a ledger as if *not* documenting this test of ours would cause his heart to pop out of his rib cage like a ripe apple. His brown wings fluttered and twitched every so often. I doubted he noticed how crazed he looked.

By the counter stood Alexander, Jaqelle and Dr. Florenne, all waiting with crossed arms and muttering comments as if this were some sport for them to spectate. Granted, Alexander had more reason than the other two to be here, being Xavier's brother, but he was the only Necrovoker here who was unable to do any of this. The blasted man couldn't even *touch* a soul. Why was he here? Nosy bunch, the lot of them... though, I supposed it was only right to make such things public. I did prefer transparency with important matters.

"You've almost got it," Xavier encouraged Lilliana, though his expression hardly looked confident in the words. "You must remember, living souls are... *thicker*, let's say, than the deceased ones. Pretend you're stitching the Seam into leather, rather than silk."

I scowled, turning to my ghost again. *Stitching into leather?* My gaze narrowed. Why, last I checked, leather required thicker thread than silk. *Thicker... I wonder.*

Curious, I pushed more Hallows through my fingertips, thickening my temporary NecroSeam. The spectral thread brightened to a more vibrant violet. Then, carefully, skeptically, I motioned to thread it into the soul.

I felt a firm *push* as it sunk in...

And it stuck.

"Bloods be good," I murmured, blinking dumbly.

The room fell Deathly quiet. I glanced about—stiffening. All heads were now turned to me, shocked still.

Xavier himself seemed want of breath. "Matt, you've... you've done it. By the Gods, you've done it!"

Her Highness urged, "Attach him to his vessel, quickly!"

Fumbling, I gripped my ghost's thickened NecroSeam and dragged him to his breathing vessel which lay beside me in his patient bed.

Xavier wheeled to the bedside, his look intent. "Ease him in! You must push further than with a corpse, it *will* be taxing."

"A...All right." I indeed pushed further, the ghost sinking into his vessel's skin. I felt the Seam vibrate against something—his heart? It was thumping in there, threatening to push the blasted soul out again, but I clamped my teeth shut, wolf ears sprouting with determined exertion, and used both hands to *shove* the Bloody thing in there.

"Thread it!" Xavier barked.

I ripped my arm left, feeling as if I pulled a two-ton boulder, then ripped right, over and over, my throat scratching sorely and sweat dripping down my brow. *Death!* This was more than taxing, it was Bloody labor work!

My arm burned like Void, but I jerked it one last time and dismissed my Hallows—

I gasped for breath and toppled to the floor, heaving for air on all fours. My elbows were shaking. "Bloody Death…" I wheezed. "I… I feel like I just dragged a mountain two feet. Did it… did it work…?"

I twisted back, hesitant.

The sleeping patient I was assigned was now sitting upright. Laughing.

Xavier clapped his hands with an incredibly thrilled smile. "You've Bloody done it!"

I was still panting when the room erupted with cheers and excited chatter. That Enlightener all but fell off his chair and scrambled over to me, asking for details on how I'd figured it out. I was far too exhausted to answer. Death, but I needed a meal and a nap.

I saw Her Highness walk to Sirra-Lynn and her lizard coworker, announcing, "The test was a success. I vow to bring your request of either a repeal or amendment to Grim's court."

GRIM

LOW RASTIRIA,
CAPITAL CITY OF THE WESTERN UNDERCONTINENT,
AND GRAND CAPITAL OF THE DEATH REALM

41

SERDIN

⌁

"These Landish rulers really don't fancy your daughter," Daniel commented as we made our way through the palace halls.

I grumbled, my wolf ears half-curled and half-draped to my neck. We'd left a conference meeting with Howllord Inion, my First Fangs here in Low Neverland. He *would* have been my daughter's father-in-law, had Willow not found Xavier alive and declined Matthiel's proposal, but I supposed life was often unexpected. Apparently, as was death, in Xavier's case.

When I'd last spoken to my daughter, she reported that Neverland's queen had declared war that night. Daniel and I needed to prepare, and soon, so consulting with my general on this continent was essential.

The queen up there was moving swiftly. It had been only three weeks since her declaration, and she'd already ordered *every* Surfacing Port destroyed in *all* cities across her kingdom. The only way up—*and* down—was through Marincia or High Everland, in the territories Lucas and Alice had claimed in my name.

It was hitting our economy impressively hard, though. With no working Surfacing Ports from Everland, all imported goods from up there were cut off. Many businesses down here relied on those imports. And now there were trapped citizens from the surface down here without funds or shelter, and the ports' employees suddenly had no work. Thousands of families found themselves with little to no income suddenly. I had Daniel do what he could to rally a relief effort campaign for those unfortunate souls, but as with all things in war time, there would always be many, many shifters unaided. And as with all things *political*, I was being blamed for not helping the poverty-stricken citizens more.

"It isn't my daughter's fault the mid-realm's leaders are all lunatics," I said. "You should have heard what that madwoman had done."

"Oh, I did," Daniel grimaced, his grown bat ears folding down. "Lilli told me the details the same night. She said Howllord Inion's son and the Sky Princess were poisoned with drinks made of Yinklît Gel. What a splendid way of welcoming house guests, eh?"

I hummed irritably. "I'm going to High Everland in a couple months to see Lucas myself and help him with his efforts there... If Willow hasn't quelled the fights above *this* continent after we finish, I'll sail there next."

Daniel nodded, running thoughtful fingers over his moustache. He hesitated. "I don't suppose... I could join you?"

I eyed him questioningly. "You sound suspiciously eager."

"Well, see, it's just that Lilli mentioned they'd found someone... interesting." He coughed into a fist. "A particular Relicblood..."

I grunted. "The Land woman?"

"Serdin, I *must* see her for myself." He was shamelessly giddy now, rubbing his thick hands together. "Five hundred years, hidden in Aspirre—*alive?*" He laughed, thumping my back. "And your wife knew about it the whole time!"

I scowled. "Don't remind me."

"I'd also like to see my daughter," he said, sighing with longing. His tone grew lonely. "I haven't seen Lilli in person for as long as you haven't seen Willow... and then, there's the news that Xavier was found alive."

"Yes, and I hear he'd lost his memories until recently." I put a fist at my side, slowing to a stop before the west wing's main stairway. "Yet, something doesn't feel right..."

"How so?" asked Daniel.

"If Xavier had been wandering the surface all this time— remembering nothing, not even his parents or his brother—I would have expected him to look completely different from Alexander now."

Daniel lifted an eyebrow. "You expected identical twins to look *different?*"

"Well, obviously I expected the same face and eyes... but the way Willow has been talking about him, he seems to be jumping back into routine with Alexander as if he never left. Would there not be some amount of... of *distance* there?" I waved a hand. "Alexander hasn't seen his brother in six years. Yet now that Xavier's suddenly here, Willow makes it sounds as if he's treating the reunion with little surprise."

Daniel shrugged. "Perhaps the dynamics of their reunion is only apparent to those currently with them?"

I brooded low. "Yes... but all the more reason to see them in person—"

"Serdin!"

We both looked at my wife when she called from up the stairway.

Myra's azure hair was frazzled, and I saw she was still in her sleepgown, even though it was early afternoon. She was holding a thin book that she kept opened to a specified page, her eyes splintered wide.

"Serdin," she said hurriedly. "Serdin, you *must* read this!"

I started up the steps skeptically. "What is it?"

"It's the first issue my mother's Chief Enlightener wrote." She briskly stepped through the upper corridor, making me rush after her. "I was given it by one of her Enlighteners here in town. It's the documentation of the Shadowblood."

The blasted woman wouldn't let me catch up. "Yes, you already explained about that. And Willow made a mention of their new Hallows months ago—"

"It's not about that," Myra contradicted, whirling on me suddenly. She slapped the back of her hand on the page she'd kept open. "It's about their life *before* knowing about their gifts. Serdin, this… this is incredible. Even *I* wasn't told about this. You must read it."

She shoved the book in my hands, and I glanced at the text warily. "Myra, I don't have my reading glas…"

She produced my reading glasses from her gown's low neckline. I sighed, slipping the eyeglasses over my nose and using the corridor's lantern light to read, the wispy fallen lights giving the pages a white wash.

I began reading. Then paused. Read longer, flipping several pages forward before my eyes ceased their scrolling.

"Myra," I said, "I have a few calls to make."

"*…still haven't mentioned why you called, Serdin,*" Lucas said from the large screen of the private conference room. "*You're being frightfully cryptic…*"

He looked worried. Even Alice beside him was trying with difficulty to hide her anxiety.

My arms were crossed over my chest, and I drummed my fingers over an arm as I waited for the second call, beside the Devouhs, to go through. Myra stood beside me, biting her tongue.

"I have something to discuss with you both," I growled, my wolf ears curled tight to my head. "And with your sons. I'm waiting for my daughter to answer her com."

Their expressions grew more worrisome. Alice cleared her throat nervously. "*Perhaps we can start without…*"

The second screen stopped its idle stirring, and once Willow's face appeared—

My breath fell away from me. So had the Devouhs'.

"Ah, Father," my daughter greeted, her eyes flicking to the corner of her screen. *"Father Lucas. Mother Alice. Is there news on High Everland's—"*

"Willow!" Myra gasped before any of us found our wits. My wife stepped closer to the large screen, clasping her hands. "You're wearing your marriage *centerpiece?"*

Willow blinked, her thoughts seeming to rewrite themselves. *"Oh,"* she said, touching the sparkling vines that dangled not from the sides of her hair, but from her forehead. *"Yes. Xavier and I have fulfilled our union."*

"What!" blustered Lucas from his screen.

Alice was utterly dumbfounded beside him. *"But we... wh–when?"*

"Three weeks prior," informed Willow.

I found my voice again and floundered. "But the wedding...?"

"We didn't hold a ceremony," she said. *"Neither of us were keen on one."*

"Who officiated?" I demanded.

"I did."

"But," Myra protested. "You're too young to marry! The age minimum..."

"... has been lowered to eighteen," I finished for her, muttering, "It was lowered along with the minimum to participate in Death's Duel. *Several* minimums were lowered. According to the new law, Willow came of age a year ago."

Willow nodded expectantly. *"Precisely."*

Alice was delighted from the other screen. *"Oh, Lucas, we've waited so long...!"*

"Too long," agreed Lucas as they exchanged an embrace in celebration. *"Nira, we have a daughter-in-law! Who took whose name?"*

"He took my name," answered Willow. *"It is tradition for the Relicbloods to keep theirs."*

Myra began tearing up, sniffling. "A new member of the Ember family. Oh, but it's still too soon...!"

Willow's tone flattened. *"It's hardly soon, Mother. We've waited ten years to wed, not to mention the months Xavier has spent inside his own..."* She trailed off, remaining silent when she glanced at Lucas and Alice.

My eyes narrowed at her. "Willow," I growled. "Perhaps you could allow your mother and I see to our new... son-in-law?"

She sighed, but walked out of whatever hut she had been in, shielding herself and the com with a waxed parasol to keep out of the heavy rain.

I watched her trudge through that campsite I'd last seen her in, when she called weeks ago. Much had apparently changed since then. Through the screen, I could see the muddy field buzzing with life, multiple blocks of soldiers training in the rain, others sawing wood at a mill-site when Willow passed, and I spied Stormchasers flying overhead in the billowing overcast.

When last I spoke with her, there were barely any shifters on the grounds. Now, there were hundreds, maybe even thousands.

Willow finally slowed, keeping her parasol overhead as—

The screen streaked when she lurched back in a startled gasp, avoiding a fist-sized globe of floating water that hovered just before her. She'd inadvertently turned the screen upward, and I saw the globe of water lift to the top of a tall pillar made of ice, where a lone figure was perched.

The man atop the frozen pillar held a glowing green hand toward the floating water ball, which zipped up to his awaiting palm, spinning in place. I could barely make out the crowned, emerald Ocean mark over his left knuckles.

A smile crossed the man's face when he noticed Willow. He tossed the ball of water aside, the parting droplets joining the rain, and he bent back until he was upside down and face to face with Willow, his long, wet hair hanging down and mismatched eyes blinking away rainwater.

"Darling!" the man chuckled, stealing her lips for an endearing moment. A marriage stud gleamed from his left ear, and I spotted the ring around his left, forth finger. *"I'm glad you're here. I've just discovered what my half of the Decepiovoking is. Watch—"*

He shut his lids and held his finger and thumb over them, the tips glowing azure for a moment as his left hand bore a crowned Dream mark, which faded when he removed his hand.

He opened his eyes, revealing a new set of matching, sapphire irises. Then one fizzled back to white, and he laughed excitedly. *"I can make colors! Just like you."*

She chuckled. *"Remarkable, love."*

He noticed the com in her hand and craned his upside-down face even further. *"Who's on com?"* he asked curiously.

She cleared her throat, bringing the screen directly before the man's face. *"Your father-in-law."*

When he met my eyes, he froze. Then he slipped off the ice pillar and hit the mud in a winded groan. He hurriedly pushed to his feet, flinging off the mud that clung to his arms.

"S-Sire...!" His smile was nervous now. *"Km-hmm, good afternoon...!"*

"Hello, *son*," I muttered, scrutinizing my daughter's new husband.

Was this truly Xavier? His heterochromia was in the right place, but he looked nothing like what I saw the last time, in High Everland. Back then, his hair had been cut short, his stubble at a minimum over his chin and jaw.

Now, his cheeks and neck were incredibly slender, sporting a fair beard, his skull's grey hair grown to his shoulders. It couldn't have grown that long in a mere few months.

"Eating enough?" I asked suspiciously. "You're looking rather thin. One would think you've been in a coma for a few years."

He swallowed visibly, the Devouhs growing rigid on the other screen.

"Xavier," another voice sounded from the screen. Alexander trotted into view behind his brother. *"Why did you stop? We're still in the middle of..."*

Alexander glanced at the screen and blinked. *"Oh. Sire."* He bowed shallowly, seeming confused as he noticed Lucas and Alice next. *"Father, Mother. Is all well overseas?"*

I stared at the brothers for a moment, realizing this was the first time I'd seen them *together*, at the same time, in years.

"I was wondering if one of you would mind clearing something up for me," I said, snatching the book Myra had had me read. "This is an interesting book... regarding the Shadowblood's upbringing."

All faces tensed.

I continued, "It says here that you, Xavier, have a strange talent with removing someone's soul with their NecroSeams intact." My glare sharpened. "And that you took out *your own* soul... Tied it to Alexander... And kept it from me for six Gods damned years."

EVERLAND

DRINELLE
NEW ALDAMSTRIA

42

LUCAS

I watched my son reach his hand to his brother's chest on their screen.

Both they and Willow had relocated out of the rain and into a private hut, where their com was set on a wooden table.

Serdin waited with grown wolf ears as he observed my sons, bristling with anger.

This was it—this was precisely what we'd been avoiding for so long. And now, somehow, Serdin knew everything. What in Bloods was that book? Who even knew enough about what had happened to *write* about it?

Alice had an incredible grip on my hand as Xavier's Death mark began to gleam on their screens, and a violet light spread across Alexander's chest.

Serdin had demanded a demonstration of Xavier's talent, to verify the legitimacy of what he'd read. Alice and I could do nothing from our end. Nothing but wait and hold our breaths.

Xavier drew out his hand on the screen, and with it came Alexander's pale soul, his body collapsing to the floor.

The light faded from Xavier's hand, and he waved to Alexander's soul unceremoniously.

From the side of the screen, Willow picked up the com and brought the view over Alexander's resting vessel, his chest rising and falling gently.

"As you can see, Father," said Willow, *"Alex is alive. He's only asleep."*

She brought the view back up to Alexander's detached soul, which gestured to a glowing thread shining bright from his translucent ribs. *"And my NecroSeam is still in one piece,"* he said.

Serdin's stare didn't soften, his colorless eyes flicking to Xavier. *"And you can bring him into a foreign vessel? One that's already occupied?"*

Xavier's lips drew into a line, almost looking like a petrified grimace, and evoked his Hallows again. He dragged Alexander's soul toward himself, and the ghost disappeared into his chest.

Xavier kept his eyes closed for a moment, silent. When his lids opened next, his eyes had switched.

"Now we're both in here." Alexander crossed his arms, and without so much as a breath, his eyes switched back to Xavier. *"We can take control individually, when we like. Though, we can't be out at the same time."*

Serdin's gaze turned contemplative. Perhaps even fascinated. He rubbed his chin. *"I assume you can replace the soul back to its original body, then?"*

Xavier shrugged. *"That's how I returned to my body, once we found it."* He pulled out Alexander's soul and placed his brother back into his rightful vessel, which blinked awake and sat up, wobbling slightly. Xavier rubbed his neck, the marriage stud in his left ear glinting in the lamplight. *"The difficult part was locating it. We didn't know if I was still alive in the first place, before then."*

I cleared my throat hastily. "But it *was* alive, as you can see. No laws were broken."

"Except the laws of magic," muttered Serdin. Then he shot a harsh glare at me. *"I only wish I'd been told all this when it first appeared, Lucas."*

I winced. And there came the guilt trip. "We didn't know what to make of it at the start, Serdin… We weren't sure if Xavier had broken any laws, so we'd taken to researching all we could. By the time we considered telling you, a year had already passed…"

Alice added solemnly, "We'd finally gotten our son back, though in an unexpected way. We didn't want to lose him again—not to mention risk losing Alexander."

On their screen, Myra laid a hand on Serdin's arm, murmuring, *"If it had happened to Willow, we likely would have done the same."*

Serdin scowled at her for a moment, but sighed. *"I… suppose. And perhaps you were right to keep it from me… I thought his death was a certainty."*

Xavier gave a dismal laugh. *"As did I. Thank Death I was wrong."*

"You're welcome," Willow said beside him, smirking. That prompted a more cheerful laugh from him.

Serdin circled his fingers over a temple, grumbling. *"Strange things are happening on Nirus, that's for certain… As for the matter of Xavier, I'm satisfied for now. My questions were answered—even if several more were raised—and you're right: no laws were broken, technically."* He looked directly at me. *"But if I find that you've kept ANYTHING else from me, Lucas, you will lose much more than your position as my Eyes."* His hurt look bit into my chest. *"You'll have lost my trust completely."*

I bowed my head, murmuring. "I understand. I... I've no excuse."

"I wish that you didn't," he begrudgingly muttered, *"but you do. Your sons were at risk... Any respectable father would likely have done the same."* His lids narrowed at me, though he seemed more curious than irate. *"When Daniel and I arrive in High Drinelle, I hope you'll grant me a more detailed story of what happened?"*

I nodded heavily, my gaze sincere. "Of course, Sire."

"And I expect the full explanation," he emphasized. *"Leave nothing out."*

"I have no more reason to, my lord," I said, and it was the truth.

He gave me a pointed look, then his screen went blank. Willow ended her call as well with Xavier and Alexander.

Now, Alice and I were alone in the private conference room of Apsonald's manor in Drinelle. I could do nothing except stare emptily at the now blank wall.

"Well... it's done," I said, "he knows everything."

Pain festered. I'd spent the last seven years lying to one of my closest friends. Too long had I dreamt of this day, waking in the night of seeing my sons killed for my mistake.

But he's letting them live, I reminded. The thought brought some relief. Serdin himself had even assessed that no laws were broken. Even if our friendship had been.

Alice rested a hand on my arm. "At least... at least we still have our family." She said, an aged smile stretching her face. "And we've gained a daughter, even."

Despite the pit in my chest, I grinned, wetting her cheek with my lips. "That we have."

My son, a married man. Nira, where did the time go?

Voices sounded from the window outside then, piercing through the rain. I moved to look down at the dark streets below, seeing several mud-covered wagons were pulling up to the manor's courtyard.

Alice came to glance over my shoulder. "The rescue party," she said softly.

I nodded, heading for the door—

A spectral, scaled head rippled through the wood. "Lucas!" the ghost—Apsonald—chuckled, bringing the rest of his translucent body into the room. "Good to see you!"

I relaxed, laughing while taking the ghost's hand and gave a firm, though incorporeal, shake. "Apson! I'm glad you made it back safely."

"It was a long trip, but yes. That Necrovoker you sent is a lovely woman, the Footrunner." He grinned to himself. "A woman Footrunner. Never seen one before."

"Not in your backwards country you haven't," I said, pointing my chin at Alice behind me. "Woman generals are rare for you up here as well, aren't they?"

"Rare?" he echoed. "There aren't *any*. Grim must be fascinating."

"Only to surface dwellers."

The ghost nodded, humming while smearing a hand over his pale chin. "True, true... I suppose, taking my current state into account, I'll have to grow accustomed to a few changes, eh?"

"Quite a few," I agreed, folding my arms. I cocked my head. "Though, I've been thinking, Apson. You now have a number of options regarding your after-life. You can choose to either take residence in one of Grim's soul communities, whichever and wherever may suit your needs, or—"

"I'd like a vassalship," he said, his creased smile sure, as if he'd not had another option in mind. "With you, if that's quite all right. The Necrovoker woman explained my options on the ride over."

I stared at him, beguiled. "You're certain this is what you want? I have no qualms, I'd be honored... but a Bloodpact will last you for—"

"The rest of your lifetime," Apson finished for me, folding white arms behind his back patiently. "She told me such details as well. I understand the terms. And I accept. Especially since I'll have more chances to see my grandson this way. I can't think of a better deal."

I exchanged a glance with Alice, then chuckled. "I suppose I can't argue with that. Very well. A Bloodpact it is."

MILANN

I shivered, my feet sticking knee-deep in the mud, rain pouring down real hard. But I stepped forward anyway and pushed through.

The muck already tooked my shoes weeks ago, so it squished all wet and cold between my toes. My stomach growled again. Maybe I should've stoled more sweet rolls at the last town these tracks went through?

My curly hair stuck to my face so much, I almost forgot it wasn't supposed to be like that. I panted, my foot sticking extra hard in the mud. I heaved—it made a *splch* noise and I toppled face first in the mud. Sniffling, hacking, I tried to wipe it off, but the rain did a better job, thunder rumbling overhead.

I was so tired... How long did these tracks *go*? I haven't seen no Reapers once since I started walking. Where were they all?

Crack!

Lightning sparked in the clouds. No, it wasn't lightning. The bolts streaked and wove in and out of the clouds like a lizard crawling through a pile of black wool. It zipped and zapped all over the place, a pair of sharp wings leaving see-through after images when it soared by.

A Shockdragon? So, that's why this storm was so strong.

A cold wind shoved me backward, so heavy I flew back and almost lost my grip on my Reaper weapon. I never let it go for more than a second. It protected me. It reminded me there was monsters out there… it reminded me that I kilt that first demon. That I… I kilt my Mum. And Mum kilt my bird, and…

My throat closed up, eyes stinging. My chest hurt so bad I couldn't move anymore. Why? Why did it feel like someone cutted out a piece of me from the inside? Why did it *hurt so much*?

The Shockdragon let out a crackling roar from the clouds, lighting up the muddy wasteland as its shiny scales brightened with a new bolt it rubbed against playfully.

Now that I could see better, what was that huge black thing up ahead? It looked like…

A city!

Thank the Gardener! Those were city walls up there all right, and real close too. If I could just get there before my stomach shriveled up…

I tightened my fingers on my Reaper weapon and waded through the thick muck, the playing Shockdragon being my nightlight.

JIMMY

The rain pelted the living Void over us, our caravan's horses trudging through the thick muck outside Drinelle's city gates. Their hooves made a suction-like *smck, smck, smck* sound from outside our shielding, wagon walls.

I pulled back a small piece of the canvas, seeing all the Reapers were running in the mud and scrambling to push one of the other wagons out of a pit as lights flickered in the storm overhead. Some of the rain was frozen, I could see tiny sparks of trapped lightning in the beads of hail as they pelted the tarp near me.

At least it was calmer than yesterday, thank Bloods. Shatter season only lasted four weeks in the middle of spring, but those four weeks had been Void since our only shelter was a piece of feral cow hide. We stopped in a small village last week when the storm hit *really* bad. For Gods' sakes, that damn Shockdragon was even still following us from that one. There it was now, snaking through the clouds like it was at a carnival and showing off its glittery pink-and-blue electric scales.

Yulia's head shifted over my shoulder, breathing slow in her sleep. Her Dream mark was gleaming blue from the palm of her thumb.

"Well, we're stuck," I said, turning to the second Yulia—her copy—who was sitting beside me, and *not* sleeping on my shoulder. "But we're here. You should probably wake up."

She hummed. "Grand timing. My original is already calling me back."

Her image faded, evaporating and phasing backward into the physical Yulia. The original's eyes fluttered, and she gently pushed off my shoulder and rubbed her eyes.

"Come on." I opened the canvas and stepped off the wagon, getting drenched the minute I walked through the curtain of rain.

She threw on her cowl and climbed down after me, the two of us sloshing through the mud toward the front of the caravan.

Only two of the wagons made it in earlier, the others were left behind, stuck in the wet muck.

I followed after the group through the city gates—

My feet kicked into something, and I damn near fell over. Luckily, Yulia was there to balance me. But when I was steadied, she wasn't looking at me. She was looking at whatever I tripped on, horror creasing her face and a hand drawn to her pale lips. What the Void was...?

I stopped cold when I looked down.

"Milann...!" I dove down and hauled the tiny sheep girl out of the muck, pulling her to my chest.

Bloods, she was covered from head to foot in this mud. Her eyes barely cracked open, the bronzed ewe looking confused. She was panting hard, wheezing, then her eyes rolled back and her head sagged, her small chest still heaving for air. "Bloods, Milann, what are you doing here?" I carried her through the gate.

Yulia hurried behind me. "You know her?"

"She doesn't know me." I kept Milann secured against my chest, keeping her warm. Land, she was freezing. "She was a client in Lindel, from my district."

Yulia was having trouble keeping up. "She survived Lindel...? But how did she make it this far alone?"

"I don't know." I evoked my dream Hallows between Milann's small sheep horns, my fingers gleaming blue. But she only wriggled in my arms, not waking up. "I need to get her inside and check on her dreams. Maybe they'll tell us a bit about what happened."

"I can care for her," Yulia offered, her cowl and snowy hair underneath already drenched from the downpour. She reached for Milann. "I can ask the High Howllord to house her."

I kept Milann's face tilted away from the shower. "She's my client. I'll look after her."

"And if she needs medical attention?" she pressed. "Last I heard, the doctors here are packed full of patients, it would take perhaps days to see her at best. If I make a request to the High Howllord, he will see her cared for immediately."

I cocked an eyebrow at her. "He'd listen to you?"

"Of course. Please." She reached for Milann again. "Trust me?"

I looked around, drew in a breath, and handed the girl over.

Plnk!

Something dropped in the mud from Milann's hand. Something that glowed.

I plucked it out of the muck and held it up for Yulia to see.

Her brow furrowed. "A scythe-sphere?"

"What was she doing with a scythe?" High Howllord Lucas questioned bitterly from his place by the window of the manor's study, turning the radiant sphere in his hand. His reflection on the window showed a low scowl on his black-and-grey bearded face.

I only shrugged. "Search me, Howllord. My guess is, she picked it up on her way here."

"She was alone?" He glanced at me skeptically. "How in Bloods did a girl that small make it all the way here from Lindel?"

"I'm not a Seer, Howllord," I muttered, scratching between my elk horns. "But Yulia's keeping watch on her dreams right now. Maybe she'll dig up some answers in Milann's subconscious."

The lord nodded, examining the scythe-sphere again with more thought. "You're sure the girl is one of ours? A Reaper? Fangs Lastings hasn't found any files on an apprentice of her description."

"She didn't have a chance to find a master." My tone soured. "Her messenger... her mother killed it the minute it found her."

His aged features sagged in horror. "Her own mother?"

"Stomped it to death right there in the street. I was there for it. So were your sons, they'll tell you the same."

The Howllord grunted and rubbed his peppered beard. "My sons know her, then..." He blew out a long, nasally breath and palmed the sphere. "Very well. For now, it seems Yulia is keen on seeing to the girl. If she wishes, the girl may stay in her care here. Perhaps once my sons return, they'll verify her lost messenger."

"Oh, they will." I folded my arms. "And I've never seen the Death Princess so angry. I get the feeling she'll remember Milann."

"I see…" He strode to the mini bar set at the back of the study, his heavy steps sinking into the sienna carpet. He rummaged through the bar's cabinet tiredly, shoulders slacked and his throat sounding hoarse suddenly. "This has been quite an evening… Care for a drink, Sir James?"

"Gin," I said, and added, "and Jimmy's fine, sir."

He nodded to the side and pulled out a bottle of gin from the cabinet. He poured the first glass and handed it to me, then poured his own glass next, downed it in one go, and filled it up again.

"You," he exhaled hard and rubbed his brow in a circular motion as if having a migraine, "are a conundrum, sir."

I cocked an eyebrow. "*I* am?"

He sipped his drink, loosening the cravat that was tucked in his shirt. "You were part of the refugee group that came with my sons, correct?"

"Yeah," I said. "I helped them out when they ran into some trouble with the locals in Lindel. Then they helped me out when it got leveled, so I figured helping their friends was fair."

He nodded, thoughtful. He gestured to a cushioned chair behind me with his glass. "May as well have a seat. I wished to discuss something with you regardless, this may be as good a time as any."

Skeptical, I lowered into the indicated chair. "All right… what is it, sir?"

He eased into a brown lounging chair himself and crossed his legs. He looked out the window contemplatively, watching the rain and small beads of hail hit the glass outside.

He stayed poised like that for a minute or two, swirling his drink. His age showed, sitting like that. Wrinkles creased his porous skin, his slightly disheveled black hair was greyed at his ears, and his beard had grown wily. He wasn't nearly as groomed as when I left.

"You know," he finally said, still watching the rain. "Twenty years I've been trying to… to encourage Yulia out of our manor. She finally did this last year, but only to accompany Alice and me to the surface. And only because my sons were leaving as well."

He let the following silence stretch on. There was a small rumble of thunder outside, then more patters of rain.

He cleared his throat, a deep guttural sound. "She refused to venture from Alice and my side the entire trip." He looked at me finally, and his leather chair made rubbing creaks when he leaned forward. "And then you come along."

What in Void is that look? "And?"

He pointed at me with his glass. "First you decide to join my sons to rescue their friends from Tanderam. Yulia followed. Next you signed up to help rescue

Apson from New Aldamstria. She followed again. *Away* from us. *Away* from my sons."

"Actually," I interjected. "She asked me to join that second time."

"Even more perplexing." He muttered, sipping his drink.

If I was supposed to say something to that, I missed the memo. So I sat there, waiting for him to go on. Bloods, waiting for him to *move*.

I put down my glass on a side table. "All right, where is this going, Howllord?" I asked. "Am I suddenly under interrogation?"

He took a minute to think, then gave a shrugging nod. "In a manner of speaking… yes."

"Why?"

"Curiosity." He tipped his glass to me. "I wanted to know who finally caught the fair Yulia's interest. I've been waiting twenty years for this, Sir James."

I grimaced. "Land, just Jimmy. *Please.*"

"You're a Dream Knight, it's only proper."

"Look, most of us have to stay in hiding in the conscious world. No one's ever called me *Sir.* I'm… well, I *was* a local Catcher."

"Have you considered going into the private sector?"

I rubbed my neck. "I've, uh… I've thought about it. But I don't exactly have any patrons lined at my doorstep."

"Then consider me the first in your queue." He leaned back in his chair, which gave more rubbing creaks.

My stare went blank. "What?"

"Give me a range for your desired salary along with your preferred working hours. You'll be given your own quarters and property, of course, as well as—"

"Hold on a minute." I raised my hands, rising. "I'm missing something. What's the catch?"

"Catch?" He scratched his scruffy neck. "I suppose… you'll have to take residence in Grim with us after we're through with the war."

"That's it?"

His head tilted. "Well… that, and perhaps… if you could keep the Lady Yulia company…"

Ah. Yep. Thought so. I slid my hands in my pockets. "Look, Howllord. I know where you're going with this, and I think I'm a *little* old to have marriage arrangements made for me, eh? I'm pushing thirty here."

"Of course, of course." He looked pressed for words, tapping his fingertips anxiously. "I only thought you would, perhaps, find interest in proposing your *own* arrangement…"

"Slow down, Howllord." I waved my hands. "Marriage is a tall order... And, uh, let's *humor* the idea that she even wanted it—you think a cushy *job* is the bribe?"

His expression brightened. "You're interested without the job?"

"Do I look like an idiot? Void *yes* I'm Bloody interested. But Bloods, I don't even know if I want to try anything in the first place."

He looked confused. "No?"

"Don't get me wrong." My tone soured. "I've just... been through some things. Local Catchers don't have the luxury of showing their Hallows to everyone they meet. We're only protected by a government law, thanks to King Dream, but most of us are still driven out of towns if the wrong people find us out." I sighed and grabbed my gin from the table, taking a swig. "I mean, my last relationship was a shit show... And only because I was stupid and thought she'd be okay with me being a Dream Walker."

"But Yulia shares your Hallows," the Howllord protested.

I pointed. "Exactly. This is... new for me. I don't have a damn clue how to approach it. So... I don't know if I want to do anything."

"But she's attracted to you!" The Howllord lifted from his own seat, troubled. "You said yourself you were interested!"

"That doesn't mean she is," I interrupted. "You're assuming she's got an attachment, but until I hear it from her, I'm not doing a Gods damned thing. I don't know what her last husband did, but I sure as Void don't want to screw up the same way."

Surprisingly, his skin paled more than I thought it could. Then his brow furrowed low. "She told you of her last husband...?"

Holy Bloods, he looked downright haunted. I gave a half-hearted shrug. "She didn't say much... except that you cut off his head."

"I did." He sat down again, chugging the last of his drink before filling up his glass again. "Bloods, his was the first beheading I was tasked to carry out in Low Everland."

"What in Void did he do?"

His chuckle was grim. "You, I'm sure, know very well what he did." He opened his mouth and started singing a gritty nursery rhyme. *"Watch your head, watch your insides, else they ride with the Death King's Eyes."*

I went stiff as the Howllord sang on, *"Death and cinder, steps like tinder, here comes Endsler the Bloody Ender."*

43

CAYDEN

The roof's rough stone was warm under my bare feet, the upcoming storm's breeze crisp and humid.

I inhaled smoothly, enjoying the night's solitary escape. Spending a month locked in the palace after every failed attempt to subtly end my father, I'd nearly become manic. Father was too well guarded. If I was to kill him, either I had to reveal myself and be killed by his guards, or I evened the numbers with my own men—however many were still left unknown in the capital. There was one man in particular I knew was still in business here, at least.

The sound of flapping wings came from my left and I threw myself behind a chimney. Peering past the side, I watched a winged Runner fly by on patrol. There were hoots and commanding yells from various Stormchasers as well, I'd seen many of them preparing their crossbows and Metaglass spheres to collect the storm's lightning.

When the roof was clear, I ducked out from the chimney's shadow and drew my hood up, making sure to adjust my eye and face mask also.

The next building, the one I sought, was separated by an alley and was one level lower. I evoked my rock Hallows and pushed off the ledge of the roof, using the *next* roof as an anchor to pull me the rest of the way, then pushed down slightly once I was near to give myself a soft landing.

Looking over the new ledge, I felt the wind pick up, sweeping threateningly as a distant rumble purred in the clouds. Shatter season was to start tomorrow. It seemed we'd hit rain on the first night, in a few hours. Perhaps even minutes.

I stayed crouched on the ledge and watched the lit streets below. Raiders and Footrunners passed in their clattering armor. They all had more weapons than usual now. For the Runners, a Shotri was issued as well as a thin saber at their side and a spear in hand. The Raider had a typical, double-edged steel blade at one hip alongside a holstered Shotri, and a Spiritcrystal sword whose light gleamed even from beneath its scabbard at the other. Without using any sealed Terravoking enchantment on the weapons to change their shape, it looked gratuitously bulky and ostentatious. But then, I supposed that was the point. Unnecessary and clunky didn't matter so long as fear was instilled in both the citizens and the enemy.

Voices sounded from the opened window below me, and my lion ears perked.

"...Best to keep that one in its sheath," said a gruff voiced man inside. "It won't cut your skin, but you won't have any skin left to cut if it slices the wrong place."

A second man grunted, the sound of metal beads clattered on a counter, and the floorboards creaked as someone walked over them. Seconds later, I saw a Raider walk out the front door, taking to the streets.

I hung over the roof's ledge to crawl into the opened window.

This attic was dim, but the small cracks in the floorboards spilled with the light from below, dust particles floating in the rays. The smell of coals and oils were pungent, and the scrape of metal on stone fell into a grating rhythm below. The door was ajar, so I slunk through and padded down the steps as softly as I could, hoping the smith's clanging work was loud enough to cover me.

Downstairs, a fire quivered and snapped from a hearth, a cast-iron pot filled with bright red coals. The smoke was thick down here, the smith's metal visor and gloves stained black as he sharpened a hatchet on his grindstone bench.

I pulled up my hood and hid in the shadowy corner near a rack of dull swords. When the smith paused his sharpening to inspect the hatchet's edge, I spoke, "Henry."

The rabbit-eared man jumped and nearly dropped the hatchet, throwing up his visor to find me in the shadowed corner. This time, he *did* drop the hatchet, jerking to his feet and ignoring the clatter the tool made when it hit the floor.

"Cayden!" He paused, his rabbit ears dropping as the man squinted at me and hissed, "Is it actually you?"

I plucked off my mask and removed my hood, letting him see my natural face. "Have I had imposters during my imprisonment in my father's palace?"

"No, but one can't be too careful these days." He peeled off his gloves and set them on a work table, going to the door and bolting the latch before drawing the curtains and setting the 'closed' sign up. "Your father made an announcement some time ago. He thinks he learned who you really are under the mask. He told the kingdom you're Linolious Rennegaurd."

I chuckled. "At least my father is stupid enough to believe our little ruse, eh? You'd think it should be simple to take him out up there... and yet, I admit, I'm finding it more difficult than planned. I need our men to pick off his guards. How many of us are left in the city? Have you made contact with anyone?"

"Not many." He massaged his arms, as if trying to loosen his strained tendons as he went to pick up the hatchet he'd dropped and set it on the table. "After Apson's execution, it looks like most have either high-tailed it out of here, died, or surrendered."

"And how's your cover so far?" I asked, inspecting his workshop. "I see you managed to set up shop, at least."

"It was a good find." He sounded smug. "I've already built a reputation with most of the king's soldiers, even. Apparently, they trip over each other to find any Blacksmiths who can forge Spiritcrystal blades."

I hummed, picking up a rather radiant sword from the rack beside me and examining it. "I don't doubt it... And I noticed the attic could be a prime location to hold meetings in private with the others."

He smirked and walked to a rug in the corner, kicking it away from the floor to reveal a hidden door. "You should see the cellar. It's why I picked this place to set up shop."

He threw open the cellar door and led the way down the dusty steps, pulling a cord hanging from the rafters to flick on the dim lamplight hanging above us.

My brow lifted as my gaze swept the expansive room. "Bloods, Henry," I said, rapping my knuckles on a nearby support beam, a puff of dust rising. "This is the perfect find."

Henry gave a bearded grin. "Isn't it? I've told most of the others left in the capital where to find it, so we'll hold meetings here at your word."

A soft pattering sounded from outside the shop's windows above us. The rain had begun.

I reached out a hand to Henry. "One more thing, before I leave. I need to borrow your com. The High Howless has been awaiting a status report, and I've been without communication for the past month. If you could?"

Henry grunted and pulled a com from his apron's pocket, handing it to me. "I've already talked with her and my niece in Neverland," he said—then he froze suddenly, a new thought hitting him. "Oh! Cayden, you'll never believe this. Vendy tells me they found—"

The com in my finger roared to life in chirping trills. Its screen of light projected to life, displaying the name of the High Howless.

"Ah!" I said and answered the call. When Fangs Alice's grey-haired head came into view on the screen, I grinned. "What timing, High Howless. I was just about to contact you."

"Cayden?" Fangs Alice greeted in surprise. *"Bloods, you certainly took your time to get back to Henry with an update."*

"I slipped out as soon as I could, Howless," I said. "Still no luck, from inside. I'll need reinforcements from the border."

"Lucas and I are making plans as we speak," she said. *"Apson will be with us in a matter of weeks. And my sons…"* There was a notable silence for a moment, then she hesitated. *"We've just heard from them. It seems they've… found Land's Relicblood."*

My very soul went numb. "Wh… what?"

Henry excitedly squeezed my shoulder. "That's what I was trying to tell you! They found Land's last reincarnation!"

"By Shel!" I gawked at him. "I—who-who is he? Where was he found?"

"Not he," Fangs Alice corrected. *"Land was apparently reborn a woman. I don't remember her name, if it was a false one or not… it was that lioness who was guarding my sons."*

"Anabelle…?" I whispered, more to myself. Gods, she'd been right there…

"She is overtaking Neverland," she went on. *"After which, Xavier has assured she will come with aid to help us here in Everland."*

I found myself smiling wickedly. "Thank you, Howless… Truly. Your sons have led us to our victory!"

It was pouring when I reached the palace gates in a full-on sprint, the rain and thunder masking my hastened footfalls as I used my Terravoking to leap perpendicular to the stone wall and run up its length, my blood thrumming in an exuberant thrill. The royal guards below the palace were too busy shielding themselves from the shower and preparing for the strengthening storm to notice me. Shatter season had arrived.

The mark of a new dawn, I thought in a heckle as I rushed unnoticed to the castle wall and walked along its side. *A new revival!*

Land had shown himself at last. Herself! Damn me, of course it was Ana! She'd been a quiet one, but by Bloods, there was more behind her gaze that she kept from the world. *My queen…* I rushed up the wall, not giving a damn about the rain soaking me head to foot as I passed by several windows, rising up the floors. *My queen is coming! To reclaim her lands!*

I needed to prepare. I needed to plan, I… I needed time—

A terrified cry jolted me out of my revere, and I halted along the wall. It'd come from a window I'd just passed. Another scream sounded there, a woman shrieking for help.

I fumbled over, and when I wiped away the fog coating the glass and peered inside, my lungs grew cold.

The screaming woman was my mother. She was in her bed in her private chambers. A dim lamp shone from her nightstand to let me see the drunken man sprawled on top of her. He was ripping off her clothes, striking her with clawed hands whenever she resisted him. She sobbed as my father held her down and helped himself to his pleasures. I watched in horror while he ravaged her, my mother's screams surely piercing enough to catch the guards' attentions outside her door? Why didn't they come? Had Father ordered them to ignore it all…?

Father was in the midst of ecstasy when I saw Mother grab the lamp at her nightstand and smash it against Father's skull. Father gave a startled roar and clutched his head as Mother scrambled off the bed and darted for the door. But Father ripped off the long, tasseled cord that was dangling from the bed's canopy and he caught her by the throat. Mother floundered, gagging breathlessly as her thin face began to blush purple.

Damn it all!

I shoved my elbow against the glass. It took a few hits before the window shattered and I threw myself inside, rain pouring in behind me as thunder ruptured from the storm. Father was distracted enough by my break-in that he released his strangle hold on Mother's neck, dropping the cord. Mother collapsed to the carpet and hacked for air.

Father didn't bother with questions and used his Terravoking to fashion a nearby marble bust into a dagger. I ducked and dodged his strikes, ripping apart a piece of a stone pillar to fashion my own knife. I snarled and slashed for Father, fury turning my blood to sizzling mist in my veins. My advance was so swift and aggressive that the nude man had no choice but to back away, dodging my blows in retreat until he was up against the window I'd broken into. I roared and charged, ready to shove him out and have the groundskeeper find this bastard's naked corpse splattered on the lawn—!

His knife bit into my shoulder, making me stagger and grunt. I ducked when he began his counter strikes, forcing me back toward the door.

The guards finally burst inside and drew their blades. *Useless idiots!* Where had they been when my *mother* was screaming for her life?

Father threw an enraged finger at me and yelled, "Assassin!"

I was disoriented for a moment, nearly forgetting I was still wearing my masks and hooded coat. I'd been so ensnared by fury, I'd thought I was killing him as myself, without a disguise.

The guards spared no time and came for me. Glancing round the room, I found the glass doors to the balcony. With father blocking my original entrance, and the guards standing between me and the doors, it was my best option. I hurtled into the glass doors and hopped onto the balcony in a shower of shards. I sprinted as fast as I damn well could across the castle wall, thanking Shel none of the guards were following me. None from that group must have had rock Hallows.

When I reached the open window to my room—one that I'd left open for this very reason—I hurriedly ripped off my damp jacket, eye mask, and mouth cloth, then jumped inside.

"Aah!" a woman screamed from the bed at my entrance—and I bristled.

Blast, I'd forgotten Revinna was here! To my aggravation, my new *wife* was already out of bed, and she jumped in fright when I landed in our chambers soaking wet, my slashed shoulder dripping blood.

"Cayden!" She rushed over, her bronze skin paling at the sight of my gash. "Bloods, what happened?!"

"Blast it, I've no time for you!" I drew my claws and tore into my other shoulder in a pained yell, then shattered a hand mirror that was on her desk and used one of the shards to slice a shallow line across my chest. I was sure Father would remember where he cut the 'assassin'. If I held the same wound in the same place, I'd be discovered. But if I held other wounds from being attacked by the same 'assassin', then I had an excuse.

I handed the bloody shard to Revinna. "Stab me."

Her fingers trembled as they were stained red from my blood. She looked sick. "W-w-what?"

I tore off my damp tunic, a streak of lightning crashing outside as I turned my bare back to her. "You weren't supposed to be awake for this, but now you may as well be of use! This shard isn't long enough to be fatal. Now hurry and *stab me.*"

"I-I-I can't! Cayden, what is hap—"

"JUST DO IT, REVINNA!"

She gave a startled cry and I felt a sharp shock above my shoulder blade, the sensation hot and agonizing. I stumbled and knocked over a vase that was on a side table, gripping anything that was near me to find an escape from the pain. I barely noticed I'd ripped the curtain from its rail at the balcony doors, the dark green drapery tumbling at my feet.

It felt like an eternity before the pain quelled, and even then, it was still at the forefront of my attention, the shard still wedged in the muscle. "G-good…" I bit down the burn, growling. "Now take it out."

She did, and I gasped in relief, the fresh wound still burning, but settled to a dull ache. I sucked in several deep breaths before turning on Revinna and seized her shoulders. "A stranger came through the window and tried to kill me. I was bathing, which is why I'm soaked. You used your mirror to try and fend him off, but he picked up a shard and attacked me."

She was blinking like a feral mouse, shuddering.

"Do you understand?" I barked, making her cringe.

The color fled from her cheeks. "I…"

The door was thrown open and a flurry of guards filed into the chamber, followed by my Father. I was thankful he'd at least thrown on a pair of simple trousers and a tunic now.

When he spotted me, his eyes bulged in horror. "Bloods, he'd been here, too…!" He rushed to touch my shoulder, and I recoiled, instinctively jerking back.

He took my disgust as something else, flinging his head at the guards. "Search the room! He may still be…"

"He's gone," I said. "He left through the window not moments ago."

"Search the grounds!" Father ordered instead. When most of the guards were gone, save for a handful which stayed outside my door to keep watch, Father glanced back at me. "Cayden, that assassin attacked your mother, also. I scared him off, thank Shel, but I fear it may be Land's Servant. He's returned to the capital."

Revinna gasped softly, her wide eyes snapping to me. *Damn it.* The connection just lit up in her eyes. The glare I sent her was the nastiest I'd ever given any woman, sending mental messages of *say a fucking word and I will kill you.*

And it must have worked, for her lips closed shut.

I turned to Father. "You're sure it was him?"

"I'm convinced," Father said. "Linus must have been a decoy to fool me… This man was a Terravoker. So was Land's Servant. And who else in that damned rebellion would be bold enough to attack my wife in our own home?"

Who indeed, I thought bitterly.

"I'll call for a Healer to tend to you." He nodded to all the cuts I fostered. "Stay on guard… he may still be in the area."

With that, Father left us with the watching honorguard, shouting for someone to find Roarlord Wales as he shut the door after him, leaving the guards outside while Revinna and I stood alone.

I exhaled all the trapped air in my lungs and went to shut the window, keeping out the rain as I sat in the nearest chair and drummed my fingers over the cushioned arm. My lion ears were curled back, my glare deadly at Revinna, who stood petrified across from me.

"Sit." I ordered.

She promptly obeyed, lowering onto the bed.

"Now," I glowered, "what to do with you?"

She swallowed visibly, blanching.

"Where do you stand?" I asked. "I assume you've deduced who I am. And I'm sure you know what I want."

Her voice was so, so soft. "You want to kill the king. Your father…"

"Correct. So… Will you get in my way, or let me do my job?"

She looked surprisingly offended. "You honestly think I want him alive?" She lifted off the bed, her fists shaking in a sudden anger. "I would have killed him myself if he wasn't so damned surrounded! Your mother tried poisoning his drink one evening, but he'd caught onto her and look where *she* ended up— caged in a lavish room with armed guards, all of whom do nothing when the king waltzes in and takes her like some twisted sex doll he pulls out of a toy box whenever it pleases him!"

My brow lifted, fingers ceasing their drumming. "She tried to poison him?"

Revinna sighed and sat back on the bed, dismayed. "*We* tried… before you came back to the palace, we'd planned it with some of your sisters. Your mother had to be the one to do it, since she shared a room with him at the time. She only had one attempt… it did not find success…" Her limbs dripped depressively. "She was able to convince your father it was an outsider's doing, but the Hand…" There was built up contempt with the last word. "Roarlord Wales suspected her immediately. He was the one to find the poison in his drink without so much as *glancing* at it. He ordered the queen to take separate bed chambers, 'for her protection'." She scoffed at the very thought. "I still don't understand how he knows so much…"

"He isn't Wales, for one thing," I grunted. "He's an imposter with a damned convincing illusion."

She frowned. "If he isn't Wales, then who is he? What does he want?"

"I have a suspicion as to the 'who'… But either way, I sure as Bloods don't want to be near enough to touch him. Every contact I've had the misfortune of having with him, I feel like I'll have a heart attack. *Physically.*"

"Let's hear your suspicion then," she said, crossing her legs and falling into a contemplative tone, as if we were having a business meeting. "Who do you think he is?"

Strange, I thought and rubbed my chin, *Of all the people in this palace to align with my own cause, this woman was certainly last on the list.*

"I think," I began, "he may be a man named Kael Treble. I've only heard of him during my time with the Devouhs, but Kael was said to be an Infeciovoker. And my sudden lapses in health every time Wales touches me makes me wonder if this imposter has infection Hallows as well. It's the only clue I have other than the Grimish accent, but then, how many men have an extinct Hallows? I've only met two Infeciovokers in person, both of whom were related. Kael was the only relative of theirs I hadn't yet met."

"An Infeciovoker..." She sounded to be mulling over a thought. "That would explain how he knew about the poison the queen slipped..."

My brow furrowed at her. "Revinna, you're admittedly more surprising than I expected... Not many people know Infeciovokers can detect diseases. I don't suppose you've been putting the palace library to use?"

She gave a devilish smirk. "I've peeked into a Grimish Hallows book or two. When I thought they'd captured you, I wanted to know what I may be up against, in case I managed to escape to find you."

My lion ears perked quizzically. "You... planned to *rescue* me?"

"Of course." She blushed slightly. "I do care for you, Cayden..."

I rubbed at the small gash in my shoulder, not sure how to feel about all this. "You don't even know who I am, Revinna. How can you possibly say you care for me when you've only just learned what I've been doing for, well, longer than you've known me?"

Her face sagged. "I... I don't care about that. Actually, I'm rather relieved. I'd just started to question everything we'd been told about the rebellion and the Reapers. All my research had shown me the Grimish culture and their respect of the deceased. What the Screens have been saying about the Reapers doesn't match the texts. I didn't know what was true anymore. But if *you're* with the rebellion, and you left to work with the Reapers..."

Her next smile was incredibly sincere. She rose off the bed and came to kneel before me, laying a hand over mine. "I know what to believe now. And I stand with you. Not only as your wife, but as your supporter and friend."

Gods damn this woman. A part of me actually *wanted* to be attracted.

A muffled voice suddenly began shouting from outside the doors. "...Bloody told you, I want to check on my son and daughter-in-law, for Shel's sake! Let me through!"

Mother. I exchanged a glance with Revinna, asking her to stay silent. She agreed with a nod. *Though, if Mother has been trying to kill Father,* I considered. *Would it be safe to tell her who I was, as well?*

The door clicked open, and Mother came quivering inside, the guards spreading through the room and keeping a careful watch on her as I hurried to my feet.

Mother had at first looked at Revinna, but noticed me and broke down in tears. "Cayden!" Her steps were hastened when she came to embrace me. "Thank Bloods, you're alive…! I-I heard he was here, and you were…"

She began sobbing, her words too choked to understand. "Mother, I'm all right…" I returned the embrace, letting out a strained sigh.

"Why did you come back?" She tried to quell her stuttering wheezes and looked up at me like a sickly pup. "Why did you come back, Cayden? Why would you ever come back to this?" Her voice dropped to a hysterical hiss in my lion ear, taking caution not to let the guards around us hear. "I-I… I know you left on your own, to find Linus…you were with him again. Weren't you?"

I went rigid. *How did she…*

"Go back, Cayden. Leave this madness." She stepped back, rubbing her eyes and strained to speak. "Please… Take Revinna with you, if you can. You, at least, have a chance at happiness. Take it…"

"I…" What was I supposed to say?

Mother's tears stained her cheeks, her eyes rimmed red. She went to the balcony and opened the doors, breathing long and slow as she let the heavy rain pelt down on her.

Mother turned to face me. "Thank you, Cayden. For being a wonderful son. My dear…"

"Mother?" My brow creased at her suddenly serene expression, a brooding sickness creeping in the pit of my stomach.

"I'm sorry," she said, taking a step backward onto the balcony, her brown hair and sleepgown soaking in the storm. "I just wanted to see you one last time. I… I can't do it anymore. Not another night of this."

"Mother, don't—!"

"It's not too late for you, at least." Her smile fractured. "Go back to him. You deserve a chance at happiness…"

Her body lurched back over the rail as her feet kicked up. My mother disappeared when the storm swallowed her.

NEVERLAND

BLACKWOOD FOREST
ROSARIA GRAND

44

HUGH

Miss Bianca handed the tiny newborn to its mother, who lay on a risen cot in the crowded clinic.

I had to stretch my neck to see over Master and Sir Alexander, finding a good view between them and peered from there. The baby had been born hours ago, but instead of sleeping, it was wide awake, his icy blue eyes huge and alert.

The father, King Dream, went to his wife's side by the cot, chuckling when his new, fox-eared and -tailed son sneezed.

I grinned. *How cute.*

Though, cute as the baby was, I had an urgent problem to relieve. I'd stayed to see the baby, but my bladder reminded me it was time to hurry.

"I'll be right back, Master," I announced to Master, making sure he acknowledged me with a nod before I took my leave.

I ran to the nearest lavatory, sighing when the danger was over. Thankfully, that Sky Prince had installed proper plumbing. Though, there was no place to wash inside. I had to go to the pump by the well for that.

I walked back out to the field and found the pump, rinsing my hands with no particular hurry before drying them on my shirt.

"Sure you don't want to tell them?" I overheard a man ask from the nearby cook's tent. "They really should know, Tavius. You've kept it to yourself long enough."

A familiar voice sighed. "I'll… tell them soon. Promise. I just don't know how to say it without freaking them out."

Wasn't that Sir Octavius? He was one of Master's friends, one of our quarter-mates.

I walked over and peeked into the tent, finding Sir Octavius speaking with one of the cooks I recognized. That was his father, wasn't it? Master introduced me a few times and explained so.

The cook shook his head. "Freak out or not, you have to tell them. I'm not sure if you've noticed, Tavius, but we're preparing for war. She's probably expecting to jump out there at the frontlines, headfirst. What part of that sounds like a good idea in her condition?"

Sir Octavius deflated, glancing down at a bowl of stew he held. "Yeah... okay. I'll think of something..."

My mouth twisted. *How odd.* What could they have been talking about—?

The tent flap slapped open suddenly, and a rabbit-eared teenager walked out. I stiffened in a blush. It was the Lady Vendy. She held a steaming bowl of stew and took care to keep it from spilling over, blowing on it before taking a sip straight from the rim.

"U-um!" I trotted up to her. "Lady Vendy...!"

She spotted me and spit out her stew in a start, folding back her rabbit ears before hurrying away.

"Wait!" I snatched her wrist. "Please, I wished to apologize! I... I am unfamiliar with your culture's way of offering favors, if I offended you, I am truly sorry, and..."

Her brow scrunched at me. "Culture? Bloods, you really *are* an idiot."

My lion ears grew meekly. "I-I... I'm sorry. If there's any way to make amends—"

She ripped her wrist free and tossed her bowl of stew to the ground. "Gardener Sow Me, Hugh—I'm *DEAD*. I'm a walking corpse!"

I shied back, my shoulder glued to my ears. "W-well... yes. And?"

"And?!" She cried, dumbfounded. "Doesn't that bother you? You can't date someone who's just a resurrected pile of bones!"

My lion ears folded down. "Why not? Being resurrected means you've been brought back to life—"

"For a TIME!" She stamped her foot, furious. "It's not permanent! It doesn't make me anymore alive, not really! I'm *dead*, Hugh. I'm bound by a Bloodpact with my *Da'torr*..." She bit her lip. "When they're done up here, I'm going back to Grim with them. You're not going to follow me all the way down there just to be with a corpse, you idiot."

I swallowed the knot in my throat, murmuring, "Why not? Mr. Treble plans to do so for his deceased wife..."

Her rabbit ears stiffened. She blushed and ripped an irritated growl, spinning on her heels and stormed off. "Stop being an idiot! Find someone who's still alive!"

She disappeared into the crowd of bustling campers, my shoulders drooping dejectedly. *So, that was why she'd been avoiding me?* I thought gloomily. *Because I was alive?* Was she right? Was I an idiot for not caring—?

A radiant woman strode past me suddenly. My attention redirected, watching her shimmering golden locks bounce in petal-like curls over her walnut brown shoulders.

Queen Anabelle.

She didn't notice me as she passed, striding ahead with her two usual bodyguards. I could never remember their names.

I hesitated. I'd been wanting to speak with her for some time now. Master had assured me he would do what he could for Sy, but if Queen Anabelle was to be the one to take her crown, bringing up my inquiry with *her* seemed safer.

She was yards away from me now. I took several deep breaths, then hurried after her.

"U-um!" I stammered when I was near enough. "Your Majesty Land…"

The bright haired queen paused, turning. Her two bodyguards glanced at me as well, making me flush.

"Oh, Hugh," she whispered. She always had such a soft voice. The few times Master brought me to see her, I'd never heard her raise her tone louder than a quiet murmur. She smiled down at me. "Good morning. Without your master today?"

"He's at the nursery with the Dream Queen and her newborn," I explained.

Her smile grew wider, ivory teeth displaying in delight. "How wonderful! Then all went well with the birth?"

I nodded. "Miss Bianca says she still needs to run a few tests to be sure nothing else need be done, but otherwise, he is healthy."

Her primary lion ears were perked with glee. "I'm glad to hear it. Please tell them I'll be over soon to see him myself. I feel as if I've gained a brother. Oh, if only Myra were here to see him…" She sighed, then turned to leave with her bodyguards. "Have a good day, Hugh."

"Wait," I called.

She twisted back, her look quizzical.

I squeezed my fingers. "I… I-I wanted to make a request… If Her Majesty would allow?"

Her golden eyes grew sad. "Is it about your sister?"

I stiffened. How had she known? Swallowing, I nodded.

She knelt and laid a gentle hand on my shoulder. "Xavier told me of your concerns… and I'm sorry you have to bear through such a conflicting burden."

"I don't agree with what Sy is doing," I said, desperate, "but I don't want to lose her either. If there's any way she can live… I-I wondered if you could…"

She smiled thinly. "I'll do what I can to spare her. Of that I promise you. But you understand that it will ultimately be her decision?"

"Yes. Master explained it. But I wanted to be sure every other option was exhausted before it came to that, s-so…"

She stroked my hair endearingly. "I'll do everything in my power to avoid that fate for your sister. Does this calm your blood?"

I exhaled. "It does… thank you, your grace."

She smiled again and rose, continuing on her original path with her guarding men.

OCTAVIUS

Okay. I focused on my breathing: in and out. In and out… *First, I'll get them both alone. Away from everyone else. Then I'll spill.*

Yeah. That was probably the best way to tell them. Though, I didn't have a damn clue where to start when I got that far, but Dad was right. They had to know as soon as possible, before any fighting started. I owed Xavier and Willow that much, at least.

I kept the steaming bowl of stew steady, careful not to spill as I crossed the campsite. There were way more people out here than when we started. I was spending most of the trek avoiding traffic, the whole place swelling with chatter and other noises as the early-morning work schedule started up. The grass was even still wet with dew, my boots were slipping and squeaking as I sidestepped around someone pushing a hover cart through the mass.

There were still some rain clouds overhead right now, even though Shatter season ended yesterday. A few drops fell on my cheeks when a light drizzle started up.

Laughing pierced through the noise and I saw Nathaniel was slapping down a hand of playing cards over a rickety table. The other resurrected players—Aiden and Dalen—groaned and threw down their own hands in a string of curses.

I passed by one of the tents and heard someone call from inside. "Oh—uh, hey! Tavius!"

I stopped and looked in. Herrin was in there, waving me over, his wings folded tiredly over his chair.

"What?" I asked, walking in.

It was a small tent, not really holding anything except a bunch of notes and books, some inkwells and frazzled quills. A fancy type writer was there, too, in the corner. It smelled like a printing house, but mixed with the humid, rainy scent, it really just smelled like soggy paper and candle wax. The last part was from the lone candle on Herrin's work desk.

"I need to ask you about some details," Herrin said.

"What kind of details?" I glanced over his shoulder at the blank page he was hunched over. It had a title at the top that read *Sir Octavius*.

"Just a few facts for me to write down before I have some of our Seers do a more formal interview with you later, so I can write it down from your perspective. What was the date when the twins first came to your town?" he asked.

My brow knitted. "Uh… well, it was on a Dualday…" I scratched the stubble at my chin, thinking back. "The twelfth of Eyesinder, I think. Last year." Land, was it really only a year ago? It felt longer.

Herrin dipped his quill in an inkwell and wrote that down. "2102 After Bloods…" he read out loud as the nib scratched over the paper.

"You're doing all this by hand?" I asked. "You know they have Scribewriters now to do that for you with the push of a few buttons and gears or whatever. And since we're with a bunch of rich folk, you could even get one of those fancy Visionwriters with the screens, the ones imported from Culatia."

"In the middle of a secluded forest during wartime?" He raised an eyebrow at me. "We might have people smuggling supplies from in town, but I don't think they can easily get away with lugging one of those heavy monsters over here… besides." He rubbed an embarrassed finger under his nose. "I don't actually know how to use one… My siblings and I didn't really stick around in one place for very long, so it's not like I could just sit down and learn. And if I do it by hand, Crysalette will have others typing it up for me anyway, so it doesn't really matter."

"Oh…" I looked at the old-fashioned quill and inkwell on his desk. "Then, why not a fountain quill without the well?"

He shrugged, smiling like a kid. "I just like the old way better. Helps penmanship, too. So anyway…" He spun forward in his chair again and readied his old-fashioned quill. "When you first met the twins, you didn't know they were in the same body, right?"

"Right," I said. "I mean, I noticed their eyes kept switching places, but they kept telling me I just had a bad memory."

He scribbled away again, and I waited awkwardly, watching a pair of lumbermen carry a long plank in the distance.

"So, uh…" I began, needing like Void to fill the silence. "What's all this for anyway? The writing?"

He put down another few words and answered, "I'm recording the lives of the Shadowblood and anyone involved with them. I already interviewed Jaq and Bianca, but I don't have your story yet."

"Is this going to be published somewhere or something?"

"Crysalette knows a few people who work in several printing houses. She asked me to record everything for the other Enlighteners. Apparently, it's part of my 'duties' as Archchancellor." He dotted a few *I*'s and dipped his quill again, scraping off the excess ink. "I'm calling it the *NecroSeam Chronicles.*"

"Not the *Shadowblood Chronicles?*"

"There were too many other voices involved," he explained. "It didn't really fit right, since it's not just a record of them, but of all of you. You guys all came together for different reasons, but it all surrounded the NecroSeam one way or another."

"Like how?"

He spun in his chair, excited. "See, their entire situation—from before—happened because *your* ancestor threw Xavier off that cliff, right?"

I grimaced at the reminder. "Yeah."

"And *that* was the catalyst that forced Xavier's power to manifest, letting him remove his own NecroSeam without reaping it." He shuffled through a stack of finished papers on the desk, looking for specific pages. "And from there, he somehow tied his Seam alongside his brother's. Then they met you, and *you* ended up being able to destroy rotten NecroSeams with your Hallows, which was thought to be extinct. Not only that, but your other ancestor had *her* NecroSeam rot and it turned her into a demon, and now she's a demon *queen.* The best part is, she was chasing you guys down the whole time without you ever seeing her until Lindel—"

"I really don't want to talk about this," I muttered.

He looked crestfallen. "But your story is probably the most important."

"Ask me after the war's over. Not while both my psychotic ancestors are still out there wanting to kill us."

I stormed out. Did he actually think I wanted to explain everything my super old relatives did? What was I going to say? *'Oh, well, I come from a long line of murderers and demon royalty, Herrin. We have Songday dinners twice a month.'*

Ugh. I was only glad my dad ended up being threatened to do what he did. At least *he* didn't have a choice.

"Tavi?"

I wheeled around, finding El behind me.

"You okay, Tavi?" El asked, her white cat ears folding down and blue wings drooping. "You looking… mad."

I rubbed my neck, blowing out a breath through my nose. "It's nothing. Uh, *za dogt…*"

"*Dogt za,*" she corrected, her brows arching back. "<And I don't believe you. What's wrong?>"

"*Za gach…*" I caught myself and corrected, "*Gach za…* uh… family problems. I don't know the word for that."

"Is *Lov'plect.* Family sickness."

I sighed and looked at my feet. "Yeah… that."

"Is Tavi's father okay?" she asked. "His mother well?"

"They're okay. *Degtta.* It's…" How the Void did I tell her about my ancestors? I don't think anyone explained that part to her. I ended up shrugging. "It's, uh… *other* family. Like, uh, uncle and aunt. Sure."

Her head cocked. "<What about them?>"

Another shrug. "I don't know. It's just… they're horrible people. Everything we've been through is actually because of them." I looked at my hand, the one that wasn't holding the stew. "And I mean, we're related and everything, so… What if *I* turn into that, or…"

"No, no." She trapped my hand in her fingers, shaking her head as she spoke in Culatian, "<You're not a bad person, Tavi. And you're not going to be. I mean, you have Hallows that can really hurt people, and it's really easy to poison them if you want, but you don't ever let that happen to people you care about.>"

I sighed, rubbing my neck. "I guess…"

—*wait.*

"Did…" My train of thought evaporated. "Did you just…" I pointed. "You know about my *Hallows?*"

She looked confused, one cat ear rotating back. "<Well, yeah. You didn't know?>"

"No, I thought…" I was having trouble focusing, and my throat dried. "H-how long have you known?"

"<Since you got me out of that desert prison in Everland. Princess Willow told me about it.>"

I gawked at her. The whole Bloody time? Even at the desert, on the ship…? Didn't she ask me to cook for her once or twice? And she was okay with touching me to get my attention, and walking around with me… and leaning on me… and falling asleep on my shoulder a couple times…

My face blistered. She wasn't letting my hand go. "You're not scared?" I asked.

Her face scrunched up in a laugh, speaking in Landish this time. "Tavi not scary! Tavi is sweet. Only hurt if friends in trouble."

"U-Um… oh…" My ears were pounding. She still wasn't letting go.

What did that mean? Most people didn't want to be near me after they found out about my infection Hallows, but she was even okay with touching me? She even called me 'sweet'…

Okay, calm down. I swallowed the knot in my throat, trying to keep my pulse steady. *I'm probably just missing something in translation.*

Yeah. That was it. I was getting better at Culatian, but I wasn't perfect.

A scratchy croak made me jolt, and I reflexively tore my hand out of hers. Shade flew down to my shoulder then, and I exhaled the breath I was holding.

El's albino messenger, Salfwy, perched on her own shoulder, making her chuckle as the raven's pale beak nuzzled against her creamy cheek, which I noticed was a little pink. Was that a blush? Maybe she *did*…

I coughed. "S-so! Uh…" I scratched under Shade's beak as a distraction, trying to remember the right words in her language. "<Have you… made choice… of, uh, Reaper…? Yes or no?>"

She glanced away. "*Tovt*… <Not yet.>"

It got really quiet for a while, the drizzle picking up. She was obviously still struggling with that issue. She was already a knighted Stormchaser—and Zyl's freaking Aide, too—so she had every reason not to join the Reapers, messenger or not. But if she didn't…

"<If El not choose Reaper,>" I said, hesitating. "<Will I… not see El longer?>"

Her answer was really soft. "<Well… no.>"

I felt sick.

"<W-well, I…>" I licked my lips and switched to Landish. "I think it'd be really cool if you came with me." *Wait.* "I-I mean us." *Damn it.*

She flushed, but cracked a shy smile. "I will think, Tavi." She let a giggle slip. "Thank you."

I gave a toothy grin. So, there was still hope. I think.

I cleared my throat and threw a thumb over my shoulder. "So, uh, the Dream Queen just had her baby," I said. "*Peiv.* <You want see?>"

She clapped her hands excitedly. "*Ûs! Ûs!*"

"—Dream baby here?" a new voice asked behind me.

I turned and saw Zyl there. "I want see, too!" she said, taking El's hand and pulling her along. She looked at me. "Where at?"

I grumbled inwardly. *Damn it.* I was hoping to just go with El… I sighed and walked forward, keeping a hold of the bowl of stew I still held. "This way…"

45

XAVIER

⌒

"He's beautiful," Willow whispered beside me, holding a finger out to the tiny, fox eared newborn that Crysalette cradled on her uplifted cot.

The baby clenched Willow's finger, his azure tail swishing while he stared with impeccably *wide* azure eyes at all the faces that surrounded him in the clinic. His icy stare was surreal, holding a strange… awareness.

He was also bafflingly quiet. He hadn't cried since his birth not hours ago. He gazed at everyone as if already knowing who we were and had no questions that needed answering.

His father, Dream, ruffled the small wisps of blue hair on the child's head, chuckling cheerily. "He recognizes us. All of us. Clever little Eryn… his prophetic Hallows will be strong."

Bianca was standing at the head of the cot, scribbling notes on a ledger.

"Primary ears and tail," she murmured, lifting the boy's arm delicately with a pen. "Royal Evocator's mark on the left elbow…" She continued her scribbles and read them aloud. "Eryn Samuel Terrance Sandist. Seven pounds, eleven ounces. Date of Birth: Lastday, 40th of Watermein, 6:23 A.M… And right on the morning of Second Spring." She smiled at the parents. "Congratulations. Our tests show he's perfectly healthy."

Dream picked up the fox kit, keeping its heavy head stable in the crook of his arm. "So many thoughts in there," he said in a laugh, brushing a curled finger over the youngling's cheek. Dream glanced at Willow and offered the boy to her.

My wife cradled him, and the child's eyes fell on me. His neutral expression faltered, now looking entranced at my face, glancing at Alexander as well, who was standing at my side.

Willow chuckled. "Your eyes must confuse him."

Alex smirked. "Let's tell him I'm Xavier and you're Alexander. It will be like the days we had substitute tutors in the Academy."

"Grand idea," I commended. "Best to start them early."

Lilli grimaced across from us. "As if that will last, with you both looking so different now." She had her hands placed over Oliver's shoulders, and she scooted him closer to Willow and the baby.

"Go on," she encouraged the blushing owl boy, "just like we talked about."

Oliver was holding a clear rubber ball the size of the baby's skull, filled with water and swirling blue glitter. Oliver presented the ball to the baby, who ogled the tumbling glitter inside.

"Um," Oliver began, sounding embarrassed to be put in the spotlight. "Mama got me one already, so… um… we got another one. It's for the visions. To keep it clear, what's real and what hasn't happened yet."

He laid the rubber ball on the baby's bundled blanket, then turned to Dream and Crysalette. He looked at Lilli for assurance before bowing to the parents. "Congra-du-lations."

Crysalette smiled warmly. "Thank you, Oliver."

Oliver beamed, seeming proud of himself. He then spun on his heels and bowed to Willow and me next. "And congra-du-lations too."

I rubbed my bristly chin. "For our marriage? You're a month late, but thank you."

Oliver's nose scrunched at me, as if befuddled. He looked ripe to say something, but he froze, his Dream mark shining for a quick moment. He pointed at the baby. "He's gunna wee."

Willow jolted and pulled her body away from the baby, though still kept a secure hold of him. Just as the rubber ball bounced over the floor, the child's swaddled cloth began dripping.

"Drat!" Dream took little Eryn back and hurried to find a new, clean blanket.

Willow checked to be sure her long sleeved tunic, trousers and boots hadn't been stained, and went to wash her hands at the sinks. "Well, that was exciting…"

Bianca retrieved a mop to swab the wet spot on the floor, chuckling. Her Barkdragon lifted its head from his pile of blankets in the corner, its skinny neck bending curiously.

The door to the hut clicked open, and a new group filed inside, led by Zylveia. "*Re, re, re?*" Zyl chimed, her grin spritely. "Where new Dream Prince be?"

Dream called back while wrapping on the new bundle, "Getting changed. Just a moment… blast it, I wish we remembered to send scouts off to find proper diapers…"

El was behind the Sky Princess, lifting to her toes as her blue wings bowed, trying to see the child. Her albino raven, Salfwy, was perched on her shoulder and stretched its neck tall to see as well.

Salfwy had recovered weeks ago, and her personality was beginning to shine through. There was no doubt that she was El's messenger. They'd been inseparable since her recovery.

Jaq was next to walk in alongside Matthiel, offering their own congratulation to the parents. Octavius entered last.

I watched Octavius peek over at the newly changed baby and smile. But that smile faded when he looked at me. His ears started growing fur, but he seemed to stop them from forming completely.

I cocked an eyebrow at him. "Something wrong?"

Octavius blushed. "Uh… fine."

There was something in his hands. It looked like a bowl of stew. "I take it your father is done with the camp's breakfast?" I asked.

"Well, uh, yeah… but that's not what this is," he admitted, scratching his nose in a sniff. He offered the bowl to Willow. "This is for you. Different stuff."

She frowned and took the bowl. "Why?"

"Well…" He squirmed, but only slightly. "It's just… well, it helps keep up your immune system. You said once that your Infeciovoking doesn't make you very immune to some diseases, since it's so diluted."

"Which makes me no different from the rest of the camp," she said, her eyes narrowing. "So why am I getting this special stew? Have I contracted something?"

He swallowed, trying to look nonchalant with an overly exaggerated shrug. "It's just in case. No real reason. My dad's just… testing out a new recipe. So…" He gave the smallest cough he couldn't stifle. "Yeah. Eat all of it. 'Scuse me."

He stepped past us to greet his resurrected mother, who had been grinding herbs in the back.

The two began whispering. *Hrm.*

I had my wolf ears grow to listen in. Let's see what this little chit-chat was about, then…

"… got to tell them sometime, Tavius," I heard Sirra hiss.

Octavius's cat ears dropped. "What am I supposed to say? It's not exactly…"

Their conversation turned into nothing but expression-shifting stares.

I glanced at Willow, whose fox ears had also grown, probably to eavesdrop as well. Her brow was furrowed at me, as if asking me for an explanation. I could only shake my head.

She looked at the stew and glowered, set it on a nearby table and walked outside. I followed close behind.

It was still drizzling, smoke from various firepits perfuming the camp, and noises of all kinds filled the humid air. Our jumbled army had recruited twenty times the number we started with, Vanessa's rebellion having grown and many realms' knights having been rescued from prisons over the last month. We were now a full blown army, if under armed and without many resources.

"Xavier," Willow began, her look worried. "Do I look ill?"

"Ill?" I inspected her face. "I suppose you're a tad paler than usual."

She ran her fingers over her lips, her brow crinkling. "Octavius has been acting strange for weeks. I... I think I have some disease. He won't say what's wrong."

"How do you feel?" I touched my fingers to her cheek. Her skin was hot, but it wasn't much hotter than her usual, Pyrovoker temperature. "Have you noticed anything?"

"No. Except, perhaps, exhaustion."

"Maybe that's why he's giving you more meals?"

"Maybe..." She bit her knuckle. "But he won't say anything. He just mentioned my ordinary immune system, but why would he bring it up? What if..." Fright tugged her jaw. "What if I've developed something? The Sky King is ill with a terminal disease, what if I have something similar? What if I'm dying?"

I gripped her shoulder. "You're fine, Willow. He would have said something if it were that serious."

"Would he, though?" she questioned. "How do you even approach the subject? How do tell someone they're dying?"

"I don't..."

"H-hey!" Octavius came trotting outside, carrying the stew she'd left behind. He placed it in her hands. "You forgot this, Willow. I *really* kind of think you should try it. My dad's really good at..."

Willow gagged when she sniffed at it. She dropped the bowl and ran around the side of the medical hut. I heard a violent retch sound, followed by the slosh of vomit.

"Willow?" I called in a panic, jogging over. I found her crouched over the mess and gasping for breath, her white hair strewn across the ground and collecting blades of soggy grass.

I knelt to take her quivering arm and lifted her up. "Death, you *are* ill."

"I-I'm fine now," she panted, combing back her hair. She took a deep breath through her nose. "It's passed. Now if you don't mind, I..."

Shouts sounded behind us. A flurry of Shotri shots echoed from within the forest behind the electric fence.

Willow's grown fox ears revolved forward. "Is that a training exercise?"

"They wouldn't be wasting what little ammo we have on training," I said, my teeth sharpening.

Willow pulled her hair stick from her tied up strands, having her scythe materialize. "Necrofera?"

"Hecrûshou and Miranda have tamed any in the area." I plucked one of my scythe spheres from my neck-chain, readying the ice building in my soul. "The only thing left would be—"

A ground-shaking explosion burst from the south end of camp. The now pluming fire engulfed our supply storage there.

"Death!" Willow raced ahead in that direction.

I sprinted after her.

"Wait!" Octavius hollered behind me. I glanced back to see he was keeping pace at my heels. He pushed faster to run at my side. "Get her back with the Healers!" he shouted. "She shouldn't be overexerting—!"

A second explosion burst from the south end, a puff of flames pouring upward.

Screams cried out, shouts and commands rippling through the camp. A team of scaled Wavecrashers came hustling past Octavius and me, evoking water Hallows and preparing their liquid into large wavering spheres.

"What's going on?" Octavius panted. "Were those from Flameglobes?"

"Let's hope so!" I growled, speeding up. "The alternative would be your ancestor!"

Fire could mean either enemy globes or Cilia. If she found us again, it could ruin all the preparation we'd spent on the takeover. But then, we had two Sentients—Ancients, even—on our side this time. If Cilia had shown up, those two could—

A Shocksphere whistled by my wolf ear, barely missing me.

Someone yelled at my front, and I saw an armored woman hefting a battle axe over her head, grunting when she swung it down at me.

I leapt back, letting the weight of the axe hunch her shoulders. I released my ice Hallows over her blade, trailing it over her arms until they were incased in the glassy frost up to her shoulders.

She grunted, her muscles flexing, and fractured the thin ice. When she twisted, the ice shattered and she was set free, though without her axe. She pulled out a sword from the scabbard at her hip and thrust it at me. I scraped my one scythe against it in a sweeping motion, then drew out my second scythe and drove it through her breast plate.

She gargled when I pulled out my now blood-soaked weapon, the woman falling at my feet.

Not Cilia, I concluded. *The queen has found us.*

I whipped my head at Octavius, who was apparently facing three women himself. He ducked and dodged their attacks, barely missing getting his face cut by the last swing from the middle woman.

The one nearest me sliced her blade at him, but I slid between them and blocked her strike with my crossed scythes. I kicked her in the sternum, making her stagger back in a winded cough.

I marveled at my brief success. How long had it been since I could over-power *anyone?* Alex's training may have been Void, but Death did it show results. Obviously, he'd inherited much of Mother's military prowess.

Octavius was clearly benefitting from it also. He only had one, long sickle, but with its exaggerated crook, he redirected both women's attacks with swift strokes and precise arches. When the far right woman stabbed for his chest, he caught the blade by the crook and forced it down as he slid his sickle up the length of her sword, trapping her wrists with the hilt.

He grabbed her throat with one bare hand, black veins sinking into her skin. She went mute, her face contorting with intense pain, skin burning away and rotting black before she dropped to the ground in a crumpled heap.

I stared at the body. There was foam bubbling from the woman's lips, her cheekbones protruding from the eaten flesh now patching her face. "Is she dead?" I asked.

His eyes met mine for a split second before darting away, as if shamed. He offered no answer.

My brow knitted. "Your Hallows is strengthening…" *Bloods.* If he could already do so much, how long before he could destroy souls? Like his ancestor…?

A yell brought my attention back to the woman I'd been fighting. She had her sword cocked back as she rushed for me, slicing upward. I dodged right and dove under her, thrusting both my scythes into her stomach and ripped upward.

The only one left of the trio was the middle woman. I caught Octavius receiving a nasty cut on his side, yelling in pain, but he grit his teeth and hooked the woman by the collarbone, the black veins of his infection Hallows spidering into her pores. She was the last of the three to drop.

Octavius clutched his bleeding side, his cat ears curled back. "Damn it…"

"How deep is it?" I asked, knowing he would be the best man to determine his own ailment, with his Hallows.

"Not too deep," he panted, wiping sweat from his brow. "I'll be fine."

I looked around the camp. Everyone from our side was scrambling to the south end, some having had the time to collect armor and weapons and others running to retrieve them. Those Wavecrashers I'd seen earlier were busy putting out the fires on the storage huts.

The Leaflite soldiers were everywhere in this quadrant. Our members had been caught by surprise, but for those still alive, we seemed to be overpowering them.

I shook my head, focusing on the two problems I now had: one was to find my wife. She'd run into that mass, and I didn't see her now. The second was to find my apprentice. Hugh had run off somewhere earlier and hadn't returned.

Looking left, I saw four figures were hustling my way. Two were my resurrected vassals, Dalen and Vendy, who were followed by Nathaniel and Aiden.

"Dalen," I shouted when he and the other two approached. "I need your help. Actually, from all of you."

Aiden pulled down the goggles on his head, securing them over his eyes as he took out an arrow and nocked it on his bowstring. "Will we be protecting someone or driving an attack forward?" Aiden asked.

"The former," I clarified. "Both Hugh and Willow are lost in there somewhere. Willow is ill and Hugh isn't ready for this. I don't want either of them in there."

Vendy grimaced, her rabbit ears falling. "Aw, Land... I'll look for Hugh." She cursed in rueful mutters and took off into the crowd, drawing her crystal sword.

Nathaniel's bear ears curled and he cracked his knuckles, summoning two puffs of fire from his hands. "Aye, lad. I'll help with the Miss'us."

"And I with Hugh," said Aiden, the robin taking to the skies. "An aerial view will serve well."

Dalen put fists at his sides determinedly. "Well, you already got wings on the kid. I'll look for your wife."

I nodded in thanks as Dalen was next to fly off. *Good,* I thought with some relief, *Dalen and Vendy can at least send updates if they find either quarry.*

"Xavier!" someone called behind me. It was Matthiel. He must have been fighting already since he was speckled with blood, his staved scythe drawn. "Where is Willow?!"

"She ran into the crowd," I said. "Quickly, help us find her. She was sick just before, she's in no condition to fight."

"You're damn right she isn't!" He freed one of his hands from his staff and shook one of my shoulders. "Sirra-Lynn just told us the news! Why in Death didn't you say anything?"

I frowned. "News?"

"Bloody Void, you don't know?" He gave Octavius a daggered look. "You haven't told him?"

Octavius paled, and my attention snapped to him now.

"Octavius," I growled, my wolf ears curling angrily. "What is wrong with my wife?"

He swallowed. "W... w-well..." He desperately waved his hands in an undefined gesture, then blew out a breath and gave up, offering instead, "Congratulations, dad."

WILLOW

I rolled my staff round my neck, slicing into a Leaflite's side. The woman crumpled, crying out when I ripped into her chest, felling her, and I winced when I heard a distinct *snap* from her Seam.

The woman's ghost rose from her vessel, looking very white and very, very startled. *Death... damned habit.*

I hated war. I hated killing. I'd been so conflicted with all of it since Tanderam, but Bloods damn it all, it was either us or them.

The world fuzzed for a moment, and the bile from earlier threatened to rise again. I clasped my mouth, holding back a gag. Death, it was hot... more than usual, my blanched hands were sleek and sweaty over my staff.

Da'torr, came the voice of my Astravoking vassal, Rosette, from my thoughts. *Are you well?*

I didn't know where she was, but I'd been coordinating with her and Nikolai for some time now during the battle. I'd seen several sparks of lightning rain down from the storm and crash onto enemy ranks, but I couldn't tell if those were her bolts or one of the Stormchasers' above us. Though, she must have been close. She sounded as though I was within her sight.

Nikolai was closer to me, just a few feet away and freezing any attacking Leaflites with his Glaciavoking. "<*Da'torr,* do we need to retreat for you?>" he asked in Marincian, his webbed ears folding in concern at me.

My head shook, speaking to both of them. "I'm fine. Don't get distracted."

"Your Highness!"

I jolted at the voice, spinning in time to see another Leaflite was charging for me with a lance. I swept my scythe to the side to hit it away and ripped my blade into her stomach, kicking her corpse down.

"Your Highness...!" Panted the voice who'd alerted me before. It was Vanessa. The resistance leader came to stand beside me with her sword held before her chest in defense. "You look sickly, Highness. Are you ill?"

I swallowed the acidic slush that burned my throat. "Never mind me. Where did these soldiers come from?"

"I don't know," she admitted, "but they seem prepared for this. They may have been scouting the camp for days, even weeks, given their numbers. They even hit our supplies first. Our food, our clothes, our tools…"

The rain picked up suddenly, almost drowning out the clamor of battle. I held a hand up to shield my eyes from the water. The winged Stormchasers were taking arms with the flying Leaflites above, Prince Roji leading the charge with incredible bolts spewing from his hands and giving his arrows a powerful boost.

"Willow, *glecht*!" came Zyl's shrieking voice to my left.

I turned to her out of reflex, and saw her draw back her bowstring and loose an arrow right over my shoulder, my hair uplifted in the following breeze. A straggled groan sounded behind me, and I looked in time to see a new woman, who'd been seconds from hurtling her steel into my skull, drop to the ground, Zyl's arrow stuck into the woman's eye.

Zyl hastily nocked another arrow in her bowstring, running to me. "You need to being the careful one, Willow," she said, loosing the new arrow into another foe in the distance. "I no have Hallows back yet, so this all I can be doing."

"More and more just keep coming…" I glared ahead at the broken fence, hearing more explosions sound from other quadrants. "How much of her army did the queen send?"

Vanessa grunted after pulling her sword out of another Leaflite. "A good portion, by the look of it," she said.

"Which may very well mean the capital's defenses are thinned…" I turned to Vanessa. "Where is Anabelle?"

"Here!" came Ana's voice from above, the lioness touching to the ground with her rock Hallows spewing from her bare feet. Her heavy steel was at the ready and coated in red, along with her armor. She must have been fighting for some time, her teeth sharp and round ears stuck to her golden hair.

Her bright eyes flicked at me. "It's time. We cannot delay a moment longer."

I nodded, as did Zyl.

Ana addressed the rebel leader. "Vanessa, oversee the effort here. Tell no one I've gone into the city. If the queen still believes I am here, she will focus the brunt of her troops in the forest while I come to take her throne before she realizes it's gone."

Vanessa saluted. "As you wish, Sire. If we succeed here, shall I send you reinforcements?"

"Only if you have no other option. I wish to keep the civilians out of the line of fire. Kurrick," she said next, and I only now noticed that her two body-guards had run up to us. "Linus. Come with me and my sister Relicbloods. It's past time we took back my country."

46

XAVIER

"*Willow!*" I screamed through the pouring rain and clapping thunder, steel and Shotri shots blurting from every direction. My pulse blistered furiously, scanning the thousands of faces that now filled the camp. My breath was ragged and heaving out gasps. "WILLOW!"

Damn it, why now? Why was this happening *now?* If these bastards could have held off another day…!

Octavius hollered for her to my right, Matthiel doing the same to my left. Nathaniel, Jaq and Alex took up the rear behind us while Lilli, El and Dalen soared overhead.

"I see her!" Lilli called down, pointing. "She's running into the forest with Ana! Toward the city!"

I threw my chin up at her. "Can you catch up to her?"

"We'll try!" Lilli called, and the winged trio flapped ahead in the storm.

We ran into the forest, cutting through the straggling Leaflites that were on the outskirts of the main battles.

—my foot caught a small dip in the mud and I skidded forward, checking my jaw, stumbling to the ground. Alex came to help me up.

"You're panicking," he said and pulled me to my feet. "That won't get you to her any faster."

"She's going to the capital expecting to fight that insane queen…!" I was wheezing now, running a sweaty hand through my hair. "Alex, if I lose her, I…!"

"We'll get to her." He squeezed my shoulder and pulled me onward. "She's my family just as well, now."

I nodded, puffing, then hurried alongside him.

CILIA

I threw myself behind a shielding tree when those twins rushed by. They were surrounded by three others. One was my descendent.

They sprinted through with such haste, I barely had a chance to fear being spotted. Where were they going? I only came this close to their camp to see what all the noise was about.

My breath fell when I noticed a group of five armored women were lying in wait in the treetops above them, their crossbows duly aimed.

No!

My claws drew and I scuttled up my tree, hopping branches toward the awaiting ambush. One of the women looked to have locked onto my descendent, and I hurtled a burst of fire at her. My flames caught her by surprise, and she yelped and lost balance, falling to her death below.

Her comrades had noticed and were looking for the cause of the sudden fire, which was doused in the rain, and I leapt from branch to branch, reaming through them like the vicious beast I was until they were all dead at the base of the forest.

Either the Reapers didn't notice or they were in too much of a hurry to examine why random soldiers were dropping from the trees. They sprinted on without pause.

My descendant was the only one to glance up. I pulled up my hood, leaping to a branch behind the trunk to hide. When I peeked round, my descendant's cat ears perked at me. There was no doubt he noticed someone was watching him. But did he know who it was…?

He glanced at his party and hurried to catch up with them, leaving me behind. I jumped down, landing with a wet squish in the mud, staring after them. *Their war has started,* I realized. *They're going to overtake the city.*

Damn. They shouldn't be going in that direction. Since this morning, a terrible ripple of several Ancient Weights had been pulsing from there. My stomach lurched faintly, since I was a good distance, but it was slowly growing heavier. I wagered they were somewhere within the capital.

"Why, Cilia," came a man's watery voice through the storm. "And here I thought such gallantry was beneath you."

I glared at Hecrûshou when he stepped forward through the rain. His glowing trident was exposed now and clutched in his smooth hands, no longer wrapped in that usual cloth.

Miranda stepped to my other side, her arms crossed expectantly as her skeletal underlings trailed her.

"Well?" the old woman asked, her white pupils glowing bright. "You seem to have a soft spot for your descendant. And he's going into hostile territory. If you want to keep him out of trouble, you may as well follow us."

"And do be on guard," warned Hecrûshou, hefting his trident over a shoulder. "I'm sure I don't need to bring the three opposing Weights to your attention? We have our own war approaching, it seems. This could be bloody. Both red and black shall be spilt."

I glowered. "A war, is it?" I cracked my neck. "Three on three are fair odds."

WILLOW

I hurried alongside Ana as we all reached the city's perimeter, puffing. How long had we been running? Bloods, it felt like an eternity.

My vision was spinning. I choked back that nagging acid churning in my stomach. Bloody Death, I felt like I'd just exerted all my Hallows stamina even though I had yet to use any of it.

Beside me, Ana too looked winded, but didn't seem nauseated. It was only me, apparently.

Her golden brows arched at me, and she touched her fingers to my clammy brow. "Are you ill? Your burn is hotter than usual."

"It comes and goes." I leaned against a tree and steadied my breath, pulling my hair behind an ear to try and cool off. It gave little relief.

Linus frowned at me, reaching for my face as well. "Have you come down with…" His hand made contact with my cheek and he stiffened. When his Dream mark gleamed blue, his expression sagged with dread as if he'd had a vision. "Oh."

"What?" I demanded, swatting his hand away. "What did you just See—?"

"Willow!" my Aide's voice called from above. She was now landing alongside El and Dalen. Lilli rushed over, frantic. "What are you doing?"

I gave her a flat stare. What did it *look* like I was doing?

"Go back and find Xavier," she ordered, gripping my hand and pulled me toward the way we came. "He's worried sick!"

I ripped free. "He can join us if he likes, but we have more important things to worry about than a damned illness." I stormed forward, the others following my lead as we approached the outskirts of the city.

There were guards lining the walls in thick layers. Though, just as we thought, most of the armies had been deployed at our camp.

"Immature teenager," I muttered to Ana, our small party crouched behind a thicket of shrubs. "A fair swordswoman she may be, but her strategy is feeble."

"A blessing for us," Ana agreed. She hesitated. "Are you sure you're well enough for this? I never thought you could pale any further."

I growled irritably. "I'm *fine*. Now how will we enter without notice?"

Ana sighed, still seeming concerned, but stomped a foot at the ground. It *clattered*, like hollow wood, instead of damp mud.

"The old tunnels have been long forgotten, two centuries back," she said, opening a hidden door that had been buried in dirt. "Kurrick and I have gone through several plans throughout the years, and this one had been a point of interest. It seems our frequent inspection has proven advantageous."

"Clearly," I commended. "I suppose a few hundred years of strategizing has its perks?"

"Of course." She smirked, then descended the stone steps.

I followed after her.

"Hold up there." Dalen snatched me by the waist—and *slung* me over his shoulder. "Just got new orders from your husband. You're comin' with me."

"P-put me *down*!" I managed to squirm out of his hold, shuffling away with a baffled scowl. "What orders?"

"To take you back." He reached to grab me again, but I leapt aside. He grumbled. "Look, it's nothin' personal. It was a direct order. Kinda can't stop my muscles from followin' through and whatnot."

I sidestepped another attempt, but he snagged both my wrists.

"Nikolai!" I barked, and my scaled vassal dashed from where he and Rosette stood puzzled off to the side. I commanded, "Stop him!"

Nikolai rushed Dalen and slammed him into a tree, the hawk's wings crushed behind him.

"Freeze him there!" I said next, starting down the steps after Ana. "Let my husband free him when he arrives. However long that will take him."

47

XAVIER

⟿

I reached the perimeter of the city gates and heard Dalen hollering off to the right.

"Y-y-yo!" He shivered from a tree he was frozen to. "Bout damn t-time! Get me outta this-s stuff-f-f!"

"Death." He'd said he was stuck, but he hadn't mentioned how *much* ice was here. The glassy crystals covered every part of him, save for his head.

Nathaniel and Matthiel thawed some of the ice at his feet while Alex willed away the frost at his neck with his Glaciavoking.

It took a few precious seconds, but after Dalen was free, he stumbled to his knees, shuddering. "B-B-Bloody… St-t-tuborn… b-bi…"

"Watch it," I warned, piqued. "That's still my wife."

Alex looked toward the city and grunted. "We should have known she wouldn't like that order."

Jaq snorted behind me. "Yeah, no kidding. 'grab her and fly her back, even though we all know she's afraid of heights'. *A plus* idea, mate."

I rubbed my eyes. "Where did she go, Dalen?"

Dalen pointed at a patch of freshly upturned dirt. "Down there."

My brow furrowed, but when I walked along the line of shrubs, I found a dirt-ridden door. *Afraid of heights,* I thought in a grumble, *so her alternative was going underground?*

Nothing for it. If that's where she went, then that's where I needed to be. I ripped the door open and climbed down a flight of stone steps that led into a large, dirt tunnel.

I couldn't see a Bloody thing at first, but once Matthiel hurried down alongside Nathaniel, they both evoked their fire Hallows and shed light into the tunnels. They both took the lead with me as the rest of our group followed.

"Hey, *Da'torr*." Dalen caught up with me, his skin still blue and shaking a bit. His voice reverberated through the tunnels. "There's somethin' else I n-need to mention."

I flicked my gaze at him. "What?"

"Well, uh, after her group came down here, someone else went after them."

"Great," I muttered, my hand reaching to my scythe-spheres reflexively. "Who was it?"

He cleared his throat, pointing ahead with his chin. "Him."

A shadowed slump was huddled against the wall, quivering. "Hugh?" I called. What in the five realms was he doing here?

Hugh's grown lion ears perked at my voice, and my apprentice leapt to his feet, perhaps out of habit. "Master?!"

He stumbled in front of me, seeming relieved beyond belief. His bronze skin was blanched, eyes wide and wild. "Bloods, I thought I would rot in here!" He shuddered. "I-I fell too far behind them and lost the light."

I looked down the dark tunnel. "You were with them?"

"I was following," he said, flushing as his lion ears dropped in shame. "I… wanted to get into the city. I know they're going to take Sy's throne, but I thought… I thought if I could talk to Sy, she could just step down and she wouldn't have to…"

"Hugh," I groaned, handing him one of my scythes. "We've discussed this. If we can spare your sister, we will. But leave that to *us*. Stay by the entrance here. Keep it secured."

He hefted the single, crooked blade with both hands, staring at its faintly glowing surface. This was the first time I'd handed him a real scythe since beginning his training. I'd had him practice with wooden substitutes until this point. I sure as Bloods couldn't risk bringing him with me, but since he was already so close to the danger, I'd be damned before I left him unarmed. *Or*, I thought after a brief reflection, *better yet, may as well assign him a guard of sorts.*

"Vendy," I said and tapped into my vassal's mental connection. "We've found Hugh. Come to the city's perimeter and find a trap door before the gate. It leads to hidden tunnels underground. Once you arrive and find Hugh, guard him."

Vendy's voice fuzzed in my thoughts in reply, *Heading over now, Da'torr.*

"But…" Hugh stammered, "but Master, I can change Sy's mind."

I clasped his shoulder. "Please, Hugh. I don't want you near any battles. Your sister may recognize you, but that doesn't mean all of her soldiers will look past your messenger." I glanced at Lady Lilac, who was huddled beside Hugh's foot behind him and shaking. "You've been improving tremendously, Hugh. I've been very impressed. And immensely proud… but it's still too soon. Stay here with Vendy when she arrives. We'll come back to get you once everything is safe. Am I understood?"

"But I—"

"Am I understood, apprentice?"

His teeth clicked shut. His face fractured, his eyes reddening, but he nodded slowly and murmured, "Yes, Master…"

"Good." I let out a stream of breath. "We'll be back soon. Nira keep you safe."

His eyes followed each of us as we passed by him, our group creeping on until Hugh was nothing but a dim glow from the scythe I'd given him. And then even that was engulfed in darkness.

It wasn't long before the tunnels came to a juncture with the city's sewer system. In the small radius of Matthiel's and Nathaniel's firelight, I could see specks of bugs scuttle across the stone walls, waste and mildew hitting my nostrils. My boot splashed in a pile of vomit—

She heaved out the acid burning her throat, not able to keep it in anymore with such a foul stench.

Though, once expelled, the sickness subsided again. She was starting to doubt how much longer she could keep going. The sewers were spinning, her stomach twisting each time a new scent intruded her nasal passages.

"Willow," Lilli hushed, rubbing her back with the utmost tenderness. "Please, you must go back. You're in no condition…"

"I'm only a little ill, for Death's sake," I muttered, waving her off stubbornly.

"Lilli is right," Linus said. "You're endangering yourself by rushing into battle like this."

She kept forward, knowing she was being stupid, but by Gods, she was not about to abandon the mission. She evoked her fire Hallows again and pushed to the front with Ana, taking the left tunnel at the fork.

"I'm feeling better now," she said, and it wasn't a lie. She did feel fine, now that the acid was out. "We can't waste any more time."

The vision vanished.

I pointed to the left tunnel at the fork. "They went this way."

Everyone followed after me, avoiding the disgusting water flow in the center of the sopping floor. Soon enough, another vision showed Willow climbing a ladder to the outside, and we copied the path.

Once at the top, I threw open the wooden door, pushing a covering rug aside, and examined the new room.

It was a dusty wine cellar. No one was here, at least for the moment, but I could hear footfalls echo from a level above us while muffled voices chatted fervently. They were too far for me to make out the exact words. The floorboards creaked overhead with everyone's weight.

I climbed out of the tunnel and helped the others up, then closed the hidden door again, throwing the rug back over it.

Jaq pushed up his glasses, avoiding a falling stream of ceiling dust that rained down at a new footstep from upstairs. "Where are we?" he hissed.

The trilling laughter of voices sounded above, and a fiddle scratched a chord as someone began playing a jig. There were so many different sounds upstairs; so many conversations from what sounded like separate groups.

Alex climbed the small staircase at the front and flattened a hand against the door. His Crest gleamed blue as his dream Hallows was evoked.

He murmured, "It's an inn. Bloods, they don't know about the battles going on in the forest."

Matthiel scoffed. "The queen must have thought she'd have us exterminated before anyone was aware."

Octavius went to join Alex by the door, putting a cat ear against the wood. "How did Willow and them get through without being seen?"

I went to touch the door next. To my satisfaction, I had another vision through Willow's eyes of what happened moments before.

"Willow gave them all new hair colors and stole a few cloaks from the corner," I explained. "They walked right through. No one even gave them more than a second glance." I waved for everyone to come closer. "We can do the same. I can change colors with illusions. Alex, can you give us new clothing?"

Alex grimaced. "I can try. My previous attempts have been less than impressive though."

"Time to test it," I said, tapping a finger between his eyebrows and evoking my illusion Hallows. His one white eye bled to the same color blue as the other, giving him a matching set. "That should last long enough until we get through. I've only been able to keep them going for three minutes, without a sealing rune."

I gave myself the same matching set of blue eyes and changed all the Grimlings' hair to different shades of brown. Jaq and Dalen needed no illusion for their hair, but I did give Jaq tanner scales.

Alex gave everyone hooded coats next, though they were stiff and grey. Not exactly laced with threads of fabric-like texture, it was a little too smooth, but someone would only notice it if they paid close attention. I changed everyone's coat colors, brown and green, in various dark shades.

Now disguised to the best of Alex and my ability, Alex returned to the door, pressing his hand on the wood.

"Clear," he hushed, and creaked open the door.

We followed him into a small corridor, taking another flight of stairs that opened into the smoky pub. We went in groups of two and three, waiting a few seconds between each pair and took different routes toward the exit. Just like when Willow's party walked by, no one thought twice about us when we passed. We were out of the inn and on the streets in less than a moment.

Though, I tensed after seeing the thick blocks of Leaflites marching through the roads. They were everywhere, stopping pedestrians who looked remotely shady and searched them for weapons.

Jaq cursed behind me, all of us stopping.

Willow, I thought intently, hoping to Gods I got another vision soon. *Where did you go from here?* I knew they obviously hadn't been caught, else there would be turmoil now—

A violent blast exploded a few streets down, smoke pluming over the rooftops.

"There!" I yelled, my voice nearly drowned by the now hysteric crowd.

We shoved through the sea of fleeing civilians, my attention locked on the black smoke. More explosions ruptured, the civilians' screams deafening.

Then I heard a familiar caw above me. My head snapped up. Chai was soaring down to me, screeching. The others' messengers came with him.

"Chai?" I panted when the bird flapped at my face. "You can't be here now. You'll give away our position."

Chai refused to leave. Our connection quivered with warning. I glanced about our group, seeing everyone's illusions were fading away. I muttered, "Death."

Skririririririririri!

A guttural shriek pierced through the screaming crowd. Then more sounded, the volume rising with each new note added to the dissonant chord. My eyes splintered at the blackened figures now swarming the city.

"What is Hecrûshou doing?" I gaped, watching as thousands of Necrofera ripped into the villagers in the farther streets. "He swore to me those things wouldn't interfere!"

"—I'd been under the impression we wouldn't take part in your skirmish," the voice of Hecrûshou grunted. The shark had apparently been one of the people I'd shoved aside, hidden under his hood. His glowing gaze was vicious and alert, his radiant trident gripped tight.

"Unfortunately," he went on, "these are neither mine nor Miranda's. It seems we Ancients are in our own war."

"Against Cilia?" asked Alex.

"Not Cilia," he denied. "They are after her as well. Do what you must with your affairs here, but be warned: no one is safe when Ancients clash. Not the Rotten, and certainly not the Clean."

He broke away, heading for the mass of Necrofera. *Willow.* My teeth gritted. *You picked the absolute worst time to run off and be a heroine.*

48

HUGH

I creaked open the wooden, trap door that led into a tavern's wine cellar, my eyes stinging at the sudden burst of light.

Screams and frightened hollers sounded from the floors above us, explosions rumbling from outside and sending a dust storm of debris down on me from the cellar's ceiling. Bloods, I'd hoped Master hadn't run into too much trouble in town, but it sounded like that hope had died long before I arrived.

My gut twisted with guilt as I climbed out of the trap door and hefted the single scythe blade Master had assigned me. I knew he'd said to wait for Lady Vendy and stay in the tunnels, but I couldn't simply sit there and do nothing while everyone else risked their lives. *And Sy...*

I blew out a determined breath and hurried to climb the stairs leading to the tavern's upper levels. Bloods, this place was in total chaos, people were rushing to board up windows and doors, all of which rattled and scratched from unseen creatures on the other side. What was happening?

I went to one of the boarded, shaking windows to get a closer look—

C-crack!

The boards split apart, and an inky, black creature dripped into the tavern and shoved me to floor. I lost hold of my scythe, the weapon skidding away as the hideous beast pinned my stomach against the floorboards with heavy, hoof-textured hands, cracking open its maw in a hungry screech—

"Idiot!"

A radiant, glowing sword flew into view above me and *sliced* off the demon's head. Its sticky skull thunking to the floor by my side.

Lady Vendy stood above me, her frazzled braid thrown over a plated shoulder as she thrust her Crystal blade into the beast's chest. She *ripped* it over its heart, and a *snap* sounded as the demon's blackened soul evaporated from its bones.

When she kicked the new skeleton off of me in a noisy clatter, she grabbed my arm and pulled me to my feet. "What in Bloods do you think you're doing up here?" she demanded, her rabbit ears folded back angrily. "You weren't supposed to leave the tunnels—*Hey!*"

I rolled away and grabbed my scythe, then leapt out of the open window in a hard sprint. "I-I'm sorry!" I called back, seeing Lady Vendy was chasing after me. "I have to stop my sister before it's too late…!"

She shouted curses at me as I veered round a corner, Lady Vendy lost in the frenzied crowd.

WILLOW

Ana tossed another hand sized globe at the charging line of Leaflite soldiers, the resulting explosion bursting in a lick of flames. She pulled out two more from her heavily pocketed belt, gripping both in either hand as she glanced around for her a new target.

Between the soldiers and the swarming Necrofera, there were plenty to choose from. Too many. Where did these things come from? Hecrûshou swore to us he would hold them back…

But then, it looked like the demons were fighting *themselves*. Had Cilia returned?

Ana hurled the Handglobes down the dangerous road, clearing a small path for us to continue on after the explosion tossed aside more soldiers and Fera. We all rushed through while we had the opportunity.

"These new globes are more effective than I expected," Ana panted as we ran. She pulled out another Handglobe, and I saw there was a divider separating it into two segments. One side held white crystal-like powder, and the other trapped active fire. "Bianca certainly knows what she's doing."

"I'm just glad as Bloods to have an Alchemist on our side," I muttered, leaping over an aged, demon corpse. "I've only read about them in history texts. I thought that branch of study was disbanded across the nations?"

"It was," Ana grinned at me. "But it seems Bianca has rekindled it in my realm."

"I should like Grim to follow her example," I said. "Those could make Fera hunts far easier. And they use less flames than nor…"

The street suddenly spun, and the ground lifted *up*ward—Lilli caught me from behind and steadied me before I collapsed. But it was too quick. The sudden stop made my stomach churn, and I bent over before clasping my mouth, swallowing vomit.

Ana and the others had gained some distance from me, but they'd skidded to a stop when Ana turned back to see I'd fallen behind with Lilli. She started back—

A skeletal figure scuttled clumsily for me, shrieking as it tried to take a bite of my arm. I jolted and drove my scythe's blade into the Fera, ripping across its sticky skull. Lilli stuck one of her dual blades into its chest and cut its Seam just as I hit another beast's eye socket with the end of my staff, pushing it away.

There were dozens surrounding us now, three pushing down my staff from the back end.

Then a curdling shout rang out, *"Away!"*

The beasts' disjointed limbs locked in place, the things backing away. A hooded woman dropped from a rooftop and *crunched* the brick under her feet. She now stood between us and the demons. The creatures shook with fright while gazing at the woman, and one by one, they scattered away.

I couldn't see her face from the drawn hood, but I recognized her guttural voice when she growled, "This is no place for you Clean Ones to be fooling around. Leave here."

"Cilia…!" Anger boiled, my grip clenched Deathly tight on my scythe. "So, you *are* still trying to kill us."

"On the contrary." She finally turned to look at me with those glowing white pupils. "I need you alive. Any demon trying to kill you now is only doing so out of accidental collateral damage, if you stay here."

She spread her hands at the new wave of skeletal beasts that lumbered for Ana and the others, and the creatures were thrown to either side of the street, slamming against buildings and scrambling out of sight.

"I can clear your path to this queen's palace," said Cilia, walking ahead with hastened steps, "but after which, I heed you stay away from the main city. I have my own war to settle with Hecrûshou and Miranda."

I stared beguiled at her. "They outnumber you two to one. If you actually expect to win, you're more a fool than I thought."

"Not against them, you thickheaded twit," she clipped. "*They* would be outnumbered without me. We face three other Ancients this day." She kept forward. "Now come. If you wish to take over this country alive, I suggest you do so quickly."

My brow furrowed. *This can't be happening.* "Why are you helping us?" I called, furious. "Do you expect praise after this? Forgiveness? You have no right…!"

Cilia paused.

"After everything you put us through…!" My fists were shaking over my scythe. "Now you decide to have a change of heart? After all the deaths and wars *you* started…!"

Cilia sighed, morose and, infuriatingly… sincere. "I know I'm not worthy of forgiveness," she said, hushed. "I won't insult you with an apology. I… am a selfish creature. I don't care for much of anything these days. But." Her expression hardened. "There is still one thing I want."

"And that is?"

Her voice fractured. "I want my husband. And I… need your help."

Excuse me? "You are a fool if you think I'd help you with anything."

"I know you will not actively help." She continued forward. "So for now, the most I can do is keep you alive. Unless, of course, you wish to die out here? Then by all means, stay."

She didn't stop again.

I glanced at the utter frenzy behind me, Necrofera cluttering every street. All avenues were blocked except for the path Cilia had cleared.

Gods… Bloody… Damn it. Damn her, damn her, *damn her*! I bit my lip, letting out a muted scream before taking off after her with the others.

49

RINGËD

⌥

"Your left!" Claude shouted at me.

I dug my heels in the mud and shot spheres at the Leaflite charging for me.

She got shocked and went stiff, the bolts lasting longer in the heavy rain. That gave me enough time to stab her in the armpit, where her armor didn't reach, with my thin sword. She went down, and I looked back to see Claude was finishing off his two girls with his own, poison-laced sword.

Damn. My father-in-law wasn't too bad with that thing. Good thing we took the time to train with them while we were here.

Shouts were heard all over the place, to the left, the right, from the dark clouds overhead… freaking everywhere. Neal was a little ways ahead, yelling at his own crew that he'd been teaching. Most of the bunch were pretty good, only a couple weren't too accurate by the look of it. Neal himself was still the best, leading his team and ordering them to pick up their ammo over and over—

Someone bumped into my back, and I whirled around, getting my sword ready and…!

I stopped cold. "Mika?"

My wife was crouched next to me, one hand clenching a curved sword that was drawn across the back of her arm toward her elbow, and the other hand hovered over a satchel stuffed with Handglobes.

I gaped at her. "What in Bloody *Oscha* are you doing out here? I thought you went to Aspirre with the Dream family?"

"I didn't go through a month's worth of ball-busting drills and sword lessons just to sit around in an empty void." Her black cat ears curled tight, wet hair sticking to her face and neck.

"Your Pyrovoking isn't going to work in this rain," I said sternly.

Her green eyes flicked me an annoyed look and she pulled out a Handglobe. This one was filled with lightning and a blue liquid, and she tossed it at an approaching cluster of Leaflites.

That group exploded with stringy bolts, their metal against the rain seeming to amplify the effect. They all went down, some twitching while others were still-as-stone dead.

Mika grabbed another globe and muttered. "Any more questions, honey?"

"Uh. Nope." Though, I had an afterthought. "Actually, yeah. Where's Kurn? I thought he was with you."

Her brow furrowed at me. "I thought you had him?"

—A crow suddenly swooped over our heads. Five more flew by, then a dozen, then about fifty more showed up. I craned my neck and gawked. There had to be thousands of black birds up there now, flocking together and practically blotting out the whole sky.

"<Onward…!>" I heard a voice squeak above me, and I looked up in time to see an elongated, feral weasel was wearing a wooden ladle for a helmet and riding one of the ravens. "<Show no fear, my dark feathered soldiers!>"

My face screwed up so damn much, the muscles hurt. Was I hallucinating? I squinted. No, that was definitely Kurn, riding Neal's messenger, Ace. Strapped to Ace's back was a small belt with two pouches on either side of him, both filled with the same Handglobes Mikani had. I watched as Kurn's head was buried in one of the pouches, popping back up to roll out one of the globes. The globe dropped to the ground right over a mass of Leaflites.

Brrrrm—POW!

The globe exploded with powerful, electric lights and showered the mass of Leaflites, the cluster of women burnt to a crisp and dropping to the mud, still twitching.

Kurn yelled in his heckling language. "<Victory is upon us! Your Emperor will guide you to fortune!>"

"What the actual…" I ducked when Ace dove over my head, and I heard Kurn give a heckling battle cry before flying off.

What in Void?

The swarming messengers were now clawing at the enemy's eyes, pecking at their skulls and necks and distracting them enough for our guys to cut them down.

Well, all right, then.

I hollered and charged alongside Mika.

WILLOW

We raced through the city with Cilia leading the way, ordering back the incredible swarm of Necrofera that came within ten yards of us.

This plan was, I hated to admit it, far easier than what we had been doing earlier. Without having to worry about demons—or the Leaflites, since they were busy trying to survive the Fera invasion—it was simple. And my nagging nausea was finally under control without the stresses of battle to aggravate it.

But Gods damn it, I thought and glared at Cilia's back. *Why couldn't it have been Hecrûshou to do this for us?*

He, at least, didn't use my image to start a war in Everland. He, at least, *helped* Sir Janson find his freedom, instead of enslaving him to kill against his will. It was all because of her. Everything we've faced was *all because of her.* And now she decides to help us? Hah! Of all the moments she could have chosen to have a self-reflection, it had to be *after* all the horrors she wreaked upon the world.

And you're a damned fool for letting her help. The thought left a hollow pit in my soul. But what choice did we have? Every other route was blocked by Fera, and with my fluctuating illness, I wasn't confident I could last long fighting all of them. And we had a different mission to keep our focus.

Cilia cut around a corner building, and we all hustled after her.

After another few blocks, she slowed to a stop, looking over the horizon, her grown cat ears perked straight up as if listening for something. Her face fell. "Land—"

She leapt back when a blurred figure *cracked* the ground where she had been standing, and all of us flinched back.

"There you are, kitty-kitty..." came a child's voice within the residual dust that now puffed in the air. "For a moment, I thought you didn't want to play?"

I had to crane my neck to spot the little girl standing in front of Cilia. Her fin-like, emerald hair was long and tied with a ribbon, her deep green eyes gleaming around white pupils.

I gaped after seeing the crowned Ocean mark on the little girl's collarbone, similar to where my Death mark was printed. *An Ocean Relicblood is a demon?* And by the cowering look on Cilia's face, I guessed this child was incredibly strong. I'd never seen Cilia show any fear, let alone bone-trembling terror.

The little girl stepped toward Cilia, and the cat fumbled away, her back hitting the nearest building. Her cat ears were stuck to the sides of her neck.

"L-L... L-L-La'lunaî...!" Stuttered Cilia, her voice cracking as she attempted a smile. "Your Grace...! My, what a s-strange coincidence! Are you also v-v-visiting Neverland on holiday...?"

"Now kitty," the little girl huffed disdainfully, putting her scaled fists at her sides. "You and I both know why I'm here. Trying to claim all the mid-realm territories with Shou and Miranda?" She *tsked*, shaking her head. "You should know better, Cilia."

"N-now, La'lunaî, let's not jump to conclu—*Ghauhck...!*"

The little girl cast a spike of ice from her hands and drove it into the cat's mouth. Cilia's jaw was wrenched from her face, the spike pinning her to the building with a squish of black blood.

"I'm already bored, Cilia," drawled the girl, pushing her spike in further and twisting. "This won't even be worth the—"

I hooked my scythe in the girl's head, making her scream, and I gave a heave while circling my catch around. I threw her several yards back, her small body shattering through a window.

I stiffened. *Death!* Why in Nira's name did I just save Cilia? Idiot! Habit must have taken over.

Shrieking curses came from inside the shattered window and the sound of shuffling shards clattered. I saw the girl rise, her glare livid at me. Then she paused. "Another Relicblood?"

She gasped excitedly, hopping into the street as she took in both Zyl's and Ana's faces next. "Three Relicbloods! All in one place, and still Clean—oh, my nest will have such power...!"

She stopped when a patch of vines ripped off the walls and wrapped around her limbs, pulling tight.

Miranda, perched on a nearby awning, leapt down. She was using her Arborvoking to yank the vines taut around the little girl.

"The Clean Ones don't concern you, La'lunaî," Miranda snarled, jackal ears curled. Her gaze flicked to Cilia. "You were unlucky, Cilia. Finding the strongest right from the start."

Cilia ripped free of her ice spike, panting as her jaw dripped back into place and sealed with sticky tendrils. "Where is Hecrûshou?" she asked Miranda, igniting her fire and standing ground beside the old woman.

"He found Khol. I imagine he'll be the easiest to kill."

"What of Shëfaux—?"

A spray of ice shot between the two demons, and both of them jumped apart to avoid it. With Miranda distracted, the little girl was released from her leafy bonds, and a voice called down from within the branches of a dogwood tree.

"Did someone call?" heckled a newcomer with leathery skin, small tusks rising from his mouth.

La'lunaî barked at the laughing man. "Have you been sitting there the whole Bloody time?"

"It was incredibly amusing," he guffawed, propping up his chin with a hand and gave a wry smile. "Did you see them jump? Oh, what fun! I love a grand entrance."

The girl muttered, "Shut it and come down here, damned ingrate."

Cilia glared at me over her shoulder and roared. "Go!"

She threw bursts of fire between us, blocking my view. I would have simply run through, but Lilli pushed me forward, running back on our original path with the others.

When we finally made it past the outskirts of the city—

Something speared through my left thigh.

I screamed, the shock bringing me to my knees. Whoever and whatever it was pulled the lance out, and the pain forced out the vomit I've been keeping down for so long.

Blearily, I found the soldier that'd suddenly appeared. The Leaflite lifted her lance over my head, then…

Someone suddenly tackled her to the ground.

Both she and the interfering man skidded over the rough road, and the interrupter cracked his elbow against the woman's temple, knocking her out. He was panting desperately, his tied hair loose and falling out of its knotted string.

It was my husband.

"Willow!" Xavier scrambled to me, holding me close as if afraid I would slip between his arms and sink through the ground. He kissed me fervently, barely leaving me room to breathe between each attack. "Are you hurt?" he demanded, wetting my cheek and brow several more times. "Please, Death, be all right…"

"Xavier, I—Please, what's gotten into—?" He shoved his lips over mine.

When he finally ceased, I was dizzy, my head tumbling even though I was sure he was keeping me steady against his chest. There were so many familiar faces around us now. Everyone was frantically running here and there, crossing blades with soldiers… Bloods, when did all these Leaflites appear?

I tried moving my leg, but the new hole it fostered shocked a pained yelp from me.

Xavier jolted at the sound. "What is it?"

"My leg…" I held back a whimper when I tried to move it again. Blast it all, if I couldn't use it, what good was I?

"Got it." He scooped me up, lifting me. Bloody Death, when did he grow strong enough to carry my weight? And with such ease?

His feet scuffed in different directions three times, his expression unsure as he scanned the terrain. "She's secured," Xavier announced to our circling team, who were still engaged in their skirmishes. "Octavius, I need a status check!"

Octavius shoved his currently wounded foe back with a heavy shove and hurried to us. He quickly waved an inspecting hand over my leg, then worked his way up to my face.

"Aside from the leg injury," he concluded, "everything's fine."

Xavier deflated in relief, leaning his cheek against my head. "Thank the Gods."

From the right, Alexander cracked his hilt against a Leaflite's skull, then looked at his brother. "Xavier, we need to get her out of here."

"Right." Xavier held me tight, staying fixed in the center of everyone. What was happening? Why was everyone acting like my personal guard?

I looked at all the familiar faces—then stiffened when I noticed one was missing.

"Ana," I gasped, squirming in Xavier's arms to look round. "Where is Ana?"

"She's moved ahead," Kurrick yelled from the right, smashing two Leaflites' heads together. "She ordered us to stay behind and see you to safety."

"Why is everyone so Bloody concerned about me, me, *me—hauh*!" I'd thrown up my hands and nearly slipped out of Xavier's hold. He drew me closer, and I had little choice but to hook an arm round his neck for both comfort and balance.

The last of the Leaflites were either down or fleeing, and our group kept their protective circle around me.

Alex cursed under his breath, throwing his head at Xavier. "We can't go back the way we came with these damned Necrofera everywhere."

"The safest place," Linus panted, his Dream mark gleaming as he watched whatever vision he was having. "Is within the palace gates. The demons are practically ignoring it, they're so focused on the battle here."

"For Death's sake!" Xavier's lips pressed into a line. "Fine. But if we can avoid any more complications, please? Alex, Linus, I need you to keep your Third Eyes open to keep us on the safest path, away from any patrolling Leaflites."

"Got it," both men agreed, taking the charge ahead as the rest of the pack moved out.

Xavier was in such a hurry that I was bounced around violently, growing queasy. I pressed a hand to my lips and gagged. Bloods, I was so tired of this bile.

"What's wrong?" Xavier asked between puffs, refusing to slow.

I muttered, "Just a bit of nausea, still…"

"Don't worry. We'll find somewhere you can rest." He paused, then laughed suddenly, his face brightening. "Odd. I just had a new memory return. Your favorite tea is spiced apple, isn't it? You said it helped you when you felt sick."

"I suppose," I said, confused. "Why?"

"I'll find you some when this is over." He kissed my crown, still chuckling as if in a delirious bliss. "Anything you wish."

"Xavier." I glared at my husband. "What aren't you telling me?"

"Willow, darling." He couldn't contain his laughter anymore. "You're carrying our child."

My eyes fixed forward. It took me several deep breaths before I found the appropriate response.

"Oh."

50

ANABELLE

I strode through the peaceful, cobbled path with regal poise.

I felt my petal-soft hair bounce over my shoulders, the stones warm and smooth under my bare feet. It was odd, to feel such peace. The strife I left behind in the city seemed to disappear while I drew closer to the palace.

Soon to be *my* palace.

Feral songbirds twittered in the blooming cherry blossoms, honey bees humming about the flowers which trailed my path. The colorful butterflies seemed to overflow here in the sanctity of the royal courtyard, as if there were no war outside of it.

There were guards lining the yard, standing with their swords drawn, though lowered, at either side of me.

Their presence did naught to my even gait. I merely stepped with light pads through the center, keeping my gaze and chin forward. I did not reach for the sword at my hip, nor for the one across my back. I let my hands fall in a natural rhythm at my sides.

I did, however, evoke my Hallows through my feet. A subtle clatter of the cobblestones as I stepped over them, a small but noticeable burst of grass and flowers sprouting up between the cracks, then drying brown as I passed… It was purely for effect, but it seemed to give the armed soldiers a reason to doubt their intended plan to apprehend me. No one dared come near. Instead, they began whispering amongst themselves. I focused my hearing on the rhythmic clatter of my armor, keeping my eyes dedicated to the plated girl waiting for me at the center of the yard.

When I was but yards from her reach, I stopped. She made no motion to approach, but drew her sword. I declined reciprocation.

"You expect a duel," I said softly, the yard deadly silent enough for me to be heard. "I am sorry. I cannot waste time with one. My people are dying."

"As are mine." The crowned girl's throat burned with vehemence.

"You misunderstand." I placed my hands before me and took a slow, saddened breath. "You have no subjects. They are all under my care. And I will ask you to stay your tongue, for I have matters of grave importance to discuss with my guard."

"Brave words from a coward." Her grip tightened on her sword and she spat at the ground. "The legendary Relicblood of Land? If you even are of the true Bloodline, I will never kneel to one who's hidden in shame for so long. You've had many a queen and king before me to overthrow. I imagine they all carried out their reign without protest because you lacked the strength to take their crowns."

My expression remained at ease. I turned to the surrounding soldiers and found the woman with the most decorated armor. She, I thought, must be the captain of this guard.

"Please assemble whatever numbers we still have at the palace," I said, hushed. "Group them according to the number of districts the city has. The Necrofera are at war with themselves. The surviving citizens are trapped in their homes and dying in the streets from the crossfires. I need them found and escorted to safety."

The scaled captain hesitated, her hand hovering over the hilt at her waist. She looked awfully familiar, now that I looked.

"How *dare* you?" The queen's voice was shrill. "Ignoring the queen is one offense, but spouting orders to my guard?!"

"They are my guard." I corrected, my gaze jaded at the adolescent. "And you are wearing my crown. I'll ask that you return it."

"Return my *brother*, knave!" She rushed for me. "You'll not touch a claw on *my*—"

I waved a hand, and in a single stroke, I focused my Hallows on the soldier's sheathed swords around me and slid them all out, many noisy scrapes ringing through the yard. Within a fraction of a second, the points of those blades hovered in a triple-layered circle around the queen's neck, forcing her to halt else she impales herself.

The soldiers all gawked at the sight, some dropping to their knees in prayer and others backing away. I feigned a calm look, though my Hallows strength was reaching its peak. I could lift an impressive amount, but my limit was approaching. I'd spent too much of my stamina on the battles before this... *I must make this short*, I decided.

"You may stay in the gardens and play with your brothers while we speak of business," I said. With a finger, I conducted one particular sword—her own, which was ripped from her fingers—and had it delicately pluck the crown from her head. The ornament slid down the weapon's blade and caught on the hilt.

I then curled in my finger and willed the blade to hover toward me, and I took it by the hilt after placing the crown atop the curls of my golden hair. I dug the sword's tip into the ground and laid my hands over the jeweled handle.

The other swords slowly hovered back to their owners, though a few soldiers didn't dare touch them, letting them drop to the grass instead.

Footfalls echoed behind me, pants and puffs bouncing about the walls of the courtyard.

The others of our party were cresting the hill to where I was. Linus and Alexander were the first to appear, stopping when they saw me, causing the rest to bump into them.

Willow, I noticed, was in her husband's arms, her leg dripping with blood. And the last to stagger up the hill, his scarred face fracturing with emotion when he locked eyes with me, was Kurrick.

I lingered on his stare the longest, but was forced to break away when the enraged girl screamed. Her clawed hands were gleaming with gold light. Around her bare feet, the grass quivered and stretched tall, tangling into spiraled knots that shot up from the dirt all around her, growing twenty, thirty, forty feet high and casting looming shadows over the courtyard.

The surrounding soldiers scattered, and my friends behind me cursed before ducking for cover themselves.

The queen thrust her hand down, aimed for me, and the colossal spires came at such speed, they cut through the air with high pitched whistles.

I slid my stance wide, ready to counter the blades with my Hallows—

"NO!" A young voice cried from behind—then a boy sprinted past me, leaping in front of the spires.

Xavier's voice ripped a desperate shout, but I didn't hear what was said. The sound of the boy's mangled gasp drowned everything else when one spire drilled through his skull. Chunks of brain matter and hair coated the twisted blades of grass.

The queen's rage vanished, replaced with terror. She yanked back the spire in a flinch, crying a choked scream when the motion made a second, disturbing noise.

They boy's single scythe blade clattered to the stones. Hugh's body tumbled down, the gritty hole in his head seeping like dark wine.

My breath was lost.

His messenger dropped from the sky beside him and let loose a wounded screech, the crow's pain tearing through the courtyard and echoing off the walls.

The queen was trembling. Whimpering. She inched her way to the boy. "Hugh…?"

Hugh did not reply. He lay slump on the ground, staring at the sun and the clouds.

"H-H… Hugh…" She crouched over him, cradling his head. An undignified squeal came from her lips, sobbing as she curled over him, crying his name.

I stood in silence, stunned. Xavier came beside me, and I glanced back to see he'd given his injured wife to Alexander. His slender face contorted sickeningly, his mismatched eyes brimmed with tears as both the girl and the crow wept over the boy. A panting Vendy came to Xavier's side then, and when she spied the boy's corpse, she choked back a sob and cupped her mouth in horror.

"Why…?" the queen cried, still clutching her younger brother. "Why defend her…? I-I don't understand…" Her bloodshot glare flicked up at me.

"*You*…" She lay him delicately on the stones, kissing her palm and placing it lovingly on the boy's head. She rose, the spirals of grass quivering back to life around her, the tangles whipping in a new, wild storm. "*You* did this. You…!"

She was cut off. I had already overpowered her spirals and taken control of them myself. I *plunged* one through her intestines, using all the stamina I had left for this last, final move.

"You." I whispered, anger boiling to a heat I'd never known before. I spread my fingers, unraveling the blades of twisted grass within her organs and conducted them upward, making her squirm and gag in agony as they slithered up her body. "Are the most unworthy." I yanked the blades up through her chest. "Unfit." Up through her vocal chords. "*Disgusting.*" The blades pierced out her neck, wrapping around her throat and cinching her adams-apple tight. "Excuse for a queen."

Her eyes dripped tears of blood, the red flooding from her lips and staining the grass.

"I pray you find humility in death." I turned my hand in an screwing motion, and the blades whirled in a circle and *sliced* through her neck.

Her head was ripped away, rocking on her throat's stub and cracked to the ground before rolling to my feet. I spat atop it, lifting my gaze to the horrified captain of the guard.

The reptile woman stood frozen for a moment, her eyes wide and incredulous. Then revelation seemed to dawn. She knelt, head bowed in reverence. The rest of the guard quickly followed suit.

Xavier was stock-still beside me, a look of shock and revulsion painting his features.

Whatever judgements he passed, I didn't care. I regretted nothing. "Xavier," I hushed, "Go to your apprentice."

He did, his steps lethargic. When he crouched over the boy, I took in a deep breath and approached the guard's captain.

She bowed her head lower when I came before her. "My liege," she said, "my women are yours to command."

I looked down at her in examination. "I remember you now. You were the one to pour the Yinklit drink over me in the palace."

"A thousand pardons, my queen." She lowered further, not daring to cast her eyes upon my face. "I was misguided. My orders were to protect the late queen. Now, I give you my sword, as her clear superior."

"You are a wise woman," I said. "The whelp was not worthy of your loyalty... What is your name?"

"Genevieve, honored lady. Genevieve Marrock."

Genevieve... that had been my mother's name. Perhaps this was no coincidence.

"Well, Sil Genevieve," I said, motioning for her to rise. "As acting captain, I will ask you to gather the generals still in the area."

"All have been deployed outside in the forest, my queen," she reported while standing. "I am the highest ranked knight here, presently."

My lion tail flicked, round ears curling. I glared at the bloody, headless corpse behind me. "That foolish girl... very well. As I have said, the citizens are in danger. Find survivors and bring them to safety. I will collect reinforcements from the forest to come to your aid."

Genevieve saluted, and I walked to where the late queen's body lay strewn, drenched in red.

Xavier had scooped up his apprentice's body, his face heavy with grief. He caught my gaze, and I bowed, whispering, "I am... truly sorry..."

He choked back another flood of tears. "I was responsible for him. I should have left more guards to watch over him. I..."

I clasped Xavier shoulder. "It was by her hand that this happened. I gave her every opportunity to walk away. She chose to decline."

He clenched his teeth when he gazed down at the boy in his arms.

"I will leave his reaping to you," I said quietly. "But leave his sister's soul undisturbed until I return. Have Spiritcrystal shackles ready." I turned my attention to Willow, who was carried by Alexander. "Your wife is wounded?" I asked.

"She's with child," Xavier whispered.

I gasped softly. That explained her illness... I nodded. "Stay with her here, away from the danger. The palace will have supplies to care for her, and all beds are available. She is free to pick whichever suits her."

He returned the nod, and I walked past him, going to Alexander and Willow next. I evoked my remedy Hallows on Willow's leg wound, sealing the entry and exit points to stop the bleeding. Then I cupped her cheek. "Congratulations... rest now. Be with your husband. We will settle the fights."

Alex carried her to Xavier, all of them walking past the headless corpse that had once been the queen and went inside. Their vassals, including Nathaniel and Aiden, accompanied them.

When they were gone, I strode to the queen's detached head and snatched it by a tuft of her cropped hair. Tears of blood stained her cheeks.

I turned to the others; to Lilli and Jaq; to El and Zylveia; to Octavius and Matthiel... to Linus... and to Kurrick. I stepped before my oldest companion.

"Come," I said tiredly. "My Hallows has been exhausted... I must return to the camp on foot and claim my armies."

Kurrick bowed. "As you wish... my queen."

From him, the words dug painfully deep. With them came the promise that he would never call me anything less again.

I inhaled... and started down the path into the chaotic city once more.

51

BIANCA

~~~~~~

Red and I ducked behind a water trough when another explosion blasted nearby, the shouts and clanging weapons ringing through my long ears.

Bazil was creaking in fright next to me, nudging his woody head under my arm like he was trying to hide. I put a hand on the Barkdragon's long snout, making sure he stayed down and out of sight.

Red had to shout for me to hear him, even though he was right next to me. "Oy, boss!" he said, "You sure this spot's any good?!"

"We'll be fine!" I hollered back.

"—Bianca!"

My head snapped to the voice. It was Dream. No, it was a copy of him, I saw a Shocksphere pass right through him, and the rain didn't touch him.

"Why in Bloods didn't you two come with us to Aspirre where it's safe?!" Dream asked frantically.

I swallowed the panic in my throat. "I—" Another blast went off nearby and I ducked, screaming.

Red and I hopped onto Bazil's long back and ran for cover behind a ruined barracks hut while I tried to choke my heart into a steady beat. "I wanted to see how our Handglobes are working!"

Dream was only more exasperated as his copy followed us hurriedly. "Don't be a fool—"

Another blast, more screams as the sound of electric bolts popped and zapped. I stretched my neck over the broken wall to see the aftermath.

Mikani was yards away from it, grabbing another Handglobe and chucking it at a new group of armed women.

I was ready for *that* blast, and was grinning hysterically. "You see that?!" I laughed and punched Red in the shoulder. "They're totally working!"

Dream's copy grimaced. "You really must be Lady Herdazicol…"

Through the ruckus, my long ears picked up a faint squeaking noise. I looked back in time to see that feral ferret of Ringëd's was scuttling up Bazil's leg, wearing a wooden ladle over its head and hopping around every time a messenger flew past him.

Frowning, I picked up the little guy and got the ladle off him. "What in Void are *you* doing out here?"

The ferret kept squeaking at the passing crows and ravens, crawling up my arm and draping himself over my shoulder. He didn't seem to want to move off of there, huffing and puffing with his tongue sticking out tiredly.

Dream motioned for us to follow him. "Come, I'll meet you both somewhere safe and…"

The swell of noise suddenly started to fade. It was a ripple effect, starting from the north end, a weird quietness spreading like an infection. Soon enough, the only sound was the pattering rain and subtle rumbles of thunder.

I saw Prince Roji swoop down from the sky in a hurry, landing in the center of a mass of people, who blocked my view of him.

I slid off of Bazil rigidly, making sure no one was fighting anymore before inching over to see what in Void just happened. Why did everyone stop?

The rain lessened to a soft drizzle, which was probably Roji's doing, and whispers started infecting the whole camp. The minute I neared the mass of people, I jumped back to avoid the shifters who almost slammed into me when they made way for someone.

My eyes splintered open.

Wearing a new crown atop her golden locks and striding past me with a deadly serious face was Ana. Her armor was spattered with blood, and clenched in her fingers was the head of the old queen.

Ana didn't notice me when she sauntered by. She didn't look at anyone or anything, just stared forward with an unamused expression. Bloods, I'd never seen her like that… She was like a totally different person.

She didn't stop until she reached the center of the shambled camp, and lifted the detached head.

"I am your queen!" she roared, fury ripping her throat. I cowered back at the sound. I wasn't alone in my reaction. Everyone gathered around her, even the Leaflites, but they all kept a safe distance away from her like they thought the ground would sink if they stepped on it.

"This war is over!" she said. "All soldiers present, from both sides, follow under my command! Those who oppose me step forward and dare to cross my blade!"

Silence. Pure, utter silence.

The drizzle finally stopped, and after seeing no one was going to move, Ana tossed the old queen's head to the mud.

"There are no rebels," she yelled. "There are no Leaflites. You are now knights of the Old Kingdom. You are the Bladesworn. Protectors of life, courage, and honor."

People started kneeling, heads dipping in the gathered mass. The only ones who didn't bow were the Reapers, Chasers and Crashers; the other realms' knights.

I blushed, bowing myself, since I wasn't really... well, anything. I was technically Landish, I guessed. Did that make her my queen, too? Or was the Death King my ruler? Bloods, this was confusing.

Someone's feet squished in the mud next to me, and I looked up to see it was Jaq.

"Jaq!" I leapt up and squeezed him tight, making him grunt. "Where the Death have you been? You guys all took off so quick..."

"Had to get to Willow," he explained, rubbing his neck. "Xavier was panicking for obvious reasons."

"No kidding..." That's right. I almost forgot Sirra told us Willow was pregnant.

It looked like everyone else had come back with Jaq. Everyone except three in particular.

"Where is she?" I asked. "And the guys?"

"They're safe," he assured. "Being guarded at Ana's new palace."

I blew out a relieved breath. "Good."

Ana hollered from the center. "But though this war is over, there is another that threatens the capital." She threw a hand in the direction of the city. "The Necrofera are at war with each other. They have invaded your homes, your businesses, your streets and schools... if they are not exterminated, your loved ones who still live will be torn to shreds in the crossfires."

A flurry of stunned and worried chatter ruptured.

"Those brave enough to face the demons, join me in taking back our city," she said, then drew out her jeweled sword and raised it above her head. "Who among you holds the courage?"

A roar erupted through the camp in response.

OCTAVIUS

I was in one of the front lines when our newly doubled army ran through the city gates.

I'd finally had time to get some plate this time, so charging in head first seemed a little less stupid with a helm hugging my skull and shoulder guards weighing down my arms.

Neal was armored too, next to me. He gripped his sickle in one gauntleted hand while his other was readying his first round of throwing scythes.

I didn't wear any gloves. I knew I'd need my Hallows for this. The gauntlets wouldn't have blocked the poison or anything, but it would have messed with the accuracy and flow. I wanted to be sure I had a clean path if the demons got too close.

Shade flapped just over me, my white-cheeked raven croaking with the rest of the messengers that followed their Reapers here. Though, looking ahead at that mass of Fera, I decided this wasn't going to be safe for Shade.

I gave him three sharp whistles, ordering him to veer off and get somewhere the demons wouldn't find him. I could hear other Reapers giving the same three whistles, the black birds falling back as we sprinted further into the city.

There was one family of locals off to my right, a father and two kids huddled behind a toppled wagon while the mother swung at a pair of demons with a garden hoe.

"Neal!" I called, breaking out of the frontlines and pulling out one of my throwing scythes. "Two o'clock!"

"Got it!" he hollered, then hurled his already prepped projectile at one creature.

The scythe hit right on point, shooting through the thing's chest with a *snap* as it cut its NecroSeam. The blackened soul evaporated and left the after-corpse tumbling to the ground.

The second demon noticed its friend drop and looked at us, forgetting about the family. It scurried after me now.

I evoked my poison Hallows and covered my throwing scythe with black, spidering veins, then launched it at the demon's clavicle. I wasn't as good as Neal, so it didn't go through, but the poison did the rest of the work. The monster gave a straggled scream of pain before it fumbled down and died.

I called for someone to escort the family out of the city. A team of Ana's soldiers came by and took care of it for me while Neal and I pushed deeper into the infested town.

Bloods, the situation had gotten way worse since we left. By the time Neal and I reached the center of the capital, I had no idea how many scores of Fera we'd killed and how many civilians we rescued. And that was just the two of us—the rest of the army must have been seeing the same numbers.

Though, killing the things wasn't as hard as I thought it'd be. Sure, there were some problems with a few, but most were too busy killing themselves, they barely noticed us.

I screeched to a stop when I saw—Bloody Land, was that *Cilia?*—leaping across roofs just over my head, blasting a violet blaze at a little girl who was countering it with water.

It looked like Cilia was running from her. Was that girl one of the other Ancients?

Neal halted with me and saw Cilia too, and he panted, "Was that our ancestor?"

"Yeah," I puffed, sliding off my helm to cool off my sweaty neck. The sun was bright and sweltering over here, which was a serious change from over at the forest.

I saw that old lady Ancient—Miranda or something?—come after Cilia and the girl, jumping over us and disappearing. *So, they were busy trying to take down the generals while we took care of the little guys...*

I set my jaw and slid my helm back on, running into an alley and climbed an iron ladder up to the roofs.

"Hey, hey!" Neal called after me. "Don't just go after them! They got it covered!"

I reached the last rung and hollered down. "If two Ancients have been fighting against that one and *still* haven't killed it, I say they're going to need some help!" I leapt onto the roof and waved him up. "Come on! If we take down the bigger ones, the rest will probably scatter!"

He cursed, but climbed up after me. I gave him a hand and pulled him up when he reached the top.

"Bloody, stupid lil' bro," he muttered, getting more throwing scythes ready. "You're going to get us killed, you know that?"

"Between the two of us," I said, grinning while coating one of my own scythes with poison. "We've got the best shot at killing the leaders. I'll provide the poison. You shoot it at them. Just like we practiced."

He spit over the edge of the roof, giving a smirk. "Well, guess if we take them down, I'll be that much more popular with our sister Reapers, eh?"

I laughed, leading the way as we hustled after the Ancients.

CILIA

I jumped to the next roof in a full on sprint, throwing back bursts of fire in hopes of slowing La'lunai's pursuit.

I could hear Miranda grunting father back. Was she injured? I glanced back as I ran.

Then I came to an abrupt halt. La'lunaî wasn't back there anymore. Miranda was incased in a thick layer of ice up against the last building we'd left behind, struggling to free herself. I doubled back and shot a green blaze at her cage, melting at least two layers. But it was too thick. It would need more to thaw—

A stream of water wrapped around my waist, the pressure growing heavy as it spread to my hands, cutting off my fire.

"I'm getting awfully tired of this game, kitty," La'lunaî sighed, the tiny Seadragon clenching her fist and bringing my watery shackles to a crushing level of pressure. *Damned Pregravokers...* separately, they weren't a threat out of water. But combined with both Aqua and Glacia, they were incredibly frightening.

Her Weight only added to the pressure, bringing me to my knees in a strained yell.

"This is what happens when you try to take other queen's territories," she said, stepping closer and pushing her tremendous Weight over me more to force me on my back. "I hope you learned your lesson. Say hello to Nira for me, when she's ripping your rotten soul to shreds—"

Something whistled through the air, and La'lunaî's face splattered with a fresh, blackened hole. Jagged veins then crawled out of the crevice her nose had once been, her screams an earsplitting howl of pain as she staggered away from me, dropping her watery hold of me.

I pushed to my feet, seeing she was starting to heal, though slower than usual.

"Taeux l'ice gingette...!" She cursed in an agonized squeal, clutching her still-gorged face. "What *is* this...?!"

My lids widened at the spidering, black veins that now crawled over her reforming scales. *Infeciovoking...?*

Two armored men suddenly hopped onto the roof with us. They wore helms over their skulls, but I saw the black strands of hair over their brows, and the matching pair of lime green eyes that glared at La'lunaî. The slightly shorter one wore no gloves, and I saw his hands were crawling with the same black veins that plagued the little Seadragon now.

"Descendants..." I wasn't sure what to say. I'd known they were here, but for them to have just fought off my predator? I wanted to cry with bliss. Were they finally accepting me...?

"An infector?" La'lunaî gawked incredulously. Her face was, for once, riddled with both fear and disbelief. "I thought they were extinct!"

I grinned, displaying my sharpened teeth. "La'lunaî, meet my Descendants."

Her gaze flicked to me. *"Descendants?"*

"Oh, did I not mention?" I had more confidence with the two brothers here, but thought it still wise to keep my distance. "My husband had been an Infeciovoker when I was alive. My line survived the extermination. And most of my family have been *powerful* Reapers over the last five centuries."

Truthfully, I hadn't known I still had family until meeting these two. I had no idea if any of my descendants before them were Reapers. But La'lunaî needn't know that.

Her finned ears flicked, and oh, did I relish that frightened look on her round face. She cursed in Marincian, then without another word, she hopped over the roof and vanished.

My shoulders dropped in a relieved laugh. "Bloody Void, she ran! You actually frighten…"

They stepped away from me and raised their glowing sickles, standing guard. My heart fell at their unwelcoming glares. *So, they still didn't trust me…* I supposed I couldn't blame them.

"I won't take you from your friends," I murmured hollowly, walking to the ledge where La'lunaî jumped off. She was nowhere to be seen. I turned back to my descendants. "She's gone for now. But there are two others accompanying her. They are weaker than she, so I suggest we track them down instead. If we lower her numbers, we may have a chance at killing her last."

"And after that's done?" the Infeciovoker questioned. "Are you gonna go back to picking us off when we get rid of your threat for you?"

My hands balled. "Does it matter what I say? You won't believe me regardless of any explanation I waste time with."

They exchanged a shrugging glance at each other, then the older one muttered, "Yeah, guess you got a point. Let's go."

OCTAVIUS

Neal and I raced behind Cilia, following her and Miranda on street-level and ducked behind alleyways to avoid notice from those other Ancients who wanted us dead.

Hated to admit it, but the path was way clearer with them leading. All they had to do was glare at the smaller, skeletal demons and they scurried away like scared rats.

I called up. "Can't you get those things to leave the city altogether? They're putting people in more danger!"

Cilia glanced back to answer me. "That's what we've been doing. The less soldiers they have, the easier it will be to fight the royals."

"The problem is," Miranda grunted beside her. "They keep getting called back here."

I growled. "Why in Land did you pick the damned city to have your stupid fight in?"

Cilia snorted. "As if it were our choice. La'lunaî is collecting fuel for her soldiers. The more souls they eat, the stronger they grow, and the harder they are for you Reapers to kill." Cilia took a pausing breath, starting again with an afterthought. "You know, I've just realized. I don't think I know either of your names, Descendants."

I scowled. "I think I'm okay with that, *Ancestor*."

Her grown cat ears folded down. That obviously hurt. *Good*. Bloody demons, switching sides whenever they Gods damn felt like it. Did she think I was just going to forget all the other stuff she did before this? We were only in this mess because of *her* in the first place. Like Void I was going to forgive her just because I shared her blood.

Cilia focused her attention ahead again, turning to Miranda. "Two equal Weights to the left," she said.

Miranda's voice was gritty. "Shou and Shëfaux…"

Cilia's brow scrunched. "I thought Hecrûshou was against Khol?"

"Either he killed Khol or lost him—"

A glowing trident shot from the roofs in front of our group and planted in the cobblestones, the staff quivering in place.

A blurred figure flew right after it, the guy's back getting pierced by the stuck staff and yelling in pain when it pushed through his stomach. *Hecrûshou!*

Another guy—must have been the other Ancient—hopped down and shot spears of ice at our group.

Neal and I dove apart while Cilia sidestepped the spears. Miranda hadn't been fast enough. She got hit head-first by the ice, slowing her down when she ripped it out and took time to mend her wound.

Cilia's hands ignited in flames and she rushed for the opposing demon. Hecrûshou, who was still impaled by his own trident, slid himself free before joining Cilia and Miranda in the fight.

I stepped up to join, but the street was suddenly flooded with the smaller Fera. Neal was on the other side of the street, cutting through his own mass of creeps while I sliced and poisoned mine from this side.

I was just about to bring my sickle to one of the things—

Fwee!

A throwing scythe flung past my ear and shot right through the Fera's chest, snapping its NecroSeam on the way out.

"Thanks, bro!" I called to Neal.

Neal ripped his sickle through a demon's chest, then looked up at me, confused. "Thanks for what?"

"Didn't you just toss that this way?"

"Does it look like I have time to throw any—"

Six more throwing scythes hurtled down from the sky, each one plunging into a different demon's chests and snapping their NecroSeams with ridiculous precision.

Holy Shel! Not even Neal could do that many so quick. Who did that?

I scanned the glaring sky, but I didn't see anyone. The Void…

Neal looked behind me and let out a thrilled laugh. "Hah, *hah*! Thought so. Figured only my best student could pull that off."

Neal's best student? Before I had time look, a winged girl landed behind me, her back turned and blue wings folding closed.

My jaw dropped. "El?"

El wasn't wearing a helm, and her white cat ears flicked back at me. But she didn't look my way. She was crouched in a defensive stance, three throwing scythes gripped in each of her hands between her fingers.

"You hurt, Tavi?" She asked. "I took a long time to find. Too much Fera all over."

"Uh…" I was still too stunned to come up with something coherent. It took me a minute to slide off my helm and sputter out, "You've been training with Neal?"

"Yea. He teach throwing to much of us."

"Many of us," I corrected in a mumble. Wait, why was I bothering with grammar? It must have been habit. "Wait," I said. "Does this mean you decided to join our Brotherhood? As a Reaper?"

One of her cat ears folded. She didn't say anything, but she briefly glanced at me and nodded.

I grinned wide. "Cool."

"Tavius," Neal called, grabbing my attention from across the street. It looked like El had killed off the rest of the Fera on this street for us. Neal pointed forward with his sickle. "The Ancients went off that way."

"Right." I looked at El and threw my head in a gesture. "Want to come with us?"

El glanced away for a second, blushing. Then she stepped up and took in a deep breath. "I want to always come with you, Tavi." Her smile was bubbly. "And Zyl tell me what 'cute' means." She leaned her face in and—

She kissed me. She Bloody *kissed* me.

I was shocked frozen, my grown cat ears jolting straight up.

When she pulled away, she giggled and ran ahead of me, Neal laughing his ass off at my blistering face as both of them trotted off.

I fumbled after them, trying to stop my pulse from exploding through my ears. "A-a... All right, then..."

I couldn't help my stupid smile.

JAQ

My chain gave a clattering hush when I reeled it in circles around an arm, having to spin in smooth, yet jerking motions to keep the momentum going.

When I'd gotten enough tension wound up, I spun the other way and unwrapped it all, then let the blade fling itself out and sink into a demon's neck.

It screamed and I hauled it toward me, plucking the scythe from its inky skin and ripped it over its chest with a solid *snap*. Its corpse fumbled down, the black tar evaporating.

I looked around the street, trying to pick a new target. Void, they were everywhere. Again. Why in Death did *we* always get the giant hordes? Can't these things invade a continent we're *not* in for once? That's just Bloody rude, right there.

I was having trouble deciding which fight to break up first. They might have been scurrying everywhere, but most of the skeletal things were preoccupied with killing each other.

A drop of sweat trickled from my head, making my scalp itch from under this stuffy helm. I pulled it off real quick to scratch at it—

I ducked when a flying Fera snapped at my head. It swooped in an arch, screeching as it dove for me again.

But a bat-winged, armored woman flew in and kicked it with her steel boots, slamming it to the ground. Then she quickly plunged her scythe blade into its chest to reap its Seam.

Lilli slid off her helmet, her black hair heavy with sweat as it stuck to her slender neck. "Are you all right, Jaq?"

I grinned in a pant. "Yeah, thanks. Got distracted."

"Not wise," she chided, glancing at the creatures surrounding us. "Well, at least most are busy fighting themselves."

"Yeah." I scratched at that itch on my scalp. "I say we let them kill each other and find civilians. If any are still alive in this district, that is."

She slid her helmet back on and nodded. Damn, she looked *sexy* in armor. Somehow, she managed to look poised and delicate even under heavy plate. Never thought someone could pull that off. *Nice.*

She started down the street past the distracted Fera and I put on my helm again before running at her side.

"You know," I said. "You should show off that plate to Alex after this."

Her brow furrowed at me, half her attention focused on looking for signs of life in the streets. "Why?"

"You look good in it," I said, no shame. "And I bet you'd snag his eye *real* quick if you wore it naked for him."

Her face turned bright red, and she shoved me with her shoulder. "I am *not* doing that."

I smirked. "Why not? He'd probably fall flat on his ass for you, then. I mean, not that I could see worth shit in Tanderam's showers, but your blur had a great figure, from what I could tell."

She rolled her eyes, still blushing. "Why, thank you, Jaq… Ever the charmer." She grit her teeth. "In any case, I don't want to *seduce* him into loving me."

"But that's the quickest way to a man's heart!"

"If he showed any interest in me, I wouldn't be in this predicament in the first place," she pointed out, sighing. "Bloods, he barely gives me a second thought as it is. I haven't even gotten any vines from him yet, and it's been months since he agreed to marry me."

My face contorted like I just tasted decayed rat. "*Still?*"

"Still," she muttered.

That Bloody idiot. Can't never trust him to treat a woman right.

"Don't worry none about that," I said, smugly pounding my chest. "I'll straighten him out."

Her tone flattened. "You don't need to intervene, Jaq. Alex has his own pace for these things."

"Yeah," I muttered, "the pace of a feral sloth. Takes him a week to scratch his own balls."

She snorted a laugh, shoving me again for the fun of it—

A window crashed behind us, and a shifter screamed in fright.

We scrambled to backtrack. A group of the fighting demons had broken into a shop, killing each other inside while the owner woman huddled in the corner behind one of the many glass counters.

One of the Fera had killed its foe and leapt onto the glass counter, shattering it as it went for the shrieking woman.

Lilli leapt inside through the broken window and slashed at the creature's back, making it screech and turn away from the shop owner.

It went for Lilli now as I rushed to the owner.

"Come on," I told the woman, "we'll get ya outta…"

I paused, glancing down at the shattered glass counter. It wasn't just a counter, apparently, it was a display case. This was a jeweler.

What caught my eye was a pair of silver vines with shiny pink diamonds and a matching center piece.

Hm.

I pointed at them, looking at the woman, "Hey lady, how much are these things? I got a buddy that needs 'em."

She didn't bother looking at the vines, her eyes glued to Lilli and the fighting demons, the bat having gained the attention of two now.

The owner's voice shivered. "Get me out of here and they're yours!"

"Deal." I swiped the box of vines, along with the matching ring and ear stud that waited in a smaller box next to it, and pocketed both. I winked at the woman. "And uh, don't say nothin' to the lady with the scythes over there, yeah?"

52

XAVIER

"Looks like you're six weeks along," reported the palace nurse, scribbling notes on a pad. "Everything looks normal… the only concern right now is that leg of yours, Your Highness."

My grip loosened on Willow's hand in relief.

Willow still seemed shell-shocked from today's events. And I couldn't blame her. After being thrown into those battles, learning of her pregnancy, and watching the disturbing scene that Ana created out in the courtyard, *I* was having trouble coming to terms with most of it. Just remembering the last bit made me sick. How could that mousey woman do something so… horrifying? And without so much as a glimmer of hesitation?

A nurse yelped in fright suddenly, and my head snapped up. Dream had just appeared out of thin air.

"Ah, perfect," the young king said, smiling at Willow and me. "Oh, congratulations, you two. Excuse me for a moment."

He disappeared right where he stood in a blinding flash.

I looked at Willow for an explanation, but she only shrugged. Seconds later, the entire clinic was suddenly flooded with people in a single instant, all having popped into existence.

It sounded like men and women swarmed the once empty corridors outside as well, the palace suddenly alive and bustling with people that, just moments ago, hadn't been there.

Dream reappeared in the same place as before, Crysalette beside him and holding baby Eryn.

Dream walked to the bed where Willow was seated. "Sorry for the crowd," he said. "I didn't know where else to take them all."

Oliver came trotting around him, reaching up his short arms and tugged the hem of Willow's blouse. "Auntie Low?" he began, looking worried. "Where's Mama?"

"She…" Willow took a breath. "She'll be here soon, I should think." By her tone, she sounded like she hoped so as well.

Alex soon pushed his way through the crowd, at first seeming baffled by the sudden number of people, but he shook his head and caught my eyes, gesturing for me to follow him.

I sighed, dropping Willow's hand. "I suppose it's time."

She nodded and slipped off the patient bed, taking a small cane that had been propped against the wall. "I'm coming with you. To pay respects."

I thought to protest, but decided against it. Perhaps it was best that she came. She was, after all, Death. Her being present seemed appropriate.

She slid her hand into the crook of my elbow, allowing me to clasp her fingers while we made our way through the dense crowd. They all parted for us thankfully, so no shoving or shoulder bumping was necessary as we left the clinic and followed Alexander.

Once we were clear of the people, Alexander murmured, "I'm sorry for the wait." He handed me a brightly glowing scythe-sphere. "It took some time to find this, but there was one left in the abandoned Reaper barracks here on the grounds."

I gazed at the sphere in my palm. It gleamed with a bright, bluish hue, so radiant and beautiful it was as if I held a piece of someone's soul in my hand. It was pure Spiritcrystal; alloyed with nothing. I curled my fingers over the ball as thin slits of light spilled between them.

Alex cleared his throat. "I have Dalen and Vendy watching over him in the gardens. All that's left now is to give our proposition and hear his answer."

I nodded, my chest heavy as we passed through the palace ballroom.

Its reconstruction had been seamless. The charred ruins we left behind a month prior had not only been rebuilt, but improved with smooth parapets, decorative columns and even taller windows which filtered in more brilliant rays of sunlight. Walking through the beams seemed almost… tangible, in the silence. It was like walking through a body of water; through an entity that surrounded us in the vast, empty space that we could feel, yet not physically touch.

Our footfalls echoed as if to give the illusion that we weren't alone, yet still reminded us that we were. The dust particles floating around us seemed to hang in a serene suspension as we stepped through them.

We stepped out to the balcony and descended the stairway. I hesitated when reaching the bottom. Vendy and Dalen stood on either side of the steps here, waiting with bowed heads—and Vendy with lowered ears.

Hugh's body lay on a stone bench in the center of the gardens. Flowers and vines of every kind dressed the surrounding pergolas and fences, the fountain in the back trickling clear water softly as feral robins preened their feathers in its small pool.

The body had been cleaned of blood since I left it here with Alexander, though the hole in the boy's skull was still there. Had Alexander washed off the blood?

That left a gnawing hole in my chest. I should have seen to that. But then, I'd needed to be sure my wife and unborn child were tended to. Alexander had offered to look after Hugh while I did what was expected of me as a husband... and soon, a father.

A father? A bolt of fear slammed through me. I couldn't be a father. Bloods, I couldn't even protect my apprentice from his own sister, how could I expect to be any better with my own child...?

Willow gripped my arm firmly. She met my eyes, her face saddened. Whatever expression I held, it only made her grasp stronger. Did I look petrified? As incredibly unsure and unprepared as I felt?

My fingers balled around the radiant scythe-sphere in my palm, and I took several deep breaths before sliding my arm out of Willow's hold and approached Hugh's body. Alexander stepped beside me.

I pressed the rune that was etched on the sphere, and it glittered with a gold light, melting in my hand and stretching like liquid glass as it took the shape of a long, staved scythe. When it solidified in that shape, I raised the shining blade over my head and inhaled.

"*Thala ul wuw shefta,*" I whispered in prayer, and swung the scythe over Hugh's chest.

As the blade ripped his clothing and passed through his ribs, fizzling through without disturbing the skin, bones, blood or muscles, I heard a soft *snap* sound.

I rested the scythe upright on its staff, hanging my head as the released soul rose out of its vessel.

Hugh's spirit gave a bleary mumble, the white specter blinking at me. "M... M-Master...?"

"Hello, Hugh," I sighed. I couldn't muster a smile. My face felt like lead.

Hugh glanced from me to Alexander; to Dalen and Vendy by the steps; to Willow in the back. When he looked at me again, he stammered, "E-everyone's white…"He found his body beneath his see-through feet and his useless breaths grew ragged. "Sy… did she…?"

"She didn't see you in time," I said. "I'm sorry, Hugh. I've… failed, as your master. I hadn't done what was needed to make sure you were safe. And it's cost you your life."

If Hugh could produce tears in his spectral form, he would be crying. "I… I-It was my fault, Master. I didn't listen…"

"Which I should have accounted for." I gripped the radiant staff in my hand, my heart somber. "Regardless, it's done. You cannot return to the living, not in any way you'd like."

His face was contorted in a pained sob. "I-I can't be a Reaper?"

"That," I hushed, "is your choice. As your master, I take full responsibility for what's happened. And I've spoken with my brother regarding a vassalship."

I glanced at Alexander beside me, who raised no protest. I went on, "He and I have agreed to take you on as our vassal, should you choose. From there, you can continue your training with me, or with Alexander. Or, I suppose, both of us."

Hugh swallowed, seeming conflicted as he looked at Alexander and me. "Well," he began, "I want another chance. With *you*, Master… no offence meant, Sir Alexander…" He looked at Alex apologetically.

Alex offered a thin grin. "None taken, Hugh. Your master and I aren't the same person. Well, not anymore."

"Though," I added. "As with Dalen and Vendy, being my vassal will make you Alexander's vassal as well. We share the same blood, if in different vessels."

Hugh nodded and rubbed his ghostly nose, though probably out of habit.

"Are you sure this is what you want?" I asked, kneeling to meet his eyelevel while keeping the scythe upright over my head. "I would be honored to continue your training, but a vassalship lasts the rest of the Necrovoker's lifetime. I'm more than glad to give you a second chance at being the knight you dreamed of, but once you reach it, you cannot leave my side, nor Alexander's. You'll have no choice but to follow us until our times come. Do you understand?"

Hugh nodded again, slower. "Yes."

"And you still wish to make a Bloodpact with us?"

"Yes." He straightened with more conviction.

"Very well…"I rose and handed the pure scythe to Alexander, then plucked one of my alloyed blades from my neck-chain. After slicing my palm and producing a line of blood, I extended the dripping hand to my student.

"Hugh Lowery," I said, "with the Goddess Nira as witness to this Pact, do you consent to serve my brother and me under our protection, our care, and our guidance?"

Hugh lifted his translucent chin high and grasped my hand, his wispy skin rippling like water under my grip. "Yes."

My blood seeped into his soul, running through him like exposed veins throughout his limbs and body. A shock thumped my chest as my blood leaked into the ghost, and I saw Alexander tense beside me, perhaps feeling the Pact bind the three of us. Even Dalen's wings yielded to a shiver, and Vendy's long ears lifted.

"Do you accept to follow us until both he and I meet our deaths?" I asked next. "Until our own Seams are reaped, under watch of Nira's hallowed gaze, and the witness of Her daughter, Death?" I gestured to Willow with the hand that wasn't grasped in the ghost's hold.

Willow stood in mourning behind us. She nodded to me.

Hugh sucked in a breath and answered, "I accept."

Once enough of my blood had dripped into his soul, the Pact was complete. I removed my hand from his, balled it into a fist, and held it to my chest in a respectful salute. Alex and I spoke in unison, "We are honored to have you with us."

Hugh pursed his white lips, about to reply…

But he was interrupted by someone sniffling behind a row of tall bushes. Then a hiccup squeezed out of what sounded like a tight throat, followed by several undignified sobs.

Dalen unfolded his arms and sidled toward the tall bushes. He eyed whomever was there, grabbed their shirt collar and yanked the young man out in the open, exposing him.

The now confused fish shifter cringed when he saw us, crawling backward on his rear and shuddering when his white pupils locked onto the Spiritcrystal scythe in Alexander's hand.

A demon!

"Dalen, get *back*!" I shouted, withdrawing one of my alloyed blades as Alex and I stepped between our vassals and the Sentient Fera. Was this one of the Ancients?

"N-n-no…!" cried the demon boy, curling into a pathetic ball and whimpering, shielding his head with his scaled arms. "Please, I-I do not want to die again…! I'll do anything! Just… just do not tell La'lunaî!"

He sniffled and blubbered over the ground, wiping his runny nose and rocking himself like a scared lunatic.

My brow hung low. "La'lunaî?"

Willow stepped up with her crutch. "That deranged little girl? The rotted Relicblood?"

"Please!" The teen curled tighter into his ball, biting his arm until it bled black. "She-she thinks I'm still down there. I'm supposed to be helping, but I-I cannot fight any of them. I'm not an Evocator. Oh, I don't want to die, not like this—I'm not ready!" His sobs grew louder as he screamed. "I didn't want to die the first time, and I don't want to now...! Oh, please, don't let her find me!"

He dove for my leg and latched on, weeping shamelessly on my foot. "Please... Please..."

I had my scythe poised over the fish shifter's head, but I paused. He was just so *pathetic*. And he seemed too frightened to attack us. Though, it could have been an act...

Keeping guard, I asked, "What is your name?"

He sucked in snot through his nose. "K-K-Khol."

Alex was next to question him. "Are you another Ancient, then?"

Khol squeaked out a laugh. "Only by age. I'm a century younger than the rest of them. But-but they're stronger. They've had more souls, and I-I do not have any magic. Oh, why was I dragged into this?" He returned to his sobbing over my leg.

So a Class 2 Ancient. Bloods, I never thought a demon could be such a sorry whelp.

Willow's fox ears curled. "Has that La'lunaî girl Marked you? Are you her slave?"

Khol hiccupped. "N-no mark. It does not work on us, if we are over three-hundred. But she can still tear my Seam and get me Cleansed if she finds out I left—"

A crash erupted from the palace roofs, stone and wooden planks bursting over the sandy shingles of the east tower.

"Death," Alex cursed next to me, reverting the pure scythe back to its spherical form. He pocketed it and plucked his alloyed blades from his neck-chain. "Was that the other Ancients, or their smaller lackies?"

Khol held onto my leg tighter and cried, "It's her, it's her...! Please—She fears the Reapers! You can get her to leave, can't you? You-you can even kill her! Please!"

I wriggled my leg free of the sniveling Ancient, growling, "Get off. If you keep to yourself, we'll leave you be, but get in our way, and *we'll* reap your soul before that other Ancient so much as breathes on you."

He recoiled when I strode past him to meet with Willow.

"Get inside," I told her. "Watch Hugh for me. If the demons find their way in, go to your grandfather and hide in Aspirre."

She looked ripe to argue, but winced when she attempted a step with her injured leg. She glanced at her bandages, then at her belly, and sighed.

"I expect you back alive," she muttered. "Otherwise, I may consider filing for divorce."

I lifted her chin and took her lips, grinning. "Stay your quill, love." My hand pressed against her stomach. "I now have two things to care for. It'd be shameful to keep both of you waiting."

I made my way to Alexander, seeing he had already resurrected Hugh's body. I tied the boy's soul within his vessel, and Hugh breathed to life once more, blinking in astonishment as he looked at his hands in wonder.

"Hugh," I said, "go inside with my wife. She's injured and carrying our child. Guard her for me, eh?" I gave him my other scythe-sphere. It was the one I'd given him before, the one he'd dropped when he was killed. "If anything happens, just think of contacting me or Alex, and speak aloud. We'll hear you. And for Gods' sakes, *stay away from the fights*. That is an order, as your master Reaper."

Hugh took the dimly glowing sphere and sucked in a breath, nodding to comply. He went and took Willow's hand to lead her into the palace.

When they were gone, I turned to Dalen and Vendy. "Back us up. We may need a set of wings and a skilled blade."

"—You'll have three pairs of each," the voice of Aiden chimed as he and Nathaniel came trotting outside from the ballroom.

Behind those two were Rosette and Nikolai. Nikolai bowed to me, saying, "*Da'torr* ask of us to help." He winced when glancing up at Dalen, who glared at him. Nikolai's webbed ears flicked guiltily. "Ah… I eez sorry for ze icing earlier…"

Dalen flapped his wings in a shrug and withdrew his Crystal daggers. "Yeah, well… I get it. Orders and whatnot. Can't control it."

Another crash rumbled from the east tower, and I rushed through the gardens. "Come on!"

Alex and I rushed up the steps of the east wing tower, Nikolai, Vendy and Nathaniel trotting at our heels. Our three winged members were taking the quicker route outside.

Got a visual, Dalen's voice reverberated in my thoughts.

Alexander must have gotten the message also because he asked, "What are we up against?"

Uh... Dalen hesitated, taking a moment before his answer came. *It looks like five Ancients.*

"Five?" I echoed skeptically. "Isn't that *all* of them?"

Alex muttered, "If you don't include that pathetic fish in the gardens, yes."

Nathaniel puffed behind us. "'ey, Lads! Now, I don't mean'ta sound discouragin', but that many Sentients would make even yer old man stop an' reconsider goin' in *head first*, it would."

Nikolai's shoulders were tense against his neck, nodding his agreement vehemently. "Zis no seem like good idea..."

Vendy panted behind us, "Yeah, can't say I'm thrilled about it either, *Da'torr*."

"I says," Nathaniel coughed, falling a bit behind on the spiraling steps. "I says we let the beasts do 'emselves in. Have 'em kill each other first an' *then* maybe run in an' pick off the rest, aye?"

I craned back to my father's winded vassal, still climbing. "We'll wait and assess the situation first, Nathaniel," I assured. "If the danger is contained by the Ancients *not* seeking to kill us, then we'll fall back and find shelter with the others."

"But if our Ancients are losing," Alex added, "then we'll be dead after them, and we might forfeit the capital altogether. If we want to keep the city, we have to help our side win."

"Aw, Bloody Void," Nathaniel wheezed, hefting after us. "Yer father ain't gon'ta be happy with me, no he ain't. He was already cross 'bout you an' the miss'us, Xavier."

My brow furrowed, panting. "About our marriage? We'd waited ten years for it already, plus the months I spent in my own body."

"It ain't the timin', lad. He says ye should have had a ceremony. An' ye should have let 'im come to it. I think ye broke his ol' heart, getting' hitched without 'im."

"As if we had a guarantee we'd be alive long enough to make it back there," I muttered. "Tell him he can attend Alexander's ceremony."

Alex laughed spitefully. "And after Nathaniel tells him Willow is carrying his grandchild? I don't think my wedding will appease him."

I grimaced, the reminder that I was going to be a father sinking in again. Bloods, Alex and I have owned a feral dog in our youth before, but a child? My son would be no pet. Or would I have a daughter—?

Crrr-brrrrmm!

The tower wall was blown open above us, stones crumbling into the stairwell. Cilia was kicked onto the steps as well by that tusked, ice slinging Ancient. Cilia's joints cracked back into place, throwing her fire at the man, who evaded and countered with spikes of ice.

"Death!" I let my own ice pour from my palms and formed a sharp lance, which Alex promptly took control of and *thrust* it into the enemy Ancient's chest with a liquid squish of black blood.

The demon screamed and reeled away, plucking out the lance, absolutely baffled when he looked at us. "What the... Clean Ones—?"

Nathaniel and Nikolai shot their Hallows at him, streams of ice and fire colliding in a spiral as Vendy charged him with her Crystal blade. The Ancient ducked out of the hole he'd made in the wall and leapt onto an attached roof.

Cilia glanced at us, nodded her appreciation, and sprinted after her foe in a flaming rage. We filed after her, keeping balance on the slanted roof.

"*Da'torr*," Dalen called and flapped to the shingles beside us. "Watch your step."

I glanced over the roof's ledge. We were high enough that a single slip would mean our deaths, the wind strong from this altitude.

"Stay by us," I told Dalen, swallowing. "In the *very likely* event that, perhaps, we happen to fall?"

Dalen gave me an uncertain look. "Bloods, if you do, I hope to Gods you do it together. I can't split myself in half here."

Alex exhaled stiffly. "Right. So, *we* stay close as well." He looked past me, and his eyes bulged. He shoved me back, and I nearly stumbled—

A body smashed into the shingles between us, directly where I had been a few seconds ago. The body, Hecrûshou, groaned and pushed himself up, using his glowing trident as support. Black tendrils slithered over his stomach, where there'd been a hole before it sealed itself back together.

He noticed us and scowled. "What in Gods' names are you doing here—?"

His head snapped forward, and he leapt several feet back as a second Ancient—a smaller, scaled girl—shoved a spike of ice into the circle of ruined shingles.

I barely had time to recover my wits before she sprang up and thrust another rod of ice at Hecrûshou, and I watched them bounce to a second rooftop above us.

Alex carefully made his way back to me, his face dreaded. "Bloods. She didn't even look at us."

"Clearly, close range is not the proper strategy." I observed. "Distance it is."

Pursing my lips, I evoked my ice Hallows. After having the frosted crystals stretch into a tall lance, I tossed it to Alex, who caught it and gave me an understanding nod.

"You supply," he began, "I shoot?"

I gave a toothy grin. "As we trained."

HERRIN

I leaned so far over the balcony's stone railing I almost fell out of the tower, stretching my wings to keep balanced.

Land, there they were! The brothers ducked and dodged the Sentient Necrofera on the roofs. Shingles went flying, ice shattered, bolts of lightning exploded, and fire raged from some other people hopping from roof to roof in the distance.

The whole freaking palace shook with small quakes every time a new explosion burst. I saw colored clouds plume everywhere, both hot and cold.

I have to write this down—

A woman from the surrounding crowd pushed her way to the front, an awestricken look on her face. "The Shadowblood…"

Wait a minute. I had to make a double-take.

She was that cardinal girl from the bookshop last month. Her auburn, feathered hair was messy and frazzled, her Harmonist robes gone and replaced with what looked like a large, ratty sack. She was covered in bruises from her bare feet to her pointed chin.

But it was her latticed arms that had me staring. Reddish-purple lacerations crawled in crisscrossed patterns from her knuckles to her shoulders in puffy, painful looking marks.

"Uh… Marian…?" I asked. "Marian Gulldread?"

Her attention ripped away from the roofs and registered me. It didn't look like she'd noticed me till now.

"Y… yes…?" she stammered, cringing away from some kind of reflex.

"Bloods, it's actually you! We've been looking everywhere…!" I thought to take her arm, but stopped after seeing those scars again. "What happened to you?"

She curled inward, glaring at me. "Who are you? Why were you looking for me?"

"My name's Herrin Tesler," I said, raising my hands in a peaceful motion. "I'm with the Enlighteners."

She stared at me. "Herrin Tesler?"

"Yeah."

"Arch*chancelor* Herrin Tesler?" Her tone was skeptical. "Chief of Knowledge, of the Enlighteners Guild?"

"Well… yeah," I said again.

She still looked disbelieving. "But you're…" She took a minute to find the right words. "*Young…*"

"Seventeen," I clarified, "I'm really not that young."

She circled confused fingers over her temple. "But I… forgive me, it's just that I was expecting an elderly man. With a beard hanging down to his knees." She made a gesture for a visual. "And a hunched back with shaking hands, who had to rely most of his weight on an ornate cane."

"Sorry." I shrugged half-heartedly. "No cane. But what in Void happened to you? We were worried the queen got to you and…"

"She did." Her voice was hollow, staring out the balcony to watch the fight. She didn't say anything else.

"You… uh…" I rubbed my neck. "Have you seen a Healer yet? With all your scars…"

She looked at her latticed skin, flakes of dried blood crusted over the auburn feathers on her arms. Looking disturbed, she tried to hide them with her hands, but that barely did anything.

"I'll be fine," she said, watching the battle overhead. "If that *queen* really is dead, then I've nothing to worry about. More so, I've been waiting so long to see the Shadowblood…"

"Yeah…" I let out a smooth breath through my nose, watching another spray of shimmering ice puff from behind the roof's tip. "It's pretty cool to see them in action finally."

XAVIER

Thunk!

Thunk!

Thunk!

I leapt back from La'lunaï's icy barrage of shards, each one sticking to the roof where I'd been standing.

Alex waved his hand over them all, snatching them in a smooth row and thrusting them right back at the little Seadragon. The shards cut across her face from both cheeks, two shooting through her torso and one sinking into her arm.

She howled, more out of rage than pain, and didn't bother to wait for her wounds to heal before coming at us again.

"Xavier!" Alex hollered, and I saw him encircle his hands, the moisture between them sucked out of the air and condensed into a wavering ball of cloudy water.

Before he lost control of it, I whipped my hand toward the ball, gripping the water from the middle with my Hallows and *yanked* it out in a twisting string as quickly as he produced it. With that hand, I drew out the water. With the other hand, I used my Glaciavoking to pour out the ice in my soul, freezing the water into a thick slush.

I splashed the little girl rushing me, tightening my grip on the water until she was caught in the slushy rope, and just as we'd done at practice, Alex came and dipped his hands in the stream, increasing the pressure to a crushing degree.

La'lunaî's bones gave audible *cracks*, her arms breaking upward and her ribs crushing as if by an invisible weight.

She roared, howling under the pain, unable to control our elements without the use of her broken hands and feet—

"*Da'torr!*" Vendy lunged for me suddenly and tackled me to the shingles, my shoulder hitting first as my supply to Alexander's water was cut off. Then an enormous pillar of jagged ice slammed into the roof where I'd been.

The second demon, Shëfaux, landed on top of it, heckling down at us.

La'lunaî was released of her bonds, panting and shying back to allow herself to heal, black blood slithering into her wounds.

Vendy pushed off of me and readied her blade as Alex ran toward us—but his foot slipped over a loose shingle and his legs slid over the edge. I seized his wrist in time, half of him dangling there until I pulled him back on the roof.

"What are you freaks?" Shëfaux laughed, scratching curiously at his head. "Grim wolves with *our* Hallows? That's a new one."

"It's *impossible*," La'lunaî spat behind him, still mending her injuries. "How do you have all three elements? Only *my* Bloodline can hold all the Blessings!"

"Not anymore," I said, crouched defensively while I held the ice in my soul, denying freedom to the coldness that itched to leak from my hands.

Shëfaux cupped a leathery hand to his mouth, hiding an amused chuckle as he smeared it down his chin and asked, "What are you Clean Ones even doing here? Our affairs don't involve you."

"It's nothing personal," Alex said beside me, drawing out one of his scythes.

"Only business," I finished and followed his example, taking out my lone scythe.

Both Ancients went rigid, staring at our radiant weapons. Dalen flew down beside us then and raised his Crystal daggers, and Vendy held hers in a defensive pose over her head, all of our weapons gleaming blue.

Shëfaux's grin vanished. "Oh, *Oscha*."

With my free hand, I let out a burst of ice, shaping them into sharp spires, and Alex took control of them and flung them at Shëfaux.

The demon dodged and took control of them himself, tossing the ice away. But we'd only used that as a distraction.

Alex and I rushed him, slicing inward at his sides. He yelped and ripped away before either of us could move in for a killing blow, and the demon hopped onto an adjacent roof—

He was blasted with fire, and I saw Nathaniel tossing more flames at him from behind Shëfaux.

Rosette soared above him then, clapping her hands together as an enormous bolt of lightning slammed over the Ancient. His screams curdled and stuttered, the stink of burnt flesh simmering even after the bolt faded.

Shëfaux started to run after Nathaniel, who was easier to reach since he had no wings, but the Ancient was blown backward off his feet by a powerful gust.

Aiden flapped down beside Nathaniel, loosening an arrow at Shëfaux that whistled in a loud burst, propelled by Aiden's Aerovoking.

Shëfaux struggled against the three vassals, Dalen even snagging a slice here and there with his daggers while Vendy managed slice at him if he escaped.

With him preoccupied, I looked at our main threat. La'lunaî hadn't moved from her post, still staring in horror at Alex and my scythes.

When she noticed me glaring at her, her finned ears flicked in fright, shoulders sticking to her neck. She glanced from me to Alexander, gave a curse in Marincian, and spun on her heels. She ran.

Ran?

I watched in disbelief as she gained distance. Then I looked to Alex for an explanation. He only shrugged at me, then took off after her. I hurried with him.

Then a thick, thorny vine wormed its way over the shingles like a feral snake. It snagged La'lunaî's ankle and wrapped all the way up her leg, yanking her flat on her face before pulling her in the air upside-down.

"Leaving so soon, La'lunaî?" Miranda's grainy voice sounded from a lower roof. I leaned over my ledge to see the old crone smirk, taunting, "Don't you like our new Reaper friends?"

"They only want to play with us," Cilia sighed next as she appeared from behind a chimney. Her smile was wickedly pleased. At her heels were three, hound-shaped masses of fire that wavered with smoke at her sides. "It would be rude to walk out on them now, don't you think?"

La'lunaî's breaths were heavy as she hung there, petrified. "H-how many Reapers do you have?!"

Cilia hummed, tapping a clawed finger to her chin curiously. "*Not* including the thousands exterminating our dumber counterparts in the city?" She asked. "I suppose… two. And their vassals, of course."

La'lunaî's emerald gaze quivered—

Something shot past my face, so quick I didn't have time to look before La'lunaî shrieked in agony. A small throwing scythe was sticking out of her shoulder, black veins squirming off the blade and into her pores. Her screams intensified.

"*Whoa!*" A voice sounded overhead.

I threw my head up, spinning. Octavius' feet kicked in the air, El's arms wrapped around him as she flapped both of them down to us. Octavius panted when he steadied, flashing us a toothy smile. "Hey guys. Did we miss anything?"

Cilia chuckled delightedly, interlacing her fingers while pointing at Octavius. "Make that four."

La'lunaî scrambled to summon a jagged ice blade, slicing Miranda's constricting vine. She thudded to the roof, tearing out the throwing scythe in her shoulder and scuttled on all fours, shying back in a panic.

She turned tail and took off again.

But a glowing trident shot from above and drove into her skull, pinning her to the roof. Hecrûshou ripped out his weapon and raised it over his head.

"*Shëfaux!*" La'lunaî shrieked, her hands shoving forward.

Something happened to our Ancients, then. I couldn't tell what was wrong. All at once, Cilia, Miranda, and Hecrûshou screamed as if pained and curled into themselves, dropping to their knees, then flattening completely as if *pushed* by the little girl's outstretched hands.

The only Ancient left unaffected was Shëfaux, who suddenly hopped in front of La'lunaî, protective.

What happened to the vassals? I thought, quickly scanning the roofs. Aiden and Nathaniel were still standing, bearing many bloody wounds, but holding their ground. Vendy fell back at my side with a puzzled look, seeming just as baffled by our Ancients' sudden distress as I was. Dalen flapped behind me, looking over my shoulder in confusion. "What's happening?" he called over the demons' pained screams.

I shook my head, puffing. "I don't know."

La'lunaî hurried to her feet behind Shëfaux and wasted no time. She fumbled away, leaping off the edge of the roof and disappeared. Shëfaux started to follow her.

"Death!" Alex cursed beside me. He put away his scythe, using both hands to summon the largest mass of water he'd created yet.

I put away my own scythe, then took the ball full-on and heaved, keeping its dense shape as it splashed over Shëfaux's head and engulfed his arms and torso.

I pulled with my Hallows and dragged him close enough for Alex to plunge his hands into the watery mass and amplify the pressure, crushing Shëfaux and snapping his arms *upward.*

My knees bent, pushed down by the weight of this dense monster that strangled the demon. I grunted when my foot slipped, and I dropped the water in a startled breath.

Shëfaux thrashed about now that he was free, his arms and ribs still mangled, but he didn't seem to care. He slammed his shoulder right into me, knocking me on my back. My skull hit the roof at full force, making my vision swim. Shëfaux's figure was still swirling when I saw him raise his newly mended arm, summoning a fractured lance of ice and thrust it down at me.

In a reflex, I lifted my shoulder away, Shëfaux's lance piercing the roof where my chest would have been, then quickly drew out my scythe and drove it into Shëfaux's right breast.

Shëfaux was shocked stiff.

I blinked when a spatter of black blood dripped on my cheek. A different scythe's tip was poking out from Shëfaux's *left* breast, an inch above mine.

I grinned, then *heaved* my scythe across his chest toward his heart at the same moment Alex cut across in the opposite direction from behind.

Snap!

I watched Shëfaux's gaze grow stale, his white pupils fading black as he gave a straggled sigh. His limbs went limp, skin turning to dust as black ichor evaporated from his barebones. His skeleton clattered over me, and I coughed when his heavy skull thudded onto my stomach.

My brother was now fully visible, grinning above me.

"Grand timing," we said in unison.

53

WILLOW

The explosions outside stopped, and my grown fox ears swiveled. I listened from my seat in the Infirmary as Hugh stiffened beside me.

Yes, the noise had stopped. Was it a good sign?

Hugh went to the door and cracked it open to peek outside. He straightened and twisted back to me. "Your friend is back, your Highness."

I slowly rose, leaning on my crutch. "Which?"

Lilli walked through the door, clad in armor, her helm tucked under her arm. Jaq was behind her.

"Willow," Lilli panted furiously. Had she run here? "The demons have retreated in town. They're gone."

"All of 'em," Jaq added in a fanged grin.

"Oh, Nira be blessed." I hobbled over and held Lilli in a tight embrace, kissing her cheek. "Thank Death you're both all right."

Lilli smiled wanly, still puffing. "I was bitten a few times, but it's not serious... where is Oliver—?"

Thwump!

The door was slammed open before I could reply. Oliver leapt from the doorway and latched onto Lilli from behind. "Mama!"

Lilli lunged back at his weight, but she took a step to maintain balance, then chuckled. "There you are, darling."

"Mama, I-I couldn't find you, and we were in that dark place again and that blue kid was *floating!* And-and there were these sandy monsters, gonna swallow us up like last time, and..."

He went on to describe his ordeal in Aspirre while Lilli and Jaq took a seat and exhaled tiredly, nodding off with soft *Mm-hmm's* and *I see's.*

If the demons in the city were retreating, I considered in silence, *then had the Ancients been killed?*

I left the infirmary and clipped out to the halls with my cane. There were so many people crowding the corridors, all murmuring about the sudden stillness. Some held hope, but others were skeptical. I shoved through the masses, looking at each face fervently.

Then the whispers rose into awed gasps, the crowd parting for a pair of men who skulked through the hall.

Xavier. He was walking alongside his brother. Octavius and El were trailing them, holding hands to my surprise, and towing that shaking, pathetic Ancient, Khol with them.

Relieved, I hurried over. When Xavier saw me coming, his face brightened, and he reeled me in by the waist to steal a kiss.

"Well, my dear," he said. "I'm still in one piece. I'm afraid you'll have to wait for that divorce."

I chuckled. "Pity. Is it done, then? Are they dead?"

Alex grunted beside him, holding up a skull he'd had tucked under his arm. "One is. The other fled."

"In a terrible rush, no less," added Xavier. "I doubt she'll be coming back anytime soon… now, for the *real* question." He held up his arm, offering it to me. When I took it, we walked on and he glanced at my belly. "Do you think we'll have a son or a daughter?"

I pressed a hand over my stomach. "Well, I… I'm not sure."

"No visions for it yet?" He sounded hopeful.

"Not that I've Seen." I eyed him warily. "You're taking this… well."

"How else should I take it?"

"With a bit more trepidation," I suggested. "Telling me it's too soon, that you're not ready."

"Oh, I'm *not.*" His laugh was nervous, his smile a little pale. But he clasped my hand and trapped it on his arm. "But it's happening, regardless. So, better to be excited than scared out of my damned mind."

"I suppose."

The crowd rippled with gasps suddenly, the hall clearing as an armored woman, Anabelle, stormed through.

"Willow." Anabelle's tone was hard, her expression tight. "Where is the body?"

Body? I frowned. "Of… the queen?"

"Have you moved her?"

My head shook. "I only just sent someone to find the proper shackles."

Ana cursed in a whisper.

My fox ears grew, and I turned to Xavier. "You say one of the Ancients fled?"

He nodded. "The younger Relicblood."

Behind me, Khol gave a choked squeal of terror, clinging to Octavius's arm. "I-I thought you said you killed her!"

Alexander glanced back at him with a raised brow. "We killed Shëfaux, not the girl."

"*Ooooh*...." He quivered and shuffled back, letting Octavius go as he glanced over his shoulder and ducked his head. "No, no, no...! She'll come back—she *always* comes back! Always... Always..."

He kept blubbering this, crouching over his knees and cradled his head in his hands, sobbing hysterically. His scene was causing a worried uproar from the people in the corridor, the Ancient's sobs echoing off the walls.

Hecrûshou pushed through the mass then and strode to the boy. "Still haven't grown a Bloody spine, I see," he said, grabbing Khol by his shirt collar and yanked him up. Hecrûshou had his radiant trident in hand, and he pushed the fork over the boy's shuddering chest.

"Well, Khol," Hecrûshou spat. "Here we are again. Though this time, I imagine slipping by like the eel you are won't prove as simple, with so many Reapers."

Khol squeaked. "W-w-wait...! Wait! I'm with you now, please...!"

"And the queen's body?" Hecrûshou demanded, the shark's teeth sharped. "Did La'lunaî take it herself, or did you drag it to her?"

"I-I-I didn't do anything...!" He blubbered. "Please...!"

Hecrûshou dropped him, letting the boy simper over the floor.

I slipped my hand out of Xavier's arm and gave Hecrûshou a sideways glance. "Are we sure that girl didn't Mark him?"

"Marking an Ancient is impossible," the shark muttered. "Any demon over three centuries rejects it."

So Khol wasn't lying. "Is he as harmless as he looks?" I asked next.

Hecrûshou sighed, rubbing his eyes. "Shamefully, yes. He's a damned pacifist... raised in a temple by Rinish Purists. He's barely had enough souls to make him Sentient. *Oscha*, when *I* first saw him, he hadn't eaten *any* souls after his awareness returned. Bloody fool, it's a wonder you've survived this long."

I let out a dismal laugh. "A demon who abhors violence. What's next?" I had a different thought and looked at Hecrûshou. "Where is Miranda? And..." My teeth barred. "Cilia?"

"They're searching for straggling mongrels," he informed. "Casting them away. Last I saw, they hadn't found La'lunaî. They'll return when they're sure the city is clear."

A bubble of hate rose, and I growled, "Cilia is not welcome here."

Hecrûshou hummed. "I thought not, no. I gave her instruction to keep out of your sight. She'll linger at your perimeters."

"She's not welcome *anywhere* near us," I clarified, my fox ears curling back. "You and Miranda—and even *this* peace-loving whelp—" I thrust a hand at the weeping Khol. "Are the only Fera I trust."

"Then trust in my judgement." Hecrûshou clipped. "You promised me citizenship to *all* Sentients, did you not?"

"All who haven't caused war on a global scale," I scoffed.

"And those who were committing those crimes by the will of a Clean One, like yourself?" He set the butt of his trident on the floor and stood tall. "Cilia is a pawn, Princess Death. She deserves a fair trial."

"She deserves to be Cleansed—"

"Were she a living shifter, would she be granted a trial if she requested?"

I paused.

"If you catch the man pulling her strings," he said, "Would *he* be granted a trial?"

"If he comes peacefully, yes," I said. "But Cilia—"

"Has cut her strings." His tone was reproving. "She poses no threat to you any longer. She has agreed to take her punishment after she has what she wants, and she will testify against Macarius as witness and victim."

My lids narrowed. "And what reason have I to trust her?"

"Considering your history with her…" He hesitated, then sighed. "I suppose you have little. But I've listened to her story. Her situation is a peculiar one. She's searching for—"

"—Her husband," I muttered, crossing my arms. "Who happens to be another murdering lunatic who has caused me, Xavier, Alexander, Octavius and his family, Anabelle, and *thousands* of other shifters five centuries worth of pain and grief. What a lovely couple they make."

"I can't argue against what they've done," he said, "just as I can't argue what mistakes *I've* made in the past. Bear in mind, you claim to have faith in me, though you're fully aware that—being what I am—I have killed thousands and eaten as many souls. But Cilia's case is unique. Where *I* was always acting on my own accord, she has been strung along by another since the beginning. And I don't doubt her husband is being equally manipulated by someone whom, I'm quite sure, you want dead far more than you want her."

I tapped a finger over my arm, pointedly silent. Hecrûshou saw my indignant expression and went on, "As I said." He waved a hand. "Cilia is a pawn. Your war against her is officially over. But that doesn't mean it's over with

Macarius. And if you have any chance of bringing down the puppeteer, you'll need Cilia on your side."

I seethed, "I'll not have that *murderer* anywhere near..."

I stopped when Xavier clasped my shoulder. He looked conflicted at me, but took a breath and turned to Hecrûshou. "How confident are you that our war with her is over?" he asked the Sentient. "How do you know it's not a bluff?"

I gaped at him. Was Xavier actually *humoring* this nonsense?

Hecrûshou shifted his weight. "Considering what Claude reported about Macarius? And about Kael?" He nodded toward Octavius behind us. "And you've seen her exclusive affection for those with her blood... My own line died off long ago. But were I to find descendants of mine this day and age?" His head shook. "I would do anything to keep them alive. To be near them... It is a hollow life, after death. It is not something I expect you Clean Ones to understand."

"Then help us understand," Xavier urged. "Why would Cilia suddenly change her mind? Why would she stop helping Macarius?"

The Ancient was quiet for a moment. Then he gazed over his shoulder, eyes growing distant.

"I was married before my death," he said, hushed. "I left my wife a widow, alone without children. After I Changed, I'd... lost my memories of her. I hadn't given her a thought, not for months. By the time I remembered her, she was already dead." His tone sagged with immense pain. "She'd given herself to the sea for me. Her soul was Reaped, so she hadn't Changed... and then, three centuries passed. I knew she'd gone back to Nira. And I..." His eyes were red and glassy. "I will never see her again."

Xavier didn't say a word. I couldn't find an appropriate response either. In the months Hecrûshou has spent with us, this was the first he spoke of his past life. Five hundred years, spent in pain? *Too long.*

The years I'd spent grieving for Xavier were barely a heartbeat's length by comparison. *And I found him alive, in the end.* I placed a gentle hand on Xavier's fingers, feeling comforted to feel their cold touch. It was a reminder that he was tangible. That he was real. That he was alive and standing here with me.

It took some time before Hecrûshou found his voice again. "But I should think," he said, "if I discovered my wife was still alive... being kept from me by someone..." His eyes flicked at me, white pupils sharp and furious. "I would do *anything* to get her back. To see her again..." His voice fractured. Then his fists clenched and his throat ripped. "And I would want the man responsible to be torn to *shreds.*"

My claws grew, tears hitting my eyes suddenly. How many times have I ripped through enemies to keep Xavier alive? To make sure he was safe? And how many more was I willing to kill to keep him that way?

My gut lurched, disgusted at how quickly that shameful answer came to mind. *Damn it.* That tiny ball of hate for Cilia curdled, warming into something more infuriating... Sympathy. *Gods damn it, no. Not for her.*

I met Xavier's gaze, his face gentle. He must have had the same thought. But Nira damn it, that didn't mean I had to like it.

54

CILIA

~~~❦~~~

My bare feet stepped over the soft grass in the palace gardens, lamps and torches lighting the many colorful flowers and marble statues, creating a soft glow in the cascading nightfall.

The air tasted warm and humid as it mixed with the salty scent from the breeze that I was sure had been picked up by the shore.

I stopped by an iron pergola, cupping a rather vibrant bloom that smelled of sweet honey and lilacs.

I remembered a table set by a window. It only held a single vase, patterned with refractory divots and peaks. Flowers much like the one I was holding spilled from the wide lip, sunlight beaming from the window as if to display their glory.

Kael had put it there for that very reason. He said that any flower grown by my hands were gems that deserved the highest praise. I'd spent years growing those blooms…

I watched as Miranda shuffled down the cobbled walkway in the distance, heading into the palace. I sighed and seated myself on a stone bench that lay beneath the pergola.

I knew I couldn't step foot inside. Not with the Death Princess and her guarding Reapers despising me so… And I deserved every ounce of it. Forgiveness did not favor me…

"You cannot erase your past," Kael whispered, clutching my hand. "But nothing is stopping you from a new life."

I remembered sitting on the strewn bed, stifling my sobs as he hushed me and brushed the tears away with his thumb.

After I'd been a fool and told my manager I wished to resign, he'd locked me in here for the last two days, beating and ravaging me as a reminder of who I belong to; of what I was—what I chose to be.

I didn't know how Kael found the keys to the lock, nor how he knew I was trapped in here. Yet there he was: kneeling by the bed where I sat, interlacing our fingers and cupping my bruised face.

"I-I can't..." I choked, leaning into his hand and pressing it to my cheek desperately. I didn't want him to let go. I needed to feel that warmth from his fingers, feel that he wasn't an illusion. My tears flooded again. "He'll have me killed. He'll find me, drag me back..."

"You needn't worry about him again." There was a deep rasp in his voice, so sure and confident in that promise. His honey eyes softened at me, and a smile broke his lips. "He cannot hunt what he does not remember."

I blinked through the tears, his meaning dawning. "Your Hallows... you erased his memories?"

"It was better than he deserved," he growled, but sighed, calming. "But you're free. That's all that matters. And..." His grip tightened on my hand. "I... I want you to be my wife, Cilia..."

The memory faded. I was still sitting on the stone bench, staring up at the flowery pergola arching over me.

I gave a long sigh. How did I ever deserve him? What had I done for the Gods to deem me worthy of someone so wonderful?

Though, perhaps I wasn't deemed so worthy. It was ripped from me so quickly...

A scuffle of feet sounded, and a young man came to stand in front of me. He wore a simple pair of loose trousers and a stained green tunic, his azure hair curled in light wisps at his cheeks. There was a crowned Dream mark at the center of his brow.

I rose, cautious. "You..." I squinted at his face, nostalgia sinking. "I know you."

"It's been a long time, Cilia," the young man said, not moving from his place on the pathway. He held something between his fingers, some sort of small, mirrored sphere. My gaze locked onto the sphere. That looked like a smaller version of the memory-holder Macarius had.

"Who are you?" I asked.

"My name is Dream," he said. "I imagine you don't remember. My daughters used to play with your son."

My son? Caleb? I took a step toward him—

But I was hit by some unseen force, pushed back. Dazed, I tried again, but was met with the same resistance. Even my hands couldn't push past it, as if a protective bubble surrounded the young man; surrounded Dream.

He hummed, unstrapping a sack that was tied to his belt, its contents clinking inside. "I suppose you *are* a demon, now, aren't you? You can't come near the Orbs anymore."

With some pause, he gently set the sack on the ground and approached me, holding up that mirrored sphere in his fingers and thought aloud, "When we didn't find you in your home back then, I knew you'd Changed... After all, what else could have happened to your body?"

Looking past him, I only now noticed there were others here, keeping their distance. I stiffened to see the Death Princess was among the group. She had her hand diplomatically clasped before her over a crutch, her hardened gaze seeming to judge every move I made. Those twins stood behind her, along with *all* my descendants: the two Reapers, the girl... the one who shared Kael's face...

"A few of your memories were simple to track down in Aspirre," Dream went on, still making his way to me, "to piece together what exactly happened before the massacre in the palace. No one was sure. Your perspective was the only one missing, in all the visions I'd had of your death. And of course, I couldn't have a vision of something you yourself didn't remember. Past perspectives are dependent on the owner's memory of it. And just when I thought Macarius had stolen that integral, linchpin memory for himself..."

He halted before me, holding up the sphere, his face burdened with intensity. "I found it."

I had trouble breathing. "Then, this is...?"

"The truth," he said, sliding the lid of the sphere open as a small glowing light gleamed from within, "through your own eyes."

His crowned Dream mark began to shine, and the ball of light lifted from the sphere. I held my breath as it floated to my face and sank into my skull with a cold, rippling touch.

Then the garden slammed out of existence.

"He's coming, mama!" Caleb pushed himself from the window and hopped at my skirts. "He's coming, he's coming!"

I pulled the roast from the oven and chuckled, ruffling the boy's black hair. "Thank you, Caleb. Now, you remember what to tell your papa?"

He threw up his hands in a giggle. "I'm going to be a brother!"

"Very good," I praised, "Now, why don't you get the door for him?"

Caleb hurried to the door, heaving it open as snow spilled inside, and he threw up his arms again. "Papa!"

Kael stepped in, sighing while lifting the boy. "Caleb, what are you doing out of bed at this hour?"

"I've let him wait for you," I called from the kitchen, a grin tugging my lips. "You'll never guess what your son has just sensed with his Infeciovoking, dear."

Kael grunted and set the boy down, unwrapping his scarf. But a thought seemed to pass through his eyes, his expression saddened, and he wrapped the scarf back on. He went to the closet and pulled out an empty pack, then sluggishly moved through the house and began stuffing belongings inside.

"Kael?" I called, baffled. "What are you doing?"

"Come, darling… Pack your things." His tone dripped. "We're leaving."

"Leaving?" I echoed. "But… where? Why?"

"I'm bringing you both to Grim," he said, as if he'd only just decided. He turned to our son and lightened his heavy tone. "Caleb, gather your things. Be quick, now. You're to meet your grandparents."

Caleb beamed. "I am?"

"You are." Kael tried a smile, but I saw it quiver. Something was wrong.

Once Caleb hurried to his room, I caught Kael's arm, stopping him from any more of his packing. "Grim, Kael?" I questioned. "Where is this coming from? What's happened?"

He wouldn't face me, as though shamed. "I will… explain on the journey there. But we cannot stay here. We cannot…" He paused, twisting his head to me. His eyes moved to my belly. "You are with child?"

I laid a hand on my belly, forcing a weak smile. "Caleb sensed it with his own Infeciovoking. We meant to surprise you."

Newly dazed, Kael ceased his packing and hovered a hand over mine, yielding to a smile. But that smile soon fell. Then his brow creased. "I *am* surprised," he said, but the words rang cold, "this is not my child."

I stiffened, watching his gaze curdle. "W… what?" I stammered. "Of course it's your child."

"Then why does it not have my blood?" He stepped away, as if disgusted. "Whose is it, then? *Whose child is that?*"

"It is *yours*." *What is he on about?* "You must be tired. Are your Hallows exhausted—?"

He slammed a fist on the wall. "*Answer me, you lying whore!*"

My throat cinched, limbs locked in fright.

The breaths through his nose staggered. "You promised me. You promised you were done with that life. And now you think you can stand there, knowing well I can feel that tainted blood in your bastard, and lie to me?"

He stormed to the door and thrust it open, a dust of snow sweeping inside.

Panicking, I grabbed his arm. "Kael, please! I am not lying, this is your child—"

He ripped out of my hold, but held his misting gaze to the ground, his voice guttural. "I know my own blood. Caleb is my blood. Not this filthy bastard you house."

"Kael, please, look at me—"

"I'd sooner see you dead than look at your face again," he barked, but retracted. He opened his mouth as though to speak again... but took a pained breath instead, looking shamed, and slammed the door behind him.

My legs were numb, staring after the door.

"Mama?" Caleb called from his bedroom door, hesitant. "Mama, why was papa yelling? Why are you crying?"

I quickly rubbed at my tears. "It's... grown up matters, dear." I had another thought, and waved for him to come. "Caleb, could you help your mama with something?"

Caleb shuffled over, his green eyes unsure. "What is it?"

I lightly took his hands and placed them on my belly. "Can you... can you feel if that child you sensed has your blood?"

Caleb's brow scrunched. "What does that mean?"

"Does it—does it feel different from you? And from papa?"

"It does," he said, puzzled. "But it still feels like Mama, so I'm still going to be a brother, won't I?"

It IS different? But how? There's been no one else.

"Thank you, Caleb..." I hushed, his face blurred through tears. "You can go back to your room. I... I suppose I ought to finish dinner."

Caleb did as told, his door swinging closed, though it didn't quite latch.

I did not finish dinner. Instead, I drifted to the kitchen table and sat. Stared at my hands.

And wept.

—the front door creaked open.

"Kael?" A familiar voice called from the doorway, a chilled gust blowing inside. "Kael, I know you're angry, but I *must* explain what I..."

Macar quieted when he spied me at the table. I was still rubbing my wet cheeks.

His face fell worried. "Cilia?" Macar asked. "What's the matter?"

"It's nothing," I said, composing myself. "It's the onions in the stew I was making."

"Onions my scales, your ears are showing." The cobra lowered into the chair beside me, his hands hesitating, as if thinking to touch my hand to console me, but deciding against it. "What's happened? Where is Kael?"

"Kael," I inhaled deeply. "Kael walked out. Something's happened, but I... I don't know what to make of it."

Macar's brow grew heavy. "Perhaps it has to do with what happened in the palace. I heard his delivery with the queen's baby was a failure... Both were lost. King Adam has just banished him."

"Banished?" Was that why he'd been packing? Talking of Grim, before he discovered I was...

I pressed my belly, squeezing my lids shut. "Why were you looking for Kael?"

He folded his scaled arms over the table. "I'm trying to convince him to help me with a... project. He keeps rejecting it. But I *need* him for everything to fall into place." He sighed, pushing up his spectacles. "If he only listened to reason, we could prevent something terrible from happening. There must be some way to convince him..."

I dabbed at my eyes again. *Something terrible?* Perhaps it had to do with Kael's—and no doubt Caleb's and my own—banishment. I swallowed the burning knot in my throat. "Is there any way I can help?"

"No, no." Macar smeared a hand over his face, uplifting his spectacles. "Not unless you can talk to him with the sweetest voice you can produce."

My laugh was more of a pained hiccup, repeating the words Kael himself had said to me. "He'd sooner see me dead than look at my face again."

Macar's face contorted. "What are you saying? You mean the world to Kael." I choked back a sob as Macar took my hand, patting my knuckles tenderly. "Cilia, whatever you've done, he would never want you dead. Bloods, if he lost you, he'd... why, he'd..."

He stopped. His eyes brightened suddenly.

"Macar?" I wiped my lids with a napkin from the table.

His gaze snapped to me, now wide and enlightened.

I asked, "What is it?"

"I... think I know how to convince Kael to help me." He rose slowly, the chair scuffing the floor. His steps toward the counter seemed aloof... almost haunted.

I pushed to my feet, confused as I went to the other side of the wooden counter. "What exactly do you need help with?"

He walked to the stove, where the roast I'd made lay untouched, the carving knife resting on the counter beside it. His back faced me as he glanced at the roast, softly inhaling the scent in an admiring smile.

"You know of my friend Dream, don't you?" he asked. "The original Relic Child?"

My brow furrowed. "Well, yes... His daughters play with Caleb, on occasion."

"When he was a child," he began, "he'd Seen disturbing visions. Visions of the End."

"The end of what?"

"Existence." He hunched over the counter and leaned on his hands, his back facing me. "I wish to prevent his vision from manifesting. There is always a way to change our future. A choice we must make… and I believe I know the solution."

He slid his hands off the counter and turned to me, arms hanging at his sides. "Dream, unfortunately, has a different opinion of how to prevent the End. But his solution won't work. It is flimsy at best. And in the matter of keeping our world alive, *flimsy*…" He hissed the word. "… will not do."

I hadn't a clue how to reply. Instead, I asked, "What will Kael do for you?"

"I need your husband to help me save the world," he said. "And I believe…" He let slip a dry heckle. "You've given me his motivation."

He lunged at me over the counter, thrusting something into my chest—

I gasped at the shock, fumbling into the table's edge. The carving knife was handle-deep in my ribs, my gown blooming crimson.

My gaze drifted to the counter, the knife by the roast gone.

An icy pain thrummed against my ribs, breaths tasting of metal. Something warm dripped from my lips.

Macar's fanged smile stretched his face as he chuckled.

"You…" I sputtered, blood drowning the words. I evoked a burst of fire from my hands, but they were quickly snuffed when I collapsed to the floor.

Then, I heard a door creak open.

Caleb peeked through the crack of his bedroom door, half his face visible.

"Ah, Caleb." Macar ripped the knife from my chest and strode to the boy. "Yes, I should think we'll want as much motivation as is available."

"N-no…" I fought the ice pushing through my veins as I summoned my fire, gave a screaming heave, and threw my weak flames at him.

Macar's sleeve was caught and he quickly swatted at the fire.

"Caleb…!" I wheezed, crawling. "G-go…!"

Caleb bolted for the door, ducking under Macar's enraged swipe, and disappeared into the snowy night.

Macar's throat clicked, his fangs growing. "Wonderful… I suppose I'll need to stage something else for him when your husband arrives." He glanced down at me. "What do you think, hm? Perhaps an illusion of someone carting him away? To show him Adam has his son, and draw him to the palace? Oh yes, I think that would be quite effective."

"You… damned…" I sputtered, my vision splotching. "Why…?"

"You must understand, Cilia." He strode to the kitchen counter and plucked the large cleaver from its drawer, idly bouncing the dull end over a shoulder.

"This is the fate of the world we speak of. You're doing a noble service to preserve us all. It's nothing personal."

"Kael… will know…"

He crouched over me, his breath hot against my cheek. "After I'm done with you, I hardly think his mind will have kept its sanity. Don't you think?"

I pushed out a snarl, summoning my fire, hands smoking—

Thnk—sqlch!

I screamed, the cleaver hitting my wrist and breaking through, the stub gushing.

Thnk—sqlch!

My other hand was separated.

He grabbed my hair and pulled my head up to face him. His grinning lips were the last things I glimpsed before the heavy blade broke through my neck.

I gasped out of the memory, falling to my knees, clutching my chest. It was still throbbing with a phantom pain, my veins pushing ice.

Dream crouched before me, saddened. "I am sorry for what he's done to you," he said. "He has Kael convinced that Adam was your killer. Kael is with him now, seeking revenge for you. He doesn't know you still walk among us."

My vision blotted, an agonized sob erupting from my lungs.

"Help me," I wheezed, my Pyrovoker's heat blazing tenfold. "Help me *kill that son of a bitch.*"

EPILOGUE
CAYDEN

⌁⌁⌁

I drifted through the palace halls like a shell, listening to the hollow sounds of my footfalls reverberating from the walls and high ceiling.

There were few bodies filling the corridors. Even my usual guards were absent. They were all attending my mother's funeral.

I was dressed in the white doublet and cape appropriate for the grim occasion, but... I couldn't bring myself to go. I'd watched her leap from my own balcony, preferring death over another moment spent in this prison.

What was worse, her soul couldn't be found. The Rockraiders had tried cutting her NecroSeam with a Crystal blade, but no ghost had risen from her corpse. It was an empty vessel.

My gaze caught another figure dressed in white walking down an adjacent corridor ahead. It was Roarlord Wales. Or rather, the man posing as him.

My lion ears curled back, teeth sharpening. I hastened my steps and turned the corner after the man.

"Strange, isn't it?" I called, making him stop and turn. "That my mother's soul was missing from her vessel."

Wales regarded me with narrow eyes, sizing me up and down. "Yes... A tragic mystery, my lord."

"I only wonder if someone was responsible," I said, slipping my hands into my trouser pockets and walking toward him. I stopped a safe distance away. "One could say it's as if her soul was destroyed. Do you think that sounds plausible, Roarlord?"

"I think you're grasping at straws made of mist, my lord. I am sorry for your loss, but I suggest you not dwell on what we cannot change. It can drive a man mad, if the wound is left to fester..."

With that, he nodded, and carried on his path.

I called after him, "Did you follow that advice for Cilia?"

His boots squealed to a stop. He whirled, shock smoldering his face. I grinned. It may have been stupid to expose my suspicion, but then, what did I have to lose? My mother was gone. Revinna and my sisters were the only risk left, but if I had to run with them in tow, I would. I was sick of this game. It ended now.

"How do you know that name?" He whispered, the echoes carrying his voice down the hall.

I kept the space between us taut. "I heard it during my months spent with the Reapers. We rescued a man named Claude, who told stories of his ancestors." My voice dropped to an accusing tenure. "You're Kael, aren't you?"

His fists balled and fell lax. Then he sucked in a breath. "He told you of Cilia."

"Actually," I contradicted. "The Reapers mentioned her first. Your wife has been quite the busy demon queen this past year. She's been giving the Death Knights a fair amount of trouble."

Kael's rising chest stilled. "Demon queen…?"

"One of the oldest recorded, from my understanding," I hummed. "She's been around for… oh, five hundred years now? Seems like a long time to still be up and about, building an army fit to kill a few Relicbloods… can you imagine—?"

He shoved me against the wall, snarling, "What are these lies?" Fury dripped from his throat. "Cilia is *dead*."

"Of course she is." My grin was spiteful. "She's a Necrofera. They're all dead. But that doesn't stop them from taking a stroll through a few cities and laying waste to its populace… especially when a certain snake has her on his leash. I wonder if he's told her *you're* still alive?"

The realization was not slow to sink in. He shoved me against the wall with more force. "What proof do you have? *Answer!*"

I chuckled. "Proof? Gods man, *Everland* is your proof. Lindel, Entrial Valley, Nulani—*demolished* by the very woman herself. Who do you think the Reapers have been fighting?"

He set his jaw, shutting his eyes and heaved in breaths.

I smirked. "You know, don't you? I'm sure you knew the cobra had a demon queen under his command. Has he bothered to mention *who* that queen was?"

His teeth gritted, giving me my answer.

He gave a final shove to my chest, slamming me into the wall before storming off down the corridor.

"Where are you going?" I called, surprised at his sudden retreat.

His glare blazed from over his shoulder. "To speak with a friend." He ripped off a gold ring from his index finger. The ring clattered to the marble floor, and I watched his brown hair bleed black, his ram horns disappearing and replaced with curled cat ears. His throat burned when he growled, "If he *is* a friend."

EVOCATOR TYPES

LAND		SKY		OCEAN	
Rock	*Terra*	Wind	*Aero*	Water	*Aqua*
Plant	*Arbor*	Rain	*Imbri*	Ice	*Glacia*
Remedy	*Healer*	Storm	*Astra*	Pressure	*Pregra*
DREAM		DEATH			
Dream	*Somnio*	Fire	*Pyro*		
Illusion	*Decepio*	Death	*Necro*		
Prophecy	*Seer*	Poison	*Infecio*		

Evocator Types in the world of Nirus

Evocators are shifters born with elemental magic, called "Hallows". There are fifteen Hallow elements in total, though most Evocators only possess one element. In rare cases, some are born with two Hallows and are known as Dual-Evocators. Only the Relicbloods (those who are descendants of the Relic Children) have ever possessed all three of their patron realm's Hallows.

Dear Readers,

Thank you so much for reading Pearl of Emerald! I hope you enjoyed it. Now that you've completed part of the Reapers' adventures, I would be extremely grateful if you would take the time to write a review.

Want to find out more about the NecroSeam Chronicles universe, including world notes, deleted scenes, character artwork, and even recorded songs from the books? Check out the necroseam.com website!

Receive announcements on new releases, upcoming conventions I'll be attending, and special promotions by signing up for my newsletter!

You can also follow me on my social media accounts below:

Twitter: @AizelleRaine
www.Facebook.com/officialEllieRaine

Thank you again!
Ellie Raine

ABOUT THE AUTHOR

Ellie Raine grew up in a family of book lovers, comic readers, and video gamers in the suburbs of Norcross Georgia where she always dreamed of making the next explosive game series that would catch fire like the Final Fantasy games, except hers would have darker themes that put the spotlight on her favorite fable: The Grim Reaper.

But that plan took a detour after she went to the Art Institute of Atlanta to make that dream happen. In the midst of her drawing classes, she made the mistake of taking a creative writing course from which there was no return. She had always loved fantasy books much like her family (she had a thing for dragons particularly), but she never thought it would end up becoming her passion. Her ongoing Scythe-and-Sorcery book series, The NecroSeam Chronicles, was originally intended to be that explosive video game series, but she's found that the book adaptation is far more fulfilling and exciting.

In 2016, her first book in the series, *Willow of Ashes*, was published under Dark Oak Press, but was later republished under her indie imprint, ScyntheFy Press, in 2018 along with the subsequent book in the on-going series. Her other works include a supernatural-noir novella titled Nightingale that was published with Pro Se Productions in 2018.

You can find out more about Ellie Raine and her books at:
http://www.NecroSeam.com